ARE WE THERE YET?

david levithan

Alfred A. Knopf

New York

THIS IS A BORZOI BOOK PUBLISHED BY ALFRED A. KNOPF

Copyright © 2005 by David Levithan

www.randomhouse.com/teens

Library of Congress Cataloging-in-Publication Data
Levithan, David.
Are we there yet? / by David Levithan. —1st ed.
p. cm.
SUMMARY: Tricked by their parents into taking a trip to Italy together, two
brothers—one in high school and the other recently graduated from college—
reflect on the directions of their own lives and on the distance that has grown
between them.
ISBN 0-375-82846-X (trade) — ISBN 0-375-92846-4 (lib. bdg.)
[1. Brothers—Fiction. 2. Conduct of life—Fiction. 3. Interpersonal relations—
Fiction. 4. Vacations—Fiction. 5. Italy—Fiction.] I. Title.
PZ7.L5798Ar 2005
[Fic]—dc22
2004061546

Printed in the United States of America

First Edition

July 2005

10 9 8 7 6 5 4 3 2 1

To Mom, Dad, and Adam
(here, there, and everywhere)

Acknowledgments

Thanks to my wonderful parents and my wonderful brother for their support far and wide. Thanks to my friends and family, who have been my faithful traveling companions, whether flying across an ocean or simply strolling through the streets of Soho. I love the moments we share.

Thank you specifically to the friends who have helped me with this book, in its valentine-story incarnation or on the road to its present form: Karen Popernik, Dan Poblocki, and Jack Lienke. Thank you also to the new friends I've found so far in my life as an author—librarians and teachers and readers and fellow writers and editors who've taken me and my writing to such incredible places. It means the world to me.

Thank you to everyone at Knopf for giving my books such a remarkable home. Thank you in particular to Melissa Nelson for her exquisite design (as always).

Thank you to the Simko Family Collection (curated by Patti Ann, John, and Zach) for the loan of their Italian Snoglobes.

Be we in Paris or in Lansing, my editor, Nancy Hinkel, is entrancing. There's no one I'd rather dance among the chandeliers with.

Finally, thank you to Jen and Paolo for showing me all of the things—especially love—that can be found in translation. As I write this, Alessandro is five days old. May he journey both close and far to discover the world.

I. DEPARTURE

The phone rings at an ungodly hour. Elijah looks at the blur of his clock as he reaches for the sound. Eleven in the morning on a Saturday. Who can be calling him at eleven in the morning on a Saturday? Cal, his best friend, stirs from somewhere on the floor. Elijah picks up the phone and murmurs a greeting.

"Oh goodness, did I wake you?" Elijah's mother asks, her voice so much louder than the dream he'd been having.

"No, no," he says, disguising his own voice to sound awake. "Not at all."

"Good, because I have some great news for you. . . ."

His mother is talking about Italy and Elijah's brother Danny and luxury accommodations. He thinks his brother has won a prize on a game show or something. Cal starts hitting his sneaker like it's a snooze button. He tells her to go back to sleep.

"What did you say?" his mother asks. "Will you go?"

"Does Danny want me to go?"

Elijah doubts highly that Danny wants him to go.

"Of course he does."

Elijah still doubts that Danny wants him to go.

Cal is awake now, rubbing her eyes. Elijah's boarding school frowns on having overnight guests, but Elijah doesn't really care if it frowns.

Elijah covers the receiver and whispers to Cal, "It's my mom. I think she wants to know if I want to go to Italy with my brother."

Cal shrugs, then nods.

That's enough for Elijah.

"Sure, Mom," he says. "And thanks."

* * *

Elijah always says thank you, and oftentimes says please.

"You're such a relic," Cal will taunt him playfully.

"Thank you," Elijah will reply.

Elijah learned quickly that saying thank you garners a variety of reactions. Some people (like his brother) can't handle it. Other people (like Cal) are amused. Most people are impressed, whether consciously or not. He'll be offered the last slice of pizza, or the last hit from the bong.

"You're a relic, not a saint," Cal will continue, dragging him to the next party, parties called *gatherings*, dances called *raves*. Where she leads, he will follow. She tousles his blond-brown hair and buys him blue sunglasses. He playfully disapproves of her random boyfriends and girlfriends, and gives her flowers for no reason. They smoke pot, but not cigarettes. At the end of most parties, they can be found woozily collecting cans and bottles for the recycling bin.

Elijah had planned to spend the summer hanging out with Cal and their other friends in Providence. At first, his parents weren't too thrilled about the idea. ("Hang out?" his mother said. "Sweetheart, *laundry* hangs out.") Now he's being sent to Italy for nine days.

"I'm going to miss you," Cal says a few nights before Elijah is scheduled to leave. They are walking home from a midnight movie at the Avon. The June night is warm and cool, as only June nights can be. The air is scored by the faint whir of cars passing elsewhere. Elijah inhales deeply and takes hold of Cal's hand. Her hair—dyed raven black—flutters despite itself.

"I love it here," Elijah says. He is not afraid to say it. "I love it here, this moment, everything." He stops looking at the sky and turns to Cal.

"Thank you," he whispers.

Cal holds his hand tighter. They walk together in silence. When they get back to school, they find four of their friends on the common room's lime-green couch. Mindy, Ivan, Laurie, and Sue are playing spin the bottle—just to be playful, just to be kissed. The moment shifts; Elijah is still happy, but it's a different happiness. A daylight happiness, a lightbulb happiness. Cal arches her eyebrow, Elijah laughs, and together they join the game.

Elijah is the first to grow unconquerably tired, the first to call it a night. Cal is still laughing, changing the CD, flirting with the lava lamp. Elijah says his good-nights and is given good-nights in return. The world already misfocusing, he makes his way to bed.

Ten minutes later, there are two knocks from the hallway. The door opens and Cal appears, brightness behind her. It is time for their ritual, their nightly ritual, which Elijah thought Cal had forgotten. Sometimes she does, and that's okay. But tonight she is in the room. Elijah moves over in his bed and Cal lies down beside him.

"Do you wonder . . . ?" she begins. This is their game—*Do you wonder?* Every night—every night when it's possible—the last thing to be heard is the asking without answer. They stare at the glow-in-the-dark planets on the ceiling, or turn sideways to trace each other's blue-black outlines, trying to detect the shimmer of silver as they speak.

This night, Cal asks, "Do you wonder if we'll ever learn to sleep with our eyes open?"

And in return, Elijah asks, "Do you think there can be such a thing as too much happiness?"

This is Elijah's favorite time. He rarely knows what he is going to say, and then suddenly it's there. Above them. Lifting.

A few minutes pass. Cal sits up and puts her hand on Elijah's shoulder.

"Good night, sleep tight," she whispers.

"Don't let the bedbugs bite," he chimes, nestling deeper under the covers.

Cal smiles and returns to the party. Elijah rearranges his pillows and fits himself within the sheets. And as he does, he wonders. He wonders about goldfish asleep with their eyes open. He wonders about Italy, about his parents, about whether the stars will be brighter in Venice. He hears voices at a distance, the lively sound of voices from the common room. Like the spots of color whenever he closes his eyes. He closes his eyes. He thinks about what a wonderful friend Cal is. How lucky he is to have such friends, all of his friends. He is happy. He is almost empty with happiness. . . .

* * *

As Elijah "hangs out" for the summer, as he smokes and dopes and lazes and does who knows what else (according to his brother), Danny toils and roils away at Gladner, Gladner, Smith & Jones. The two senior Gladners (of no relation—they sat next to each other at Harvard Business School) have taken Danny under their wingtips. Their secretary saves him a seat in the boardroom and provides him with an ample supply of Mark Cross pens. He walks the halls with a boy-wonder halo, the recipient of enough gratitude to deflect all but the pettiest begrudgements. He is twenty-three years old.

People at work pay attention to Danny Silver because he single-thoughtedly saved the Miss Jane's Homemade Petite Snack Cakes account (Gladner, Gladner's largest). Danny specializes in crisis control, and the crisis faced by Miss Jane's was a doozy: a bored and crusading *Washington Post* reporter discovered that the neon-pink frosting on Miss Jane's most popular snack cake ("the Divine") was made with the same ingredients as the nation's bestselling lipstick ("Pink Nightshade"). Consumers were not pleased. Miss Jane's stock plummeted; the company's profits seemed poised to go the way of a dung-coated Twinkie.

Enter Danny Silver. (Imagine this to be a grand entrance— the boardroom door opens, Miss Jane's directors all turn in unison to see their fair-haired savior. In truth, Danny Silver first appeared to the cupcake conspirators via e-mail, and his hair isn't fair. But the effect was the same.) While others advised refusal and rebuttal, Danny suggested humility and humor. A

7

press conference was announced, during which the company president expressed shock and dismay, and pledged an overhaul of the Divine, wherein the frosting would be made from purely organic sources. He also made clear that the rest of the snack cakes in the Miss Jane's family were "one hundred percent cosmetic-free." As soon as Danny heard the reporters laugh with this, he knew everything would be okay.

But *okay* wasn't good enough. The company had to emerge triumphant.

In a mere thirty-nine hours, Danny had come up with his masterstroke. It came to him as he paced his Upper East Side apartment, throwing clothes into the hamper, figuring out which kind of pasta to boil for dinner. (He loves to tell this story; it's one of his best stories.) As Danny paced, he thought of cakes, cream fillings, cafeterias, and childhood. The idea appeared. It wove itself brilliantly within him. He did not hesitate. He called Jones, who called Smith, who paged Gladner, who woke up Gladner at his girlfriend's apartment in the Village. Three hours later, the bigwigs gathered—a war room—as Danny bounced among them. A conference call was placed to "Miss Jane" (aka Arthur Swindland, 61, renowned throughout the world for his collection of celebrity polo sticks).

A scant two weeks later, America and Europe witnessed Miss Jane's First Annual Bake Sale. (The rest of the world would continue to eat lipstick frosting.) Miss Jane's employees and certain grandmothers-for-hire set up tables in supermarkets across the land, all selling snack cakes. The profits would go to the newly formed Miss Jane's Homemade Petite Snack Cake Center for World Peace. Katie Couric herself bought a snack cake on live television. Oprah invited Miss Jane to be her guest on a program stressing "corporate responsibility in the kinder, gentler age." (When Mrs. Silver saw this show, she knew her son had arrived. Making corporate billions was one thing—but to be on *Oprah!* was true accomplishment. Elijah didn't bother to watch.) Miss Jane (née Mr. Swindland) was so impressed with Danny that he earmarked .01% of the MJHPSCCWP's profits to the charity of Danny's choice. (The rest would be distributed to Shriners organizations around the world.)

As his star rises, Danny finds himself working longer and longer hours. By the time he leaves the office, the wastebaskets have been emptied and the floors have been vacuumed. He has begun to forget what his apartment looks like. (His friends might say the same about him.) Gladner and Gladner (both devotees of Ted Newness, the management guru) tell Danny they will give him a raise—as long as he takes a vacation in the month of July.

Three days later, Mrs. Silver calls with her offer.

Danny Silver doesn't doubt for a second that he's being tricked into taking a trip to Italy.

"It's all *prepaid*," his mother proclaims. "I know this is such short notice. But I just don't think that your father can go. Italy isn't a place for sitting. And his leg—well, you know your father's leg. We had hoped it would be okay by now. But who can know such things?"

Danny's father is fine. The day before, he played eighteen holes of golf.

"How are you feeling, Pop?" Danny asks once his mother has passed over the phone.

"Oh, I don't know. The leg's been acting up."

"But you were playing golf yesterday."

"Yes, yes, yes. I must have overextended myself. A damn shame. About Italy, I mean. But Mom tells me you and Elijah are going to go. . . ."

Aha, Danny thinks. *The hitch.*

There is a whisper and a shuffling noise as Mrs. Silver takes back the phone.

"I know, I know," Danny's mom says as her husband recedes to the couch. "I hadn't mentioned that part. But it's only fair. We have two tickets. Two sons. And it's prepaid. Nonrefundable. Your father can't go. So I can't go."

"Ask the Himmelfarbs," Danny offers. "They're your best friends, after all."

"The *Himmelfarbs?* Do you know how much this trip *costs?*" Mrs. Silver takes a deep breath. "No. You and Elijah should take the tickets. It's a week. Nine days."

Nine days with Elijah. Nine days with Quiet Boy, Mr. Virtue, Boy Misunderstood. Elijah, who never seemed to change. Not since he was ten or so and started to grow quiet. His mind seems to be working on two levels at once—*pass the salt* and *contemplate the pureness of the clouds.* He is always dazed, and he is always kind. Faultlessly kind.

Danny can't stand it.

"Have you asked Elijah how he feels about this?" Danny is hoping that Elijah might still say no. Since Elijah is still in high school and Danny is in the Working World, the two of them rarely have to see each other.

"Yes," his mother replies. "He thinks it's a great idea."

Danny can hear his father chuckle in the background. He can imagine his father giving his mother a thumbs-up sign and his mother smiling. *Prepaid. No refunds.*

His mother continues. "It's over the week of July Fourth. You'd only have to take six days off from work. And you haven't been *anywhere* this year."

"Okay, okay, okay," Danny relents. He wonders if it counts as being tricked if he knows what's really going on.

"You'll go?"

Danny smiles. "There is nothing in the world I would rather do."

There is still a chance that Elijah will back out. . . .

* * *

But no.

At one in the morning the night before departure, Danny wakes up with a start.

He hasn't talked to Elijah since their mother made the offer. He should have talked to him, and has tried to, but whenever he's called, someone else has answered. Probably some pothead incapable of taking a message. Danny wants to be well-Fodored and well-Frommered by the time he sets down on Italian soil. But what will Elijah want to do? What does Elijah *normally* do?

I'll have to talk to him. For a week. Nine days.

But about what?

How's life? (Two-minute answer.) *How's school?* (Five minutes, tops.) *How's life with the dope fiends?* (Maybe not a minute—maybe just a Look.) *What do you want to do today?* (That one could stretch out—maybe twenty minutes each day, depending on the repetition of shrugs.) *So isn't this a fine mess we're in?* (Rhetorical—no help.)

Danny gets out of bed, switches on the light, and squints. He counts his traveler's checks; he's bringing extra spending money, assuming Elijah won't have any. He takes out the list of gifts he has to buy, makes sure it's in his wallet, and makes sure his wallet is on the bureau by the keys.

He knows he is missing something. He is always missing something. He can never get past the first step of finding it, which is knowing what it is.

He stays up most of the night, doing things like this. He doesn't want to forget anything. And, more than that, he wants to think of something to say.

* * *

    Seven years apart. Danny can remember the moment his father called to say Elijah had been born. Elijah can't picture Danny younger than ten, except from the photographs that hung around the house long after Danny left for college.

    They never had to share a room, except when they went down to the shore. Spending the day by the pool, broken by stretches of playing on the beach. Danny was the Master Builder of sandcastles, Elijah his ready First Assistant. No two castles were the same, and in that way no two days were ever the same. One day would bring the Empire State Building, the next a dragon. Danny always sketched it first on the surface of the beach. Then Elijah dug, providing sand and more sand and more more sand until he hit the water beneath and had to move a little bit over to start again. As Danny created windows out of Popsicle sticks and towers out of turned-over buckets, Elijah would wander wide to collect shells. Sometimes the shells would be decoration, and other times they would become the residents of the castle. Extended shell families, each with a name and a story. As Danny dipped his hand in water to pat the walls smooth, Elijah would explain what went on inside, making the shape and the hour more real than Danny could have ever made alone.

    There would always be extra shells, and at night Elijah would line them up on the dresser, sometimes according to size, sometimes according to color. Then he would crawl into his bed and Danny would crawl only two feet away into his own bed. From there, Danny would read Elijah a story.

13

Whatever older-kid books Danny was reading—Narnia being chronicled, time being wrinkled—he would send through the stillness to his brother. This was supposed to put Elijah to sleep, but it never did. He always wanted to find out where his brother would take him next.

* * *

Cal drives Elijah down from Providence in her bitchin'
Camaro. It was buck-naked white until she and Elijah covered it with the primary-color handprints of all their friends.
It's a 1979 model, the transmission is crap, and it goes from 0
to 60 in just under four minutes. But, man, once it gets to 60!
The Camaro is, joyously, a convertible. Cal and Elijah zoom
down I-95, blasting pop from the year of the car's birth,
swerving from lane to lane. When they can hear each other
over the wind and the music, they speak Connecticut: *I will
not Stamford this type of behavior. What's Groton into you? What
did Danbury his Hartford? New Haven can wait. Darien't no place
I'd rather be.*

As they reach the New York state line, Elijah feels the
urge to turn back. He can't pinpoint why. It seems the wrong
time to be leaving. He doesn't want to step out of the present, this present. Because once he does, there will be college
applications and college acceptances (just one will do) and
the last of everything (last class, last party, last night, last day,
last goodbye), and then the world will change forever and he
will go to college and eventually become an adult. That is not
what he wants. He does not want those complications, that
change. Not now.

He tells himself to get a grip. Cal is driving him forward.
Cal and everyone else will be here when he returns. It's like he's
traveling into another dimension. Time here will stop. Because
he is entering Family Standard Time. None of it will carry over
to Cal, to the Camaro, to the state of Connecticut.

15

He will go with his brother. He will have a good time. Life will be waiting for him when he gets back. Not a bad deal.

Elijah smiles at Cal. But Cal isn't looking. Then she turns to him as if she knows. She smiles back and blasts the music louder.

* * *

Danny's mother drives him. He lives in New York City. Therefore, he doesn't have a car of his own. When he wants to travel far, he signs out a company car. But this time, his mother won't hear of it. Those are her exact words—"I won't hear of it"—as if it's news of an ignoble death.

"Just be nice to him," his mother is saying now. He's heard this before. *Just be nice to him.* He heard it after he dared Elijah to poke the hanger in the socket. After he put glue in Elijah's socks, telling him it was foot lotion. After he turned off the hot water while Elijah was in the shower. For the fifth time.

Elijah could have retaliated. But he never even tattled. Elijah has always taken his mother's words to heart. Elijah can just be nice. Sometimes, Danny thinks this is all Elijah can be.

"I *mean it*," his mother stresses. Then her tone shifts and Danny thinks, *Yes, she does mean it.*

"I worry about you." She looks straight ahead while turning the radio down. Danny thinks it remarkable that she still doesn't look old. "Really, I do worry about you. I worry about you both, and that you won't have each other. There aren't many times that I wish you were younger. But when I remember the way the two of you would get along—you cared about him *so much.* When he was a baby, you were always feeling his head and coming to me and saying he had a fever. Or you'd wake us up, worrying he'd been kidnapped. All night, I had to reassure you that he was okay. Staying up with the older son instead of the baby. But it was worth it. In the middle of the night, when you couldn't sleep, you'd beg me to take you to Eli's room. And when

17

I did, you would sing to him. He was already asleep, and still you wanted to sing him a lullaby. I would whisper with you. It was so wonderful, even if it was three in the morning. For a few years after, you watched over him. And then something happened. And I wish I knew what it was. Because I'd undo it in a second."

"But, Mom—"

"Don't interrupt." She holds up her hand. "You know it's important to your father. It's important to me. It's also important to *you*. I don't think you realize it yet. You both can be so nice and so smart and so generous. I just don't understand why you can't be that way with each other."

Danny wants to say something to assure his mother. He wants to tell her he loves Elijah, but he's afraid it won't sound convincing.

So they remain silent. Eventually, Danny turns the radio up a little and Mrs. Silver shifts lanes to make the airport turnoff. She asks Danny if he's remembered his traveler's checks, his passport, his guidebooks.

"Of course I remembered them," Danny responds. "I'm your son, after all."

That gets a smile. And Danny is happy, because even if he can't do anything else right, at least he can still make his mother smile.

* * *

Cal doesn't want to stay for the Silver family reunion. After she speeds away in the bitchin' Camaro, Elijah waves goodbye for a full minute before entering the airport.

He finds his mother and brother easily enough.

"So where's your girlfriend?" Danny asks as Mrs. Silver hugs Elijah tightly.

"She's not my girlfriend."

"So where is she?" Danny is wearing a suit. For the airplane.

"She had to go." Elijah can't stand still. His sneakers keep squeaking on the linoleum. He doesn't know whether it's the suit that makes Danny look old or whether it's just life. He is *filling out*, as their mother would say, as if the outline of his adult self was always there, waiting. Elijah thinks this is scary.

"I brought you danish," Mrs. Silver says, handing Elijah a white box tied with bakery string.

"You're the greatest," Elijah announces. And he means it. Because he knows the bakery, he can see his mother holding the number in her hand, hoping against hope that they'll have blueberry, because that's his favorite.

Mrs. Silver blushes. Danny gazes intently at a newsstand.

"I need to buy gum," he says.

"Oh, I have gum." Mrs. Silver's purse is opened in a flash.

"Yeah, *sugarless*. I don't want sugarless. I'll just go get some Juicy Fruit, okay?"

"Oh," Mrs. Silver sighs. "Do you need money?"

Danny smiles. "I think I can afford a pack of gum, Mom." Then he's off, dropping his bag at Elijah's feet.

19

"I'll take some Trident," Elijah offers.

Mrs. Silver rummages again and unearths a blue pack and a green pack.

"Sorry, no red," she says with a smile as she hands the gum over.

"No problem. Thanks." Elijah tucks the gum into his pocket. He doesn't like either blue or green, but he doesn't mind taking it. Someone else on the plane might want some.

While Danny buys his gum (and newspapers and Advil and a hardcover legal thriller), Elijah asks about his father's leg, and she tells him it's getting better. He thanks her again for the trip—he is *sure* it's going to be great, there are *so many* things he wants to see. She thinks his hair is a little too long, but doesn't say anything. (The telltale look at his collar gives her away.)

"So are we ready?" Danny is back.

"Ready as we'll never be," Elijah replies. Danny's tie is caught in his shoulder-bag strap. Elijah is inordinately pleased by this.

* * *

There's an issue that has to be resolved immediately. Danny, bearer of the tickets, brings it up as soon as he and Elijah are through security.

"So," he asks, "do you want the window seat or the middle seat?"

"Up to you."

Of course. Danny knew this was going to happen. Clearly, the window seat is preferable to the middle seat. And politeness decrees that whoever chooses first will have to choose the middle seat. Elijah *must* know this. Typical Elijah. He *seems* so kind. But really, he is passive-aggressive.

(*"Why can't you be more like your brother?"* his parents would ask when he was seventeen.

"Because he's ten!" Danny would shout before slamming his door closed.)

"You don't have any preference?" Danny asks. "None whatsoever?"

Elijah shrugs. "Whatever you want. I'm just going to sleep."

"But wouldn't it be easier for you to have the window seat, then?" Danny continues, a little too urgently.

"It's no big deal. I'll take the middle seat if you want me to."

Great. Now Elijah is the martyr. Danny can't stand it when Elijah plays the martyr. But if it gets him the window seat . . .

"Fine. You can have the middle seat."

"Thanks."

At the gate, they have to cool their heels for almost an hour. Danny is bothered despite his desire not to be bothered. (It

21

bothers him even more to be bothered against his will.) Elijah reads a British music magazine and listens to his headphones. Because Elijah slumps in his seat, Danny doesn't realize they're now the same height. All he notices is Elijah's ragged haircut, the small silver hoop piercing the top of his earlobe.

Danny tries to read the book he bought, but it doesn't work. He is too distracted. Not only because he's bothered. He is slowly crossing over. He is realizing for the first time that, yes, he is about to go to Italy. Every trip has this time—the shift into happening. Before things can go badly or go well, there is always the first moment when expectation turns to *now*.

Danny relaxes a little. He puts away his book and takes out his *Fodor's Venice*. Minutes later, there is a call for boarding. Danny gathers his things for pre-boarding. Elijah pointedly makes them wait until their row is called.

"You're sure you don't want the window seat?" Danny asks as they walk the ramp to the plane.

"Not unless you want the middle seat," Elijah answers.

Danny waves the subject away.

Elijah charms the flight crew from the get-go. He asks the flight attendants how they are doing. He looks at the cockpit with such awe that the pilot smiles. Danny maneuvers Elijah to their seats, then has to get up again to find overhead compartment space (the rest of the row illegally pre-boarded).

Once they settle into their seats, Danny expects Elijah to strike up a conversation with his aisle-seat neighbor. But Elijah keeps a respectful distance. He says hello. He tells his neighbor to let him know if his music gets too loud. And then he puts on his headphones, even though he's supposed to wait.

Danny offers Elijah a guidebook. Elijah says he'll look at it later. Danny doesn't want Elijah to wait until the last minute (so predictable), but doesn't bother to say anything. He just sits back and prepares for the flight. He is ready for takeoff. He loves takeoff. Takeoff is precisely the thing he wants his life to be.

As the plane lifts, Danny sees that his brother's teeth are clenched. Elijah's fingers grip at his shirt, twisting it.

"Are you okay?" Danny asks as the plane bumps a little.

Elijah opens his eyes.

"I'm fine," he says, his face deathly pale.

Then he shuts his eyes again and makes his music louder.

Danny stares at his brother for a moment, then closes his own eyes. *Fodor's* can wait for a few minutes. Right now, all Danny wants to do is rise.

* * *

Elijah tries to translate the music into pictures. He tries to translate the music into thoughts. The plane is rising. Elijah is falling. He is seeing himself falling. He is blasting his music and still thinking that the whole *concept* of flying in an airplane is ridiculous. Like riding an aluminum toilet paper roll into outer space. What was he thinking? The music isn't translating. New Order cannot give him order. The bizarre love triangle is falling falling falling into the Bermuda Triangle.

Enough. This will have to be enough. The takeoff is almost over. The plane is flying steadily. Elijah inhales. He feels like he's gone an hour without breathing. Danny hasn't noticed. Danny is in Guidebook Country. Danny doesn't think twice about flying. He doesn't think twice about Elijah, really.

And if the plane were to crash . . . Elijah thinks about those final seconds. It could be as long as a minute, he's heard. What would he and Danny have to say to each other? Would everything suddenly be all right? Elijah thinks it might be, and that gives him a strange, momentary hope. Really, Cal would be a better doomsday companion. But Danny might do.

Imagining this scenario makes it okay. Elijah is okay as long as he can picture the wreck.

The captain turns off the fasten-seat-belt light. Danny unfastens his, even though he doesn't have to get up. Elijah leaves his on.

There is a tap on his shoulder. Not Danny. The other side.

"Excuse me," the woman next to him is saying. He takes the headphones off his ears, to be polite.

"Oh," the woman says, "you didn't have to do that. I have nothing against New Order, but it was getting a little loud, and you said to let you know. . . ." She trails off.

"You like New Order?" Elijah asks.

The conversation begins.

* * *

Elijah loves *the conversation*. Whatever conversation. The tentative first steps. The shyness. Wondering whether it's going to happen and where it will go. He hates surface talk. He wants to dive right through it. With anyone. Because anyone he talks to seems to have something worthwhile to say.

The first steps are always the most awkward; he can tell almost immediately whether the surface is water or ice. The dancing of the eyes—*Are we going to have this conversation or not?* The first words—the common ground. *And how have you found yourself here? Where are you going?*—two simple questions that can lead to days of words.

"You like New Order?" Elijah asks.

The woman laughs. "In college. I loved New Order, but I had a Joy Division boyfriend. I wanted to hang out, he wanted to hang himself. We were doomed from the start."

The conversation continues.

*   *   *

Danny can't help but overhear them. Elijah is, after all, sitting at his elbow, taking up the armrest. Chatting away with the woman about disco groups. Unbelievable. Talking about college and girlfriends and Elijah's prom. ("She disappeared after the second song, but that was okay. . . .") Danny usually assumes that lonely people are the only ones who have conversations on airplanes. Now he is faced with a dilemma: Is he wrong, or is Elijah lonely? To sidestep the issue entirely, Danny decides that Elijah is an exception. Elijah, as always, is being unusually kind. While he himself is not lonely, he doesn't mind talking to lonely people. He is the Mother Teresa of banter.

Danny silently waits for his introduction, the moment when Elijah gestures to him and says, "This is my brother." Danny plans to put his guidebook down, smile a hello (taking a good look at the woman, who's about ten years older than him, but still attractive), and then make a hasty retreat back to *Inns & Hotels*.

But the conversation never drifts his way. Instead, they are talking about *Roman Holiday*. Danny can't believe it when Elijah says how much he loves Audrey Hepburn. He can understand it, but he can't *believe* it, for it's an adoration that he himself shares. Danny isn't used to having something in common with Elijah, however slight. Their last name is the rope that ties them together. And now there is also this tiny thread. Audrey Hepburn.

Danny thinks about this for a moment. (If Elijah were to look over, he would notice his brother hasn't turned the page in the past ten minutes.) As Elijah and this stranger discuss the ending of *Roman Holiday* and how it makes them feel (sad, happy), Danny wonders whether it's true that *everyone*, at heart, likes Audrey Hepburn. So the similarity isn't that strange at all. It's as commonplace as the desire to eat when hungry. It doesn't link the two brothers any more than that.

That is something Danny can believe.

"So this is your brother?" Penelope whispers, pointing over Elijah's shoulder. He doesn't know why she is whispering. Then he turns and sees that Danny has fallen asleep on his tray table, the edge of his shoulder spotlighted by the overhead lamp.

"Do you think he needs a pillow?" Elijah asks.

"No. He'll be all right."

Elijah reaches over the armrest and presses the lightbulb button. Then he turns back to Penelope and asks her if she has any brothers or sisters. She has three sisters, one of whom is getting married in a matter of months.

"She's older than me, thank God," Penelope says with a sigh. "I have to wear this hideous dress. I told her—I said, '*This dress is hideous.*' Her dress is gorgeous, by the way. Bridesmaids only exist to make the brides look good. I don't care what anyone says. It's not an honor. It's a mockery.

"Her dress has a train. When I saw it, I just started to cry. Not because I'm not the one who's getting married. I can handle that. But to see my sister in a white satin train—it was like we were playing dress-up again. She'd always let my mother's dresses trail behind her. Of course, I'd jump on them and try to trip her up. And I was always the one who got in trouble for the footprints—it didn't matter that the bottom was also covered with dust. Anyway—seeing her at the fitting, it struck me that I can't jump on her dress anymore. I can't pull it over her head and show her underwear to the congregation. I can't even tell her that it isn't hers, that she has to put it back in the closet before our mother comes home. No, it's hers. And it's *her.*"

Penelope shakes her head.

* * *

Boys never dress up as grooms, Elijah thinks. *They never practice their own weddings like girls do.* But there are other kinds of pairs. He remembers Batman and Robin. Luke and Han. Frodo and Aragorn. Cowboy and Indian.

There was only a year or two for those games, before Danny started dressing up in a different way. This time, the character he was playing was the cooler version of himself, shopping at the mall for the perfect costume, trying to blend in and stand out at the same time. It was never explained to Elijah, and he wasn't old enough to figure it out. All he knew was that one day his brother stopped wanting to be a superhero, stopped wanting to save their backyard world. Elijah stopped dressing up then, too. He retreated to the realm of his room, to his drawings, to his stuffed animals.

It wasn't the same.

Sisters dress up to rehearse for what will really happen to them. But brothers, Elijah realizes, are never rehearsing that way. They rehearse their own illusions, until reality takes a turn and they are asked to rehearse for other things. You go to school. You graduate. You sell snack cakes. You hang up your cape and put on a suit.

* * *

Danny wakes up into the strange timeless nighttime of air travel. The window shades are drawn. The flight attendants float down the aisle like guardian angels. The guidebook has fallen at his feet. A woman is talking.

". . . And then, it was the strangest thing, I walk into the room and *there's Courtney Love*. Have I told you this? No? Good. So I can't believe it. Now, this is after she was the lead singer of—what was it called?—Hole. Don't think I'm *that* old. I'm not that old. So it's after Hole, and I walk into the room, and there she is. I can't believe it. So I walk over to her and offer her a joint. Real cool. I can tell that my boyfriend's real impressed at how smooth I am. And she says yes. *But neither of us has a match.* I'm fumbling around, pulling the rolling papers and the dope out of my pockets, and I can't find a light! So my boyfriend just leans over, Courtney looks up at him, and all smooth, he lights her up. I'm still there fumbling. She says thanks to him, offers him a puff, and when he's done he *doesn't even offer it to me*. Because now they're talking and *sharing* and it's like I'm not even there. I say his name, and he just gives me one of those side smiles. I can't believe it. Some other guys join the conversation and I'm out of the circle. And I'm sure Courtney has seen me. But does she say anything? No. Not a word. My boyfriend's treating her like the Pope and my head's all screwed up, so I just say real loud, 'Well, why don't you just kiss her ring!' Everyone stares at me. Like, it makes perfect sense to me, but I'm the only person in the room with the context. I have to get out of there. Right away. My boyfriend's staring at me like I just called his mother a whore. And everyone else thinks I'm insulting Her Highness Courtney Love. So I run out of the room. But I'm not looking where I'm going—I crash into this guy in the doorway—*and that's how I met Billy Corgan.*"

It's the woman next to Elijah. Danny is paralyzed by her talking.

"No way!" Elijah exhales in admiration.

"Uh-huh."

Danny tries to fall back to sleep. He can't believe they're still awake.

* * *

Penelope sleeps soundly on Elijah's shoulder. Which is to say, soundlessly. He doesn't mind, even though it makes his arm sore. *Pins and needles,* Elijah thinks, and then he figures that having an arm full of pins and needles would hurt a hell of a lot more than this.

Danny stirs on the other side of him, waking up and turning to Elijah, his eyes unaccustomed to the simulated day. He registers Penelope on Elijah's shoulder and smiles groggily. *It's not like that,* Elijah wants to tell his brother. But he doesn't want to wake Penelope up.

It's like comfort, Elijah figures. Being a comfort is itself pretty comforting. Having someone find a place on your shoulder and be able to rest. Not seeing her face, but picturing it from her breath. Like a baby sleeping. Feeling her breath so slightly on his arm. Breathing in time. Comfort.

The quiet times are the ones to hold on to. In the quiet times, Elijah can think of other quiet times. Staring at the ceiling with Cal. Driving home from a concert, the road silent, the music in his head. Sharing a smile—for a moment—with a beautiful stranger passing in a car.

Beside Elijah, Danny shifts in his seat and signals to the flight attendant for another Diet Coke.

Danny would never let a stranger sleep on his shoulder, Elijah thinks. *Danny would be afraid of the germs.*

He closes his eyes and tries to drift off.

* * *

Amazing. Danny thinks it's amazing to be moving so fast without feeling movement. To be sitting in an airplane, traveling as fast as he's ever traveled, and still it feels like he's in a car, steadier than a train, not even as fast as sliding down a slide. *How can this be?* Danny wonders. He wants to ask someone. But who can he ask? Elijah, even if he were awake? The girl on Elijah's shoulder? (Isn't she a little old for him?) The pilot? No one. There's no one to tell him how it can feel so slow to go so fast.

The phone is embedded above the fold-down tray. He could make a collect call from above the Atlantic Ocean. He could slip the corporate card into the proper slot and dial any area code around the world. He does it—slips in the card—just to see what the dials are like. Thinking, *Wouldn't it be funny to slip your credit card into the slot, ten thousand miles in the air, and find a rotary phone?* But no—just the usual buttons. He can pretend it's home. Just a local call.

He pauses before dialing. He pauses too long. He pauses long enough to realize that no one comes instantly to mind. He doesn't have anyone instant. He doesn't have anyone worth a twenty-dollar-a-minute call.

Quietly, Danny places the phone back in its receiver. He presses a little too hard, and the woman in front of him rustles in her sleep. Danny looks at Elijah. He looks at Elijah's eyelids and tries to tell whether he's awake. He used to do that all the time when they were kids. Elijah would be faking sleep—he didn't want to leave the car, he didn't want to go to school—and

Danny would catch the small, betraying twitches. He would try to point them out to his mom, and Elijah would mysteriously pop out of sleep before Danny could finish his sentence. Their mom would shake her head, more annoyed with Danny's tattling than with Elijah's fakery. Or so it seemed to Danny. Back then, and still.

Now Danny concentrates—staring into his brother's closed eyes. Waiting for one eye to open, to see if anyone's looking. Waiting for a telltale giggle of breath, or the twitch of an itching finger. Instead, he observes Elijah and the woman both breathing to the same silent measure. Crescendo. Diminuendo. Rise. Fall. Speed and slowness.

* * *

Danny remembers the nightmares he would have. The strangers climbing through the window and stealing Elijah from the crib. He remembers waking the house without waking the baby. Running to Elijah's room to make sure. Because if Elijah was okay, that meant everything was fine.

* * *

Elijah travels in and out of sleep, like the airplane traveling in and out of clouds. Moments of fleeting wakefulness, dream-like. The rituals of airline travel, meant to guard against your fears. Words of conversation. The echo of the in-flight movie from too-loud headphones many rows behind. The wheels of the beverage cart and the crisp opening of a soda can. The pad of feet in the aisle. A child's questions. The flipping of a magazine page. Penelope's breathing. The sound of speeding air. The realization that clouds sound no different than air.

He dreams of Cal's Camaro, and of driving to Italy.

Then he wakes up, and he is there.

II. VENICE

The plane lands impeccably. Danny is up and angling for the aisle before the captain's announcement can tell him to keep his seat belt on. Elijah watches him with a certain degree of embarrassment. He can't see what the rush is. It's not like they can leave the plane any faster. All it means is they'll have their bags in their laps for that much longer. Even the flight attendants are still strapped in; they can't make Danny sit down. Along with the rest of the passengers, Elijah hopes a sudden stop will jolt Danny to the ground.

Elijah remains in his seat until the plane has come to a complete stop. Danny passes over their carry-ons. Penelope leans over and says she can't believe she's finally in Venice.

Elijah nods his head and looks out the window.

Venice.

But not really Venice. The airport.

It is raining outside.

* * *

Elijah can't help it. He scans the crowd at the gate outside of customs, looking to see if someone is waiting for him. As if Cal could truly drive the bitchin' Camaro across the Atlantic Ocean and wait with a lei, just to be inappropriate.

"Let's go," Danny says, hiking his bag higher on his shoulder. "And tie your shoelaces."

Elijah doesn't care about his shoelaces, but he ties them anyway. He nearly loses Danny in the airport rush. He doesn't care much about that, either, except for the fact that Danny has the money and the name of the hotel. (Typical.) Elijah nurtures a half-fantasy of disappearing into the crowd, making his own way to Venice, living by his wits for a week and then returning at the end of it all to share the flight home with his brother. He can't imagine that Danny would mind.

But Danny has stopped. Danny is waiting and watching— watching his watch, tapping his foot, prodding Elijah forward. International crowds huddle-walk between them. Families with suitcases. A girl who drops her Little Mermaid doll.

Elijah returns the doll and makes his way to his waiting brother, who asks, "What took you so long?"

Elijah doesn't know what to say. Shrugs were invented to answer such questions, so that's just what Elijah does.

*   *   *

Italy should make Danny feel rich, but instead it makes him feel poor. To change 120 (dollars) into 180,000 (lire) should make a man feel like he's expanded his wealth. But instead it makes the whole concept of wealth seem pointless. The zeros—the measures of American worth—are grotesque, mocking. The woman at the exchange bureau counts out his change with a smile—*Look at all the money you get.* But Danny would feel better with Monopoly chump change.

He leads Elijah out to the vaporetto launch. It's quite a scam they're running—the only way into Venice from the airport, really. It's one of the worst feelings Danny knows—the acknowledgment that he's going to pay through the nose, and there's nothing he can do about it.

"One hundred twenty thousand lire for the men," the vaporetto driver (the vaporetteer?) says in flawed English.

Danny shakes his head.

"Best price. Guarantee," the driver insists. Danny can tell he's been brushing up on his Best Buy commercials. Probably has his American cousins videotape them.

Danny tries three other drivers. Other tourists gratefully take the vaporettos he discards.

"You really expect me to pay one hundred and twenty thousand lire—*eighty dollars*—for a vaporetto ride?" Danny asks the fourth driver.

"It is not a vaporetto. A *water taxi,* sir."

Elijah steps into the boat.

"Sounds great," he tells the driver. "Thank you."

* * *

It is pouring now. Cold and rainy and gray.

Elijah can't see much through the clouds and mist. Still, he's thrilled by the approach—thrilled by the wackiness of it all. Because—he's realizing this now—Venice is a *totally* wacky city. A loony idea that's held its ground for hundreds of years. Elijah has to respect that.

The buildings are *right on the water*. Elijah can't believe it. Sure, he's seen Venice in the movies—*Portrait of a Room with a View of the Wings of the Lady Dove*. But he'd always assumed that they picked the best places to show. Now Elijah sees the whole city is like that. The buildings line the canals like long sentences—each house a word, each window a letter, each gap a punctuation. The rain cannot diminish this.

Elijah walks to the front of the taxi and stands with the driver. The boat moves at a walking pace. It leaves a wider canal—Elijah can't help but think of it as an avenue—and takes a series of narrow turns.

Finally, they arrive at the proper dock. The driver points the way, and Danny and Elijah soon find themselves maneuvering their suitcases through the alleys of Venice. The Gritti is smaller than Danny had pictured. He looks at its entrance suspiciously, while Elijah—unburdened by expectation—is more excited.

An elaborately dressed bellman glides forward and gathers their bags. Danny, momentarily confused, resists. It is only after Elijah says thank you that the suitcases are relinquished and the steps toward the registration desk are taken.

"May I help you?" an unmistakably European man asks from behind the counter. He wears an Armani smile. Elijah is impressed.

"Yes," Danny starts, leaning on the desktop. "The name is Silver. A room for two. Originally the room was under my parents' names, but they should have switched it to mine. Danny Silver. We need a room with two beds. On the canal side."

"If that's possible," Elijah adds. Danny swats him away.

The manager's smile doesn't falter. He opens a ledger and types a few keys on his computer. A temporary concern crosses his brow, but it is soon resolved.

"Yes, Silver," he says to Danny. "We have a room—a beautiful room. Two beds. That is what you requested in March. One room for Daniel and Elijah Silver."

Elijah thinks this sounds great. But Danny doesn't look happy.

"Wait a sec—" he says. "What do you mean, March? The initial reservation should have been for Rachel and Arthur Silver, not for Daniel and Elijah."

The manager checks the ledger again.

"We have no record of a change," he tells Danny. "Is this a problem?"

Danny shakes his head severely. "You see," he says to the man behind the desk, "my parents made me think this had been *their* vacation. But now you're saying that it was *our* vacation all along."

"Which is great," Elijah assures the still-confused manager. "It's just a surprise. For him especially."

"I see," the hotel manager intones, nodding solemnly. After the paperwork is completed, he produces a pair of golden keys.

45

Elijah says thank you. Danny continues to shake his head and mutters his way to the elevator. The hotel manager smiles a little wider as he hands the keys to Elijah. Beneath his coutured appearance, his sympathy is palpable.

Elijah says thank you again.

*   *   *

"I can't *believe* it." Danny also can't stop hitting the side of the elevator.

"What's the matter?" Elijah asks as they walk to their room.

"What's the matter?!? They tricked us, Elijah. Our own parents. Tricked us. I mean, I knew they meant for us to come here together. But to have had that plan all along . . ."

They are being led into the room now. It is beautiful. Even Danny has to shut up for a second, just to look out the windows at the canal. Now that the rain has been reduced to a sound, it is moodily atmospheric, mysteriously foreign.

Elijah puts his suitcase on the bed closest to the windows as Danny tips (no doubt undertips) the bellman. When Danny returns to the windows, the spell has been broken. His tirade continues.

"I just can't believe they'd be so . . . manipulative. I can't believe they could stand there and lie to us, all these months."

"I think it's kind of nice," Elijah mumbles.

"What?"

"I said it's kind of a surprise."

Elijah knows, from years of practice, that it's best to just ride the conversation through. Unpack. Nod occasionally. Pretend that Danny's right, even if he's acting like he's been set up on a hideous blind date.

The trick is, Danny doesn't particularly like to hear himself talk, especially in monologues. Halfway through a sentence, he'll realize there's no reason to go on. His point has been made, if not accepted. Like now:

47

"If only they'd . . ." Danny says with a sigh. Then he pauses, and listens to the rain outside. He realizes he's in Venice, and that his parents cannot hear him. He walks to the closet and hangs up his coat. His last sentence dangles in the air, until it is forgotten.

*   *   *

Naps and dinner. Naps and dinner. It seems to Elijah that
every family vacation revolves around naps and dinner. This vacation does not appear to be an exception. As soon as Danny
has unpacked, he kicks off his shoes and tears off the bed-
spread, thrusting it aside in a vanquished heap. They have just
arrived—they have just been sitting for countless hours—and
still Danny feels the need to lie down and close his eyes. Elijah
is mystified. Danny's behavior is perfectly predictable, and perfectly beyond understanding.

"I'm going for a walk," Elijah says.

"Be back for dinner." Danny nods for emphasis, then nods off.

Because the sky is gray and the time zones are shifty, Elijah
finds it hard to gauge the hour. He never wears a watch (his
own rebellion against time, against watching). He must rely on
the concierge to supply him with a frame of reference. It is four
in the afternoon. Two hours until dinner.

Upon leaving the Gritti, Elijah is presented with one of the
most exquisite things about Venice—there is no obvious way to
go. Although St. Mark's Square pulses in the background, and
the canals hold notions in sway, there is no grand promenade to
lead Elijah forward. There is no ready stream of pedestrians
to subsume him into its mass. Instead, he is presented with
corners—genuine corners, at which each direction makes the
same amount of sense.

Elijah walks left, and then right. And then left, and then
right. He is amazed by the narrowness of the streets. He is
amazed by the footbridges and the curving of paths. He sees

49

people from his flight and nods hello. They smile in return. They are still caught in the welcomeness rapture; they've deposited their baggage, and now they wander.

We are like freshmen, Elijah thinks. The incoming class of tourists. The upperclassmen look at them knowingly, remembering that initial rush, when every moment seems picture-perfect and the tiredness distorts the hours into something approaching surreality.

Elijah feels giddiness and delight—although he is now in Venice, he is still high on the anticipation of Venice. The trip has not settled yet. It hasn't officially begun. Instead, Elijah is staking out the territory—sometimes circling the same block three times from different directions—somehow missing the major squares and the more famous statues. Instead, he finds a small shop that sells shelves of miniature books. The shopkeeper comes over and shows Elijah a magazine the size of a postage stamp. Elijah wants to buy it for Cal, but he's forgotten to bring money. He wants to come back tomorrow, but doesn't know if he will ever be able to find the store again. He could ask for the address, but he doesn't want to travel in such a way. He wants encounters instead of plans—the magic of appearance rather than the architecture of destination.

Seconds pass with every door. Minutes pass with every street. Elijah never realizes that he's lost, so he has no trouble finding his way back. Three hours have gone by, but he doesn't know this. Night has fallen, but that seems only a matter of light and air. When Elijah returns to the hotel, he doesn't ask the concierge for the time. Instead, he asks for a postcard. He draws a smile on the back and sends it to Cal. He cannot describe the afternoon any other way. He knows she'll understand.

* * *

Danny is still asleep when Elijah returns to the room. But only for a moment.

"What took you so long?" he asks, stretching out, reaching for his watch.

"Are you ready to go?" Elijah replies. Danny grunts and puts on his shoes.

Map in hand, Danny leads the way to St. Mark's Square. His movement is propulsive, unchecked by awe or curiosity. He knows where he wants to go, and he wants to get there soon. Elijah struggles to keep up.

(*"What is taking you so long?"* Danny is on his way to the arcade and supposed to be watching his ten-year-old brother. Danny has agreed to drive Elijah and his friends to the movies and waits impatiently by the car. Danny is walking ten feet ahead to the bus stop and wants to get to his friends. Elijah is holding him back. That is the clear implication of the question. It is Elijah's fault. Elijah is left behind because he's too slow.)

As they approach St. Mark's, the streets become more crowded. Danny weaves and bobs through the fray, dodging the men and women who walk at a more leisurely pace. Elijah follows in Danny's wake, without enough time to wonder if these couples are lovers, or if the children are playing games. Finally—too soon—they arrive at the Caffè Florian. Danny barks out their name and says, "Reservation, table for two." The maitre d' smiles, and Elijah can sense him thinking to himself, *American.*

51

The restaurant unfolds like a house of mirrors—room after room, with Danny and Elijah stumbling through. Menus are procured, and the Silver brothers are shown to their table. Before he has even been seated, Danny orders wine and asks for some bread. Elijah studies his menu and wishes he knew more Italian.

The waiter is gorgeous—the kind of man, Elijah thinks, who would sweep Cal off her feet. It isn't just that he's beautiful but that his movements are beautiful. If all men looked like this waiter, there wouldn't be any need for color—just white shirts and black pants, black shoes and black ties.

Danny is more interested in the waiter's grasp of the English language (mercifully adequate). Even though Elijah is a vegetarian, Danny does not hesitate to order a rack of lamb. Elijah tries not to notice and orders penne. When it is pointed out to him that the pasta course is an appetizer, he assents to a grilled vegetable plate. The waiter seems pleased, and Elijah is pleased to have pleased him.

"So what are we going to do?" Danny asks, breaking off a piece of bread and searching for the butter.

Elijah is not sure how big this question is. He assumes it is a matter of itinerary, not relations.

"I'd like to go to the basilica," he answers, "and the Academy."

"Well, of course. Those are givens. But what else? And where's the butter?"

Elijah points to the dish of olive oil. Danny is not pleased.

"I'll never understand why people do that—olive oil is so far removed from butter. It's a totally different sensory experience, you know? It's like substituting salt for cheese. Doesn't make any sense." Danny puts down the bread. "I'd like to go to the old Jewish ghetto tomorrow morning, if that's okay with you."

Elijah is surprised. He had expected less of his brother—a search for the nearest Hard Rock Cafe, perhaps.

"We can go to the Academy when it opens," Danny continues, "and then take a vaporetto to the ghetto. The whole Sunday thing shouldn't be a problem there."

Elijah agrees, and is glad when the food comes—no need for further conversation. Which isn't to say the brothers don't talk. They do. But it's hardly conversation. Instead, it's filling the time with idle words—Danny returns to the topic of their parents' deception, and Elijah shifts gears by mentioning movies, one of the only things they can talk about easily. Even if Danny feels it's his masculine duty to disparage Merchant Ivory, at least it's something to talk about. Elijah realizes this strain in conversation now, and Danny has the same thought a few minutes later. But there is no way for the two of them to know that they have this feeling in common. It doesn't come up at the dinner table, and instead the brothers teeter in their consciousness of being together, and apart. Danny takes out his Palm Pilot and shows Elijah all of the things it can do, most of them work-related. There is something about this that strikes Elijah as familiar—Danny always loved having the latest toys. Elijah tries to share in the marvel. The main course arrives, and he tries to avoid the sight of Danny gnawing at the bones.

They do not stay for dessert. By the end of the night, all they can say is how tired they've become.

On the walk back to the hotel, Elijah realizes this is his first real adult trip. Even though he considers himself far from an adult, he can see that the trip marks some change. No parents. No teen tour counselors. No teachers chaperoning. This is what adults do. They book tickets and they travel.

If Elijah is reluctant to see himself as an adult, or even as a potential adult, seeing Danny as an adult comes easily enough. In Elijah's eyes, Danny has always been a grown-up. Less of a grown-up than their parents, but still much more of a grown-up than Elijah's friends.

Danny was always so far ahead. None of Elijah's friends had a brother who was that much older. They would gather at the Silvers' house and become Danny's congregation, Elijah included. When they played basketball in the driveway, Danny always counted as four people, so the games were six on three, five on two, four on one. He always knew how to use the right curse words at the right time. If he wanted to change the channel, they would let him. Because he thought their shows were childish, and they didn't want to be childish. They wanted to know how to solve the secret puzzles the next few years would bring.

And then there was the armpit hair. Elijah spotted it one day when Danny was wrapped in a towel, finished with the shower. He raised his arm to deodorize—and there it was. Elijah told his friends, and the next time there was a pool party, Danny was the main attraction. He had no idea why the kids kept throwing the beach ball just over his head. Armpit hair was fascinating and scary and, more than anything, grown-up.

Danny's voice was beginning to sound like he was chewing ice cubes. His body grew taller and taller, like celery shooting.

He was thirteen then, Elijah almost seven. Now, ten years later, Elijah realizes he's older than Danny was. That all of those changes have happened to him, too. The changes that nobody has any say over. The biology—"growing" and "up" as a physical matter. The changes after—Elijah has to believe they're a matter of choice. Looking at Danny used to be like looking at the future. Now looking at Danny is like looking at a future he doesn't want.

His thoughts turn to Cal, to his friends, to home. He wishes that time was a matter of choice. That you could live your life controlling the metronome—speed it up sometimes, but mostly slow it down. Stay at the party for as long as you like. Prolong the conversation until everything is known.

To feel such a longing for his own life, even as he's living it—he wonders what that means.

* * *

Elijah falls asleep as soon as he returns to the hotel. In fact, he falls asleep a few turns from the hotel, but some mental and physical anomaly conspires to keep him upright until the door of the room closes. Danny is a little more fastidious before his own collapse. He hangs up all of his clothing and studiously brushes his teeth. Then he stands for a minute in front of one of the windows. He opens it wide, so the sounds of the canal and the laughter from the bar downstairs can segue into sleep.

* * *

Danny dreams of soldiers, and Elijah dreams of wings. They wake numerous times during the night, but never at the same time. Elijah thinks he hears Danny get up to shut the window, but when he wakes up, the window is still open.

*   *   *

Morning.

Breakfast.

"You fool," Elijah says, glancing at the menu.

"What?" Danny grunts.

"I said, 'You fool.' "

Danny looks at the menu and understands.

"No," he says, "I won't quiche you."

"Quiche me, you fool! *Please!*"

"If you say that any louder, you're toast."

"Quiche me and marry me in a church, since we cantaloupe!" Elijah is giddy with the old routine.

"Orange juice kidding?" Danny gasps.

"I will milk this for all it's worth."

"You *can't* be cereal."

"I can sense you're waffling. . . ."

Danny looks up triumphantly. "There aren't any waffles on the menu! You lose!"

Elijah is surprised by how abruptly disappointed he is. *That's not the point,* he thinks. He turns away. Danny pauses for a second, watching him, not knowing what he's done. Then he shrugs, picks up an *International Herald Tribune,* and begins to read.

* * *

Danny and Elijah are both museum junkies, each in his own way. It is hard to entirely escape all vestiges of a shared parentage. From an early age, both of the Silver brothers found themselves folded into the backseat of the family car for Sunday-morning excursions to the museums of New York. There was never any traffic—driving through the city was almost like driving through a painting, the streets wider and cleaner than any New York street is supposed to be. An uncrowded city is a form of magic . . . and the magic only intensified as the museums neared. Sometimes the Silvers would walk amidst dinosaur bones and hanging whales. But most of the time, they made pilgrimages to color and light, brushstrokes and angles. Elijah saved the buttonhole entry tags from each museum as if they were coins from a higher society—the nearly Egyptian M for the Met, the hip capitalization of MoMA, each visit in a different color from the time before.

Danny fell in love with *Starry Night* long before he knew he was supposed to. Elijah would bring his *Star Wars* figures to the MoMA sculpture garden and have Princess Leia and Han Solo make a home in the smooth pocket of a Henry Moore. As they grew older (but not too much older), the brothers would hatch Saturday-night schemes to make the museums their home. As their babysitter looked on with amusement, Danny and Elijah would pore over *From the Mixed-Up Files of Mrs. Basil E. Frankweiler* as if it were both guidebook and bible—a map and a divination. Sometimes the museums' floor plans would also be consulted, the bathrooms carefully marked and noted. As the ten o'clock TV shows said their eleven o'clock goodbyes, Danny and Elijah would whisper their plans, each more elaborate than its predecessor. *We'll hide in the second-floor men's room, and when the janitor comes, we'll stand on the toilets so he can't see our legs. We'll hide under the bench in the room with the splatter painting. We'll spend the night in King Tut's tomb.*

The Sunday-morning trips began to ebb as Little League, summer camp, and adolescent resentment appeared. Danny became a teenager, which Elijah couldn't begin to understand. (Danny told him so. Repeatedly.) All plans were off, because Danny had new plans of his own. The Silvers still went to the museum together, but with the near-formality of a special occasion. These were Big Exhibition trips—mornings of Monet and afternoons of Acoustiguided El Greco.

Later on, Danny and Elijah made their own excursions into the city, sometimes with friends but most of the time alone. Danny loved MoMA, with its establishment airs and Big Artist dynamics. Elijah was more partial to the Whitney, with its Hopper despair and youth-in-revolt aspirations.

Strangely, neither Danny nor Elijah felt a strong affinity for the Met. Perhaps the Temple of Dendur fails to amaze after the twentieth visit. Perhaps the museum itself is too palatial, too expansive to ever really know.

It should be taken as a measure of Danny's true New York soul that his first reaction upon entering the Academy is a vow to spend more time at the Met, in the Renaissance rooms.

Elijah's response is a much more succinct (yet also more entire) "Wow."

There is a danger in living on a steady diet of Rothko and Pollack, Monet and Manet and Magritte. Danny and Elijah have an inkling of this now, almost immediately. They are struck, more than anything, by the details in the Academy's artwork. The faces in a painter's stonework. The downturn of a Madonna's eyes. The arrow's angle as it tears into Sebastian's side.

They do not know the stories behind all the paintings—such things weren't taught in Hebrew school. Perhaps that adds to the mystery and helps them approach in a strange state of wonder. Elijah is drawn to the paintings of Orsola—is she a martyr or a dreamer, a saint or a princess? He has no way of knowing. He asks Danny, and Danny mumbles something about enigmas. There is a happy complicity in their ignorance.

After an hour and a half, the Madonnas begin to look too much alike, and the Jesus babies are growing more grotesque in their bald adultness. Danny and Elijah are both losing sight of the details—it is harder to focus, and Danny is becoming restless. He wants to get to the synagogue in time for the noon tour. There will be more time for Art later.

They both agree on this.

A city presents many different faces, and it is up to the traveler to assemble the proper composite. Venice seems, at first, to be a simple enough city to render. It is the canals, the basilica, the shutters on the homes. It is the gondolier's call and the beat of the pigeon's wing and the church bell that chimes to mark the passing of an hour. To many people, this is all, and this is enough. A tourist does not want to be weighed down by realities, unless the realities are presented as monumental stories.

It takes a traveler, not a tourist, to search for something deeper. Travelers want to find the wavelength on which they and the city connect.

Danny is drawn to the ghetto. None of his immediate ancestors ever set foot in Venice (or Italy, for that matter). None of his friends have ever spent time there. He has never read or dreamed about life in such a place. And yet this is the destination he has chosen within a city of destinations.

(Elijah comes too and is moved and affected, but not in the same way. This is not what he has visited for. For him, the city is much more elusive, and will not know where he wants to be until he actually gets there.)

According to the museum in the ghetto, eight thousand Italian Jews were sent to concentration camps during the Holocaust.

Only eight of them returned to Venice.

This is the fact to which Danny attaches himself. If the ghetto itself is the bell, this fact is the toll.

The word "ghetto" comes from the Venetian *jeto*, which means "foundry." The island upon which the Jews originally settled was formerly a foundry area (Danny learns). But the Jews, newly arrived from Germany and Eastern European countries, couldn't pronounce the soft *j* and instead called it *geto*. In the sixteenth century, the Jews were locked in from midnight to dawn; they became usurers because most other businesses were prohibited. (*Hence Shylock*, Danny thinks. *The Merchant of Venice* was the closest he came to finding meaning in Shakespeare in college.)

At one point in the ghetto, Jews had to wear yellow hats or scarves whenever they went out. Danny notes the color yellow—how can he not? The past reverberates so clearly, later on. Yellow hats, yellow stars.

As Elijah waits in the courtyard, Danny stands in the shade of a Sephardic synagogue—still in use, saved from the World War II bombings by an ironic alliance made between the Germans and the Italians. People begin to gather for the tour—a small, quiet group, almost all of them American.

The inside of the synagogue is dominated by black wood-work and red curtains. There is a separate section for women—a shielded balcony, high beyond the pulpit. The guide jokes that this means women are closer to God. Only the men laugh.

The guide goes on to say that there are now 600 Jews in all of Venice. Danny feels his somberness confirmed—how else can one feel when surrounded by such a majority of ghosts? You can find sorrow in the arithmetic, and you can find a bittersweet hope.

After the synagogue, Danny sees things differently. It's not that he's religious—at best, he would like to believe in God, if only he could believe it. Instead, his identity asserts itself. He sits in the plaza outside the temple and thinks about the 600 and what a crazy life they must lead. He wonders what it must be like to live in a place where Christ is in every doorway—well, maybe not *every* doorway, but he's sure it must seem that way. In American terms, it must be like living in the Bible Belt— with Christmas all year round.

Danny has these thoughts, but he doesn't share them. He can see that Elijah isn't in a similar space. Instead, he is sitting (shoelaces untied) in the sunniest corner of the plaza, watching a little redheaded girl in pink plastic sunglasses as she charges an unsuspecting flock of pigeons. There is a flash-flutter of wings—Elijah hunches over as the birds throw themselves skyward and fly thoughtlessly over the bench where he sits.

There is a small Judaica store open off the square. Danny walks to the window, but he doesn't go inside. Instead, he looks at the stained-glass kiddush cups and the tiny scrolls of the translucent mezuzot. Women from the synagogue tour step in- side the store and touch the cases reverently. Danny turns away. He wants to go inside, but he doesn't want to go inside. It's his place, but it's not his place. Elijah is walking over now, and Danny allows this to be a cue to leave.

They walk for some time without speaking. But this is a dif- ferent non-speaking than it was before. Danny is still deep in his thoughts, and Elijah is letting him stay there.

Finally, Danny speaks, and what he says is, "It's incredible, really." Then he stops and points back to the synagogue and says he can't imagine. He just can't imagine. Elijah listens as Danny wonders how such things can happen, what lesson could possi- bly be learned.

"I don't know," Elijah says. He thinks of their parents, and how they'd be glad that their sons were here, thinking about it.

"All this history . . . ," Danny says, then trails off. Lost in it. Feeling it connect. Realizing the weight of the world comes largely from its past.

Although it is such a singular word, there are many variations of *alone*. There is the alone of an empty beach at twilight. There is the alone of an empty hotel room. There is the alone of being caught in a throng of people. There is the alone of missing a particular person. And there is the alone of being with a particular person and realizing you are still alone.

Elijah parts with Danny in St. Mark's Square and is at first disoriented. The courtyard is filled with thousands of people, speaking what seem to be thousands of languages. People are moving in such an everywhere direction that there is simply nowhere to go without firm resolution. Elijah's first instinct is to steal a quiet corner, to purchase a postcard from a hundred-lire stall and write to Cal about all the people and the birds and the way tourists stop to check their watches every time the bell tolls. He would sign the postcard *Wish you were here,* and he would mean it—because that would be his big threepenny wishing-well birthday-candle wish, if one were granted by a passerby. Cal would make him smile, and Cal would make him laugh, and Cal would take his hand so they could waltz where there was no space to waltz and run where there was no room to run. He thinks about her all the time.

Elijah finds a postcard and sits down to write, drawing a picture of the basilica above Cal's address. Then he files the postcard in his pocket for future delivery and wonders what to do. The alleys leave little room to think. So Elijah makes a decision not to decide. He steps into the crowd and gives in.

It is Elijah's rare talent—a talent he doesn't realize—to be surrounded by strangers and not feel alone. As soon as he steps into the rush of people, he is engaged. He is amazed through the power of watching, bewitched by the searching. As he is led from St. Mark's to the walk beside the canal, he scans the crowd for beautiful people he will never know. He smiles as large groups struggle to stay together. Young children swoop beside his legs as old men lazily push strollers. Vendors sell the same cheap T-shirts at five-foot intervals. A band from a canal-side hotel plays, and mothers call their daughters away from the sea.

If you wanted to reassemble Elijah's afternoon, you probably could do it by stringing together all the photographs and all of the frames of videotape that he walks into. Always a passerby, he is immortalized and unknown.

Farther from St. Mark's, the people fall away and the noise dies down. Strange sculptures appear—enormous anchors and acrobatic steel beams. Elijah figures these are just part of the landscape—the New City's wink at the Old City.

And then he finds the Biennial.

* * *

One night, deep in December, Cal had asked: *"Do you won-der why we wander?"*

The answer, Elijah now realizes, is: *Discovery.*

In an age of guidebooks, websites, and radio waves, discov-ery has nearly become a lost feeling. If anything, it is now a mat-ter of expectations to surpass—rarely a matter of unexpected wonderment. It is unusual to find a situation that appears with-out word, or a place that was not known to be on the road.

As Elijah buys his ticket and enters the Biennial exhibition, he feels not only discovery but also a discovery of discovery. It's a spiritual rush, and it leaves him buoyant. He feels the antithe-sis of alone, because he is in the company of circumstance.

This is so cool, he thinks—this is his vocabulary of rhapsody. He has entered (for lack of a better reference) an Art World EPCOT Center, each country's pavilion beckoning him for-ward. The afternoon is growing late, and the crowd has thinned out to a devoutly quiet core.

Elijah walks into the Spanish pavilion and stands before an abstract angel made from golden wire. Even though it doesn't move, Elijah can feel the angel lift. Serendipity is a narcotic, and Elijah is under its sway. He stares at the angel until he can feel it watermark his memory of the day. Then, giddy and awed, he moves on.

Whether keenly striking or laughably awful, contemporary art is rarely unentertaining. Within its elaborately constructed pavilions, the Biennial demonstrates this appropriately. In Belgium, Elijah finds a series of open white (plaster?) containers. Luxembourg is populated by lawn chairs with the word "SAMPLE" placed in the corner (*perhaps*, Elijah thinks too easily, *they were desperate for artists from Luxembourg*). Holland features films of a girl flipping off a wall (her bloomers show) and of a man showering gratuitously. In addition, lightbulbs with nipples (there's no better way to describe them) litter the floor.

Elijah finds this more amusing than any so-called amusement park. Then he enters the strange world of the Japanese exhibit. Its lower level is devoted to repetitive photos of black-and-white cells. Elijah walks upstairs, and there is a burst of color—brilliant spectrum cellscapes viewed from a wooden walkway on the outskirts of an inner lake. Elijah is dazzled. He goes through three times and then makes his way to the French pavilion, which is filled with smashed auto cubes.

Elijah wants to call Danny, because he feels it's near criminal to allow his brother to miss such a strangely magical place. But Elijah doesn't know the phone number of the hotel—he doesn't even know how to make a call from an Italian phone booth. So he vows to make Danny come tomorrow, and even decides to accompany him, if need be.

The epigram for the Russian exhibit is "Reason is something the world must obtain whether it wants to or not." At the center of the pavilion is a container (large, metal) with a hole in it—the sign above it reads, *Donate for artificial reason*. Elijah reaches into his wallet and pulls out a crumpled American dollar. Then he moves on—to delicate paintings of violent acts and sculptured mazes scored by ominous music.

The narcotic of serendipity numbs his sense of time. The afternoon is over before Elijah has a chance to recognize it. An announcement is made in five languages—the exhibition will soon be closing. Elijah wanders to the gift shop and buys a few more postcards for Cal. Then he steps through the gate, back into the expected world. He looks to the exhibition sign and learns that the Biennial is closed tomorrow. Danny is out of luck. Elijah is disappointed. And at the same time, he is relieved. Not because the experience will solely be his (really, he wants Danny to see it). But instead because he knows deep in his heart that it would be foolish to return.

Discovery cannot be revisited.

* * *

"Do you wonder why we wander?" Cal had asked.

It was the night of the first snow; you could hear the branches bending and the icicles falling outside the window, beyond the wall.

They were warmth together. They were hot breath and blankets and wrapping themselves close.

And Elijah had thought, *I wonder why I never kiss you. I wonder what would happen.*

But he didn't say anything out loud.

*　*　*

Danny and Elijah had been walking the back way to school—even though Danny's first bell rang twenty minutes earlier than Elijah's, they usually walked together, with Danny dropping Elijah off at the playground before heading to middle school.

The back way went by the brook, by the strand of trees that the boys could call a forest without feeling any doubt. Sometimes along the way they found signs of trespass—teenage beer cans, hand-smashed or misplaced intact; gum wrappers folded into the ground; once, a high-heeled shoe.

That morning, they found a large spool of red twine. Elijah picked it up, the twine end pointing out like a tail.

"Let's tie the trees together," he suggested.

And Danny said, "Sure."

They tied the tail end to a branch—Elijah looping it like a shoelace, Danny double-knotting so it would hold. Then they ran randomly from tree to tree, sometimes throwing the spool high to get a branch that was just out of reach, other times dipping low to let the lowest of bushes in on the action.

They laughed, they looped, they were hopelessly late for school.

There was no way to explain it, so neither of them tried.

* * *

As Elijah wanders through the Biennial, Danny is in an-other part of town, altering his concept of nationality. At first, he thought he had it figured out: the American tourists were the loud walkers with Chicago Bulls T-shirts, and the Euro-peans were the teeter-walkers with an unfortunate propensity toward dark socks. But no. That was not the case at all.

Take baseball caps. Danny initially assumed that anyone wearing a baseball cap was from the U.S.—after all, baseball is not exactly America's most exportable pastime. But does that matter? No. Alongside postcards and Venezia T-shirts, street vendors are flush with New York Yankees, Washington Redskins, and Dartmouth (*Dartmouth?*) paraphernalia.

Even in the Doges' Palace, things are askew. Danny stands beside an Ethan Hawke look-alike who is clearly a semester-abroad NYU student. Then Ethan opens his mouth and speaks an unintelligible language. Danny retreats to the side of a glam-orous woman with a Spanish complexion and raven hair. She speaks fluent Brooklyn, albeit with a curator's vocabulary. (To her, the subtle curve of a David is a "mask-uline ref-rence to thuh fem-nin ark-uh-type.") Danny is confounded—the Europeans are trying to be American, the Americans are trying to be European, and the Japanese are furiously upholding their stereotype by taking a horrendous number of snapshots for no clear reason.

Internationality is a German teenager in Venice wearing a Carolina Panthers jersey. (Danny passes three of them as he leaves the museum.)

73

And if this is internationality . . . where does that leave nationality? Danny has a fierce desire to identify Americans. Finally, he realizes: you can tell an American not by the American-ness of his T-shirt but by the level of its obscurity. For example, if the shirt reads "Snoopy" or "New Jersey Sports" or (especially) "U.S.A.," odds are it's not an American. But if the shirt says "Lafayette College Homecoming Weekend" or "Paul Simon in Central Park," odds are it's an American in front of you.

Danny takes comfort in a stranger's Habitat for Humanity T-shirt as he walks back to the hotel. It is his way of keeping in touch with home.

* * *

Elijah leaves the Biennial and walks straight into an adjacent park. There are flowers everywhere. Elijah knows it's quite simple, but such things make him happy anyway. Old people sit on benches and talk boldly to one another. The women in particular make an impression on Elijah—old women in America don't seem as loud and animated and free. On the streets of Manhattan, it always seems like they travel alone, stooped, on their way from the grocery, toward somewhere equally unpleasant. But the Italian women don't look like abandoned grandmothers. They appear in flocks. They seem to know more.

Walking slowly, Elijah passes a man taking a picture of someone else's clothesline. It is, like all snapshots, a stolen image. The man clicks the shutter, then leaves guiltily.

The afternoon has now dimmed into evening. Candles are lit on cafe tables. The alleyways grow ominous, the crowds more unruly. It is as if twilight unleashes a darker undertow. Elijah feels the turn as the day goes from wistful to stark. The streets are so narrow they cry for confusion and claustrophobia. They desire speed, the rush of running through a maze. *It is like a movie*, Elijah thinks. *A James Bond movie.* There is no speed limit for pedestrians. It isn't like he's poolside—*no running allowed*. Unencumbered by packages, still high on the day, Elijah decides to bolt.

Bystanders are surprised. Elijah has been casually walking along. Now he runs as if he's being chased by KGB agents. It isn't entirely like a James Bond movie—he is careful not to knock down passersby or vendors of fruit.

As he gains speed, the streets seem to narrow further. The buildings threaten to cave in on him. The corners are sharper than before. The back of his coat trails in the air. Elijah wants to whoop with joy—running every which way, catapulting himself over bridges, a fascinating streak in a photo that will be developed weeks from now. He is tired, but he's free. He is living, because he's in motion.

Exhilaration.

Acceleration.

Exhilaration.

Acceleration.

Stop.

He almost runs into the wall of people. He is flying along, and then the crowd looms like a dead end. He could turn around, but curiosity encourages momentum. He touches the back of the crowd and then makes his way forward.

"Doctor? *Medico?*" a small female voice cries from somewhere in the front. Elijah pushes forward some more and then sees the girl and her distress. She is holding the same travel dictionary that Danny carries. "*Può chiamare un medico, per favore?*" From her accent, it's clear she took French in high school.

At her feet, a guy lies bleeding. Elijah steps back. He stares at the wound and then traces its trail to the pavement. The guy and the girl, both easily American, are no more than a year older than Elijah. The guy is bleeding, but he's also trying to smile. Elijah immediately feels a kinship and offers help.

He looks at the young man's wound. It doesn't seem too serious—the girl explains that he tripped on a wet stone and hit his head. She wonders whether he should be moved. No one in the crowd seems to have the answer—many are starting to walk away.

The young man rests his head on an L.L. Bean backpack. Elijah introduces himself and pulls a Kleenex out of his pocket to help stanch the flow of blood. The young man—Greg—is calmer than his partner—Isabel. As she frantically procures a handkerchief from a shopkeeper, he tells Elijah it's really not so bad.

"Liar," Isabel says. "The shopkeeper said help is on the way. Do you know what the Italian word for 'stitches' is? It's not in this stupid dictionary."

Just then, help arrives. Elijah almost laughs. The "ambulance" is a wicker chair placed on a wheeled cart. Elijah moves away from Greg as two men lift him into position. The blood has now spread over his shirtfront in baby-food dribbles. Despite his Eddie Bauer wardrobe, Greg looks like a bloodied prisoner being taken to the gallows. Isabel steps from one side of the chair to the other—she doesn't know where to be. Elijah hands her the backpack and stands to follow. But the paramedics are already on the move, with Isabel running hastily behind them. Greg looks over, one hand holding the Kleenex to his brow, the other hand raised in a Tom Hanks salute.

Elijah watches the chair disappear around a corner and immediately feels a loss. He can't believe that you can meet a person in this way and then lose touch with them forever. He could check all the hotels in Venice and look for a Greg and an Isabel, but he knows he won't. He wants to, though. Because he wants to believe in sudden fate.

The crowd has dispersed. People are obliviously stepping

across the lines of blood, turning them into streaks and foot-prints. Those people who didn't see the incident look at the stain with disgust and dismay. Elijah just stares—his momen-tum is over, his giddiness lost. A hand touches his shoulder.

"I'm sure he'll be fine," a voice says. Elijah turns around, and there she is—easily one of the loveliest girls he's ever seen. She has short brown hair—light brown—and dazzling azure eyes. Her complexion is smooth. (Elijah, who never notices these things, not even when stoned, suddenly notices them now.) She isn't wearing any make-up. She looks twenty, give or take a year. And she is concerned about him. He sees that right away.

Elijah is afraid to speak, for fear that any word he says will come out as "uh."

"What you did was very nice," the girl continues.

"Thank you."

They hang on a pause. Elijah looks to the ground, looks back up, and she's still there.

A second pause will lead to departure. Elijah wants her to stay, so he gives her his name.

"I'm Elijah."

"Nice to meet you, Elijah. I'm Julia."

A bell chimes. Then three bells, and five bells, and seven bells at once.

It is six o'clock.

"Oh my God, I'm late!" Julia's eyes flash a genuine panic. Then they refocus on Elijah.

She touches his forearm.

"I'll see you soon. I promise."

And there is, that moment, a shock of recognition. Elijah doesn't even know yet what he is recognizing. There is only the shock. The sense. That feeling of something happening that was meant to happen. Two people fitting in a space and time.

For a moment.

Julia smiles *sorry* at him and then is gone.

Elijah stands still. Julia is the kind of person who leaves a vapor trail. Traces of an accent, carried into memory. A perfume of kindness and expectation. A strange sense of certainty.

Elijah cannot explain it. The *I'll see you soon* could be mistaken for a generic farewell. The *I promise* cannot be.

Julia knows she will see him soon.

He hopes she's right.

* * *

It is quiet when Elijah returns to the room. It is quiet, but not completely silent. Danny's breathing is as barely noticeable as the rise and fall of his body.

As Elijah steps gently over the floorboards, a bigger sound arrives. Underneath the hotel windows, a gondolier begins to sing with great passion, to cheers from all along the waterway. Elijah peers out and watches as other gondoliers move closer to be nearer to the first gondolier's boat. An accordion begins. Elijah opens a window wide. The only smell is the breeze. Even though the water is a churnish brown, for a moment Elijah can imagine it's a sapphire blue. That is how he feels. The gondolier is passing by, leaving the sound of the waves and an undertow from the Gritti's cafe.

This is why we go on holiday, Elijah thinks. *You can't get moments like this at home. The familiar can only bring another kind of wonderful.*

Even though the sun is lowering, even though there are dinner reservations to be upheld and clothes to change, Elijah lets Danny sleep. He pulls a chair to the window and takes Dickens's *Pictures from Italy* from his bag. He reads five pages and then, on his sixth page, he finds these words:

"Sunday was a day so bright and blue: so cloudless, balmy, wonderfully bright . . . that all the previous bad weather vanished from the recollection in a moment."

And Elijah thinks, *That is exactly it.*

The serendipity of the printed page.

* * *

Danny wakes up as Elijah turns the twenty-first page of that day. He is happy until he looks at his watch (sitting guiltily on the bedside table). Then he becomes frantic.

"Why didn't you wake me?" he accuses as he pulls on his pants. He can't help it—he feels sabotaged.

"I'm sorry," Elijah says in a tone that isn't sorry at all.

Danny hustles Elijah out of the room and orders the concierge to call the restaurant and pronounce a delay. Elijah is glad he spent the afternoon wandering, because Danny sprints him to the vaporetto so fast that there isn't much time to look at anything. Even on the boat, the air between them is tense and time-concerned. Elijah wants to let go of Danny's thoughts—after all, no amount of grimacing will make the boat go faster. But Danny's aggravation is inescapable. It imposes.

Elijah closes his eyes and thinks of Julia. He tries to count the number of words they exchanged—whatever the number is, it is unbelievably small. There is no real reason for Elijah to be thinking about her with such wistful longing. And yet, it is exactly because there's no real reason that the emotion is more intriguing.

After a time—a time filled with water and alleyways—they arrive at Antico Capriccio. It is a tiny restaurant, on the corner of somewhere and nowhere. It has been recommended by a friend of a friend of Danny's. He had to mention the friend of a friend's name when making the reservation—the Continental equivalent of a secret handshake.

They are greeted at the door by an old man named Joseph.

It soon becomes clear that he is owner and waiter, maitre d' and busboy. Whenever possible, he stays out of the kitchen. That is his wife's territory.

Joseph doesn't speak much English, and doesn't care to hear it anyway. Danny starts to ask if Visa is accepted, but Joseph brushes the question away like a foul odor. Chatting amiably, he seats Danny and Elijah by an ancient fireplace. They are the only ones in the restaurant—or, at the very least, the only ones they can see. Joseph brings them wine before they even see the menus. Danny tries to protest—he prefers white to red. But Elijah takes the wine gladly; just the sight of it makes him feel warm.

The menus are entirely in Italian. Danny and Elijah both feel the need for Danny's travel dictionary, but they are too abashed to take it out. It doesn't matter anyway—when an answer isn't immediately forthcoming, Joseph pulls the menus from their hands and orders for them. He clearly revels in their confusion, but not in a mean-spirited, French way. *Let me take care of you,* his smile says. Elijah relaxes and submits willingly after it is made clear that he is *vegetariano.* Danny has never been able to submit willingly to anything besides his boss's whims. He is not about to start now. He asks if the fish is good. Joseph laughs and walks away.

"So how was your day?" Danny asks, his fingers tapping the table.

"Fine."

"Where did you go?"

"Around."

"The weather was good?"

"Yeah."

"It didn't rain?"

"Nope."

"That's good."

"Yeah."

Talking like this is like throwing small, round stones—nothing can be built from them, except perhaps the cairn of a lost conversation. Neither brother is trying. Instead, they are filling the space, united by their mutual dislike of awkward silence.

Joseph returns to light a candle. Elijah spots a medal on his lapel and asks if he's ever been in a war. This is clearly the right question to ask. Joseph takes the medal from his jacket and lets Elijah hold it in his hand. In a river of Italian broken by crags of English, he talks about his days in the military—*il paese, il fiume, la morte.* Elijah hears the word *diciannove,* but cannot tell whether it is an age or a number of years.

As Joseph leaves to compel the first course, Elijah finds himself thinking once more about Julia. It surprises him—to be hearing an old man's reminiscence of the war one moment, and to be recalling her eyes in the next. The segue is in the storytelling—he sees Joseph's words as something he wants to share with Julia. He doesn't know whether he'll ever see her again, but still he feels the need to tell her things.

How strange, he thinks. *How very strange.*

His hope to see her again is prayerful—not because it is addressed to a spirit, but because it is mysteriously drawn from an unknown part of his soul.

My soul. How very strange.

"So how's your girlfriend?" Danny asks. Elijah is jarred—how could Danny know about Julia—and why would he call her that?

Danny sees the confusion on Elijah's face and tries again. "You know—what's her name—Cat?"

"Cat?"

"You know, the girl you hang out with."

"Oh. Cal."

"Yeah, Cal."

"She's not my girlfriend."

"Whatever you say."

Elijah thinks about Cal and feels a vague sort of distance. For the first time, she seems out of reach. All of their Wonder Twin Telepathic Powers have failed him. "*Whenever you need me*," she'd say, "*wiggle your ears.*" Elijah never had the heart to tell her he couldn't wiggle his ears. He'd just smile and nod, and know (wiggle or not) they would never have distance, even when they were apart.

But now—what does it mean? Cal is suddenly a home-movie presence. The feeling of non-feeling is inescapable. Elijah assumes it will pass. He reasons it out—in a corner of a restaurant in a corner of a city, it is natural to feel Away and Apart. As soon as he gets back to the hotel, he'll be able to pull out his Magic 8 Ball keychain and conjure Cal from the radio-waved ether. Simple as that.

As Elijah drifts off and Joseph mercifully brings the first course, Danny's thoughts also turn to the distance from home. He thinks about voice mail and conference calls, even though he hates himself for doing so. He's not so far gone that he doesn't know such thoughts are inappropriate. But such thoughts bring urgency to his life. Without them, he would have no clear game to play.

"Remind me to call Allison when we get back to the hotel," he tells Elijah.

"Allison?" Elijah echoes with a distinct question mark.

"Yes. She's working on the ranch-dressing account with me. I need to check in with her. See what's going on."

"Oh." Elijah's curiosity deflates.

"We're supposed to get the shooting script in for this great ad. Spike Lee might direct it."

"Oh."

You'd think I had the most boring job in the world, Danny sighs to himself. *You'd think I was an accountant. Or a dentist. I mean, Spike Lee's a big deal. Advertising is as creative as being a snotty English-major-in-training.* Elijah's problem, in Danny's mind, is that he has no sense of what it takes to make a living.

Danny's problem, in Elijah's mind, is that he has no sense of what it takes to make a life.

When Danny mentioned Allison's name, Elijah had been hoping she was a girlfriend. Danny used to have dozens of girlfriends, most of them nicer to Elijah than Danny himself. In high school, Marjorie Keener had brought along an extra flower for Elijah when she picked Danny up for the prom. Angelica, Danny's freshman-year college girlfriend, had spent most of their spring break playing Boggle with Elijah until the wee hours of the morning. (Danny never played, because Danny always lost.) Sophie—from junior year—had been cool, even if Elijah had spotted her eating disorder before Danny ever noticed. That relationship didn't last very long.

Now Danny didn't have anyone. He had Allison—an office full of Allisons. No doubt the only thing he ever shared with them was an elevator ride.

"So how's your job going this summer?" Danny asks. He's already plowed through his pasta. Elijah has taken two bites.

"It's okay," Elijah replies. He'd almost forgotten about working in his school's admissions office. It was that kind of job.

"So you sort through applications?"

"Nah. We just file last year's applications. There was this one girl—she painted her whole room the school colors and sent in a photo with her holding a paintbrush. Just to get in."

"Did she get in?"

"Yes, actually."

"And that's all you do all day—file? Will that get you into college?"

"Well, we can't all be in *advertising.*"

"What is *that* supposed to mean?"

"Nothing."

Elijah bends back over his pasta. Danny tries to signal Joseph for more wine, but Joseph is nowhere to be found.

Danny and Elijah are both struck by the abruptness of their conversation. They both know they've gone a little bit too far. They've broken their unwritten agreement—they are allowed to gibe each other, but it's never supposed to get too personal.

Danny had always been too old to beat up Elijah. Even to a ten-year-old, a seven-year difference seems unfair. Danny was not above using force to get his way—an arm twist for the remote control or a shove to get the front seat. But it was not the habitual violence symptomatic of a usual brother-brother relationship.

Instead, Danny showed Elijah the depth of his disdain.

There were times of pure love, for sure. But when Danny wanted to strike out, he did it with a shrug, not a fist. If he wanted to, he could pretend Elijah wasn't there. Elijah could preen or caterwaul—whatever he did, he only made it worse in Danny's eyes. Eventually, Elijah gave up. He found his own private universe. And he learned his own form of disdain.

The bad can be found in anything. It is so much easier to find than the good. So when Elijah hears *advertising*, he thinks *sellout* and *phony* and *liar*. Most of all, he thinks, *My brother is so different from me. He is so wrong.*

And when Danny hears *I'm going to be an English major when I get to college*, he thinks *pothead fallback* and *no sense of reality* and *penniless.* He thinks, *Anything but me.*

Perhaps Joseph senses this divide as he brings the main course. He has brought them different dishes, but knows they will not share. There is sadness in his eyes, because he knows they will not experience the full joy of the meal.

The meal is, in fact, one of the best they've ever had. Even Elijah, who never thinks of food as something that can be enjoyed like a CD, is enraptured.

It is an experience they will talk about for years to come. And, more important, it is a meal they can talk about for the rest of the evening, all the way back to the hotel.

Elijah is nervous when the time comes to pay the check and leave the tip. But Danny surprises him by leaving thirty percent. They both chorus Joseph with thank-yous before they leave into the night. Joseph smiles and pats the two brothers on the back. He watches as they slowly walk to the vaporetto station. Then he returns to their table and pushes the chairs together before he leaves.

* * *

They are due to visit Murano the next morning.

Elijah cannot believe it is already their last day in Venice. He feels like he's only just arrived. The prospect of Florence (and furthermore Rome) excites him, but not as much as before. It is the traveler's great dilemma. When he arrived, Elijah had felt he was wandering over vast sands. Now he realizes he's been in an hourglass the whole time.

Will that get you into college?—Danny's words from last night. His question. The ever-present question.

The applications lie in unopened envelopes. Cal has put them in alphabetical order on his desk. She scribbles comments under the postmarks, the things she's found from visits he hasn't made, information sessions he hasn't even considered.

He knows he's supposed to hate high school. Everybody says they hate high school. The cliques, the insecurity, the pressure. But Elijah has somehow found a place that he loves. It is not childhood. It is not adulthood. It is now, and it too resides in the hourglass.

He'd chosen a high school his brother had never been. Teachers who had never heard Danny's name. Hallways that wouldn't bear his echo. He hadn't been sent away, although maybe he'd made it sound that way to the friends he was leaving back home. But he had wanted to go. He had wanted to live there and sleep there and wake there. He had wanted to be somewhere entirely new. Not because of Danny or his parents, who were at first a little sad about him going away, but then felt better when he said it was about getting a different experience, not about escaping. Funny, but at the time it had seemed like a grown-up thing to do. *Planning for your future*, his father had said. Once he got there, though, the future was the last thing on his mind. When he went home to his parents and his old friends, that was the past. And Cal and Ivan and the others were the present. The future? Maybe Danny was the future. But less so. The avoidable future.

Elijah lies awake for an hour before he rises from the hotel bed. He drifts from the past to the near past. He wishes memory could be as easy as breathing.

Thoughts of Julia begin to blur within the air.

The sound of small waves seems to bring on the daylight.

* * *

Danny has trouble waking up. The time zones have finally caught up with him. Reluctantly, he gets dressed and plods his way to breakfast with Elijah. He realizes he has become a full member of the Society of Temporary Expatriates—the dining area is filled with people from their flight or from the synagogue or from loud American conversations on the street. Danny feels a displaced sense of community. Even on the vaporetto ride to Murano, he spots a teenager from the plane, who was wearing a Wolverines T-shirt yesterday and now pledges sartorial allegiance to the Bulls.

Murano is an island known throughout the world for its glass. Danny is surprised to find that most of its buildings are stone. With jet-lag weariness, he allows himself to be led to kilns and hammerings. He admires without touching. He is amazed when color appears from the wand of the glassblower. He expects to find the glass clear, but instead discovers it rimmed with red or blue.

By the third stop, Danny is ready to leave. He feels very much like his reflection—worn out and only vaguely present. Elijah is kept awake by his wonder. Danny subsides.

"A nap," he says. But Elijah isn't listening. He is looking around, as if for someone else.

"Who are you looking for?" Danny asks.

"No one," Elijah replies, focusing now.

Yeah, right, Danny thinks. He figures his brother is looking for some old lady he helped to cross the street. Or maybe that girl from the plane who wouldn't shut up about herself.

"Do you want to go back for a quick nap before we leave?" Danny asks, even though it's only eleven.

Elijah nods. He wants to go back.

But he doesn't have any intention of napping.

* * *

The laws of gravity vary from city to city. In Venice, the laws state that no matter where you want to go, you will always be drawn back to St. Mark's Square. Even though you know it will be immensely crowded, and even though you have nothing in particular to do there, you will still feel yourself drawn.

Elijah diverges from Danny at the gates of the hotel and finds himself gravitating. He moves as if he knows the place. It is a spiritual familiarity.

Past the coffee bars and through the crowds of pigeons, Elijah heads for the basilica. It is busy, as it always is. There are numerous signs prohibiting photography. Some tourists rankle at this and fail to put their cameras away. Others would never imagine taking a photograph in such a place. They stand solemnly before the statues and say prayers of thanks or pain.

Elijah pays his admission and walks into the entryway. Immediately he is amazed by the floors. Marble of every color—triangles and squares dancing in greater shapes. As others rush past, Elijah kneels down. He runs his hand over the marble. Other people stop to watch him, and it is only then that they too see the floors. Elijah is overwhelmed by the sheer fact of all the people who have walked over this very spot. As he watches Nikes and loafers glide past, he tries to fathom the feet of centuries ago. A person could stay in this same place his whole life and meet millions of people from all over the world. But instead, everyone moves on, and meets no one.

From the floor, Elijah looks to the ceiling—all gold tile and mural, epic scenes and godly interventions. The ceilings speak a different language from the floors. Both are art, but the ceilings are story while the floors are mathematic. People walk between, every single one of them a foreigner.

Elijah stands back up and re-enters the flow. He veers toward the corners, delicate shrines that counterbalance the immensity of the building. He stops in front of a saint he doesn't know. Candles flicker at her feet. Elijah loves the ceremony of candles—his mother waving her hands over the flames on Shabbat, or the two memorial candles that beacon through the house on Yom Kippur. This is, of course, a different context. Yet Elijah is tempted to light a candle, just the same. He puts three thousand lire in the box and pulls a candle from its stand.

He'll light one for Cal. She's Christian, so that must be legal.

He wonders what she'd wish for. He wonders what she'd want to tell the saint.

He touches the wick against another candle. He wonders if its wish transfers with the flame.

The wax drips onto his hand. An old woman shuffles up and takes a candle for herself.

Cal. Cal. Cal.

"Happiness," Elijah whispers. Then he places the candle at the altar. The wax cools on his hand as he pulls away.

The old woman lights her candle, and a smile flickers across her face. Elijah thinks of birthdays, and wonders why birthday wishes aren't made when the candles are lit. If he could have his way, candles would never be blown out.

After a few minutes of candle staring, he drops some extra coins into the candle box. Not for the candle, but for all candles. No payback necessary.

* * *

Back at the hotel, Danny realizes too late that it's too early to take a nap. He wrestles across his bed and tries to contort himself into sleepfulness, but it's no use. After a half hour of impatient waking, Danny shifts to the side of the bed and picks up the phone. It takes a showdown with a contentious operator (who seemingly wouldn't know an AT&T calling card if it rode a gondola up to her desk) for Danny to place a call to his voice mail. There are nine new messages, which makes Danny happy, even as he mentally chastises all the people who have left him messages when his outgoing message clearly states that he is away.

*4 to save, *6 to delete, *1 to respond. These dialing commands have become an essential part of Danny's being, his voice-mail mantra. Even after a live phone conversation, Danny finds himself hitting *6 to erase what he's just heard. Now he plows through the messages with corporate efficiency. He is happy to hear that there aren't any emergencies, and he is happy to hear that not much else is happening, either. Message six is from Cody in Legal, who informs Danny that one of his catchphrases has just been registered for trademarking. Danny smiles at that and forwards the message to Allison. He tells her he loves to be working in a country where the phrase "All the Oil You Need" can be owned.

After listening through the messages (sometimes twice), Danny faces a different set of options. *1 to record a message, *8 to change a message, *3 to listen to saved messages. Danny *1s his work-friend John, just to say hey. Then he *1s Allison to tell her all is well and that he hopes work isn't too chaotic with him gone. As soon as he's hit the # key to end, he realizes he has something more to say, so he *1s her again and tells her he hopes she's not working too too late. Then he phones his assistant and says the same thing. He thinks about *1ing Gladner or Gladner to thank them for the time off. But even he sees how ridiculous this would sound, especially since they've sent him away to think of things other than work.

Impulsively—reluctant to hang up quite yet—Danny hits *3. Then he lies back on the bed and closes his eyes.

You have eight old messages, the voice-mail femail says. *Your first message is one year, five months, and twelve days old.*

Cue: The *Twilight Zone* theme. Starting with a click of the tape recorder, then growing louder.

"Yes, folks, we've entered a world of bright lights and big cities . . . a world of wine, women, and thongs . . . a world where debutantes still roam the SoHo plains in search of the perfect two-hundred-dollar T-shirt bargain. Yes, we have entered . . . the Danny Zone! Do-do-do-do Do-do-do-do. My name is Enigo Montoya, but you can call me Will for short. I will soon be entering the Danny Zone and need to arrange the peculiars. So PLEASE give a call back at 415-66—hell, you can use your ESP to complete the number. I eagerly await your call. If you don't call back in fifteen seconds, I will self-destruct. Fifteen. Fourteen. Thirteen . . ."

One year, five months, and twelve days old. Which would make it one year, five months, and two days since he last saw Will, his best friend in the whole wide world—until the whole wide world intervened. He had flown in five days after the message, while Danny was caught in a tempest of work.

"Can you make time?" Will had asked.

"I can't make time," Danny had responded, "but if you know someone who does make time, I'd be more than happy to buy a lot of it from him."

95

Before the call, it had been another year since they'd seen each other. In that year, Danny had stayed in the same place and had progressed in the same job. Will had lived in Spain, Nebraska, and California. He'd been a playwright, a computer consultant, and a door-to-door salesman. He had a million stories to tell. Danny only had one or two. He didn't want to bore Will with the details of his work, and at the same time he resented the way such details became boring. Will wanted to stay up late and go to clubs where the barmaids were playfully cruel. He wanted to hit galleries and pawnshops and diners where a grilled cheese still cost two dollars and the tomato came free. Danny didn't know such places. After two days, he felt he didn't know the city at all.

"What have you been *doing?*" Will asked with mock exasperation.

And the only answer Danny could think of was, *Living my life.*

Will wanted Danny to cut work. Danny felt he couldn't. Will wanted Danny to get a tattoo. Danny wouldn't.

They parted on good terms, but it felt like parting, and it felt like terms. Danny hadn't meant to lose touch with Will—but all it took was one lost change-of-address card and the fact that Will refused to have e-mail. Danny heard word through friends of friends—Will was now a potter in Oregon—but he knew it wasn't enough to send word back. After all, Will knew where Danny was. It wasn't like he'd moved.

*Please press *4 to save, *6 to delete, or *7-3 to listen to this message again,* the voice-mail femail insists. Danny hits *4.

*1—to respond—is only an option for internal calls.

* * *

While Danny dials transatlantic, Elijah walks to the top of the basilica. Not to the dome, but to the balcony. Touched full-force by the sun, he watches over the square, tourists moving like rivulets of water, birds shifting like newsprint fingerprints. A string band concertos to the left, while a trumpeter blasts from the right. Strangely, the two sounds complement rather than conflict.

The bell tower begins to ring. The time is marked.

Elijah breathes. He breathes deeply and tries to pull his sight into his breath, and his hearing into his breath, and his feeling into his breath.

He knows this will be his goodbye to Venice. The rest will be walking and packing and checking out. This is the height. This is the time for thanks.

He thinks of Julia, the stranger, and says goodbye to her as well.

He thinks of Julia, and she appears.

She doesn't see him at first. She steps out onto the balcony and walks to the edge. She leans against the railing and dangles her head over. She is smiling at the square, like a child tummy-down on a swing, pretending to fly.

Elijah knows he is not part of this picture. He knows he is seeing more of her than he would be brave enough to give of himself.

Wonder lights her face. She stands up straight again and shakes her head in a barely perceptible motion. She is watching sunset, even though the sun is still high in the sky.

Then, with another shake of her head, she moves a step back. Her smile is now self-aware. She knows she is a bit loony in her wonder, but she doesn't really mind.

Elijah walks over before he can think about it. He walks over because what he feels is strange enough to be a dream, and in dreams ordinary rules do not apply.

"Hello again," he says.

She turns to him and looks momentarily surprised. Not displeased. But surprised.

"Hello," she says. "Isn't this wonderful?"

He looks back over the square.

"Absolutely."

"It makes me want to—"

"—fly?"

Julia laughs. "Yes! Exactly! How did you know what I was going to say?"

And the answer is: *Because I was going to say the same thing.*

Elijah feels the electric rush that comes when coincidence turns into coinciding. He feels nervous and comfortable, disbelieving and amazed.

He does not need to know what is happening in order to know something is happening.

"Where are you from?" he asks.

"Toronto," she replies, her inflections now explained.

"Have you been here long?"

"No. You?"

"No."

They are not looking at each other. Instead, they stare out into the square, each extremely aware of the other's every breath, every move.

This doesn't make sense, he thinks.

Her arm brushes his, and when she turns to see him, loose strands of her short hair blow over her eyes.

"I'm going to Florence," he says.

And she says, "I am, too."

III. FLORENCE

Since Danny can stand Elijah's driving even less than Elijah can stand Danny's, it is Danny who drives the rent-a-car. Within five minutes, they are lost on a road where it's prolongedly impossible to make a U-turn. In response, Danny swears like a drag queen with a broken heel as Elijah bends and folds the map into something approaching origami.

It is not a good moment.

Danny swerves through the lanes, dodging the European cars that whiz by at incomprehensible speeds. Elijah wonders how guilty his parents will feel when both their sons get trapped in a fiery wreck in the middle of a prepaid vacation.

We are going to die, Elijah genuinely thinks. *Or, at the very least, we are going to kill a cyclist.*

He takes some comfort in the fact that the stop signs still read STOP.

Eventually, the road they're on turns into the road they had meant to get on in the first place. Once on the highway, Danny relaxes behind the wheel. Elijah puts a CD in the stereo—Paul Simon's *Graceland,* something they can agree upon.

Once the music is in, Elijah decides to close his eyes. If he can't see, he won't be scared.

He thinks of Julia and the hour they'd managed to steal before Elijah had to leave Venice. A spare cafe hour of signals and conversation, sharing the arcane facts of their lives, touching upon the founding of Rhode Island and the temperature of a Toronto summer day. Finally, he'd had to leave, their goodbye drawn out over a number of goodbyes and one-last-things to say. He didn't know where he'd be staying in Florence, but she had been able to write down the name of her *pensione*. He promised to be there as soon as she arrived.

Danny had not been happy when Elijah returned so late. When Danny demanded to know why he was so tardy (such a schoolteacher word), Elijah disguised Julia in a fit of mumbles and evasions, saying quite simply that he'd been lost. Danny could believe this easily enough.

Now they are making up for Elijah's delay, as Danny fulfills all of his test-drive fantasies. Even with his eyes closed and the music playing, Elijah can sense the impatient speed. There are two kinds of drivers, he thinks: those who see the world around the road, and those who fixate on the road itself.

We'll end up where we want to be. We always do.

Elijah reclines in the melody of "Under African Skies" and thinks once more of Julia. The promise of Florence has become the promise of their next encounter. But unlike Danny, he is not in a rush. He wants to feel the nervous sweetness of expectation, if only for a little while longer.

* * *

"Open your eyes."

Elijah hears Danny's voice and wants to reject it. He's been safely, happily asleep, dreaming of a gondolier who sings love songs to a maiden on a bridge. Surely, Danny doesn't need to wake him. Surely, he can read his own map. Why can't he leave Elijah to his reverie?

"I mean it. Open your eyes."

Elijah stirs and groans. He opens his eyes and sees the plastic wood of the dashboard. *Graceland* has now played twice around.

Danny smiles in amusement and says, "Look outside."

Elijah turns to the window and is startled straight into joy. A field of sunflowers surrounds the road, devout yellow heads bent, an oceanic congregation. Elijah cannot see beyond them. There are so many, and they are all so bright. Sunflowers as far as the eye can see.

"I wonder," Danny says, "are sunflowers called sunflowers because they look like the sun, or because they follow the sun? Either one would be a perfectly good explanation, and there are so few things that deserve two perfectly good explanations."

The sunflowers are retreating now—Elijah turns back to look at them, his wonder nearly dreamlike in its intensity and disbelief. He feels a strange gratitude toward his brother, for he knows he could have slept through the whole thing.

So instead of answering Danny's question, he says, "I met a girl named Julia in Venice." And he tells a little bit of the story. Not the good parts. But enough to let Danny know what's going on.

* * *

A girl, Danny thinks. *Elijah has met a girl.*
He doesn't know how he feels about this.

* * *

Florence is not quite what Danny or Elijah had been expecting. Venice, in many ways, has misled them into thinking that the past can remain fully intact. And yet here is Florence, a city of the past with a city of the present imposed right atop it. (The future is nowhere to be found.) Benettons grow in the cracks between cathedrals. Moped-clad citizens run on caffeinated fumes. Crosswalks are suddenly necessary. Ghetto-blaster teenagers skateboard past multinational newsstands. The Arno River shrugs by.

For a moment, traffic makes Florence seem like anywhere else. As Danny curses and stops and starts and struggles for direction, Elijah takes drive-by snapshots of the city and its contradictions. Venice was a museum city; Florence is a city with museums. There is, Elijah thinks, a big spiritual difference between the two.

Danny and Elijah are staying a little outside the city, at the Excelsior on the Piazza Ognissanti. There is a message waiting for them at the desk. Elijah's heart lifts when he sees the envelope, wondering how Julia could have known.

But the message is from Mr. and Mrs. Silver—*Hoping you're having a lovely time!*—signed with *Much Love*. Danny grumbles a little (he still has not entirely forgiven his parents' trickery) and hands Elijah the note. The porter brings their bags to the room, and they immediately depart. (Elijah takes a piece of the hotel stationery with him, just so he'll know where he's staying.)

Elijah wants to track Julia down immediately. But Danny is so antsy that he's willing to forgo his afternoon nap. This day is

107

not supposed to be a Transportation Day—it is supposed to be a Florence Day, and Danny is willing to take the necessary steps to see it before sundown.

They taxi to the center of the city in the most rushed hour of the day. Danny is reminded of home—men with their leather briefcases jostle down the sidewalk, exuding a barely concealed hostility. A woman with a stroller crosses against traffic; horns blare in response.

"Where have you been?" the taxi driver asks. "Where are you going?"

Danny looks down and notices Elijah's shoes are untied.

"You'd better tie them," he says.

Elijah scowls and makes a double knot.

The driver nods and turns up the radio.

Elijah stares out the window, somehow expecting Julia to be there, waving.

* * *

The Duomo is closed, so Elijah and Danny must be content with walking around its brilliantly traceable exterior.

"Not bad, for a church," Danny says. Elijah is elsewhere.

"Where's she staying?" Danny asks.

"Here," Elijah replies, pulling out an old bank receipt with an address written in red ink on the back.

"Then I guess we'd better go there and ask her to dinner."

* * *

It is, by all means, an awkward situation. Because Elijah has no intention of sharing his time with anyone but Julia. But at the same time, he must be grateful for his brother's gesture. As they wait in the lobby for Julia to appear, Elijah tries to conjure somewhere else for Danny to go. But it's no use . . . for now.

The elevator teasingly discharges passengers who are markedly not Julia. Danny laughs to himself as they disembark, imagining that one of the sixtysomething dowagers is the woman for whom Elijah has so obviously fallen. He almost doesn't notice when Julia arrives. It's from Elijah's beaming that Danny can tell.

So this is Julia, he thinks. She isn't really attractive—rather boyish, with her hair so short and no make-up. No breasts to speak of. In fact, no real curves of any kind. And what is a girl without curves if not, well, a boy? Danny is confounded by his brother's choice.

"Julia, this is my brother, Danny. Danny, this is Julia." She doesn't have a label yet. She is just Julia.

"Nice to meet you."

"Nice to meet you."

Elijah doesn't know what to do. He doesn't know what to say, doesn't know where to put his hands, doesn't know how familiar to be with Julia, especially with Danny watching. Julia sends him a winking look—something for them to share—and suddenly Elijah feels okay with the situation. Danny is harmless. Julia is everything.

It is, by European standards, obscenely early for dinner—

not yet seven o'clock. This makes it easier for them to change their reservation from two to three. It also ensures that the few other people in the restaurant will be English-speakers like themselves.

Even though most of the tables are empty, they are seated right next to a family of six. Their acquaintance is soon enough made—the youngest child, age three, grabs Elijah's shirt as he goes to sit down. The mother apologizes profusely, while Elijah profusely declares that it's no problem whatsoever. Soon enough, introductions are made, and Mrs. Allison Feldstein of Commack, Long Island, is telling the story of the Feldstein family's day in Pisa:

"We were worried that we'd be driving all that way for nothing—like those poor souls who drive halfway through South Dakota to see Mount Rushmore. You know what I mean? But Davey has a Sno-globe collection—don't you, Davey?—and he really wanted to have one from the leaning tower. And there's a restaurant two towns over from ours named The Tower of Pizza, so the kids wanted to go on account of that, ha ha. So we got in the car and drove there—it wasn't as long as we thought it would be. The drive was actually enjoyable. And when we got there, the town itself was a very pleasant surprise. It's so strange to see something in person that you've been seeing all your life. I mean, everyone knows the tower leans. But it's not until you're standing right there that you can truly understand what a spectacular kind of thing this is. It's really quite striking, especially when you're looking at it from behind. I mean, buildings just aren't meant to lean away from you, so it's startling when they do. The little one here was terrified it would fall, and I have to tell you, the thought crossed my mind, too. It probably crosses everyone's mind. It shakes the fundamental trust we have in buildings. And it's a beautiful building—that's something you never hear about. It would be worth seeing even if it wasn't leaning. And the cathedral next to it—who even knew there was a cathedral? But it's really one of the most striking ones we've seen. It was all white and shadow. I loved it. And believe you me, we've seen more than enough cathedrals on this trip. . . ."

As Elijah listens to this, Danny shoots a look at Julia—who rolls her eyes right back. They have become prisoners of Jewish Geography, inextricably bonded to these similar strangers in a strange land.

Mrs. Feldstein's children grow restless before either she or Elijah does. They are swapping itineraries—the Feldsteins are on their way to Venice and have just come from Rome. Danny begins to play with the remnants of bread on the tablecloth. Julia laughs at this and begins to flick crumbs his way. Elijah turns back to the table aglow with conversation—only to find his brother and his newfound love skirmishing playfully. It is the first time in a long time that he feels like the more mature brother.

As soon as he's back, Julia's attention returns to him, and he feels all right again. Danny feels the center slip away from him. He is once more a hypotenuse.

"How was your drive?" Julia asks, and even though it could be meant for either of them, both of them know it is Elijah's place to answer.

"Fine," Danny says.

"If your idea of 'fine' is being trapped in a car with the Red Baron driving," Elijah adds.

"You're mixing your transportation metaphors."

"It's not a *metaphor*, it's a *reference*."

Julia smiles. "I think I'm getting the picture," she says, and the two of them are reduced to silence.

"You'll have to pardon us—we're brothers," Danny says after a moment.

"Yes, I've noticed. I have four brothers of my own."

Four brothers. Neither Danny nor Elijah can imagine having four brothers. Separately, they wonder if it's harder or easier than having just one.

From this point on, Julia owns the conversation. Elijah admires the fact that she is charming enough to make the people she is with act charming as well. Danny's and Elijah's words suddenly run in paragraphs, not sentences. They tell her of their parents' trickery, of their lives back home. Danny talks about work, and even Elijah isn't bored—not totally. Julia seems interested, and Elijah is interested in the way she is interested.

The Feldsteins leave, with Mrs. Feldstein writing down a list of sites they have to see in Rome. The language of the restaurant slowly shifts to Italian. As the other patrons arrive, Danny, Elijah, and Julia lean into their table to offer critiques.

"What I want to know is this," Julia begins. She has been drinking wine casually, and the effect can be heard in her voice. "All of the young Italian men are so gorgeous, right?"

"I hadn't noticed," Danny sniffs.

"Liar!" Elijah cries. "They are absolutely beautiful, and you know it."

"Okay," Danny concedes.

"Exactly!" Julia smiles. "They all have this perfect proportion, this delicate balance of divinity and boyishness. I can hardly manage to walk down the street without kissing a dozen

113

strangers. When I'm around them, I feel like such a woman. So my question is this: What happens? You see all of these beautiful young men . . . and all of the old men are at least two feet shorter, round, and balding. There's *no trace* of the young men in the old men. None whatsoever. It's like they dance at the ball until they're thirty, then—poof!—the midnight bell chimes. They shrink back to size, and their Fiats turn into pumpkins."

"What an awful thing to say!" Danny gasps in his most scandalized voice.

"But true, eh?"

"Absolutely true."

There is a pause, and then Danny asks, "So what brings you here?" He is still thinking of her walking down crowded narrow alleyways, kissing strangers.

"It's an old story," Julia says, leaning back in her chair. "Only for me, it's new. I went to school for industrial design. All my life, I've been fascinated by chairs—I know it sounds silly, but it's true. Form meets purpose in a chair. My parents thought I was crazy, but somehow I convinced them to pay my way to California. To study furniture design. I was all excited at first. It was totally unlike me to go so far away from home. But I was sick of the cold and sick of the snow. I figured a little sun might change my life. So I headed down to L.A. and roomed with the friend of an ex-girlfriend of my brother's. She was an aspiring radio actress, which meant she was home a lot.

"At first, I loved it. I didn't even let the summer go by. I dove right into my classes. Soon enough, I learned I couldn't just focus on chairs. I had to design spoons and toilet-bowl cleaners and thermostats. The math never bothered me, but the professors did. They could demolish you in a second without giving you a clue of how to rebuild. I spent more and more time in the studio, with other crazed students who guarded their own projects like toy-jealous kids. I started to go for walks. Long walks. I couldn't go home because my roommate was always there. The sun was too much for me, so I'd stay indoors. A certain kind of indoors—the anonymous indoors. I spent hours in supermarkets, walking aisle to aisle, picking up groceries and then putting them back. I went to bowling alleys and pharmacies. I rode in buses that kept their lights on all night. I sat in Laundromats because once upon a time Laundromats made me happy. But now the hum of the machines sounded like life going past.

"Finally, one night I sat too long in the laundry. The woman who folded in the back—Alma—walked over to me and said, 'What are you doing here, girl?' And I knew that there wasn't any answer. There couldn't be any answer. And that's when I knew it was time to go.

"I had saved some money—not much, but enough. I was far from home, and my first decision was that I couldn't go back. I chose Europe because it was somewhere else, and I'd always wanted to go there."

"You thought you'd be happier here," Elijah says.

Julia shakes her head. "Not really. But I figured if I was going to be miserable, I might as well be miserable for different reasons."

"And are you miserable?" Danny asks.

"Strangely, no."

He can't help but look her in the eye and ask more. "And have you found what you're looking for?"

Julia looks at him quietly for a moment, then shrugs. "I don't even know what I'm looking for, although I hope I'll know it if I find it along the way. Sometimes I want to simplify my life into a single bare thing. And other times I want to complicate it so thoroughly that everything I touch will become bound in some way to me. I've become quite aware of my contradictions, but there's no true resolution in that."

The waiter returns, a conversational semicolon. Dessert and coffee are deferred. Danny tries to look Julia in the eye again, but she is studying the tablecloth, finger-tracing lines around the remaining silverware.

Elijah reaches over and touches her hand. He feels nervous and brave. She looks up and doesn't pull away.

Danny takes care of the check.

Outside, night is just beginning. The sun has been down for some time, but the Italians use another definition for night. As Elijah and Danny leave the restaurant, they take turns holding the door for Julia. She murmurs thank you to each and lifts on her toes when her face first touches the night air.

"Now what?" Danny asks.

Elijah is taken aback. He thought it was obvious.

"We're going to go for coffee," he says discreetly.

Danny's energy fades at once, confronted with a "we" that doesn't include him.

"Oh," he says. "Of course." Then, "Do you need money?"

"No. Thank you."

Danny waits for a moment. He wants to see if Julia is going to say anything. If she wants him to stay, he will.

But Julia remains silent, swaying from foot to foot.

Elijah wants to ask his brother what he's going to do, but is afraid it will sound too cruel.

"Don't wake me when you come back," Danny says instead. Then he turns to Julia and tells her it's been nice to meet her.

"Absolutely," she replies. "Thank you for dinner. I'm sure we'll see each other again soon."

"I'm sure."

Danny moves his hand in a little wave and makes his departure. After he's walked a block, he turns around and sees Julia and Elijah in the same lamplight frame, discussing where to go next. Their bodies are not touching, but their expressions are.

Danny turns back to the street and heads for the hotel.

* * *

"He seems nice," Julia says, some minutes later.

"Well, I wouldn't call him naughty, if that's the other choice," Elijah replies. They are walking alongside the Arno— the sidewalk is also a river, of men in jackets and women with jewelry headed out into the evening. The last thing Elijah wants to talk about is Danny.

"So the two of you don't get along?"

"Not really."

How many times has Elijah heard this question before? Even though it's a question, it contains the speaker's own observation: *I've seen the two of you and know you don't get along. Isn't that true?* Elijah could say so much more than a simple "not really." He could compile lists of incidents and spites. But then, when he recited them, he would sound bitter and mean—in other words, he would sound just like Danny. One of the worst things about Danny is the tendency to take on Elijah's qualities when talking to or about him. Elijah can hardly bear it. So ignoring it—ignoring *him*—seems like the best idea.

But Julia persists. "Still, he seems to care about you."

Elijah wonders what observation *this* statement could be based upon.

"Not really," he mutters again.

"I think you're wrong."

Elijah is growing impatient—Danny is souring the conversation from afar. "*Look*," he says, and immediately modifies his tone. "I guess you just haven't known us long enough. He doesn't really care about me at all. Not in any way that matters."

118

"Why do you say that?"

"Here's an example." Elijah stops on a street corner and points to his shoes. "My shoelaces. I know they come untied a lot. I am aware of the situation. But every chance Danny gets, he's telling me to tie my shoes. At least once an hour, sometimes more frequently. And I wouldn't mind it—I swear I wouldn't mind it—if he was actually concerned about my well-being. If he was worried about me tripping into traffic, I would tie them every time. But no. He doesn't care whether or not I fall on my face. He wants me to tie my shoelaces because untied shoelaces *annoy* him. They *embarrass* him. They *get on his nerves.*"

"How do you know?"

"Believe me, I know. If you live with someone all your life, you can tell when you are annoying them. Their face just shuts down. Their words sound almost mechanical, because they are reining in all the other emotions. I think I'd also know if I made Danny happy, but I never make him happy. Ever."

Elijah's never said these exact words before, and now that he's said them, they seem even more real. They are so real, they scare him. Because Elijah fundamentally wants everyone to be happy. With everyone else, he still tries. But he gave up on Danny long ago, for so many reasons that they add up to no clear reason at all.

Julia takes his hand. He thinks the subject is finished, but then she asks, "When did that start?"

She seems so genuinely to want to know the answer that he finds himself talking again. "I guess it was high school," he says.

"So when he was your age now?"

That sounds strange to Elijah, but he guesses it's true. He nods. "About my age. And I was eleven or twelve. Just starting it all, you know. And Danny became a closed door to me. Literally. Wherever he went, the door closed behind him, and that's all I'd see. Like I'd done something. When he'd open the door, when we actually saw him, he was always grouping me with my parents, always saying I was taking their side or scamming to get into their good graces. That I was the good son. But the thing is, he'd been good, too. Then the doors started closing. And it wasn't even like he was doing anything so crazy. I mean, he wasn't shutting himself in his room and smoking up or looking at porn or sneaking in girlfriends. He wasn't hiding anything but himself. And I just didn't get it."

"Do you get it now?" Julia asks.

"I don't know. I don't have a little brother, I guess. It's different at my school. I like having the door open."

They have walked past the busier part of town and are now in a streetlight that barely glimmers above the river darkness.

"He's cute, you know," Julia says.

"He is?"

"In that isn't-doing-what-he-wants-to-be way. A look like that, you just want to help."

"In what way?"

"I don't know," Julia says. "You just want to tell him it's okay to be himself."

"And me?" Elijah asks.

Julia arches an eyebrow. "You? You're much easier. You're cute in a cute way."

"Really?"

Julia smiles.

"Really."

Elijah slowly feels lucky again.

＊　＊　＊

Danny has deliberately lost his way. He feels it is too much
of a defeat to return to the hotel so early. He is suddenly concerned about what the concierge will think.

So he wanders through Florence, which doesn't feel like Venice
at all. He walks down to the Arno, to be by the water. He leans
against the railing and stares at the other side, thinking of home. A
few minutes later, he is distracted by an eager conversation, spoken
in a foreign tongue. Not ten feet from him, a young couple talks in
an embrace. (*Young* being seventeen or eighteen . . . this has become
young to Danny, and he hates that.) The boy is not beautiful,
merely good-looking, wearing (of all things) a beret. The girl has
long hair that shifts every time she laughs. To them, Danny is as real
as the river or the city—nice, incidental music behind the conversation. Danny turns away, obtrusive in his own eyes. The couple is
taking in all the magic of the moment for themselves. They have
left Danny with nothing but scenery and air. And the air is beginning to chill.

Danny moves away from the river, back to the streets. Paying closer attention, he realizes the packs that pass him are all
American. A succession of American collegians—all having the
same conversations ("And so I told her to . . ." "Are you telling
me I should . . . ?" "Get out of here!"). They are all attractive, or
trying very hard to be attractive. Danny chuckles at this endless
parade of semesters abroad. He doesn't feel at all like one of
them. He doesn't have their gall or revelry.

It seems entirely fitting when the fluorescent logo of a
7-Eleven rises before him. Amused, Danny steps in—just to see

if a 7-Eleven in Florence is any different from a 7-Eleven in Connecticut or California. Slurpee is spelled the same in any language, and while some of the beverages are different, the beverage cases still mist if he opens the door for too long. Struck by impulse, Danny tracks down the snack cakes. And indeed, there it is: the all-new, cosmetic-free Miss Jane's Homemade Petite Snack Cake—translated into Italian.

Danny reads the name aloud, mispronouncing most of the syllables. He grins and beams—these are words that he wrote at a desk thousands of miles away, not even knowing they'd be translated into a language he'd never spoken. Something that travels so far must be, at the very least, a little important.

There are only three snack cakes left. Danny buys them all—one for his parents, one for his office, and one for his own delight. He can't wait to show people. He wishes Elijah were with him. He wishes he were with someone who would understand—not just the seventeen-year-old cashier, looking embarrassed in his maroon, orange, and white uniform (such a combination has never before appeared in Italy, especially not in polyester).

Buoyed by his discovery, Danny returns to the hotel. But he's not ready for the night to end—not quite yet. Elijah isn't back, so Danny heads for the bar. Since he thinks there is something disreputable about drinking a bottle of wine alone, he drinks by the glass until the world goes soft. He drinks, even though drinking always makes him remember rather than forget. He tells the bartender about the snack cake. The bartender smiles happily and congratulates him.

Danny is happy in return.

* * *

With the right person, you can have a late-night conversation at any time of the day. But it helps to have it late at night.

Elijah and Julia are back in Julia's room, in Julia's *pensione*. Elijah touches the blanket and stares at the pictures on the wall, which he thinks of as hers, even though they are not hers at all. All of her possessions are still in a suitcase.

"I didn't have time to unpack," she explains. "You were here so soon."

"I'm sorry if I disturbed you."

"Don't worry—I was already disturbed."

She takes off her shoes, and he follows suit. Although there are chairs in the room, they are far too rigid for casual conversation. So Elijah and Julia sit on the floor, leaning on the same side of the bed.

"I wish we had candles," Elijah says.

"What if we turn the lights off and leave only the lamp on?"

As Julia rises to get the switch, Elijah closes his eyes. He can feel her moving across the room, he can see the change from light to dark, and then the small step back to light. He can feel her returning to him. Sitting next to him. Breathing softly.

"Relax," she says, and the word itself is relaxing.

Do you wonder?

"Who are you thinking about?" Julia asks quietly.

"Nobody. Just my best friend. Wondering what time it is over there."

"Is he back in Rhode Island?"

"Yes."

"Then the night is just beginning."

Elijah opens his eyes, and finds that Julia has closed hers.

Their voices travel at the speed of night.

* * *

It takes three tries for Danny to fit his key into the lock.

"Elijah?" he asks. But the bed is empty, and the room is alone.

* * *

Slowly, Elijah and Julia begin to lose their words. They fall from the conversation one by one, lengthening the pauses, heightening the expectation. Her hand moves from his arm to his cheek. He closes his eyes, and she smiles. He is so serious. The first kiss is clear, ready to be set for memory. The second and the third and the fourth begin to blur—they are no longer singular things, but part of something larger than even their sum.

"Thank you," Elijah whispers in one of the moments of breath.

"You're welcome," Julia replies, and before he can say another word, she kisses him again.

They kiss and touch and trace themselves to sleep. They will wake at sunrise, in each other's arms.

* * *

Danny goes to sleep easily, and wakes up two hours later. Nausea infuses every pore of his consciousness. Part of him wants to throw up and get it over with. And part of him remembers what he had for dinner—veal, asparagus, tomato bread soup—and wants to keep it in. Finally, he decides ginger ale is the way to go, and overrules his inner cheapskate to take a swipe at the minibar. Sadly, ginger ale is nowhere to be found. Fanta will have to do.

"Elijah—are you sleeping?" Danny fumbles for the bottle opener and cuts his hand on the cap. He follows the rug to the lip of the bathroom, then liberates four Tylenol from his travel kit. The first Tylenol falls down the drain, but the other three hit their mark, drowned in a tide of too-sweet soda.

Danny still feels sick. But he falls asleep anyway.

* * *

In the morning, the phone winks red at him.

"Meet us at the Uffizi," Elijah's voice says. "We'll see you at eleven."

* * *

It's Julia's dope and Elijah's idea to go to the museum stoned. Julia rolls him a joint, and then—seeing the happiness in his smile—gives him a little extra to go. After they've smoked, they hold hands through the lobby. The *pensione's* owner nods a good morning. Julia and Elijah giggle and smile in return. When they reach the door, they break into a skip.

It is eleven-fifteen.

* * *

Danny waits by the entrance, and then he waits on line. He searches for his brother, and then he gives up. Perhaps Elijah is already inside. Perhaps he won't show at all. Danny is not in the mood for empty minutes. He can barely stand it when he wastes his own time; for someone else to waste it is unconscionable.

The line is very long and very slow. Danny is bracketed by American families—restless children and desperately agreeable parents. The walls of the museum are touched by graffiti: KURT 4-EVA and MARIA DEL MAR 4/4/98 and CLARE 27/03 FRANCESE . . . TI AMO JUSTIN. One of the American families is accompanied by an abusive tour guide, who takes the children's listlessness to task. "Boredom is a dirty habit," she mutters. The American mother has murder in her eyes.

Five minutes and no Elijah . . . fifteen minutes and no Elijah . . . the ticket taker asks Danny to enter, and he does not argue. He decides to start at the beginning of the museum and work his way through history. Elijah will no doubt meet him somewhere in the middle, without realizing he's late.

* * *

Elijah isn't surprised that his brother hasn't waited. Really, it doesn't matter. Elijah is happy to be here, is happy to be with Julia. His buzz is just right—enough so things seem real close, but not so much that things seem real far away. He and Julia are surprised by the length of the line; luckily, Elijah strikes up a conversation with the trio of Australian women in front of them, so the time passes quickly. Maura's fortieth birthday is three days away; Judy and Helen are planning to take her to the most expensive restaurant in Siena, bringing at least four bottles of wine. They are legal secretaries—they met in high school and their fates have been tied together ever since. They ask Elijah and Julia how long they've been together, and Elijah revels in the fact that they've seen fit to ask.

"It's been ages," Julia replies, wrapping her arm around Elijah and snuggling close.

"At least three hundred years," Elijah adds.

Once inside the Uffizi, Elijah is dizzied by the ceilings. Julia has to remind him to watch where he steps. A guard looks at him curiously, so Elijah says hello, and the guard suddenly becomes less guarded.

There are so many paintings, all with the same plot. Mary looks stoned, and the Jesus babies are still scary. It's the glummest Sears Family Portrait in history. The angels are all the same person, and the skies are always the same blue.

"Come here," Julia whispers, pulling Elijah to his first Annunciation of the day. "Look closely. I love this scene. Gabriel is telling Mary the story of the rest of her life. Every artist has a different take on it. Like this one."

Elijah leans closer. Indeed, Mary's slight boredom—all too evident in the mother-son shots—has disappeared. In this painting—by someone named Martini—Mary looks uncomfortable. She's not sure about what she's being told. Gabriel, meanwhile, wears a pleading expression. He knows what's at stake.

"Let's see all the Annunciations," Elijah says, a little too eager, a little too loud.

"Absolutely," Julia agrees.

Elijah takes one last look at Mary and Gabriel. Mary winks at him and tells him to move on.

*   *   *

Danny's guidebook talks about Piero della Francesca's "daring search for perspective"—and, quite frankly, Danny doesn't get it. How can you discover perspective? Why did it take thousands of years for artists to discover a third dimension? How can you discover something that is already there?

It's only the fifteenth century and already Danny is getting tired. All these people in robes, with their wooden pastures and wooden expressions. Then the burst of Botticelli. The people are no longer bloodless; Danny can almost believe they have hearts.

"Hey there," someone says. Danny assumes she's talking to someone else. Then he feels a hand on his arm. He turns to find Julia.

"Where's Elijah?" he asks.

"Oh, around. I figured I'd try to find you."

"He didn't want to join you?"

"I don't think he realizes I left. He's rather transfixed."

"Good for him."

Julia gestures to the painting, Perugino's *Crucifixion*. "I wonder about the red hat on the ground."

Danny nods. "I was just thinking the same thing."

"I also wonder why they're so clean."

"As opposed to what? A pornographic crucifixion?"

"No. I mean *clean*. Think about it. People in the sixteenth century—not to mention in Jesus's time—didn't look like this: perfect skin, perfect hairdos, spotless clothes. These are people who went to the bathroom in the street, for God's sake. There's no way they looked like this. But that's how we're going to re-member them. Our alabaster past. When nothing else is left, art will become the truth of the time. Then people will get to the nineteenth and twentieth centuries and wonder what hap-pened—how we all became so imperfect."

Danny doesn't know what to say to this, and Julia becomes immediately self-conscious.

"Sorry," she says, ducking her head down. "Shove me into shallow water, you know."

"No—you're absolutely right. I've never thought of it that way."

Danny sees that Julia can't decide whether he's being true or whether he's just being kind. It doesn't occur to her that the two can be one and the same.

   *   *   *

Elijah figures Julia has made her way to the ladies' room or something, so he continues on his trail of Annunciations. *Primavera* momentarily gets in the way—Elijah is shocked at how dark it has become. Elijah has always looked to the painting for joy, but now the dark angel in the corner gains prominence. The right-hand maiden is trapped in his grasp. The woman in the center of it all seems detached, resigned.

Still, people flock to her. Elijah stands in front of the tourist flashbulbs, trying to protect her. A torrent of foreign words tells him to move. But he will not. Each time a camera is raised, he gets in the way. There are signs everywhere saying not to take pictures. And yet everyone acts like he's the one doing something wrong.

Once the latest tour group has passed, Elijah returns to Mary and Gabriel. In Botticelli's version, Mary seems demure, almost faint. Gabriel looks like a woman—perhaps an easier way to convey the news, with a flower held like a pen in his hand. Elijah wishes Julia were around to ask—*How did Gabriel persuade her? Why isn't she frightened by the sight of his wings?* In the frame, Mary sits on the edge of what looks like a tomb. *Isn't she surprised the angel is kneeling at her feet?*

DaVinci's *Annunciation* is almost like a sequel to Botticelli's. Gabriel is in the same pose, but Mary seems to be acknowledging him. She has become regal, undoubting. She is no longer sitting in a room, with the wide world merely alluded to through a window. It is the opposite now. Elijah does not like this Mary. She is too steely, whereas Botticelli's is too weak.

A few galleries later, Elijah gazes again at the ceiling. The details are surreal. A knight stands atop a dragon, about to swing his sword at an armless angel who has breasts, a tail, and a mermaid limb that trails off into a small tree.

"Man, that's so messed up," Elijah murmurs.

It's like the ceiling has dredged the dope back into his bloodstream. The paintings are going freaky. Caravaggio's *Medusa* is a scary, screaming bitch.

A very papal-looking portrait watches over *Slaughter of the Innocents*. Elijah can't believe how sexy the slaughter seems. He's strangely turned on. Gentileschi's *Santa Caterina d'Alessandria* holds her breasts in a very provocative way, leading Elijah to wonder what kind of saints they had, way back when.

The rooms are beginning to tip a little. Elijah sits on a bench and stares again at the ceiling. A woman plays violin as a dog and a donkey sit and listen. A man raises a hammer to a bull's head. Three naked women dance, while human heads are superimposed onto the wings of a red butterfly.

"There you are," Julia's voice calls. Elijah is afraid to turn to her, afraid that she too will be written on the wings of an insect, poised to fly away. The dog and the donkey are getting up to leave now. The hammer falls short, and the bull laughs and laughs. Julia sits down next to him and asks if everything is okay.

Elijah closes his eyes and opens them. All the variations go away. Julia is the only real thing he can see.

"I found Danny," she says.

"Good for you. How annoyed is he?"

"Not that annoyed."

"That's probably because I wasn't with you."

136

Julia sighs. "I told him we'd meet him by Veronese's *Annunciation*."

"So now he's into Annunciations, too?"

"No. It was just a place to meet."

Elijah knows he's being a drag. So he concentrates hard to send the bad vibes away. He can feel them disperse, like dark angels dipping away to the sky.

"I'm glad you're back," he says.

They both stand and kiss briefly in front of a small tree that floats on a cloud.

Then Julia pulls away and leads Elijah to his brother.

The three of them stand in front of Veronese's *Annunciation*. Danny doesn't say a word to Elijah about being late. Elijah assumes this is because of Julia's presence.

Mary seems beautifully anguished as a cloud of angels and souls falls onto her. Gabriel is fiercer than before, his finger jabbing upward, the flowers spilling from his hands.

"I guess you have to feel sorry for her," Elijah says. Julia nods, but she's barely listening. She's still studying the painting, her eyes following the flowers' paths.

"Did Mary have any friends?" Danny asks.

Julia turns to him. "What?"

"I'm the first to admit that I don't know that much about the whole Mary thing. But didn't she have friends? She always seems so alone in these paintings. And then once she has the baby, it's like her previous life never happened."

"I don't know," Julia says. "But it's a good question."

"She probably had friends," Elijah chimes in. "They just didn't want to be in the picture."

Julia has nothing to say to that.

*   *   *

After skimming the rest of the museum and dipping into
the gift shop for a moment (trying to avoid the *Primavera* mouse
pad and the *Birth of Venus* outerwear), Julia looks at her watch
and makes an announcement.

"I'm afraid I have to leave you for a little bit," she says. "I
have plans to meet an old girlfriend for the afternoon." She sees
the look on Danny's face and laughs. "Not *that* kind of girlfriend, Danny. Man, you boys are going to need to work on
those hang-ups of yours. I'm meeting an old friend from high
school who's doing some curating work here. She's going to tell
me all about the floods."

Danny is surprised by how sorry he is to see her go. He is
not surprised by how sorry Elijah seems. Danny keeps a respectful distance while his brother asks Julia when she'll be
back and when they can meet again. Julia touches his cheek and
says it won't be long. They make plans for their next encounter.

"So now what?" Elijah asks as Julia heads away. He watches
her disappear into the human traffic. He would wave, if only she
would see him.

The brothers decide to fall back on tourism, heading to the
Duomo and its environs. The austere interior doesn't at all
match the delightful exterior, which is itself darkened by car
fumes and other modern pollutants. Elijah hangs by the candles,
while Danny paces the baptistery and admires the windows.

Elijah cannot believe how tired he feels. It hits him fully,
now that Julia is gone. She'd buoyed him into wakefulness. Now

he's wrapped in fatigue, all of the sleepless hours catching up to him.

"Maybe we should go back to the hotel? To take a nap?" he suggests.

"Good idea," Danny replies. He too is feeling the full breadth of his tiredness. It's a different tiredness from home— less workmanlike, more atmospheric.

They walk for ten minutes in silence. Then Danny asks, "So what time are you meeting her?"

"About four. You don't mind, do you?"

"Of course not. It's not as if I thought I was going to have dinner with you."

"What do you mean?"

"Nothing. Just a joke. A bad joke."

"Are you sure?"

"Absolutely. I have my book. And I should probably get some sleep tonight."

Elijah can see his brother is bluffing, but he can't think of anything to say besides, "Okay."

"Just be ready to leave for Rome tomorrow afternoon."

"Okay."

"She seems very nice."

"She *is* very nice."

"I know. That's what I just said."

Back at the hotel, Elijah grabs his toiletry kit and heads straight to the bathroom. Danny realizes he's forgotten about lunch. But really, he's not in the mood. Sleep will taste much better.

The water turns on and off. Elijah leaves the bathroom and puts his kit back in his bag.

"What about your girlfriend?" Danny asks.

"Huh?"

"You know. Cal."

"She's not my girlfriend."

"But weren't you going to write to her?"

"I did," Elijah says flatly. But he feels guilty when he says it. It's the truth when measured against the question, but it's hardly the truth when measured against his original intentions. He'd meant to write to Cal every day. He'd meant to live his days as letters to her—turning the trip into a story as he went along. Now the story has become something he can't quite share.

If he sent a letter now, it would get to Providence after his return. The end of the story would precede the beginning. Just the fact that he'll be home in less than a week fills Elijah with dread. He would put off his return for a month, if it meant more time with Julia. He wishes he could conjure a future where Julia came back with him to Providence, and the three of them—Julia, him, Cal—frolicked and conversed for the remainder of the summer. But he knows this can't happen. For a variety of unarticulated reasons.

Danny is already snoring. Elijah looks to his brother and feels a genuine guilt. He hadn't intended to abandon Danny so blatantly. He feels bad about it. But the alternative is to not see Julia at all. And that's impossible.

He hopes Danny will be okay and wonders if there's anything in Danny's life that would help him to understand.

Elijah spots two snack cakes at the foot of Danny's bed. *He just can't escape America, can he?* Carefully, Elijah moves them to the dresser so they won't get stepped on.

He tries to sleep. He closes his eyes and sees ceilings.

Melting faces, black woodwork. Saints, inscriptions, murders. Gold, angels, nightmare Popes.

There are good angels and bad angels. There are trees that become clouds.

Julia is gravitating toward him, sliding along in the half of a shell. He is wrestling demons to get to her. Wedding bells ring and children throw crosses in the air.

Only an hour has passed when he wakes up. Danny is still solidly asleep. Quietly, Elijah puts on his shoes and leaves the room. Then he comes back, writes a note thanking Danny for being so cool about everything, and leaves again. He is hours early, but he cannot wait. He will find the bench nearest to Julia's *pensione*.

Then he will wait for her to appear.

*   *   *

Danny is relieved to find it's still daylight. Naps can be devils of disorientation. He is glad to have gotten free before the day has ended. He is not surprised to find that Elijah has gone. But he is surprised by Elijah's note. It's not something Danny would've thought of at seventeen. Danny knows that at that age he would've left without a word.

Part of him can't even believe that Elijah is about to go to college, about to enter that world. Danny still thinks of him as twelve, their parents' favorite, so sure of what is right. But now he's off with a college girl. Or, more accurately, a dropped-out-of-college girl. Something Danny would have only dreamed of when he was seventeen. And maybe still does, from the other end.

Picking up his college copy of *A Room with a View* (never read, alas), he resists the call of CNN and heads to the park square across from the hotel. Most of the benches are already taken. (*Don't these people have jobs?* Danny thinks.) Finally, he finds a spot in the shade. He cracks the paperback spine and settles in. After an hour, he's utterly absorbed and utterly despondent.

Danny puts the book in his lap and searches the park for echoes of Forster. He tries to harken back to a time when being abroad meant something. He searches for a traveler sketching a scene or writing in a journal, as Forster's characters did each afternoon. But instead he sees cell phones and shopping bags, camcorders and an occasional hardcover.

Travel is no longer a pursuit, he thinks. There is something inherently noble about that word—*pursuit.* Life should be a pursuit. But Danny doesn't feel like it is. Or, at the very least, that it's a pursuit of the right things.

The daylight dims, and the people scatter like birds. Danny sits still, watching.

He doesn't know what to do. He heads off to find the statue of David, and figures he'll go from there.

*   *   *

Statues was one of their games. There was Statues, and Runaround, and Penny Flick, and TV Tag. And others now forgotten, invented only for a single afternoon before they disappeared with sundown.

Danny remembers the first time their mother walked in on them playing Statues. They couldn't have surprised her more if they'd been dripping with blood. But instead they were absolutely still, absolutely silent, fully clothed and striking classical poses. A Frisbee for a discus. A Lincoln Log for a javelin. Not looking at each other, because then it would become a staring contest, and they would both crack up. So instead they stared into space until a single arm fell or a single leg wobbled.

It couldn't have lasted for longer than a minute. They couldn't have done it that many times. But still, Danny remembers. And when he sees the statues in Florence, he remembers the way he would try to turn himself into carved stone. The way, when Elijah was young, he would secretly be hoping that his younger brother would win. The times he dropped the Frisbee, just to give Elijah that satisfaction. Their mother walking in, not believing her eyes.

In the museum, he tries to mirror one of the statues. He tries to compete again. But it's not the same. He can stare off now for hours. He can avoid moving a muscle. But it doesn't mean anything without someone beside him. It's not a game if he's the only one playing.

Eventually, it's time for dinner. Danny realizes he should have given Elijah and Julia the dinner reservations. He is in no mood to eat alone at a fancy restaurant. Nor is he ready to concede a room-service defeat. So he grabs the travel dictionary and heads to a nearby trattoria. Forster keeps him company.

When he returns to the room, nighttime now, he calls the office to check his voice mail. There are no new messages, not even in response to the messages he sent yesterday.

It is a terrible thing to not feel missed.

Danny can no longer read. His head has started to ache again. The Tylenol is no longer in his bag—he must have put it in Elijah's by mistake. In the dim hotel light (why can't hotel rooms ever be well lit?), he opens Elijah's kit and finds a plastic baggie of pot on the top.

"What the—!" Danny cries out, dropping the bag. Then he picks it back up for examination. There's no doubt. Clearly weed.

He cannot believe it. He absolutely cannot believe it. *Elijah is traveling with drugs. He went through customs with drugs. He left drugs in our hotel room. He didn't bother to tell me that we could be arrested at any time.*

It's not the drugs themselves that bother Danny—he's inhaled his share, albeit a while ago. No, it's the *stupidity* that gets to him. The all-out stupidity of the thing.

Danny imagines the phone call he'd have to make to his parents: *"Thanks for the trip, Mom. But, Dad, we need a little help. You see, we're stuck in jail on a narcotics charge. Do you happen to know any lawyers in Florence?*" Elijah does not care. Everybody thinks he cares. Everybody thinks he's thoughtful. But he's as selfish as anybody else. His kindness has a motive, and kindness with a motive isn't really kindness at all. He pretends to be considerate, and then he leaves his brother to eat alone and sleep alone and pay for every check. He says thank you, but with Danny he never can manage to do something thanksworthy in return.

Why do I bother? Danny wonders. *What holds us together?* Because even though they spent almost every hour of their childhood together, and even though they come from the same town and the same parents, and even though they once genuinely liked each other, Elijah has somehow ended up half a world away from Danny.

"Stupid stupid stupid." Danny puts the drugs back in the kit, and the kit back in Elijah's bag. He's not going to risk throwing them out. Just his luck, he'd get nabbed by an undercover *carabiniere* as he left the hotel.

No, Danny has to sit still. He has to wait for Elijah to come home.

And then he will yell.

He hasn't yelled for years. But now he feels like yelling.

Before he can calm down—before he even has time to settle—he hears the key in the door. He stands his full height. He doesn't care how late it is. He doesn't care if Elijah is in some dreamy foreign-girlfriend bliss.

Elijah will have to answer for what he's done.

There is no thank you that can get him out of this.

The door opens.

Danny reaches for the evidence.

But it's not Elijah.

It's Julia.

"Is this a bad time?" she says. "I didn't want to wake you, so I borrowed the key."

She closes the door.

"Where's Elijah?" Danny asks. Has he known somehow to stay away—to stay in the hallway, even?

"Oh, he's asleep. He forgot to take extra clothes, and I was in the mood for a walk. So I decided to come here. You don't mind, do you?"

"No. Sure. Whatever."

It's too late for Danny to tuck in his shirt or to pick up his dirty socks from the floor. Julia doesn't seem to mind. She starts moving for Elijah's bag—Danny stops her.

"Allow me," he says, and puts Elijah's kit on the pillow, taking out the necessary clothes from underneath.

"Thanks." There is a nervous edge to Julia's voice. Danny wonders if his behavior has given the whole secret away. Even though he's angry, he doesn't want to get her involved.

"It's really nice of you to come all this way," Danny says awkwardly. "I mean, I'm sure Elijah doesn't mind wearing the same clothes two days in a row. . . ."

"That's not why I came here." Julia has stepped back now. She's looking Danny straight in the eye.

"Oh." Danny is holding out one of Elijah's shirts. He doesn't know what to do with it.

"I came here to see you."

"Oh."

"Which is entirely crazy. So I'll go now."

Flustered, Julia moves to the wrong door and heads straight for the closet. Then, realizing her mistake, she doubles back.

"Look," she says, "I don't mean to complicate things. I mean—I know this is complicated. And I'm not sure why I came here. I just wanted to see you and see what happened when I saw you. And now I have, and I've made a complete fool of myself, so I'm going to go, and you can just pretend that it never happened."

Danny puts Elijah's shirt on the bed. He studies this strange girl. And maybe it's because he's angry, or maybe because he's tired, or maybe because he's intrigued—whatever the case, he says, "You haven't made a complete fool of yourself."

"Yes, I have."

"I just don't understand." He wants clarity. He wants to define the situation. Even as he reads it in her eyes.

"You mean, about Elijah?"

"There's that."

"I don't know. I like him. Really, I do. But today in the museum, I thought that maybe . . ."

"Maybe?"

"I swore to myself when I came to Italy that I wouldn't let chances go by. You know?"

Danny nods.

"You see," Julia continues, "Elijah doesn't know lonely. *You* know lonely, and I like that."

She has come a little closer now. Or maybe he's the one who's moved—in all the confusion, it's hard to tell. Danny is undeniably attracted to her. He wouldn't have predicted it, but there it is. She is not his type, but she makes him wonder if he truly knows what his type is. He is conscious of her breathing, and his own. One more step will be too close, and not close enough.

"I was hoping that we could . . . I mean, I want you," she says.

He is not used to hearing the words. The tone.

It's nice.

You know lonely, and I like that.

He moves away from her to turn off the lights. He wants to see her in shadow. He wants to know what he wants.

There is still light from the street lamps that dangle over the park outside. She is a whisper now, her expression turned entirely to words.

"Come here," she says. It doesn't seem real. His senses are jangling and his temperature is rising and this is a girl he hardly knows, who has appeared as if conjured, bringing everything wrong and everything right.

He doesn't want to mention Elijah's name. Not because he is afraid it will turn her away. No, he is afraid that she will dismiss it, say it doesn't matter. He is afraid he will believe her, and of what he will then do.

Elijah.

Alone in a hotel room—a neat role reversal. While Danny is here with his temporary girl and his stupid drugs.

Elijah.

Julia is close enough to kiss. Her scent is all over the moment. Her eyes are watching his. She is as uneasy and vulnerable as he feels.

"Come here," she says again. "It'll be all right."

It would be so easy. To whisper, "I know." To lean into the embrace. To let the lighting dictate the future. To shut off the sense of anywhere but here.

It would be so easy.

And yet Danny turns his head. He breaks the stare. He pushes the moment away.

"What is it?" she asks.

And again, he can't say Elijah's name. Because she will give him a reason to get past it. She will give him the reason to go on.

It would be so easy.

"I can't" is all he says.

She nods. She backs down.

She shivers.

"It was crazy to come here. I'm sorry."

"It's okay."

"No, really."

"Really."

Go back to my brother.

Stay away from my brother.

She gathers herself and leaves the room. The hallway brightness flashes, and then it's dark again.

Come here.

Go away.

Please.

* * *

Elijah is an atheist, but he prays. In the quiet, pre-sunlight morning, he is thankful for the path that has led him to this moment, to this bed. He is not thankful to anyone or anything specific. He does not bargain—or even hope—to make the moment longer. He believes in everyday graces. He believes that nothing is arranged, but everything is an arrangement. The angle of Julia's naked shoulder is not preordained. But he is thankful just the same. The lift and release of his breath is not something to be measured. And he is thankful nonetheless.

He will not wake her, and he will not sleep. He will lay in wonder, and he will daydream.

* * *

"Can I come to Rome with you?" she asks, as soon as she opens her eyes.

"Of course," he replies.

* * *

Danny is amazed that he's slept. Of all nights to sleep. The emotions that would have singularly kept him up—anger, lust, confusion—combined to exhaust him into submission. Now he's awake, and the evening returns to him like a movie remembered—every word was said, but none of it seems real.

He thinks about home, and about going home. Every vacation has a shelf life, and maybe this one will expire before Rome.

He doesn't expect Elijah to come back anytime soon. But, strangely enough, the door opens a little after nine. For an instant, Danny hopes that Julia has returned. He closes his eyes and recognizes that the footsteps aren't hers. Elijah is back, packing up.

Danny feigns sleep. Elijah is careful, quiet. Danny knows this could be seen as respectful. But really, Elijah doesn't want to get caught.

Danny waits until Elijah is close by. At the foot of the bed. Hovering over his clothes.

Then Danny opens his eyes and says, "I found your drugs."

Elijah stops what he's doing and turns to his brother. "You found me drugs?"

"No. I found *your* drugs."

"Oh, you mean the pot?" Elijah is rooting through his bag, looking for something. "Feel free to take some."

Danny sits up now. "You're kidding, right?"

"No, really. Go crazy. I think Julia can get us more."

"So they're Julia's drugs?"

"They're not *anybody's* drugs, okay? They're, like, community property."

Elijah is so laid-back—feeling generous, even. Danny wants to strangle him.

"I have just one question," he says. "Do you ever *think?* For just one moment out of your dippy happy life, do you ever think about things? About little things like international laws, or my feelings, or our parents."

"Our parents aren't little things, Danny."

"DON'T DANNY ME," Danny yells. "We have to talk. Right now. About you. And thinking. Because I don't want some Italian cop pulling us over and busting our asses. And I'm not sure that you should be spending all your time with this Julia."

Now he's got Elijah's attention.

"What do you mean, *this Julia?* Don't drag her into your guilt trip, okay?"

Danny's on his feet now. "I haven't dragged her into anything. You have."

"I have?"

"Yes."

They're facing off now. They haven't done this in so long.

"So what are you saying?" Elijah asks.

"Are you sleeping with her?" Danny asks back.

"WHAT?"

"I said, are you sleeping with her?"

"Are you saying I have to sleep with someone in order to be with them?"

"I'll take that as a 'no.'"

"Take what you want. I'm going." Elijah has his notebook now and moves to the door.

Danny blocks him. "Not so fast. I want to talk to you about Julia. I'm just not sure you're seeing everything."

"I thought you liked her."

"I do. I did. It's just that—"

"I'm spending too much time with her. Which means I'm not spending enough time with you. But you know what? I *enjoy* myself when I'm with her. I do *not* enjoy myself when I'm with you. And neither do you. So consider Julia a blessing."

"In disguise."

"What do you mean?"

Danny is so close to telling. He is so close to shattering Elijah into little lovelorn pieces. But he can't. Invoking the moral high ground somehow makes you lose it. Using a secret as a weapon makes you almost as bad as the transgressor.

He will not tell.

Elijah will never know the only good gesture Danny can make.

"Doesn't your wistful romanticism ever get tiring?" Danny sighs.

"No," Elijah says. "*You* get tiring. Look, I'm sorry. But I have to go."

"Where are you going?"

"To Rome. With Julia. We'll take the train."

"Don't be silly."

"I'm not being silly at all. I'm *thinking*, Danny. Isn't that what you want me to do?" In two short minutes, he packs his bag— no hard thing, since he was never around enough to unpack.

"You don't have to do this," Danny says as Elijah reaches the door.

"You don't have to say that," Elijah ricochets. "You don't have to start being nice now. It doesn't suit you. I know where we're staying. I'll see you in Rome."

With that, he leaves.

As he does, Danny realizes his shoelaces are untied.

It is too late, though, for Danny to say anything about it. If Elijah trips, there's nothing he can do. If Elijah falls, he will still feel in some way responsible. For having noticed too late.

IV. ROME

As Danny drives the Autostrada del Sole toward Rome, he cannot help but think of everything that's happened. From Julia's hello to Elijah's nonexistent goodbye. The flicker of Julia's glance, the barely bridled fury in Elijah's eyes. For once, Danny wanted Elijah to come right out and say *I hate you,* if only so he could say, *Well, I don't hate you* back.

The cars swerve past him, but this time Danny isn't in a rush. Everything seems so precarious to him. Like driving. Like the fact that all you need to do is move your hand a quarter of an inch and you will be in the next lane. Crashed and dead. So easy.

Concentration. Driving requires concentration, but Danny isn't quite there. He is driving by instinct, like the other thousand strangers upon whom his safety depends. Towns and street signs whiz by, and Danny tries to recall Julia's exact expression. He knows he did the right thing. But still he feels like he's done himself some wrong.

At this very moment, Elijah and Julia are on a train. Or maybe they're still in Florence, dancing along the Ponte Vecchio. Elijah is ignorantly grinning, laughing at the performance. But who is Julia thinking about? That is what Danny wants to know.

He tells himself it's just a summer thing. *Fling* is such an apt word—it casually throws you. Then life resumes.

Danny drives. He wishes he could tell the truth to someone, so it could be recognized.

"It's good to share a life." His mother had said this to him not too long ago. He had come home for Sunday dinner, something

he tried to do once every month. His parents, as always, were on their best behavior—only minimal discussion of Elijah, and virtually no mention of future weddings or grandchildren. Many of Danny's friends—especially his female friends—faced a terrifying litany every time they stepped into their parents' home: *Aren't you getting old? We're not getting any younger. Isn't Alexandra a beautiful name for a baby girl?* But Danny's parents were good. Either they had faith that they didn't have to interfere, or they'd already given up hope. The only marriage reference came after dinner while Danny's mother washed and Danny's father dried. They had done this for as long as he could remember, with the radio turned on to the news.

"Don't you ever want to dry?" Danny had asked his mother.

And she'd smiled and said, "It's good to share a life."

Making it sound so easy.

Danny was approaching Rome now. He could see Coca-Cola signs and Mel Gibson billboards. The return of the common culture. Something he could be a part of. Larry King nightly in seventy countries worldwide. Star Wars chat rooms on the Internet. Madonna in any language. The closeness and the emptiness of it all. And Danny in his Avis rent-a-car, turning on the radio, hoping it will help.

It's good to share a life—and it's good to share minutes and hours, too, Danny thinks. With a wife. With a husband. With a boyfriend, girlfriend, best friend. With a fling. With a brother.

* * *

For a moment, one brief moment, Elijah and Julia run out of things to say. They are on the train, headed south through Tuscany. They have just been talking about windmills, even though there aren't any windmills in sight. Julia was recalling Amsterdam, and Elijah drew her outward. He asked her about tulips, then asked her about windmills. He himself has never seen one. But they've appeared in his dreams, each a different color, swirling as they spin.

"Ah, the windmills of your mind," she says. Then falls silent.

He doesn't know what to say next.

She stares out the window—he can see her reflected over the moving countryside. Her eyes aren't fixed on any one place. They are fixed on the blur.

Her expression is the kind that shifts the air into stillness and cold.

"Julia," he says gently, throwing her name into the breach.

It takes her a second to turn. Then she smiles tenderly.

"You have no idea how confused I am," she says.

"So give me an idea."

She just shakes her head.

"I don't want to taint you. I want you to remain clear."

Can't you see you're confusing me already? Elijah wants to say. But he doesn't. He wants to unburden her, not the opposite.

He lets her turn back to the window. He takes out *Pictures from Italy.* As she looks out the glass, she reaches back for his hand. He lets her take it. The book rests against his chest, open and unread.

Elijah feels like a grown-up, with a grown-up love.

* * *

Danny gets lost, so incredibly lost on his way into Rome that he almost pulls off to the side of the road and abandons the car. His hotel, d'Inghilterra, must be on some obscure street, since everyone he asks just shrugs or points vaguely. Hemingway once slept there, but that doesn't help.

It's always a low when life begins to imitate an old Chevy Chase movie. He circles the same roads at least ten times, searching for any sort of direction. He vows never to rent a car in a foreign country again. Next time, he'll take the train, or a taxi between cities, if that's what it takes.

Danny curses up a storm. And feels stupid. Because cursing in front of company at least generates an effect. Cursing alone is like taking a Hi-Liter to futility.

At the seventy-eighth red light, Danny leans over and asks directions from a cab driver. The cab driver, amazingly, says, "Follow me." In just two short minutes, Danny is in front of the hotel. He tries to run out and pay the driver, but the taxi is gone before he can even make the gesture.

"Your reservation is for *due*," the stark man behind the reception counter says, his voice carrying through the grand hallway before being absorbed by the curtains.

Danny nods.

"And the other party?"

"Is coming."

"*Oggi?*"

"I believe so."

Danny is perversely afraid that word will get back to his

parents: *Your sons didn't check in together. They must have had a fight.*

Danny knows this will be viewed as his failure.

"What did you do?" his mother will ask, followed by a dollar-a-minute pause.

"Nothing," he'll reply.

And then she'll say, *"That's exactly what I thought."*

* * *

As they pull into the Stazione Termini, Julia turns to Elijah and says, "It's okay. I'm here now."

"But where have you been?" he cannot help but ask.

"It doesn't matter," she replies. Even though it does.

*   *   *

With all due respect to d'Inghilterra, Danny decides he is sick of Italian hotels. There is something to be said for opulent lobbies, but he would trade in every last ornamentation for a well-lit, generously bedded room where the towels are not made of the same material as the tablecloths.

All of the driving has taken its toll, and although Danny refuses to nap, his senses are blunted as he walks outside the hotel. *I am in Rome,* he says to himself, trying to muster the vacation's last waning pulse of enthusiasm. It is too late and too gray to go to the Pantheon—he wants more celestial weather for that. So instead of the Usual Attractions, Danny shifts gears and decides to go shopping. Not for himself. He can't imagine anything more boring than shopping for himself. But his gift list must be reckoned with. He must lay his souvenirs at the altars of his co-workers, lest they think he hasn't been thinking of them while he was away.

The list is still neatly folded into his wallet. Gladner and Gladner. Allison. Perhaps John. Mom and Dad, of course. His assistant, Derek.

Since his hotel is near the Spanish Steps, Danny decides to duck his head into the posher stores. Especially for Gladner and Gladner. He thinks it would be most appropriate to buy them ties. And maybe a tie for his father.

So he heads to the men's stores and is met with gross indifference. Clearly, a customer is not important unless he or she is Japanese. Danny has never been able to stand disdainful salespeople, but after he storms out of four stores, he realizes he

167

must accept his least-favored-nationality status if he's going to get Gladner and Gladner something classy.

The prices are extraordinarily high. But Danny thinks, *If you're not going to buy an expensive gift for your bosses, then who are you ever going to spend money on?*

He thinks this for a good five minutes as he shuffles through the tie racks. Then he asks himself, *What the hell am I doing?*

Gladner and Gladner already have ties. They have closets full of ties. And most of them are spectacularly dull. Polo stripes and wallpaper prints.

When Gladner and Gladner go away on vacation, they don't bring anything back for Danny. Not even a pen with a floating Eiffel Tower or a paperweight of the Sphinx.

Danny steps away from the tie racks. He steps out of the store. The salesmen do not nod a goodbye. He is not even there to them. He is nobody.

The street is aswarm with people. Danny stands like a hydrant and looks over his list. It is so short, really. Take off Gladner and Gladner, and he is left with five people. Two parents. One co-worker. One assistant. One work-friend.

The question blasts through him. Paralyzes him.

How did my world get so small?

A pack of students pushes him aside. Two girls giggle at his slow reaction.

Two parents. One co-worker. One assistant. One work-friend.

This is not my life, he thinks. There are college friends, and Will, and his high school girlfriend Marjorie, who he meets for lunch every now and then.

They're just not on the list.

But they could be.

Danny shoves his hands in his pockets, digging for a pen. He needs a new list.

Allison, yes. Derek. And John, without a question mark this time. And Will. And Marjorie. And Joan and Terry, even though they live in California and the gift will have to be shipped.

No Gladner. No Gladner.

Allison first. Allison, who puts up with him. Allison, who smiles and kvetches and asks him out for a beer, even though he's technically the boss. He wants to buy her something special. Not chocolate—he's always brought her chocolate, even when he went to Houston and other areas not known for their confectionary. No, he wants to find her something that she especially would like. So she can know that he has an inkling of who she is.

Three stores later, he finds it: a hand-sewn journal, its cover a painted river.

And for John, a pair of opera glasses.

And for Derek, a tie more expensive than Gladner's or Gladner's.

And for his mother, a scarf made of seven fabrics, woven with gold threads.

And for his father, an antique deck of cards.

And for Will . . .

Danny doesn't know.

Is Will the same person now, or would any gift bought for Will be one year, five months, and now five days out of date?

Is the Jesus night-light still appropriate? The clapping nun? The blue-glass lamp that glows rather than burns?

They all seem right, but uncertainly so.

So Danny returns to his room, takes out the hotel stationery, and begins to write a very long letter.

* * *

Meanwhile, Elijah and Julia are in another hotel room, in another part of town. Elijah is feeling amorous, but Julia fends him off with her *Let's Go!* guide. Relenting, Elijah says he wants to go stoned to the Vatican. Julia vetoes this idea. Her rebellious streak goes only so far.

"You've offended my inner nun," she says, slipping her wallet into her bag.

"You have an inner nun?"

"Of course. Every girl has one. Some are just louder than others."

Elijah pauses for a moment, packing his backpack. "Even Jewish girls?"

"*Especially* Jewish girls. Thank Julie Andrews for that."

Outside, it is a strange combination of hot and cloudy. Taking hold of Elijah's hand, Julia leads the way. She does not slow down to talk or to point out any of the sights (the shop entirely devoted to chess sets, the man who is putting birdseed on his shoulders to attract the pigeons). Elijah can tell she is determined, but he can't say exactly why.

"Hold on." He's trying to slow her down a little. But she takes it a different way, and holds his hand tighter, pulling him along.

Something has changed between them. The challenge for Elijah is to find out what exactly it is and what it means. They have left the first stage of romance—the rhapsody of *us*. Where everything is *you-me* or *me-you* or a giddily tentative *we*. Now *him* and *her* are asserting themselves, each given a private, pensive depth. Within the rhapsody of *us*, Elijah could think, *I don't really know you, but I will*. Now he is not so sure.

But he will not stop trying. She is still here, and that means something. She is still smiling, and he doesn't wish that to be gone.

The Vatican, Elijah has always been told, is the size of Central Park. And the crowds therein, he soon learns, are akin to a free concert on the Great Lawn. Although it's possible he's seen so many people in one place before, he's never seen them levered into an art museum—pushing, wending, photographing, grasping onto children and purses. It is hard to stand still, not to mention contemplate.

The art is overwhelming. It is overload. There is too much of it to be truly breathtaking. Instead, it comes across as bragging. Or perhaps only the non-Catholics feel that way.

It's disorienting. Julia and Elijah try to trace a coherent path, but the building defies them. There are more twists in the halls than there are angels on the ceiling. Packs of foreign-exchange youth and tough gangs of elderly pilgrims block the corridors as they listen to their overenthusiastic guides.

It's only in the Sistine Chapel that the quiet returns. The hushed, respectful movements subdue most of the flashbulbs.

"It's amazing," Julia whispers, and Elijah has to agree. The creation of Adam is surprisingly small—Elijah had always assumed it took up most of the ceiling. But no, there is so much more. It doesn't even stand on its own—it is part of a history, part of a story. The triumph is the space between the fingers: if God exists anywhere, he exists there. That almost-but-not-quite touch.

Elijah and Julia drift slowly through the chapel. And when they are through, they walk backward and drift through again.

Outside, Elijah debates going into the gift shop. He can hear Cal saying, *"Don't do it, don't give them a penny."* So he saves his postcard money, but doesn't say anything when Julia buys a souvenir book.

"Who knows when I'll be back?" she says.

"Tomorrow?" Elijah offers. "A week from now?"

Julia shakes her head and smiles.

"A month from now?" Elijah pursues.

They are walking through St. Peter's Square, which is actually something of a circle. Elijah is not asking the question he wants to ask, but Julia picks up on it anyway.

"I don't know what I'm doing next," she says. "I don't know where I'll be."

"You could stay here."

"I could."

"Or go back to Canada?"

"Not an option."

"California?"

"Ditto."

"How about the East Coast?" Elijah asks, his voice a nervous suitor. "I know this great town in Rhode Island. You'd really like it."

"You're sweet," she says, patting his arm.

And it's funny the way she says it, because he'd always assumed that *sweet* was a good thing.

Now he's not so sure.

* * *

It is July twilight by the time Danny finishes his letter to Will. His hand is raw—he is not used to writing like this. Not on such a scale.

He has told Will everything he could think of and, in doing so, told himself many things that he hadn't thought he'd known.

Whenever I am asked about my life, I invariably answer with a reference to work.

At work I feel needed in a way that I've never been needed before.

My parents tricked me into coming to Italy.

I think they are worried about me.

I don't know.

Elijah is somewhere else in the city. Perhaps that's for the best. Perhaps it's enough that one of us is happy. I can give him that much, and not much more.

It's so strange to have words mean exactly what they're supposed to mean. No manipulation, no subtext, no enticement to buy.

Danny puts the letter in an envelope. He puts the envelope in a book. He puts the book in his bag.

Then he looks around the hotel room, his glance settling on the second, still-made bed.

He wonders where Elijah is. And Julia. But more Elijah.

He imagines Elijah as he is back at his boarding school, the center of his friends' orbit. Always there for a midnight call. Always ready to listen. Voted Most Likely to Succeed—not because he is the most likely to succeed, but because everyone likes him the most.

It is a dangerous thing with brothers, to think that you could be as strong as them, or as wise as them, or as good as them. To believe that you could have been the same person, if only you hadn't gone a different way. To think that your parents raised you the same, and that your genes combined the same, and that the rest of what has happened is all your triumph . . . or failure.

This is why so many kids want to believe that their siblings are adopted. So that the potential isn't the same. So that you can't look at your brother and say, *I could have been like him, if only I'd tried.*

Danny doesn't want to be as strong as his brother (Elijah is basically a wimp) or as wise as his brother (Danny has no desire to read Kerouac). It is the goodness that grates. Even if it's mostly false (Danny would like to believe, but doesn't really), Elijah has the gift of talking to people, of being liked by people, and Danny can't help but wonder why he didn't turn out the same way.

Restless, he leaves the hotel. The shops are more welcoming now that they're closed. Danny examines the windows of the Via Borgognona and the Via Condotti. Then he has a leisurely dinner; he is getting used to eating alone in public. He watches the people at the other tables and drinks plenty of wine.

After dinner is over, he wanders farther. He keeps expecting to bump into Elijah and Julia. Instead, he comes to Trevi— the fountain of youths. Teenagers from various nations are perched around its rim, cackling and flirting and preening. It is a point of convergence for those who are not wearied by midnight and everything after.

Danny stands to the side and watches the swagger, banter,

and anguish. The packs of girls and the packs of boys collide and separate at will. For Danny, it is like visiting a neighborhood where he once lived. The familiarity and the distance of it.

He is no longer young, and he is far from old.

They laugh so hard around the fountain. He misses that acutely. Not the folly of entanglements or the drama of indecision. But the laughter. The bold bravado that can take you through the night.

Danny doesn't want to be them, and he doesn't even want to stay and watch them. He only wants to find an intensity to match their own.

Elijah and Julia go to a French movie with Italian subtitles. Then, as the languages intermingle in their memory, they return to the hotel.

That night, the rhapsody of *us* returns, in physical form. They have a conversation of movements, silent from the moment they walk in the door. They undress each other completely—tracing, gliding, holding. Only the bodies whisper. Breath signals. Fingers entwine.

It is almost like floating. It is that simple, that understood.

Elijah closes his eyes. Julia kisses his eyelids. He flutters them open, and Julia whispers *"no."* So he closes them again, and the moment continues.

Elijah feels colors, and wonders if he's in love.

* * *

The next day is July 4th. Danny wears a red-and-white Polo shirt and a pair of blue shorts. He can't help himself.

In the morning, he heads to the ruins. He thinks he will beat the midday heat, but in this he is wrong. The day is scorching, the lack of shade relentless. Danny loses interest quickly. The area he sees, with its rows and rows of broken columns, must have once been grand. But now it is only rows and rows of broken columns. They are not even beautiful. They are merely, admirably, old. Danny takes a few photos, but it's more for historical reasons than out of any visual pleasure.

It is soon unbearably hot. Danny throngs to a streetside vendor in search of Evian. The line is long, but Danny doesn't see he has a choice. As he waits, a hand taps him on the shoulder.

"Danny Silver?" a voice asks.

Startled, Danny turns—and is even more startled to see Ari Rubin, from Camp Wahnkeemakah.

"Ari?"

It must be—what—seven years? More?

"So it *is* you. That's unbelievable."

Ari looks amazing. Tan, tall, his hair no longer in a bowl cut. From Camp Wahnkeemakah. Ages ago.

He doesn't look at all the same. Except it's recognizably him.

"What are you doing here?" Ari asks.

"Vacation," Danny replies, still stunned. Ari was his best friend for three straight summers. They were pen pals for two summers after that, and then drifted apart.

Seven years? More like ten.

Danny has to turn away to buy his bottles of water. But when he turns back, Ari is still there, beaming.

"And what are you doing here?" Danny asks.

"Working."

"Business?"

"Pilot."

Danny laughs. *Of course* Ari is a pilot. Ari, whose mother would send him a new model airplane every week. Ari, whose bunk smelled like Krazy Glue and balsa wood.

A pilot.

"I can't believe I recognized you."

"Me neither."

They lost touch because Danny lived in New Jersey and Ari lived in Ohio, and neither of them liked to talk on the phone. But when they'd been at camp, they were nearly inseparable. They planned all their activities together, requested the same bunks, and even tried to be on the same Color War teams. There was one time, the second summer, when Danny had been stuck in the infirmary with a flu bug. The only thing to do in the infirmary was watch videos. Which would have been an unparalleled delight, except the only two movies they had were *Annie* and *Predator*. Danny would have gone absolutely bonkers if Ari hadn't come to his window at every available break, telling him what was going on and making jokes to count away the hours.

Danny can see that Ari is as amazed by this surreal reunion as he is. They lost touch because of the distance between New Jersey and Ohio. Now they meet up in Rome. Of course.

Ari seems genuinely thrilled, but there's also a flicker of worry, a consciousness of time in his eyes.

"You have to be somewhere?" Danny guesses.

Ari nods.

"Now?"

"Yes—but . . . are you free tonight?"

"Absolutely."

Dinner arrangements are made. Danny cannot stop shaking his head at the coincidence of it all. Ari says goodbye, and as he leaves, Danny can see that he's shaking his head, too.

Still smiling, Danny heads to the old Jewish ghetto. For at least another fifteen minutes, he doesn't even think about the heat.

* * *

Elijah awakens to the sound of rain. Or at least he thinks it's rain. It's really the hotel's ancient air conditioner, struggling unsuccessfully against the heat of the day.

Julia is nowhere to be found. It is eleven o'clock in the morning, which means Elijah slept for at least four hours. The bathroom door is open and all the fixtures are silent—Julia is not in there, either. Elijah rolls over and throws on some clothes. After a few minutes of vague worry, he hears the key in the door. Julia walks in.

"Where have you been?" he asks.

"Thinking," she replies, and it is to Elijah's credit that he realizes: *To Julia, thinking is indeed a place.*

He remembers that it's July 4th, but that seems like a rude thing to mention to a Canadian. So instead he wishes her a very happy Friday, and she in turn looks at him with an almost resigned curiosity.

"Let's go to the Colosseum," she says, and indeed they do. Strangely enough, it is not as intact as Elijah had thought it would be. He'd imagined a full and complex building with part of the rim chipped off. But instead it looks like something unearthed from the Planet of the Apes.

"People died here," Julia whispers.

Elijah pulls her into the shade and begins to kiss her. Almost immediately, he sees he's done the wrong thing. Although Julia's body doesn't move away, it feels as if she's left it. Elijah says, "Well, then," and the two of them move on.

They walk through the ancient city without really saying a word. Elijah wants to go to the Pantheon, but that's where Julia went while he slept. So instead they head to the Piazza Navona, in the hope of sitting down to eat. In the hope of conversation.

Elijah can see that Julia is troubled, and it is the core of his nature to want to make it better. Whenever he says *"I'm sorry,"* she tells him it is not his fault. He knows this. But he is sorry just the same.

He blames time, for there are only two days left until he must return to America. Two days left to answer the question: *And now what?*

The two of them sit on a bench. Julia leans her body into his and closes her eyes. He takes this as a good sign. Although it is wretchedly hot, the sun feels good as it shines across his face. Careful not to shift away from Julia, Elijah studies his surroundings. The fountain at the heart of the piazza is beautiful, topped by an obelisk inscribed in languages from a different time. A blond boy with a pink teddy bear—he must be about six—points at an overweight couple sitting on slim cafe chairs. There is a breeze. It is nice. A group of fifty or so young Italian women passes by, trailing talk. Another boy chases pigeons. He is running in circles. Elijah closes his eyes and stays still. He and Julia are picture-perfect statues. The fountain splashes in murmurs. The breeze continues. The tourists fade away. A clock that no longer works watches over them.

Minutes pass. Elijah opens his eyes as a bride walks by. Her long gown glides across the stone, picking up the dust of the square. She smiles at Elijah smiling. Or perhaps she doesn't see Elijah at all.

A photographer arranges the full wedding party in front of the fountain—bride, groom, and an assemblage of family members, each with a paper fan to rustle away the heat.

Julia pulls away from Elijah and stands. She stares for a moment at the bride and the groom. The expression on her face is a different language to Elijah. And he cannot ask for a translation, for fear of exposing an ignorance that love can't conquer.

Love?

Julia is walking, then waiting for Elijah to follow.

"Julia," he says. But she is already too far away.

*   *   *

The Jewish ghetto makes Danny feel hope and sadness. Hope because the Sinagoga Ashkenazita is still there. Sadness because it must be guarded by *carabinieri* armed with machine guns.

After a tour of the Jewish Museum, Danny heads to the Piazza Navona. He has heard that the fountain is beautiful, and it does not disappoint. A wedding party is having its picture taken in front of the obelisk. From the ragged state of their smiles, Danny can tell they've been at it for a little while. The photographer is manipulating the group into preposterous poses, using a lamppost as a prop. The groom lovingly arranges the bride's dress so that she may sit. In this heat, the bride is no doubt wishing she'd worn a miniskirt. The groom is clearly itching to take off his jacket and dive into the water.

Tourists take pictures of the photographer taking pictures.

Danny sits on a bench and watches. In a nearby cafe, a lunchtime guitarist is singing "Knockin' on Heaven's Door," only the refrain sounds much more like "Knock, knock, knockin' on lemon's door."

Soon the song turns to another song. And another. Danny sits and listens and watches as the people pass by.

At long last, the wedding photographs are done. Joy returns to the faces of the bride and the groom. He lifts her up and swings her through the air. The photographer fumbles for his camera, but he is too late. As the bride and groom parade back through the square, the bride looks at Danny and gives a little smile and salute. Danny smiles back, and wonders where such familiarity came from.

* * *

"Let's get dressed up for dinner," Julia says. It is the end of the day—all the ruins have been visited, all the squares have been crossed. Elijah is exhausted.

"I'm not sure I have anything to wear," he confesses.

"Didn't you bring a suit?"

"I'm not sure I own a suit."

"I'll bet Danny brought a suit."

"I'll bet Danny couldn't travel without one. Just in case there was, you know, a business emergency."

Julia pulls a sleeveless black dress from her bag.

"Do you have anything that would remotely go with this?"

"What's the occasion?"

"Isn't it your Independence Day? Or maybe I just want to take you out to a wonderful dinner. Do you think you could deal with that?"

"I think I could manage."

Elijah triumphantly pulls a tie from the bottom of his bag. Julia applauds and slips off her clothes. Before Elijah can react, she is putting on the dress.

She looks even more beautiful with it on.

*　*　*

Danny is nervous that Ari won't show up. He has been looking forward to this too much—he is relying too heavily on a random encounter. He paces the sidewalk in front of the restaurant for twenty minutes—fifteen minutes before Ari is supposed to show and five minutes after. Danny is worried that he misheard the directions. He is worried he is waiting at the wrong place, for the wrong person.

Then Ari appears, apologizing the five minutes away. He shakes Danny's hand and ushers him in the door. The maitre d' seems to know him, and the table they get has a spectacular view of the nighttime alleyways.

"I'm so glad I found you," Ari says, sitting down.

"Likewise."

It has been so many years, but they plunge into them quickly. Danny says he can't believe Ari is already a pilot, and Ari tells him how it came to be. He dropped out of Harvard for flight school, which caused his parents no end of grief.

"Is your mom still in Ohio?" Danny asks.

Ari nods. "Same house. Same life. Her gallery keeps getting bigger and bigger—she just bought out the jeweler next door, so she can expand again."

"And your father?"

"What wife was he on when we last wrote to each other?"

"The second, I think. No wait—he was just starting with . . . Laureen."

"I can't believe you remember her name!" Ari exclaims. (Neither can Danny, for that matter.) "She actually never made

185

it to the altar. Dad left her for Gail. Now he's with Wanda, soon to be wife number four."

"Do you like her?"

"I like that she's his age."

"Does your mom still make those raisin cookies?"

"Yup. You are still, to this day, the only person who liked them without raisins."

"I didn't appreciate raisins back then."

"You always wanted chocolate chips."

The waiter makes a third pass at the table, and Danny and Ari finally take up their menus. Danny steals glances at Ari as Ari carefully reads the selections. He wasn't a particularly attractive kid, but he's grown up to be an attractive man. Not that Danny can really tell. But he takes some satisfaction that it's not only the bastards who get good looks. Danny remembers back when they were in camp—every body change seemed like an event, shocking and fascinating, the prelude to such alien phenomena as sex and shaving. Now they've crossed over to that other world. They are comfortable within their own skin (or at least Ari seems to be).

Did they even think about the real future back then? Did they just assume they'd be friends forever?

Danny cannot remember what his younger self foretold.

* * *

Julia takes Elijah to a room lit only by candles. There are other people within it, but they are only flickers in the background, sounds in the air.

"This is wonderful," Elijah says. He had tried to stop at an ATM on the way, but Julia wouldn't let him. "It's my night," she had said.

The owner gave Elijah a jacket at the door. Julia said it made him look dashing. Like a film star.

Now she watches intently as he unfolds his napkin and places it on his lap. She is taking him all in.

He picks up the menu, but she waves him down.

"Allow me," she says.

The waiter approaches. His hair is the color of burnt embers. Julia orders for them both, her Italian faltering in parts.

The waiter nods, understanding. Two minutes later, he is back with the wine, which Julia sips to her satisfaction. The room is warm, and Elijah can feel himself settling into the candlelight glow. The waiter pours the wine. Julia smiles secretly.

"A toast," she says, raising her glass. "To the end."

"I was engaged once," Ari tells Danny. "I really thought she was the one. I really thought, *This is it*. I met her while I was in school—we volunteered at the same shelter. Perfect, right? She was a nurse, so that made scheduling a little hard. But we managed. For three years, we managed. I proposed to her the first time she flew with me. My instructor lent me his Cessna. At first, Anna was really nervous—she wasn't a big fan of flying. But I asked her to trust me, and she did. I took her up over the Rockies—it was a gorgeous day, you could see everything. When we hit ten thousand feet, I put on the autopilot, pulled the ring from my pocket, leaned over to her, and asked her to marry me. Right away, she said yes.

"I thought that was the hard part, but I was wrong. We moved in together, which was great when we were both there, but we weren't both there a lot. I graduated, and Continental picked me up. Denver was still my home base, but I had to go wherever they wanted me to go. At first, Anna understood this. She supported it. But after a while it wore us both down. Finally, one night I came home—it must have been two in the morning—and she said it was too much. She said she wasn't sure she was old enough to be anybody's wife. And she sure as hell wasn't old enough to be a pilot's wife. I couldn't argue with her. We both realized we'd gotten as far as we could go, and that the only way to go from there was backward. And neither of us wanted to go through that."

Ari pauses and takes another sip of his water. "How about you? Anything like that?"

Danny shakes his head. "Nothing."

"Not even a little?"

"Not even a little."

* * *

At first, Elijah thinks he's misunderstood her. Or that she's misunderstood him.

"To the end?" he asks.

"To the end," she repeats, taking a sip of wine.

"But tomorrow's my last night. I leave Sunday."

"I know."

He still doesn't get it.

"So why is this the end?"

Julia puts down her glass and says, simply, "Because it is."

* * *

Danny is amazed that he feels so comfortable. He is amazed that while there are some people you can see every day and not say a word to, there are other people whom you can see once a year—or once a decade, or once a life—and say anything.

"How's your brother?" Ari asks. "God, he must be old now, right? I remember you writing to me about how you were going to teach him multiplication, even though he was only four. You were going to make him the smartest kid in his nursery school class."

Danny starts off by saying Elijah's fine. Then he finds himself telling Ari everything that's happened—from the moment he got his parents' call to the moment Elijah left the hotel room in Florence. He remembers that Ari has two brothers of his own—two brothers and three stepsisters.

Ari listens carefully. Danny isn't just talking to say things aloud. He is talking directly to him.

"I don't know how we got this way, Ari. I don't know when I stopped wanting to help him, or even when I stopped wanting him to be smart. I *dreaded* coming here with him. I really didn't want him to come—I figured I'd be happier alone. And I don't know whether it's because he was here and then he left, or whether I was just wrong in the first place, but right now I wish he was here. Not at this table with us. But I just wish I knew where he was."

"It's hard."

"Yeah, it's hard."

Ari puts down his fork and looks right into Danny's eyes.

"Brothers are not like sisters," he says. From his tone, Danny can tell this is something he's learned. "They don't call each other every week. They don't have secret worlds to share. Can you think of two brothers who are really, inseparably close? No, for brothers it's a different set of rules. Like it or not, we're held to the bare minimum. Will you be there for him if he needs you? Of course. Should you love him without question? Absolutely. But those are the easy things. Do you make him a large part of your life, an equal to a wife or a best friend? At the beginning, when you're kids, the answer is often yes. But when you get to high school, or older? Do you tell him everything? Do you let him know who you really are? The answer is usually no. Because all these other things get in the way. Girlfriends. Rebellion. Work."

"So this is normal?" Danny asks.

"Don't go for normal," Ari suggests. "Go for happy. Go for what you want it to be instead of settling for what it is."

* * *

Elijah doesn't see how he and Julia can go on with the meal, but they do. She asks him about home, and he finds himself telling her about the time Mindy got fired from her temp job at the Gap because she couldn't fold properly, and the time his friends Max and Cindy got caught making out in Cindy's parents' bed. Her parents never said a word about it, but her mother threw out the sheets.

Julia is laughing, and Elijah is smiling, and to any other person in the room they must look like a happy couple. But all Elijah can think is, *It's over.* And there's nothing in Julia's face that says anything different.

"What do you want?" Julia asks over dessert.

"From what?" Elijah asks.

"From love. I mean, from the person you're with."

"Love is enough," Elijah answers.

Julia shakes her head. "It's more complicated than that. I know I'm only, what, three years older than you? But let me tell you, it can get so complicated. Try to keep it simple. Here's what I think. We all want someone to build a fort with. We want somebody to swap crayons with and play hide-and-seek with and live out imaginary stories with. We start out getting that from our family. Then we get it from our friends. And then, for whatever reasons, we get it into our heads that we need to get that feeling—that *intimacy*—from a single someone else. We call that growing up. But really, when you take sex out of it, what we want is a companion. And we make that so damn hard to find."

193

When dessert is over, Julia pays with a Gold Card. Then she touches Elijah's hand and tells him it's probably time to get his things.

She seems sad when she says it. But he can tell he's not going to change her mind.

* * *

Ari walks Danny back to the hotel. He has an early flight
the next morning, otherwise they'd probably walk all night.
They are talking tangents now, but somehow the tangents connect. Ari is talking about all the places he's been. Danny feels
like they are all the places he wants to go. The Sahara. Bu-
dapest. Sydney. New York.

Danny pulls Ari into a 7-Eleven and shows him the Italian
translation of his work. Ari is amused, and asks if the snack cake
is suitable for framing. Danny says he doesn't think so—but perhaps that can be the slogan for the new Pop-Tarts campaign.

Ari wants to buy one of the Divines, but Danny is afraid he
might actually try to eat it. So instead they get Slurpees—their
own shamelessly American way of celebrating the Fourth of July.

"So your job sounds like fun," Ari says as they leave the convenience store.

Danny nods. "I'm afraid that's the problem. Maybe I enjoy
it too much."

"I know what you mean."

"Someday we'll have a balance, right?"

"Someday. Yes."

Across Rome, towers chime midnight. Danny raises his
Slurpee in a toast.

"To reunions," he says.

"To reunions," Ari echoes.

The Slurpees don't taste the same as they used to. Maybe
that's because it's a foreign country. Maybe it's because nothing

ever tastes the same as it did when you were ten. Or maybe the 7-Eleven syrup has changed.

Danny and Ari ponder this and soon ponder other things. Before they forget, they exchange addresses and phone numbers and e-mail addreses. Danny promises they will keep in touch.

At the hotel, Ari hugs Danny goodbye. Danny is not used to being fully hugged—just the sports-guy hugging-without-touching. But this is the real thing, the hug that lets you feel held.

They say goodbye at least five times, and then Ari leaves. Danny heads straight back to his room—he's had a wonderful night, and he doesn't want to press his luck. He sticks his tongue out at himself in the mirror and finds that it is still the color of a neon sky. He remembers how he and Elijah would have contests to see whose tongue could stay blue the longest. Hours without drinking, trying not to swallow needlessly. This makes him smile now. He realizes it will always make him smile, if he can hold on to his brother in some way. If he can make his way through all the distractions, back to what they once shared. And still share.

He takes a shower and heads to bed, ready for a good night's sleep. Then, at the last minute, he thinks of something else to do.

He reopens his letter to Will and adds another page.

He writes about how things have changed and how things don't have to change. He can't go back to the past, he knows. But maybe there's a chance of getting Elijah back.

* * *

Elijah's possessions haven't been scattered far, so it doesn't take him long to gather them. Julia keeps asking him if he's sure he knows where Danny is staying. She offers to call, to let Danny know Elijah is coming. Elijah tells her not to bother.

She won't give him an explanation about what's happening, and why he has to leave. All at once, he's realizing she's not the kind of person who gives explanations. She might not know herself.

He wants to ask, *Are you sure?* But he's afraid the line between a yes and a no would be frustratingly unclear.

Soon his bag is packed. There's nothing else to do. The maid has already cleaned up. There's just the matter of leaving.

"So goodbye, I guess."

Julia hands him a slip of paper.

"My parents' address," she says. "You can always reach me there."

"Oh."

"Look, I know this probably isn't what you thought would—"

"It's okay. Really. I just have to go."

Julia hovers in front of the door. "I mean, when I said it was the end, it wasn't—oh, I don't know. The end doesn't have to be the end, you know. You can stay, if you'd like."

"No. It's okay."

"I see. No, you're right. Can I get your address?"

Elijah writes it down for her. It feels like an empty gesture now, whereas once he thought it would be the key to their future.

"I'm sorry," she says. She hasn't opened the door, but she's no longer standing in front of it. "Tell Danny I'm sorry, too."

"For what?"

"For ruining your holiday."

Elijah knows that any goodbye kiss won't end up being a goodbye kiss. So he just bows his head a little and thanks her for dinner. Then he opens the door and leaves. In the hallway, he stops for a moment and waits to hear her turn the lock.

She doesn't, but he heads to the street anyway.

＊　＊　＊

Elijah needs to walk. He needs to forget about destinations and meanings and plans. He feels like a door has opened and he has walked into a world filled with his own mistakes.

Once, when he and his friend Jared were on acid, they stumbled across a pad of Post-its. Immediately, they began to label everything they encountered: DOOR and BOOK and HAND. Each Post-it bestowed a cosmic sense of clarity. The door was a door because the writing said DOOR. The floor was a hand because the writing said HAND. It seemed, for a moment, that they could live their lives that way, as omniscient identifiers and casual illusionists.

Elijah wishes he had the acid now, and the Post-its, so he could make Julia the JULIA he wanted her to be, and his life the LIFE that he had thought he had been living. He wants to bend time backward, so he could write dozens of postcards to Cal, so he could label as SORRY the very things he's now done. If Danny's Post-it said BROTHER instead of DANNY, would that work? Could Elijah take an eraser to ROME and suddenly make it HOME?

He is not angry with Julia. He is confused by her actions, and his own. As he walks through the midnight streets, he tries to reach into her side of the conversation, to pull out the cardinal truths.

He keeps picturing Cal in Providence, walking to the P.O. box, hoping for some word from him.

He imagines them building forts.

He thinks of his parents, and how concerned they'd be to see him walking where all the stores have long since closed.

He imagines Julia back in her hotel room, sitting absolutely still, or moving completely on.

There can be no destination. He can't go back to her, and he can't go on to Danny. He doesn't want to have to account for himself right now. Either Danny will say something and Elijah will explode, or Danny will say nothing and Elijah will disappear completely.

It's not about the city, it's about the walking. Really, he could be anywhere now, because he wants to be nowhere. Rome is lost on him. It's the time of night when no one walks alone. Couples eye him warily, as he walks with his bag slung over his shoulder. He finds himself on the same street he and Julia took to the Colosseum, only it's totally different now.

Every ounce of his soul tells him this will make a good story to tell his friends—an anecdote in the biography, an incident in the life. But part of the sorrow he feels—and it is that—comes from the distance he sees between himself and the storytelling, the hole that has ripped open between the here and the there. He hasn't been thinking of there nearly enough. He hasn't been a good enough friend.

I'm sorry, he says to Cal, and to his parents, and to Julia, and to Danny.

Because he doesn't know what else to say.

"*Stai bene?*" a voice asks.

He has been standing still on the sidewalk. Now he looks across the street and sees a young woman and her date. The man wants to keep walking, but the woman has stopped.

"I don't understand," Elijah explains.

"Are you all right?"

"Oh, yes. Thank you."

"Are you lost?"

"I'm not sure."

"Where are you going?"

"The Pantheon?" Elijah says. It's the first building that comes to mind. "I'm supposed to meet someone outside the Pantheon."

The man laughs and takes hold of the woman's elbow. She shrugs him off, whispering, "*Un attimo.*" Then she crosses the street, pulling a pen from her pocketbook. Her mouth is all lipstick, her eyes dark as the lashes.

"Give me your hand," she says. Elijah holds out his palm. She takes hold of it and draws a map. At the end of the map is a star.

"That," she says, "is the Pantheon."

"*Sofia!*" the man calls. With a curious smile, she turns and runs back across the street.

"Thank you!" Elijah shouts.

"*Avanti diritto!*" she calls back, and is gone.

Elijah stares at his hand. It is a complex map, without any names. Just a beginning, an ending, and a path.

Remarkably, he finds his way. Never once closing his fingers. Never once looking anywhere but where he is.

By the time he reaches the Pantheon, there are hints that the sun will soon rise. He sits on a bench and stares at the building's exterior—rather plain, with only a hint of what's inside.

As he waits for it to open, he falls asleep.

* * *

Danny arrives first. Elijah arrives second. This time they are separated by minutes, not years.

The Pantheon is empty.

Danny does not notice. He is staring up into the eye of the sky. He is standing in the golden beam of light that falls to the floor. The lifting dome, a chorus of geometry. Crowned by the circle of air, the eclipse of architecture. An opening where nobody would ever imagine one to be.

Elijah wakes up on the bench, gathers himself together, and walks inside. At first he is overwhelmed by the building. The silence. Then he sees the one figure standing there. And knows immediately who it is.

He walks over, puts a hand on his brother's shoulder. Danny turns, and Elijah is moved by the relief that rises to his face. Danny is about to say something, but Elijah gestures him to be quiet.

The two of them look around.

No one but the statues.

Nothing but the space.

They cannot believe it. They marvel at the emptiness. As if the building has been waiting for them, preparing for this moment and this moment only.

The guard stands by the door, unaware.

The sunlight streams down on them as they look up and ponder the tiles that reach toward blue. The quiet is extraordinary.

Elijah walks into the shadows, his footsteps keeping time

over marble. Danny begins to circle, too, until suddenly they are in orbit around each other, reverently floating through the room. They look at statues and cornices and old-spoken words. They look at the colors that fall under their feet—white marble, red marble, black marble. They look at the dome and the intimation of air. They wait for someone else to walk in the door, but no one does.

They look at each other and share a smile of disbelief and wonder. Their orbit becomes more pronounced, and now they are truly circling each other, not speaking a word, not daring to look away. It is like a dance, because they are partners. It is like a dream, because there is nothing else.

They will have this.

Danny stands in the center of the light, so the sun can stare down at him. Then he closes his eyes and extends his arms. He can feel the space of the building, like he can feel the building itself beneath his feet.

Elijah stays in the shadows. He too closes his eyes. He holds them closed for a minute, maybe two. For he knows that when he opens them, things will not be as they once were. Tourists will arrive. A cloud will cross the eye. They will no longer be alone together. But they will still be together.

Slowly Elijah opens his eyes and walks to his brother. He thinks of the Statues game. He thinks of red twine spinning from trees, and his brother's hands as they pushed him on the swing.

Elijah extends his arms so that his fingertips touch his brother's. Then, just once, they spin like children.

This is what is lost.

This is what is never lost.

"Where have you been?" Danny asks. His tone is not accusatory; it is genuinely concerned. They are standing in the undirected light of day now, next to a postcard vendor outside the Pantheon.

"Just around," Elijah replies. He knows he must look like a total unbathed freak.

"Where's Julia?"

"In her hotel room, I think. Back there, in the Pantheon, did you . . . ?"

Danny nods.

"So it wasn't just me?"

"No. It wasn't just you. It was just us."

"Wow."

The pleasure on Danny's face flickers. "Are you going back to Julia's now?" he asks.

"No," Elijah says. "We, um, said goodbye."

This is not what Danny was expecting to hear. "Oh," he says. "For good?"

"For good."

Elijah is surprised by how angry he doesn't sound.

Danny wants to hear more of the story, but he doesn't really have the grounds to ask. He's never asked before, so it would seem strange to ask now. He also wants to know whether or not Elijah found out about Julia's late-night visit. Elijah doesn't look as if he's found out, but maybe he's just hiding it.

In the end, Elijah will never know, and Danny will never know whether or not Elijah knows.

"So where have you been?" Danny asks. "Where do you want to go now?"

"How about the ruins?"

"Sure."

"You haven't been there already?"

"Nope," Danny lies. (Elijah won't know this is a lie until a month later, when Danny drives up to Providence and brings along his few vacation photos.)

They both take a minute before leaving the Pantheon's sight. Elijah buys a few postcards. Danny takes out a pen, and they write to their parents, thanking them. Then Danny gets out his camera, and they ask the postcard vendor to take their picture. Just to prove they've been here. Together.

As they head off to the ruins, Danny asks Elijah what he's written on his hand.

And Elijah tells him a true story.

*   *   *

When they get to the ruins, it begins to rain. Neither Danny nor Elijah has an umbrella, and neither will admit he wants one. So instead they dart from overhang to overhang—and end up standing without cover, daring to be drenched.

Elijah is inexplicably moved by the broken columns and fragmented floors. He cannot help but find a meaning and a message in their poverty of stature. *This is what remains,* he thinks. It seems a valuable lesson on a day when card catalogs are dying, communications are deleted, and buildings crumble under the weight of society's expectations.

Danny sees Elijah's remorseful expression and doesn't know what to think. Does such an expression come from knowledge or innocence? Sometimes it's so hard to tell the difference.

The rain will not let up. For a moment, Elijah thinks he sees Julia, and his feelings zigzag. But it's not her—not her at all. She is no longer a person in his life; instead, she is a person that other people will remind him of.

Danny and Elijah run to a cafe, the dirt of Italy slowly gathering on their shoes and their legs. A bad case of the doldrums seems to have hit the natives along with the rain—the waiters look glum, almost forlorn. Although Danny has picked up enough Italian to place his order, he is afraid that if he speaks a few words in Italian, the waiter will assume he knows more than a few words. So he sticks to English, thereby assuring that the waiter will not smile in return.

"So where do you want to go next?" Danny asks Elijah after the waiter has departed.

"I'd love to see the statue—you know, the one with the face that you can stick your hand in."

"The one from *Roman Holiday?*"

"Yes. Exactly. How did you know?"

Soon they are talking loudly, animatedly, impersonating Gregory Peck. They are reliving the movie and debating its finer points, agreeing only upon the ending.

How strange they must seem to the unimpressible Italian waiters and the pop-star Spanish teens and the Japanese image collectors and the umbrella-sticked British pensioners—two grown American brothers, talking about how Audrey Hepburn makes them cry.

*   *   *

Danny proposes a nap, and this time Elijah doesn't disagree. He is surprised when Danny stops at the door of the hotel.

"What the hell?" Danny shouts.

"What is it?" Elijah asks. Then he sees what Danny is seeing—a small swastika, drawn on the door of the d'Inghilterra. What's inexplicable is not just that it was put there, but that the hotel hasn't noticed—or has even kept it up.

Danny immediately pulls a pen from his pocket and begins to cross it out. Elijah keeps watch, but nobody stops them. The door is bleeding ink—Danny is pressing so hard that he is chipping off the paint.

"It's gone," Elijah tells him. And indeed it is—replaced by a dark, ugly blot.

Danny goes to complain to the manager, who appears sympathetic. Then the Silver brothers return to their room. Danny heads straight for the shower. Elijah writes belated postcards to his friends and waits his turn. He starts one postcard to Cal, then writes three more. Even though he'll see her tomorrow, he wants to give her something she will be able to keep. He tries not to think about Julia, and in the act of trying, he thinks about her. But she seems vague now. Not a part of the real story.

"All yours," Danny says when he gets out of the shower. He is wearing one of the hotel robes.

Elijah is gratified to find there's still hot water. He closes his eyes and breathes in the steam. When he looks down at

the drain, he sees a small ring of hair. Danny's hair. It is ir-
refutable proof, but still Elijah asks himself, *Is Danny losing
his hair?* This would mean that Danny is growing older. Is
changing.

So strange.

Elijah's inner snapshot of Danny is long out of date. But he
hasn't realized it until now.

"What are you looking at?" Danny asks when Elijah steps
from the bathroom and stares at his hairline. (It looks fine. Although there *is* a little gray. . . .)

"Nothing," Elijah says. "I can't believe we're this old."

"Tell me about it."

Danny is already under the covers. It is two in the afternoon. Sunlight filters through the window, but Elijah gets into
his bed anyway.

"We'll walk around a little before dinner," Danny continues
driftily. He is turned away from Elijah, but entirely conscious he
is there. "You can tell me what you've been up to."

"Okay." Elijah closes his eyes and imagines that afternoon is
night.

"And then we'll have a nice dinner."

"Sounds good."

"And walk around some more."

"Sure."

"And then I'll teach you multiplication."

Elijah smiles. "Perfect."

"I'm glad that you're here."

"So am I. I'm sorry about—well, what happened."

"So am I."

Danny thinks this will be the end of the conversation, but then Elijah (thinking of Julia, thinking of Cal, thinking of college applications, thinking of the confusion and elation and mistakes of the past week) asks, "Is this what growing up is like?"

And Danny answers, "I think so."

They will stay together until they leave the next day.

V. ARRIVAL

After they get through customs (Elijah's pot having been left for the maid service in Rome), they are confronted by a throng of eager, peering faces. Danny scans the crowd and sees his parents a little way off. His mother is reading a magazine and his father is staring at the flight listing.

A little closer, Danny spots Elijah's friend—no doubt the one who dropped him off. This time, she's wearing a chauffeur's cap and jacket, the cap tilted at a Dietrich angle.

Elijah hasn't seen her yet.

"Hey, isn't that your girlfriend?" Danny asks.

Elijah takes a look and beams. Cal sees him and beams in return.

"She's not my girlfriend," he tells his brother.

"Well, maybe she should be," his brother advises.

Elijah doesn't know what to say to that. Because now Cal is jumping the queue, running over and giving him the most fabulous hug.

"Speak Italian to me!" she cries. "Welcome home!"

"What are you wearing?" Elijah asks gleefully.

"You will not believe how many seventy-year-old men I had to hit up before I could get me one of these. I should go return it. I'll be right back."

With that, she jets off again. Danny's gaze follows her—sure enough, she is handing the cap and jacket back to a shirt-sleeved older man.

Elijah keeps hearing Danny's words—*Well, maybe she should*

be. He wonders if it could really be that simple. If something so obvious could actually be right.

"Elijah! Danny!" Their mother is calling them now. She, too, is beaming.

"C'mon," Danny says. Elijah picks up his bag and continues down the arrival pathway.

After the hellos, the thank yous begin. The word "trickery" does not come up. Danny doesn't even think it anymore.

When Mrs. Silver asks her sons what their favorite part of the trip was, they overlap and finish each other's sentences.

"Oh, it had to be—"

"The Pantheon was the most incredible—"

"—thing I've—"

"—*we've*—"

"—ever seen. You wouldn't—"

"You wouldn't believe it."

Mrs. Silver and Mr. Silver share a knowing look.

Elijah and Danny continue on—the telling makes them realize what a good time they've had. Danny talks about gondoliers and Joseph and meeting Ari again, while Elijah tells them about the balcony over St. Mark's Square, the floors and the ceilings, and the woman on the plane ride over who once met Billy Corgan. Julia is not mentioned—she is, momentarily, forgotten.

Mr. Silver asks if all the hotels were okay. Mrs. Silver asks if they had a chance to see the synagogues.

Elijah and Cal walk arm in arm as they all head to the garage. The conversation falls back onto the usual post-vacation topics—what the weather was like here, what the weather was like there, what's been on the news. Cal clearly has other news to tell Elijah, but it will have to wait for the car ride home.

214

Danny overhears her telling Elijah that Ivan and Meg had a falling-out in the middle of ballroom dance, and the implications are *huge*.

Finally, they reach the point where Cal's car is one direction and the Silvers' is the other.

Mr. and Mrs. Silver's desire to have Cal and Elijah over for dinner is overruled by their desire to have them drive home before sundown. Plus, Elijah has to be at work early the next day. ("Early" being ten o'clock.)

Elijah says thank you again and again. He hugs his mother and father . . . as does Cal. Then he comes over to Danny, and the two of them shake hands.

"Give me a break," Cal moans.

"Tell me about it," Mrs. Silver puts in.

Elijah and Danny laugh and go for a hug. They hold on longer than either would have expected. When they let go, they thank each other and smile.

"Good luck."

"You, too."

Then, with a wave, Cal and Elijah walk away.

Danny watches them go—arm in arm, fading into the garage.

As Elijah walks back into the land of the student, with its late-night coffee conversations and application anxieties, and as Danny returns to his voice-mail, e-mail, direct-deposit, pulse-driven existence, Danny wonders when he'll next see his brother. And what it will be like.

There is the distance of miles, and the distance of brothers, to overcome. He can feel the world coming between them again.

But the world is so much smaller than it used to be.

david levithan

è l'autore di *Boy Meets Boy* e *The Realm of Possibility*. Attualmente egli vive nel New Jersey e viaggia spesso al di fuori dei suoi confini. David non parla Italiano, e se voi non capite questo paragrafo, anche voi non parlate Italiano.*

To find out more about him, check: www.davidlevithan.com.

*David Levithan is the author of *Boy Meets Boy* and *The Realm of Possibility*. He currently lives in New Jersey and travels outside of it often. He does not speak Italian, and if you don't understand this, you don't speak Italian, either.

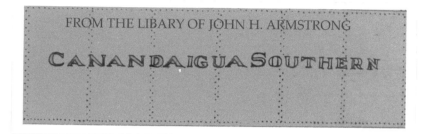

Railway Pricing Under Commercial Freedom: The Canadian Experience

**T.D. Heaver and
James C. Nelson**

Centre for Transportation Studies
University of British Columbia
Vancouver, Canada

Second printing–1978
Copyright © 1977 by:
THE CENTRE FOR TRANSPORTATION STUDIES
University of British Columbia
Vancouver, Canada V6T 1W5

Heaver, Trevor D., 1936–
    Railway pricing

    (Centre transportation series)
    ISBN 0–919804–020

    1. Railroads – Canada – Rates. 2. Freight
and freightage – Canada. I. Nelson, James
C., 1908– II. Title. III. Series:
University of British Columbia. Centre for
Transportation Studies. Centre transportation
series.
HE2135.H429   385'.1'0971   C77–002098–4

LC 77–75583

THE CENTRE FOR TRANSPORTATION STUDIES

is funded by the Canadian Ministry of Transport through the Transportation Development Agency. Its purpose is to improve the quality of transportation education through a variety of educational endeavors.

The TDA grant makes possible many of the Centre's activities. It underwrites seminars, symposia, and other gatherings of interest to academicians, to government officials, and to the business community. It enables the University to bring distinguished visitors to the campus, thus enriching the classroom experience. By providing for fellowships, assistantships, and other financial aids, the Centre makes it possible for good students to learn about transportation and to prepare themselves for useful careers in this field.

Central to the Centre's activities is its program of research. Faculty members associated with the Centre have undertaken a substantial number of research projects dealing with many facets of transportation. Some of these projects are funded by the business community. Others are supported by the provincial government, by the Canadian Ministry of Transport, or by other organizations. Some research is supported entirely by funds from the TDA grant.

The Centre sponsors seminars and symposia for a variety of reasons. Sometimes the purpose of a symposium is to disseminate information. Other seminars are organized to facilitate discussion and interchange of information among well informed participants. Still other seminars seek to bring together a small group of specialists to focus on a particular problem so that their knowledge and expertise can be shared with many people who cannot be present at the seminar itself.

This book results from a research project funded by the Transportation Development Agency under its program of negotiated research grants. It had the wholehearted support of the Canadian Transport Commission, both of the Canadian transcontinental railroads, and a number of important shippers.

To our children and students for the stimulus to look at the world afresh and to our mentors for reminding us of the lessons of history.

PREFACE

In 1967, the Parliament of Canada enacted the National Transportation Act, which largely freed Canadian railways of restrictive regulation of their pricing. The fact that the railways had lost the monopoly power in transport markets which they once enjoyed had been persuasively argued by the MacPherson Royal Commission in 1961. The 1967 Act was the outgrowth of the philosophy set forth by that Commission. Regulatory powers over the railways were reserved, basically, for those few instances where railway rates could be unreasonably high because real monopoly power still remained and where important questions of the public interest were involved.

This system seemed to be working reasonably well, but in 1973 at the Western Economic Opportunities Conference, the Premiers of the four Western Provinces raised serious challenges about the working and desirability of the National Transportation Policy and associated regulations. The complaints raised at that Conference set into motion a number of studies and programmes of discussions to examine the effects of certain changes in National Transport Policy and in the relevant Acts, and to ascertain certain facts about the Canadian transport system.

This study was initiated against this background and on the premise that insufficient documentation was available on the working of the railway pricing system under commercial freedom as allowed by the legislation of 1967. It was obvious that foreign visitors were curious about Canada's reliance on competition to regulate railway rates and how well the system had worked. It was also obvious that there was no adequate literature available on the subject.

The study has been made feasible by the financial support provided by the Transportation Development Agency of Transport Canada. Without the programme of financial support to university programmes administered by the Transportation Development Agency for the Federal Government, it is most unlikely that this project would have been initiated and quite inconceivable that it could have been accomplished on the scale achieved. We are most indebted to the Agency for its financial support and to Mr. J.H. Morgan of the Agency for his encouragement and assistance.

The research for the study has benefited from the considerable assistance provided by visitors to the Centre for Transportation Studies at the University of British Columbia. Dr. Martin Christopher of the Cranfield Institute of Technology gave valuable assistance during the development of the interview programme for the case studies in the spring of 1975 and undertook much of the

v

research concerned with the organization of the marketing and sales activities of the railways. He was assisted in this by Mr. Chris Jurczynski, a former graduate student in the Faculty of Commerce and Business Administration. Professor A.A. Walters of the London School of Economics and Political Science prepared a background paper during the summer of 1975 which has been most helpful in the preparation of Chapter IV and in providing guidance for the study of the detailed workings of competitive forces within the broader framework of economics. Throughout the research, we benefited from the counsel of Professor F.W. Anderson of the University of Saskatchewan and former President of the Western Transportation Advisory Council.

The interview programme and much other research was undertaken by students of the Faculty of Commerce and Business Administration. The students who conducted the field interviews were Mr. Wm. N. Fritz, Mr. N. Lafrance, Mr. S. MacKay, and Mr. P.D. Wing. Students who assisted with other phases of the research were Mr. R.R. Horne, Mr. L. Olsen, Mr. T.H. Oum and Ms. K.G. Watson. The assistance of these students is gratefully acknowledged.

Our greatest indebtedness, however, is to the large number of managers in the railways and manufacturing and distribution concerns who gave us their time and were very cooperative in providing us with necessary information. In view of the time pressures on shippers and railway personnel during the summer of 1975, the cooperation given to the interviewers was extraordinary. Naturally our demands focused more heavily on the railways than shippers. In particular, we acknowledge the assistance provided to us by Mr. J. Gratwick, Mr. J.C. Gardiner and Mr. A.H. MacPherson of Canadian National Railways and Mr. H.M. Romoff, Mr. W.G. Scott and Mr. D.W. Chapman of CP Rail. We have also received notable assistance with information and helpful suggestions from Mr. J.C.R. Hanley and Dr. K.W. Studnicki-Gizbert of the Canadian Transport Commission. To the hundreds of other persons who have also given us their time and assistance, we are most grateful.

The research could not have been conducted effectively or the manuscript completed so quickly had it not been for the excellent and friendly secretarial assistance provided by Leslie Anne Dureau and Mrs. Betty Perry of the Centre for Transportation Studies. The preparation of the book, especially when completed to meet tight time constraints, placed many demands on our wives and families. To Joan, who also assisted with the preparation of the manuscript, Peter and Sandra, and also Helen, our thanks for their assistance and support.

While we appreciate the wide and valuable assistance which we received with the study, sole responsibility for the contents of the book rests with the authors.

Vancouver
December, 1976

Trevor D. Heaver
James C. Nelson

TABLE OF CONTENTS

CHAPTER I

INTRODUCTION

In the transport sectors of Canada and other countries, the monopoly organization and markets characteristic of the 19th Century have largely been replaced by competitive organizations and markets. This gradual change has resulted from the development of new modes of transport, particularly the air, highway and pipelines modes, and thus new intermodal carriers to compete with the dominant railways. Public enterprise in the air and highway fields, public aids and subsidies, and limited or non-existent regulation during initial development greatly stimulated the economic growth of air and highway transport, resulting in a continual increase and widespread incidence of competition in transport markets, so that today competition can be described as pervasive in Canada, the U.S.A., and such other developed countries as Australia, Great Britain and Sweden.

Basically, then, the overall problem of public transport policy is to adopt policies that will enable competition in transport to work efficiently. Public policy must ensure that adequate supplies of the many and diverse transport services demanded are available, with as low unit costs and rates as are feasible, and with sufficient returns to the carriers and modes so that facilities will be forthcoming as needed and will be technologically modern and productive. In line with the competitive organization of transport industries, Canada liberalized her regulation in 1967. Australia and Great Britain have deregulated all or much of their intercity transport, and the U.S.A., is currently considering additional deregulatory policies, having recently enacted the Railroad Revitalization and Regulatory Reform Act of 1976.[1]

The emergence of predominantly competitive conditions in transport, however, has not meant that all of the former problems with which public transport policy was primarily concerned a century ago have disappeared. For 50 years, during the final quarter of the last century and the first quarter of the present century, public transport policy in Canada and elsewhere was largely concerned with monopoly in railroads and the economic regulation of railway rates and services. In that period and until relatively recently, the view was widely held that competition within the railroad industry and between other

1

modal carriers and the railways was insufficient to insure the public that railway freight rates would behave as competitive prices or be reasonably equitable between shippers, communities, regions and ports. The existence of market and producing area competition as powerful forces limiting railway freight rates and adjusting them so that differently located producers could market their products in common markets was well known and welcomed by shippers and consumers as protective of their interests. Also, water carrier competition along and between the coasts, on the river systems and on the Great Lakes further limited railway rates, but the market influence of water competition was uneven geographically and yielded lower rates to and from port cities than to and from interior ones not advantaged by such intermodal competition. Competition between railways existed in services and at times in rates, but the railways, both of Canada and the U.S.A., ultimately developed institutions for conferring and agreeing on rates. Thus, with monopoly in areas where only one railroad was available to shippers, and as a result of cartelized rate bureaus, the railways could and did design their rate structures on value-of-service or discriminating principles. Dissatisfaction by shippers, communities and regions with many types of rate and service discrimination by the railways brought about public regulation of maximum rates, of discriminatory rates (including long-short haul rates in the U.S.A.), and established standards for reasonable and nondiscriminating rates, to be administered by the Board of Railway Commissioners in Canada and the Interstate Commerce Commission in the U.S.A.

Some of the railway rate issues of the 1875-1925 period still demand public policy attention in both countries, as transport competition is not present and effective in all railway markets, even today. For example, there are complaints in Canada from some shippers that they are captive to the railways without sufficient regulatory remedies, and the Prairie Provinces still complain that higher rates for shorter hauls to the Prairies than for longer hauls to the West Coast and higher rates on processed commodities than on the raw materials are retarding industrial and economic development in the Prairies. Hence, although the MacPherson Royal Commission in the early 1960's comprehensively reviewed the growth of intermodal competition in Canadian transport and reported that competitive conditions had become dominant and that consequently less regulation of the railways was necessary to protect the public interest, Transport Canada, the Trudeau Administration, and the Provinces have been conducting inquiries and research on how the liberalized regulation under the National Transportation Act of 1967 has been working out in practice.[2] As the railways were granted a great deal of commercial freedom in rate making by the Act and some previous enactments, in effect the present comprehensive policy review seeks to determine whether competition within and with the rail transport mode has been effective in limiting rail freight rates, in stimulating the

2

efficient operation of transport modes, and in assuring adequate investment to meet the future needs of commerce. Additionally, it seeks to ascertain whether railway rates have been regionally and otherwise equitable.

Commercial Freedom for Railways by the 1967 Act

In Canada, the railroads have been freed from most of the significant public regulatory constraints under which they had operated for more than 50 years before the 1967 Act was enacted. This followed gradual elimination of economic regulation of the railways in Great Britain and its relaxation in several other countries. As early as 1938, Canada allowed her railways to meet the growing intermodal competition from road, pipeline and water carriers by negotiating agreed charges with shippers, with loyalty provisions insuring the railways all or a percentage of their business for a year and with conditions to protect shippers who might be unjustly discriminated against as the result of an agreed charge.[3] Nevertheless, although the legislative process of freeing the railways to compete with other modes started earlier, the enactment of the National Transportation Act of 1967 truly brought about a large reduction in the regulation of railway pricing by the Canadian Transport Commission (formerly the Board of Transport Commissioners). Indeed, the Canadian railways were given, in recognition of the widespread competitive markets in which they operate and sell their services, almost complete freedom to make and change their rates, subject to the requirement of Section 275 of the Railway Act that rate increases must be filed with the CTC 30 days before they become effective, though rate reductions can become effective immediately and filed afterwards with the CTC.

The Canadian railways today have freedom to make and file rates without their being subject to suspension for a period to allow CTC investigation of their lawfulness under the standards of The National Transportation Act and The Railway Act. The railways are largely free to raise their rates as commercial considerations make desirable so long as they meet the filing and waiting-period requirements. In addition, the earlier specific constraints on rate and service discrimination on the basis of undue discrimination or preferences were eliminated by the 1967 Act.[4] However, Canadian railways are still subject to some maximum rate and public-interest control of rates under Section 278 of the Railway Act and Section 23 of the National Transportation Act. The Canadian railways have never been constrained in meeting rate competition from trucks or in engaging in other modal operations as have the American railroads. The minimum rate regulation provided by the 1967 Act (Section 276 of the Railway Act) prescribes variable cost as the rate floor. This insures that railway price competition with highway transporters does not assure the road carriers "a fair share of the traffic", or an arbitrary allocation of the market based on a parity of truck and rail rates and service competition as in the U.S.A. In short, the Canadian railways have wide discretion in making their rates and in engaging

3

in rate and service competition with other modes. Whether the residual regulation of railway rates is adequate as conducted by the CTC is, of course, one of the key issues of national transport policy in Canada.

The significant effect of the 1967 Act in reducing economic regulation of railway rates is evidenced by the small number of formal cases that have occurred in more than a decade. There have been no minimum rate cases acted on by the CTC. Only one maximum rate appeal has been taken to the CTC, and that case (the Domtar Case) did not progress to a decision. As of May 1976, three public-interest appeals have been taken to the CTC, one of which (the Rapeseed Case) resulted in a CTC decision in 1973. Some of this case's issues were appealed to the Governor in Council for further consideration.[5] One case (the Newsprint Case) was nearing a decision by the CTC, and the other (the Prince Albert Pulp and Paper Case) was withdrawn by the applicant after successful negotiations between the parties on an agreeable rate and the ICC decision removing the undue preference and prejudice in the U.S.A. rates also involved.[6] The substantial rate increases of 1976 have given rise to another Section 23 appeal being filed with the CTC and it is possible that further cases may arise. The small number of formal cases since 1967 contrasts sharply with several general rate level railway cases and numerous minimum rate and undue discrimination cases heard and decided by the ICC in the U.S.A. in the same period.[7] It is evident that the frequency of regulatory interference with railway pricing has been greatly lessened in Canada.

Notwithstanding the large amount of commercial freedom existing Canadian regulation accords to the railway firms, they are still subject to the severe limitation of statutory rates and to rate level holddowns, some of which have been compensated by rate subsidies by the Federal Government.[8] The most significant case of statutory rates results from the Crows Nest Pass Agreement of 1897 and an amendment to the Railway Act in 1925, which insure that rates on grain and flour traffic moving from the Prairies to Thunder Bay, to Vancouver and other Pacific ports for export, or to Churchill on the Hudson Bay for export, are held to the 1897 level of 0.5 cents per ton-mile.[9] No direct subsidy compensation is paid the railways for these unprofitable Crows Nest Pass rates, although government compensation for maintenance of branch lines in the Prairies for the grain trade offsets the deficits from export grain traffic, at least partially. Feed grain rates, too, have been subject to a federal subsidy.[10] From 1958 until 1967 there was a rate-level holddown under the Freight Rate Reduction Act with compensating subsidy payments to the railways.[11] From July 1973 through December 1974 the railways held down non-negotiated rates at the request of the Minister of Transport. The railways were compensated by subsidy payments for this holddown.[12] In addition, railway rates from and within the Maritimes have been held down by subsidies through the Maritime Freight Rates Act of 1927 and subsequent amendments and the Atlantic Region Freight Assistance

4

Act of 1969. The latter Act extended subsidies to common carrier truck rates, in the continuing effort to aid the Maritime Provinces develop their industries in spite of their distances from the markets of Central Canada and beyond.[13] The general effect of such legislated or government-requested rate holddowns has been to shift part of the constant, and possibly variable, costs of railway facilities and services to the Canadian taxpayers or, in the case of the Crows Nest Pass grain rates, to other shippers who use Canada's railways, including shippers of manufactured products throughout Canada, but especially long-haul shippers, for example, to and from the Prairie Provinces.

In Canada, then, the position is significant liberalization and deregulation of railway pricing, modified by a continuation of traditional statutory holddowns on grain rates, by the subsidization of feed grain rates and the Maritime rates, and by the 1973-74 holddown of non-negotiated rail rates. The very large amount of commercial freedom granted the railways is, therefore, legislatively constrained to apply to all freight traffic except statutory grains. The extent to which direct statutory regulation of railway rates and the exercise of Executive power have been employed to limit rates in Canada is in substantial contrast with government action on railway freight rates in the U.S.A. There, direct statutory rate regulation has been avoided, even though some ICC regulatory decisions and influences have long held down key long-haul rates on some agricultural products and raw materials to fairly low levels, even to below out-of-pocket costs in some instances.[14] The employment of Executive power to hold down railway rate increases during recent inflationary periods in Canada is also strikingly different than in the U.S., although in the latter country the Departments of Agriculture, Commerce, Transportation and other executive agencies have appeared before the ICC to present evidence that some general railway or other modal rate increases should be limited in whole or in part.

However, although Canada's Government exerts much more legislative and executive influence toward limiting railway rates than does the U.S.A. Government, Canada's present-day regulation of the railways and other land modes is far less comprehensive and restrictive than U.S.A. regulation and far more designed to allow the competitive forces in freight transport markets to operate freely and fully. It is for this reason that a lively and sustained interest exists in the U.S.A. among ICC-watchers, shippers, carriers and academic and government economists in developments in Canadian transport and railway pricing under the 1967 Act. They are interested in whether the competitive forces that have been freed to operate have actually been workably competitive and beneficial for the public. Because both actual and potential competitive forces now are given their play through shipper-carrier rate negotiations, interest in the U.S.A. is also high in the rate negotiating process in Canada and its successes and failures. Countries that have deregulated, including Australia, Great Britain, Sweden and others, are interested in what has happened in Canada

5

for comparison with their own experiences, and countries which have not deregulated much or at all, including France and West Germany, are interested in Canadian experience for the light that it might throw on the case for reform of their regulatory policies. Finally, micro theorists and other economists everywhere will be interested in an exposition of the competitive influences in the pricing of a railway duopoly, the CNR and the CPR.

Issues over Commercial Freedom and the Complaints of the Provinces and Shippers

Canada is a large country with railway service provided largely by two large railways with hauls up to 4,000 miles to some markets. The agriculture, fishery and the extractive mineral and wood products industries are important, especially in the outlying Provinces. Manufacturing industries and population are concentrated in southern Ontario and southwestern Quebec. In this setting and in view of the long-standing regional conflicts over transport and industrial policy, it cannot be surprising that significant issues continue to exist over transport policy and that the Prairie and Maritime Provinces continue to make complaints about railway rates. In fact, many of the complaints traditionally voiced by the Prairie Provinces when railway regulation was comprehensive under the Board of Transport Commissioners continue to be pressed in negotiations with the Federal Government Departments, in Parliament in Ottawa, before the CTC, and before the public in general. For example, complaints of long-short haul discrimination against the Prairie Provinces continue to be heard as before 1967 when railway regulation was far more comprehensive.[15]

Leaving the particular complaints of the Prairie Provinces aside for the moment, it is the issue of the workability and effectiveness of transport competition that has become the overall and basic question concerning the 1967 Act in Canada. Competitive forces of one kind or another have to be present in transport markets if they are to limit railway rates and rate discrimination as would be desirable. While such forces do exist in most markets, the realities are that in some markets the traffic can move efficiently only by railroad, the number of competing railways is usually limited to two or three, and some areas and many points are served only by one railway. Hence, if competition is to work effectively as to railway prices, the shippers must negotiate effectively in terms of their intermodal, intramodal, and locational alternatives and utilize potential competition in a sophisticated manner in their negotiations with the railways. At times, they must deal collectively with the market power of the railways with the countervailing power of all shippers in an industry.

Were all transport industries organized as many-firm industries with almost all costs variable with output, competition would obviously be effective on the seller's side of the market. In Canadian freight transport, that condition is met

6

only in highway transport, and even in that industry only on the dense-traffic routes and where Provincial restrictive entry and operating authority control has not severely limited the number of competing firms. As there is no Federal regulation of entry into inter-Provincial motor freight transport in effect in Canada and entry regulation by the Provinces varies from none in Alberta to rather strict entry controls in some other Provinces, the number of for-hire highway competitors to the railways has not been rigorously limited in Canada as in the U.S. But although the MacPherson Royal Commission emphasized the widespread and growing intermodal competition to the railways, especially from the truckers, as justifying relaxation of railway regulation, the Commission recognized that there are commodity markets in transport in which the highway alternative is absent or quite limited. The extent of the markets in which railway service provides the only viable alternative is not known precisely, although the present Minister of Transport in Ottawa has stated that about 40 percent of railway rates are not fixed by competition.[16] Needless to say, this estimate will be uncertain until sufficient facts are available to confirm or modify it. Nevertheless, there are market areas in which intermodal competition from trucks or water carriers is not viable, so the question becomes one of whether market competitive forces can effectively limit railway rates in such markets.

Whatever percentage of the Canadian railway freight traffic is not subject to intermodal competition, it clearly is important to ascertain two things before conclusions are drawn that all such railway freight is priced under monopoly conditions and without limitation by competitive forces. As market competition of various kinds and intrarailway competition can be present and effective in transport markets, two questions arise. First, to what extent does market competition from imports, from the same or substitute products from other producing areas, and from logistical changes that some shippers can make to change their production source for a given market, limit the railway rates not restrained by intermodal competition? Second, to what extent do the two or three railways, sometimes enlarged to more firms in the market when the competing U.S.A. railways are considered, actually engage in meaningful service, technological, cost and rate competition in the markets in which viable intermodal alternatives are not available to the shippers?

Specific Complaints of the Prairie Provinces

Although the Prairie Provinces have long had the benefit of low statutory rates on grain and related products, they have complained of high and discriminating railway freight rates since before completion of the Canadian Pacific Railway in 1885. Their contention that railway rates have restricted economic and industrial development in Alberta, Saskatchewan and Manitoba have continued to be pressed since enactment of the 1967 Act. Indeed, at the

7

Western Economic Opportunities Conference (WEOC) in Calgary during July 1973 between the Prime Minister of Canada and the Premiers of the four Western Provinces, they sharpened their attack on railway rate discriminations and claimed that "the development of the Western region of Canada is inhibited by the lack of positive policy direction and the discrimination inherent in our present system of freight rates".[17]

The overall complaint of the Prairie Provinces is that because of the lack of competition to the railways for their supplies and shipments, the Prairie Provinces have to bear more than their fair share of the revenue contribution to the constant costs of the railways. This, of course, assumes that there is some economic and equitable way to determine the appropriate contributions of specific traffic to fixed costs other than by giving weight to the varying elasticities of demand for rail transport in the marketplace. Saskatchewan is probably the Province most subject to any lack of alternative transport, as Manitoba is close to the Great Lakes and Alberta is near the West Coast, in both cases more within the spatial range of truck competition to the railways. But locationally, all three Prairie Provinces are relatively affected by long distances to populous markets and are highly dependent on rail transport to market their products. These conditions and their dependence on agricultural and extractive industries and on exports account for their deep interest in railway pricing.

The specific rate complaints of the Prairie Provinces are of three railway rate relationships. The first one alleges that their industries are charged higher rates on finished or processed goods than on raw materials and that this discriminatory rate relationship impedes the development and growth of plants in the Prairies to process raw materials produced there. The Section 23 appeal to the CTC that the rates on rapeseed meal and oil produced in the Prairies were too high in relation to the rates on rapeseed well exemplifies this cateogry.[18] The second category of complaint alleges that because Prairie communities are assessed by the railways higher rates on steel products, canned goods and other manufactured goods than the rates on the same commodities for the longer hauls from Central Canada to Vancouver, this long-short haul discrimination favors the location of wholesaling, jobbing and manufacturing on the West Coast rather than in the Prairies. Here, the distance advantage of the Prairies to and from Central Canada is disregarded in railway ratemaking, it is contended.[19] A third complaint is that the Prairies do not enjoy the advantage of blanket or group rates to the extent that the railways have arranged such rates for Central Canada. Hence, while group rates that give the smaller population centres within a group the same rates as the large centres may encourage industrial development in small cities in Central Canada, it is argued that the lack of similar application of group rates in the Prairies hinders development at the smaller cities and towns in that region. Allegations of these kinds, which were made at WEOC in July 1973, were subsequently investigated by the CTC. The report to the Minister of

Transport in December 1973 was made public in 1975.[20]

The continuance of markets in which intermodal competition is absent or ineffective and dissatisfaction with the regulatory remedies achieved both before and after the 1967 Act have prompted the Western Provinces to negotiate at WEOC and in subsequent discussions for changes in the National Transportation Act and its policy principles. In particular, the Prairie Provinces emphasize the goal of greater equity in railway freight rates, a goal that appears to mean less discrimination in railway rates, that is, more attention to costs of service in ratemaking and less attention to value-of-service considerations. In an attempt to hasten change in this direction, Alberta proposed at WEOC *"The Equitable Pricing Proposal"* which would have related railway rates to variable costs, necessitating Government subsidies to the railways to cover their constant costs.[21] This would have assured that the rates to and from shorter hauls contained within longer hauls would be lower than the long-haul rates as railway variable costs rise with distance; and that the rates on processed products and on the related raw materials would be the same if the variable costs were the same by railway. But such rates would have required large government subsidies to the railways to cover their constant costs, and the proposal raised investment problems with respect to future railway capacity for the growing Canadian economy. Manitoba proposed the "Destination Rate Principle", which advocated that the lowest basis of railway rates for any commodity to a particular destination would become the rate basis for all other originating points shipping that commodity to that destination.[22]

If adopted, either of those proposals for bringing about greater equity in freight rates, as viewed in the Prairies, would have greatly limited the railways in assessing rate increments above variable costs according to the relative inelasticitics or elasticities of demand in order to recover constant costs. Obviously, the railroads have been strongly opposed to such pricing standards, and the proposed standards raised a host of problems for the Federal Government and other shipper groups. Though investigated by a group of consultants, such standards seem unlikely to be adopted in Canada. The consultants' study concludes, "It is clear, however, that general rate policies, as exemplified by EPP and DRL, are exceptionally costly to the railroads and for-hire trucking, will provide excessive benefits to areas and producers not in need of such assistance and may perversely influence the Western industrial structure."[23] Nevertheless, the advocacy of such railway pricing standards by the Prairie Provinces reveals that a key issue in railway freight rates concerns value-of-service pricing as traditionally and currently practiced and whether its distribution of the burden of constant costs among commodities, shippers and regions has been equitable. As will be noted, this is an issue that has also been raised by some industrial shippers located elsewhere than in the Prairies, both because of their necessary dependence on railway service and their perception of

9

the indirect effects of the low statutory rates on grains on the rates on manufactures.

Rate Concerns of the Atlantic Region

Concern with transport facilities and rates is also traditional in the Maritime Provinces, located as they are far away from the large markets of Central Canada. A large rise in freight rates during and after World War I and the dissatisfaction of those Provinces prompted Parliament to enact the Maritime Freight Rates Act in 1927. This provided a 20-percent subsidy on rail traffic movements within a defined area of the Maritimes (called the Select Territory) and on the westbound rail traffic that moved from that territory. Further complaints by the Maritime Provinces induced Parliament to increase the outbound western subsidy to 30 percent in 1957. In 1969, these rate subsidies were extended to truck common carriers to equalize competitive conditions between road and rail and provisions were made to reduce the subsidy to 15 percent on movements within the Select Territory, with the subsidy savings to be used for alternative forms of transport assistance, including the upping of the subsidy on selected westbound shipments to 50 percent. The cost of such subsidies amounted to $36 million in 1974.[24]

The long-standing subsidy assistance on freight rates and the increased rate of subsidy on westbound movements in the Select Territory have not completely subdued the complaints of the Maritime Provinces as to freight rates. Since small-scale manufacturing generates a large proportion of small shipments in that region, there have been recent complaints that the rates on small shipments are too high. Though it is somewhat difficult to document their specific complaints concerning railway rates under the circumstances of subsidy assistance, the Atlantic Premiers stated in 1975 that the reliance on competition in the 1967 Act "is not practical in the Atlantic Provinces where there is limited competition, lack of facilities, a low volume of traffic, and long distances which are sparsely populated".[25] As in the Prairies, the view is common in the Maritimes that freight rates unfairly discourage industrial growth in the Atlantic Region.

Concerns of Industrial Shippers Dependent on Railway Service

Although generally industrial shippers support the commercial freedom granted the railways by the 1967 Act and its emphasis on competition, they, too, have questions regarding railway rates and statutory and commission regulation of them as it exists in Canada today. Thus, industrial shippers generally argue that the long-continued statutory rates on export grains means that the railways run deficits on grain traffic, which is a substantial proportion of all railway freight traffic in Canada, and that this necessarily presses the railways to place the burden of such losses and of contributions to constant costs upon other shippers, especially on the shippers of high-value

10

manufactures.[26] This complaint, of course, is not of the 1967 Act. Some industrial shippers, particularly those which largely or wholly depend on the railways to reach their markets, contend that the 1967 Act needs some change to make the maximum rate remedies for captive shippers more workable.[27] They tend to advocate a clearer definition of the conditions when a shipper becomes captive to the railways and some narrowing of the range for prescription of maximum rates from the present 250 percent of variable costs under a complicated formula involving carloads of 30,000 pounds. In short, such industrial shippers desire greater limitation of the ability of railways under the 1967 Act to assess revenue contributions on a value-of-service basis to defray the constant costs, although they seldom, if ever, advocate cost-based rates throughout the railway rate structure. Such shippers also contend that the existing regulatory remedies under Section 23 of the 1967 Act and Section 278 of the Railway Act are too slow, costly and difficult to invoke under existing CTC procedures. Among industrial shippers expressing some discontent with these features of the 1967 Act are the large companies which are largely dependent on the railways because their manufactured products are resource-based and their plants are located in remote areas close to the raw materials or hydro power essential to their operations.

It should be noted, nevertheless, that the dissatisfactions of the industrial shippers with the liberalized regulation of the 1967 Act is not as harsh nor as general and vocal as the rate dissatisfactions expressed by the politicians of the Prairie Provinces. Rather than a basic change in the commercial freedom granted railways by the Act, the concerned industrial shippers desire some government effort to make the regulatory remedies already provided more effective, less time-consuming and costly to realize, and more certain of achievement. Generally, they do not question commercial freedom and competition, but only the undue exercise of that freedom by the railways when intermodal or other competitive forces are absent or ineffective.

Problems of Shippers in Negotiating Rates

Shippers, particularly those with large volumes of traffic and those marketing through cooperatives or marketing agencies, have long been active in negotiating initial rates and changes in rates with the railways and other modes. Extension of rate making freedom to the railways by the 1967 Act has made it easier for the carriers to respond to specific competitive or cost-related arguments of a particular shipper or group of shippers without fear of facing extensive unjust discrimination cases. However, the added flexibility of the railways is not an unmixed blessing for shippers. In earlier periods, the dissatisfied shipper could complain to the Board of Transport Commissioners and request that rates be investigated as to their lawfulness under the undue discrimination standards of the regulatory law and seek to have rate changes suspended during investigation

11

of their lawfulness under those or the reasonable rate standards provided by the regulatory statutes. Today, though the shipper can appeal to the CTC on the grounds that rate filings did not allow the required 30-day notice for rate increases, that he is a captive shipper and that this circumstance justifies a fixed maximum rate, or that the rates in question involve public-interest issues under Section 23, he must rely far more on his own, or his industry's, ability to negotiate with the railways for the needed rates or rate adjustments. In practice, this situation requires a shipper or shippers to have actual or potential alternative ways to ship the products to markets, including by private carrier vehicles. The shipper must be aware of alternative sources of supply, locations for plants, and possibilities of shifting or exchanging production sources. Usually, all of these activities, including keeping up with alternative costs, rates and services and measuring the effects on the shipper's business of alternative methods of shipment, require a traffic or transport management organization.

Obviously, small shippers generally have less knowledge of transport markets than the large shippers and less organizational ability to study transport alternatives and to negotiate with the railways. Their lesser traffic volumes also may make their custom less important to the railways, although collectively their traffic may be significant to a railway. For those reasons, and because railway regulation originally sought primarily to protect the small shippers, the question of how well small shippers fare in their negotiations with the railways is of considerable interest in a country that has significantly deregulated railway transport, as has Canada.

But the problem does not end there. For if the competitive forces which the 1967 Act's policy relies on are to have their limiting and equalizing effects on railways rates, all shippers, both large and small, must be able to present their shipping, locational and logistical alternatives effectively to the carriers. Where good actual or potential intermodal alternatives exist, shippers can often moderate railway rate increases or even get them withdrawn or delayed by shifting or threatening to shift their traffic to alternative modal carriers. Where intermodal alternatives are not available, shippers can moderate rate increases by showing that both they and the carriers will lose business because of market competition if the rate increases are not limited. Where neither type of competitive force is viable, shippers have a more difficult problem in rate negotiations and may have to relocate plants or their markets or resort to the residual regulatory protections still afforded by the 1967 Act. In such cases, shippers may be able to show they are actually captive to a railway or the railways.

Objectives and Scope of the Study

The National Transportation Act of 1967 granted a great deal of commercial freedom to the Canadian railways in ratemaking and relied heavily on intermodal and other competitive forces on transport markets to bring about reasonable railway rates. As a result of the concerns of some Provinces and shippers as outlined above, substantial research and extended discussions have taken place, particularly since WEOC in 1973. In June 1975, Transport Canada (the new name for the Ministry of Transport) issued Interim Reports on freight and passenger transport in Canada and a Summary Report, *Transportation Policy, A Framework for Transport in Canada.*[28] While discussions between parties affected by transport policy have considered the nature and role of rate making extensively, no published information on the working of rate making under the freedom provided by the 1967 Act is available. The research program on which this monograph is based was commenced in late 1974 partially to fill the void.

Consequently, the broad general objectives of this study are as follows: (1) To ascertain how the competitive forces in transport markets in Canada have worked out under the 1967 Act and whether reliance on competitive forces has been beneficial to consumers and the major parties involved: and (2) to throw light, on the basis of the experience with liberalized regulation and wide commercial freedom for the railways, on how transport competition can be expected to work out in other economies with comparable or roughly comparable conditions and institutions.

To ascertain how Canadian shippers actually negotiate with the railways with respect to initial rates or rate changes, to learn whether they are knowledgeable and well organized for that purpose, and to find out how rate negotiations work out in practice in terms of carrier and shipper needs, more than 80 shipper interviews were conducted during the summer of 1975 and more than 60 case studies of railway rate negotiations were prepared for this study. The bulk of the rate negotiations had been conducted during 1972-1974, although some went back as far as the early 1960s and some negotiations were concluded in late 1975. Consequently, the negotiations generally dealt with rate increases as the majority took place during an inflationary period. Interviews were held with shippers or receivers in all provinces outside of the Maritimes. Although the shippers interviewed were not selected as a representative sample, they covered a wide variety of commodity groups and firm sizes. Interviews were held with the shipper representatives involved in the negotiations with the railways, and in most instances interviews were also held with the railways personnel who had been involved in the rate negotiations.

From those interviews and from separate studies conducted on the internal organizations of the railways for marketing and ratemaking, a great deal of useful knowledge was obtained. It sheds much light on whether, and the extent to which, the heavy reliance of the 1967 Act on shipper-carrier negotiations for the implementation of the competitive forces to limit railway freight rates has been working out well and beneficially. The results found will be disclosed at several points in this monograph.

13

As the title of the study suggests, the study's scope has been limited to the processes and economic factors in railway ratemaking and negotiation and to the closely related public policy questions. The latter pertain primarily to whether the liberalization and deregulation steps taken by the Parliament in enacting the 1967 Act were basically correct and enlightened or whether they were wrong and should be reversed. As there is a widespread world movement toward deregulation of the railways and other modes for freight traffic, the conclusions reached on the basis of the Canadian experience will be meaningful elsewhere. Should this study show that the course of public policy taken in 1967 was essentially sound with or without somewhat greater residual regulation of maximum and discriminating railway rates than was provided in that Act, the conclusion reached and the supporting experience documented could be very helpful in public regulatory policy formation, both in solving the current issues in Canada and in revealing to outsiders the residual and viable role that may be left to economic regulation by the growth of transport competition.

In Canada and other countries, much statistical work has been done to show the extent of development of intermodal competition in recent decades. Though in large countries such as Canada and the United States, there are still gaps in statistical knowledge of the extent to which noncompetitive markets and markets captive to the railways still exist, there are even greater lacks in knowledge about how, and with what results, shippers and carriers negotiate with respect to rates in actual practice.[29] As rate negotiations will continue to be the market devices through which competitive alternatives will have their influences on freight rates, it is important to have greater knowledge of the rate negotiation process, its successes, and its failures. This study of what happens in actual transport markets was designed in part to add to existing knowledge of institutions and processes through which competitive forces operate in transport markets.

On the other hand, this monograph was not conceived as a complete study either of all public policy issues in transport in Canada or of the economic problems and future of the railways. The study does not examine the significant questions of user fees for public transport facilities and whether the modes competing with the railways pay fully the public and social costs of their use of highways and other public facilities. It does not address itself to many of the specific problems of the economic development of the transport modes in the several regions of Canada in order to meet the needs of commerce, industry and government in those regions and for Canada as a whole. Though this study can throw some light on the question whether the present competitive and regulatory conditions in Canada bring about an efficient division of freight traffic between the railways and other modes, it was not designed to examine or to measure the extent of misallocations of resources within transport and between transport and other industries in Canada. Rather, it has been limited to finding out how competition in transport works out under liberalized regulation and wide commercial freedom for the railways, and to examining the processes through which competition works as it bears on railway freight rates. In doing this and in throwing considerable light on shipper-carrier rate negotiations and the problems involved, it can be helpful in settling some of the outstanding issues of regulatory policy in Canada.

Chapters II through IV give preliminary but essential background information for analysis of the workability of competitive forces in the limitation of Canadian railway rates. After a brief description of the railway rate structure and the changing significance of different types of rates in terms of traffic and revenues, Chapter II presents a statistical analysis of the basic factors that influence railway freight rates to be as they are. This throws some light on the relative extent to which such rates are based on cost of service and on value of service. Chapter III explains the internal organization of the railways and the location of responsibility for marketing and pricing, and the institutional adaptation that has taken place to technological change and the growing competitive environment, including some decentralization in the pricing organization of the railways. The types of communications between shippers and railways and between the railways on rate matters and the rate negotiating process are described, with appropriate attention accorded to shipper organization for negotiating rate and service adjustments. Also in Chapter III, the present roles of the CTC and the Provinces in the regulation of railway rates are broadly described as conditioning factors supplementary to the forces of competition. Chapter IV describes the dynamic nature of transport competition, the forms that competition can take in transport markets, and briefly reviews the theory of pricing under various relevant market states, including pure or perfect competition, duopoly, and oligopoly of a few firms. Its role is to indicate the theoretical considerations in railway rate making and its regulation, with appropriate explanation of the roles of discriminating rates and of uniform rates in efficient and equitable railway pricing.

Chapters V through VII present the evidence, from the case interviews with shippers and from other sources, on how, and with what effects, competition works in limiting rail freight rates. Chapter V treats market competition in its various forms, and shows that market competitive forces were strong competitive factors in railway rates before and during the period of comprehensive regulation and that they continue to be today. Chapter VI discusses the principal and most widespread form of transport competition today, intermodal competition between truck and water carriers and the railways, and shows that actual or potential use of private or for-hire trucks is a competitive alternative that many, if not most, shippers can employ to advantage in rate negotiations with the railways. Chapter VII examines case interview, rate case, and other evidence on the kinds of market situations in

15

which the railways, even where only two exist in the market, do engage in service competition and even in price competition. The barriers to price competition between railways, both economic and institutional, are also discussed.

The last three chapters discuss in more detail the regulatory and governmental influences that condition railway freight rates and influence the efficiency and equitability of railway pricing in Canada. Chapter VIII discusses the prices and price policies which are allowable under the changed regulatory rules prescribed by the 1967 Act. It also examines and evaluates the several formal cases which have been made pursuant to Section 23 of that Act and Section 278 of the Railway Act, referring to limitations on discriminating and maximum railway rates, respectively, and it discusses the role of the CTC in handling and mediating information complaints from shippers about railway rates. Finally, it summarizes the statutory and executive rate freezes that have vitally limited railway rates in Canada. Chapter IX reports on the economic effects of the commercial freedom granted the railways in 1967 under the minimal regulation of the 1967 Act, as found in this study. It also comments on the general attitudes of shippers toward negotiation of rates under commercial freedom and in the light that the study throws on this subject. Chapter X gives the authors' conclusions on the policy implications of the study for Canada's transport regulation in the future, and states the direction that any revision of the National Transportation Act of 1967 and other legislation should take to improve the overall efficiency and equitability of railway pricing of freight traffic. It also states some observations on the implications that the Canadian experience with commercial freedom for the railways may have for other countries, with particular reference to the U.S.A.

FOOTNOTES

1. Public Law 94-210, 94th Cong., S. 2718, approved February 5, 1976.
2. See the *Report of the Royal Commission on Transportation* (Ottawa: The Queen's Printer, March and December 1961), Vols. I and II; and Transport Canada, *Transportation Policy, A Framework for Transport in Canada, Summary Report,* June 1975. Accompanying the latter were two other reports by Transport Canada, *An Interim Report on Freight Transportation in Canada* and *An Interim Report on Inter-City Passenger Movement in Canada,* both issued in June 1975.
3. Agreed charges were first authorized in 1938 by Part IV of the Transport Act of 1938, and followed authorization of similar but less restrictive legislation by the United Kingdom in the Road and Rail Traffic Act of 1933. See *Report of the Royal Commission on Transportation,* W.F.A. Turgeon, Chairman (Ottawa: The King's Printer, February 9, 1951), pp. 89-95; and *Report of Royal Commission on Agreed Charges,* W.F.A. Turgeon, Commissioner (Ottawa: The Queen's Printer, February 21, 1955), pp. 9-13, 21-22, 25-38 and 47-48.
4. A.W. Currie, *Canadian Transportation Economics* (Toronto: University of Toronto Press, 1967), pp. 226-229.
5. *In the Matter of the Application and Appeal of Saskatchewan Wheat Pool, Agra Industries Limited, Co-op Vegetable Oils Ltd. and Western Canadian Seed Processors Ltd.,* pursuant to Section 23 of the *National Transportation Act,* File No. 30637.2, decided by the CTC June 27, 1973. On March 15, 1974, the original applicants appealed to the Governor in Council under Section 64(1) of the National Transportation Act to vary in various respects the Orders of the CTC made pursuant to that decision.
6. *Prince Albert Pulp Co., Ltd. v. Canadian Natl. Rys.,* 349 I.C.C. 477 (1972) and on reconsideration, 349 I.C.C. 482 (1974). With respect to through international rates on newsprint, see *Anglo-Canadian Pulp & Paper Mills, LTD v. A&RR Co.,* 351 I.C.C. 325 (1975).
7. See the ICC's *88th Annual Report,* Fiscal Year Ending June 30, 1974, (Washington: U.S. Government Printing Office), pp. 31-34, 66 and 75-82.
8. For a review of the historical background, the original purposes and the evolution of various rate subsidies to the railways, see Howard J. Darling, *The Structure of Railroad Subsidies in Canada* (Toronto: York University Transportation Centre, October 1974). See pp. 29-33 and 58-61 for the evolution and subsidy cost of another statutory set of rates similar to the Crows Nest Pass Rates, the grain and flour rates for export through the Canadian Atlantic ports (known as "At and East Rates").
9. H.L. Purdy, *Transport Competition and Public Policy in Canada* (Vancouver: University of British Columbia Press, 1972), pp. 175-182. These statutory rates also apply to certain by-products of the milling, distilling and brewing industries, and also to certain feed products and to rapeseed but not to rapeseed products.
10. *Ibid.,* pp. 153-155. Products covered are wheat, oats, barley, rye, bran, shorts, middlings, and feed screenings.
11. *Ibid.,* pp. 158-162; and Howard J. Darling, *op.cit.,* pp. 33-36, 42-45 and 65-71.
12. Authorization for 1973 payments to the railways of the Governor General in Council on the recommendation of the Minister of Transport and the Treasury Board, pursuant to Vote 45, The Appropriation Act, No. 1, 1974, P.C. 1974 — 2/801, April 9, 1974; for 1974 payments to the railways, pursuant to Vote 45, The Appropriation Act, No. 5 1974, PC 1974 — 9/2876, December 20, 1974; and for payments to for-hire trucking companies, pursuant to Transport Vote 50a, Appropriation Act No. 4, 1975, P.C. 1976-503, 2 March, 1976.

RAILWAY PRICING UNDER COMMERCIAL FREEDOM

13. H.L. Purdy, *op.cit.,* pp. 163-174; and Howard J. Darling, *op.cit.,* pp. 13-23 and 53-55. In 1970, the intraterritorial subsidy was reduced to 17 1/2 percent (later to 15 percent) and in 1974 the reductions in rates on specific interterritorial movements were increased from 30 to 50 percent.

14. James C. Nelson, *Railroad Transportation and Public Policy* (Washington: The Brookings Institution, 1959), pp. 36-40; and Ann F. Friedlaender, *The Dilemma of Freight Transport Regulation* (Washington: The Brookings Institution, 1969), pp. 21-23.

15. For a concise perceptive background, see K.W. Studnicki-Gizbert, *Issues in Canadian Transport Policy,* Part I, "Historical Background" (Toronto: Macmillan, 1974).

16. According to the *CP News Summary,* January 23, 1976, Transport Minister Otto Lang was quoted in the *Financial Post* as stating: "We have studied this very closely and found that, by and large, 60 per cent of the freight and passenger rates are set against competition. In other words they do reflect the alternatives available. It is the other 40 per cent where they [the railways] can get away with charging a lot because there really isn't any alternative."

17. Submittal of the Premiers of Saskatchewan, British Columbia, Manitoba and Alberta, *Transportation,* to the Western Economic Opportunities Conference called by the Federal Government, Calgary, July 24-26, 1973, p. 3. See Howard J. Darling "Transport Policy in Canada: The Struggle of Ideologies versus Realities", in *Issues in Canadian Transport Policy, op.cit.,* pp. 3-46.

18. A decision was reached by the CTC in *The Rapeseed Case* on June 27, 1973, but some issues were appealed to and decided by the Governor in Council—see Chapter VIII. Also see the reply of July 19, 1973 from E.J. Benson, President, CTC, to the then Minister of Transport, Jean Marchand, regarding federal handling of freight rate appeals under Section 23 of the National Transportation Act.

19. This long-standing issue was specifically heard before the two Turgeon Royal Commissions and was also presented to the MacPherson Commission. See the reports of the Turgeon Commissions in 1951 and 1955, pp. 96-101 and 38-46, respectively. Long-short haul discrimination was only broadly considered in Volume II of the report of the MacPherson Commission, December 1961, pp. 43-121 and 159-178.

20. Report to the Honourable the Minister of Transport pursuant to his Request of July 19, 1973 under the Provisions of Section 22 of the National Transportation Act. See Appendix "A" for the letter from the then Transport Minister Jean Marchand requesting investigation of 22 railway freight rates involving rate issues discussed at WEOC.

21. F.H. Peacock, Minister of Industry and Commerce, Government of Alberta, *"The Equitable Pricing Proposal"* presented to the Western Economic Opportunities Conference, Calgary, July 24, 1973. This presentation was supported by a 103-page study by the Transport Research and Development Division of that Department, *The Equitable Pricing Policy, A New Method of Railway Rate Making,* Edmonton, July 1973.

22. Province of Manitoba, "Destination Rate Principle", a proposal to WEOC, at Calgary, July 1973.

23. See *Two Proposals for Rail Freight Pricing: Assessment of Their Prospective Impact,* a Report to the Federal-Provincial Committee on Western Transportation, by P.S. Ross & Partners, MPS Associates Ltd., R.L. Banks and Associates, Inc., Trimac Consulting Services Ltd., the M.W. Menzies Group Limited, and George W. Wilson, Indiana University, September 30, 1974, pp. 12-18.

24. The Select Territory includes New Brunswick, Nova Scotia, Prince Edward Island and Eastern Quebec; Newfoundland was included when it entered Confederation in 1949. John Heads, *Transport Subsidies and Regional Development,* Ph.D. thesis at the

University of Manitoba, 1976.

25. *Ibid.,* p. 5.
26. The Canadian Industrial Traffic League, "A Statement of Position Prepared for the Honourable Otto Emil Lang, P.C., M.P., Minister of Transport Concerning Transportation Policy — A Framework for Transport in Canada, January 13, 1976, pp. 4-6.
27. *Ibid.,* p. 9. See Arthur V. Mauro, "Conglomerates — Is Regulation Necessary", *ICC Practitioners' Journal,* September-October 1970, pp. 955-962.
28. *Transportation Policy, A Framework for Transport in Canada, Summary Report,* Transport Canada (Ottawa: Information Canada, 1975).
29. John C. Spychalski, "Criticisms of Regulated Freight Transport: Do Economists' Perceptions Conform with Institutional Realities", *Transportation Journal,* Spring 1975, pp. 5-17.

CHAPTER II

RAIL FREIGHT TRAFFIC AND RATES IN CANADA

The purpose of this chapter is to describe the main features of Canadian rail traffic and the rate structure. The chapter provides the background for rate making in Canada and introduces some general evidence of the influence of competitive forces on railway rates. Some particular features of the rate structure of concern to shippers and governments are also described.

The chapter is in five main sections. The first outlines the main features of Canadian domestic and Canada-U.S.A. rail traffic. The second section describes the types of rail rates in Canada and the changing importance of the various types of rates since 1951. The third section presents the results of a statistical analysis which examines the influence of various rate-making factors on the level of rates. The fourth section shows rate-level changes from 1959 to 1976. The chapter concludes with some examples of the controversial aspects of rates in Canada.

Significant Features of Canadian Railway Traffic

Canada is a vast country in which the production of basic farm, forest and mineral products is highly important. It is not surprising, then, that rail transport has played and still does play an important role in the political and economic well-being of the country.

The railways in Canada still carry a substantial proportion of intercity freight. Unfortunately, the last comprehensive estimate of the share of Canadian traffic carried by rail was produced as long ago as 1969. Table 1 shows the relative importance of rail traffic in terms of ton-miles over the period 1944 to 1968. The share of the ton-miles carried by rail declined rapidly between 1944 and 1961, but then stabilized at 53 percent and increased slightly to 55 percent in 1967 and 1968. Railways carried a major share of intercity ton-miles of freight and were dominant over truck transport. However, in terms of tons carried the trucking industry was of equivalent importance to the railways by 1968.

During the 1970's, two important developments have occurred. The first is the rapid growth of a limited number of major bulk commodity movements by rail, particularly coal, potash and sulphur in Western Canada. The expansion of this traffic along with the continued growth of other bulk rail traffic has given

21

rise to major concerns about the adequacy of rail capacity to support the over-seas export positions in Eastern and Western Canada.[1] The second major development has been the continued extention of the influence of trucking competition, especially for non-bulk freight, but also for bulk freight over short hauls.

As a result of these developments, the physical output of rail transport has increased relative to truck. It was estimated by Transport Canada that the railways and intercity trucking industry transported between them 397.4 million tons of freight in 1972.[2] Of that tonnage, 57 percent was carried by the railways. However, the market value of the rail service, as indicated by freight revenue, was less than that of trucking. The gross revenues earned by rail and the for-hire section of the trucking industry during 1972 totalled $4.26 billions, of which $2.23 billions or 52 percent, was earned by for-hire trucking.[3]

Table 2 shows the changes which have taken place between 1969 and 1974 in the movement of major commodities by rail. (1969 is used as the base year as the Standard Commodity Classification system was adopted then in the *Waybill Analysis*.) Over this period, the total ton-miles of traffic in the Waybill sample increased by 42.3 percent. In 1974, nine commodities each accounted for more than two percent of ton-miles and a total of 50.6 percent of all ton-miles. These commodities accounted for 41.8 percent of the ton-miles in 1969. This increased concentration is accounted for in large part by the increase in bituminous coal, potash and sulphur from 14.5 percent of the ton-miles in 1969 to 22.7 percent in 1974. Of the other major movements, container traffic also shows a notable increase in its share of the ton-miles.

Relative Amounts of Domestic and Trans-border Traffic

The relative importance of the modes of transport varies regionally as the transport requirements of the regional economies vary. The differences in the regional requirements for rail traffic can be described most conveniently by examining in some detail the composition of Canadian rail traffic. This description is based on two reference papers on rail commodity flow published by the Traffic and Tariffs Branch of the Canadian Transport Commission.[4] The statistics in those publications as used here account for approximately 60 percent of the total originated revenue tonnage of railways in Canada.[5] The exclusion of certain types of traffic appears to result in a significant distortion of traffic data in only one local case.[6]

Domestic traffic accounts for about 73 percent of revenues of the total Canadian rail freight traffic shown in Table 3. International traffic is, therefore, an important component of rail traffic in Canada. The volume of trans-border traffic is important as a source of intramodal rail competition and as shown in Chapter VIII, as a source of problems associated with the regulation of international rail rates.

Rail freight revenue to the U.S.A. is substantially greater than that from the

Table 1

Intercity Freight by Mode of Transport
(excluding pipelines), 1944-68

(Billions of ton-miles and percent of total by each mode)

	RAIL		ROAD		WATER	
Year	Ton-miles	Percent	Ton-miles	Percent	Ton-Miles	Percent
1944	65.93	74	2.67	3	20.31	23
1948	59.08	68	5.19	5	23.20	27
1952	68.43	63	8.90	8	30.87	29
1956	78.82	61	10.61	8	39.41	31
1960	65.45	56	13.84	12	36.87	32
1961	65.83	54	16.10	13	39.38	33
1962	67.94	53	16.58	13	42.95	34
1963	75.80	53	16.70	12	50.12	35
1964	85.03	52	17.47	11	59.19	37
1965	87.19	53	18.20	11	57.82	36
1966	95.10	53	18.95	11	64.41	36
1967	94.10	55	19.54	11	57.15	34
1968	96.86	55	21.13	12	58.11	33

Source: Calculated from the Dominion Bureau of Statistics, Special
Release, April 1969.

Table 2

Commodities Accounting for More Than Two Percent
of Rail Ton-Miles in 1969 and 1974

Commodity	Rank in 1974	1974 Ton-miles		1969 Ton-miles	
		Millions	Percent	Millions	Percent
Wheat	1	124.5	13.6	92.6	14.4
Bituminous Coal	2	97.8	10.7	42.5	6.6
Potash	3	57.2	6.3	36.1	5.6
Sulphur	4	51.9	5.7	14.8	2.3
Barley	5	34.4	3.8	26.7	4.2
TOFC	6	33.3	3.6	24.7	3.8
Lumber	7	24.7	2.7	19.2	3.0
Freight Forwarder and Shipper Associations	8	21.2	2.3	12.3	1.9
COFC	9	18.6	2.0	0.2	-
Total of Commodities Above		463.6	50.6	269.1	41.8
Total of All Rail Traffic		915.5	100	643.6	100

Source: Canadian Transport Commission, Waybill Analysis, 1974 and 1969.

23

Table 3

Canadian Domestic and Trans-Border Rail Traffic, 1972

	Tonnage (000)	% of total tonnage	Ton-miles (000)	% of total ton-miles	Revenue (000)	% of total revenue
Canada-Canada	128,826	79.4	72,803,549	77.9	930,387	72.9
Canada-U.S.[a]	33,504	20.6	20,603,208	22.1	346,135	27.1
Total	162,330	100%	93,406,757	100%	1,276,522	100%

Note:

[a]Data for Canada-U.S. traffic refer only to mileage from place of origin or destination in Canada to the international border.

Sources: Calculated from Canadian Transport Commission, Reference Paper 1, Canadian Carload All-Rail Traffic, 1968-1972, Tables I and II; and Reference Paper 3, Carload All-Rail Traffic Between Canada and the United States, 1968-1973, Tables 13 and 14.

Table 4

Distribution of Canadian Originated Rail Traffic, 1972

	Origin			
	B.C.	Prairies	Ontario & Quebec	Maritimes
% of originated tonnage	13.5	37.8	39.5	9.2
% of originated ton-miles	18.6	49.7	27.0	4.7
% of originated revenue	17.3	32.1	44.3	6.2
Av. length of haul (mi.)	806	771	401	298

Note:
The numbers in the first three rows represent the traffic originated in the specified region as a percent of total originated traffic. The figures include both national and international traffic.

Source: Calculated from Canadian Transport Commission, Reference Paper 1, Canadian Carload All-Rail Traffic, 1968-72, Tables I and II; and Reference Paper 3, Carload All-Rail Traffic Between Canada and the United States, 1968-1973, Tables 13 and 14.

U.S.A. In 1972, the southbound revenue of $261 million was 3.1 times the northbound revenue. The dominant commodity group in both directions was manufactured and miscellaneous products, and that traffic contributed 54 percent of the revenue southbound and 69 percent of the revenue northbound.

Regional Traffic Flows and Lengths of Haul

Data in this chapter on regional traffic and rates are derived from two sources in which the regional definitions differ. Therefore, the regions in Tables 4, 5 and 6 are groupings of provinces. The regions in Tables 9, 10 and 12 are those used in the *Waybill Analysis* published by the CTC. The regions are shown in Figure 1.

Table 4 gives a breakdown of Canadian originated railway traffic in 1972 by region of origin. The Provinces of Ontario and Quebec originated the greatest volume of tonnage and revenue. Nevertheless, the Prairie Provinces originated the greatest volume of traffic as measured by ton-miles. The large proportion of ton-miles originated in the Prairies, in comparison with the proportion of revenue and tons originated there, is accounted for largely by the importance of grain moving long distances to the ports of Vancouver, Thunder Bay and Churchill at low rates set by the Government of Canada.[7] The average length of haul is longest for B.C., 806 miles, and shortest for the Maritime Provinces, 298 miles. Considering the size of the country, average distances are not great because for each region except the Prairies the majority of rail traffic is intraregional.

Table 5 shows the destination of rail traffic by region of origin. Only 20 percent of the tonnage originated in the Prairies is intraregional traffic. About one-third is destined for B.C. (mainly to Vancouver for export), and one-third for Ontario and Quebec (a considerable portion of the volume being grain to Thunder Bay). Intra-regional traffic accounts for more than 71 percent of the tonnage in the Maritimes and Ontario and Quebec. Traffic to the U.S.A. is of the greatest relative importance in B.C. The average length of haul of this traffic is 1,320 miles, indicating that much of it moves over Canadian lines as far as Winnipeg, Manibtoba before moving south.

The data for all of Canada in Table 5 show the dominance of Ontario, Quebec and B.C. as destinations of rail traffic. In Ontario and Quebec, the concentrations of terminating traffic are at the ports on the Great Lakes, especially Thunder Bay, and at the large population centres. In B.C., the terminating traffic is heavily concentrated in Vancouver, for export and local consumption.

Commodity Composition of Railway Traffic Overall and in Regions

A further contrast in the rail traffic of the four regions is shown in Table 6. The characteristics of the regional economies are evident in this table through the relative importance of the commodity classes shipped. In B.C., the volume of forest products (which is understated because of the exclusion of B.C. Railway

25

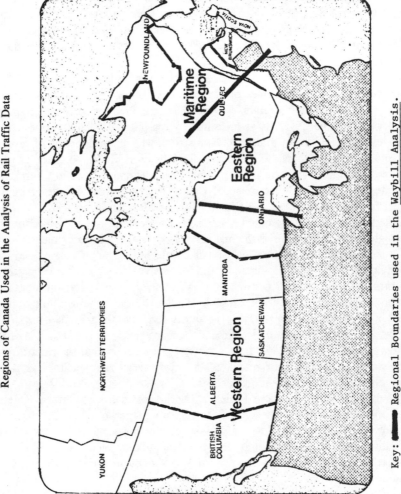

Figure 1

Regions of Canada Used in the Analysis of Rail Traffic Data

Key: ▬▬▬ Regional Boundaries used in the Waybill Analysis.
      ✍ Regional Boundaries constructed from data by province in the
         CTC Reference Papers on Carload Traffic.

Table 5

Destination of Canadian Originated Rail Tonnage,
by Region of Origin, 1972

Destination

Origin	B.C.	Prairies	Ontario & Quebec	Maritimes	U.S.
B.C.					
% of originated tonnage	59.8	12.3	4.8	0.4	22.7
Av. length of haul (mi.)	451	745	2,721	3,592	1,320
Prairies					
% of originated tonnage	31.9	19.6	33.4	0.6	14.4
Av. length of haul (mi.)	942	307	909	2,489	674
Ontario and Quebec					
% of originated tonnage	1.3	3.3	71.4	6.8	17.3
Av. length of haul (mi.)	2,790	1,676	244	945	416
Maritimes					
% of originated tonnage	0.1	0.3	16.3	75.4	7.9
Av. length of haul(mi.)	3,678	2,553	861	107	840
Total (Canada)					
% of originated tonnage	20.7	10.4	42.9	9.9	16.1
Av. length of haul (mi.)	722	557	498	406	696

Sources: Calculated from Canadian Transport Commission, Reference Paper 1, Canadian Carload All-Rail Traffic 1968-72, Tables I and II; and Reference Paper 3, Carload All-Rail Traffic Between Canada and the United States, 1968-1973, Tables 13 and 14.

27

data) and mineral products reflects the importance of forestry and mining. A significant component of manufactured goods also is attributable to forestry. Traffic originating in the Prairie Provinces is concentrated in agricultural products, predominantly grain. Traffic originating in Ontario and Quebec is relatively diversified in volume, but is predominantly in manufactured goods when measured by revenue; more than 70 percent of the revenue from originating traffic comes from manufactured goods. Manufactured goods are also an important source of revenue in the Maritime Provinces.

Table 6 highlights the importance of manufactured goods as a predominant source of rail revenue for Canada in general and for most regions. The products of agriculture and forestry jointly make up 65 percent and 64 percent of originated tonnage and ton-miles, respectively, but only 37 percent of revenue. Manufactured and miscellaneous commodities, on the other hand, make up 24 percent and 28 percent of tonnage and ton-miles, but 52 percent of revenue. These figures cannot be interpreted directly to reflect the profitability of various traffic categories as they give little indication of the costs associated with performing various services. However, at the least they cast some doubt on two common notions about freight rates. The first is that agriculture, forestry (and mining) bear an unduly large burden of rail constant costs. The second is that the advent of severe intermodal competition, particularly between rail and truck, has resulted in the total elimination of profitable price discrimination by the railways on manufactured commodities.

Types of Rail Freight Rates
and Their Changing Importance

The railway freight rate structure as a whole is made up of a very large number of different types of rates and individual commodity and regional rate structures. These have evolved in response to the need to provide rates on all commodities between all pairs of rail points, the necessity to meet carrier competition effectively, and the profit stimulus for adjustment of rates to the marketing requirements of products as far as is practicable. Within the different types of rates, three special structures are common even though deviations from the structure have been necessary to meet the varied competitive conditions.

Basic Kinds of Rate Structures

The three basic kinds of rate structure are found in distance-related rates, group rates and base-related rates.[8] Distance rates are appropriate in cases where specific competitive conditions are not major factors. The uniform mileage scale for class rates in Canada was established first in 1952, following the recommendation of the Turgeon Royal Commission.[9] However, that Commission did not recommend the establishment of a mileage structure for other types of rates for which local or regional considerations significantly affected rail costs or competition.

28

Table 6

Percent of Domestic and International Rail Traffic by Region
and Commodity Group, 1972

	Agriculture		Animal		Forest		Mineral		Manufactured & Misc.		Total	
	1[a]	2[a]	1	2	1	2	1	2	1	2	1	2
B.C.												
% of tonnage	0.5	1.2	0.1	0.1	52.1	2.9	33.4	57.6	13.9	38.2	100	100
% of ton-miles	0.9	0.4	0.4	0.2	52.4	0.7	24.3	61.8	22.0	37.0	100	100
% of revenue	2.1	0.5	0.6	0.2	28.3	0.8	29.1	68.0	39.8	30.4	100	100
Av. length of haul (mi.)	1,221	452	2,246	2,312	659	305	478	1,414	1,038	1,279	656	1,320
Prairies												
% of tonnage	57.8	0.7	0.9	0.2	27.7	57.9	0.8	3.3	12.8	37.9	100	100
% of ton-miles	63.4	1.0	1.9	0.1	23.7	55.7	0.4	4.7	10.7	38.5	100	100
% of revenue	42.5	1.0	7.7	0.2	24.3	53.7	0.9	5.8	24.7	39.3	100	100
Av. length of haul (mi.)	863	1,009	1,678	374	673	651	353	1,020	657	673	787	674
Ontario and Quebec												
% of tonnage	6.0	2.5	0.2	0.1	45.5	17.9	10.8	6.2	37.4	73.3	100	100
% of ton-miles	12.9	2.5	0.5	0.1	18.5	18.0	8.6	6.1	59.6	73.3	100	100
% or revenue	6.1	2.2	0.9	0.1	13.0	10.7	6.4	7.6	73.6	79.4	100	100
Av. length of haul (mi.)	849	426	1,071	444	161	418	316	407	632	417	398	416
Maritimes												
% of tonnage	3.7	0.2	0.3	0.1	52.1	2.4	12.1	6.5	31.7	90.8	100	100
% of ton-miles	8.9	0.3	1.0	0.1	16.7	1.9	8.0	4.1	65.4	93.8	100	100
% of revenue	10.5	0.3	1.8	0.2	14.9	1.2	10.6	5.5	62.3	92.8	100	100
Av. length of haul (mi.)	609	983	924	816	80	650	164	524	519	867	251	840
Total												
% of tonnage	25.0	1.5	0.5	0.1	40.1	27.9	9.9	15.1	24.4	55.3	100	100
% of ton-miles	38.1	1.1	1.3	0.1	26.1	23.3	6.4	25.8	28.2	49.6	100	100
% of revenue	17.9	1.2	3.2	0.2	18.9	19.6	8.0	25.1	52.0	53.8	100	100
Av. length of haul (mi.)	859	525	1,551	706	367	581	356	1,192	651	624	565	696

Notes:
[a]Sub-column 1 represents Canada-destined traffic; sub-column 2 represents U.S.-destined traffic.
[2]The "% of tonnage", "% of ton-miles", "% of revenue" figure for each commodity group for each
destination (Canada or the U.S.) indicates the tonnage, ton-miles and revenue of that commodity
group as a percentage of the total tonnage, ton-miles and revenue moving from the region to the
specified destination.

Sources: Calculated from various Tables in Canadian Transport Commission Reference Paper 1,
Canadian Carload All-Rail Traffic, 1968-72; and Reference Paper 3, Canadian All-Rail
Traffic Between Canada and the United States, 1968-1973.

29

Group rates, or blanket rates, are rates which are uniform over a traffic originating or terminating area. They are a common form of rate to meet the need of various producers to compete in a large common market area. Conversely, consumers in those areas are given a wide choice among suppliers. An example of a group rate is the tariff on lumber from the Pacific Northwest and B.C. to the U.S.A. midwest and east coast. The rate to any point between Chicago and New York is the same amount for a particular commodity.

Base-and-related rates are made up of a base rate for a point or group of points to which are added or subtracted a rate differential or arbitrary rate. This differential rate recognises to some extent differences which apply over distance in either cost or competitive conditions.

The evolution of the structure of transcontinental rates in the U.S. has been explained well by Daggett and Carter.[10] They show how the strucutre in particular class and commodity rate scales evolved over time in response to varied competitive conditions affecting the railways and their customers. Experience in Canada has been the same and the result is a complex pattern of rate structures and types of rates which make a general description of freight rates difficult. A 1974 study of freight rates in Canada quoted an earlier characterization of railway rates as a "collection of numbers gratuitously referred to as the 'rate structure'."[11] However, as the Turgeon Commission found, the very responsiveness of freight rates to heterogeneous conditions precludes the existence of a general or simple pattern or structure of rates which can be readily described.

General Types of Railway Rates and Waybill Classification

The distribution of railway traffic by type of rate may be reported in various ways because there are many different types of tariffs. The actual designation of a rate may be related to a specific commodity or group of commodities in commodity rates or it may relate to a class rating or classification in class rates. However, in spite of the simplicity in the actual quotation of a rate, there is considerable complexity in the types of tariffs in which the rates are found.

By far the most common method of describing the distribution of traffic by rate type in Canada is to use the classifications and data available in the annual Waybill Analysis published by the CTC.[12] The first three types of rates given there are related to the categories of rates as specified in Section 274 of the Railway Act, but they are described in the Waybill Analysis under different terminology. The terminology used in the Waybill Analysis has given rise to some confusion.

A class rate is simply a rate applicable to a class rating to which articles are assigned in the freight classification. In the Waybill Analysis, the traffic in this category is that which moves under the Canadian Uniform Class Rate Tariff (except in the Maritime region where special tariff provisions apply). These class rates provide rates for every commodity that moves, or might move, between all points in Canada served by the railways. They provide a general rate structure for all commodities and shipments and, in effect, are the ceiling for railway rates.

The second type of rate defined in the Railway Act is a commodity rate. A commodity rate is one applicable to a specific article or group of goods described or named in the tariff containing the rate. The term "commodity rate" was adopted in the Railway Act of 1951. It replaced the old "special freight tariff" set down in the Railway Act of 1903. Commodity rates are tailored rates, designed to enable producers to meet competitive conditions in the markets for their products. Therefore, commodity rates are commonly set and/or adjusted after negotiations between the railways and shippers. Many low-value bulk commodities subject to severe market competition move under these rates, for example, coal, sulphur and potash. In the Waybill Analysis these rates are referred to as "non-competitive commodity rates". The railways prefer to use the term "normal" commodity rates.[13]

A competitive rate is defined in the Railway Act as a class or commodity rate that is issued to meet competition. That is, the rate may be made by assigning a commodity to a lower class rating than would otherwise apply or by quoting a commodity rate on the commodity within the competitive tariff. Competitive rates are established by the railways to meet competition from other modes of transport, and they are often arrived at by negotiation between the railways and shippers. The quotation of these rates today on the basis of class ratings is exceptional. In the Waybill Analysis, they are classified as competitive commodity rates.

The designation of some rates as "non-competitive" or "normal" and others as "competitive" can prompt an unwarranted conclusion that competitive conditions are not present in the setting of "normal" commodity rates. The competition present is market competition rather than direct intermodal competition, but the force of competitive pressures is still important in making such railway rates.

The fourth type of rate in the Waybill Analysis is the agreed charge. Agreed charges were made legal in Canada by Part IV of the Transport Act of 1938. The rate in an agreed charge is made on the established basis of rate making and is expressed in cents per hundred pounds or some other unit of weight or measurement as is appropriate. Under an agreed charge, a rate is agreed to between the carrier and shipper either for an agreed period of less than a year or for at least a year after which time either party may withdraw on ninety days' notice. Prior to 1976, the general interpretation of Section 32(12) of the Transport Act was that an agreed charge had to be made for a minimum period of a year. The section is now interpreted to allow agreed charges of less than one year as long as an expiration date is stipulated. Other shippers may become a party to the agreed charge with the consent of the carrier, but they must meet the same terms as the original signatories and, under these conditions, the railways have allowed other shippers to become a party to existing agreed charges. The CTC may fix rates for shippers judged unjustly discriminated against by agreed charges.[14]

Agreed charges might be arranged by carriers under any market conditions that make it desirable to enter into a contract with a shipper or a group of shippers. The railways have employed them mainly to meet intermodal competition, but they are also used in market competitive situations. They are not used as rate competitive devices to further intramodal competition in Canada as the Transport Act requires agreement in writing between, or joint participation by, competing railways before an agreed charge can be made to, from or between competitive railway points.[15] A major provision in an agreed charge is that the shipper provide a certain amount of his business to the railway. In practice, this is usually prescribed as a percentage of a shipper's traffic, but it may be based on an actual physical volume.

The fifth and last type of rate listed in the Waybill Analysis is the statutory rate. These are rates on grain and related products which were first introduced into the Railway Act in 1922. This was done to resolve a dispute about the application and implication of the Crows Nest Pass Agreement of 1897 between the CP* and the federal government. The CP received a subsidy amounting to $3.4 million for building a line through Crows Nest Pass in the Rocky Mountains. In return, the railway agreed to reduce its rates on "settlers' effects" and to reduce existing rates on grain and flour by three cents per hundred pounds and to maintain that rate "hereafter". "Not suprisingly, those Prairie interests benefiting from the agreement maintain that the 'hereafter' in it meant just that".[16] Subsequent controversy arising from the application of that agreement only to the lines in existence in 1897 resulted in a 1925 amendment to the Railway Act applying the Crows Nest Pass Rates to "all such traffic moving from all points on all lines of railway west of Fort William to Fort William or Port Arthur over all lines now or hereafter constructed by any company subject to the jurisdiction of Parliament". (RS. 1952, Railway Act, Sec. 328(6)). Decisions by the Board of Transport Commissioners and some voluntary extensions by the railways have extended the Crows Nest Pass rate level to apply to about one-fifth to one-third of the ton-miles of domestic carload traffic.

Changing Breakdown of Railway Traffic by Rate Category

Table 7 shows the breakdown of railway traffic by rate category for the years 1951, 1963 and 1974 as given in the Waybill Analysis. In 1951, class rates accounted for 22 percent of rail revenue, non-competitive commodity rates 53

*Throughout this book, the designation CP is used for CP Rail or CPR. Corporate reorganisation and the change of names took place in 1968.

percent and competitive rates and agreed charges a total of 13 percent. During the 1950's and 1960's, the upsurge of trucking led to a rapid increase in the number of competitive rates and agreed charges. In 1974, they accounted for 40 percent and 23 percent, respectively.

Table 7

Distribution of Traffic by Rate Category,
1951, 1963, 1974

		Class	Commodity		Agreed Charge	Statutory	Mixed
			non-comp.	comp.			
millions	1951	29	169	28	3	79	4
ton-miles[a]	1963	8	124	62	77	141	-
	1974	11	333	262	143	165	-
% of	1951	9%	54%	10%	1%	25%	1%
total	1963	2%	30%	15%	19%	34%	-
ton-miles	1974	1%	36%	29%	16%	18%	-
revenue,	1951	.9	2.2	.4	.1	.4	.09
million $	1963	.9	1.9	1.6	1.5	0.7	-
	1974	.5	3.9	5.8	3.3	.8	-
% of	1951	22%	53%	10%	3%	10%	2%
total	1963	5%	32%	26%	25%	12%	-
revenue	1974	3%	27%	40%	23%	6%	-

Note:
 [a]The waybill Analysis is a one percent sample of carload traffic. The sample figures are reported here.

Source: Canadian Transport Commission, Waybill Analysis, 1951, 1963, 1974.

Agreed charges have been used extensively by the railways to meet intermodal competition, and it is generally recognized that they have been successful in retaining or capturing traffic for the railways.[17] Table 8 shows the use of agreed charges as measured by the number in effect during the years 1939 to 1975. A significant increase in the number of agreed charges did not occur until 1956, following modification of the Transport Act on the recommendations of the Royal Commission on Agreed Charges, 1955. The highest annual average number of agreed charges in effect was during 1966. Agreed charges accounted for their greatest percentage of rail revenues in 1969 when they accounted for 28.9 percent of rail revenue.[18] The number of agreed charges in

33

Table 8

Use of
Agreed Charges in Canada

| | Agreed Charges | | |
	Becoming Effective	Terminated	Avg. No. In Effect[1]
1939	4	–	3
1940	11	5	6
1941	11	3	16
1942	2	2	19
1943	1	2	17
1944	1	1	17
1945	1	1	17
1946	4	1	19
1947	2	2	20
1948	1	–	20
1949	5	2	23
1950	2	4	22
1951	1	–	22
1951	3	2	24
1953	12	1	29
1954	23	4	44
1955	45	6	67
1956	77	17	129
1957	135	13	210
1958	210	21	372
1959	311	34	615
1960	253	40	860
1961	259	52	1,077
1962	202	78	1,144
1963	222	51	1,387
1964	191	97	1,520
1965	194	134	1,590
1966	109	88	1,632
1967	194	245	1,545
1968	78	197	1,519
1969	86	169	1,411
1970	67	208	1,306
1971	74	161	1,190
1972	74	142	1,061
1973	76	144	998
1974	28	92	936
1975	40	436	728

[1]Total number in effect each month divided by 12.

Source: Records of Canadian Transport Commission

34

effect has shown a steady decline during the 1970's and has decreased drastically during 1975. At the end of 1975, there were only 503 agreed charges in effect, that is, 52 percent of the number on effect at the end of 1973.[19]

The main reason for the rapid decline in the number of agreed charges has been the reluctance of the railways to commit themselves, during a period of rapid inflation, to rates for a twelve-month period. Rail costs have been less predictable than previously and truck rates, against which many agreed charges are set, have also been increasing. As a consequence of the decline in agreed charges, a significant increase has taken place in competitive commodity rates. Some of the characteristics of the move to competitive rates will be considered in more detail in later chapters. However, it may be noted here that many of the provisions formerly characteristic of agreed charges (limitation to named shippers, volume requirements, and penalty charges for a shortfall in volume or other requirements) are now being published in open tariffs.

Regional Rate Levels and Problems of Statutory Rates

In Canadian transport studies, it is essential to draw attention to the characteristics of the traffic carried at statutory rates. In 1974, this traffic accounted for 18 percent of ton-miles but only 6 percent of freight revenue. It is generally accepted that this traffic imposes a substantial financial burden on the railways. The MacPherson Royal Commission accepted that the railways incurred a loss on statutory traffic and recommended the payment of a subsidy to the railways.[20] Unfortunately, opposition of Prairie interests prevented actions which might have led to a long-run solution of the issues raised by the statutory rates. A provision proposed for the National Transportation Act that the CTC study the costs of moving traffic under these rates was defeated in Parliament. Further, the payment of a subsidy to the railways for the operation of unremunerative branch lines kept open in the public interest, made it less clear than would otherwise have been the case that the railways have incurred substantial losses annually on the carriage of one-fifth to one-third of their business. It has been left to the Snavely Commission to document the size of the losses incurred by the railways. The Commission estimated that for 1974 the loss incurred by the railways was $89.3 million.[21]

The unremunerative statutory traffic is significant to the pricing of other traffic in Canada because of the impact which it has on the net revenue of the railways and on the perceptions of shippers. The loss which the railways incur on the traffic reduces the net revenue of the railways to the detriment of other shippers. The perception of both the loss and the impact is also very important for other shippers who believe that they are paying a subsidy to the statutory traffic. These shippers are concerned that, when the railways need extra revenue from them to cover rising costs, the costs to be covered by higher rates be costs which might be attributed to their own traffic and not be the result of carrying grain at rates below variable costs.

35

It is important to view the impact of statutory rates and rate levels in general within a regional framework, as many complaints about freight rates are regional in nature. Only limited regional data are tabulated here as the presentation and comparison of simple averages can be misleading. Full consideration of regional differences in rates must take into account the impact of heterogenous traffic, changes in average hauls, and environmental and other conditions.

Table 9 shows the distribution of traffic originated in the three regions given in the Waybill Analysis by type of rate. In the Western Region, the most important rate categories in ton-miles are the non-competitive commodity and the statutory rates. In marked contrast, in the Eastern and Maritime Regions the competitive rates and agreed charges account for more than three quarters of the traffic by revenue and ton-miles. The relative lack of competitive rates in the Western Region gives rise to the complaint that rates are not set on the basis of competitive forces and that because of this Western Canada is at a disadvantage in the matter of freight rates.

Table 10 shows the average revenue per ton-mile by region and for Canada in 1974. Apart from statutory rates, at 0.50 cents per ton-mile, the lowest rates are the non-competitive commodity rates in the Western Region with an average rate of 1.06 cents per ton-mile. The low level of these rates is explained by the efficient movement of bulk commodities, especially coal in unit trains, in keeping down costs and by the influence of market competition in keeping down the rates. Even excluding the statutory traffic, the average revenue per ton-mile of traffic originating in the Western Region in 1974 (1.37 cents) is less than that in the other regions. However, such a simple comparison is possibly misleading because it does not take into account the various traffic conditions such as difference in average lengths of haul. The difficulty in using the Waybill Analysis data without performing significant statistical work to segregate important traffic features that influence differences in average freight rate is one reason that neither the railways nor the federal government has been able to allay the fears of the Canadian West concerning the undue burden of freight rates on Western Canadian industry and consumers.[22]

Statistical Analysis of Factors in Canadian Freight Rate Levels

A statistical analysis of Waybill data can provide evidence on the influence of diverse traffic characteristics on rate levels and on regional differences in rate levels. The Waybill data are used generally to demonstrate changes in the average level of rates over time and changes in the percentage of traffic moving under various categories of rates. A major deficiency of such presentations is that they provide little or no analysis of the extent to which changes or differences in freight rate levels are to be explained by differences in the nature of commodities moved, the volume moved, the length of haul or other traffic, cost,

Table 9

Percentage Distribution of Rail Traffic,
by Rate Type and Region, 1974

	Maritimes		Eastern		Western	
	Ton-Miles	Revenue	Ton-Miles	Revenue	Ton-Miles	Revenue
Class	5.0	8.6	2.9	5.4	0.1	0.5
Non-Competitive Commodity	12.7	13.6	14.2	10.8	47.9	44.8
Competitive Commodity	47.6	47.6	52.8	50.4	16.5	29.8
Agreed Charges	34.7	30.2	30.1	33.4	7.8	12.7
Statutory	--	--	--	--	27.7	12.2
	100	100	100	100	100	100

Source: Canadian Transport Commission, Waybill Analysis, 1974.

Table 10

Rail Revenue Per Ton-Mile, by
Rate Type, by Region and for Canada, 1974

	Maritimes	Eastern	Western	Canada
Class	3.64 cents	4.42 cents	5.18 cents	4.33 cents
Non-Competitive Commodity	2.27	1.84	1.06	1.17
Competitive Commodity	2.12	2.31	2.05	2.20
Agreed Charges	1.85	2.70	1.84	2.33
Statutory	--	--	0.50	0.50
	2.12	2.42	1.13	1.56

Source: Canadian Transport Commission, Waybill Analysis, 1974.

and market circumstances.

The results of a basic statistical analysis are presented here.[23] They show that over the period 1956 to 1972, the Canadian railway rate structure appears to have become more cost oriented as competitive forces increased, and that the railways' pricing practices have been equally responsive to cost levels and competitive forces in all parts of the country.

Agreed charges, most competitive rates, and major commodity rates are set by negotiation (oral or written) between the railways and shippers and/or receivers. This process does not provide statistical information about the relative importance of cost and competitive variables, though the influence of competition is illuminated more than that of cost changes and unit costs. Therefore, an analysis of the changing rate structure which discerns the influence of the forces shaping it must rely largely on the published Waybill data. Appendix I describes the data used in the analysis conducted in this study and points out some of the limitations associated with the use of Waybill statistics. No commodity moving at a statutory rate was included in the sample of commodities for statistical analysis.

The data are analysed by using a logarithmic form of regression model. This model conforms with the expected non-linear form of relationships between the rate making factors and the rate, and gives a better statistical fit than any other familiar functional form. This form of regression also has the convenience that the logarithmic regression coefficients indicate the proportionate changes in the freight rate with respect to changes in the rate factors. The model used is specified in Appendix I.

The variables included in the regression analysis are the rate per 100 lbs., the length of haul, the commodity class, the load per car, the number of cars in the sample for the year, the value of the commodity per ton, the regional origin and destination and the car type (tank car, refrigerator car and other equipment). With three regions, Maritime, Eastern and Western Regions, nine links are possible.

Proportionate Changes in Rates to Changes in Available Rate Factors

Table 11 shows the regression results when the data are analysed for short-haul and long-haul links separately. The short-haul links are the three intra-regional movement patterns which averaged a length of 394 miles in 1972. The three long-haul links are Western to Eastern, Eastern to Western, and Western to Maritimes; the average length of haul for these links was 2,269 miles in 1972. The regression results show some interesting differences.

The explanatory powers of the regression equations for all regressions is high as shown by the R^2 coefficient. Between 82 percent and 95 percent of the difference in the rate per ton for commodity classes can be related to the variables in the equations. This does not mean that the causal explanation is simple, as the statistcal relationships observed may have various explanations.

Table 11

Regression Results for Short-Haul
and Long-Haul Links, 1956, 1963, 1972

Year	Intercept[a]	Length of Haul	Tons per Car	Number of Cars	Dollars Per Ton	M/M Link	Regrigerator[a] Car Variable	R^2	No. of Observations
				Short-Haul Links[b]					
1972	2.13 (4.93)[c]	0.6002 (13.65)	-0.4648 (5.67)	-0.1131 (4.70)	0.0539 (2.73)	--	--	0.8909	72
1963	2.08 (4.79)	0.5950 (12.62)	-0.5050 (6.48)	-0.0930 (3.62)	0.0590 (3.06)	-0.2032 (2.05)	--	0.9117	66
1956	1.26 (2.65)	0.6896 (14.95)	-0.3780 (4.95)	-0.1408 (5.26)	0.0671 (3.63)	-0.2151 (2.28)	--	0.9491	66
				Long-Haul Links[d]					
1972	2.98 (3.70)	0.4749 (5.17)	-0.4844 (5.12)	--	0.0678 (2.93)	N.A.	0.2502 (2.44)	0.8176	40
1963	4.15 (2.71)	0.3633 (2.24)	-0.6134 (5.66)	--	0.0707 (1.79)	N.A.	--	0.8522	19
1956	2.12 (2.37)	0.6511 (5.20)	-0.6934 (6.70)	--	0.0791 (2.40)	N.A.	--	0.8528	20

Notes:
[a] All variables except intercept, links and refrigerator car variables are logarithims.
[b] The links are M/M, E/E, W/W.
[c] Numbers in parentheses are t- statistics.
[d] The links are W/E, E/W W/M.

39

For example, the length of haul may be related to the rate level because of its influence on railway costs and/or because it is related, in general, to the effectiveness of trucking competition.[24] However, comparison of the results of the regressions for the short- and long-haul links provides some useful insights into the influence of the factors on freight rates.

The numbers shown for the length of haul, tons per car, number of cars and value per ton are the proportional change in the freight rate associated with a proportional change in these independent variables. For example, on the short-haul links in 1972, a 10-percent increase in the length of haul was associated with a 6.0-percent increase in the freight rate; a 10-percent increase in the number of tons per car was associated with a 4.6-percent decrease in the freight rate; a 10-percent increase in the value per ton was associated with a 0.5-percent increase in the freight rate.

The proportionate change in rates in response to a change in the length of haul is greater for movements over a short distance than a long distance. This is consistent with the taper of rates with respect to distance. The impact of distance on rates has declined over time for long- and short-hauls. However, the absolute and relative amount of the decline has been greater for long-haul movements. This statistical result would be consistent with a greater rate of increase in competitiveness on long-haul traffic and with the presence of railway cost saving in line-haul operation. The results suggest that the effect on Western Canada of distance from market has been diminishing over the period analyzed. The extent to which this trend may continue will be influenced by increases in resource costs, particularly fuel, and the extent to which the railways can continue to improve their line-haul performance by technological innovation and operational changes.

The weight carried per car consistently shows a negative relationship with the freight rate. The amount of saving due to an increase in the carload weight, and passed on to the shipper in the form of a rate reduction, has been increasing for short-haul movements but decreasing for long-haul movements. The latter is not consistent with the study's expectations. However, the divergent trends have resulted in the elasticity of the freight rate in response to tons per car moving closer together for long-haul and short-haul traffic. The substantial difference which existed in 1956 is not one which would have been expected on the basis of either railway cost characteristics or the impact of intermodal competition. Therefore, the divergent trends may represent a rationalization of the structure of incentive rates as incentive rates have become more common.

The impact of the value of commodities on the level of freight rates has decreased in both sets of markets over the time period, although the value of the commodity is consistently more important on the long-haul movements than on the short-haul movements. This can be explained by the presence of less stringent competitive forces on the long-haul movements which allows the railways to practice a greater degree of price discrimination. However, in comparison with the other variables the value of the commodity is still of limited significance.

The number of cars in the sample is only of statistical significance for the short-haul links. The greater the number of cars of a commodity moved per year, the lower the freight rate. No significant change in the importance of this factor has taken place over the time period. For the long-haul links, no statistically identifiable impact is evident; however, few of the commodity movements on the long-haul links were of substantial volume.

No link pattern is statistically significant except for the Intra-Maritime traffic. This suggests that with this exception, the pricing practices of the railways in the various regions of the country are similar, and that no statistically significant variations exist for commodities moving east or west in Western Canadian trade.

Regression analysis using all of the link data confirms that the level of rates is explained by an equal level of responsiveness to cost and competitive forces for all of the links with the exception of those affected by the Maritime Freight Rates Act.[25] Table 12 draws on the system-wide regression (presented in Appendix I, Table I-C) to show the relationship between the statistical results and changes in the level of subsdiy. Table 12 shows the responsiveness of the freight rate level to changes in the subsidy policy. In 1956, when the subsidy on traffic moving west was 20 percent, the rates on the commodities in the sample were 15 percent below the national level. In 1972, when the subsidy was 30 percent, the rates were 28.5 percent below the national level. Only for 1972 do the results show no statistically significant difference in the level of rates on intra-Maritime traffic and that on other links beyond that explained by the other variables in the analysis. This change may be explained by the reduction in the subsidy and its availability to truckers.

In the absence of direct measures of the extent of intermodal or market competition, those variables were not included in the system-wide analysis. However, a measure of those variables is available for three links, Western to Western, Western to Eastern and Eastern to Western, for 1972. For each commodity class on each of those links, a rating was obtained from railway marketing personnel for the degree of intermodal and market competition. The regression result is shown in Table 13.

The intermodal competition variable is not statistically significant. In part, this results from the correlation between intermodal competition and other independent variables, especially length of haul and the value of the commodity. It may also result from the difficulty of fitting the degree of competition to an ordinal scale from 0 to 3.

The level of market competition is shown to have a significant effect on the freight rate. Calculations using the coefficient for market competition in Table 13 show that, if the rate on a commodity subject to no market competition is

41

Table 12

Rate Subsidy Provisions and the Estimated
Freight Rates Levels of
M/E and M/M Links as Percent of Normal Rates

Year	Links[a]	Percent of Normal Rate[b]	Effective % of Subsidy
1956	M/E	85.2%	20%
	M/M	85.2%	20%
1963	M/E	77.6%	30%
	M/M	80.2%	20%
1972[c]	M/E	71.5%	30%
	M/M	--	17.5%

Notes:

[a]The links are Maritime to Eastern (M/E) and inter-Maritime (M/M).
[b]Calculated from the link coefficient reported in Appendix I, Table I-C.
[c]In 1972, the same percentages of subsidies were also applied to the trucking industry under the Atlantic Provinces Freight Assistance Act of 1969.

Table 13

Regression Analysis for Selected Links
Including Competitive Variables for 1972.[a]

Length of Haul	Tons per Car	# Cars	$ per Ton	Market Comp.	R^2
0.75[b]	-0.35	-0.06	-0.04	-0.13	0.93
(14.58)[c]	(4.01)	(2.06)	(1.8)	(2.46)	

Notes:

[a]Data are for the links Western to Western, Western to Eastern and Eastern to Western.
[b]Coefficients are in logarithims except for the coefficient for market competition.
[c]Numbers in parenthese are t- statistics.

expressed as 100, the rate on commodities for scale 1 to 3 (low to high market competition) are 87 percent, 77 percent and 67 percent, respectively.

Implications of Regression Results with
respect to Regional Rate Issues

These regression analyses have many limitations. In spite of these limitations, the analyses carried out provide the basis for three conclusions. First, the railway's pricing practices have been consistent across the country in their response to cost levels and competitive forces. The only regional differences in freight rate levels evident in the analyses are to be explained by the effects of the rate subsidies provided by the Maritime Freight Rates Act and the Atlantic Provinces Freight Assistance Act. Second, over the period 1956 to 1972, the freight rate structure became more cost influenced or cost based, as would be expected with growing competition. Third, statistical analysis of Waybill data can be an effective means of analyzing the influence of cost and competitive factors on freight rates and throwing considerable light on broad questions related to public policy.

Rate Level Changes, 1959-1976

Changes in the level of rates over time show the effects of traffic characteristics, technology and marketing innovations, and more recently, of inflation on the general level of charges faced by shippers. General changes in rate levels are shown normally by using revenue per ton-mile figures. The revenue per ton-mile is an extremely crude figure when given for wide categories of traffic as its level is subject to change with many changes in traffic composition. These include changes in the commodity mix, the load per car and the average length of haul. The ability of the railways to reduce their rates and the revenue per ton-mile is dependent on cost reductions, resulting from new technology, as well as on the effect of competitive forces causing rates to move closer to costs. Therefore, the significant reduction which has been achieved in the general level of rates since 1959 does not *prove* conclusively that reliance on market forces has worked well or been responsible for the general rate reduction. However, it is certainly strongly supportive evidence.

Table 14 shows the revenue per ton-mile by category of freight rate for four years. The first year, 1959, is the year the MacPherson Royal Commission was established and also the year in which the revenue per ton-mile for all traffic was at its highest level in the post-war period to 1974. The second year, 1967, was the year in which the National Transportation Act was passed. The third year, 1971, was the year in which the revenue per ton-mile for all traffic was at its lowest. The 1974 data are from the most recent *Waybill Analysis*.

The actual level of revenue per ton-mile for all traffic declined by 24 percent from 1959 to 1971 in spite of inflation during that period. Between 1967 and 1971, revenue per ton-mile declined for non-competitive and competitive

43

Table 14

Revenue Per Ton-Mile by Rate Category,
1959, 1967, 1971 and 1974

Category of Freight Rate	Revenue Per Ton-Mile (Cents)				Percent of 1959 Level			
	1959	1967	1971	1974	1959	1967	1971	1974
Class Rated	4.59	4.03	4.35	4.33	100	88	95	94
Commodity, Non-competitive	1.95	1.52	1.20	1.17	100	78	62	60
Commodity, Competitive	2.77	2.65	2.07	2.20	100	96	75	79
Agreed Charges	2.37	1.87	1.90	2.33	100	79	80	98
Statutory Grain Rates	0.50	0.50	0.50	0.50	100	100	100	100
All Traffic	1.79	1.54	1.36	1.56	100	86	76	87

Source: Revenue per ton-mile obtained from Canadian Transport Commission, Waybill Analysis, 1959, 1967, 1971, and 1974.

Table 15

Average Revenue per Ton-Mile, 1973-1976
(Calculated from Railway Operating Statistics)

Year	Freight Revenue ($ millions)	Ton-Miles (billions)	Revenue per Ton-Mile (cents)	Annual Percent Change in Revenue per Ton-Mile
1973	1,741.2	125.5	1.39	--
1974	2,051.1	133.6	1.54	+10.7
1975	2,169.8	131.0	1.66	+7.9
1976	1,435.3	76.1	1.89	+13.9

Source: Statistics Canada, Railway Operating Statistics, Statistics Canada, 52-003, Monthly.

Table 16

Return on Net Railway Investment of CP Rail; in Percent, 1959-75.[a]

1959	2.7	1963	2.8	1967	3.1	1971	4.1
1960	2.5	1964	3.5	1968	3.2	1972	4.6
1961	2.9	1965	3.2	1969	2.6	1973	4.7
1962	2.3	1966	3.9	1970	3.3	1974	5.5
						1975	4.7

Note:

[a] Data exclude investment in and revenue from all non-rail operations.

Source: Office of Comptroller, CP Ltd., Montreal, 1976.

44

commodity rate traffic, although it increased for class and agreed charge rated traffic. Between 1971 and 1974, the only important category of traffic to show a decrease in revenue per ton-mile was that moving under non-competitive commodity rates.

During 1975 and 1976 the railways selectively increased many of their rates, by considerable percentages or amounts to adjust for the effects of inflation in those years and to catch up for the rate freeze of 1973-74 on non-negotiated rates. Such rate adjustments will not be reflected in the ton-mile revenue figures in the *Waybill Analysis* until the data for the years subsequent to 1974 became available. The rate increases may be documented by noting changes in specific tariff levels,[26] or by the use of other data. Table 15 shows railway freight revenue and ton-miles from Statistics Canada data, and shows a significant annual increase in rates. It must be remembered that these percentage increases, like the percentage decreases in average revenue per ton-mile in earlier years, were realized when the freight rates on export grain and related movements, amounting to twenty to thirty percent of rail traffic, were held at a statutory level.

The earnings of the railways over the period 1959 to 1975 have been low, as shown by Table 16. The Table shows that some improvement in earnings has been realised under commercial freedom, but it must be remembered that the cost of capital has remained substantially higher than return on capital throughout the period. As the railways have been largely free of regulatory constraints in their pricing, one would suppose that they would have raised their rates and ton-mile revenue yield after 1967. This is not evident as a general trend until 1972, by which time the pressure of cost increases in labour and supplies necessitated rate increases. As the railways only achieved low earnings over the period, only one inference is possible. That is that the railways have been forced to pass on savings to shippers by competitive pressures. This appears to be particularly true of the market competitive pressures on the non-competitive commodity rates, many of which apply on heavy-volume resource commodities moved at low rates to enable the producers to compete in world markets.

Characteristics of Railway Rates Subject to Regional Complaints in Canada

If a unique basis exists for complaints about freight rates in Western Canada, it does not lie in the general results of the present-day rate making process.[27] It seems likely that complaints arise from four sources. First, fundamentally different views of the role of transport in the national political economy may exist. Second, a misunderstanding of rate making and the role of transport in the political economy may exist. Third, persons may treat a number of "anomolous rates" as though they are characteristic of the whole rate structure. And lastly, a greater reliance on market competition in the West than in other regions for negotiating rates may give rise to some distinctive regional perceptions about the monopoly power of the railways.

It seems likely that all four phenomena are present in Western Canada. The presence of a large volume of bulk traffic with long hauls to market, lacking intermodal competition except over short hauls, results in greater importance being attached to market competition in Western Canada than in other regions or provinces. Therefore, it is particularly important for Western Canada that the rate making process is organized and conducted in a manner that allows market competition to be reflected properly in rates. (The statistical analysis suggests that it is *a* factor.) The working of market competitive factors will be considered in later chapters.

The presence of specific rate anomalies has also been a matter of concern. Some were cited at the Western Economic Opportunities Conference.[28] It is not the purpose of this chapter to review in detail the so-called "anomalies", but a number of particular characteristics of railway rates can be reviewed to provide a better background with respect to the level and relationships of freight rates in Canada.

The complaints of the Western Provinces about freight rates have often been general. Even in 1973, the Western Premiers claimed that "The lack of competition in certain regions of the West places railways in a position of significant monopoly, leading to rail rates and pricing policies which are a major barrier to economic development and diversification".[29] There has been little evidence to substantiate these claims; on the contrary, the evidence suggests that while there may be specific instances of freight rates detrimental to industries, the present rate structure does not hinder economic development.[30]

However, in 1973 the Western Provinces also brought forward a number of specific examples of rates which they considered to be anomalies detrimental to the development of industries in Western Canada. The rate anomalies or rate inequities cited were examples where rate differences were not, or did not seem to be, related to differences in the cost of providing the rail service. The complaints focused on certain aspects of rail rates which arose from, or were believed to be caused by, value-of-service pricing. The main complaints of the Western Provinces dealt with the relationship between the rates on finished goods and the raw materials from which they were produced, the relationship between long- and short-haul rates, and the existence of larger zones in Eastern Canada than in Western Canada for the application of zone or blanket rates. In addition, the Western Provinces have been concerned about the relative level of eastbound and westbound rates.

Long- and Short-haul Rates

Long- and short-haul pricing refers to the practice of charging higher rates to intermediate points than to more distant points on the same commodities moving in the same direction and with the shorter distance being included in the

46

longer distance. On the surface, this pricing seems contrary to common sense and has been the source of considerable controversy.[31] It is justified by its supporters as being necessary to enable the railways to retain or obtain traffic in their more competitive terminal markets at reduced profit margins without having to forgo profits in their less competitive interior markets by reducing rates there. It is pointed out that where the railways are responsible for their own earnings in a competitive environment, it is necessary to give them the freedom to respond to the incidence of competitive forces even if this results in long- and short-haul discrimination. Further, the notion of the unreasonable cost disadvantage inflicted on intermediate locations by long- and short-haul pricing may arise from traditional notions of spatial relations based on air or railway mileages whereas relative location in effective economic terms must be measured in time and transportation costs. In this sense, points far removed from one another but connected by water transportation may be closer in economic terms than centres closer together but dependent on higher-cost transport.

Arguments against long- and short-haul discrimination are that it is inefficient and inequitable. Such rate discrimination is thought to be inefficient and inequitable because freight rates are not directly related to the variable costs of the rail service; industries at intermediate points may be adversely affected; and the competition to other modes serving the long-haul points may be injurious to these modes.

If it is accepted that railway enterprises have the responsibility for their commercial viability and that they must ordinarily practice freight rate discrimination to be viable, then determination of the reasonableness of long- and short-haul discrimination must rest on the judgement, in a case-by-case basis, as to whether the competitive circumstances surrounding the movements warrant the resulting price differentials.

In Canada, long- and short-haul discrimination has been the subject of several investigations.[32] Following the recommendation of the Turgeon Royal Commission in 1951, a limit was placed on the amount by which short-haul rates could exceed long-haul rates where the shorter distance was included in the longer distance. The One and One-Third Rule prohibited short-haul rates from exceeding long-haul rates by more than one-third. The short-term effect was that the railways increased some of their long-haul rates and lost some traffic, but this was subsequently regained by the introduction of Agreed Charges.

In 1958, Alberta Phoenix Tube and Pipe Limited of Calgary obtained a fixed rate under Judgement and Order No. 94129 of The Board of Transport Commissioners on the basis of unjust discrimination under Section 32, (10) of the Transport Act caused by agreed charges from Eastern Canada to Vancouver. The agreed charges enabled skelp from Eastern Canada to be processed into pipe in Vancouver at a landed transportation cost of $1.295 per 100 lbs. This compared with a total freight charge under normal commodity rates on skelp from Eastern Canada to Edmonton and pipe from Edmonton to Vancouver of $3.165 per 100 lbs. This difference the Commission found unjustly discriminatory and set the rates on pipe and the skelp for its manufacture so that the rate to Vancouver on pipe manufactured in Edmonton totaled $1.34 per 100 lbs.

In spite of submissions against long- and short-haul discrimination to the MacPherson Royal Commission, the Commission recommended, and the 1967 Act implemented, treatment of long- and short-haul discrimination simply under the regulatory controls remaining applicable to any other traffic. The constraint of the One and One-Third Rule was removed.

The full extent of long- and short-haul price discrimination in Canada is not known. Controversy over the practice is focussed in Western Canada where the railways report that the rates on two groups of commodities, iron and steel products and canned goods and packaged food products, make up 90 percent of the traffic moving under long- and short-haul rate structures.[33] The 1973 report by the CTC on rate matters lists 26 commodity groups moving under such tariffs, including glass, paint, linoleum, petroleum products and fish meal.[34]

The situation of steel has been well documented for 1972.[35] The lower rail rates to Vancouver than to Prairie cities had been negotiated by the railways with Canadian steel producers to assist the Canadian industry to compete effectively against foreign competition for the Pacific Coast market. Even with the low rates, a significant portion of the B.C. market was served from off-shore sources, as shown in Table 17.

Table 17

Steel Consumption in B.C. and the Prairies, 1972

B.C. Steel Consumption

	Tons	Per Cent
Total B.C. Steel Consumption	777,326	100.0
Canadian Production	282,916	30.0
Foreign Imports	541,410	70.0

Prairie Steel Consumption

	Tons	Per Cent
Total Prairie Steel Consumption	897,268	100.0
Canadian Production	886,749	98.8
Foreign Imports	10,522	1.2

Source: Railway Freight Rates, A Source Book (Montreal: CN & CP, 1973).

By 1974, the world demand and supply situation for steel had changed so radically that Canadian steel was some of the cheapest steel in the world and could be landed in Vancouver significantly more cheaply than Japanese steel. As a consequence, very substantial rate increases were introduced on iron and steel goods to B.C. and the extent of long-short haul discrimination was reduced. However, in the long run off-shore steel appeared likely to return to its preferred position in the coastal market. While the freight rates on steel are the subject of much political attention, it seems likely that should market conditions warrant it, long- and short-haul discrimination may become greater again. Certainly, since 1973 other instances of long- and short-haul pricing have persisted and, in the case of glass, at least, the absolute and relative size of the rate difference has increased.

Rate Groupings for Blanket or Zone Rates

Rate groupings, like long- and short-haul rates, have been the subject of many studies because they are frequently the source of complaint about unjust railway rate discrimination.[36] A rate group exists where the rail rate is the same for all origin points within an area or to all destination points within an area. For some traffic, particularly resource-based commodities, there may be both origin and destination groups. The EPP proposal of the Government of Alberta stated that "The absence of industrial rate groups in the West seriously impedes the geographic dispersion of industry and provokes higher costs in the smaller population centres."[37] The 1951 Turgeon Commission investigated the complaints of Alberta with respect to rate groupings and recommended no legislation on the subject.[38]

Four types of rate groups may be recognised.[39] In the first type, rates are fixed in blocks of a number of miles to avoid a multiplicity of point-to-point rates. The size of the blocks increases as hauls get longer. The uniform class rate scales are based on this principle. The second type is compelled by competition, usually water competition, which can affect a relatively large area. The railways are forced to establish uniform rates over an area in order to remain competitive. The third type of rate grouping is created to meet the needs of producers, or sometimes distributors, who are diffused throughout an area and for whom it is desirable that they all be treated alike to avoid significant competitive transport advantages among them. This often applies to homogeneous resource-base products for which differences in transportation costs may be significant in marketing. The fourth type is really a combination of the previous two. Situations exist where intermodal competition affects an area in which some producers are located, but the competitive rate zone is extended beyond the competitive area to encompass the larger area in which other producers are located.

The class rate mileage scale, which was first prescribed by Order No. 83242 of

The Board of Transport Commissioners in 1954, consists of 5-mile blocks up to 60 miles, 25-mile blocks for distances between 61 and 1,500 miles, and 50-mile blocks thereafter. The two major exceptions are rates on movements between Eastern and Western Canada, for which rate groups exist between Montreal and Windsor, and rates on movements to and from the Maritimes. The use of the 50-mile block applies to Western Canadian traffic moving east under commodity tariffs, except for the major resource movements and truck competitive traffic.

Resource-based products, such as sulphur, liquified petroleum gases, woodpulp, lumber, potash and saltcake, are the most important commodities by volume that are grouped both for origin and destination points. For most of these commodities, a single rate applies to eastern Canada from all origins, although for woodpulp the rate from coastal mills is reduced by an arbitrary for inland mills in a "group and related rate structure." Destination rates are commonly at two levels. There is one level of rates to eastern water competitive points to meet import competition, for example, on potash, and a higher level of rates to the points where a rail or truck haul is required from water to the inland point. (It is not clear whether the West has complained about this example of long- and short-haul discrimination.)

Truck competitive tariffs do not frequently have rate groupings. The reason is that truck rates must reflect mileage due to the greater variability of truck costs than rail costs with mileage.

In Eastern Canada, a substantial part of southern Quebec and Ontario has large origin rate groups for traffic moving to Western Canada. These rate groups in the East are explained by the early competitive influence of St. Lawrence and Great Lake shipping services, and they have been preserved in large part by the stabilizing influence of developed industries and by the competitive influence of rail services through the U.S.A. from cities within the Ontario peninsula.

A contrast which exists in the rate groupings of Eastern and Western Canada is that the western resource industries enjoy larger origin and destination groupings than do the comparable resource industries in Eastern Canada, but the grouping structure available for western manufacturing is more limited than its eastern counterpart. This pattern appears to be consistent with the market, intra- and intermodal competition forces present. Some of the Western Provinces desire to have more rate groupings, especially for manufacturing. Whether or not this would favour the development and dispersion of industry is not clear. The averaging of freight rates between the more favoured large cities and the more remote small communities may make the large cities less desirable locations, and it is in those locations that the West has the greatest opportunity to attract new secondary industries. Therefore, perhaps a means other than rate groupings would be more effective in bringing about industrial dispersion.

Differences in Eastbound and Westbound Rates

It is often asserted in Western Canada that the directional level of freight rates accentuates the concentration of manufacturing activities in Eastern Canada. It is suggested that the rates on westbound goods are lower than the rates on similar commodities moving east. To make such comparisons requires a careful analysis of tariff provisions and the volume of traffic actually moving under those tariffs. This has not been done for this study. However, the evidence which is available does not support the assertion.

Calculations from the 1974 Waybill Analysis show that the average rail rate into Western Canada from east of Thunder Bay was $52.62 per ton compared with a rate of $32.87 per ton in the reverse direction. The average rate on competitive commodity and agreed charge rates for the same directional movements were $51.27 and $37.17 per ton, respectively. However, those comparisons of averages may be as misleading as they are useful, for they can be interpreted only in the light of the extremely complex and heterogeneous conditions of the traffic and tariffs. The data can only be regarded as casting doubt on the validity of the general assertion that freight rates are lower westbound than eastbound on comparable commodities. The evidence from the statistical analysis that the impact of rate making factors is the same on traffic in each direction is more significant and again negates the assertion.

A recent study includes some data from an examination of the particular commodity classes in the Waybill Analysis. It reports in part as follows:

> An examination of a number of TFC 3-digit product categories from the 1971 Waybill Sample indicated that for the following manufactured commodities, the revenue per ton from western provinces to eastern provinces (mostly Ontario) was systematically below the revenue per ton in the opposite direction: plastic materials, paint and related products, steel bars and rods, structural shapes and steel piling, pipes and tubes (iron and steel), construction and maintenance machinery and equipment, electrical lighting, distributing and control equipment, and metal containers. For the remaining manufactured commodities no systematic pattern was discernible. Given the broad categories characteristic of the Waybill Sample, as well as other problems inherent with its present composition, too much should not be read into the above. However, the available evidence does not support the view that freight rate differences by direction *sytematically* prefer industries located in the East over those in the West. More detailed research at lower levels of aggregation is clearly in order.[40]

51

The research into the rate making process through shipper interviews does not support the notion of discrimination against eastbound as compared with westbound movements. Further consideration will be given to this after the information from the case studies has been presented.

Rates on Raw Materials versus Rates on Finished Products

The effects on industrial location of the relationship between rates on raw materials and rates on the finished products made from them are not central to the objective of this Chapter, which is to describe the general level and structure of rates. However, the relative level of rates is a matter of substantial concern in the West and is considered briefly here as well as in the later chapters.

The Turgeon Commission reported that

> "Alberta referred to a relationship in freight rates which would not discourage producer location as the 'critical' relationship, one which, if properly balanced, would be neutral in its effect upon the location of industries."[41]

In 1950 and in 1973, Alberta was particularly concerned about the effect of freight rates on the location of the meat packing industry. This industry, therefore, is the example which will be given prime attention here.

Comparison of the level of railway freight rates alone is inadequate as a method of assessing the effect of rates on the location of industry and the reasonableness of that rate. Differences in rate levels may reflect real differences in rail costs per 100 lbs. and/or competition from other modes. Further, freight rates on raw materials must be equated with rates on comparable weights of products in assessing the impact of the rates. For example, to consider the effect of freight rates on the location of meat packing, a rate per 100 lbs. of livestock must be compared with a rate on less than 100 lbs. of meat because of the weight loss during process.[42]

Taking this matter into account, three recent studies conclude that unjust discrimination in rail rates is not a factor detrimental to the development of the meat packing industry in Alberta. The CTC review of rate anomolies for the Minister of Transport showed that the rates complained of were truck competitive rates and much of the traffic, in fact, moved by truck.[43] If a problem exists, it was not "caused" by indiscriminate railway pricing.

Two studies specifically on the livestock and meat industries are of even more relevance. The Commission of Inquiry into the Marketing of Beef and Veal, 1976, concludes that "freight rates are not a significant deterent to the location of packinghouse activity in Western Canada".[44] This conclusion is consistent with the more detailed findings of a special CTC report.[45]

However, both of these reports do recognise that holding down grain rates to the statutory level does have a distorting effect on the location of industry. "The combined effect of statutory grain rates (Crow's Nest Pass rates), feed freight

52

assistance, and the 8 cent tariff per bushel on U.S.A. corn imports may explain the heavy outflows of feeder calves from Western Canada...."[46] The distorting effect of the statutory rates has been recognised even more explicitly in the case of the rapeseed processing industry. Only partial resolution of this problem has been reached in spite of a decision generally favourable to the western rapeseed processing industry from the CTC and despite appeals to the Minister of Transport. (This case is considered in some detail in Chapter VIII.) The explanation for this is the unwillingness of the Government of Canada to impose an extension of unremunerative services on the railways through legislation. The desirability of removing the distorting effect of the statutory rates is recognised. In a statement to Parliament on Transportation Policy in July 1976, the Minister of Transport stated:

> "I have, therefore, said with regard to the Crowsnest pass rates that if this benefit were confined more directly, and if we did not pin it on the rate, we would not only benefit the region as much in terms of dollars, but a lower-cost-over-all transportation system would be brought about because we would be shipping the goods which it makes more sense to ship, instead of goods which are shipped because of the artificially lower rate upon those goods.[47]

Therefore, with the exception of the effect of statutory rates, there is no general disadvantage to the development of industry in Western Canada caused by unjust discrimination in freight rates, although on a case-by-case basis and from time to time issues may arise. It is to be hoped that the negotiating process between the railways and shippers would resolve such matters and that, failing commercial resolution, the regulatory process would be effective in resolving matters on a case-by-case basis. The research reported in later chapters throws light on these matters.

Conclusions

This chapter reviews some of the major characteristics of Canada's rail traffic and freight rates. The statistical analysis provides general evidence of the changing influence of various rate making factors on the level of rates. In particular, it provides general evidence of the reduced power of the railway to practice price discrimination because of the spread of competition, and it does not reveal any difference in the application of the rate making factors in Western Canada than in Eastern Canada. Only the Maritimes enjoy rates with a unique impact of the rate making factors, and this is explained by the Maritime Freight Rates Act.

The particular characteristics of the rate structure considered are those raised by the Western Provinces at WEOC. The characteristics are perennial sources of complaint, but do not appear to be bases for basic revisions of the rate structure and National Transport Policy.

What is possible, as Professor F.W. Anderson has suggested in more moderate terms, is that the absence of an effective mechanism to deal with specific and relatively minor issues as they arose, finally resulted in a political polemic.[48] If this is the case, it lends weight to the importance of studying the rate making process in detail as it may be there that problems arise and could be most readily resolved. Certainly, attempts along those lines have been made over the last decade, as is documented in the next chapter.

RAIL FREIGHT TRAFFIC AND RATES IN CANADA

FOOTNOTES

1. Canada, Transport Canada, *An Interim Report on Freight Transportation in Canada* (Ottawa: Information Canada, 1975).
2. *Ibid.,* Exhibit 4.
3. *Ibid.,* p. 9.
4. Canada, Canadian Transport Commission, Reference Paper 1, *Canadian Carload All-Rail Traffic, 1968-72* (Ottawa: Information Canada, 1974); and Reference Paper 3, *Carload All-Rail Traffic Between Canada and the United States, 1968-1973* (Ottawa: Information Canada, 1975).
5. The following types of traffic are excluded from the data: LCL; express; lake-rail and rail-lake-rail; container and piggyback; freight carried on company service; interline traffic for Canadian origin and destination traffic; traffic originating (Canada to U.S.A.) and terminating (Canada-Canada) on lines other than CN and CP.
6. In British Columbia, the importance of forest products appears to be less than is actually the case because of exclusion of the British Columbia Railway which originates considerable forest products traffic.
7. For a more detailed explanation, see A.W. Currie, *Canadian Transportation Economics* (Toronto: University of Toronto Press, 1967), Chapter 4.
8. This section is drawn from W.G. Scott, "Evidence Before the Railway Transport Committee of the Canadian Transport Commission in the Prince Albert Pulp Co. Ltd. case", CTC File No. 26901.97.1.
9. Canada, *Royal Commission on Transportation* (Turgeon Commission), (Ottawa: Kings Printer, 1951).
10. S. Daggett and J.P. Carter, *The Structure of Transcontinental Railroad Rates* (Berkeley: University of California Press, 1947).
11. G.W. Wilson, "The Effects of Rate Regulation on Resource Allocation in Transportation", *American Economic Review,* Vol. 54, 1964, p. 170, quoted in P.S. Ross and Partners et al., *Two Proposals for Rail Freight Pricing: Assessment of their Prospective Impact,* A report to the federal-provincial committee on western transportation, 1974, p. 4-2.
12. Canada, Canadian Transport Commission, *Waybill Analysis* (Ottawa: Information Canada).
13. *Railway Freight Rates, A Source Book* (Montreal: CN and CP, 1973).
14. Canada, *Transport Act,* Part IV, Section 32(10).
15. *Ibid.,* Section 32(2).
16. H.L. Purdy, *Transport Competition and Public Policy in Canada* (Vancouver: University of British Columbia Press, 1972), p. 176.
17. See for example, MPS Associates Ltd., *The Influence of Truck-Rail Competition on Rate Patterns* (Ottawa: Canadian Transport Commission, 1973).
18. Waybill Analysis 1971, *op.cit.*
19. Records of the Traffic and Tariffs Branch, Canadian Transport Commission.
20. Canada, Royal Commission on Transportation (MacPherson Commission), Vol. I (Ottawa: Queens Printer, 1961 and 1962), pp. 65-66.
21. *The Commission on the Costs of Transporting Grain by Rail,* Carl M. Snavely, Jr., Commissioner, Report to the Governor in Council (mimeographed), Volume 1, October 1976 (released December, 1976), p. 207.
22. For a railway presentation using Waybill Analysis data, see J.H. Morrish and D.P. MacKinnon, *The Only Thing Wrong with Simple Solutions is the Lack of a Simple Problem,* Address to the Canadian Industrial Traffic League, Winnipeg, Manitoba, February 1974.

23. The research was carried out under the direction of Dr. Trevor D. Heaver by S.D. Shepherdson and T.H. Oum, graduate students at the University of British Columbia.

24. For a more detailed consideration of the possible effects of the various factors on rates, see T.D. Heaver and T.H. Oum, "A Statistical Analysis of the Canadian Railway Rate Structure", *Logistics and Transportation Review,* Vol. 12, No. 5, 1976 (forthcoming).

25. Under the Maritime Freight Rates Act of 1927, rail rates on traffic (except express) moving within and westbound from the region have been held down to reduce the disadvantage of the region because of the Canadian rail line mileage from the rest of Canada. For further information, see H.L. Purdy, *op.cit.,* Chapter, 10, and A.W. Currie, *op.cit.,* Chapter 5.

26. See Ken W. Stickland, "Freight Rates in Western Canada", Alberta Rural Development Studies, sponsored by the Rural Education and Development Association and Alberta Agriculture, Edmonton, Alberta, October 1976, pp. 7-9 and Appendix I.

27. This view is corroborated by the conclusion, reached at a conference attended by many shippers, that transportation problems in Western Canada are not unique. *Transportation Policy: Action in the West,* Summary of a Workshop, Saskatoon, May 1975 (Vancouver: WESTAC, 1976).

28. *Western Economic Opportunities Conference Transportation Paper,* jointly submitted by the Premiers of Saskatchewan, British Columbia, Manitoba and Alberta (Calgary, 1973).

29. *Ibid.,* p. 1.

30. P.S. Ross et al., *op.cit.,* p. 12-12; and John Heads, *Transport Subsidies and Regional Development,* Ph.D. thesis at the University of Manitoba, 1976.

31. For an excellent treatment of long- and short-haul rates in the U.S.A., see Ralph L. Dewey, *The Long and Short Haul Principle of Rate Regulation* (Columbus, Ohio: Ohio State University Press, 1935.)

32. For a brief summary see, T.D. Heaver, "Wrong Way to Solve Ill-Defined Problems" *Executive,* July/August 1973. For a review of forces affecting long- and short-haul pricing in Western Canada, see D.L. McLachlan, C. Ozol, *Transportation Problems Relating to Manufacturing Industry in the Calgary Area* (Ottawa: CTC, Research Publications, 1973), pp. 19-27.

33. *Railway Freight Rates, A Source Book, op.cit.,* Part 6.

34. Canadian Transport Commission, Report to the Minister of Transport under Section 22 of the National Transportation Act, December 1973, Appendix E.

35. *Railway Freight Rates, A Source Book, loc.cit.*

36. Currie, *op.cit.,* pp. 234-235.

37. *The Equitable Pricing Proposal,* Government of Alberta, (Edmonton: July 1973), p. 10.

38. *Turgeon Commission, op.cit.,* pp. 109-111.

39. This follows the classification used by the Turgeon Commission, *loc.cit.,*

40. P.S. Ross, et.al., *op.cit.,* p. 12-9. After the text was completed, during the Fall of 1976, the MPS Associates Ltd. Report for the Federal Ministery of Transport, *Transport and Regional Development in the Prairies,* Vols. I and II, December 1975, was released by Transport Canada as a contribution to discussion of the issues in the Transport Policy Review initiated early in the year. Thirteen theoretical case studies in food products industries, metals products industries, and miscellaneous industries were made to determine whether the cost of transport for inbound and outbound commodities for the same "average plant" located in the Prairie Provinces and in Central Canada would significantly influence industrial development. The study found that the level of rates would be higher for a plant located in the Prairies than for the same plant located in Central Canada, particularly for selling manufactures in the national Canadian market. This conclusion comes as no surprise, however, as the estimated rates for the alternative

regional plant locations reflected distance differences only (the so-called rate anomolies were eliminated or averaged out); and given the basic economic geography of Canada, the Prairie locations for industrial plants are far greater distances from the populous national markets than are the Central Canada locations.

41. *Turgeon Commission, op.cit.,* p. 116.
42. For an example, see *MacPherson Commission,* Vol I, 1961, Chapter 8.3, Table IX, p. 128.
43. CTC, Report to the Minister of Transport, *op.cit.,* pp. 3-13.
44. Canada, *Report of the Commission of Inquiry into the Marketing of Beef and Veal,* (Ottawa: Minister of Supply and Services, 1976), p. 141.
45. Canadian Transport Commission, *Transportation Factors and the Canadian Livestock and Meat Industries* (Ottawa: CTC Research Branch, 1975), ESAB, 75-19.
46. *Commission on Beef and Veal Marketing, op.cit.,* p. 142.
47. Hon. Otto E. Lang, Minister of Transport, *Commons Debates,* June 11, 1976, p. 14,419.
48. F.W. Anderson "The Philosophy of the MacPherson Royal Commission and the National Transportation Act: A Retrospective Essay", in *Issues in Canadian Transport Policy,* ed. K.W. Studnicki-Gizbert, (Toronto: Macmillan of Canada, 1974) pp. 47-72.

APPENDIX I

The main source of data for the regression analysis is the *Waybill Analysis.*[1] Table I-A shows the data identified in the *Waybill Analysis* for each commodity class. In the 1972 data, approximately 300 commodity classes are listed. For each commodity class, national and regional data are provided. Canada is divided into Maritime, Eastern and Western regions (defined in Table I-A), so that nine regional movement patterns, or links, are possible. The commodity classes used in the *Waybill Analysis* are much broader than the commodity classifications found in railway freight tariffs. Therefore, a Waybill commodity class usually includes commodities subject to different rates in a tariff or tariffs. Further, the data are the totals for carload movements of the commodity class in a regional pattern. Movements of a commodity under different tariffs, with different loads per car and different lengths of haul are summed together.

The *Waybill Analysis* does not include some very important types of data for the analysis of the rate structure. The most important of these is the value of the commodity carried. This commodity characteristic is generally agreed to be the single most important commodity characteristic influencing the ability of a commodity to bear a transport cost. Data on the value of certain commodities are available from Statistics Canada.[2] To combine data from this source with data from the *Waybill Analysis* required drawing a sample of commodities for which data are available in both source documents. The list of commodities used in the analysis is in Table I-B. A sufficient number of commodities is available for analyses of all regional combinations with the exception of the link from the Maritimes to Western Canada.

The use of average data imposes constraints on the objectives of a statistical analysis. Differences in rates between types of tariff rates cannot be examined. The absolute impact of various factors on rate levels cannot be expected to be equivalent to those which would be obtained if individual movement data were analyzed. However, these avearge data can be expected to give a very reliable estimate of the overriding relative importance of various factors in explaining differences in freight rates at one time, over time and for different regional movements. These various data are utilized in regression analyses to examine the significance of the following factors on the rate level: the regional origin and destination (the link); the length of haul; the load per car; the number of carloads in the sample; the total weight moved; the value of the commodity; and the car type used. The rate per 100 lbs. was calculated from the revenue per ton-mile given in the *Waybill Analysis.*

A logarithmic form of regression model is used. The results of applying the model to system-wide data is shown in Table I-C. The model combines log-log and semi-log functions, as follows:

Table I-A

Extract from the Annual Waybill Analysis, 1972

Class No.	Commodity Class	Region[a] From	To	No. of Carloads	Weight (Tons)	Revenue ($)	Ton-Miles	Car-Miles	Length of Haul (Miles)	Average Load Per Car (Tons)	Revenue Per Ton-Mile (¢)	Per Car-Mile ($)
124	Pre-cooked Frozen Food Preparations	Maritime	Maritime	2	65.0	931	8,395	247	130	32.5	11.09	3.77
		Maritime	Western	3	95.6	7,268	263,718	8,251	2,759	31.9	2.76	.88
		Eastern	Maritime	2	29.8	1,271	32,870	2,206	1,103	14.9	3.87	.58
		Eastern	Western	2	53.8	3,531	136,431	4,779	2,536	26.9	2.59	.74
		Western	Maritime	2	44.5	2,520	87,935	3,988	1,977	22.3	2.87	.63
		Western	Eastern	2	65.4	2,593	111,636	3,451	1,707	32.7	2.32	.75
		Western	Western	6	153.9	2,728	65,981	3,004	428	25.7	4.13	.91
				19	508.0	20,842	706,966	25,926	1,392	26.7	2.95	.80

Notes:

[a]The Maritime region consists of the Maritime provinces and that part of Quebec east of Levis and Diamond, Quebec. The Eastern region consists of the remainder of Quebec and that part of Ontario, east of Thunder Bay and Armstrong, Ontario. The Western regions consists of all territory west of Thunder Bay and Armstrong, excluding the Yukon Territory.

Source: Canadian Transport Commission, Waybill Analysis, 1972.

59

Table I-B

*Total List of Commodities Included
in the Regression Analysis of the
Various Regional Movements*

Class Number	Commodity
10	Meat, fresh or chilled
16	Fish and marine animals
18	Butter
20	Cheese
54	Apples
62	Grapes
70	Pears
78	Fruit juice and fruit juice concentrates
86	Sugar beets
88	Cabbage
94	Onions and shallots
108	Sugar
114	Coffee
120	Shortening and lard
122	Soups and infant food
128	Hay, forage and straw
148	Ale, beer, stout and porter
150	Wines and fermented alcoholic beverages
156	Tobacco, unmanufactured
204	Copper ore and concentrates
208	Iron ore and concentrates
210	Lead ore and concentrates
216	Nickel ore and concentrates
222	Zinc ore and concentrates
238	Bituminous coal
248	Asbestos, crude, unmanufactured
258	Sand, N.E.S.
274	Barytes, natural
276	Gypsum
280	Nepheline Syenite
288	Liquid sulphur
330	Woodpulp
516	Portland Cement
528	Lime, Hydrated and Quick
580	Toiletries

Source: Canadian Transport Commission, *Waybill Analysis.*

Table I-C

System-wide Regression Results
1956, 1963, 1972

Year	Intercept[a]	Tons per Car	# Cars	$ per Ton			Refr.[a]	R^2	No. of Observations
1972	2.23 (7.99)[b]	-0.5202 (24.48)	-0.0867	0.0510	-0.3341	-0.2259	0.1612	0.9272	

Table I-C

System-wide Regression Results
1956, 1963, 1972

Year	Intercept[a]	Length of Haul	Tons per Car	# Cars	$ per Ton	Links[a] M/E	M/M	Refr.[a]	R^2	No. of Observations
1972	2.23 (7.99)[b]	0.6108 (24.48)	-0.5202 (9.71)	-0.0867 (5.14)	0.0510 (3.72)	-0.3341 (3.41)	-0.2259 (2.38)	0.1612 (2.13)	0.9272	138
1963	2.04 (6.00)	0.6188 (18.51)	-0.5495 (9.78)	-0.0794 (4.08)	0.0710 (4.55)	-0.2522 (2.17)	-0.1611 (2.05)	--	0.9275	99
1956	1.52 (4.40)	0.6604 (19.01)	-0.4669 (7.01)	-0.0994 (4.44)	0.0675 (4.06)	-0.1611 (2.05)	--	--	0.9347	105

Notes:

[a] All variables except intercept, links and refrigerator car variables are natural logarithms.

[b] Numbers in parenthesis are t- statistics.

[c] In 1956, there was no significant difference for the M/E and M/M links. The coefficient shown for 1956 is for M/E and M/M links combined. In 1963, a significant difference exists between the separate M/E and M/M coefficients. In 1972, the M/M coefficient is not statistically significant.

61

$$\log R_i = a + d \log D_i + t \log T_i + c \log C_i + v \log V_i + \sum_{k=1}^{n} b_k S_{ki} + G_i$$

where

i represents the ith observation

a, d, t, c, v, and b_k are parameters to be estimated

R is the rate in cents per 100 lbs.

D is the average miles hauled

T is the average load per car

C is the number of carloads in the sample

V is the value of the commodity per ton in dollars

G is the residual

S_k represents the kth dummy or ordinal variable

"n" is the number of dummy variables included in the model

The dummy variables are:

special car type (tank car and refrigerated car)

regional movement pattern (intra-Maritime, Maritime to eastern, eastern to Maritime, intra-eastern, eastern to western, western to eastern, western to Maritime, and intra-western*)

FOOTNOTES

1. Canada, Canadian Transport Commission, *Waybill Analysis,* Annual.
2. Statistics Canada, *Retail Prices and Living Costs,* Service Bulletin, 62005, February, 1975, Table 2; and *Prices and Price Indices,* DBS 62-002, June 1956 and June 1963.

*The dummy variable for the intra-western link was omitted in the model in order to avoid singularity of the data matrix.

CHAPTER III

RATE MAKING INSTITUTIONS AND PRACTICES IN CANADA

The changes in the railway rate structure outlined in the previous Chapter have been associated with radical changes in the environment in which, and the procedures by which, freight rates have been made. The most important change in the transport environment has been the growth of intermodal competition. However, the significant increase in bulk traffic and the relaxation of regulatory controls have also been important.

These changes in the environment within which railway freight rates are set have been associated with changes in the organization and procedures of both the railways and shippers. Shippers have been more sophisticated and more likely to take group action in the negotiation of rates than they were prior to 1967. The railways have developed the organization, procedures and personnel to meet the need for more information and responsiveness with respect to changing rates on a selective rather than an across-the-board basis. It is necessary to describe the organization and procedures of the railways before proceeding to consider the evidence of the case studies in later chapters. It is also appropriate to describe the main constraints and influences of Government on rate making. The constraints established by legislation and the organization of the negotiating parties must be established before the conduct and effectiveness of negotiations can be examined.

Description of the institutional background in which freight rates are set is the first purpose of this chapter. The second purpose is to document the dynamic response of both the railways and shippers, but especially the former, to the development and pricing of services in a competitive environment in which the railways have wide commercial freedom. For the railways, the need to respond to continually widening competitive pressures and their substantial measure of freedom to respond through commercial means have been associated with the development of modern and sophisticated marketing organizations. The extent to which this has led to innovative activities in pricing and service development will be of interest to persons in other countries concerned with the effects of regulations on innovative activity. The third purpose of the chapter is

63

to identify those changes in transport policy and regulation which were of greatest concern to shippers, to the provinces and to carriers competing with the railways in 1966 when the National Transportation Act was being debated. An understanding of the concerns in 1966 may be important to understanding some shippers' concerns with existing legislation and to determining what, if any, change in the legislation is appropriate. The final purpose of the chapter is to describe some of the main features of shipper/carrier negotiations. The effectiveness of the negotiating process is crucial to a transport policy which relies heavily on the working of market forces.

Rail Freight Marketing Organization in CN and CP[1]

The CN and CP are multi-modal transportation companies in which a considerable degree of autonomy has been given to the individual modes of transport within those organizations for several years.[2] Changes in the organization structure of the two companies over the last decade have increased the amount of autonomy given to the modal organizations. In CP, separate subsidiary companies have been established. In CN, at the beginning of 1976 five operative divisions were established. They are Rail, Trucking and Express, Telecommunications, Passenger Services and Hotels, and Grand Trunk Corp., the holding company for CN's U.S. rail operations. Each division is a profit centre and has a chief executive who is responsible for the performance of his unit in much the same manner as a president is responsible for the performance of his company.

The treatment of the individual modes in CN and CP as separate profit centres means that the organization of rail freight marketing is largely unaffected by the multi-modal nature of the corporations. The only evident advantages which the rail organizations realize is first-hand knowledge of other modal costs and services and a somewhat greater ease in developing integrated transport services for specialized movements. Such integrated arrangements are commonly made through personnel in the Industrial Development Department of the railways. The departments responsible for intermodal services in both the CN and CP are primarily responsible for piggyback and container services.[3] Intermodal services do not consist of rail service integrated end-to-end with another mode of transport except in the case of container or piggyback service.

Development of Railway Freight Marketing in the CN and CP

The organization of rail freight marketing in the CN and CP has evolved in a corporate structure dominated traditionally by Operations, as is characteristic of all North American railways.[4] In the 1940's, the railways had Traffic Departments whose main functions were the setting and quotation of rates and personal selling and customer service. The rate-making activity was highly centralized because of the system-wide nature of pricing and because of the tradition of centralization in the railways.

64

The shift in corporate policy to a modern competitive marketing philosophy was a gradual evolutionary process rather than a definitive undertaking made at a particular point in time. The evolutionary process commenced in the work of the Research Departments, set up in the case of the CN in the 1930's. The Research Departments had responsibilities chiefly in operations research when established, but came to be of considerable importance for their costing studies and industry studies. The former allowed the railways to examine the profitability of various traffics. The latter allowed the railways to analyze the traffic potential and the transportation needs of certain industries.[5] In 1955 at CN and in 1960 at CP, new Traffic Research Departments were set up as the availability of computerized internal railway accounting data made it possible regularly to produce information valuable for marketing activities. Originally, Traffic Research at CP, for example, was required to do revenue forecasts, to undertake traffic studies and to determine the information needs for market and rate research using the new computer installation. The organization of the traffic function of CP at that time is shown in Figure 2. The special requirements of foreign freight and piggyback services were reflected in the separate departments for those activities. The dominant functional group was Freight-Traffic in which the regional managers were responsible to the General Freight Traffic Manager in Montreal.

The new Traffic Research Departments were expected to perform marketing functions in a more formalized fashion than previously and to study ways and means to facilitate competition with other transport modes, mainly trucking, by differential competitive pricing techniques and by improved services. Contemporaneous technological developments in yard operations, diesel locomotives, rolling stock and communications, and the development of more sophisticated costing techniques, were important. The railways were viewing their services as merely one component of shippers' distribution systems so that service level was recognized as being potentially of more importance to shippers than rates, at least in the case of high-value goods.[6]

The number of tasks of Traffic Research in CP increased, and in 1963 that Department was formally broken down into three functional groups. They were Market Development, which was concerned with external data sources and with product development; Sales Analysis, which analyzed internal data and produced revenue forecasts, sales quotas and traffic analyses; and Pricing, which did sensitivity studies related to rate adjustments. W.G. Scott, who was the Manager of Traffic Research in 1960, explained the CP's philosophy of marketing, as follows:

> We recognise the increasing importance of the marketing concept, which starts with the customer and his needs, and ends only when those needs are filled in a way which is

65

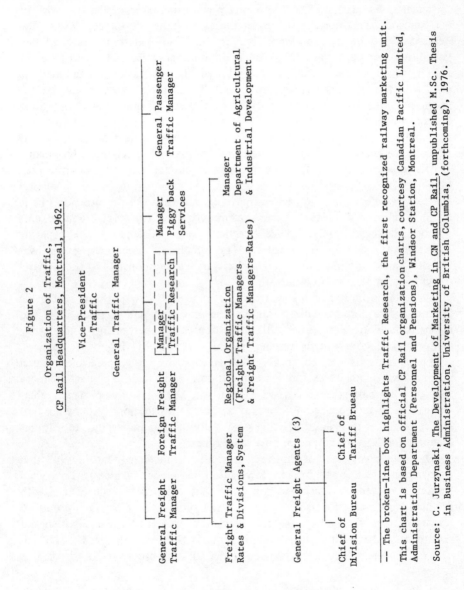

Figure 2

Organization of Traffic,
CP Rail Headquarters, Montreal, 1962.

-- The broken-line box highlights Traffic Research, the first recognized railway marketing unit.

This chart is based on official CP Rail organization charts, courtesy Canadian Pacific Limited, Administration Department (Personnel and Pensions), Windsor Station, Montreal.

Source: C. Jurzynski, The Development of Marketing in CN and CP Rail, unpublished M.Sc. Thesis in Business Administration, University of British Columbia, (forthcoming), 1976.

beneficial both to him and to our Company. It is the objective of our research programme to try to predict future changes in transportation demand well in advance and effectively adapt our rates, service and sales policies to meet them.[7]

Scott went on to outline six components which he expected to see coordinated in the marketing approach. They were "customer research, design and development of a product or service, pricing, promotion, sales and market studies".[8] The development of these activities was essential to provide the railways with the capability to respond to the new localized nature of competitive forces. It was the lack of this price and service responsiveness and flexibility which had been a hinderance to the railways in the 1950's, and which had caused the railways to rely on insensitive across-the-board freight rate increases.[9]

From the mid-1960's on, the organization and personnel profiles changed frequently as marketing functions were added to the historical pricing and sales functions. Coordination and integration of these functions came later, and has been difficult to achieve effectively.

Concurrent with the evolution of marketing activities during the late 1950's and the 1960's, both the CN and CP were moving away from the centralization characteristic of railway management. In this respect the Canadian railways appear to have been different than American railways, which Wyckoff notes have moved to a more centralized management.[10] CP decentralized line responsibility for operations to the regions in 1959, but it was not until 1968 that line responsibility for regional marketing and sales was transferred to regional Vice Presidents from the system Vice President, Marketing and Sales. CN moved to decentralize both Traffic (Sales) and Operations in 1961, and took this process not only to the regional level but also to a new area level. Many revenue responsibilities on the Sales side and cost responsibilities in Operations and Maintenance were delegated to the five Regional Vice-Presidents and, below them, to the eighteen Area Managers. However, this system did not work well, and in 1971 the CN moved to the two-level format so that today the CN and CP in general have comparable levels of decentralization.

The devolution of responsibility to the regions has not occurred uniformly in all marketing functions. The extent of decentralization and the responsibilities of the various departments can be summarized by reviewing the recent marketing organization of one of the railways. Slight difference exist between the CN and CP and even within each railway between the regions, but a review of the CP system and Pacific regional organizations gives a representative picture of the current structure of marketing activities.

Current Railway Freight Marketing Organization in the CP

Figure 3 shows the 1975 organization of CP's Marketing and Sales at headquarters in Montreal. (At CN, the title "Marketing" is used.) Reporting to the Vice President are seven departments, five of them responsible for marketing functions, two of them responsible for market sectors, overseas trade and intermodal services. Responsibility for pricing intermodal services rests with the headquarters staff throughout the CP system. Information on regional market conditions affecting intermodal services is provided to headquarters by a sales representative and a rate officer specializing in intermodal services in each region. Overseas trade decisions also tend to be more centralized than decisions on domestic freight, although the Regional Managers, Overseas Trade, report to the Regional General Managers, Marketing and Sales. The five departments with functional responsibility at headquarters are responsible for four main functions; they are Sales, Market Development, Pricing and Marketing Information. Pricing is divided into two departments, one concerned with general matters of pricing economics, the other with research and economics related to specific commodity pricing issues.

The regional organization of CP, Pacific Region, for 1975 is shown in Figure 4. Integration of pricing and marketing functions was achieved by having both activities report to the Manager, Market Development. The activities of freight selling and customer service were the responsibility of the Manager, Freight Sales.

The relationship between the activities of Headquarters departments and those of regional Marketing and Sales varies with the functions. Marketing Information has a centralized function and is a part of the large Corporate Management Information System. The manager is responsible for developing traffic information and disseminating it to the various Marketing and Sales Departments, so that these departments can better measure and control their activities in sales, pricing, market research, traffic analyses, special studies, equipment utilization and forecasting.

Sales functions at headquarters are supportive of the regional sales activity where interaction with customers naturally takes place. Marketing and Sales at headquarters provides salesmanship training programs and develops promotional campaigns for salesmen across the entire system. The old notion that the total level of rail traffic is dependent almost entirely on general swings in the economy is no longer accepted. The sales representatives in the region are expected to spot marketing opportunities or problems for action by Market Development.

The functions and levels of responsibility between headquarters and the regions are less clear in the areas of Pricing and Market Development. In both of these areas, not only does headquarters provide the more specialized and supportive activities necessary for effective work at the regional level, but it

Figure 3

Organization of Freight Marketing and Sales,
CP Rail Headquarters, Montreal, 1975.

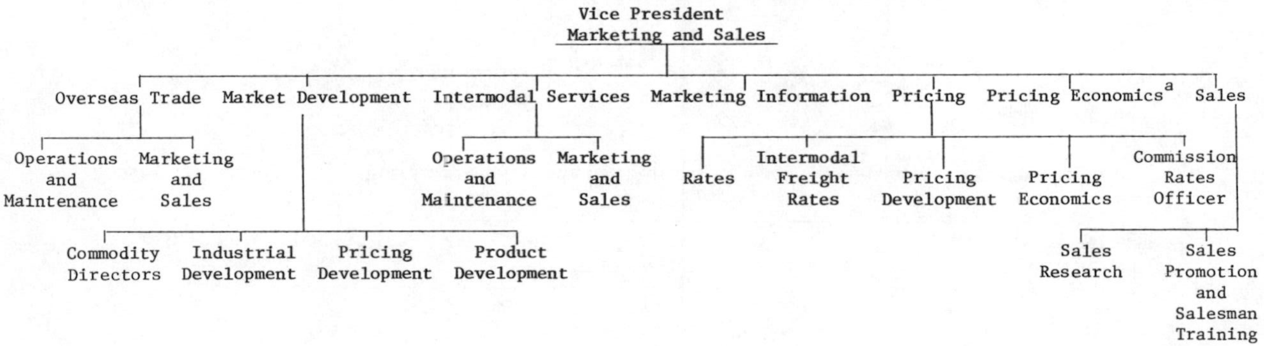

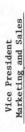

Note: [a]The General Manager, Pricing Economics was W.G. Scott. He was responsible for general matters of pricing economics. The Department of Pricing Economics reporting to the General Manager, Pricing was responsible for research and economics related to specific pricing and rate issues.

Source: C. Jurczynski, The Development of Marketing in CN and CP Rail, unpublished M.Sc. Thesis in Business Administration, University of British Columbia, (forthcoming), 1976.

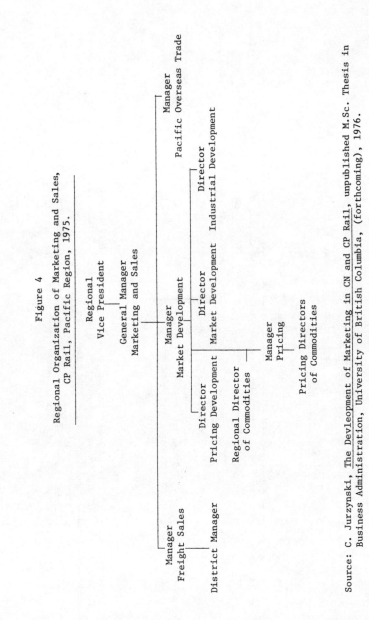

Figure 4

Regional Organization of Marketing and Sales,
CP Rail, Pacific Region, 1975.

Source: C. Jurzynski, The Devleopment of Marketing in CN and CP Rail, unpublished M.Sc. Thesis in Business Administration, University of British Columbia, (forthcoming), 1976.

has a system-wide responsibility for some activities also performed at the regional level. At the regional level, a number of Pricing Directors responsible for commodity groups report to the Manager, Pricing. At headquarters, a comparable organization by commodity groups has only been established by CP in 1976, although the functions of system pricing managers were performed previously. (The CN has a number of Freight Rates Officers, each responsible for certain commodity groups.) The need for this apparent duplication at system and regional levels is to ensure an adequate system-wide rate structure and to deal with issues of interregional pricing. The level of regional autonomy given to the regions appears to be greater in CP than in CN, but it varies by region and commodity. This structure means that, in practice, no precise general explanation of the communication which takes place on pricing matters between the region and headquarters can be set forth. However, the level of responsibility in the regions appears to be greater than is perceived by many shippers. Headquarters support functions are essential for regional pricing activities. For example, the estimates of the variable cost of traffic necessary for pricing decisions are supplied to the regions through the computer costing programs which are the responsibility of headquarters Pricing Research.

The Managers of Market Development in the regions are responsible for the integration of general market intelligence, from the product Marketing Directors or Representatives, with industrial development opportunities and pricing issues. The development of new services and the servicing of new firms or industries is the responsibility of the Director, Industrial Development. If a new service requires significant equipment or transportation planning, then the headquarters Product Development group will be involved substantially. Examples of the work of Product Development include the development of high-reliability freight services, run-through services, and various equipment modifications.

This organization structure provides the shipper with a number of probable contact points with the railways. The first is the sales representative, who is generally concerned with customer service and problems. For many small firms, this is the only contact with the railways' marketing organizations. However, for larger firms in particular, contact with a Pricing Director would be normal on rate matters. Any firm may work with the Director of Industrial Development if its situation involves new service aspects. If a shipper is considering container or piggyback service, he will deal with a local intermodal representative, but the responsibility of headquarters is greater than if the service were all-rail or rail-truck or rail-water service.

The effectiveness of the railways' marketing efforts and the perceptions of shippers are greatly influenced by the capabilities of the railways' personnel. When reorganizing their marketing program in the 1960's, the railways deliberately undertook to upgrade the quality of their personnel. The upgrading of personnel has been achieved by the railways recruiting more widely and more

71

highly educated employees, including university graduates, for sales and marketing functions, and by increasing the general promotion potential for persons in the marketing field. The effectiveness of this has been recognized by shippers, who often acknowledged in the case studies done for this research effort that the quality of railway personnel in marketing has shown a radical improvement since about 1969. A survey of Canadian shippers in 1972 reported that several respondents mentioned that both railways "now have good new marketing people".[11]

Examination of the changes in the railways' organization structures, the improved quality of their marketing personnel, and the general recognition by shippers of the improved railway marketing personnel, make it clear that by the early 1970's the CN and CP had achieved a major institutional adjustment to the competitive transport environment of the modern era. The change was in response to, and not in anticipation of, the new competitive environment and the widened commercial freedom afforded the railways. However, the slowness of human institutions in changing is commonplace and appears to apply as much to shippers as to the railways, as will be seen later.

Joint Rate Making Practices of the CN and CP

The organization of the individual railways is crucial to the effective marketing and pricing of rail services and, therefore, to the working of the National Transportation Act. However, the relationship between the railways is also very important and is significantly different in Canada than the U.S.A., where the railways may not confer and make rates jointly in the ways permitted in Canada. In Canada, the railways are permitted under the Railway Act, Section 279, to exchange information when establishing rates and to negotiate jointly with shippers, and in the case of agreed charges are required by Section 32 (2) of the Transport Act to agree in writing or be a party to an agreed charge from or to a competitive point.[12]

As a result of these powers and requirements, after the railways have established separately the rate they require on a new commodity movement or the amount by which they wish to adjust an existing rate, rate officers in the two railways usually confer to establish the rate they will publish or present to shippers. Negotiations with shippers are normally conducted jointly or with one railway representing both railways. Exceptions to this procedure do occur but joint rate making and negotiation is most common. Rate bureaus play no part in the negotiation of domestic rates in Canada, although the Canadian Freight Association is involved in publishing tariffs and some administrative work.

The Canadian Freight Association

The Canadian Freight Association (CFA) was established to assist with the establishment, publication and administration of rates, rules and other conditions of carriage governing the movement of freight traffic. It is empowered by member lines to examine shipping documents to see that rates and rules agreed upon are followed. Inspection officers employed by CFA check on shippers' records to make sure they are conforming with the provisions of agreed charges, check inbound and outbound records for in-transit processing, and check on car loading performance. CFA has two sections, one located in Montreal, the other in Winnipeg, and has various committes, for example the Tariff Committee, the Bill of Lading Committee and the Weighing Committee. CFA publishes tariffs in Montreal and distributes its own and CN and CP tariffs from both the eastern and western offices.

The Tariff Committee of CFA consists of the Chairman of the Association and rate officers of member lines. Docketed rate items are confined to international rates. The Chairman of CFA in Montreal frequently is responsible for sending letters to shippers informing them of domestic as well as international rate proposals. These letters are drafted by the railways and replies sent to the CFA are dealt with by the railways. In spite of the appearance of active involvement in the domestic rate making process by CFA, its function is purely administrative.

Shipper Organization for Railway Rate Negotiations

No attempt has been made in the research for this study to document either the organization of traffic and distribution departments in industrial and commercial firms or the development of industry associations involved in transportation matters. However, through interviews with the shippers' representatives involved in rate negotiations and from the general literature on physical distribution management, it is clear that during the 1960's the organization of shippers with respect to transport functions has changed to take advantage of the potential of physical distribution management. One of the stimuli to physical distribution management has been the development of a variety of improved transportation and communications alternatives as these make effective control of distribution costs and service not only a complex undertaking, but also a potentially profitable one.

The recruiting of experienced railway personnel into industrial traffic departments has often played a significant role in the development of expertise in distribution management and has aided firms in developing negotiating positions. For many firms, rate negotiations during the 1960's were new in the extent to which they relied on presentation to the railways of evidence of the alternatives to rail service available to the shipper. The increase of competitive commodity and agreed charge rates is evidence of this activity. The experience gained by shippers, as well as the railways, has increased the capability of the traffic departments.

The large shipper firms interviewed in the case studies carry out many of their rate negotiations from the central traffic office. In no instance was a decentralization policy found, although shipper firms often allowed purely regional movements to be negotiated at the regional level. However, traffic movements which were interregional or involved major volumes were negotiated from head office. Consequently, for large shipper firms with head offices in Toronto or Montreal, such as the oil and chemical companies, the decentralization of railway rate making may make negotiations less convenient if the responsible railway rates officer is located in the traffic-originating area.

Joint Negotiation by Shippers

The most noticeable development in the organization of shippers for negotiations has been the increasing role of formal or informal committees over the last fifteen years.[13] In several instances, informal committees were established in the early 1960's for the purpose of bargaining, and they now have become permanent committees. Four reasons have been identified for this trend, but it is not possible to assign a clear ranking of them.

The first reason is the benefit which shippers perceive they derive from using the countervailing power of an industry in negotiations with the large railway corporations. However, neither many shippers nor railway rate officers believe that significant benefits are derived by shippers on the basis of size alone. The power of shippers is based primarily on the alternatives they have to avoid the use of the railways with whom they are negotiating. The case studies support the proposition that, apart from volume-based rates which have been made for a few individual firms, size per se of the negotiating shipper or shippers is not a substantive factor in negotiations. Irritation was even expressed by one large shipper that it seems easier for small shippers to get rate adjustments on the basis of letters alone than for a large shipper who has to engage in time-consuming preparation and presentation of his case to the railways.

The second and very important reason is that a joint negotiation is an effective means of ensuring that all shippers who wish their rates to be closely related or based on the same factors get the same or satisfactorily related rates. Shippers, particularly of homogeneous commodities competing in a single market, are very much concerned with the comparative level of rates. The individuals negotiating the rates for shippers are very concerned that the published rates show that they do just as good a job as other negotiators in the industry. The railways, for their part, prefer not to be faced with a series of requests for different concessions from a number of shippers when the final rate structure is one which will be the same or very similar for all firms.

The third reason for industry negotiation is the convenience that the system creates for all parties. When an industry has a formal negotiating committee, whether it be for an agreed charge or other rate, the railways can be assured that notification of an impending rate change to that committee will reach all shippers effectively. Without the formal structure, the case studies show that errors or delays in informing some firms in an industry of an impending rate change can cause irritation. This occurs for large and small firms. The negotiating process and, for the shippers, the preparation of position papers can often be accomplished more effectively on an industry basis than with several firms working separately and making separate submissions.

The fourth reason for industry negotiations is to increase the number and potential impacts of transport, distribution and location alternatives to rail transport. For example, in homogeneous commodities such as cement and some petroleum products it may be practical for firms to engage in product exchange if freight rates become too high. For instance, firms A and B are located in different parts of a market area but compete throughout the market area. Rather than cross-hauling into each others market territories, they can elect to exchange products. Also, various economies of scale may be achievable if shippers are willing to ship collectively. For example, back-haul movements may be economically possible, economies of utilization in rail operation may be feasible, or bulk transport by water may be an alternative. Examples of corporations being set up to be responsible for commodity transportation for participating firms are Canpotex for potash; Sultran for sulphur; Torman Assembly based in Toronto, as agents for the Canadian Retail Shippers' Association; and Western Assembly, based in Vancouver, for the transport of merchandise for certain retail stores.

Considerations in Joint or Individual Company Negotiations by Shippers

Individual shippers must assess the costs and probable benefits of negotiating within a joint committee or a more formal individual arrangement such as a company. Individual shippers may not be able to press their particular advantage or concern as far as they would like in group negotiations, and they may have to accept a rate structure which is better suited to the average condition of the shippers than to their own particular circumstances. These differences arise because shipper firms in the same industry can and often do have different commodity mixes, different plant locations and different market areas. For example, the proportion of lumber and plywood shipped by British Columbia forest product firms varies, but railway rates on these commodities, subject to somewhat different competitive forces, are negotiated together by the Transportation Committee of the Council of Forest Industries of B.C. A firm with a higher proportion of plywood in its product mix than other firms may be less satisfied with a truck competitive rate achieved through the Committee's actions, than a firm shipping mainly lumber, because competition from trucking has a more significant influence on high-value plywood than on lumber. In the case of automobiles, only General Motors and Ford can negotiate rates to the West Coast of Canada on the basis of their alternative of supplying loaded cars from assembly plants in California (Freemont and Los Angeles, respectively)

75

rather than from plants in eastern Canada. Nevertheless, an overall industry rate structure is maintained.

Therefore, among shippers negotiating as a group there are competitive pressures and differences of opinion. The joint negotiations will only go on for as long as the individual firms perceive that the benefits of the group system of negotiation exceed the costs. The case studies provide no evidence that the trend for shippers to negotiate collectively is changing.

Two firms with American parent companies expressed concern about engaging in joint negotiations because of the parent companies' general concern about antitrust legislation. One of these companies, although active in rate negotiations, opposed a formal negotiating committee for the group.

From an economist's perspective, it is expected that the shippers will find it beneficial to negotiate collectively as long as they have a similar elasticity of demand for rail transport; for example, as long as the impact of freight rates on plywood is not too dissimilar from the impact of rates on lumber. Also, as long as elasticities are similar, railways would find little advantage in negotiating with individual shippers as there would be no differences in demand elasticities to be translated into differential freight rates.

Role of Canadian Industrial Traffic League

Before leaving the topic of shipper organization special mention should be made of the role of the Canadian Industrial Traffic League. The League estimates that its members pay about fifty per cent of Canada's total freight bill of road and rail carriers. Through its regional organizations, the League can represent a wide cross-section of shipper opinion in representations either to Government or the railways. The League does not become involved with carriers on the matter of freight rates which may only affect some of its members but is active in matters of general concern. For example, the League made active representations to the railways on proposed changes in demurrage regulations and in regulations governing the responsibilities of the shipper and carrier for third-party liability. During 1975 and 1976, the League has been important in helping effective communication between the railways and a large number of shippers and in giving shippers a means of expressing their views to Government.

Legislative and Other Government Constraints on Railway Rates Since 1967

The organizations of the railways and shippers are important to the effectiveness with which railway rates are established. The evolution of these organizations and the effectiveness with which they work are influenced by the constraints placed on rates and rate making by Government. Therefore, before reporting on the workings of the rate making process, it is necessary to establish the major constraints which Government has placed on rate making. This section reports briefly on the major provisions of regulatory legislation affecting railway rates and rate making since 1967 and explains how Government has exerted its executive type of influence on railway rates.

The General Principles of Canadian Transport Policy, 1967

The Minister of Transport responsible for the passage of the National Transportation Act and the first President of the Canadian Transport Commission was J.W. Pickersgill. He explained the basis of the National Transportation Policy on many occasions. On one of these, he stated:

> Competition between the modes is the essential ingredient of the national transportation policy. ... The major regulatory responsibility is to prevent unduly high rates in conditions of monopoly or, in conditions of competition, unprofitable rates that may throw an unfair burden on other traffic or undermine a more efficient mode. ... We have attempted in the National Transportation Act to bring our whole approach to transport development in Canada up to date: to regulate when necessary but only when necessary. Otherwise the interplay of competition forces will fashion the variety and standard of the services offered and the level of rate of the competing modes.[14]

The principle is set down in Section (3) of the National Transportation Act. In addition to placing reliance on competitive forces, this section of the Act also recognises that government policies and actions must not burden or benefit particular modes of transportation. The statement of National Transportation Policy in the 1967 Act is given in Appendix III-1.

Neither in 1966, when the National Transportation Act was being debated, nor today, is there unanimity of views concerning this statement of policy. A fundamental issue is whether there should be a transport policy concerned primarily with the efficiency with which the transport sector can provide demanded services or whether there should be a national policy in which transport is regarded as an instrument or tool for the achievement of national social and development goals. In 1966, the National Farmers Union, which favours the nationalization and integration of the entire Canadian rail system, stated that, "the objective of interprovincial transportation should remain an instrument for the development and maintenance of a viable economic and political nation."[15]

In 1973, the four Western Provinces proposed a change in the policy statement "to clearly place regional economic development as one of the basic objectives of national transportation policy".[16] In 1975, Transport Canada issued a report in which a new set of policy principles were set out. The first

77

policy objective states:

> A total transportation system for Canada, providing accessibility and equality of treatment for users, is an essential instrument of support for the achievement of national economic and social objectives.[17]

How far transport will be used as an instrument for the achievement of other economic, social and political policies is unclear. Certainly, both the carriers and the shippers generally are opposed to the practice. The Canadian Industrial Traffic League has informed the Minister of Transport that:

> CITL is fearful that more Government involvement in transportation and the use of transportation to attain national objectives, may very well put too much reliance on transportation for the development of various regions of Canada.

> This could lead to disproportionate benefits being expected from transportation alone and could possibly detract from the real needs of a region.

> While the League is in general agreement with the three objectives stated, it does have some concern over the degree of involvement by Government in attaining them. The League is convinced that these objectives, to a large degree, are being realized under the National Transportation Act in response to the normal pressures of the competitive system.[18]

How the present Government will attempt to resolve the policy question and the program implementation of the relationship between transportation and regional economic development is not clear. It appears that in those areas where "an objective of commercial viability including cost-recovery, both in the operation of transportation services and in the provision of facilities and services for direct support of transportation"[19] is possible, this principle will be followed.

Wide Pricing Freedom of the Railways

A major concern of several shippers with the National Transportation Act in 1966 was the repeal of Section 317 of the Railway Act which had enabled shippers to protest against rail rates on the grounds of unjust discrimination. Substituted for that provision was Section 23 of the National Transportation Act. This important new Section requires shippers to demonstrate a *prima facie* case of injury to the public interest before a consideration of redress can be obtained from the CTC. Section 23 of the National Transportation Act is given in Appendix III-2.

Section 23 does not limit the definition of public interest. The Section is not limited to rates, but also applies to any act or omission of a carrier. The scope of this wording has been significant for the rate making process as it has been used to ensure that the process of consultation and negotiation of transportation rate and service matters has been adequate. As documented and discussed in Chapter VIII, it has also been used to test whether alleged rate discriminations and alleged unreasonable levels of rates which are, however, below the maximum permitted level of rates, are contrary to the public interest.

In 1966, a number of shipper and regional submissions spoke strongly against repeal of Section 317 of the Railway Act dealing with limitation of unjust discrimination. The view was expressed that in the absence of intermodal competition the railways would engage in pricing prejudicial to particular shippers and regions. For example, the Mining Association of Canada stated:

> As far as freight traffic is concerned, Bill C-231 removes from the Railway Act all references to unjust discrimination, undue preference and just and reasonable rates.

> It is presumed that this action is based on the assumption that rates which are established by free competition between the railways and the other modes of transport must by definition be just and reasonable and that the forces of competition in themselves will prevent unjust discrimination and undue preference.

> We cannot bring ourselves to believe that such an assumption is realistic and valid. The whole history of rate-making demonstrates, in our submission, that even where some element of competition exists between various modes of transport, statutory protection for the shipper against unreasonable prejudice and discrimination is necessary. The removal of that protection simply invites the railways to introduce, where they consider it necessary or desirable, discriminatory practices and preferences which have hitherto been prohibited by law. To say this does not, and is not intended to, impute to the railways bad faith or other unworthy motives. It is simply likely to be the case that, in the face of their overall circumstances and in the absence of adequate statutory restrictions, the railways will feel compelled to introduce practices which are unreasonably preferential or prejudicial to particular shippers or to particular localities in the field of rates, car supply, car service, transit arrangements or other aspects of the shipment of their

goods.[20]

What this position overlooks is the mutual interest of the railways and shippers in freight rates which enable the movement of traffic which can make a contribution to rail revenue beyond the variable cost of the traffic in question. The case studies reveal some concern with the working of Section 23, but not with the principle on which it is based, that is, that there is to be CTC interference only where the public interest is involved and has been proved. The case studies also reveal that significant flexibility in pricing has been provided to the railways by the removal of Section 317. The railways have felt more able to respond to specific local competitive forces, to share with shippers economies derived from volume movements, and to enter into long-term agreements through letters of intent.

The National Transportation Act did not remove the criterion of unjust discrimination from the Transport Act applying to agreed charges. Part IV of the Transport Act, dealing with agreed charges, is shown in Appendix III-3. Part IV of the Transport Act has given shippers, in Section 32 (10), the opportunity to protest an agreed charge as unjustly discriminatory and to obtain a fixed charge set by the CTC. Section 33 (1) of the Transport Act has given shippers, any body representative of shippers and any carrier or association of carriers, the right to complain to the Minister of Transport that a rate, which has been in effect for at least three months, is unjustly discriminatory. The Minister may refer the complaint to the CTC. If the CTC finds that the agreed charge is undesirable in the public interest, Section 33 (4) provides powers for it to vary or cancel the agreed charge or to make such other order as it considers appropriate. No complaint has been referred to the CTC by the Minister, nor has the CTC dealt with any application for a fixed rate on the grounds of unjust discrimination. The absence of such cases is noteworthy in view of the importance of agreed charges.

Other than rates for grain and related products only three specific constraints were placed on rates by changes in the Railway Act introduced through the National Transportation Act. They specify the level of rates for small shipments, and the minimum and maximum level of rates in general.

Section 264 of the Railway Act allows the CTC to prescribe tolls on traffic moving in less-than-carload quantities under five thousand pounds. There have been no cases under this section and there is no less-than-carload traffic in Canada outside Newfoundland today. Small shipments now are carried by other modes in Canada, primarily by truck and air.

Section 276 requires that all rates be compensatory, that is that they exceed the variable cost of the traffic concerned as determined by the CTC. The Commission may investigate a rate on its own motion or on complaint under Section 277 of the Railway Act. No investigation of minimum rates has been

80

carried out under this Section.

This reflects the lack of predatory pricing by the railways, and the fact that the main concern of shippers is with low rates established by government statutes and rate hold-downs and not with non-compensatory rates established by errors of judgement by the railways. Undoubtedly, some railway rates have been established at non-compensatory levels through errors or have become non-compensatory because of inflation. The magnitude of rate increases for heavy cars during 1975 and 1976 has been explained in part as necessary because charges in effect before the increases were non-compensatory. It is generally acknowledged that the first rates on coal moving in unit trains to Vancouver for export were soon recognized as unremunerative as inflation affected costs and as the railways learned more of the effects of heavy trains on track maintenance. Also, the rates for some industries based on resource developments have been held down and may have become unremunerative during start-up periods when the projects experienced unexpected start-up problems. However, overall, there is no evidence that the railways have made errors of judgement or responded so generously to shippers' requests for low rates that rates below compensatory levels, except those established or caused by government action, have been cause for concern.

Section 278, the so-called captive-shipper section, of the Railway Act states the conditions under which the CTC may specify and prescribe a maximum rate and the method by which the rate should be calculated. Section 278 is shown in Appendix III-4. The section was the subject of considerable debate in 1966. The views of that time are significant because they provide some accurate description of the rail freight market, express the fears of some shippers, and are evidence of confusion over the intention of the maximum rate section.

The National Transportation Act followed the recommendation of the MacPherson Royal Commission closely with respect to maximum rate control.[21] However, while the Commission was very clear in its explanation of the development of intermodal competition and in the general rationale for its policy recommendations, it did not make clear the importance of market competition, as well as intermodal competition, in the setting of maximum rates. The report emphasized the general pervasiveness of intermodal competition, and recognized that the influence of competitive forces were not uniform for all commodities or locations. It did not make explicit the importance of market competition for many commodities.

The need for effective shipper protection was recommended when the monopoly power of the railways was sufficient to permit an unacceptable spread between railway cost and revenue.[22] That is, the MacPherson Commission did not use the absence of competing modes as its criterion for the need for maximum rate protection. It used the ability of the railways to charge rates "many times higher than costs"[23] because of the absence of competitive forces, intermodal, intramodal and market competitive forces. The Commission's position is explained more fully in Chapter V when considering the significance of market competition.

The interpretation of the Commission report by many shippers and Provinces was that maximum rate protection should be available to shippers lacking intermodal competition. However, the principle on which Section 278 of the Railway Act was based, is that protection should be available to shippers who lacked competitive forces, whatever their nature, so that the railways could not take advantage of their real monopoly power and charge rates many times greater than costs. Section 278 was not designed to protect the shipper of bulk commodities on which railway rates are low because of market competitive forces, even though that shipper may lack the availability of intermodal competition.

The fundamental difference between protecting shippers paying very high rates because of limited competitive forces of any type and protecting shippers lacking intermodal competitive forces is still not a difference which is clearly understood. Section 278 is worded to apply where "no alternative, effective and competitive service by a common carrier other than a rail carrier" is available. However, the *level* of the maximum rate applicable is deliberately set to afford protection only to those shippers also lacking market competitive forces to hold rates down to a "reasonable" level. This was made clear by both the railways and Mr. Pickersgill during discussion of the National Transportation Act.

Mr. Sinclair, President of the Canadian Pacific Railway, stated that the bulk shipper dependent on rail service "would never make use of the captive shipper provision. He has other protections which are much greater than any the law can give."[24] Later he stated "Economic sanction is the greatest protection in the world."[25]

Mr. MacDougall, General Solicitor for the Canadian National Railways, gave the following replies to questions:

> We do not look on that man [a bulk shipper with alternative production location] as a captive, or somebody who needs protection against bearing too great a share of the overhead in rates. The purpose of the captive shipper scheme is to ensure that those people who are really captive are not going to be imposed upon by having an excess portion of overhead placed on their shoulders. This man is not in that position, therefore there is a large group in the non-competitive commodity rate area whom we cannot visualize coming forward as captives, or whom this scheme was ever designed to protect. There may be some of them in there but I would say, generally, in answer to your question, Mr.

Olson, that the majority of them would be in the class rate group.

Mr. Olson: Accepting, just tentatively, your contention that there are other forces that can be brought to bear in negotiating a rate with the railway for a company that is intending to set up an operation, do you contend that these same kind of forces are applicable where an establishment is now in place?

Mr. MacDougall: Very definitely, sir. We repeatedly have emissaries from industries of that kind, who are coming every so often seeking different rate concessions, or adjustments in rates, to meet the problems and difficulties which they have to face from day to day and year to year in their own business. The first thing they do when they are looking for some assistance is to come to us to see if they can chip a little off the rate. This is going on all the time with existing industries as well as new ones. It is very much in our interest to keep those people in business, if we can, at a rate which returns a new dollar for an old dollar.[26]

Mr. Pickersgill stated the position as follows:

...I think it is a very hard argument to refute, namely, that if a shipper already has sufficient bargaining power that he does not pay the maximum rate under the law now, his bargaining power is not going to be reduced by the passage of this bill ... It was never contemplated that many shippers would, in fact, pay the maximum rate because nearly all shippers today have really an economic bargaining power at least as great as the railways, and in many cases greater, and there is surely no need for us to prescribe regulations in cases of that kind.[27]

The greatest concern with Section 278 was expressed by the Western Provinces and some shippers. They sought to have maximum rates available to all shippers, and to bring down the level of the maximum rate so that it would be effective for additional shippers. Many groups such as the Coal Operators Associations, the Canadian Pulp and Paper Association and the Canadian Manufacturers' Association proposed flexibilitty in the setting of maximum rates. The latter Association stated:

We submit that the free judgement of the commission, relying on its own fact-finding facilities, is the proper authority to analyze the case and fix a rate.[28]

The Government resisted these pressures which were very explicitly recognized by Mr. Pickersgill. He stated:

> No maximum rate formula that we could possibly devise is going to be satisfactory in dealing with the big shippers with commodity rates. We do not want — certainly I do not want — to provide shippers of that kind with an advantage written into legislation in bargaining against the carriers. It seems to me that we ought to leave them free.[29]

Later, Mr. Pickersgill attempted to clarify the intent of the Act further, as follows:

> It is perhaps unfortunate that we could not have thought of a different phrase than 'captive shipper' because it suggests the normal usage which Mr. Southam has just used, that someone is a captive shipper who cannot ship any other way except by rail [for example a shipper of coal] ... A very large proportion of all the shippers in Canada are captive shippers in that sense. They have no other way to ship than by rail. [However] in the sense in which the term 'captive shipper' is used in this bill ... it is a subjective state. You cannot be a captive shipper under the proposed law unless you make yourself one ... Maybe we should try to think up a different term so it will not mislead people — a 'protected shipper' or something of that sort — because I think it has created a lot of misunderstandings in our discussions. Two different meanings have been put on the phrase 'captive shipper' and both could be considered proper meanings.[30]

The effect of Section 278 has been to leave rate making free to market forces. Only one shipper has applied to the CTC under Section 278. Application was made for the probable range in which a maximum rate would fall by Domtar Ltd. in 1971, but no decision has been handed down by the CTC on whether the shipper was captive as required by the Railway Act and, therefore, eligible for a maximum rate, [see Chapter VIII]. The wide freedom of pricing under the Railway Act has meant that considerable importance has attached to Section 23 of the National Transportation Act.

In addition to these specific sections of the Railway Act, Transport Act and National Transportation Act, dealing explicitly with the powers and responsibilities of the CTC with respect to the level of rates, analysis of rate negotiations has revealed that other sections of legislation affect railway rates and service. Legislation affecting the level of intermodal and intramodal competition, directly or indirectly, through such measures as user charges or

84

motor vehicle weight limits are important to the setting of rates. These features of existing statutes are considered primarily in later chapters. However, two specific constraints on the level of intramodal competition are noted here as they are provided for in the Transport Act and Railway Act.

First, as explained earlier, the railways are required to agree on agreed charges involving competitive railway locations under the Transport Act, Section 32 (a), and may confer on rates under Section 279 of the Railway Act. Second, Canadian railways are afforded protection against competition with U.S.A. railways by Section 382 of the Railway Act; this Section is shown in Appendix III-5. Under this Section all goods originating in Canada and moving over a continuous rail route through the U.S.A. to a Canadian destination are subject to a thirty percent customs duty unless a joint railway tariff has been filed with the CTC. This precludes the use of combination rates. Therefore, unless the Canadian railways agree to the publication of a joint rate on Canadian traffic moving through the U.S.A. rather than over Canadian lines, a prohibitive thirty percent duty applies. The constraint which this imposes on intramodal competition is considered in Chapter VII.

Flexibility in Implementation of Rate and Tariff Changes

Prior to the National Transportation Act, Canadian railways had considerable freedom in introducing rates. This freedom was extended considerably by repeal in 1967 of the old Section 328 of the Railway Act which had given the Board of Transport Commissioners wide powers to postpone the effective date of a tariff or to suspend any tariff pending investigation. Under the revised Railway Act, Section 275, tariffs must be filed in accordance with the Act and directions of the CTC, and tariffs so filed are effective unless and until they are disallowed by the CTC under one or more of the substantive rate controls still provided under the 1967 Act, as summarized previously.

In effect, this change extended to the railways the freedom to introduce rate increases on the basis of meeting filing requirements which the railways had in practice long experienced for rate reductions. The filing requirements continue to require the railways to file tariffs increasing rates thirty days before they become effective, but competitive tariffs reducing rates may continue to be put into effect immediately on their issuance and before they are filed with the CTC. The significant flexibility available to the railways to meet competition has been important in allowing the railways to negotiate with shippers and to respond to transport competition effectively.

The regulations of the CTC governing the construction, filing and posting of tariffs are set down in Tariff Circular 1-A, issued originally by the Board of Transport Commissioners in 1960. Rule 38 of the regulations was introduced in 1962 and permits the railways to publish Limited Freight Tariffs, which are effective as soon as they are published, as are competitive rates, but limited in duration to a maximum of sixty days. Limited Freight Tariffs are single-page tariffs amending tolls in regular tariffs, in which changes are required by market circumstances to be brought into effect promptly. Ease of publication have made them popular with the railways to meet short-run competition from trucking and to accommodate short-run shipper requirements, for example, the inventory location problems in a large distribution system. (It is possible that such a short-run rate, based on the short-run operating conditions of the railway, might be judged non-compensatory by the long-run variable cost standard of Section 276 of the Railway Act.)

Although the 1967 legislation removed Section 278 of the Railway Act which had given the Board of Transport Commissioners power to suspend rates, Section 59 of the National Transportation Act gives the CTC wide powers to forbid certain actions by the railways. Section 59 of the National Transportation Act states:

> The Commission may, if the special circumstances of any case so require, make an interim *ex parte* order authorizing, requiring or forbidding anything to be done that the Commission would be empowered, on application, notice and hearing, to authorize, require or forbid; but no such interim order shall be made for any longer time than the Commission may deem necessary to enable the matter to be heard and determined.

This power might be used by the CTC to ensure that prior to changing a rate the railways had engaged in reasonable communication and negotiation with shippers and considered the effects on other parties.

Statutory Rates and Subsidies

Consideration of the impact of the National Transportation Act on rate making must deal with the provisions affecting statutory rates and subsidies. These not only affect certain rates directly, but influence the overall cash flow of the railways and, therefore, the level of rates and quality of service for other shippers.

The general philosophy of the 1967 Act is that the railways should receive compensation from the government for services which cannot be provided commercially, but must be maintained in the public interest. A program for subsidies is established by Sections 252-261 of the Railway Act, inclusive, under "Abandonment and Rationalization of Lines or Operations". Under this program, the railways can receive a subsidy to make up all the loss as calculated by the CTC for the operation of unremunerative branch lines and eighty percent of the loss on unremunerative passenger services, after a hearing has been held concerning an application by a railway to abandon a line and/or service. The working of this section of the Act has not been satisfactory. The railways have faced strong opposition when applying for abandonment although their goal may have been to obtain a subsidy. They have not been able to apply for the abandonment of as many lines or services as they have desired. And, the payment of only eighty per cent of the loss on passenger services has placed a financial burden on the railways and shippers in maintaining passenger train services. Notwithstanding the dissatisfaction of the railways and many shippers with the revenue shortfall experienced by the railways for unremunerative services required in the public interest, the amount of the subsidy has grown at a rate frightening to taxpayers. In 1971, payments to Canadian railways under the National Transportation Act were $53.5 million; in 1975, they were $237.4 million.[31]

With respect to statutory rates, Mr. Pickersgill commented on the first day of the Standing Committee's proceedings as follows:

> I want to say a word about the Crowsnest rates. It is probably unnecessary because I went into the matter half a dozen times [in the House] and I do not think I could have been more categorical but I do not think the record would be complete if I did not say it again: that there is no intention whatsoever of making any change at all or permitting any change to be made in the Crowsnest rates.[32]

The Section of the Railway Act dealing with Crows Nest Pass rates is Section 271. In addition, Section 272 of the Railway Act froze rates for export grain and flour to certain eastern ports at the level applying on the 30th of November 1960 and the 30th of September 1966.

The possibility that the 1967 Act would lead to an early analysis of the financial implications of the statutory rates for the railways was lost when a section of the proposed Act was defeated. That proposed section of the Act would have required a review of the statutory rates and the related costs within three years after the passage of the Act. As noted in Chapter II, the financial impact of the statutory rates on the railways has been under study by the Snavely Commission during 1975-76. The report of this Commission was submitted to the Minister of Transport in late 1976 and at the time of writing is awaiting publication. The findings of this Commission are of vital importance. Should the Commission find that the statutory rates impose a financial burden on the railways, as is expected, swift action to relieve the railways of this burden is crucial to the interests of the railways and shippers.

General Powers and Influence of Government

The legal powers of the government over the railways are those provided by the various statutes, particularly the National Transportation Act and the Railway Act. The fact that the CN is a Crown Corporation has little bearing on the day-to-day influence of the government on the running of the company. The

Government appoints the chief executive officers and members of the Board, and Parliament must approve the annual budget. However, Government does not appear to exert a significantly greater influence over the CN because it is a Crown Corporation than it does over the CP, which is a major privately-owned national company significantly affected by the public interst.[33]

However, because of the traditional importance of transportation to the economic and political well being of Canada, the record of the 1970's shows that the Government is able to exert substantial powers of persuasion with the railways. Although the railways had not increased their class or general commodity rates for some time, they acceded to a request of the Minister of Transport to freeze the rates following WEOC in 1973. The understanding between the railways and the Minister was informal, but was generally interpreted by the railways to apply to non-negotiated rates. The rate freeze applied until the end of 1974, but during 1974 increases in some negotiated rates which the Minister had believed frozen took place and remained in effect in spite of the Minister's statements that they would be rolled back.[34] The CN and CP refused to act on the Minister's request on this occasion. Had the railways refused to accede to the request of the Minister in 1973, political pressures would no doubt have been great but the railways might have avoided the difficulties encountered with shippers when they attempted to catch up with past inflation by raising the rate levels during 1975 and 1976.

The willingness of the railways to freeze their non-negotiated rates is a measure of the influence of government opinion over the railways. It is also a measure of the strength of feeling and political power of the Premiers of the Western Provinces concerning the inequities they believe to have continued under the existing National Transportation Policy, and a measure of the railways' concern with these views. However, as reported in Chapter II, the strong general complaints of the Prairie politicians have not been substantiated by subsequent studies nor have they been supported by shippers. Shippers seek adjustments to the regulatory constraints on railway rate making, rather than substantial revision of transport policy and regulations [see Chapter VIII].

Rate Making Procedures and Rate Negotiations

The institutional setting is vital to the opportunity for competitive forces to be able to work. Government constraints and corporate organization affect the opportunity for competitive forces to work and influence the effectiveness with which they work. However, the actual operation of competitive forces on railway rates is also dependent on the attitudes and actions of individuals. Therefore, to examine how effectively reliance on competitive forces in making railway rates has worked, it is necessary to examine the actual rate-making and negotiating process. The purpose of this chapter is to describe the general nature of the process before considering, in later chapters, the use by shippers of particular arguments and transport alternatives available to them for the negotiation of rates and service issues with the railways.

Service Considerations in Rate Making

The price of any service, and transportation is no exception, must be viewed in conjunction with the quality of service provided. The shippers' concern with service was found in the shipper interviews to take many forms. There was a common recognition that rail rate increases have been essential in recent years to cover rising railway costs and to enable the railways to maintain and continue to expand and improve upon the services which they provide. However, a wide range of specific considerations was also found to be important in negotiations. For example, general shipper complaints about car quality, car supply, loss and damage experience and transit time reliability were arguments presented in several rate negotiations. These arguments were used not only in the hope of getting better service, but also to provide a graphic example of poor rail service in comparison with trucking which might, therefore, be a viable alternative to rail service even if the truck rate were higher than the rail rate. On occasion, significant service provisions are included in letters of intent, which may be entered into when rates are set. These may place obligations on shippers to free cars within a certain time and to ship certain volumes over particular periods, and obligations on the railways to provide certain types and numbers of cars, or to achieve car placement at certain times. Negotiations may also be on the basis of the effect of the ownership of cars or sidings, or the responsibility for insurance, on the freight rate to be paid. Therefore, when considering rate making and rate negotiations, it is important to remember that while attention may seem to be focussed on the freight rate, in practice, rates and rate making are significantly linked to service considerations in both the long- and short-run.

Diversity of Rates for Negotiation

The diversity of negotiations is not only accounted for by the presence of various service characteristics but also by the diversity of rates and rate patterns for negotiation. Rates may be open tariff rates with no contract provisions, they may be open tariff rates made with accompanying letters of intent, or they may be contract rates, agreed charges, with or without further letters of intent. Agreements in letters of intent can be crucial. For example, they may contain escalation clauses or may deal with the duration over which a rate will apply, service levels and performance requirements for both the shipper and carrier.

The number of parties involved in rate negotiations can also vary greatly. Negotiations may involve one or more shippers concerned with one or more origins and/or destinations and be with one or more railways, either domestic or trans-border. Consequently, rate negotiations may be as simple in structure as a mining company negotiating with the only railway serving its site for the carriage of the product to a single predetermined destination, for example, coal or copper from a mine in British Columbia to Vancouver for export. Or the negotiations may affect many producers over a large area served by many railways moving one or more products to large market areas served by many other producers and railways. For example, the case of railway rates on newsprint from eastern Canada into the U.S.A. involves many producers and a number of railways. Rates on such a movement have given rise to an appeal to the CTC under Section 23 of the National Transportation Act. This case is described in Chapter VIII.

About two-thirds of the rate negotiations researched in this study were initiated by the railways seeking rate increases to offset rising costs and to adjust the level of rates which had been held down by the partial rate freeze of 1973-74. In the cases investigated, those initiated by shippers more often involved substantive quality of service questions than was the case in the negotiations initiated by the railways, or they were for new or significantly expanded movements. When the shippers initiated negotiations, the first shipper contact with the railways was usually with the sales representatives and involved more pricing and service development activity than when the railways came forward with proposed rate increases. However, in general no substantive difference in the actual process of rate negotiations existed between railway-initiated and shipper-initiated discussions.

The Pricing Practices of the Railways

General requirements for rate increases are established through corporate budgeting procedures which yield forecasts of revenue requirements. With this general requirement in mind, rate increases on particular traffic are estimated on the railways' marketing and pricing officers' perceptions of the current and expected value of service to the shipper. On traffic subject to contracts these estimates are normally made about four months before contracts expire. Pricing research involves thousands of costings each year so that rate officers are aware of the cost floor for rates.[35] For minimum levels, the railways have general goals, for example, rates should be at least the variable cost plus twenty-five per cent. However, the rate first proposed to shippers by the railways does not always attain this level. Indeed, during 1975 rate officers gave the impression that because of increases in input costs and the move to replacement costing, several rates proposed were significantly below the overall guidelines. The rate position presented to shippers may be the rate the railways expect to apply, or in the case of some shippers who are known to require rate concessions, may be above the target level.

The procedures observed for the setting of target rates is entirely consistent with the pricing procedure explained by the railways in 1966. Mr. J.C. Gardiner stated:

> ... we use the variable cost estimates provided by the

90

costing section just to make sure that we do not come down so low that we go below our variable costs. We do not rate competitively on the basis of cost plus ... We use the variable cost to determine whether we should stay in that type of business. That is all. We do not start with a variable cost and build on that as much as we can, because the market sets the price for us.[36]

Initial Rail-Shipper Communication

Communication of the rate changes to shippers takes place by various means and this diversity is one source of confusion among shippers as to exactly who are the responsible railway pricing officers.

Shippers usually learn first of an impending change in an agreed charge by a letter from the CFA, signed by the Chairman of the CFA. It is exceptional for a railway pricing or marketing officer to make initial contact. The letters from the CFA are impersonal. Over the last few years, they have emphasized the need for rate increases because of rising costs and, often, the need for an increase in rail cash-flow to support new rail investment. An example of such a letter is given in Exhibit 1. CFA is acting in an administrative capacity in sending out these letters; and if replies are sent back to the CFA, they are dealt with by railway officers although replies may again be channelled through the CFA.

From the shipper's standpoint, this procedure has three deficiencies. First, the impersonal nature of letters is conducive to the view that the railways are "high-handed". Second, for small shippers and those who may be unfamiliar with rate negotiations even though parties to an agreed charge, the letters do not direct the shipper's attention to the appropriate railway officer to contact concerning problems. Third, letters from the Montreal office of CFA give the appearance of a centralized rate-making process, and, for shippers outside central Canada, one that is far removed. For shippers who, for various reasons, may be unfavourably disposed to railway pricing practices, these problems are further irritants.

The explanation for this centralization of procedures for agreed charges but not the responsibility for the negotiation or for rate making, appears to be the requirement under the Transport Act, Section 32 (2), that competing carriers confer. This Section is shown in Appendix III-3. Control over this, as with administration of the volume agreements in agreed charges, is exercised by CFA. Before an agreed charge can be published the CFA in Montreal requires confirmation in writing that competing carriers concur with the rate.

Letters are also sent out by the CFA, as well as directly by the railways, to shippers concerning changes in open tariffs which are normally negotiated. While no instance was found in the case studies, the railways, since 1974, have made greater efforts than formerly to inform shippers with non-negotiated rates that they are willing to negotiate. The Canadian Industrial Traffic League has published a number of these letters; for example, see Exhibit 2. In the case of the removal of LCL tariffs in the Maritime Provinces, the Atlantic Provinces Transportation Commission expressed its "consideration to the railways, and more particularly to the CNR who were most actively involved, for the excellent cooperation so far extended as a result of which many difficult problems were resolved."[37]

The trend to reliance on selectively applied rate increases, with negotiation common, is characteristic of the changes in railway pricing over the last twenty-five years. The open encouragement by the railways for shippers to discuss any problems has been furthered by the concerns of the Western Provinces and the position adopted by Federal Minister of Transport Jean Marchand that horizontal percentage freight-rate increases are undesirable.[38]

While the approach of the railways to shippers is usually joint, instances were found in the case studies where individual railways believed they knew of a traffic potential and approached a shipper singly. In one instance, this was new rail traffic for which the railway initiating the rate might expect to obtain much of the traffic. In another case, the movement could be integrated into a rail and export terminal handling contract.

Freight sales representatives do not normally inform shippers of impending rate increases. Some shippers feel that railway salesmen know nothing about rates, although others believe that salesmen know a shipper's business and are good intermediaries with pricing officers.[39] A number of cases revealed freight salesmen, working effectively to bring service and/or rate problems of shippers to the attention of pricing officers or market development officers. The role of a freight salesman varies from industry to industry. In industries characterized by large firms which negotiate on an industry basis, the salesman does not usually have a role in the rate-making process.

Shipper Negotiations with Individual Railways

In cases where shippers initiated contact with the railways on pricing matters, a number of situations were found in which the shippers approached the railways separately and continued to negotiate on this basis. This has been the case for the majority of copper mines which have developed in British Columbia over the last decade. Since their experiences are exceptional and even contrary to the explanation of senior railway executives that the railways "never compete on rates", the case of rate making for the copper producers deserves special attention.

In the early 1960's when the first copper mines were approaching the production stage, the mining executives, who were mining engineers with no experience in rail transport, approached buying transport in much the same way as they approached contracting engineering work. They expected independent bids from which they would select the best one. In an early instance, the CN and CP submitted a joint bid, would not negotiate separately, and were surprised to learn subsequently that they had lost the traffic to a trucker. Subsequently, the CN, CP and British Columbia Railway (BCR) have negotiated separately, often to develop and price integrated truck-rail movements. These negotiations have proceeded to the detailed aspects of five-year contracts. It appears that four features of the copper concentrate traffic led the railways to negotiate separately. First, there was the strong sentiment of the shippers that they should negotiate separately. Second, there was the presence of intermodal competition so that the traffic could be lost. Third, the transportation contracts required certain facilities to be built and were to be of a long-term nature, about five years, so that the negotiations were in an "all or nothing context". Fourth, either railway had the capacity to perform the carriage from origin to destination.

The inability of the railways to share the traffic once a rate has been established appears to be a particularly important aspect in the success of some shippers in approaching the railways separately. The pricing of single movements of special equipment or of traffic for construction sites was found on occasion to be based on rates requested separately of the railways and acted on by them competitively.

The Arguments of Shippers in Negotiations with the Railways

The working of competitive forces is achieved through the research and other functions of the railway personnel in the planning and pricing of railway services and through the communications and negotiations of the shippers with the railways. The direct communication of the shippers with the carriers often can increase the railways' knowledge of details of competitive and other factors, more than is possible through the railways' research. The interviews with the shippers and the railways revealed a wide variety of arguments used by shippers. The details of the types of arguments and the response of the railways to them are considered in Chapters V to VII. Only the general nature of the arguments are considered here.

The dominant basis for shippers' arguments is that, unless the railways accede to the shippers' requests, the railways will be less profitable than would otherwise be the case. Shippers argue either that the railways will lose profitable traffic because of the alternatives available to the shipper, or because the shipper will be priced out of a market he will not be able to ship the good at all, or shippers argue that by carrying the freight in ways and at rates different than those proposed by the railways both the shipper and carriers will benefit. Equity arguments of various types are used by shippers, but not often, as explained in the latter part of Chapter VII.

Shippers relying primarily on the availability of alternatives to particular railway services when negotiating the level of a railway rate and the quality of railway service, utilize the availability of alternative carriers and alternate markets, sources of supply and location of production. Such alternatives may be currently or potentially available to shippers. While the present availability of an alternative may make the possible loss of traffic immediate, the potential availability of an alternative can be equally, if not more, pressing. For example, once a firm commits itself to private trucking, to a new system of distribution with more or fewer warehouses, or has changed markets or locations of production, it will be very difficult for the rail carrier to win back this traffic.

In their negotiations, shippers present the alternatives available to them as constraints on the railways actions. In a great many instances, the shipper will mention the for-hire trucking rates and services available to him and the fact that he has already been shipping by truck or has tried out trucking service. Or he will state that efficient private carrier trucking can be developed or increased if the railway rates are not adjusted downward or his service requirements are not met. In some cases, a shipper seeking a point-to-point rate will negotiate independently with two or more railways in position to carry his traffic or to expand facilities for that purpose. In some instances, truck-rail or water-rail alternatives will be mentioned in arguing for lower rates or service improvement. A shipper may show that he can serve alternate markets, or that he can rearrange his production and distribution to supply a market from the nearer of his plants and save ton-miles and transport cost in doing so. In some complex cases, a shipper's alternatives involve several types of competition: intermodal, intramodal and market.

Many shippers of bulk commodities, in particular, cannot confront the railways with arguments about the alternatives available to them. The frustration of a shipper under those conditions is undersirable. No buyer likes to be confronted with the market power of a single seller. However, unless the railways are willing to be responsive to the market competitive pressures faced by the shipper, neither the shipper nor the carrier may enjoy the business. Therefore, shippers often present very sophisticated arguments about the constraints of market competition on their pricing and thus on railway rates. The lack of intramodal, intermodal or other alternatives, then, does not mean that the results of the negotiation process necessary will be unfavourable to the shipper. Indeed, if, with the benefit of hindsight, the level of rates on Kaiser Resources coal traffic carried by CP is considered, rates set on the traffic for the early 1970's were not unfairly high, but uneconomically low. (This example is cited in more detail in Chapter V.)

Finally, a shipper may negotiate arrangements with the railways by which traffic may be handled in different ways to reduce railway costs and enable some of the benefits to be passed along to the shippers. The benefit to the shipper may be in the form of reduced rates, smaller increases in rates than would otherwise be necessary, and/or improvements in service.

The availability of arguments to a shipper and the effectiveness of them are influenced by the negotiating strategy of a shipper. If a shipper negotiates jointly within an industry group, the probability of rivalry between the carriers within the negotiations is reduced. Further, a number of firms negotiating together probably provides a different mix of alternatives and market competitive forces than if any one of the shippers were to negotiate individually because of the diversity of plant locations, product mixes and markets served.

Shipper Negotiating Strategy

The majority of shippers do not think of negotiating with the railways separately on rates or believe that it is possible when both the CN and CP could carry the traffic. It is simply accepted that the railways negotiate jointly. There is often good reason for this. First, many individual movements involve interline arrangements, although on a smaller percentage of movements in Canada than the U.S.A. because of the extensive coverage of Canada by both the CN and CP. Second, the negotiation of rates by a firm may involve multiple origins and/or destinations, some served by both carriers but others by only one carrier. No shipper interviewed considered the possibility of different rates on different routes dependent on separate negotiations with a carrier, although under the Railway Act and National Transportation Act independent negotiations and different rates would appear to be legal. Third, groups of firms, whether in formal shipper organizations or not, may prefer to negotiate with the railways as an industry.

Some shippers have expressed the view that it would not be in their long-run interest to attempt to get the railways to compete on rates. However, shippers who expressed this view were involved in industry-wide negotiations and could not contemplate a rate structure free from traditional zone relationships. Shippers also recognize that in a duopoly of railways aggressive independent rate making is not likely to take place in many situations. Shippers, on the whole, do not believe that presently the railways *would* negotiate separately nor that shippers would generally derive identifiable benefits from negotiations with single railways. The case studies provide considerable evidence that "some shippers actually prefer the continuation of railroad cartels".[40]

However, this was not the unanimous view of shippers. In one case, a large shipper having regular traffic flows negotiated with the CN and CP in Central Canada on the basis of giving one of the carriers all of the traffic from a plant, rather than dividing it between them. The negotiations proceeded separately for several weeks before the pricing executives at main headquarters became aware of the situation and refused to negotiate separately any further. Presumably, if the shipper had settled sooner, he would have moved the traffic by one carrier.

What the implication of this would have been for subsequent negotiations is a matter of speculation, in view of the current right of the railways to negotiate jointly.

From an economic perspective, shippers might expect to negotiate with the railways jointly when they perceive that the railways have similar elasticities of supply. That is, the traffic levels and other operating conditions of the railways make them equally eager for the traffic. If there are significant differences between the supply elasticity of each railway, it might be worthwhile for the shipper to negotiate with each railway separately. However, when the railways negotiate jointly, the position which they individually bring to the negotiations will be derived from their own individual supply elasticity.

The position of shippers as to the negotiation of railway proposals for rate increases ranged from acceptance of an increase as reasonable to expectation that haggling and delaying negotiations to postpone and minimize rate increases should always take place. Both of these positions were exceptional. The most common approach was for the shipper to verify what competitive forces existed and to use them in a reasonable way to reduce rate increases. Negotiation was not viewed as a repetitive bidding process. Most shippers considered it important to maintain their long-run credibility with the carriers.

Shippers have often undertaken substantial studies to establish the feasibility of alternate transport methods, for example, the use of shipping rather than rail service, or the economics of decentralized rather than centralized production. In some instances, those studies were provided to the railways. In contrast to detailed studies for the design of new logistics systems, arguments involving the availability of truck competition were commonly confined to shipper quotation of trucking rate figures to the railways, with the latter having to estimate whether such trucking rates really existed and for how much tonnage.

In spite of the importance of competitive alternatives to shippers, on several occasions shippers reduced their own scope for negotiation on rates and services by making plant or routing decisions prior to a determination on the freight rates. In many instances, a mining company has little alternative but to prove the commercial viability of a mine before negotiating a freight rate. However, in two cases a mine faced with an excess of ore for smelting and with two refineries available, signed the refining contract before investigating the freight rates. In another case, a manufacturing firm in the Prairies purchased a warehouse in a new market before holding any discussions on rates with the railways. It is not clear that the outcome of the negotiations would have been different with different strategies, but the importance of maintaining negotiating flexibility was recognized by shippers generally. Some shippers believed that it was important to maintain alternatives to a rail route readily available, for example, by using another mode of transport for a part of the traffic, or by utilizing a diversity of sources of supply using the services of different carriers. These shippers argued that even if such action was costly in the short-run, it enhanced the apparent level of competition and maintained the institutional framework for making a change away from a particular rail route should it become desirable.

Shippers Reactions to Railway Negotiations

Shippers generally acknowledged the substantial improvement in the ability and knowledge of railway marketing and pricing officers in recent years. Several of the case studies demonstrated the responsiveness of the marketing departments of both railways to opportunities to innovate through integrated as well as intermodal services. However, the view was common that to have the railways acknowledge problems with rail service, the shipper must devote excessive time and effort to the documentation of the problems.

The main concern of shippers undoubtedly was with respect to the railways' response in negotiations. Two main shipper complaints were found. The first was that, even in cases prior to 1973, the railways provided little information during the negotiations. Basically, they received and responded to information. This frustrated the shippers, but so long as the railways responded in the way shippers wanted, the railways' responses gave rise to no significant problems. The second complaint was that the more recent explanation of the railways for rate increases as being essential to cover cost increases and to provide the cash flow needed to support capital investments have not been supported to the shippers' satisfaction. The railways' emphasis on cost increases and capital needs have given rise to significant concerns by many shippers.

Apart from the very general references to cost shown in the railway letters, little further evidence was provided by the railways of cost increases. Consequently, shippers had some reason to doubt that the figures quoted by the railways applied to the particular business of the shippers whose rates were being raised. Such shippers also feared that they were being asked to subsidize capacity expansion for other shippers and to subsidize unremunerative railway services such as the export and related grain traffic and passenger services. These critical views have been aggravated by the tone of letters sent by the railways and speeches of executives.

Different shippers, and even individual shippers, have adopted radically conflicting positions in explaining their reactions to the railways. On the one hand, they may complain about the unwillingness of the railways to divulge meaningful information on how the cost of the traffic in question has increased. On the other hand, they may acknowledge that rates are necessarily made on a value-of-service basis and not on a cost-plus basis, and that the forced disclosure of railway cost is undesirable. Shipper concern has undoubtedly been heightened by a belief that the railways have been attempting to pass on costs for which the shippers in question were not responsible and which were being forced onto the system in total by services required in the public interest but subsidized by other shippers and not by government payments.

Shipper Attitudes and Negotiations During a Period of Substantial Rate Increases

During 1975 and 1976, the concern of shippers with the magnitude of rate increases and the apparent lack of responsiveness by the railways to shipper dissatisfaction became significant. Shipper reaction must be viewed against the background of decreasing rates over the period, 1959-1971, and, then, a substantial rate of increase, especially in 1975-1976, which was the combined result of inflation and the rate catch-up on previously frozen rates, as noted in Chapter II. During 1975-1976, some shippers faced substantial increases, in extreme cases more than one hundred percent in two years. The concern of shippers resulted in a meeting being called by the Canadian Industrial Traffic League with the CN and CP. The League summary of the meeting reveals that:

> There was a growing concern amongst our membership that the railways were being "hard nosed" in their approach to negotiating with shippers, and in fact a number of shippers believe that the railways are not negotiating at all but are in fact assuming a "take it or leave it" stance.

> Further, some members believe the railways do not appear to be concerned over losing traffic to a competitive mode or to be concerned whether a manufacturer will lose his business because of market competitive forces. Other members have indicated that the personal level of past rail/shipper negotiations "has gone out the window" and that the present day attitude seems to be one of strictly dollars and cents and the need for a certain return on investment with headquarters staff, as well as local railway rate officers, being curtailed to such a "dollar and cents" attitude with little or no flexibility.

> Firstly, Messrs. Lawless and Morrish thanked the League Officers for calling the special meeting indicating their desire to get the thinking of shippers through the League and wished to continue to do so.

> In defense of their purported past actions the railways indicated:

> i. They had taken a fairly "hard nosed" approach to rate increases, particularly on those rail rates which had been frozen, when the freeze was lifted in January 1975, because of the need for quick action.

> ii. Their approach to rate negotiations are based on "return on

98

investment" which is a requirement if the railways are to remain viable and for them to continue to expand, purchase replacement equipment etc. to serve the needs of the shipping public.

iii. They advised that the railways in Canada, not unlike other Canadian industries have been faced with severe increases in labour costs, purchased equipment costs, fuel etc. and recent rate increases were required to recover such increases, to ensure a fair return to them, and to provide services required by their customers.

iv. Their approach today is that all traffic must pay its way.

In concluding our discussions the railway executives indicated while they agreed that they had been forced to act rather quickly in the past, they wanted to maintain an open door policy in rate negotiations and they are willing to review all the facts of a specific shipper proposal.

In addition the railways indicated that they would dedicate more attention in all forthcoming negotiations.

The League indicated to the railway executives that in their view there was a distinct need for better P.R. on the part of the railways in their relationship with shippers by their more fully explaining their problems, their needs to remain viable, and why certain requests of shippers can or cannot be met.[41]

The need of the railways for recent rate and revenue increases can be seen from data on their net revenue position. The railways' net revenue position by month for the period January 1973 to July 1976 is shown in Table 18. The combined impact on net rail revenue of the rate freeze, cost increases and a decline in traffic is evident in the low monthly earnings and the losses of early 1975. However, while the magnitude of proposed rate increases was due to the railways' revenue needs, the following facts are important to an understanding of the apparent lack of responsiveness of the railways to shipper complaints that the increases would adversely affect the level of rail traffic. First, large and frequent rate increases can obviously be frustrating to shippers and give rise to shipper complaints. Second, periods of rising costs have their greatest impact on low rates that are close to cost and leave little room for the negotiation of these rates. Unfortunately, for both the railways and shippers, the commodities most affected can be the low-rated commodities with a fairly high sensitivity to transport charges. Third, the railways have been carrying out more careful economic analyses than in previous years before engaging in major rate negotiations. As a consequence, they have been in a better position to assess the probability of losing traffic. Rate officers have not responded to some shipper arguments used previously because of this better information as well as the pressure on them to increase rail revenues.

Table 18

Monthly Railway Net Income,
In Canada, January 1973 to July 1976
($ millions)

	1973[a]	1974[a]	1975[a]	1976
January	7.3	-1.0	-12.0	-10.0
February	7.7	-1.6	-11.9	15.5
March	14.3	0.2	-14.9	12.3
April	7.1	5.7	-0.3	8.5
May	6.8	4.3	-8.7	-11.9
June	7.2	-2.5	-4.7	3.2
July	0.0	2.2	61.7	2.0
August	-34.0	4.8	8.9	
September	0.7	1.0	11.8	
October	20.2	-0.3	16.9	
November	17.7	1.2	8.3	
December	38.9	39.3	-103.3[b]	

Notes:

[a] Figures to and including July 1975 are revised figures.

[b] The size of the loss is accounted for by a change from a cash to an accrual basis in accounting for government payments under the National Transportation Act.

Source: Statistics Canada, Railway Operating Statistics, Monthly, Statistics Canada 52-003.

Rising rail costs have undoubtedly resulted in some loss of rail traffic. For example, the railways were unable to match the competition in rates and service on beer traffic from trucks and recognized explicitly during negotiations that they would have to lose this traffic. This attitude of railways is adequately explained by a letter to the Canadian Industrial Traffic League in 1975 by the General Manager, Express and Intermodal Services, of the CN concerning the minimum charge per piece:

> Our experience since the introduction of this item has shown that any attrition in gross revenues has been more than offset by real savings in equivalent terminal handling expense. Given this result we quite naturally have no thought of removing the application of a minimum charge per piece from our marketing package.[42]

The level of shipper concern with rate increases during 1976 has given rise to another appeal to the CTC under Section 23 of the National Transportation Act and shipper consideration of the desirability of filing some additional cases under that Section.

During the 9½-month period between October 14, 1975 and July 31, 1976, the CTC received fifty-nine complaints or enquiries with respect to increases in freight rates in relation to the requirements of the Anti-Inflation Legislation introduced in Canada during 1975.[43] Of these complaints, eight were enquiries about the impact of the Anti-Inflation Legislation on freight rates and five were very general complaints without reference to specific traffic. Seventeen complaints were withdrawn because they were settled by negotiations between the shipper(s) and the railway(s).[44] Five of the increases were alleged by the railways to be necessary to make the rates compensatory. The remaining twenty-four complaints are either under investigation by the CTC, or the investigation has been completed. The results of these factual investigations are reported to the shippers, when completed.

The CTC reports that forty out of the fifty-nine complaints or enquiries related to products used as industrial inputs and to bulky articles. The rates on most of these items are low per 100 pounds and the report notes that, "during a period of inflation, variable costs tend to rise faster than overhead costs, with resulting pressures on freight rates that are at the lower end of the freight rate spectrum".[45]

In spite of the "very substantial increases in freight rates" which have taken place in 1975 and 1976, the CTC found that the CN and CP have been operating within the Anti-Inflation Guidelines which require that corporate pre-tax net profit margins be no higher than 95 per cent of the average net profit margin over the past five years.[46]

Difficulties in the Negotiation of Long-Term Contracts

A special difficulty exists in some negotiations because of the desirability of a long-term contract. This was found particularly for resource developments, but also for other movements involving specific investments in terminals or rolling stock. Three problems were evident. The first problem was to establish the general terms under which the railways would be willing to enter into a long-term contract. For example, the ownership of rolling stock and terminal facilities and the level of guaranteed contract volumes were difficult to agree upon. The long-term contracts which have been entered into because they were "essential" to project development have required escalation clauses. The second problem was over reaching agreement on an index to use on which to base an escalation clause. In some cases, Indexes of Railroad Material Price and Wage Rates put out by the Association of American Railroads were used. The question of the applicability of these data to Canada gave rise to some dissatisfaction. The absence of a Canadian rail cost index has also increased the difficulty of the railways in persuading some shippers, with rates in long-term contracts made in the early 1970's, that the rates in those contracts should be renegotiated. The third difficulty was over reaching agreement on the use of available indices. The railways often wished for an escalation clause to apply to total costs so that the revenue earned would allow for equipment replacement. Shippers wished to tie escalation to only those variable costs for which cost increases were identifiable. The railways may have been influenced by a desire to ensure a particular revenue — variable cost ratio, for example 1.4:1.0. To do this, they would need to inflate fixed as well as variable costs over time for both the ratio in the first year, which they look at closely, and the ratio in subsequent years to equal 1.4:1.0. The railways' capital budgeting and pricing decisions were not investigated in depth, so that it is not clear whether the methods of analysis used by the railways (or shippers) for long-term contract evaluation are consistent with capital budgeting theory.

Shippers' Use of Regulatory Constraints

Between 1967 and the end of 1976, very few formal appeals were made to the CTC on railway rates and even fewer decisions issued. These cases are reviewed in Chapter VIII. The purpose of this section is to examine the significance of the existing regulatory constraints in terms of making improvements in the effectiveness of the rate-making and negotiation process.

It appears that little consideration has been given by shippers or carriers to the wide interpretation possible of Section 23 of the National Transportation Act (see Appendix III-2). If the basic objective of transportation policy is taken to be the development and maintenance of an economically efficient transport system consistent with the commercial viability of the carriers, some broad interpretations affecting shipper-carrier relations are possible.

For example, in one case investigated, a shipper needed specialized rail equipment which was being prepared for hauls from different origins by both the CN and CP. The shipper became faced with a surplus of CN cars in one location and a shortage of cars at a CP local point. The shipper proposed the use of CN cars at the local CP point rather than using trucks. Unfortunately, the railways were unable to reach an agreement on a usage charge and the length of the haul on CN and CP lines. The movement took place by truck to the disadvantage of the railways, the shipper and the economy. The shipper was unaware of specific provisions in transport legislation which could cover his problem. Yet it would seem that the public interest section should be applicable when both the efficiency of the transport system and the commerical position of the railways could be improved if a rail/rail negotiating impasse could be resolved.

One broad interpretation of Section 23 has been used by shippers in two cases. That is, that reliance on the free market system to establish rates requires reasonable behaviour on the part of the railways in setting rates and that includes research and negotiation, if necessary, to establish the impact of proposed charges. This was the basic argument used by the Canadian Pulp and Paper Association in the case which they filed with the Canadian Transport Commission in 1973 to stop reduction in free time through a change in demurrage regulations.[47] The Association's brief quotes from three separate places in the decision of the Railway Transport Committee of the CTC in the Rapeseed Case as follows:

> However, in the absence of effective competition for traffic, as was the case here, rate negotiations must be conducted in an atmosphere of fairness, of give and take, with information being freely exchanged, so that the parties can bargain on a basis of equality. The National Transportation policy requires at least that much, if not more.[48]

> There was no real attempt by railway freight rate officers to make available to the applicants the facts on which the railway companies based their rate determinations; the process was one sided with all the emphasis on the factors favourable to the Railway companies.[49]

> We have earlier stated our view that the evidence in this case revealed a persistent unwillingness on the part of railway freight rate officers to react clearly, promptly and unequivocally to requests from the applicants for more favourable rates. Such behavior, in our view, cannot be condoned and is contrary to the objectives of the National Transportation Policy. We consider that freedom in rate making is conditional upon a responsibility to the shipping public in keeping with the objectives of that Policy. That responsibility includes the duty of reasonably prompt responses to shipper requests that are clear and unequivocal. Further, we consider that such requests must be met with adequate explanations based on facts known to the railways,

in cases where the railway companies consider that they are
unable to accede to such requests in whole or in part.[50]

Following scheduling of a public hearing by the CTC on the Association appeal,
the railways withdrew the proposed tariff changes and a joint Industry/Rail Task
Force was established. Subsequent to the completion of the Task Force's work,
reductions in free time were introduced in a manner generally satisfactory to
shippers.

In the second case, the receivers felt it necessary, in order to develop effective
negotiations, to make reference to the requirements imposed on the railways
under Section 23 to achieve a full understanding of the impact of a rate change
through effective negotiation. In this case, a change in negotiating responsibility
between shippers and receivers had, perhaps, resulted in some confusion on the
part of the railways, but the threat of a Section 23 appeal was enough to lead to
negotiation which produced results satisfactory to the receivers.

In five additional case studies shippers gave consideration to, or took some
steps toward, regulatory action. In three cases, informal enquiries were made to
the CTC. In one case, a shipper sought to have a commodity classification
changed. In another case, the shipper was seeking a means to avoid a fifteen
percent rate increase. In the third case, the shipper disputed the expiration date
on an agreed charge in a somewhat complicated case. In the first two cases, the
CTC advised the shippers to negotiate with the railways. In the third case, the
CTC advised the shipper of the facts from the railways' filing record. No
consideration was given to a Section 23 case by the shipper, his lawyer or the
CTC. In the final two cases, the shippers considered the possibility of a Section
23 case, but decided against it primarily on the basis of the length of time and
cost associated with such a case.

Informal use is made by shippers of the officers of the CTC, although no
record exists of the number of occasions on which shippers discussed rate
matters with them prior to 1975. The informal role of the Commission is
evidenced by the Canadian Industrial Traffic League keeping the Commission
informed of one of its disputes with the railways. During 1975, the CN and CP
proposed to hold shippers liable for third-party damages caused by their
products while in the custody of the railways. The railways withdrew this
proposal, but not before the League had conducted communications with the
CTC.

The case studies and shipper actions cited comprise evidence that the
regulatory powers in the 1967 regulatory legislation and the presence of the CTC
officers have played some role in achieving an effective resolution of shippers'
rate and service problems. This might not have occurred in the absence of any
regulatory body. However, in two respects the actions of shippers appear to
have been very limited in terms of the possibilities that seem to exist.

First, shippers appear to have given no or very little consideration to the use of an independent mediation approach to help resolve an impasse in negotiations before proceeding to litigation proceedings. This approach would provide the opportunity for a knowledgeable and practical transport economist to throw a fresh light on a dispute in the hope of providing a basis for a settlement. Recently, there has been some consideration of the mediation approach, using officers of the Canadian Transport Commission. However, it was only in 1976 that the executive of the Canadian Industrial Traffic League became aware that the CTC could deal with shippers' complaints on rate matters in places other than in Ottawa.[51]

Second, shippers have not attempted to develop their own arguments based on "the public interest". Rather, they have attempted to seek specific clauses in the legislation to apply to their own situations as they formerly did with the Railway Act and the decisions of the Board of Transport Commissioners prior to 1967. Attempts to interpret the general economic implications of Section 23 have been lacking from shippers, lawyers and academics. Therefore, the wide opportunities provided by Section 23 to bring forward cases when the railways have made errors in acts or omissions have not been fully appreciated.

If the CTC is to be expected to respond quickly and effectively in granting a hearing under Section 23 on the acts, omissions or rates of the railways which shippers believe are contrary to the public interest, it is incumbent on the shippers to present a line of argument with at least some supporting evidence sufficient to warrant the case proceeding to a hearing. It does not seem to provide an adequate basis for a CTC decision to hold a hearing, merely to describe a freight rate increase, for example, and to assert that the increase is "punitive", "unfair" and "prejudicial". Some reasonable explanation supporting the contention that the rate is against the public interest, and some reasonable evidence that it is so, should be present.

The difficulty of individual shippers being able to present arguments based on "the public interest" was recognized in the 1966 debate of the proposed National Transportation Act. Mr. Rae of the Canadian Manufacturers Association stated, "It is submitted that an individual, a company or industry could face insuperable difficulties in attempting to prove that public interest had been wronged ..."[52]

Cooperative Activities of Shippers and Carriers

Consideration of railway rate-making practices can all too easily focus on the adversary nature of rate making. On the one hand, carriers may appear to be always working to force rates upward. On the other hand, shippers may appear always to be working to get rates reduced. While these forces are certainly present, cooperative activities are very important. They flow from the fact that, in the long-run, the profitability of the railways is dependent on their ability to provide a service which is remunerative and which meets shippers' needs and enables the business of shippers to expand. Three examples of cooperative and developmental work by the railways are appropriate.

First, the market development activities of the railways are responsible for a number of service improvements and cooperative service developments. For example, the railways have planned and managed integrated transport systems for shippers and have worked cooperatively in the development of specialized equipment and services. The development of seasonal rates for the movement of potash, unit train systems, block car movements, and the development of terminal and transport systems are examples of developments which have required cooperative development.

Second, the railways participate in shipper-carrier committees and undertake joint studies of both specific and general rail transport problems. For example, the CN and five pulp and paper companies in Eastern Canada worked on a "Newsprint Distribution Research" project between 1971 and 1974. This project investigated the economics of setting up a producer-sponsored Newsprint Distribution Company that "would co-ordinate, on behalf of its participants, all 'mill-to-customer' distribution functions related to the shipping of Eastern Canadian produced newsprint to the U.S. market."[53] (The cooperation evidenced in this study did not prevent the newsprint companies from filing an appeal with the CTC in 1970 under Section 23 of the National Transportation Act in connection with rates from Eastern Canada into the U.S.A.) An example of cooperative shipper-carrier work in Western Canada is the Forest Industry Transportation Advisory Committee in Vancouver. It is composed of members of the railways and the forest industry. Traffic managers with forest products firms acknowledge that it has been effective in improving car utilization and in designing new cars.

Third, the railways have promoted the concept of physical distribution management to shippers. CP has established consulting organizations, CANALOC Distribution and Canadian Pacific Consulting Services, and CN, CANAL Distribution, to offer shippers total physical distribution studies.

Cooperative efforts by shippers and carriers do not mean that shipper/carrier relations are not without acrimony at times. However, the necessity for a shipper to appeal to the CTC on an issue does not mean that shippers wish to forego the right to negotiate or to force the railways to forego this right. The views of shippers concerning changes in legislation affecting rates and rate making are discussed in the final chapters after the evidence of the case studies is considered.

FOOTNOTES

1. This section draws extensively on research carried out by C. Jerezynski. M.Sc. student in Transportation, Faculty of Commerce and Business Administration, University of British Columbia, and Dr. Martin Christopher of the Cranfield School of Management, England, while Visiting Research Fellow, Centre for Transportation Studies, University of British Columbia, 1975.

2. T.D. Heaver, "Multi Modal Ownership, The Canadian Experience," *Transportation Journal,* Fall, 1971, pp. 14-28.

3. In CN pricing, intermodal services are under a General Rates Officer responsible for piggyback services, domestic container services and, on the West Coast, foreign container service. In CP, Intermodal Services, which is a separate function reporting to the VP Freight Marketing and Sales, is responsible for all movements of trailers and containers on flat cars, and all pricing except overseas container traffic.

4. For a description of early railroad organization in England and the U.S.A. and of the development of railway organization in the U.S.A. to the present day, see D. Daryl Wyckoff, *Railroad Management* (Lexington, Mass.: D.C. Heath and Co., 1975).

5. Examples of early reports by the Research Department, CP, include, "Summary of the Working Papers for the Study of the Costs of Handling Grain and Grain Products in Western Canada", 1948, and "The Trucking Industry in Western Canada", 1952.

6. For example, in a speech, "New Look in Traffic Prices", given to the Canadian Industrial Traffic League, Toronto, February 15, 1962, I.D. Sinclair, then V.P. of the CPR, made reference to "the application of the new concept of total distribution costs".

7. W.G. Scott, "Traffic Developments in the 60's", Address to the Peterborough Traffic Club, Sept. 21, 1960. The Annual Report of the CNR, 1960 also recognized the need to adjust to the competitive environment: "The experience (1960's financial record) served to highlight the necessity for pressing forward with programs designed to mould the System into an instrument better able to adjust and respond to both the prevailing business climate and the shifts and new challenges of a highly competitive transportation market".

8. Scott, *op.cit.,* pp. 5-6.

9. D.W. Carr and Associates, "Truck-Rail Competition in Canada", *Royal Commission on Transportation,* Vol. III, 1961, especially pp. 63-79.

10. Wyckoff, *op.cit.,* pp. 3, 7-8. Wyckoff recommends decentralization; see pp. 127-128.

11. B. Mallen and J.F. Pernotte, *Decision Making and Attitudes of Canadian Freight and Cargo Transportation Buyers* (Montreal: Faculty of Commerce, Sir George Williams University, 1972), p. 27.

12. Section 279 of the Railway Act states:

> Railway companies shall exchange such information with respect to costs as may be required under this Act and may agree upon and charge common rates under and in accordance with regulations or orders made by the Commission.

Section 32(2) of the Transport Act states:

> No agreement for an agreed change for the transport by rail from or to a competitive point, or between competitive points, on the lines of two or more carriers by rail shall be made unless the competing carriers by rail consent thereto in writing or join in making it.

13. The following shipper organizations were responsible for or involved in negotiating some issues affecting rates in the cases studied: Brewers Association of Canada, Canadian Canners Assoc., Canadian Fertilizer Institute, Canadian Food Processors': Assoc.,

Canadian Meatpackers Council, Canadian Millers' Assoc., Canpotac, Council of Forest Industries of B.C., Import Car Assoc. of Canada, Motor Vehicle Manufacturers Assoc., Petroleum Traffic Committee, Pulp and Paper Assoc. of Canada, and the Rubber Association of Canada.

14. J.W. Pickersgill, "Canada's National Transport Policy", *Transportation Law Journal,* January 1969, pp. 79-86.

15. Canada, House of Commons, 27th Parliament, 1st Session, Standing Committee on Transport and Communications, Minutes of Proceedings and Evidence, October 27, 1966, p. 2,127.

16. *Western Economic Opportunities Conference Transportation Paper,* jointly submitted by the Premiers of Saskatchewan, British Columbia, Manitoba, and Alberta, (Calgary, 1973), p. 3.

17. Canada, Transport Canada, *Transportation Policy, A Framework for Transport in Canada* (Ottawa: Information Canada, 1975), p. 28.

18. Letter from A.A. Landry, President, Canadian Industrial Traffic League, to Mr. N. Mulder, Transport Canada and to the Hon. O.E. Lang, Minister of Transport, July 8, 1976.

19. *Transportation Policy, A Framework for Transport in Canada, op.cit.,* p. 29.

20. Standing Committee, *op.cit.,* pp. 2,521-2,522.

21. Canada, *Royal Commission on Transportation,* known as the MacPherson Commission, (Ottawa: Queen's Printer), Vol. II, 1961, Chapter 4.

22. *Ibid.,* pp. 47-48.

23. *Ibid.,* p. 48.

24. Standing Committee, *op.cit.,* p. 1,977.

25. *Ibid.,* p. 1,981.

26. *Ibid.,* pp. 1,760-1,761.

27. *Ibid.,* p. 2,107.

28. *Ibid.,* p. 1,931.

29. *Ibid.,* p. 2,594.

30. *Ibid.,* p. 2,804.

31. Statistics Canada, *Rail Transport, Part II Financial Statistics,* (Statistics Canada, 52-208) 1975 and 1971.

32. Standing Committee, *op.cit.,* p. 1,668.

33. For a discussion of the status of the CN and other Crown Corporations, see C.A. Ashley and R.G.H. Smails, *Canadian Crown Corporations,* (Toronto: MacMillan, 1965). See especially Chapters 5, 6 and 10.

34. A negotiated settlement on freight rate increases on iron and steel products was reported in the *Vancouver Province,* March 9, 1974. These increases stayed in effect in spite of the public announcement by Federal Transport Minister Jean Marchand than he would have the increases rolled back, *Vancouver Province,* March 14, 1974. (A number of statements attributed to Mr. Marchand during 1974 and 1975 implied powers beyond those possessed by the Minister of Transport!)

35. Between 1961 and 1965 inclusive, the railways performed the following numbers of point-to-point costings: 13,200; 18,000; 24,700; 21,300; 21,900; R.A. Bandeen, Standing Committee, *op.cit.,* p. 1,723.

36. J.C. Gardiner, Standing Committee, *op.cit.,* p. 1,808.

37. Atlantic Provinces Transportation Commission, *LCL Rate Cancellation,* Circular No. 75-3, February 14, 1975, p. 5.

38. Provincial concern with horizontal percentage increases was expressed in the WEOC Transportation Paper, *op.cit.,* p. 2. Mr. Marchand's opposition to "across-the-board"

freight rate increases was made clear following a meeting with the Western Provinces; see *Vancouver Province,* February 25, 1975; and "Joint Communique Federal/Provincial Ministers Meeting on Western Transportation", Transport Canada, *News,* November 10, 1975.

39. Dissatisfaction of shippers with freight sales representatives of all modes has been expressed elsewhere; see Mallen and Pernotte, *op.cit.,* pp. 30-33, and "Editorial" in *Traffic Management,* August 1976, p. 9.

40. Discussion of paper by A.L. Morton in *Perspectives on Federal Transport Policy,* ed. James C. Miller III (Washington D.C.: American Enterprise Institute for Public Policy Research, 1975), p. 51.

41. Canadian Industrial Traffic League, *Traffic Notes,* Issue No. 4772, July 29, 1975.

42. *Ibid.,* Issue No. 4796, January 20, 1976, p. 8.

43. Canadian Transport Commission, *Monitoring of Increases in Railway Freight Rates Under the Anti-Inflation Act and Regulations,* Railway Transport Committee, Anti-Inflation Report No. 1, August, 1976, p. 16.

44. *Ibid.,* pp. 16-17.

45. *Ibid.,* p. 18.

46. *Ibid.,* pp. 18-19.

47. Canadian Transport Commission, *An Application by the Canadian Pulp and Paper Association for an Order Pursuant to Section 59 of the National Transportation Act,* 27 July, 1973.

48. Canadian Transport Commission, *Saskatchewan Wheat Pool et.al. v. Canadian National Railways et.al.,* Railway Transport Committee, Decision, File No. 30637.2, 1973, p. 44.

49. *Ibid,* p. 46.

50. *Ibid.,* p. 53.

51. Canadian Industrial Traffic League, "CTC Regional Transportation Advisory Officers" *Traffic Notes,* October 14, 1976.

52. Standing Committee, *op.cit.,* p. 1,928.

53. *Distribution of Eastern Canadian Newsprint to the United States Market,* Project Report of Newsprint Distribution Research, September 1974, p. 1.

APPENDIX TO CHAPTER III
EXTRACTS FROM CANADIAN STATUTES

APPENDIX III-1
Statement of National Transportation Policy
(National Transportation Act 1966-67, c.69, s.2, Section 3.)

3. It is hereby declared that an economic, efficient and adequate transportation system making the best use of all available modes of transportation at the lowest total cost is essential to protect the interests of the users of transportation and to maintain the economic well-being and growth of Canada, and that these objectives are most likely to be achieved when all modes of transport are able to compete under conditions ensuring that having due regard to national policy and to legal and constitutional requirements

(a) regulation of all modes of transport will not be of such a nature as to restrict the ability of any mode of transport to compete freely with any other modes of transport;

(b) each mode of transport, so far as practicable, bears a fair proportion of the real costs of the resources, facilities and services provided that mode of transport at public expense;

(c) each mode of transport, so far as practicable, receives compensation for the resources, facilities and services that it is required to provide as an imposed public duty; and

(d) each mode of transport, so far as practicable, carries traffic to or from any point in Canada under tolls and conditions that do not constitute

(i) an unfair disadvantage in respect of any such traffic beyond that disadvantage inherent in the location or volume of the traffic, the scale of operation connected therewith or the type of traffic or service involved, or

(ii) an undue obstacle to the interchange of commodities between points in Canada or unreasonable discouragement to the development of primary or secondary industries or to export trade in or from any region of Canada or to the movement of commodities through Canadian ports;

and this Act is enacted in accordance with and for the attainment of so much of these objectives as fall within the purview of subject-matters under the jurisdiction of Parliament relating to transportation.

110

APPENDIX III-2
Public Interest Section of the National Transportation Act
(National Transportation Act 1966-67, c.69, s.2, Section 23)

23. (1) In this section "carrier" means any person engaged for hire or reward in transport, to which the legislative authority of the Parliament of Canada extends, by railway, water, aircraft, motor vehicle undertaking or commodity pipeline;
"public interest" includes, without limiting the generality thereof, the public interest as described in section 3.

(2) Where a person has reason to believe
> (a) that any act or omission of a carrier or of any two or more carriers, or
> (b) that the effect of any rate established by a carrier or carriers pursuant to this Act or the *Railway Act* after the 19th day of September 1967,

may prejudicially affect the public interest in respect of tolls for, or conditions of, the carriage of traffic within, into or from Canada, such person may apply to the Commission for leave to appeal the act, omission or rate, and the Commission shall, if it is satisfied that a *prima facie* case has been made, make such investigation of the act, omission or rate and the effect thereof, as in its opinion is warranted.

(3) In conducting an investigation under this section, the Commission shall have regard to all considerations that appear to it to be relevant, including, without limiting the generality of the foregoing,
> (a) whether the tolls or conditions specified for the carriage of traffic under the rate so established are such as to create
>> (i) an unfair disadvantage beyond any disadvantage that may be deemed to be inherent in the location or volume of the traffic, the scale of operation connected therewith or the type of traffic or service involved, or
>> (ii) an undue obstacle to the interchange of commodities between points in Canada or an unreasonable discouragement to the development of primary or secondary industries or to export trade in or from any region of Canada or to the movement of commodities through Canadian ports; or
> (b) whether control by, or the interests of a carrier in, another form of transportation service, or control of a carrier by, or the interest in the carrier of, a company or person engaged in another

111

RAILWAY PRICING UNDER COMMERCIAL FREEDOM

form of transportation service may be involved.

(4) If the Commission, after a hearing, finds that the act, omission or rate in respect of which the appeal is made is prejudicial to the public interest, the Commission may, notwithstanding the fixing of any rate pursuant to section 278 of the *Railway Act* but having regard to sections 276 and 277 of that Act, make an order requiring the carrier to remove the prejudicial feature in the relevant tolls or conditions specified for the carriage of traffic or such other order as in the circustmances it may consider proper, or it may report thereon to the Governor in Council for any action that is considered appropriate.

APPENDIX III-3
Agreed Charge Legislation
(Transport Act. R.S., c.271, s.1, Part IV.)

AGREED CHARGES

32. (1) Notwithstanding anything in the *Railway Act* or in this Act, a carrier may make such charges for the transport from one point in Canada to another point in Canada of goods of a shipper as are agreed between the carrier and the shipper.

(2) No agreement for an agreed charge for the transport by rail from or to a competitive point, or between competitive points, on the lines of two or more carriers by rail shall be made unless the competing carriers by rail consent thereto in writing or join in making it.

(3) Subsections (1) and (2) do not apply to a railway company incorporated in the United States and owning, or operating on, a railway line in Canada (in this section called a "United States carrier") except as between points on its lines in Canada served exclusively by such carrier.

(4) Notwithstanding subsection (3), where an agreement for an agreed charge has been made by a carrier by rail, whether before or after the 28th day of July 1955, and the railway of a United States carrier

(a) operates at a point of origin or destination named in the agreement for an agreed charge or between such points, and

(b) constitutes, or forms part of, a continuous route by rail established between such points, entirely in Canada or partly in Canada and partly in the United States,

the United States carrier is entitled to become a party to the agreement if all the railway companies over whose lines the continuous route is established concur, and the United States carrier files with the Commission a notice of intention to become a party to the agreement.

(5) Where an agreement for an agreed charge is made by a carrier by rail any carrier by water that has established through routes and interchange arrangements with a carrier by rail shall be entitled to become a party to an agreement for an agreed charge and to participate in that agreed charge on a basis of differentials to be agreed upon in respect of the transport from or to a competitive point or between competitive points served by the carrier by water

113

of goods with regard to which the carrier by water is required by this Act to file tariffs of tolls.

(6) An agreed charge shall be made on the established basis of rate making and shall be expressed in cents per hundred pounds or such other unit of weight or measurement as is appropriate; and the car-load rate for one car shall not exceed the car-load rate for any greater number of cars.

(7) An agreement for an agreed charge shall be prepared and executed in tariff form, and a duplicate original thereof shall, in accordance with regulations prescribed by the Commission, be filed with the Commission within seven days after the day the agreement was made, and the agreed charge takes effect twenty days after the day the agreement therefor was so filed.

(8) The agreement for an agreed charge, after it has been filed with the Commission, shall be published in the manner provided by subsection 275(1) of the *Railway Act*.

(9) Where an agreement for an agreed charge has been made between a carrier and a shipper, any other shipper may with the consent of the carrier become a party to the agreement by filing a notice of intent with the Commission in accordance with regulations prescribed by the Commission, and the agreed charge takes effect in relation to such other shipper on such day, not earlier than the day the agreement was made, as the carrier and such other shipper may agree upon.

(10) Any shipper who considers that his business is or will be unjustly discriminated against by an agreed charge may at any time apply to the Commission for a charge to be fixed for the transport by the same carrier with which the agreed charge was made of goods of the shipper that are the same as or similar to, and are offered for carriage under substantially similar circumstances and conditions as, the goods to which the agreed charge relates, and, if the Commission is satisfied that the business of the shipper is or will be unjustly discriminatd against by the agreed charge, it may fix a charge, including the conditions to be attached thereto, to be made by the carrier for the transport of the goods of the shipper, and may fix the day on which those charges shall be effective, not being earlier than the day on which the agreement for the agreed charge was made.

(11) Where an agreement for an agreed charge or any amendment thereto has been filed and notice of the issue of the charge has been

114

given in accordance with this Act and the regulations, orders and directions of the Commission, the charge shall conclusively be deemed to be the lawful charge in respect of the transport of the goods referred to in the agreement until it expires or is otherwise terminated, and after the day on which the agreement takes effect, until it expires or is otherwise terminated, the carrier shall make the charge as specified therein.

(12) Notwithstanding anything in an agreement for an agreed charge, any party to the agreement, if it has been in effect at least one year, may withdraw from the agreement by giving written notice of withdrawal to all other parties thereto at least ninety days before the day upon which the withdrawal is to become effective.

33. (1) Where an agreed charge has been in effect for at least three months

(a) any carrier, or association of carriers, by water or rail,

(b) any association or other body representative of the shippers of any locality, or

(c) any association or other body representative of the motor vehicle operators of Canada or of a province thereof

may complain to the Minister that the agreed charge is unjustly discriminatory against a carrier or a motor vehicle operator or a shipper or places his business at an unfair disadvantage, and the Minister may, if he is satisfied that in the public interest the complaint should be investigated, refer the complaint to the Commission for investigation.

(2) The Governor in Council, if he has reason to believe that an agreed charge may be undesirable in the public interest, may refer the agreed charge to the Commission for investigation.

(3) In dealing with a reference under this section the Commission shall have regard to all considerations that appear to it to be relevant, including the effect that the making of the agreed charges has had or is likely to have on the net revenue of the carriers who are parties to it, and in particular shall determine whether the agreed charge is undesirable in the public interest on the ground that it is unjustly discriminatory against any person complaining against it or places his business at an unfair disadvantage or on any other ground, and, if so directed by the Governor in Council in a reference under subsection (2), whether the agreed charge is undesirable in the public interest on the ground that it places any other form of transportatin

115

services at an unfair disadvantage.

(4) If the Commission, after a hearing, finds that the agreed charge is undesirable in the public interest on the ground that is is unjustly discriminatory against any person complaining against it or places his business or any other form of transportation services at an unfair disadvantage or on any other ground, the Commission may make an order varying or cancelling the agreed charge or such other order as in the circumstances it considers proper.

(5) When under this section the Commission varies or cancels an agreed charge, any charge fixed under subsection 32(10) in favour of a shipper complaining of that agreed charge ceases to operate or is subject to such corresponding modifications as the Commission determines.

34. Nothing in this Part affects any right or obligation granted or imposed by the *Maritime Freight Rates Act* or by Term 32 of the Terms of Union of Newfoundland with Canada, or by subsection 265(8) or section 271 or 272 of the *Railway Act*.

35. This Part dos not apply to the transport by water of goods in bulk on waters other than the Mackenzie River.

APPENDIX III-4
Maximum Rate Regulation Through Application For A Fixed Rate
(Railway Act, Section 278)
(Railway Act. R.S. c.234, s.1, Section 278.)

278. (1) A shipper of goods for which in respect of those goods there is no alternative, effective and competitive service by a common carrier other than a rail carrier or carriers or a combination of rail carriers may, if he is dissatisfied with the rate applicable to the carriage of those goods after negotiation with a rail carrier for an adjustment of the rate, apply to the Commission to have the probable range within which a fixed rate for the carriage of the goods would fall determined by the Commission; and the Commission shall inform the shipper of the range within which a fixed rate for the carriage of the goods would probably fall.

(2) After being informed by the Commission of the probable range within which a fixed rate for the carriage of the goods would fall, the shipper may apply to the Commission to fix a rate for the carriage of the goods, and the Commission may after such investigation as it deems necessary fix a rate equal to the variable cost of the carriage of the goods and an amount equal to one hundred and fifty per cent of the variable cost as the fixed rate applicable to the carriage of the goods in respect of which the application was made (hereinafter in this section referred to as the "goods concerned").

(3) In determining the variable cost of the carriage of goods for the purposes of this section, the Commission shall
(a) have regard to all items and factors prescribed by regulations of the Commission as being relevant in the determination of variable costs;
(b) compute the costs of capital in all cases by using the costs of capital approved by the Commission as proper for the Canadian Pacific Railway Company;
(c) calculate the cost of carriage of the goods concerned on the basis of carloads of thirty thousand pounds in the standard railway equipment for such goods; and
(d) if the goods concerned may move between points in Canada by alternative routes of two or more railway companies, compute the variable cost on the basis of the costs of the lowest cost rail route.

117

(4) Where a fixed rate is made under this section, the Commission shall forthwith notify the shipper of the rate so fixed, and if within thirty days of the mailing of the notice to the shipper by the Commission, the shipper enters into a written undertaking with a railway company, in a form satisfactory to the Commission, to ship the goods concerned by rail in accordance with this section, the company shall file and publish a tariff of the fixed rate which shall be effective upon such date as the Commission may, by order or regulation, direct.

(5) When a shipper enters into a written undertaking as provided in subsection (4).

(a) the shipper shall cause to be shipped by rail, for a period of one year from the date the fixed rate takes effect and for so long thereafter as the fixed rate as originally fixed or as altered under paragraph (8)(a) remains in force, all shipments of the goods concerned except such shipments as the Commission may from time to time authorize to be shipped for experimental purposes by another mode of transport; and

(b) the charges for any shipments of the goods concerned in the standard railway equipment for goods of that type shall be

(i) except in any case coming under subparagraph (ii) or (iii), at the fixed rate on the basis of a minimum carload weight of thirty thousand pounds, and for shipments under thirty thousand pounds, at the prevailing rate under the tariffs of the company for goods of that type unless the shipper assumes the charges for a shipment of thirty thousand pounds at the fixed rate,

(ii) except in any case coming under subparagraph (iii), if the carload weight of a single shipment of the goods concerned is fifty thousand pounds or more, at a rate to be determined by deducting from the fixed rate an amount equal to one-half the amount of the reduction in the variable cost of the shipment of the goods concerned below the amount of the variable cost with reference to which the fixed rate was established, but rates need be determined under this subparagraph only as required and then for minimum carload weights based on units of twenty thousand added to thirty thousand and a rate for a carload weight in excess of fifty thousand pounds and between any two minimum carload weights so established shall be the rate for the lower of such minimum carload weights, or

(iii) at such rate less than the fixed rate, on the basis of such

118

minimum carload weight, as the shipper may negotiate with a railway company at the time he enters into the written undertaking or at any time thereafter, and every such rate so negotiated shall be filed and published in accordance with regulations, orders or directions made by the Commission.

(6) The Commission may require any shipper for whom a rate has been fixed under this section to supply any information to the Commission, or to make available for the inspection of the Commission, shipping books, shipping records and invoice records of every kind for the purpose of verifying that the shipper has complied with paragraph (5)(a); and where it is shown to the Commission that the shipper has contravened that paragraph, or where the shipper defaults in giving the Commission any information required by it, the Commission may authorize cancellation of the fixed rate in respect of the goods concerned.

(7) Where a fixed rate has been cancelled pursuant to an authorization under subsection (6), the company may recover from the shipper for all goods shipped at the maximum rate the difference between charges at the maximum rate and charges based on the rate in effect on such goods immediately before the effective date of the maximum rate, and, in addition, the company is entitled to liquidated damages at the rate of ten per cent of the maximum rate on all goods shipped by the shipper otherwise than in accordance with the provisions of the written undertaking referred to in subsection (4).

(8) At any time after the expiration of one year from the date the fixed rate became effective in respect of the carriage by rail of the goods concerned,

(a) the Commission may, upon being satisfied of a change in the variable cost in relation to which a rate was fixed under this section, alter the fixed rate as the Commission may specify;

(b) the shipper may give notice in writing to the Commission and to any railway company with whom he had shipped the goods concerned that the shipper no longer desires to be bound by the written undertaking entered into in respect of the goods concerned on and after a date specified in the notice, not being earlier than ten days from the date of the notice, and thereupon his undertaking is terminated as of the date so specified, and the fixed rate shall be cancelled in respect of the goods concerned; and

(c) where the Commission is satisfied that there is available to the shipper in respect of the goods concerned an alternative, effective and competitive service by a common carrier other than a rail carrier or carriers or combination of rail carriers, the Commission by order may, upon the application of a railway company, authorize the cancellation of the fixed rate as originally fixed or as altered under paragraph (a) in respect of the goods concerned, upon such date, not being earlier than ten days from the date of the order, as is stated in the order.

(9) An application under this section shall be in such form and contain such information as the Commission may by regulation or otherwise require and without limiting the generality of the foregoing,

(a) an application under subsection (1) shall be accompanied by copies of all letters and documents exchanged between the shipper and any railway company in respect of the negotiations between the shipper and the rail carriers for an adjustment in the rate applicable to the goods to be shipped or received by the shipper; and

(b) in the case of an application under subsection (2) the shipper making the application shall pay to the Receiver General for the use of Her Majesty such fee, if any, as may be determined by the Commission but not exceeding in any event twenty-five dollars.

(10) This section is subject to the *Maritime Freight Rates Act* and Term 32 of the Terms of Union of Newfoundland with Canada.

(11) This section does not apply in respect of any freight rate in effect upon the 1st day of August 1966, including any freight rate payable by a shipper at a level provided for on the principles of the *Freight Rates Reduction Act,* until that freight rate advances above the level payable by a shipper as of the 1st day of August 1966.

(12) If the goods of a shipper pass over any continuous rail route in Canada operated by two or more railway companies, the expression "company" as used in this section shall be taken to mean each such company.

(13) In this section "shipper" means a person sending or desiring to send goods between points in Canada or who receives or desires to receive goods shipped between points in Canada.

(14) Notwithstanding subsection (11), where immediately before the 23rd day of March 1967 a reduced freight rate was in effect pursuant to section 468 of chapter 234 of the Revised Statutes of Canada, 1952, an advance in that rate shall be deemed not to be an

advance in the freight rate payable by a shipper until that freight rate advances to a level beyond any level authorized by the Commission under section 412.

(15) Subsection (11) expires two years after the 22nd day of March 1967 unless, before that date, a later date is fixed for its expiration by proclamation of the Governor in Council in which case that subsection expires on such later date.

(16) As soon as practicable after the expiration of four years from the 22nd day of March 1967 the Commission shall, after holding such public hearings as it may deem expedient and hearing the submissions of interested parties, report to the Governor in Council on the operation of this section and matters relevant thereto and, having regard to the national transportation policy, shall make such recommendations to the Governor in Council with respect to the operation of the section as the Commission considers desirable in the public interest.

APPENDIX III-5
Rail Traffic Subject to Customs Duties
(Railway Act. R.S., c.234, s.1, Section 382.)

382. (1) All goods carried or being carried over any continuous route, from a point in Canada through a foreign country into Canada, operated by two or more companies whether Canadian or foreign, are, unless companies have filed with the Commission a joint tariff for such continuous route, subject upon admission into Canada, to customs duties, as if such goods were of foreign production and coming into Canada for the first time.

(2) Such goods are subject to a customs duty of thirty per cent of the value thereof, if they would not be subject to any customs duty in case they were of foreign production, and coming into Canada for the first time.

(3) If any such duty is paid by the consignor or consignee of such goods, the same shall be repaid on demand to the person so paying by the company or companies owning or operating so much of such continuous line or route as lies within Canada.

Exhibit 1

An Example of a Letter of May, 1975, from CFA for a Change in an Agreed Charge

Dear Sir:

Subject: Agreed Charge CTC (AC) No XXX

This agreement has been of mutual benefit in the past and the rail carriers would like to continue to participate in the movement of your traffic. At the same time, I am sure you are aware of the significant cost increases the rail carriers have incurred in recent months in all aspects of their operations. These escalations have become more frequent of late, and it is likely this upward trend will continue for an indefinite period in all sectors of industry.

In this uncertain economic environment, the rail carriers, facing spiralling increases in labour, fuel and material expenses, find it most difficult to enter into long term commitments in tariff rates. This is made the more difficult when numerous changes and unforeseen increases are taking place on a monthly basis in their own operations. Because of these features, the carriers are, wherever possible, cancelling Agreed Charge publications and publishing rates in open tariff.

Consequently, they regret that they have no alternative but to give Statutory Notice in compliance with the terms of this Agreed Charge contract to cancel the rates effective August 31, 1975.

However, it is recognized that in certain instances, an Agreed Charge arrangement will better serve the interest of the rail carriers and shippers even in these troubled times. This agreement falls into this category and the carriers are prepared to continue it in effect with the application of a XX increase effective September 1, 1975.

Inasmuch as these rates have not been increased over the past twelve months, we trust you will appreciate that an increase is required to offset rising costs.

Since it is necessary that the new rates be on file with the Canadian Transport Commission at least three weeks prior to the effective date, you will understand that in order to do all the preparatory work, it is essential that the attached supplement be signed and returned to reach this Association no later than June 23, 1975. If you do not wish to remain a party to the contract, will you please advise within the same period of time, in which event open tariff rates will, of course, be available.

In the past, your co-operation in enabling us to comply with the required procedures has been most helpful and appreciated and we look forward to your further assistance to ensure continuation of the Agreed Charge.

Yours truly,
P.J. Lavallee, Chairman
Canadian Freight Association

123

Exhibit 2

Joint Letter of Canadian National Railways and CP Rail Concerning Proposed Rate Increases, 1975.

In a joint letter Canadian National Railways and CP Rail have announced a 20% freight rate increase to impact on a host of bulk items including in a later letter, plastics. You will note that the rails say that they will give careful consideration to any submissions made by interested parties.

"Freight Rates covering the movement of Chemicals, Gases other than Petroleum, Acids, Salt, Salt Cake, Soda Products, Alcohols, Calcined Alumina, Crude Barium Sulphate, Barytes, Insecticides and Fungicides in the tariff Items outlined in the attached statements, moving within Canada, were maintained at the same level from February 1972 until 1 January 1975, when they were increased by an average of 25% in two stages.

An analysis of the effects of current inflationary conditions on the Railway's costs indicates the cost of labour will have increased an average of 68%, and the cost of materials consumed by the Railways will have increased an average of 89% from the end of 1971 until the end of 1975. On the other hand, our rate adjustments since 1 January 1972 have averaged only 32%.

Furthermore, the Railways have reached the point in time when large capital investments in equipment, power, terminals and rail network must be made to provide sufficient capacity and maintain adequate levels of service. The investment required to sustain a viable freight service is substantial, and will necessitate a marked increase in cash flow if it is to be commercially sound.

We believe you will appreciate that the additional revenues required to offset the increases in our costs of doing business and the money required to sustain and improve our rail systems must be secured from the users of rail service by means of freight rate increases.

It is essential that we secure additional revenues as soon as possible if we are to ensure that a viable operation is maintained, and to this end we intend increasing freight rates on commodities moving within Canada. This is to advise you that freight rates outlined on the attached statements will be increased by 20% to become effective 12 June 1975.

We appreciate that costs in general have increased for all concerned over the past several years, and as such the increase may affect certain movements more seriously than others from a market or mode competitive standpoint. In such situations, we are naturally quite prepared to carefully review any submission made, or if discussions are required, arrangements will be made to meet with interested parties. We would suggest that your submissions be presented to our Regional Pricing Officers involved, who shall be pleased to deal with them.

We trust you are aware that in publishing freight rates the Railways must allow sufficient lead time so that at least 30 days advance notice of increases in freight rates is given to the Canadian Transport Commission. In view of the notice required, it is essential that those parties desiring discussion make their positions known as soon as possible in order that scheduling of meetings can be arranged."

Source: Canadian Industrial Traffic League, Traffic Notes, Issue No. 4759, April 29, 1975, pp. 5-6.

CHAPTER IV

DYNAMIC COMPETITIVE FORCES IN FREIGHT TRANSPORT

How the mix of competitive and monopolistic forces in transport markets actually do work, given the commercial freedom that exists, is a difficult matter to analyze, trace out, and test for accuracy. Among other things, the effects of the forces on services and their availability, on prices for transport services of various kinds and under varying conditions, on utilization of scarce resources and human labor, on the rate of innovation, on the rate of return to capital and investment, and on social considerations all have to be determined from voluminous and complex market, industry organizational, and cost and pricing facts. Not only are the data for analyzing those aspects generally insufficient or deficient, but all of the transport industries are dynamic, always in a process of change and movement. Sophisticated statistical methods are required for sampling, analysis and testing of the data that can be assembled. And, of course, the relevant economic theory must be applied. At best, analysis of the effects and workability of competition in particular industries leaves much to be desired. Yet this task must be undertaken as well and as accurately as possible in order for a society to know whether to promote free or regulated markets.

It is helpful, therefore, to look to the economic theory of markets, at least briefly, for guidance as to how competitive forces tend to work under various states of market organization and assumptions. How competitive forces work in ideal competitive markets to relate price to cost and to bring about efficient output at least cost, can give highly useful standards for analyzing the economic performance of industries and markets in the real world in which markets generally fall short of being ideal ones, either in organization, in market conduct, or in accomplishment of economic results. However, such standards from perfect competition alone do not suffice for this analysis.[1] It is also necessary to review what microeconomic theory reveals as to the price, output, cost and profit tendencies under conditions of monopoly, duopoly, oligopoly and cartel organization of markets, as these states are found more frequently than perfect or pure competition in the real world and in transport industries.

But useful as theory can be, alone it cannot be relied on to predict how the

127

competitive forces in Canadian transport markets have been working out in practice or what the economic results are that will flow from the operation of such forces in the future. To draw conclusions on how competitive forces work in actual markets, then, attention must be given to the extent to which the factors favorable to effective competition actually exist[2], to the facts pertaining to shipper-carrier rate negotiations and organizations, as given in Chapter III, and to the nature and effectiveness of the actual and potential transport, supply and locational alternatives available to shippers as bases for the negotiation of railway rates. Indeed, the attitudes, perceptions and actions of individual competitors, as well as of buyers, can influence the operation and results of competitive forces significantly. In Canadian transport, the ability and vigor of the shippers in exploring intramodal, intermodal, market and locational alternatives have much to do with whether or not railway rates behave like competitive prices. To an extent, the aggressiveness of individual railways on the sellers' side of the market in exploiting market opportunities will influence railway pricing along competitive lines, even in markets served only by railways.

Much can be learned about the feasibility, operation and effects of competitive forces in Canadian transport by an analysis that combines the relevant economic theory with exploration of the dynamics and conditions of competition that actually exist in Canadian freight markets, including those for railway freight services. Theory shows how effectively competitive markets could be expected to work in limiting rates and in influencing service offerings and efficient production, but only an analysis of the competitive conditions and dynamic forces that actually exist and are developing in Canadian transport markets can reveal whether the expectations of theory are substantially or fully realized by policies that allow and promote competition in transport. Hence, this Chapter, in addition to reviewing briefly the expectations of the relevant theory, will describe the factors influencing the nature of competition in transport and the dynamic competitive conditions that exist today and are likely to continue in the future. If the prerequisites of effective or workable competition are found substantially to exist in Canada, then a reasonable inference might be that the beneficient effects of competition would be substantially achievable without the restrictive influences of comprehensive government economic regulation.

Pricing Under Different Market States According to Theory

The economic theory of the firm provides guides to profitable and economic pricing for transport firms.[3] The model of perfect, or pure, competition is usually regarded as a standard by which a firm's pricing can be judged, even when the industry under consideration does not have firms which exhibit all of the rather stringent assumptions that theory requires of the truly competitive firm. Employment of the perfectly or purely competitive model is justifiable because it reveals clearly the price-cost relation and output conditions required

128

for allocative efficiency, even for the few industries that are best organized as government-regulated or government-operated monopolies.

Pricing under Perfect or Pure Competition

Under the perfect or pure competition model, there must be many sellers and buyers in the market so that no seller or buyer can influence the market price by withdrawal of supply or purchase. Output of the firms must be homogeneous. There must be no barriers to entry or lack of mobility of scarce resources. Both sellers and buyers must be knowledgeable about supply and demand conditions and they must be rational in their market actions. That is, sellers seek to maximize profits and buyers seek to maximize consumer satisfaction and other gains. Of course, these are rigorous conditions seldom found completely in real markets, including in transport. Notwithstanding, the model does reveal how competition, when ideally present and effective, works to fix price to cost and to maximize output and efficiency in the use of scarce resources.

Under this ideal model of perfect or pure competition, price is fixed through the interaction between supply and demand in the market place. In the short term, therefore, the competitive firm can be making more than normal rates of return on particular products or less than normal rates of return. However, the tendency will exist for prices always to return to levels approximating minimum average total unit costs and returns to move toward normal rates of return. In the long run, when the firm and industry are in competitive equilibrium, price will be equal to marginal cost and also equal to average total unit cost, and marginal revenue (the competitive price) will be equal both to marginal cost and to average total unit cost. Output will be at the ideal level, for any greater output would have a marginal cost greater than marginal revenue and any lesser output would have a marginal cost less than marginal revenue. Firms will be operating at the optimum size for the firm and at the optimal rate of output. Finally, the returns for the different products or services produced would tend to be the same, providing the risk to capital were the same and equilibrium conditions could be maintained.

The output and price-cost relations just described are found most frequently in industries whose firms have conditions of constant costs or increasing costs. Firms whose costs are almost totally variable with output will tend to lack significant economies of scale in size of firm, will lack high ratios of fixed to total annual costs, and will not have chronic excess capacity; as output expands, their unit costs will tend to be constant. In industries, including some modes of transport, in which such cost conditions obtain, entry and exit of firms will be easy and there will be many competing firms, especially in the large markets. Hence, given rational conduct and knowledgeable buyers and sellers, the presence of many firms and many buyers in the markets will assure that competition will work to yield as low prices as possible, nondiscriminating prices

129

except in true joint-cost conditions, good-quality products and services, efficient production and returns to capital that are no greater than necessary. Obviously, competition works ideally for the consumers and the general public when such conditions hold in an industry or an economy.

Pricing under Monopoly

Simple monopoly exists in a market or industry when there is only one seller facing many buyers of his products or services. Bilateral monopoly exists where there is only one buyer facing one seller. Obviously, in these types of market which occur far more rarely than markets of imperfect competition having elements of monopoly, the many-firm condition of perfectly or highly competitive industries does not obtain. Hence, the monopolist, say one railroad or one public utility serving a market, is not constrained by the rivalry of other similar firms in his pricing or other activities except in the form of substitute products of services. However, the monopolist may be constrained by the buyer in bilateral monopoly. The behavior of the buyer in bilateral monopoly can influence the price fixed by the monopolist seller, a complicated market situation in which the outcome depends on the bargaining skill of the parties. Seldom does a monopolist have unlimited power to fix prices, but the buyer's position is weak under simple monopoly because his alternatives are not very good or nonexistent.

In the simple monopoly situation, the monopolist fixes a uniform price on the demand curve but limits output to that which equates his marginal revenue with his marginal cost. Since the monopolist is the only seller, the demand curve that he faces is the community demand curve, a downward sloping one with the marginal revenue less than price. Like the competitive firm, the monopolist seller seeks to maximize his profits. But he can do this by limiting his output to that fixed by the intersection of his marginal revenue with his marginal cost and by setting his price above his average total unit cost for that output. If the monopolist has decreasing costs with increasing utilization, his marginal cost will be below his average total unit cost. But as the price for the limited output will be above that average total unit cost, the monopolist will earn monopoly profits even though his output will be below the quantity which would be produced under competitive conditions. However, if the monopolist could achieve economies of scale over those any competitive firm could obtain if the market were organized with more firms, the monopolist could achieve his monopoly profit maximization objective by producing more output at a lower price than competitive firms could (the natural monopoly situation). So long as the monopolist maintains his monopoly position and the demand for his product or service continues, there will be no direct competitors to exert rivalry by quoting lower rates or by other means. However, the monopolist's price will be somewhat or significantly limited if good substitutes exist or if there are other

130

types of competitive forces in the market that do not depend on two or more firms being present as direct competitors.

The monopoly price described above would be a uniform price for all buyers. But a monopolist, if he could separate his markets sufficiently into those with greater or lesser demand elasticities, could increase his monopoly profit by discriminating in his prices between the classes of buyers so defined.[4] If he could discriminate perfectly, the monopolist could take all the consumers' surplus; he could absorb less of it if his monopoly power were limited by substitutes or other competitive forces or by government regulation. Railways the world over have discriminated in rates, though they usually have not had a complete monopoly of their markets. Cost and utilization-of-plant conditions can make discriminating monopoly prices economic for both railways and society if they are appropriately limited by the competitive or regulative forces so that monopoly profits are not earned.

Except in those cases in which a cartel acts like a monopoly, monopoly firms are found in industries (a) in which there are economic barriers to entry – a very large investment may be required; (b) the supplier is connected with its customers (as in the case of a gas pipe line); or (c) there are significant economies of scale as regards a firm which presently dominates a particular market and there are no prospects that the size of the market will increase. Railroads and other public utilities have many of these monopoly characteristics.[5] Nevertheless, there can be competitive organization that is efficient, at least for the railways, when the market is of such size as to support two or more competitive firms, a condition that exists in many of the large railway markets in Canada and to an even greater extent in those in the U.S.A. Even so, railways are firms having a high ratio of constant costs to total costs, substantial excess capacity over long periods of time, and average total unit costs that decrease as output expands to utilize existing capacity. Hence, railway prices will not necessarily be equated with both marginal and average total unit costs as is the case for highly competitive firms having constant costs. When output is less than ideal, as when significant excess capacity exists, marginal costs will be below, possibly far below, average total unit costs. The unit costs that are relevant for pricing in this situation are the relevant marginal or incremental costs. Constant costs that do not change with variations of output are not allocated in fixed proportions when pricing specific services; but, if budgetary equilibrium and profitable operation are to be achieved, each price must make a revenue contribution to constant cost, with the amount of that contribution determined by the elasticity of demand. The practice of price discrimination in railways is explained also by the existence of areas of common costs that are extremely difficult to trace to specific outputs and some areas of true joint costs. Uniform prices as in truly competitive industries are seldom, if ever, found in railways, and these prices would be irrational, given that the railways' long-standing

131

economic, cost and utilization characteristics continue in the future.[6]

Pricing under Duopoly

Duopoly is a market state in which two sellers face a large number of buyers. Obviously, this condition describes many of the Canadian railway markets served by both the CP and the CN. How pricing actually occurs in duopolistic railway markets, therefore, is of great interest in Canada.

Unfortunately, little can be said definitely from formal economic theory about the precise outcome of competitive rivalry in duopoly markets. As with bilateral monopoly, much depends on the strategy and tactics of the sellers. If, as Cournot considered, one duopolist is passive while the other duopolist adjusts his output to the optimum quantity and price, then the former one will follow, both will charge the same price (assuming identical products or services), and they will share equally in the market if both experience the same cost conditions. In this case, there would be no inducement to engage in price competition. If, however, the two duopolists have different marginal costs, the one initiating a move would cut price to expand his output and this would be met with a further cut if the other duopolist's marginal cost were below his marginal revenue. This process would continue so long as the marginal cost of each duopolist were below the marginal revenue, but would stop when equilibrium outputs resulted in marginal revenue being equal to marginal cost in each case.[7] In this instance, the market shares would be different, with the duopolist having the lower marginal cost taking a larger market share.

As it is unlikely that one duopolist would be passive during each round of price fixing, the model is not very useful for predicting pricing in the real-world cases of duopoly. Yet it reveals that under some conditions duopolists will price compete. In fact, this has been found to happen at times in the CP and CN duopoly markets.

Pricing under Oligopoly

Oligopoly is a market state in which there are more than two sellers in a market, but so few that each competitor's price and output actions will have an appreciable or significant effect on the market. Oligopolies of a few competitors usually refer to four or five firms, but there are oligopolies with more firms. However, as the number of competing firms increase, the influence of each on the market decreases until the market becomes purely competitive, i.e., there are many firms, none of which has a significant effect on the market. In Canada, there are oligopoly railway markets of three or more firms where regional Canadian railways and/or U.S.A. railways are in the market with CP and CN.

Pricing under oligopoly of three or four firms can be like that under duopoly if passive behaviour on the part of all oligopolists in a market is assumed except for one. But in such cases, the other firms can often foresee the competitive move of an aggressive competitor, and their shares of the market will be large enough so that they will be injured by a price cut if they do not meet the price competition immediately. This perception by one or all of the competing oligopolists will also be surmised by the oligopolist considering a competitive thrust in price. Under such assumptions, little price competition will occur in the market as all oligopolists would perceive that after the price competition had occurred each would be worse off with less revenue from the lower price but with the same share of the market. Competition would then be concentrated on product differentiation, advertising and selling effort.

But while this outcome of oligopoly of the few can and does take place, oligopoly can also be more active in terms of price competition among the oligopolists. This will occur when an aggressive firm thinks that it can gain market share and profitability by cutting price because it will take considerable time for other oligopolists to find out about the price cuts and react to them, or when the act of price-cutting makes the buyer "loyal" to the price-cutting firm. Independent action is more likely when it takes the form of not going along with a price increase, because no further "rate cutting" is likely to follow. Therefore, in times of inflation this can be very important.

Where price cutting can take sophisticated forms, as in railway markets, aggression may be regarded profitable. Where new technology is involved that will lower unit cost and will not be available to all competitors immediately, an oligopolist may perceive gain in price cutting. Hence, under oligopoly of few firms there are likely to be self-imposed restraints on price competition, but the incentives from mutual interaction will not prevent price competition altogether. And the more the number of firms or the competitive influences from the outside such as market competition, the greater the prospect that price competition will occur. Under oligopoly, pricing can be either along monopoly lines or along competitive lines. Much depends on the circumstances in the market and the strategies of the participants.

Pricing under Cartels

Where oligopolists or other competitive firms can get together and agree on prices for an industry, they can often make greater profits than they can make as individual oligopolists or competitive firms in a competitive struggle. When they can form an effective cartel or other pricing organization, they price as a group against the downward-sloping community demand curves for their products or services, and so attain, in effect, the market position of a single monopolist facing many buyers. In Canada, the railways are permitted to confer and agree on rates and thus, subject to the intramodal, intermodal and market competitive forces in many of their markets, can elect to price monopolistically in certain of their markets.

Cartels price like simple monopolies. In theory, they find the marginal cost curve of the collective of firms. They can then maximize the cartel profit by producing a cartel output determined at the level where the market marginal revenue curve is equal to the cartel's marginal cost curve. As the cartel price will generally be above the level of price in competitive oligopoly or in highly competitive markets, the collective profits of the cartel will normally exceed those of a collection of oligopolists or of competitive firms under competition. Accordingly, the cartel members can be made better off than they would be under oligopolistic rivalry or under many-firm competition. But cartels tend to break down because each cartel member would find it in his interest to increase his output and sell more at the going cartel price, which would be above his marginal costs. If not limited by production quotas, market-sharing agreements, pooling or other devices, this incentive to produce will cause overproduction in terms of the cartel price and will drive the price below the cartel profit-maximizing level. Where an industry is composed of many small firms and entry is easy, an effective cartel can be formed only when restrictive entry control by government is exercised, as in the case of regulation of interstate motor carriers in the U.S.A.[8] In spite of the difficulties, there is evidence that cartels, when effective, do charge higher-than-competitive prices and yield monopoly profits. Obviously, this is accomplished by limiting price competition, directly or indirectly.

The General Nature of Competition in Canadian Transport Markets

In the real world of Canadian transport, no one market state describes all freight markets and their pricing, not even all those in railway transport. In the latter, however, duopoly is the most common occurrence, though oligopoly of the few is also found. Even so, railway freight markets are widely subject to the forces of actual or potential truck and other intermodal competition, market competition, and to locational influences that also limit railway rates. Moreover, competition takes place in other forms of rivalry of importance to shippers and consumers besides rivalry in price. Hence, neither the extent, workings, nor effects of competition in railway markets can be predicted by basing them on one state of market organization and its theory presuppositions and predilections. An ecclectic analysis of competition is necessary and it must be in terms of the dynamics of competition.

Dynamic Competition in Canadian Railway Freight Markets

In his *Competition as a Dynamic Process,* published by The Brookings Institution in 1961, John Maurice Clark sought to explain competition in all its diverse dynamic aspects and to appraise its effectiveness as a regulative force in the modern economy. Clark sought to shift "the emphasis from competition as a mechanism of equilibrium to competition as a dynamic process."[9] This statement reflects his view that the models of perfect and pure competition, although useful as models of how competition would work and create benefits under conditions of perfection in markets, could not describe the competitive forces that actually and potentially persist in the real world of today, more pervasively

134

and effectively than many theorists and others perceive. Clark recognized that competition has changed its character with the vast changes in industrial organization and the productive processes that have come in the last century, and that competitive market forces are loaded with imperfections. Nevertheless, the preservation of the constructive features of competitive forces is desirable, Clark held, "because they have somehow managed to combine competitive incentives with mass production and applied science that are nowadays essential to dynamic progress. And for appraising dynamic progress, 'perfection' is an irrelevant criterion."[10]

Clark emphasized the point that competitive forces in the modern economy will evidence themselves in many forms or dimensions. Clark noted that the selection and design of a product or service, the selling effort to bring it to the favorable notice of potential buyers, and price are the principal forms that competition can take, and that any one of them can change without change in the others or in combination with changes in the others. Because the ability of firms to produce efficiently enhances the effectiveness of their selling inducements, Clark considered cost reduction under competitive pressures as a fourth means of competitive appeal.[11] Giving attention to all types of competitive appeals instead of price alone, Clark found that competition can be dynamic and effective in spite of the fewness of firms and the presence of product or service differentiation. Conditions arise that give some competitors an incentive to take aggressive actions that others will have to meet, as when prices are materially above the minimum prices at which the industry would supply the amounts demanded of the various grades and types of products or services it produces.[12] Competition is dynamic both in the several ways that rivalry and competitive appeal can be expressed and in the fact that its occurrence arises from continually changing market, cost and technological conditions. When changing conditions make competition in price, product quality, selling effort or cost a real potential, the force of competition will be a factor in market price, the conditions of sale and other aspects of a firm's product or service.

The availability of efficient carrying equipment, the timing and dependability of delivery, the care of the shipment when goods are fragile and valuable, the speed of transit and flexibility of delivery and the availability of capacity for large volumes or special shipments are very important traits of transport service to shippers. Hence, competition among carriers and modes is important to shippers even though price competition may be absent for one reason or another or take place only occasionally when conditions are ripe for competitive thrusts in price. Competition in freight transport in forms other than price tends to be far less wasteful than in the production and sale of many consumer goods where monopolistic competition often prevails. This is true because the buyers of freight services are rational, are usually experienced in making comparisons of

135

rate and service alternatives, and have real needs for the product and service differentiation that takes place under the stimulation of nonprice competition.

Some ways in which carriers continually exert rivalry for traffic can illustrate the dynamics of competition in transport. Carriers in different modes are continuously exerting rivalry in the specific services and service qualities they offer shippers against other carriers in the same mode as well as carriers in another mode. They frequently and aggressively call on shippers served by other carriers and modes to offer their services and their expertise for solving the distribution and logistical problems of the shippers. They quote and design rates to influence a switch by the shipper to their services, sometimes below those of the existing carrier or carriers sharing the traffic, sometimes at the existing rates with reliance on service quality to attract the shipper's custom, and sometimes above the rates of the alternative modal carriers when their services are distinctly preferred by the shipper for significantly lowering his other costs. Often, the truckers and other carriers seek out back hauls to lower their ton-mile cost, or take other productive action having the same effect, so that they can become rate-competitive with the carrier or mode that presently has a shipper's traffic.

Individual carriers indicate willingness to enter into contracts or commitments to make terminal, equipment or way investments in order to handle a shipper's volume expeditiously and efficiently. Such willingness with respect to furnishing facilities and designing distribution systems is often a key competitive element when railroads are in competition with other railroads, when truck-rail intermodal groups compete with other such intermodal groups or when a shipper's plant investment plans depends on efficient special facilities and competitive service. Equipment capacity can be the significant factor when truckers compete with the railways, as when there are shortages of rail freight cars or when truck equipment for back hauls is insufficient to handle the volume a shipper expects to ship. Even flexibility and quick adjustment of services, equipment and facilities to the special needs of particular shippers can be a significant element in the rivalry between carriers and modes. As technological developments that affect the productivity, cost and service capability of carriers and modes are continually taking place, many opportunities arise over time for specific types of dynamic competitive rivalry to express themselves in intramodal and intermodal markets. Market competition from new or expanding sources of materials or products also introduces dynamic competitive forces in railway markets from time to time. In many ways, potential, as well as actual, competition exists, and potential competition that may become actual competition at any time is a dynamic competitive force in railway freight markets.

In one respect. Clark's conditions for effective dynamic competition are not always present in transport markets. Clark stipulated that firms act independently in pricing, as a condition for such competition to occur when

136

only a few firms are in the market.[13] In Canada, the railways generally confer on rates, often make rates jointly and frequently notify shippers of rate adjustments by joint letter, or alternatively, through the Canadian Freight Association. And some groups of Provincially regulated truckers agree on rates through rate bureaus as do both the railways and regulated truckers in the U.S.A. Only infrequently do the two major Canadian railways quote rates separately and against each other. Normally, differences of position on rates are resolved confidentially by the railways before a joint front is presented to a shipper. When alternative rail routes or combinations of rail with truck or water services are available, a railroad may take independent action on rates when in disagreement with another railroad or railroads.[14] Likewise, individual truckers in rate associations as well as independent truckers often act independently by cutting rates, and private carrier truckers engage in cost-rate competition with for-hire carriers regularly.

Independent action is the rule as to other forms of competitive rivalry. These include car supply, innovations in equipment and services, delivery schedules, provision of capacity, logistical and distributional planning, and efforts to produce transport services more efficiently. Overall, the conditions favorable to Clarkian dynamic competition generally obtain in Canadian freight markets, though to a very limited extent with respect to price competition between the two major railways.

Factors in Transport Competition in Canadian Freight Markets

As noted, the theory of the firm indicates whether there will be competition and how competition and monopoly will work to fix prices and output in several different assumed states of the market. It specifies the prerequisites for competition or for monopoly and yields the theoretical effects of market forces in the hypothetical markets analyzed, not the actual effects in real markets. To find out how competition actually works in transport markets, it is essential to take into account the actual conditions that exist in those markets and the market conduct that takes place in them, as is undertaken in Chapters V, VI and VII.

The character, amount and effectiveness of competition in freight markets depends on the presence or absence of a number of market conditions that can be favorable or unfavorable to effective or workable competition. Among these are the number of firms in the market, the homogeneity or heterogeneity of the services of the carriers within a mode or between modes, the presence of fixed costs and excess capacity, the relative levels of unit costs of the modes, the feasibility of back loads, the distance that goods have to be shipped to market and the extent and character of value-of-service rates. In addition, the progress of transport technology and the knowledge, strategy and agressiveness of carriers and shippers will influence the dynamics of competition in transport markets.

137

The number of firms in the market. As was noted above, generally the more firms that are competing in markets, the less will the competitive actions of one firm affect the market opportunity of other firms and the more effective competition will be. Where there are many firms, there will be more price competition and, probably, less service competition than where only two or a few firms are in the market. In the latter cases, price competition will be subdued but not necessarily eliminated and product or service competition and other forms of nonprice competition will be emphasized. Free-entry conditions, low economic barriers to entry, and lack of dominance by one or a few large firms facilitate effective competition. And carriers in different modes add to the number of competing firms whenever their services are substitutable[15] at the relative rates prevailing in the marketplace.

The homogeneity or heterogeneity of services. Competition, given the other conditions for its effective working, works most effectively when the competing firms all produce and sell the same commodity or service. Perfect competition presupposes homogeneous output by the competing firms. In the real world, competing firms adjust their products and service, selling efforts, and conditions of sale as competitive appeals, and they often seek to differentiate their products or services in order to induce buyers to prefer them to competing products, even at higher prices. In other words, they seek ways to monopolize market demand or portions of it. Where such efforts are successful, monopolistic competition can work to raise prices and costs and to reduce efficiency in the use of scarce resources. Of course, as Clark holds, some forms of nonprice competition can help make dynamic competition work effectively as well. This is true of freight transport where the shippers are knowledgeable and discriminating in procuring freight services.

Within a given mode or a specialized group of carriers within a mode, the services tend to be highly homogeneous among the competing carriers. Though some carriers render better service than others, they as a group tend to render standard services and any one carrier can ordinarily meet the standards of those offering superior services at the time. Thus, competing railroads generally offer about the same services in terms of the number of days required for carload deliveries, the types of cars supplied, free time for loading and unloading and care of traffic. Similar standard services and service conditions exist in the trucking of general freight and in each specialized field of trucking. Such homogeneity conditions are favorable to competition if other necessary conditions exist, and individual carriers offering higher quality services may spur other carriers to follow and to innovate so as to promote dynamic competition and its benefits.

Carrier services tend to be considerably different or heterogeneous in competition between modes. For example, trucking services are generally more flexible, speedier and more protective of cargo than railway service, though this

138

is not always true. Superior services can be superior in speed of shipment transit and delivery, off-rail delivery and pickup capacity, care of the shipment from loss and damage during transit or in terminals and greater reliability as to on-time deliveries.

The modal carriers or groups offering the services most desired by shippers or consignees, and most capable of reducing shipper costs other than rate costs, will emphasize service competition. Nevertheless, service differences among carriers and modes do not necessarily prevent price competition from occurring in intermodal markets. When carriers in differnet modes compete in price to reflect their different ton-mile cost levels as well as in service, their differentiated services often become highly substitutable to the shippers, price competition becomes workable and traffic and resource misallocation is avoided.

The cost characteristics of the carriers and modes. Modes, or specialized fields within a mode, whose operating costs are mostly or completely variable are those most likely to experience price competition, providing restrictive entry control does not limit entry, expansion and exit of firms. Entry will be comparatively easy as economies of scale in size of firm will be negligible, and there will be many firms except in small markets. If excessive entries occur in a period of general depression or because of ignorance of costs and business acumen, there may be excessive competition at times, a condition that tends to be self-corrective and not ruinous of competition.[16]

On the other hand, modes whose carriers have high fixed costs and much excess capacity are less likely to exhibit price competition. This is because there will be fewer competitors in the market; each will tend to view price competition as bringing prompt retaliation, as the actions of one competitor will have a significant impact on the others; and, if utilization of fixed capacity is very low, the condition of marginal costs being far below average total unit costs could lead to ruinous competition, that is, to competition that eliminates itself and establishes monopoly firms or cartel conditions. Historically, railways exhibited these characteristics.[17] As railways operate closer to full utilization today, the outcome of ruinous competition from price rivalry is far less likely. Consequently, the railways' cost characteristics today are more conducive than they were historically to the occurrence of some intramodal price competition.[18]

The relative levels of unit costs of the modes. Especially for traffic in bulk commodities moving comparatively long distances and in large shipments, the ton-mile cost level of different modal carriers is a significant factor in the choice of mode. For such traffic, transport cost is a large factor in the commodity's destination value, so that the demand for transport tends to be price elastic. Hence, the modal carriers with the lowest rates will be accorded the traffic and the high-cost modal carriers will usually be unable to compete in the market.[19]

Often, too, the low-cost mode will have greater supply capacity, such as unit trains, for accommodating huge flows of basic commodities, while competing modes will not. These factors tend to narrow competition to the carriers within the mode or modes having low ton-mile costs, as in the case of the westward movements of coal, potash and sulphur for export that move almost wholly by rail from the Prairie Provinces or Southeastern British Columbia to Vancouver.[20] In such cases, carrier competition is limited to intramodal railway competition, although there are forces of market competition as to these raw materials from other producing countries that powerfully limit railway rates, even in the instances in which only one railway serves the Canadian producers.

In the case of high-value traffic, differences in ton-mile cost between the modes are not as significant in the choice of modal carriers as in the case of the transport of bulk commodities. This is because the demand for transport of high-value goods tends to be relatively inelastic, though the demand for one type of modal carrier can be very elastic when two or more modes are engaging in active price competition. Also, such traffic and often, other traffic moving in small shipments, are far more sensitive to service quality offered by different modes than are bulk commodities. If service quality is important to the shippers in terms of demand creation or cost reduction, they will often be willing to pay higher rates for the service of the high-quality modal carriers.[21] In such cases, high ton-mile-cost modal carriers can enter into competition with low ton-mile cost modal carriers. Historically, the truckers have successfully competed for high-value manufactured traffic with the railways even when their rates were higher because of higher ton-mile costs. Hence, it cannot be concluded that significant differences in unit costs for different modes will necessarily prevent competition; although if transport competition were entirely to consist of price competition, the high-cost modal carriers would eventually be eliminated from the market. On the other hand, if one mode's ton-mile costs are too high compared with those of the low-cost mode and there are no service considerations that justify payment of higher rates to the high-cost mode, then that mode can exert competitive rivalry only if the low-cost mode quotes very high rates for its services, as under motor-rail rate parity pricing and regulation in the U.S.A.

The relative unit cost levels of carriers in different modes are subject to change in ways that might increase or lessen the extent of intermodal competition. For example, the improvement in the main highways in Canada in recent years and the permission given for employment of larger and heavier truck combinations and for operation at higher speeds, along with technical advances in truck equipment and power units, have substantially lowered truck ton-mile costs in relation to railway rates and unit costs. The lower levels of truck rates that this facilitates have extended both the distance and commodity range of road-rail competition, even to some bulk commodities when the distances are not too great. Thus, the Trans-Canada Highway and the Interstate System in the U.S.A. have made cost competition between truck and rail carriers far more a reality, especially over long transcontinental hauls and for some less valuable commodities, than heretofore.[22] On the other hand, the invention and the use of the tri-level railway cars for hauling new automobiles has reduced ton-mile costs by railroad in relation to highway carriage so much that the long-distance trucking of new automobiles has virtually been eliminated.[23] Relative unit cost levels, being subject to change, are therefore a factor in dynamic competition between the modes as well as in the forms that competition will take over time.

The feasibility of back hauls. An important factor in the continued tendency for truck competition with the railroads to increase its mileage and commodity range is the active search of truckers for back-haul traffic. The high variable and unit cost characteristic of trucking enterprises makes it very important for truckers to seek out freight so that a high utilization of truck capacity can be achieved on all legs of routes. The successful search for compatible freight to facilitate a high round-trip truck utilization can even enable the carriage of relatively low-rated freight in both directions, with a sufficiently high equipment load and mileage utilization that rates can be reduced to levels significantly competitive with rail service.[24]

The extent of the competitive influence of truckers cannot be judged by examining overall trucking statistics. Even on routes in which the preponderant traffic flow is in one direction, it is quite likely that particular truckers will have a deficiency of traffic in that direction, caused by the use of specialized equipment or by the characteristics of the particular segment of the market they serve. They often seek out traffic compatible with their own equipment and service needs at back-haul rates and, in so doing, provide some shippers with an effective alternative to rail service.

The influence of distance from the market. Canada is a continental country with long distances between most of its principal cities, ranging from 500 to 700 miles to 4,000 miles.[25] Between the Western Provinces and the heavily populated and industrialized Central Region dominated by Toronto and Montreal, many transcontinental hauls of 2,000 miles or more are involved. Within the principal cities of Southern Ontario and Southwestern Quebec, the hauls are shorter, about 300 miles between Toronto and Montreal. Within metropolitan areas, hauls are short.

Competition to the railways from road carriers is most intense in markets in which the hauls range up to 500 or 600 miles. For local movements and short intercity hauls possibly up to 200 miles, truck unit costs often are below railway costs and trucks have distinct service advantages as well. The precise length of haul at which rail unit costs generally are below trucking costs on carload and truckload quantities is difficult to specify, but this almost certainly is the case for transcontinental and other very long-distance movements in carload quantities.[26] Where hauls are long and trucking costs are relatively high, the traffic moves by truck only where value-of-service rates by rail are quite high or the service advantages by truck are significant to the shipper.[27] The low unit costs obtainable when truckers can arrange full loads for the back haul have significantly increased the competitiveness of trucking to the railways over very long hauls in recent years. Notwithstanding, truck competition becomes weaker the longer the haul beyond the range in which truck costs are below rail costs, and for many very long hauls of service-insensitive commodities it is absent except as a potential competitive force should railway rates rise greatly. But where this is the case, market competition or U.S. rail competition can be powerful rate-limiting factors.

The nature of the traffic. As noted, bulk commodities move most efficiently in large shipments up to full trainloads or shiploads, and seek the lowest rates because of elastic demands for transport. These requirements become even more pressing as the distances of shipment increase. For those reasons, bulk commodities in Canada move largely by rail and water — only short distances by truck, usually to intermodal loading stations or to ports. For this traffic, competition is largely between the railways or between them and water carriers, though here, again, market competition can be present as an effective limiting factor on rail freight rates.[28]

For competition between truck and rail, a number of traffic characteristics are important. Some of the most important characteristics are whether the traffic is bulk-handled in large shipments or packaged or palletized in small shipments; low-value or high value; heavy or light per unit of space; perishable or non-perishable; and low or high in loss-damage risk. For small shipments and for carload or truckload quantities of manufactured and other high-value goods, trucking becomes a vital and widespread competitive force to the railways, except for quite long hauls.[29] Even for such hauls, trucking can be an effective alternative to railways where service quality is highly significant to shippers.

The railway share of the market. The rail share of the market can also be a factor in the competitive responses of the railways to intermodal competition from trucks. Historically, when the railroads have had a very high share of the market in high-value commodities, they did not engage in aggressive price competition against the truckers. This may have been because they concluded that revenue-wise they were better off with higher rates and less of the traffic, and/or because they lacked the organizational flexibility to compete with trucking on a local basis.

It was not until the railways had lost a significant share of the high-value freight market that they pursued aggressive competitive courses to retain the traffic which they still had and to recapture that which they had lost. In Canada they did this by various actions, including the purchase of trucking companies, particularly after 1957, the development of new services such as piggyback, container and merchandising services, the use of aggressive pricing with agreed charges and the development of a more decentralized and service-orientated marketing organization.[30]

In the U.S.A., the railways remained unaggressive in their competition with trucking for a longer period. The railways operated under a rate parity policy sponsored and implemented by "fair-sharing" minimum rate regulation by the I.C.C.[31] This policy cost the railways much traffic and revenues over the long run and did not bring down the high value-of-service rates until the urgent concern of the railways over their diminishing market share induced them to engage in price competition and in innovating activities within the constraints allowed by regulation.

The influence of value-of-service rates. Traditionally, the railways have assessed discriminating, or value-of-service, rates. This practice sets rates on traffic regarded as having inelastic demands high above railway variable costs or even above the full costs, and it assesses low rates, at times as low as the short-run marginal costs, on traffic believed to have elastic demands for transport. Thus, high rates were placed on manufactured goods and other high-value goods and low rates were assessed on low-grade bulk commodities and some agricultural products. With the advent of good roads and trucking, this rate structure enabled the truckers, often with much higher unit costs, to engage in service competition, and even in price competition, with the railways. It also facilitated their extending competition to medium and long hauls for high-rated goods in the rail rate structure. For many years, but for longer in the U.S.A. than in Canada, the railway value-of-service rate structure, in effect, held a rate umbrella under which truck competition could expand to the detriment of the railways even when railway ton-mile costs were far lower and the distances of haul fairly long.[32]

The railways have been in a dilemma over what to do about their high value-of-service rates. On the one hand, they invite more trucking competition for the railways' best-paying traffic. On the other hand, the railways, with their fixed cost and excess capacity characteristics, require such value-of-service rates for good utilization of their facilities and for obtaining adequate revenues and profitability. In Canada, the railways are also motivated to place very high rates on high-value commodities in their noncompetitive traffic areas because of the government rate holddowns on export grains and other traffic. Yet the practice invites extension of truck competition and shipper and regional displeasure.

The Presence or Absence of the Prerequisites of Competition

Ideally, all of the requirements for competition to work under the models of pure or perfect competition should be present if competitive forces are to bring their full benefits in transport markets as in other markets. As noted above, among the theory requirements for the ideal states of competition are a large number of sellers and buyers in the market, sellers and buyers as price takers instead of price makers, conditions of constant or increasing costs, strictly homogeneous products or services, mobile resources, and full information on the part of all who enter the market. Such conditions do not generally exist throughout the transport industries or throughout the entire economy, although certain cases do exist, including the world ocean tramp shipping industry, and exempt for-hire trucking in the U.S.A., where the prerequisites of pure or perfect competition are tolerably well met. But, as Clark emphasized, perfection in the underlying conditions for competition cannot often be expected in the modern industrial economies; and though market imperfections create problems, dynamic competitive forces can still be present and can accomplish the principal gains expected of competition in all industries in which they can operate. The question is: Are the prerequisites for competition sufficiently present so that competition can be workable in most Canadian freight markets and an effective force in the development, selling and pricing of Canadian railway services?

The extent of the existence of the prerequisites for effective competition in the public-facility modes. These modes are those whose carriers operate their vehicles on ways provided by the public or provided naturally, and thus do not confront the way facility investment barriers to entry and the fixed or constant costs associated with way investments as do the railways and pipelines. The principal public-facility freight modes are the highway truckers and the towboat, barge and water carriers on the Great Lakes, coastal waters, and inland waterways.

Except on low-density rural routes, the trucking industry, where not restricted by entry control, exhibits most of the prerequisites for effective competition. Under free-or easy-entry conditions such as obtain in Alberta and some other Provinces, the number of for-hire trucking firms can adjust flexibly to the traffic densities in specific markets and to the economics of scale in size of firm. Since such scale economies are limited in trucking, there are many competing for-hire truckers over all routes of dense traffic between the principal cities of Canada.[33] With unrestricted private carrier operation of trucks the wide employment of private carriers adds to the number of firms competing in the market. With some exceptions, the number of competing truckers can be sufficient for truckers to be price takers and for excessive dominance in the market to be avoided except on routes of low traffic offerings or in traffic-specialization areas such as household-goods carriage. In terms of the number of firms required for effective competition, then, that condition normally is met in the important trucking markets.

Investment in equipment is the principal capital requirement for operation of a trucking firm. Regular route hauliers of small shipments also invest in terminal facilities. And truck equipment is highly mobile, is in units of small capacity and has a relatively short service life. Because of these characteristics and the labor-intensiveness trait, trucking costs are largely variable with output, as indicated by the very high operating ratios with which trucking firms can operate profitably. Without high ratios of fixed cost, truckers can generally avoid significant excess capacity and marginal costs significantly below their average costs.[34] Consequently, truck rates under unrestricted competition can be equal to, or close approximations of, their marginal and average costs, as in the perfect or pure competition models. As in other competitive industries, prices tend to be uniform prices rather than discriminating prices except as to back hauls involving true joint cost conditions where discriminating pricing will occur even under perfect competition.

Within any natural subdivision of the trucking industry such as common carriage of general commodities, the same types of vehicular equipment will be employed by the different firms, the speeds of the rolling trucks will be the same on given highways, the same conditions of congestion will be met and the drivers will all be working under comparable union conditions except for owner-drivers who operate mostly as independent entrepreneurs. For these and competitive reasons, the trucking firms engaged in hauling the same commodities and types of loads in the same markets will render highly homogeneous services. Thus, another condition for effective competition, including price competition is commonly present.

In the depressed 1930's, the view was commonly held that excessive entries and exits of firms occurred in the trucking industry under free-entry conditions. This view was based on the low financial requirements for entry and an assumed lack of knowledge by entrepreneurs of how to operate a competitive enterprise, particularly with respect to costs and pricing. Excessive competition was believed to occur, and it probably did occur under the extremely large unemployment of that period, when many otherwise unemployed people sought to enter the fields of easy entry. Even though the expectation of a recurrence of excessive competition persists today in some quarters, conditions have changed since the 1930's. Full or near-full employment conditions have been the rule, the cost of entry into trucking with one to three combination units has risen, hours-of-driving regulations have been more general and effective, and trucking is now highly organized with industry associations that make much cost and technical information available. Hence, under present-day circumstances there is little ground for the assumption that excessive competition will inevitably occur and that the entering firms will have seriously inadequate knowledge of their costs for profitable pricing. As in other competitive fields, there will be mistakes in entries and bankruptcies will occur. But these conditions are essential to effective competition under dynamic conditions.

Clearly, then, the essential prerequisites for effective competition generally

145

prevail in Canadian trucking. While this means that most significant trucking markets can be organized competitively, it does not mean that all such markets will be or are so organized. Entry and operating authority control in some Provinces has lessened the number of competitors,[35] and many rural markets will not support more than one or a very few firms. Nevertheless, competition of several or many firms is the general situation in Canadian trucking. And this industry supplies thousands of firms in a country as large as Canada to compete with the railways except for bulk commodities and some other commodities carried most efficiently in very large shipments over long distances.

Similarly, there is reason to anticipate that water carriers, where available, will operate in a largely competitive manner. This may be less so of the Canadian Great Lakes where some of the firms are large enterprises and are highly integrated with other modes. Water carriers, too, avoid large fixed facility investments. Except for some terminals, their investments are largely in equipment units which, although large individually, can be increased or reduced in number with traffic conditions. Except where fixed schedules are held to, water carrier costs are largely variable.[36] Hence their rates, except in some package services, tend to be uniform competitive prices rather than discriminating prices. There are usually enough competing firms to assure competitive pricing and competitive forces that limit rail rates. Geographically, however, this occurs only where navigation facilities and waterways exist.

The extent of the existence of the prerequisites for effective competition in the fixed-cost modes. The ideal conditions for competition according to the perfect or pure competition models exist to a far less extent in the oil pipeline and railway industries. Although there is market competition between Canadian and U.S.A. pipelines serving the same eastern consuming markets, the oil pipelines are the closest approach to natural monopoly requiring regulation in intercity freight transport. They operate with significant economies of scale, both in utilization and in size of pipe. Because of the huge initial investments required, ownership tends to be by the major oil companies and potential competition is muted. Pipeline rates conform to simple monopoly pricing, and pipelines engage in less price discrimination than the railways. With large-diameter pipes, pipeline unit costs become so low that they command all of the volume traffic except where large tankers can be operated. Hence, in volume markets, they are not a limiting factor on railway freight rates.

Over the principal traffic routes of Canada, the transcontinental and Central Canadian routes, two railways, the CN and the CP, comprise the effective competitors in that mode.[37] To and from many intermediate points along the lines of either railway service is available to shippers from only one railway. At markets in Canada to which American railway lines extend, such as Vancouver and Winnipeg, or at markets that can be reached by short intermodal trucking hauls, there are additional railway firms in the market. And in certain regions, a

146

third Canadian railway is in some railway markets, as the BCR in British Columbia and the Ontario Northland Railway in Ontario.

The duopoly or oligopoly-of-few-firms conditions in railway organization neither meets the firm-numbers nor the firm-dominancy tests which make the selling side of railway freight markets highly price competitive. Generally, though, there are many buyers on the buying side of the market. Though much service competition and some intramodal price competition occurs, the Canadian railways, by themselves, are not organized as a basically competitive industry. Neither is this industry organized as a natural monopoly. Rather, it is best characterized as an imperfectly competitive industry, with some markets, generally the larger railway terminal cities subject to some or considerable intra-railway competition, while the small centers and intermediate points often have no intrarailway competition. This is not to say, however, that other competitive forces, such as intermodal and market competition, are not present, as one or the other, or both, clearly are in most Canadian markets for railway service.

The railways provide their own way and terminal facilities. Hence, they initially displayed considerable economies of scale in size of firm, though this characteristic is doubtful for firm sizes that are typical in the industry today.[38] Railways do have high initial and continuing durable and long-lived investments; they often continue to experience relatively high ratios of fixed costs to total costs, especially when their capacity is greatly or significantly underutilized, and thus they frequently have marginal costs below their average total unit costs and decreasing average costs with fuller utilization. Consequently, railway prices have not conformed to the uniform prices of perfect or pure competition, but rather have been highly discriminating prices from the beginning of railroading. And railroad executives typically view price competition among themselves with considerable skepticism; in Canada the two major railways typically discuss and agree on rates when changes are under consideration. As noted in Chapter III, railway management personnel are experienced and well informed, and the Canadian railways engage rather vigorously today in conducting market development, costing and pricing research.

Because of these features, railroads do not comply well with the set of conditions specified for perfect or pure competition. Nevertheless, they are not natural monopolies in a relevant sense, as the condition of greatly increasing utilization of their main lines over the last few decades has eliminated sharply increasing returns and, therefore, much of the historical tendency to engage in ruinous competition. Even so, the Canadian railways engage in intramodal price competition in only a limited number of market situations that are favorable to this form of competition. On the other hand, they do engage in sharp competition in furnishing modern equipment, in supplying an adequate number of cars to shippers, in shortening freight schedules, and in introducing technological changes that bring significant benefits to shippers. Hence, even though the railways utilize price competition mainly in their rivalry with other modes, dynamic competitive force, including price competition occasionally, do exert themselves in intramodal railway markets.

The extent of the existence of the prerequisites for effective intermodal competition. The above analysis suggests that in the markets in which the railways are important, the principal sources of carrier competition to the railroads, particularly in terms of price, will be the other modes. Thus, except for market competition and locational and logistical alternatives that frequently exist, shippers of freight by railway will look primarily to intermodal competition to obtain the benefits of competition in limiting railway rates and stimulating good service. But will competition take place between road and rail freight carriers in view of the small number of railways in the market, their size and market dominance, the heterogeneity of the services rendered by carriers in different modes, and other factors?

Notwithstanding the imperfections in the conditions underlying transport competition within the several modes and between the modes, intermodal competitive forces can be effective in limiting railway rates and in bringing the ordinary gains of competition to shippers and consumers. There are two basic reasons for this. First, though rail and truck services are far from homogeneous in terms of speed, off-route pickups and deliveries, care of the shipments, on-time service reliability, and schedule frequency, in the real world there is often high substitutability between truck and rail services. This is especially true where the railways reduce their rates on high-value goods while truck rates remain the same or are forced to be significantly higher than rail rates because truck ton-mile costs are higher, as has frequently, though not always, been the case.[39] Though the railways have been reluctant to reduce their high value-of-service rates when they continue to have a large share of a specific market, in time they will take competitive rate action when the facts show that their market share of profitable traffic has slipped significantly and will continue to fall unless such action is taken. Although the unique services of the truckers provide them some insulation from railway competition, the demand curve facing the individual trucking firms will be close enough to the horizontal that they will lose traffic and revenues quickly when the railroads engage in aggressive price competition and service improvement.[40] The truckers' competitive strategy has always been to divert traffic and revenues from the railways, primarily by service competition but also by shaving the railway prices whenever they are high and service competition is not effective. Thus, the market differences in road and rail freight services do not create permanent pockets of non-competitive traffic except for small shipments and special services that the railways cannot render unless they enter trucking. Effective intermodal price and service competition occurs extensively between road and rail carriers.

148

Water carrier services are distinctly inferior to railway services. However, since water carrier unit costs enable them to quote rates differentially below the railway rates, the rail and water services are substitutable and vigorous intermodal competition occurs in markets such as the Great Lakes.

A second reason that effective intermodal competition takes place is that the introduction and development of the newer modes of transport have added significantly to the number of actual and potential firms competing in the markets for freight. Instead of having two railroads to depend on and negotiate with, most shippers in Canada today have as many railways as during the railway era, a number of for-hire truckers in addition, and also the important alternative of operating their own or leased trucks. Some shippers can also utilize or operate water carrier services in serving their domestic or American markets to obtain favorable rail rates. Even the potential use of trucks or vessels can be effective in limiting railway rates. For the movement of general commodities between large cities up to 600 or 700 miles apart, there will be up to ten, and often more, for-hire truckers competing actively with the railways.[41] Hence, except for bulk commodities moving efficiently only in large shipments over long distances and some other rail-bound commodities moving long distances from remote resource-orientated production locations, in Canada transport markets today are many-firm markets far more often than they were during the railway era. This condition is favorable to both price and service competition since at prevailing prices the differentiated intermodal services are substitutable in the marketplace. And the variable cost characteristic of the additional modal carriers in the market further reinforces competitive action between the modes.

Clearly, the ideal prerequisites for effective competition according to the perfect or pure competition model do not exist in all intramodal and intermodal markets in Canada. Nevertheless, the structures of the intramodal markets for trucking and water carrier services and those of the intermodal road-rail and water-rail markets are conducive to dynamic competitive forces, including price competition. Moreover, the regulatory climate in Canada today is favorable to allowing the dynamic competitive forces inherent in the market structures to work rather freely, in view of the wide commercial freedom of the railways to set their rates above variable costs and to engage in price competition against trucks and water carriers down to their own variable costs, and even to operate trucking and shipping firms. This does not mean that in Canada there are no markets in which there are no other modal carriers available as alternatives to the railways, with comparably low unit costs and rates and capacity to serve huge flows of traffic. This analysis of the extent of existence of the prerequisites for effective competition does imply, however, that most freight rates in Canada are probably set by actual or potential intramodal or intermodal competition alone or in combination with the forces of market competition. Indeed, many of the freight rates on rail-bound bulk commodity movements or on shipments of resource-based enterprises far from their markets are limited by market competition.

Market and Producing Area Competition

Up to this point, only occasional mention has been made of another type of very significant competition that has a strong impact on railway rates, even in many markets in which the traffic wholly or largely moves by railway. This is the force of market competition.

Although fuller explanation and examples are given in Chapter V, this competitive force typically takes place where there are two or more producing areas for a product or for substitutable products that are geographically separated and often different distances from common markets. When the producers in different producing areas attempt to sell their products in the same large distributing or consuming market, the products from the different producing areas compete with one another in that market. Carriers serving the different producing areas will therefore adjust their rates to enable their shippers to sell profitably in the common market. If a producing region is farther away from the market than another such region, the competitive pressures from the distance-disadvantaged producers and the traffic and revenue incentives for the carriers will motivate the railway or railways serving that region to reduce the rates in relation to those from the nearer, distance-advantaged producing regions. An interesting feature is that market competition can compel railroads to undertake competitive rate making even when they are not physically close to one another and do not serve the alternative producing areas. For example, the CN and the CP are in competition with American railways even when their routes are hundreds of miles apart, because Canadian lumber, newsprint, paper and potash producers market their products in the same American markets as American producers.

In Canada, there are many situations, including export markets, in which the competitive force of market competition limits substantially the rates on railway traffic that otherwise would be subject to monopoly rate fixation by the railways. When added to the intermodal and intramodal competitive forces that prevail under the competition-prerequisite conditions discussed above, there is a strong logical presumption that railway rates in Canada are generally limited by the dynamic forces of actual or potential competition.

The Continued Role of Price Discrimination in Railway Transport

Though the impact of competitive forces on railways has increased profoundly in recent times, railways continue to employ discriminating rates to attain budgetary equilibrium and modest rates of return or to lessen their losses. In theory, under equilibrium conditions, competitive pricing equates price with marginal and average total unit costs, results in uniform prices rather than discriminating prices except in true joint-cost situations, such as the back-haul,

150

and promotes production by the optimal size firm at the optimal or least-cost level of a firm's output. Does the continuance of discriminating rate structures after widespread competition has developed in freight transport mean that the railways are engaging in uneconomic pricing and should be compelled to utilize uniform prices? Or is it that, though competition has made railway freight rates behave more like competitive prices, the conditions requiring discriminating rate structures for profitable and efficient railroading still substantially continue to exist? In view of the complaints of the Prairie Provinces and some shippers of inequitable rate discriminations, and Alberta's advocacy of basing rates on variable costs, these are significant questions for policy as well as for the railways in Canada.

Discriminating rates, not only in true joint-cost conditions but throughout the railway markets for freight, have been the histroical and normal pricing for the railway industry in every country, whether railways have been privately-owned or publicly-owned.[42] This pricing system for railways has not been arbitrarily imposed on society, but for 150 years has been regarded, even by economists and public regulators, as normal and efficient pricing for the railways. The historical and continuing support for discriminating pricing for railways has been based on the original necessary overbuilding of railways, the continuing excess capacity from expansion or technological modernization and their special conditions of wide areas of common and fixed costs, considerable underutilization of fixed factors, especially track capacity, and the multiple nature of their output.[43] With respect to Canada, the MacPherson Royal Commission on Transportation called attention to the economic case for discriminating rates for railways, as follows:

> ... Under this system of differential pricing the railways hauled bulk commodities which had a relatively low value per pound such as grain, coal, ore, gravel, etc., at low rates which sometimes covered little more than actual "out-of-pocket" costs, and recovered most of their overhead costs from the high rates applicable to more finished goods with a much higher value per pound such as clothing, tobacco, hardware, machinery, etc. Without the low rates a good deal of the bulk traffic would not have moved at all because transportation costs would have been too high in proportion to the value of the commodity to make their shipment profitable — whereas the finished goods, because of their greater value, could and did move at the higher rates. The railways thus obtained a volume of traffic which might not otherwise have come into being and they did so with the active encouragement of the Federal Government which saw in the low-rate policy a further means of stimulating the development of primary production

151

in Canada. The rate classification system which developed on this basis allowed rates to vary from a low of as little as one-half cent up to as much as ten cents per ton-mile and they bore little relation to the cost of performing the service; a rate was considered "just and reasonable" if it displayed what seemed to be an equitable relationship to the remainder of the rate structure. The traditional principle of ratemaking, then, represented a form of cross subsidization under which some users of rail service contributed through higher rates a relatively greater amount to the total transportation bill than did others − on a sort of capacity-to-pay basis. It was a system that seemed eminently suited to the needs of the developing Canadian economy as well as to the needs of the railways for the maximum volume of traffic consistent with adequate revenue returns − and if there were certain shippers who questioned the reasonableness of the rate structure there was, in the transportation environment of the day, very little they could do about it.[44]

Discriminating pricing for railways has long been judged in economics as socially efficient pricing, as a second-best pricing solution to that of having all prices equated with marginal costs. This is because it has encouraged traffic flows sufficient to enable railways to be constructed in undeveloped regions, has continued to facilitate higher utilization of fixed facilities to lower the average costs and the rate level compared to what they would be under uniform rates, and eliminate the necessity of taxation to cover the fixed costs and to attract capital.[45] If railway rates had been made uniform competitive prices under the excess capacity conditions that have generally obtained, freight rates would have been based on variable costs when these were below total average unit costs. Consequently, the total revenues to the railways would have been less than their total expenses and the deficits would have to be made up by taxation. This would have raised a welfare problem because through taxation people not in the market for railway services would have been taxed to defray the fixed costs.[46] Thus, discriminating pricing, if adequately limited by selective government regulation or competitive market forces to contain it to the requirements of the necessary rates of return and to ensure protection of the public interest, is the economic pricing scheme for railways so long as the conditions that make it inevitable and socially beneficial continue.[47]

For uniform prices to be efficient for the railways, they, like competitive firms, would have to be able to operate regularly with traffic in sufficient volumes to utilize their capacity, including track capacity, optimally so that their marginal costs would equate with their total average unit costs. Then, at uniform rates, except in true joint-cost situations, the railways could operate efficiently with normal profitability at their least-cost levels of output. Such ideally efficient conditions for railway pricing have not existed except rarely in the past, and are not likely to take place in the future. How close the Canadian mainline railways are to being operated regularly at optimal utilization rates, is, of course, a factual question. However, such data as are readily available do not indicate that the Canadian railways can anticipate a full-utilization-of-capacity operation continuously, and, of course, the unbalanced traffic in different directions that create true joint costs as to the back hauls will continue in large measure as in the past.[48] It follows that discriminating railway rates will continue, though the advent of widespread and forceful competition from other modes and other sources no doubt will continue to lessen their range and amount as competitive forces have done in the past.

The preceding analysis of the extent to which the prerequisites for workable competition exist in Canadian freight transport makes it evident that any expectation of realizing the ideal pricing, output, efficiency and allocative results from competition in its purest competitive market state would not be realistic for Canadian conditions, particularly for Canadian rail transport. But this is equally true of many other industries and sets of markets in the economy.[49] As concluded above, the prerequisites for workable competition do appear to be sufficiently present in Canadian freight transport to make reasonable the presumption that effective competition generally exists. At issue is whether under appropriate (or liberalized) regulation, the vital, forceful and widespread dynamic competitive forces that do exist in today's transport markets can bring a large measure of the benefits that ordinarily accrue from effective competition wherever it takes place. To answer this question requires a close examination of the operation of the marketing and pricing of railway services. The next three chapters throw light on this question. Therefore, detailed conclusions on the effects of competitive forces in Canadian freight transport are reserved for Chapter IX.

FOOTNOTES

1. J.C. Bonbright, *Principles of Public Utility Rates* (New York: Columbia University Press, 1961), Chaps. III, VI and XVII-XX.
2. See Joe S. Bain, *Industrial Organization,* 2d ed. (New York: John Wiley & Sons, Inc., 1968); and for an excellent application of the market factors favorable to effective competition in air transport, see Richard E. Caves, *Air Transport and Its Regulators: An Industry Study* (Cambridge, Mass.: Harvard University Press, 1962).
3. A paper by Alan Walters, "Problems of Oligopoly, Bilateral Monopoly and Strategic Behavior", drafted while he was at the Centre for Transportation Studies, University of British Columbia during August 1975, was very helpful in summarizing the relevant theory in this section. However, the responsibility for this statement is wholly that of the authors of this monograph.
4. For a simple demonstration, see Charles F. Phillips, Jr., *The Economics of Regulation,* rev. ed. (Homewood, Ill.: Richard D. Irwin, Inc., 1969), pp. 303-310.
5. Dudley F. Pegrum, *Transportation, Economics and Public Policy* (Homewood Ill.: Richard D. Irwin, Inc., 1963), pp. 140-144. See Chaps. 7 and 8 for some of the theory models for pricing and the cost complications in the theory of pricing for transport.
6. James C. Nelson, "Toward Rational Price Policies," in *The Future of American Transportation,* edited by Ernest W. Williams, Jr. (Englewood Cliffs, N.J.: Prentice-Hall, Inc., 1971), pp. 125-130; and see European Economic Community, *Studies, Options in Transport Tariff Policy,* by a group of distinguished university economists headed by Professor Maurice Allais, National School of Mines, Paris, Transport Series No. 1, Brussels, 1965, pp. 9-10, 140 and 147-148.
7. Alan Walters, "Problems of Oligopoly, Bilateral Monopoly and Strategic Behavior," *op.cit.,* pp. 3-5. See "Memorandum on Transportation by Dr. H.A. Innis" in *Report of the Royal Commission on Transportation,* W.F.A. Turgeon, Chairman (Ottawa, King's Printer and Controller of Stationery, 1951), pp. 297 and 300-302.
8. See George J. Stigler, "The Theory of Economic Regulation," *The Bell Journal of Economics and Management Science,* Spring 1971, pp. 3-21; Richard A. Posner, "Theories of Economic Regulation," *ibid.,* Autumn 1974, pp. 335-358; and James C. Nelson, "New Concepts in Transportation Regulation", *Transportation and National Policy,* National Resources Planning Board, Washington, May 1942, pp. 197-237. The last paper documents the formation of a cartel by regulated American truckers after entry control was established by the Motor Carrier Act of 1935.
9. John Maurice Clark, *Competition as a Dynamic Process* (Washington, D.C.: The Brookings Institution, 1961), p. 2. See also his "Toward a Concept of Workable Competition," *The American Economic Review,* June 1940, pp. 241-256.
10. *Ibid.,* p. 2.
11. *Ibid.,* p. 16.
12. *Ibid.,* pp. 15, 18, 21, 70-72 and 465-490.
13. *Ibid.,* pp. 15-16 and 18.
14. Compare Milton Moore, *How Much Price Competition?, The Prerequisite of an Effective Canadian Competition Policy* (Montreal: McGill-Queen's University Press, 1970), pp. 43-44.
15. Ernest W. Williams Jr., *The Regulation of Rail-Motor Rate Competition* (New York: Harper & Bros., 1958), pp. 210-212 and 221-222; and James C. Nelson, *Railroad Transportation and Public Policy* (Washington, D.C.: The Brookings Institution, 1959), pp. 40-66, 142-147 and 349-351.
16. John R. Meyer et.al., *The Eonomics of Competition in the Transportation Industries*

(Cambridge, Mass.: Harvard University Press, 1959), pp. 215-222. For a critical review of studies of economies of scale in size of firm in trucking, see John R. Felton and Dale G. Anderson, "Impact of Motor Carrier Deregulation on Agriculture, Rural Shippers, and Receivers," paper before the National Symposium on Transportation for Agriculture and Rural America, New Orleans, Louisiana, November 15, 1976, pp. 2-7.

17. See Paul W. MacAvoy, *The Economic Effects of Regulation: the Trunk-Line Railroad Cartels and the Interstate Commerce Commission Before 1900* (Cambridge, Mass.: The M.I.T. Press, 1965); and Robert M. Spann and Edward W. Erickson, "The Economics of Railroading: The Beginning of Cartelization and Regulation," *The Bell Journal of Economics and Management Science,* Autumn 1970, pp. 227-244, particularly p. 243. MacAvoy shows that in the U.S.A., periods of active price competition broke down cartel arrangements from time to time in the final quarter of the 19th Century.

18. See Kent T. Healy, *The Effects of Scale in the Railroad Industry,* Committee on Transportation, Yale University, 1961; George H. Borts, "The Estimation of Rail Cost Functions," *Econometrica,* January 1960, pp. 108-131, particularly pp. 126-128; and Theodore E. Keeler, "Railroad Costs, Returns to Scale, and Excess Capacity," *The Review of Economics and Statistics,* May 1974, pp. 201-208.

19. See the comparative cost levels by type of freight carrier and their general effects on methods of movement in Marvin L. Fair and Ernest W. Williams, Jr., *Economics of Transportation and Logistics* (Dallas, Tex.: Business Publications, Inc., 1975), pp. 169-181; and John R. Meyer et. al., *The Economics of Competition in the Transportation Industries, op.cit.,* Chap. VI.

20. See H.L. Purdy, *Transport Competition and Public Policy in Canada* (Vancouver: University of British Columbia Press, 1972), pp. 18, 69 and 72; Pacific Transportation Advisory Council, *Proposed Organization and Terms of Reference,* prepared for the Striking Committee, June 2, 1972, pp. 6-8; and Transport Canada, *An Interim Report on Freight Transportation in Canada,* June 1975, pp. 8-9 and Exhibit 4.

21. Alexander Lyall Morton, "Truck-Rail Competition for Traffic in Manufactures," Transportation Research Forum, *Proceedings-Twelfth Annual Meeting* (Oxford, Ind.: The Richard B. Cross Company, 1971), pp. 151-168, particularly pp. 167-168.

22. H.L. Purdy, *op.cit.,* pp. 69-73; and *An Interim Report on Freight Transportation in Canada, op.cit.,* Figure 3B and pp. 22-24.

23. Interstate Commerce Commission, *Transport Economics,* May 1969, pp. 1-2; December 1968, pp. 1-3.

24. See D. Daryl Wyckoff and David H. Maister, *The Owner-Operator: Independent Trucker* (Lexington, Mass.: Lexington Books, D.C. Heath and Co., 1975), Chaps. 2, 3 and 8. In the U.S.A., owner-operators, operating much like tramp ships on the oceans, frequently take circuitous circular or triangular routings back to their home bases if essential to back-haul loadings.

25. *Transportation Policy, A Framework for Transport in Canada, Summary Report, op.cit.,* Introduction.

26. Marvin L. Fair and Ernest W. Williams Jr., *op.cit.,* pp. 175-176.

27. James C. Nelson, *Railroad Transportation and Public Policy, op.cit.,* pp. 57-60.

28. Marvin L. Fair and Ernest W. Williams Jr., *op.cit.,* pp. 171 and 178-180.

29. *Ibid.,* p. 177.

30. For an excellent discussion of truck-rail competition in Canada, see D.W. Carr and Associates, "Truck-Rail Competition in Canada", *Royal Commission on Transportation* (Ottawa: Queen's Printer, 1962), Vol. III, pp. 1-93.

31. James C. Nelson, *Railroad Transportation and Public Policy, op.cit.,* pp. 43-47, 50-51, 63, 138-147, 348-349 and 367-369.

32. Ann F. Friedlaender, *The Dilemma of Freight Transport Regulation* (Washington, D.C.: The Brookings Institution, 1969), pp. 66-69 and 98-99.
33. H.L. Purdy, *op.cit.*, pp. 70-71; and *An Interim Report on Freight Transportation in Canada*, Exhibit 12B. See also Canadian Transport Commission, *The Canadian Trucking Industry: Issues Arising out of Current Information*, ESAB 75-5, April 1975, pp. 3, 7, 11-13, 20-26 and 30-32.
34. John R. Meyer et.al., *The Economics of Competition in the Transportation Industries, op.cit.*, pp. 86-101.
35. James Sloss, "Regulation of Motor Freight Transportation: A Quantitative Evaluation of Policy, " *The Bell Journal of Economics and Management Science,* Autumn 1970, pp. 327-366, particularly pp. 334-341. See Richard Schultz, "Intergovernmental Cooperation in Transportation: The Case of the Extra-Provincial Motor Carrier Industry in Canada," paper before the Joint Session of the Transportation Research Forum and the Canadian Transportation Research Forum, Toronto, November 4, 1975.
36. John R. Meyer et.al., *The Economics of Competition in the Transportation Industries, op.cit.*, pp. 111-126, particularly p. 112.
37. See *An Interim Report on Freight Transportation in Canada, op.cit.*, p. 7 and Exhibit 2A.
38. Kent T. Healy, *op.cit.*, pp. 1-5.
39. James C. Nelson, *Railroad Transportation and Public Policy, op.cit.*, pp. 50-51 and 367-369.
40. H.L. Purdy, *op.cit.*, pp. 90-91; and Marvin L. Fair and Ernest W. Williams Jr., *op.cit.*, pp. 287 and 289-291.
41. *An Interim Report on Freight Transportation in Canada, op.cit.*, pp. 23-24 and Exhibit 12B. See also E.J. Benson, "The Unknown Industry", an address before the Annual Convention of the Canadian Trucking Association, Toronto, November 24, 1974, pp. 3 and 6a-8.
42. John R. Meyer et.al., *op.cit.*, pp. 169-188; Ann F. Friedlaender, *op.cit.*, pp. 63-64; and H.L. Purdy, *op.cit.*, pp. 91-92.
43. James C. Nelson, *Railroad Transportation and Public Policy, op.cit.*, pp. 151-171.
44. Royal Commission on Transportation (MacPherson Commission), (Ottawa: Queen's Printer, 1961), Vol. I, pp. 4-5.
45. D.P. Locklin, "The Literature on Railway Rate Theory," *Quarterly Journal of Economics,* February 1933, pp. 167-230; and D.H. Wallace, "Joint and Overhead Cost and Railway Rate Policy", *Quarterly Journal of Economics,* August 1934, pp. 583-619.
46. Nancy Ruggles, "Recent Developments in the Theory of Marginal Cost Pricing," reprinted from *Review of Economic Studies,* Vol. 17 (1949-50), pp. 107-126, in *Public Enterprise,* edited by R. Turvey (Baltimore: Penguin Books, 1968), pp. 11-43.
47. EEC, Studies, *Options in Transport Tariff Policy, op.cit.*, p. 148; and William J. Baumol and David E. Bradford, "Optional Departures from Marginal Cost Pricing," *American Economic Review,* June 1970, pp. 265-283, particularly pp. 265-267, 271-272 and 277-280.
48. *An Interim Report on Freight Transportation in Canada, op.cit.*, pp. 8-13, 31-32, and 37-41.
49. John R. Meyer et.al., *op.cit.*, pp. 238-241 and 270-273.

CHAPTER V

MARKET COMPETITION AS A COMPETITIVE INFLUENCE ON RAILWAY RATES

The demand for transport is a derived demand, derived, in the case of freight, from the needs of producers and distributors to move products in a timely and reliable way from origins to destinations, where they have higher value. The difference between the cost of the goods at their origin, including a return on capital, and their value at destination is a measure of the value of the transportation service.[1] It follows from this that carriers must be concerned with the extent to which their services meet the constraints of the time and place utility associated with the movement of particular commodities over their routes. The concept of the value of transportation service links together the demand for the transportation of a commodity and the demand for the commodity itself. Anything which restricts the demand for a commodity to be moved restricts the demand for the transportation of that commodity. The constraint placed on the value of transportation service by competition between alternate sources of supply of a commodity, or between a commodity and substitute commodities, is the force of market competition.

Market competition becomes the form of effective competition in the absence of direct intramodal or intermodal competition in transport markets. Intramodal or intermodal competition is effective when carriers within a mode or in different modes of transport are willing to transport freight at a rate below the value of the service to the shippers. In the presence of effective intramodal and/or intermodal competition, the need for examining the degree of market competition as it affects freight rates is lessened. If direct carrier competition is weak or only present in some markets for the movement of a shipper's freight, both modal and market competition may be important in negotiations.

Market competition, like direct carrier competition, may exert a strong competitive pressure on a carrier, so that the rate charged must be close to the relevant cost of the service and only a small contribution to the carrier's constant costs can be earned. In other instances, the margin between the cost of the good at origin and the value of the good at destination may be great, so that

157

the rate charged by the carrier makes a substantial contribution to the carrier's constant costs. In this case, it should be noted that if the carrier did not earn this margin it would accrue to the shipper. In other cases, the level of market competition may become so great that the value of service is less than the carrier's cost so that neither the production nor the transportation of the good at a given origin can take place profitably.

The limit placed on freight rates by market competition varies among commodities, among regions and over time. The situation which raises the greatest difficulty for carriers, producers and society is that where a service changes from having a value in excess of the cost of carriage to having a value less than the cost of carriage. This means that a service which was commercially viable has become unprofitable with the associated serious consequences. Society may be faced with the choice of allowing the economic forces to run their course through the commercial system, leading to the failure of a part or all of a shipper's, and perhaps a carrier's, business, or society may choose to intervene by subsidies, for example, if the public interest is found to warrant such action.

General Views on the Role of Market Competition in Canada

The extent and effectiveness of market competition in Canadian rail transport markets has been given far too little attention. Unfortunately, the shortcoming has been in existence since before the MacPherson Royal Commission. The importance of market competition as a limit on the monopoly power of the railways was not explicitly recognized in that Commission's report. It is, perhaps, because of this omission that amibiguity has arisen about the protection intended by the Commission for shippers relying mainly on rail service. It is desirable to review the conclusions of the MacPherson Commission in order to indicate how market competition fits into that Commission's rationale. It is also appropriate to consider the views on market competition and its relevance to maximum rate protection expressed in 1966. The discussion prior to the passing of the National Transportation Act indicated that a number of fears existed about the effects of relying on market competition where intermodal competition was lacking. Examination of the experience since 1967 can reveal how far the undesirable effects anticipated have actually materialized.

Monopoly Power as Viewed by the MacPherson Commission

The MacPherson Commission argued persuasively that the extension of intermodal competition had reshaped, and in 1961 was still radically and quickly reshaping, the nature of the transportation industry and the internal organization and practices of the railways. Although it was recognized that the level of intermodal competition varies, the Commission concluded that "the average degree of monopoly which the railways have today is not itself significant and would not itself justify elaborate and expensive rate regulating machinery".[2] Therefore, the Commission was less concerned with the possibility "that the railways are exploiting all shippers than with the possibility that a significant element of monopoly may still persist in a few cases".[3] The Commission was very much concerned with the criteria by which to judge whether the degree of monopoly power warranted regulation of maximum rates. It concluded that

> ... in the case of railway shipments, the degree of monopoly power for each [shipment] could be measured by the difference between rate and cost divided by the cost. Alternatively, the same effect could be obtained by expressing the rate as a percentage of cost. It is essentially this relationship of rate to cost which provides the basis for our proposals regarding maximum rate control.[4]

The Commission went on to recognize that some shippers are dependent on rail service for most or perhaps all of their traffic. For those shippers no "feeling of escape presents itself"[5], and for such shippers a need for some upper bound imposed on freight rates was accepted as desirable. However, to balance the revenue needs of the railways and the need for protection of shippers, the level of the maximum rate was selected at a high level, clearly well above the level of the major non-competitive commodity rates. The Commission did not make clear that the level of those rates were held down by market competition. The Commission recommended that the eligibility of a shipper to receive the protection of the maximum rate was to be dependent on the decision of the shipper "to seek captive status" by confining all of the traffic in question to the railway at the maximum rate.[6] The state of captivity was seen by the Commission as a part of the process for establishing the applicability of maximum rate control, not as a precondition for its application.

The maximum rate control recommended by the Commission and conceived as desirable by the Government was one which would set an upper limit on rates, but would not be the effective rate-setting factor for most captive shippers. The Government showed, during debate on the legislation in 1966, that it understood that the majority of captive shippers were given as effective a protection, or even more effective protection, against high rates by market competition as were other shippers by intermodal competition. Nevertheless, the Government made the maximum rate section apply only on traffic for which there is "no alternative, effective and competitive service by a common carrier other than a rail carrier or a combination of rail carriers..."[7] This restriction of maximum rate control has made it difficult to determine the eligibility of shippers and, in that sense, has reduced the availability of the control as perceived by the MacPherson Commission. It seems likely that this restriction will be removed as a result of the 1973-76 policy review.

159

Support for the Effectiveness of Competition in 1966

In presenting evidence to the Standing Committee on Transport and Communications in 1966, shippers made representations to seek modification of sections of the bill which they believed contrary to their interests. Without exception, those appearing wished to see the control of rates changed to produce lower maxima. However, few large shippers made such representations, as was noted by Mr. Pickersgill, the Minister of Transport. He stated that if

> ... I had a large business, shipping bulk commodities over a long period and I felt that the protection I now had in the present Railway Act was being taken away by this legislation, I would be here with the best lawyer I could hire to say that that protection should not be taken away or that some equally good protection should be put in its place. The fact, again apart from the Wabush Case and the coal operators, no such person has done that, suggests to me that most of these large shippers of bulk commodities have already made pretty satisfactory deals with the railways from their own point of view and they are not worried about the legislation. Now, that is the conclusion I draw from the set of facts.[8]

One of the few views of support for the responsiveness of the railways to market competitive arguments was made by Mr. Mauro, Q.C., representing the Government of Manitoba. He stated:

> ... I could not permit this opportunity to go by without complimenting the railways, particularly in the past, on the fact that they will sit down and talk to you and attempt to discuss these problems to see if they can be helpful in development situations. I do not want my brief to suggest for a minute that this is the province of Manitoba arraigned against some pirate type adversary who is attempting to break our economy. I think that the railways are trying to do a good job. I think the railways are the first to admit, though, there have to be some rules to the way the game is played. The railways are most helpful in trying to determine whether or not they can assist in resource development to their own benefit and to the benefit of the provinces.[9]

However, the major argument concerning the effectiveness of market competition came from the railways or Mr. Pickersgill and some of his colleagues. Some of these views were quoted in Chapter III. In essence, they argued that the relationship between the demand for the good and the demand for transport necessitates that the railways be responsive. It might be said that the captivity of the railways to captive shippers requires a setting of rate and service matters to their mutual advantage! Mr. Gordon, President of the CN, explained how the process works. He stated:

> ... if a particular shipper — let us say he is a manufacturer — comes to us and says, look, I have to reach Chicago, and I am meeting competition in the Chicago market, and on the basis of my costs of production and so forth I can not stand your freight rate, well then we will sit down and we will analyze that and find out what our own costs are, and we can then determine whether or not we can temper the wind to the shorn lamb, if you want to put it that way, and give him a rate that will still show us a profit but which will enable him to meet his market competition.[10]

Reliance on the railway managers to determine whether or not they could establish a rate to enable a shipper to meet his market competition gave rise to a number of concerns.

Concerns of Shippers about Reliance on Market Competition in Rate Making in 1966

In spite of the support given to the responsiveness of the railways by the Province of Manitoba, the view was expressed that the railways were not responsive. Mr. Whittaker, the Manager of the Coal Operators Association of Western Canada, stated:

> ... when we first started to develop the competition of oil and gas and we had discussions with the railways about lower freight rates, and because the railways would not move, for reasons best known to themselves, we lost the business. After we lost the business the railways told us that they would be prepared to do something. We have had some actual concrete experiences where we have lost substantial business just by this attitude.[11]

The Association was clearly concerned about the responsiveness of the railways. Recognition that by error, lack of information or some other reason the railways may prevent a shipper from being able to meet competition was one of the reasons for the broad wording of Section 23 of the National Transportation Act. Cases under this Section have dealt with situations where railway rates have been considered by shippers to be a major impediment to their sales in competitive markets (see Chapter VIII).

It appeared that some persons were concerned about the railways' ability to charge according to railway conceptions of the value of service, even if the traffic could still move. For example, Mr. Cantelon, a member of the Standing

161

Committee, stated:

> The point I want to make is that this leaves the railway quite a lot of leeway. For instance, if the potash can be produced in Saskatchewan — let us just use some fictitious figures — at $2 a ton which, of course, it is not, and it has to go onto the world market at $5 a ton, the railway can charge up to $2.90 to get it on that world market. That puts it on the world market then at $5 a ton. This allows the railway quite a lot of power, I think, in its negotiation; and to me this does not show that the potash company is a non-captive shipper. They are captive to the extent that the railway can charge as much as the traffic will bear and, if I know anything, the railway will charge as much as the traffic will bear.[12]

Concern about the level of railway earnings because of the "monopoly position" of the railways over captive shippers was expressed by the Province of Alberta and Dr. E. Williams, a witness for Alberta, Manitoba and the Maritime Provinces.[13] The difficulty of applying a rate-of-return approach to a part of the railway system was noted by Mr. Pickersgill.[14]

The responsibility of the railways to respond to market competition was a concern because it was perceived that the railways would have the ability to direct industrial expansion in Canada by discriminatory pricing. Mr. Mauro, Q.C., stated, "they could charge one person 10 per cent above out-of-pocket costs, charge the other fellow 150 per cent and effectively close the other chap out of the market."[15] Mr. V. Stechishin, when summarizing the brief of the Winnipeg Chamber of Commerce, said, "... I think what is overlooked is that a large number of shippers who are now moving under the so-called non-competitive commodity rates are getting the rates because of the discrimination section [in the pre-1967 Railway Act.]"[16]

In view of the limited information on the workings of market competition in Canada, it is important to examine the evidence of the case studies and other evidence since 1967 to see how market competitive forces have worked to affect freight rates and service. Have shippers of bulk commodities by rail been afforded effective protection by market competition, as implicitly expected by the MacPherson Commission in 1961 and as anticipated by the Government in 1966? Have the railways responded to the needs of shippers for rates which allow the shippers to compete in distant markets? Have the railways behaved responsively in setting rates where market competition exists or have they taken advantage of the absence of an explicit constraint on unjust discrimination?

Evidence on the Workings of Market Competitive Forces

The case studies provide considerable evidence on the importance and working of competitive forces. It is the judgement of the authors that the evidence is sufficient for the conclusions drawn, although it is not claimed that the case studies are representative in any statistical sense. It is difficult to judge whether shippers deliberately concealed negotiating situations in which the railways had been unresponsive, but that seems unlikely, in view of traditional concerns about railway rates and rate making, and in view of the general cooperation of shippers during interviews.

The investigation of the negotiations between shippers and carriers required long interviews during which the confidential files which the firms maintained were normally available for reference and were commonly reviewed. Because of the confidential nature of the rate negotiation process the specific case data are confidential, so that references to specific negotiations can report only information or ideas which have become common knowledge. The review of evidence on the workings of market, and other, competitive forces draws on information both from the case studies and from other sources.

Market competitive forces on railway rates can be very complex and may take several forms. Therefore, for ease of description, the examples of market competition found in the case studies are placed in three categories. They are, first, competition between different producers for a common market; second, market competition in the location or expansion of plants; and, third, market competition through the use of alternate markets or sources of supply. These categories are based on the thrust of the market competitive conditions cited in the arguments presented by shippers to the railways. The differences among the categories may arise from the depth to which an argument was developed or the time period over which it was applied. For example, it may be that reducing the competitiveness of a shipper in a market will affect the size of his plant compared with that of his competitors over the long run. However, the particulars of the competitive conditions at a particular time may only lead the producer to be concerned with his ability to sell his current output in a market. He may not raise any question about the long-run effect on his growth opportunities.

Market Competition between Different Producers for a Common Market

The most frequent form of market competition is that between separately located producers competing for a common market. The working of market competitive forces applies to Canadian products competing in foreign markets, to the competitive influence of imports in Canadian markets and to the competition between Canadian producers selling in the domestic market.

Competition of Canadian products in overseas markets. The form of competition affecting more traffic than any other form in Western Canada is the market competition faced by Canadian products in world markets. This force is particularly important for the railway movement of bulk products in large volume for which no alternate form of transportation is practicable in view of the quantities to be moved and the distances involved. The major commodities affected are coal from eastern British Columbia and western Alberta, sulphur from Alberta and potash from Saskatchewan. The development of each of these commodity trades has required the investment of hundreds of millions of dollars, and they are major resource developments in Western Canada. In spite of important differences between the economic characteristics of the development of the three resources and the relationships between the producers and the railways, there are a number of important similarities.

The development of coal, potash and sulphur production has increased to major proportions only since the late 1960's. Coal has been produced for decades, but it was only in 1970 that the first bulk export movement to Vancouver took place by unit train. The first production of potash in Saskatchewan took place in 1962, but, since that time, the increase in production from that Province now places Canada second to Russia as a producer of potash.[17] Sulphur is produced in Alberta as a by-product of the cleaning of sour natural gas, that is, natural gas with a high sulphur content. During the 1960's, it was produced and shipped by a number of plants in Alberta separately in single or multiple-car lots to Vancouver for export. The system was not well-coordinated and had limited storage facilities. During and since 1969, the development of an improved transportation system has been concomitant with the growth of sulphur exports. Data in Table 2 in Chapter II show that the car-miles of traffic for coal, potash and sulphur in Canada have increased between 1969 and 1974 by 130 percent, 58 percent and 250 percent, respectively. This record of growth shows that the railways have established rates which have enabled these resource industries to expand, in spite of their virtual dependence on rail transport to ship their product to North American consumers or to tidewater for export.

The growth of this traffic has been associated with the development of integrated bulk rail and terminal handling systems, which have reduced rail costs and enabled rates to be reduced and/or held down when they might otherwise have increased. The conditions affecting the development of well-coordinated transport systems differ among the commodities. The conditions warrant brief description.

In the case of coal, the mines developed so far are only accessible by one railway and the mining companies have had to work with that railway to plan the unit train system. The design volumes at each mine are sufficient to support a unit train operation, so that the major requirement has been for effective integration between a mine, a railway and a terminal operation. The characteristics of handling potash and sulphur have similarly required the development of bulk handling systems, but the systems have been much more difficult to develop and operate. Companies have had to agree to commodity standardization and mixing of output to achieve design volumes sufficient to warrant bulk shipping and terminal handling systems.

In the case of overseas shipments of potash, which comprise about 25 percent of the industry output, effective coordination of transportation to Vancouver was brought about through Canpotex Ltd., an industry-organized, Saskatchewan Government approved, agency for handling all offshore potash sales. It was originally set up in 1970, and in 1972 deliberate policies of the Provincial Government forced all companies to join it.[18] The nine producing companies in Saskatchewan were, in part, brought together by Provincial Government pressure for the purposes of prorationing output and maintaining a minimum price.[19] The transportation responsibility of Canpotex during and since 1973 has made the planning and operation of the overseas transportation system more efficient than it would have been if the companies had been acting individually. The rates on potash are on a carload basis and the tariffs do not specify an annual volume commitment.

The development of the sulphur handling system has involved complex factors influencing the utilization of rail equipment. These include annual tonnage commitments and agreements concerning the time required for loading and unloading. Negotiations of rates for the producers have been the responsibility of a negotiating committee in which major companies, such as Shell, and the agents of other producers, for example Trimac Ltd., have been important. Often, it has been difficult to achieve the throughput and performance objectives agreed to and in 1976 a new company, Sultran Ltd., was established to be responsible for the administration of transportation. It is not clear how many of the producers will join this organization.

The joint efforts of the producers and railways have been important to the efficiency of the rail transport, but they have not prevented difficult negotiations of rail rates. The importance of the rates have been shown in various ways. Two instances warrant brief description. The first involves coal, the second, potash.

The first rate for the movement of coal by unit train in Canada was established by CP for the movement of coal from the Kaiser Resources mine near Fernie, B.C. to the port of Roberts Bank, Vancouver, at a base rate of $3.50 per ton. This rate was negotiated with the Japanese buyers of the coal. The price of the coal, f.o.b. Vancouver, was about $13 per ton. In subsequent negotiations between Crows Nest Industries (who had previously owned the property developed by Kaiser Resources) and Kaiser Resources with the CP, the railway indicated that the rates would have to be higher for subsequent contracts. In an attempt to avoid higher rates, Crows Nest Industries proposed to construct a railway, the Kootenay and Elk Railway, eighty miles to the American border to connect with the Burlington Northern so that coal could

165

move over that railway to Vancouver. The construction of this line was opposed by the CP, and the regulatory case initiated in May, 1969, involved hearings before the CTC and the Supreme Court of Canada.[20] Following a decision of the Supreme Court on May 1, 1972, it appeared that no obstacle remained to the construction of the line and construction began on April 26, 1973. On April 28, 1973, the Premier of British Columbia announced that the Government of British Columbia would deny the railway permission to cross the Elk Forest, which is on provincially-controlled Crown land.[21] Premier Barrett felt that the possible loss of railway jobs by employees of the CP to employees of the BN was a more important matter of public interest than was the power of the CP in setting rates for the coal producers of the area. Subsequent events proved that both the rail rate and the price of the coal had been set too low. Both the rail rate and the coal price were renegotiated with the Japanese to what appear to be profitable levels.[22]

The negotiation of rates on Saskatchewan potash is unusual in the extent of involvement of the Provincial Government. The extreme use of Government power is demonstrated by the events of 1970. The rate on potash from Saskatchewan to Vancouver was $9.00 per ton. It had been set at that level by the railways in 1958 as a "development" rate based on the rate from Carlsbad, New Mexico to Long Beach, California of $9.60 per ton.[23] In 1970, the railways proposed a rate increase of six percent which was countered by the Province with a request that the rates be reduced. Apparently, under a threat that the Province would increase mineral taxes on railway-owned property, the railways reduced the rates by eleven percent, including the six percent increase.[24] There is no evidence that this government action was taken on the initiative of the producers. At least, subsequently, the producers appear to have had more difficulty with Federal and Provincial tax policies and nationalization by the Province than they had in negotiating rail rates.[25]

The freight rates on coal are negotiated and set for each mine. The rates on potash and sulphur are zone and zone-related rates. In the last three years, the level of rates on these commodities has increased substantially, but by substantially smaller amounts than the increase in value of the commodities. The record of sulphur rates is given, as an example, in Table 19.

The table shows the wide and sudden variations in the sulphur price. In contrast, the variations from year to year in the freight rates have been small. The first notable change in the level of freight rates is the reduction in 1968, and again in 1969, associated with the introduction of volume-based rates, as allowed by the National Transportation Act. In view of the high price of sulphur, particularly during 1968, there is no evidence that the railways took advantage of any monopoly power. Indeed, in view of the price of the sulphur, produced as a by-product from natural gas, and the record of low railway earnings, it could be considered surprizing that the level of rates did not rise in 1968, or at least

Table 19

Sulphur Prices and Freight Rates, 1965-1976

	Freight Rate[a]		Estimated Sulphur Price at Plant		Freight Rate as percent of Plant Price
	$ per short ton	Change from Previous Year	$ per short ton	Change from Previous Year	
1965	9.00	-	13.88	-	65
1956	9.00	0	21.55	+7.67	42
1967	9.00	0	30.42	+8.87	30
1968	7.50[b]	-1.50	34.55	+4.13	22
1969	5.12[c]	-2.38	16.13	-18.42	32
1970	5.12	0	8.92	-7.21	57
1971	5.37	+0.25	7.23	-1.69	74
1972	5.64	+0.27	5.70	-1.53	99
1973	6.15	+0.51	5.50	-0.20	112
1974	7.27	+1.12	13.88	+8.38	52
1975	8.40	+1.13	30.00	+16.12	28
1976	11.50	+3.10	30.00	0	38

Notes: [a]Freight rates are from Southern Alberta to Vancouver for export.

[b]The first multiple car rates were introduced in 1968. They ranged from $8.10 per ton on 10 cars to $7.50 per ton on 50 cars.

[c]The first trainload rates were introduced in 1969. The $5.12 per ton rate applied on tonnage up to 500,000 tons; the $6.31 per ton rate applied on additional tonnage. The lower rate is shown for the years subsequent to 1969.

Source: The freight rates are from the records of CN and CP. The prices are estimated from data reported occasionally in Canadian Chemical Processing and from estimates of sulphur prices made by CP pricing officers.

167

stay constant, even with the volume-based rates. Since 1970, the freight rates have been increasing; slowly until 1973, and with a notable jump in 1976. Notwithstanding the last increase, the current value per ton at the plant is comparable with the high values realized in the late 1960's.

The attitude of bulk shippers in Western Canada to reliance on negotiation with the railways is reported in a recent study.[26] The study shows that there is uncertainty concerning the amount by which freight rates will increase, there is frustration in dealing with the railways in an inflationary period when the railways do not accede to shippers' requests for lesser increases and there is concern over the reasonableness of the railways' explanations for increases. The study states:

> Many bulk shippers exhibit feelings of frustration in dealing with the railroads on the subject of freight rates. This is reflected, in part, by their desires to be assured that rate increases are really justified on the basis of cost increases to the railroads.[27]

Shippers also expressed concern over the length of time it sometimes takes the railways to quote rates. However, the report gives no indication of whether complex factors were present in those cases when the railways were slow in quoting rates. One potash shipper is reported to have pointed out that

> ... shipping costs tend to rise and fall with world market prices, while rail rates rise. This places Canadian producers in an insecure position, since Canada's internal transport requirements for potash (from mine to port) are among the heaviest in the world.[28]

This view appears to give support to more value-of-service pricing than the railways now practice, but the majority of shippers seemed concerned over whether rate increases have been justified by railroad cost increases. However, these complaints and concerns about railway pricing were made at a time of very rapid rate increases. Further, the interview program on which the report was based was intended to find out what shippers and others saw as uncertainties and problems in the development of the transport system in Western Canada. In spite of the specific concerns of the shippers, the general conclusion of shippers concerning reliance on commercial negotiation without further government intervention is clear. The report states:

> Some representatives from the commercial sector in the west, notably bulk commodity producers, terminal operators, and railways are strongly calling for *less* government involvement in their activities. There are strong desires for less government "interference" in free enterprise activities, including marketing, pricing and terminal operations.[29]

With specific reference to rate making, the report states:

> While shippers also experience uncertainty with respect to rail freight rates and pricing policies, they generally feel that rate negotiations should continue to take place on a one-to-one basis, and that new mechanisms (such as suggested above for capacity concerns) are not required. However, some shippers do feel that the existence of a new process for communication and information exchange between shippers and carriers would generate knowledge useful in rate negotiations, and at the same time help to reduce some mistrust and misunderstandings which presently exist.[30]

The record of the growth of exports, the record of technological developments and investments of producers, railways and port authorities and the support of shippers for the present rate making process are evidence that the railways have established rates on coal, potash and sulphur so that these commodities can compete effectively in world markets. Indeed, during the early development of the coal trade the railways established rates so close to their costs, so that the Canadian producers would be competitive, that their rates were soon non-compensatory.

While resource developers may be concerned that freight rates be set low enough and be stable enough for resource development to proceed, a strong public concern has evolved over the last five years that Canada should receive a reasonable share of the profits earned from resource developments. In this sense, there has been a growing concern to insure that railway rates are set high enough and, certainly, at compensatory levels.

The examples in this section have focused on the market competitive forces affecting rates in Western Canada on natural resource commodities moving in bulk. However, the presence of greater competitive constraints on export rates than on domestic rates has been recognized for many years. Currie explains this as follows:

> ... as a rule export rates are much lower than local ones. Lower export tolls are published in order to stimulate the sale of Canadian staple commodities overseas and can be justified under the principle of value of service. The export rate is the amount which is not in excess of that which the railway believes the Canadian producer selling in the export market can afford to pay and still market his goods in competition with suppliers in other countries. It is designed, as far as railway rates can be, to bring prosperity to the export trades and business to railways.[31]

Competition of off-shore imports in Canadian markets. Low rates on imports

169

are less common than those on exports. Where low rates on imports exist, they are often explained by the necessity of competitive rates to draw traffic from the competing port and railway systems of the USA. Canadian manufacturers are often concerned about the relationship between domestic and import rates and will request the railways to raise rates on imported traffic.

The availability of imported goods at Canadian ports is an important source of market competition for domestic traffic. The responsiveness of the railways to this type of market competition has given rise to a number of cases of long- and short-haul rates. The case of steel rates to Vancouver was explained in Chapter II. In 1973 it was estimated that, had the Canadian railways not priced this traffic competitively, the loss of the Canadian producers' share of the British Columbian steel market would have cost the producers in Eastern Canada $50 million in annual sales and the railways $3.6 million in freight revenue per year.[32] The desirability of responding to the competitive pressure is not questioned. What is difficult to explain is the complexity of the resulting rate structure.

The effect of imports on domestic rail rates on glass are also evident. In 1974, the rates on glass moving from Toronto and Concord under agreed charges varied between $2.03 per 100 lbs. to Winnipeg, $3.20 per 100 lbs. to Calgary and $2.56 per 100 lbs. to Vancouver.[33] The explanation for the inconsistency in rates lies in the availability of imports in Vancouver. In 1974, of the total weight of off-shore imports of sheet glass into the four Western Provinces, 93 percent was for British Columbia.[34]

Although examples of the responsiveness of railway rates to imports has focussed on cases involving long- and short-haul discrimination on the West Coast, the availability of imports is important in the Maritimes and in the St. Lawrence area. For example, rates on potash to coastal points have been influenced by potash imported through the Gulf ports, which at one time came from New Mexico but has more recently come from Europe.

Market competition for Canadian products in the U.S.A. Canadian exports to the U.S.A. by rail are an important source of rail traffic for Canadian railways. Figures given in Chapter II show that in 1972 Canadian rail traffic into the U.S.A. contributed 20 per cent of Canadian rail revenue. Many of the commodities involved experience significant competition in those parts of the U.S.A. where they no longer enjoy proximity to their own plants. Several exmaples of this are well known. Cases involving forest products have been well documented before the CTC and ICC. These cases are considered more fully in Chapter VIII, but one example is given here.

Prince Albert Pulp Company has a sulphate woodpulp mill in Prince Albert, Saskatchewan. Its principal market is the States of Minnesota, Wisconsin, Michigan and Ohio. It competes in that market with other producers in Eastern and Western Canada as well as in the U.S.A. In 1970, the company filed a complaint with the ICC on the grounds that the small differential between its rates and those of its competitors much further west, and that the large differential between its rate and those of its competitors further east but only slightly closer to the market, failed to give due recognition to the geographical advantage of the Prince Albert location. In this case, the Province of Ontario and North Western Pulp & Power, Ltd., of Hinton, Alberta intervened on behalf of the defendant railways. The evidence produced for that case demonstrates quite clearly that the general structure of rail rates evolved in terms of market competition. The Statement of Facts in the ICC decision states:

> To keep Canadian mills competitive with western U.S. mills, the rates on woodpulp from western Canada have been based in large part on the U.S. transcontinental rate structure. The transcontinental rate structure is unique in that distance "is to a large extent disregarded and there is no other rate adjustment in the country with such extensive blanket or zone rates." *Grand Junction Cham. of Com. v Aberdeen & R.R. Co.*, 190 I.C.C. 233,252 (1932). Its underlying purpose has been to promote the free flow of commodities produced in excess of the needs of western markets to the population and manufacturing centers of the East and Midwest.[35]

The structuring of rates to allow shippers to meet market competition is not always successful, nor is it always viewed with favour by all of the competitors in the market. Further, a change in the market competitiveness of firms that is caused by decreases, but more particularly by increases, in freight rates can change traditional relationships and give rise to market competitive cases. Such has been the case in the Eastern Newsprint Case, discussed in Chapter VIII, and it was the basis for the opposition of the Council of Forest Industries of British Columbia to an increase in freight rates on lumber into the U.S.A. during 1976.[36]

The role of the expanding potash production in Saskatchewan raised two notable examples of market competitive forces. The first was the establishment, in 1969, of a railway rate structure, as well as an industry pricing policy, which would give both the Saskatchewan and the New Mexico producers satisfactory access to and prices in the American middle west markets.[37] The second was the refusal of the CN and CP to break a zone rate structure for International Minerals and Chemical (IMC) of Chicago. This has been explained as follows:

> IMC would have been in a better position to retain its market hold had it been able to work out a favourable agreed charge with the railways. The company argued that the greater proximity of the Esterhazy complex to the US border called for a freight rate lower than that accorded to the Saskatoon

171

area mines. The CN and CP refused to give IMC such an edge, arguing that this would be betrayal of other producers who proceeded with large investments on the basis of being on an equal footing in transportation costs.[38]

In retaliation IMC made an arrangement to truck to the Burlington Northern Railway just beyond the border, in the U.S.A. It is not clear whether IMC has cut its costs through this routing or not.

Market competition from American products imported into Canada. The competitive effect of imports from the U.S.A. on domestic rail rates is important. The influence applies across the country but has been found to be especially important in the case studies in Western Canada. The distance of Western Canada from Eastern Canadian manufacturers allows sources of supply in the Western U.S.A. to be competitive and to hold rates down.

For example, the availability of automobiles, chemicals, salt cake and foodstuffs from California and other Western States has influenced the level of rates, particularly to Vancouver, but also to other points in Western Canada. Examples of the influence of rates being held down in Eastern Canada on products moving east include rates on sulphur and potash to water competitive points to meet the competition of waterborne imports from the Gulf of Mexico, and rates on fruit, particularly apples from British Columbia.

In the latter case, the Canadian railways have not been successful recently in meeting either American rail or Canadian truck competition. Until 1968, the rates to Eastern Canada were maintained at a level equal to that applicable to other west coast origins, particularly California. Following withdrawal from the U.S.A.-related rate structure, Canadian truck-competitive rail rates were lower than the rates in the U.S.A. for some time. However, superior truck service and rising rail costs and, therefore, rates on specialized equipment, have caused the railways to lose much of the traffic to trucking, as well as to raise their rates to levels above those in the U.S.A. The higher rate of inflation in Canada than the U.S.A. will make it difficult in this and other cases for the Canadian railways to be as competitive in the future with market competition from and in the U.S.A. as they have been in the past.

Since market competition is based on the total landed price of goods, the competitiveness of imports is influenced by the application of tariffs. For example, in one case the rate which the Canadian railways were required to meet was $7.08 per 100 lbs. Of this rate, $4.12 per 100 lbs., or 58 per cent, was an import duty. In this instance, the tariff was providing an umbrella for railway pricing as well as protecting the domestic producers.

Market competition among Canadian producers in the domestic market. The railways are faced also with market competition among Canadian producers. This type of market competition raises particularly difficult issues for the railways. First, with their interest in profit maximizing, they must be

172

concerned about the impact of a rate for one domestic shipper on the volume of traffic of the competing Canadian producer. They would see little advantage in reducing a rate from A to B to build that traffic, if the result were to be a reduction of traffic from C to B. Therefore, the interests of the railways are less likely to coincide with those of the shipper than in other cases where the railways stand to gain or protect traffic without offsetting losses. Second, the railways have, do and presumably will receive arguments from shippers seeking more favourable rates to assist them in their market competition with other producers. The case studies suggest that the railways are very conscious of the influence of their rates on the competitive position of shippers and that they try to be "fair".

In view of the diverse pressures on the railways, it is difficult to generalize about the pattern of market competitive pressures within Canada. One common situation is where competing firms of comparable size are competing in a market and wish to maintain an equality or established relationship in freight rates. An example is the competition between eastern and western processors of imported sugar in the Manitoba market, which for many years has been the "divide" between those competing processors.

Competition between producers in different locations in a common market may well be associated with competition between different railways. For example, a case investigated for this project revealed that the CN and CP quoted rates independently on a proposed movement of chemicals from alternate locations to one buyer. Although each supplier only had one railway available, there was competition between the railways as well as the suppliers. Such independent action would be less likely on an established movement with an established rate relationship. In such a case, the railways would probably confer, but not necessarily agree, on the rate action to be taken.

A particular concern in Western Canada, involving competition between producers in different regions, is the possibility that the railways will grant favourable rates to large eastern producers to the detriment of small western producers. The case studies revealed no action of this type. The case studies involving rates for eastern producers shipping into the West were instances where rate increases were introduced which gave added protection to small producers for a local market. The rates for the western producers were increased in a manner consistent with the changing long-haul rates, but so that the competitive position of the local firm improved slightly. No case was found where shippers felt that they were being unfairly treated in comparison with their competition located in Eastern Canada.

The increase in freight rates can be expected to increase the competitive advantage for the firm serving a local market. In Western Canada, the protection afforded local steel production by freight rates is a good example. The pricing of steel reflects the competitive position of steel produced by the large plants in Eastern Canada. Thus, during periods when steel is in short supply, base point

173

pricing practices have been found.[39] During such periods, the Ipsco plant located in Regina charges as its base price the Algoma base price plus freight from Sault Ste. Marie to Regina, so that Regina becomes the base point. A customer outside Regina pays that price plus freight even though he may be located east of Regina.

From the viewpoint of the long-haul shipper, in general, the inflationary pressure on railway costs has made it increasingly difficult for the railways to maintain traditional relationships. In 1974, one shipper reported that he had been able to negotiate an absolute rate change comparable to that of his competitor closer to the market. In 1975, the same shipper found that the railways claimed they were unable to maintain the rate relationship because of cost increases which made increases of comparable percentage amounts necessary. The interests of the railways and shippers were similar because the long-haul traffic might be lost in favour of truck competitive short-haul traffic.

The concern of the railways to respond to market competition does not imply that the railways will make rates for firms in an unfavourable location comparable with those in a more favoured location. For example, the presence of intermodal competition in one place does not result necessarily in a competitive rate being established from non-competitive locations. However, what is the reasonable relationship between rates for competing firms when one has the benefit of intermodal competition and the other does not, is a matter of judgement on the specifics of the case. In some instances, the localized benefits of intermodal competition are extended by zone rates. For example, the rates on lumber from the coastal regions of British Columbia to Eastern Canada became based on water competition during the 1960's and, through a zone rate system, the benefits of that competitive force were extended to inland mills beyond the extent warranted by strictly competitive factors. The use of zone and related prices to accommodate market and other competitive factors is common in the rate structure. Determining either the profit maximizing rate structure for the railways or the most "equitable" structure for competing producers is difficult. Achieving the right balance between these concepts in the rate structure is even more difficult. It is for this reason that a general regulatory protection of the "public interest", such that as provided by Section 23 of the National Transportation Act, is necessary and desirable.

Market Competition of New or Expanded Production

The forces of competition evident between existing producers competing in a market are similar to those based on the development of new production capacity. However, the long-run importance of capital decisions to shippers and the railways gives them special importance. The arguments may affect the development of facilities of competing firms or the location chosen by a firm which intends to increase its plant capacity in one of alternate locations.

Market competition among firms for expanded production. With market growth, the competition among firms progresses from a short-run concern about the immediate profitability of their market shares to the long-run ability of that profitability to support new capital investment. In competitive markets, trends in freight rates can cause the economic advantage of one region to change in favour of another. Competing firms are concerned about such trends. Common concerns are over the relationship between long-haul and short-haul rates. In the former case, whether the processing of raw materials or manufacture of goods is located close to markets or close to raw materials is influenced by the transportation costs on the raw as compared with finished products. In the latter case, the level of rates influences the comparative advantages in transportation of the firm with the short haul.

The relationship of rates on raw materials and finished products has been a source of controversy in Western Canada. The relationship between the rates on rapeseed and rapeseed products has been considered in a case before the CTC and is considered more fully in Chapter VIII. However, it is appropriate to present some evidence from that case here. Table 20 shows a summary of rate data affecting rapeseed and rapeseed products as presented by D.C. McLachlan and C. Ozol.[40] The rates on rapeseed, which were much lower than the rates on rapeseed products were felt by the western producers to place an undue disadvantage on the expansion of the industry in the West. Many factors affected the rates structure, including the costs of transportation and intermodal competition, but the most significant factor was the impact of the Crows Nest Pass Rates, which apply on rapeseed but not on its products.

McLachlan and Ozol explain that the decision of Western Canadian Seed Processors, Ltd. in the late 1950's to locate in Lethbridge, Alberta, was made on the basis of data on numerous facts, including freight rates, as they existed then. It was only after the plant came into operation that the rate on rapeseed was reduced to the statutory level, thereby affecting the economics of plant location. McLachlan and Ozol explain:

> One of the main parties pressing for this privileged treatment for rapeseed was the Government of the Province of Alberta. It would appear that the zeal with which the statutory rate for rapeseed was pursued blinded the government at the time to the possible implications of the privileged rate for the rapeseed processing industry in the Province.[41]

Only some of the unfavourable effects of the rapeseed rates have been removed by the judgement of the CTC and the order of the Governor in Council to reduce certain rates on the rapeseed products (see Chapter VIII).

The impact of freight rates on the location of the livestock fattening and

Table 20
Comparative Rail Transportation Costs in Shipping
Rapeseed and Rapeseed Products from Lethbridge in 1973

Comparative Rail Transportation Costs Involved in

(a) Crushing 100 lbs of rapeseed at Lethbridge and
shipping the resulting oil and meal to Montreal;
and

(b) shipping 100 lbs of rapeseed to Montreal.

(c) Crushing 100 lbs of rapeseed in Lethbridge and
shipping the resulting oil and meal to Vancouver
for export; and

(d) shipping 100 lbs of rapeseed to Vancouver for
export.

From	(a)	(b)	Excess of (a) over (b) as %	(c)	(d)	Excess of (c) over (d) as %
Innisfail, Alta.	135.7[a]	72.5	87	69.6[a]	22.5	209
Innisfail, Alta.	118.6[b]	72.5	64	63.2[b]	22.5	181
Lethbridge, Alta.	128.9[a]	70.5	83	72.6[a]	23.5	209
Lethbridge, Alta.	111.8[b]	70.5	59	66.2[b]	23.5	182

Notes: [a]30 ton tank car used for oil movement
[b]72 ton tank car used for oil movement

Source: Information supplied by Western Canadian Seed Processors
Ltd., Lethbridge.

Quoted in D.C. McLachlan and C. Ozol, Transportation
Problems Relating to Manufacturing Industry in the Calgary
Area (Ottawa: Canadian Transport Commission, 1973),
Appendix 9, p. 78.

176

meat processing industries has also been a matter of considerable concern in the Prairies. It has been felt that the freight rates have been unduly favourable to the movement out of the Prairies of feed grain rather than cattle, and live cattle rather than meat. Thus one of the particular rate relationships which the CTC was asked to investigate in 1973 was the relationship between the rates on livestock and meat.[42] These rates have been subject to further analysis in two more recent studies.[43] The structure of freight rates and their impact on the location of the livestock and meat processing industries are complex. Not only must studies take into account the actual levels of rates and carriers' costs but also the effect of the impact of rates on plant location through such factors as freight rate subsidies, weight loss and gain associated with processing, and the availability of alternate sources of supply. The conclusions of all three studies indicate that the pricing practices of the railways have not been an impediment to the development of processing in the Prairies, although public policy measures in holding down freight rates on grain have discouraged cattle fattening and the raising of hogs and poultry in the Prairies. The public policies have been the application of Crows Nest Pass rates on grain to Thunder Bay and the payment of freight rate subsidies to the purchasers of feed grain under the Feed Freight Assistance Act of 1941. The Commission of Inquiry concluded that:

> The fuller utilization of existing facilities and the opportunity to develop a stable beef finishing and processing industry in the West is placed in jeopardy by the dramatic spread that now exists between Crow's Nest Pass rates and all other transport costs.[44]

Some producers of meat in the West have been concerned about the reasonableness of the rates on livestock and meat. However, the studies have shown that the relationship between these rates is favourable to the shipment of meat and not livestock and, further, that the contribution made above the relevant variable costs is greater on livestock than meat.[45]

In spite of the concern of meat processors in the Prairies concerning the level and relationships of rates, the case studies did not reveal that the railways had been unresponsive in meeting industry needs. The introduction of large-capacity, mechanically cooled cars enabled transport cost savings to be passed on to shippers in the form of reduced rates during the 1960's.[46] This may explain the view of one traffic manager involved in the shipment of meat from the Prairies and interviewed during the research for this book that "the meat packing industry has really had no complaint with the rates". He also noted that increases in freight rates on meat could be expected to be accompanied by the shipment of boxed beef rather than hanging carcasses.[47] The transportation of boxed beef by rail is subject to highly effective competition from trucking over the road and via piggyback service. However, in the case of the development of both the rapeseed-processing and the meat-packing industries in the Prairies, a major factor leading to unfavourable effects on those industries is the government policy of holding down the rates on grain.

In instances where the railways are faced with arguments dealing with the differences in rates for competing firms, they appear to respond reasonably by maintaining traditional rate relationships subject to the constraints of their costs, transport competition and important economic conditions affecting shippers. For example, a manufacturer of sulphuric acid requested a low rate on the basis that the customer could produce sulphur acid as a by-product but at a high cost from some of his operations. If the railways wanted the business, they had to establish a freight rate such that when the rate was added to the cost of producing sulphuric acid in bulk, the laid down cost was less than the cost of producing the acid on a small scale. A low enough rate was established for the movement to take place.

Market competition through alternate locations of a firm. Arguments concerning the economics of centralized versus decentralized production were found in several cases. Arguments were presented by shippers that either rates had to be reduced or increases lessened or it would become economic to decentralize production. In one case, a shipper indicated to the railways that a new plant was to be built to serve a local market but that the number of products to be produced there was dependent on the level of freight rates. A reduction in the rates on several commodities meant that the production line in the new plant was narrower than would otherwise have been the case, and total costs were held down.

In any instance where firms competing in a common market have different plant locations and distribution systems, negotiations are likely to involve market competitive arguments. For example, petroleum-based products such as grease and lubricants formerly were shipped into Alberta from Eastern Canada, under an agreed charge first established in the mid-1950's. The growth of the western market led some firms to locate processing plants in the West, for example, Imperial Oil in Edmonton. This then placed other suppliers under increased competitive pressure to move their products at relatively low rates or to establish new plants. As the market has continued to grow and the railways have been less able to hold down rates, the economics of new plants in the West have become more attractive.

Comparable situations have occurred in Eastern Canada. For example, the flour-milling industry, which has been declining in the West under the influence of the Crows Nest Pass rates, has been growing in Ontario and Quebec. As firms have opened new plants in major markets, for example, Montreal, this has increased the competitive pressure on other firms and on the railways serving that market from plants in Ontario. Firms with plants in both areas, but with different product lines in each, are able to negotiate freight rates on the basis that they could change the product mix in the plants, should freight rates becomes high enough that less traffic would move. In essence, instead of regional specialization and distribution of the product by rail, the firms would adapt the capacity of the plants so that more production for the local markets would take place.

Market Competition through Alternate Markets and Sources of Supply

Without changing the output of any one plant, a firm may be able to shift its sources of supply or markets away from those served by the rail carrier(s) with whom the shipper is negotiating. For example, rates on some petroleum-based products produced in Alberta can be shipped either to Eastern Canada or exported via Vancouver. If the eastbound freight rates become too high, it will be more efficient for the western plants to use the shorter westbound route, perhaps using rail or truck, to serve the export market. Several instances of the impact of imports from the U.S.A. were cases of Canadian manufacturers having alternate sources of supply. They would avoid the use of the Canadian railways unless the domestic rates could be established at a level which would allow the total cost of the Canadian product at the destination market to be competitive with that from the U.S.A.

It is noted in Chapter III that some shippers, with the potential to negotiate on the basis of alternate markets, were unable to do so because they had entered into contracts or purchased facilities prior to the negotiation of rail rates. In two cases, these were mines seeking to sell some output beyond the need of their main purchaser. Since resource-based industries lack some of the locational flexibility of manufacturing firms, it would be desirable, from the shippers' standpoint, to maintain the flexibility of markets as long as possible.

Developmental Rates

The counsel for the Province of Manitoba is quoted in Chapter III as being supportive of the railways in their establishing rates to assist the development of industry. Several shippers interviewed in the research for this study acknowledged that reasonable rates had been introduced by the railways to assist development. In one case, in Eastern Canada a large pulp mill had serious start-up problems, and during this initial period the rates in the agreed charge were held down. The railways felt that their ability to retain the low rates without undue pressure from other producers for comparable rates, was because they ensured that the agreed charge was viewed as "a package" of rates and requirements for the inbound and outbound rates for the mill. However, some shippers who enjoyed developmental rates, while acknowledging that they had low rates initially, felt that the railways had not been justified in the amount by which rates had been increased subsequently.

Related to the attitude of the railways on developmental rates is the position they adopt when a shipper claims he is in serious financial difficulty. In one case in Western Canada, the railways deviated from a zone rate to establish a lower rate for a shipper who, because of short-run problems, faced bankruptcy. The annual freight revenue of the shipper was worth about a million dollars. Although the end use of the product was different than that of other shippers, the railways were subsequently placed under considerable pressure to extend the rate level to other shippers. The railways did not do this until the commercial position of the shipper improved so that rates could again move into line. This example is exceptional because the railways are naturally reluctant to change the competitive relationship between competing Canadian firms and to reduce their own profit margins in cases where the explanation for a firm's problem is its poor location or management.

Examples of Cases where the Railways were Largely Unresponsive to Shippers Requests

In some of the cases researched in this study the railways did not respond to a shipper's request for a lesser freight rate increase than that proposed. In each of these cases the position adopted by the railways was taken after giving careful consideration to the factors involved. First, the railways did not respond by lowering rates or holding down increases when rates were close to relevant costs. This response has become more common since 1973. A complaint of shippers in this situation was the absence of evidence, acceptable to them, that costs were, in fact, close to rates. Second, the railways were not responsive when they believed that traffic volumes would remain largely unaffected even if the shipper profit margins were reduced. This was often a matter of judgement and the railways' position was influenced by the quality of evidence provided and their assessment of the credibility of the shipper with respect to a particular type of argument. In complex markets of heterogeneous products, it was much harder for a shipper to assess and to present evidence on the effect of a freight rate increase than it was in the case of a homogeneous raw material which competes in a market largely on the basis of price. Third, the railways were reluctant to change rates when it would change a traditional rate relationship unless it was necessitated by cost or other competitive factors, such as intermodal competition. Fourth, the railways were reluctant to change rates when the gain on one part of the system would be offset by losses on another. Fifth, the railways attempted to avoid cutting their own rates to a minimum for shippers who had established plants in a poor location and wished to compete with better located plants.

The lack of responsiveness by the railways did not seem to be related to the size of the shipper. In one case of very important traffic to both the railways and the shippers, the president of the American parent of the Canadian company wrote to the presidents of the CN and CP in an attempt to persuade the railways to reduce the amount of a proposed increase, but the increase was left unchanged. The case studies made clear that in the negotiation of rates the presence of the competitive forces of intermodal, intramodal or market competition is crucial, even to the negotiating position of large shippers. The impact of the countervailing power of large shippers or an association of shippers is realized through the relevance of competitive forces to large blocks of traffic and not merely through the presence of a large volume of traffic per se. Indeed, large shippers may often feel compelled to present better reasoned and documented studies than small shippers to obtain rate adjustments, as the railways are becoming better informed of the conditions affecting major industries through their product-marketing specialists.

The only case researched for this study in which a shipper indicated that dissatisfaction with the outcome of rail negotiations had played a role in the location of a plant, in this instance the location of a plant expansion, involved a multi-national company. However, that shipper admitted that the question of freight rates was only one of a very large number of considerations. Dissatisfaction with the site of the first plant in terms of dependence on one railway alone was as much a factor as the actual rates negotiated. The manufacturer felt that, in the long run, dependence on rate negotiation with one firm and on the economics of rail transport would be too risky in view of the alternative available. Plant expansion was possible at a location offering effective intramodal and intermodal competition so that both the level and stability of rates and service quality would be more satisfactory in the long run.

Conclusions on the Significance of Market Competition

The evidence is clear that market competition in its various forms is a significant controlling factor on the level of railway rates throughout the country and on a wide range of commodities. Its applications go beyond the pressures of producers competing with one another for common markets, although these instances are the best known because these competitive pressures give rise to appeals to regulatory bodies. The constraint of market competitive forces also encompasses the alternative plant locations and logistical arrangements available to shippers which they may use in their negotiation of rates and related matters with the railways. The constraint on railway rates through the possibility of losing traffic through market competition is as real as the constraint of losing traffic for any other reason. The evidence is clear that the railways are responsive and establish mutually acceptable rates with the shippers when the railways can see that they will lose profitable traffic or when they can see the potential for the development of profitable traffic.

This chapter shows that market competitive forces effectively limit the monopoly power of the railways in setting commodity rates for substantial volumes of rail traffic in Canada, particularly for raw materials moving in bulk.

Therefore, the designation of rates which are not set on the basis of intermodal competition as "non-competitive rates" can lead to a serious misunderstanding about the nature and extent of competitive forces in rail transport markets. The presence of market competition may not be as readily observable as are some aspects of intermodal and intramodal competition where traffic is shared among carriers. Nor do the pressures of market competitive forces work as simply, because of the possible conflict of interest among shippers. But, powerful competitive constraints operate on the 36 percent of rail ton-miles designated in the Waybill Analysis as non-competitive commodity rates (see Table 7, Chapter II).

However, the bases on which the railways judge the appropriate rate to charge in the face of market competition are necessarily very imperfect. In many instances of market competition, even the shipper has only a rough idea of what the effect of a freight rate increase will actually be on his profitability over the next year because of uncertain prices, other costs and sales volumes. The information collection and analysis of the railways over the last few years has become much more sophisticated than formerly, and has aided them in assessing critically the effects of rate changes claimed by shippers. It appears from the case studies that if, as a generalization, the railways had erred in their assessment of market competition, they have not been unresponsive to it. Rather, it has been that they have been overly responsive to market competition. However, that is not to deny that there have been cases, particularly in the last two years, in which the railways have not responded as the shippers have requested.

On occasion, the unwillingness of the railways to respond to a market competitive argument is frustrating to shippers. However, while shippers have been aggravated at times by the information provided by the railways during negotiations, they do not feel that the railways significantly misjudge the impact of market competitive forces nor that, based on the railways' misjudgement, a change in the regulatory process is desirable. It is significant, however, that prior to 1976, when inflation and substantial rate increases have given rise to additional appeals to the CTC under Section 23 of the National Transportation Act, the three cases heard under Section 23 all involved highly complex cases in which market competition figured prominently. In these cases, there were conflicting interests between shippers and between railways as well as between the complainant shippers and the railways.

Market competitive forces apply throughout Canada to raw materials and finished goods and on eastbound and westbound freight. Certainly, the market competition which is easiest to identify is that applying on the raw materials competing in world markets. The constraint placed on the profit margins on coal, potash and sulphur has certainly been more severe at times than the level of competition caused by intermodal comeptition on much traffic more highly valued and highly rated than the raw material exports.

The particular fears expressed in 1966 about reliance on market competitive forces have not been realized. The railways have been responsive to market competitive forces and have not been accused by shippers of gouging the maximum revenue possible on the basis of value-of-service pricing. Nor have they been able to turn whatever monopoly powers they may have to monopoly profits overall. On particular traffic, only one shipper has proceeded to ask the CTC to indicate the range for a fixed (maximum) rate, so that presumably no, or, more likely, little, traffic is carried at rates above the level which would be set if the shipper sought and obtained a fixed rate under Section 278 of the Railway Act.

To the extent that price increases during 1976 have given rise to more complaints during that year than in previous years, there is some evidence of the undesirable effects on shippers, and often on the railways, of cost increases, but those complaints alone are not evidence of unreasonable pricing, as the investigations of the CTC have shown. If cost increases should affect the railways in the future more than their shippers, a shift in the share of profits from the production and distribution activities of producers to railways will have to be examined on the circumstances of the particular cases.

Finally, the railways have not used their powers to practice discriminatory pricing in ways to direct arbitrarily the location of industry. They have responded to market competitive forces and in so doing have established rates that influence industrial location and development. That, however, is the very essence of response to market competitive forces. The response of the railways has resulted in the efficient evolution of manufacturing and distribution systems and in the growth, particularly in Western Canada, of major resource industries selling in intensely competitive world markets. The presence of long- and short-haul rates is merely one product of the responsiveness of the railways to market competition in Canada. It is clear that the railways do at times have the power to influence the location and development of industry contrary to the efficient use of resources and development of the Canadian economy. It is for this reason that some residual regulatory provisions, such as Section 23 of the National Transportation Act, are necessary. Fortunately, because of the effectiveness of shipper/carrier negotiations, they have been used little since 1967.

To conclude this Chapter, it is appropriate to comment on a practice which has not been found as much as might be expected. That is, the railways do not attempt to gear their rates to the cyclical value of service. They may take advantage of periods of high commodity prices to raise rates, but they do not do this as much as might be expected. During periods of low commodity prices, on the other hand, they have not reduced rates unless changes in methods have enabled cost reductions. The relative insensitivity of rates to the value-of-service factors means that the impact of the business cycle is reflected in the railways' revenue, mainly in its effects on traffic volumes and the traffic composition, but not through the changes in the values of the individual commodities carried. From the standpoint of railway profitability, the question is whether or not the railways would be better off experiencing a wider fluctuation of revenue from more discriminating pricing. The question cannot be answered easily because of the effect on the long-run expected rate of return of shippers on traffic volumes, if the railways were successful in achieving a higher income through more discriminating pricing.

A simple means by which the railways could practice such discriminating pricing, in the case of homogeneous raw materials, would be to establish a rate directly related to value. Such a value-related rate is applied to the concentrate of Pine Point Mines, a lead-zinc mine in the Northwest Territories. The mine is a subsidiary of CP Ltd., but it is served by the CN. The rates applicable during 1976 have ranged from $41.41 per short ton through a total of eleven rate levels to $63.24 per short ton, depending on the value of the ore, which range from $70.00 to $250.00 per short ton, and when the annual shipments are up to and including 215,000 tons.[48]

It is not suggested here that such pricing would necessarily increase railway revenue in the long run. Nor is it to be implied that such pricing would be politically acceptable in view of traditional railway pricing, nor that it would be practicable today in view of resource taxation policies. It is merely pointed out that while the rate structure, in general, is intended to price on the basis of the value of service, in practice, this principle has not been applied as might have been expected to those shippers who, lacking alternatives, were benefiting from exceptionally high short-run prices and profits. It might also be pointed out that some of those shippers, while no less important to the Canadian economy than the railways, are large corporations with higher rates of return than the railways and a higher level of foreign ownership or control.

FOOTNOTES

1. The concept of value of service is complex when considered in a dynamic economic system; see D. Philip Locklin, *Economics of Transportation* (Homewood, Illinois: Irwin, 7th ed., 1972) pp. 157-162.
2. Canada, Royal Commission on Transportation (MacPherson Commission) (Ottawa: Queen's Printer, 1961), Vol. II, 2nd Printing, 1966, p. 48.
3. *Ibid.,* p. 47.
4. *Ibid.*
5. *Ibid.,* p. 49.
6. *Ibid.*, pp. 52-53.
7. Canada, *Railway Act* R.S., c.234, s. 1, Section 278(1).
8. Canada, House of Commons, 27th Parliament 1st Session, Standing Committee on Transport and Communications, Minutes of Proceedings and Evidence, November 24, 1966, p. 1,876.
9. *Ibid.,* p. 2,613.
10. *Ibid.,* p. 1,773.
11. *Ibid.,* p. 2,151.
12. *Ibid.,* p. 2,798.
13. *Ibid.,* pp. 2,818 and 2,846.
14. *Ibid.,* p. 2,762.
15. *Ibid.,* p. 2,609.
16. *Ibid.,* p. 2,477.
17. B.M. Litvack, *The Canadian Potash Industry* (Ottawa: CTC Report 62, 1973), p. 7.
18. *Ibid.,* p. 59.
19. "Can Ross Thatcher Solves the Big Potash Mess" *Executive,* August, 1970, pp. 18-23.
20. Canadian Transport Commission, Railway Transport Committee, *Decision in the Matter of Files 49311 and 49311.1,* August 20, 1970; Canadian Transport Commission, Railway Transport Committee, *Decision in the Matter of File 49311, 49311.6 and 49311.5,* May 13, 1971 and *Order No. R-11708,* May 13, 1971; Supreme Court of Canada, *Kootenay and Elk Railway Co. and Burlington Northern, Inc. v. Canadian Pacific Railway Company et.al.,* Opinion given May 1, 1972.
21. *Vancouver Province,* April 29, 1973.
22. F.S. Burbidge, "Canadian Pacific: Whipping Boy in the West", *Winnipeg Tribune,* October 27, 1976, Mimeographed reprint.
23. *Executive, op.cit.,* p. 23.
24. *Vancouver Province,* September 22, 1970; and *Transportation Newsletter,* (Vancouver: Westrade Publications), November 16, 1970.
25. "Potash Takeovers Can't Be Refused", *Financial Post,* June 19, 1976, p. 38.
26. *Elements of Uncertainty in Western Transportation* (Vancouver: Western Transportation Advisory Council, 1976).
27. *Ibid.,* p. 66.
28. *Ibid.,* p. 65.
29. *Ibid.,* p. 14.
30. *Ibid.,* p. 30.
31. A.W. Currie, *Canadian Transportation Economics* (Toronto: University of Toronto Press, 1967), p. 219.
32. D.L. McLachlan and C. Ozol, *Transportation Problems Relating to Manufacturing Industry in the Calgary Area* (Ottawa: CTC, Research Publication, 1973), p. 26.
33. Rates in Agreed Charges 118 and 500 for minimum weight of 80,000 lbs. in standard box cars.

34. Statistics Canada, *Imports, Province of Customs Clearance,* Special Tabulation, Unpublished, 1974.
35. *Prince Albert Pulp Co. Ltd. v. Canadian National Railways, et.al.,* 349 ICC 477, 456 (1973).
36. This case has been a part of the *Increased Freight Rates and Charges — 1976,* Ex Parte No. 318, Council of Forest Industries of B.C. statement before the ICC, April 9, 1976.
37. *Executive, op.cit.,* pp. 20-21.
38. *Ibid.*
39. Canada, *Steel Profits Inquiry* The Honourable Mr. Justice Willard Z. Estey, Commissioner (Ottawa: Queen's Printer, 1974), pp. 31-32.
40. D.C. McLachlan and C. Ozol, *op.cit.,* p. 78.
41. *Ibid.,* p. 38.
42. Canadian Transport Commission, *Report to the Honourable Minister of Transport Pursuant to his request of July 19, 1973 Under the Provisions of Section 22 of the National Transportation Act,* mimeographed, pp. 4-10, and Appendices B, C and D.
43. Canadian Transport Commission, *Transportation Factors and the Canadian Livestock and Meat Industries* (Ottawa: Research Branch, CTC, Report ESAB 75-19, 1975); Canada, *Report of the Commission of Inquiry into the Marketing of Beef and Veal,* 1976 (Ottawa: Minister of Supply and Services, 1976).
44. *Commission of Inquiry into the Marketing of Beef and Veal, op.cit.,* p. 142.
45. *Transportation Factors and the Canadian Livestock and Meat Industries, op.cit.,* pp. 33-37.
46. *Commission of Inquiry into the Marketing of Beef and Veal, op.cit.,* pp. 93-94.
47. The opportunity to improve processing and distribution for meat is also noted in other studies. *Ibid.,* p. 94; and a statement of the General Traffic Manager of Burns Foods Limited, Calgary, quoted in Canadian Transport Commission, *Report to the Minister of Transport,* 1973, *op.cit.,* p. 8.
48. Further details of the rate are in the tariff, 5th revised page 65, Tariff CTC(F) W.2934, CNR W. 186-M.

CHAPTER VI

INTERMODAL COMPETITION AS A COMPETITIVE INFLUENCE ON RAILWAY RATES

The influence of intermodal competition on railway pricing has been well documented by the MacPherson Commission and other studies.[1] Demonstration of the extensive impact of intermodal competition usually involves some evidence of the relative and absolute amount of business done by the various modes, measured either in physical terms, such as tons or ton-miles, or in the dollar value of the services performed. What such measurements do not reflect is that the dynamic competition between the modes is dependent on the threat of losing business, or the promise of gaining business, facing the managers of carrier firms. The potential for traffic to shift from one mode to another, or the competition between modes for new traffic, occurs when the modes can be substituted for one another. Since the mere existence of two modes operating between two cities does not mean that the use of either mode is possible for a particular traffic, some emphasis has been given to the fact that competition between modes is "at the margin".[2] That is, competition occurs over that range of service levels and rates for which the modes are alternatives, but not necessarily over their entire range of output.

The managers of transport firms decide whether or not to adjust their prices and services offered in terms of their perception of the threat of losing business or the promise of gaining it. Many factors influence the credibility and importance which they attach to these pressures and opportunities. One of these is whether a competing service is currently in existence. However, it is the probability of a competing service actually being used by their shippers which is important, not merely whether it currently exists. If a competing service does not exist, the manager of the existing carrier can be expected to take price and/or service actions to prevent its development. Currie notes:

> It is not good business practice for a concern to keep its prices high until a competitor comes in to force reductions. On the contrary, the wise businessman keeps his prices as low as he can with the object of discouraging competition. It is better

187

> to choke off potential competitors before they get started
> than to wait until they are well established before dealing with
> them. The Board [of Transport Commissioners] has recognized
> the economic soundness of the policy. ...[3]

Under dynamic competitive conditions, the threat of losing business is a powerful "compelling incentive" for management to take competitive action.[4] What action is warranted, if any, is a matter of judgement. Often, the manager requires considerable knowledge of the various competitive forces, of the prices and of the costs of his own and other enterprises to determine what should be done.

The range of competitive alternatives available to shippers in Canada is considerable, and it encompasses actual as well as potential services. Railways are in competition with shipping along the Great Lakes and the St. Lawrence River, with coastal shipping on the Atlantic and Pacific coasts, and with shipping via the Panama Canal on traffic moving between British Columbia and Eastern Canada. Pipelines for natural gas and petroleum, despite their far lower ton-mile costs which tends to remove the railways from competition, may still be effective competitors with rail service, and in some instances the transmission of electricity may be an effective alternative to the carriage of coal. Railways compete with truckers almost everywhere in Canada, and truckers engage in a great many long hauls, as well as in short hauls, in competition with the railways. Highly competitive services which involve both the railways and truckers are available in piggyback services, officially known as Trailer on Flat Car services (TOFC). The widespread influence of these competitive services on railway rates and services was the main reason for the significant change in railway regulatory policy in 1967, following the recommendation of the MacPherson Commission.

Intermodal Competition and Transport Regulation since 1967

The competitive relationships among the modes of transport in Canada are influenced not only by the regulations affecting the railways, but also by the economic conditions and regulations pertaining to the other modes. Some of the regulations affecting the railways were described in Chapter III, and the regulations affecting other modes were mentioned briefly in Chapter IV. The objective here is to review the major provisions in the regulation of railways relevant to intermodal competition and to describe briefly the regulations affecting the trucking industry and waterway operators.

Regulatory Constraints on Competitive Actions by the Railways

The major regulatory provisions affecting railway rates have been described in Chapter III. The principle of allowing the railways to compete freely with other modes, and, particularly, trucking, was supported generally in 1966. Moreover, the use of variable cost, as defined by the CTC, was not opposed as the level for minimum rates for the railways. In 1966, Mr. Magee, Manager of the Canadian Trucking Associations, stated:

> I agree that low rates are advantageous to the economy of the west. Our point is that competitive forces should be left to work out the rate situation, the railways and the trucking industry competing with each other, and that there should not be an artificial intervention by the injection of subsidized reduction of freight rates.[5]

The Canadian Trucking Associations did express dissatisfaction with the requirement that to obtain a fixed (maximum) rate under Section 278 of the Railway Act, the shipper has to commit all of the affected traffic to the railways for a minimum period of one year, with the exception of experimental shipments by other modes as approved by the CTC.[6] The fixed rate remains in effect for a minimum period of one year, and is then subject to cancellation after ten days either on notice by the shipper or on determination by the CTC that an effective, competitive alternative by a common carrier of another mode exists. The Canadian Trucking Associations wished to have it made much easier for trucking to participate in the high-rated traffic, even when a fixed rail rate had been set.

The trucking industry was concerned with three other aspects of the 1967 transport policy. First, the industry was concerned about extension of the ownership of trucking by the railways. Recognition of the potential disadvantage for the public interest of the ownership by one firm of controlling interest in the operation of services in more than one mode of transport, resulted in Section 27 of the National Transportation Act. Under this Section, where an objection is made to the CTC of a carrier under federal jurisdiction acquiring an interest in any undertaking whose primary business is transportation, the CTC must investigate the matter to determine whether the acquisition is in the public interest. A number of investigations involving trucking, aviation and shipping have been held under this section. However, while the individual cases have raised important questions about the influence on the public interest of the corporate structure of particular markets, the freedom of the railways to control firms in other modes of transport has not had a material influence on intermodal competition. No evidence has been produced to show that the multi-modal ownership structure of the CN and CP is, in general, against the public interest.

An extensive investigation of the ownership and the operation of the railway-owned trucking operations was completed by the CTC during 1976.[7] The study was carried out by the CTC's Motor Vehicle Transport Committee in conjunction with an investigation resulting from an objection by the Trucking Association of Quebec to the CN acquisition of Chalut Transport Inc., a trucking firm based in Joliette, Quebec. The Motor Vehicle Transport Committee found no grounds for disallowance of the acquisition of the trucking firm. The Committee further reported that the CN and CP owned or controlled 18 of the 6,774 for-hire trucking companies involved in intercity truck transport in Canada during 1974. These 18 companies had 9.9 percent of total trucking industry revenues; of this amount CP controlled companies that earned 6.4 percent.[8] The Committee found that although the railways had a "meaningful foothold" in the trucking industry, there was no restriction of competition "let alone an 'undue' restriction of competition".[9] The report confirmed that the railways' trucking activities were carried on in a completely separate way from the railway operations.

The second concern of the truckers was that they could face difficulty in competing with rail piggyback operations through the provision of poor facilities for truckers. Section 265(8) of the Railway Act was added in 1967 to require the railways to provide truckers with the same piggyback facilities at the same rates as those applicable to vehicles operated by the railways.

The third concern of the truckers was with the Canadian practice of attempting to achieve general public goals through the subsidization of rail service by the Federal Government. The Canadian Trucking Association recommended amendment of the Maritime Freight Rates Act and other rate subsidy programmes so that truckers could become eligible for subsidies, thus avoiding an inequity and a source of economic inefficiency in resource allocation in transport. The extension of subsidies to truckers in the Maritimes was accomplished by the Atlantic Region Freight Assistance Act of 1969. The principle of providing rate subsidies for truck as well as rail movements has also been extended to subsidies for the movement of feed grains in Western Canada. Notwithstanding these measures, the concern of Federal and Provincial Governments in 1973 over transport matters led them to request a freeze on rail rates, perhaps without giving adequate consideration to the serious repercussions of this action on the trucking industry. However, when compensation was arranged to be paid to the carriers for the 1973-1974 rate freeze, it was given to both the railways and the highway carriers (as noted in Chapter VIII).

Regulation of Trucking in Canada

In Canada until 1954, the regulation of the trucking industry was carried on as though all trucking fell under the jurisdiction of the Provinces. In that year, the final decision in the Winner case determined that regulation of inter-provincial trucking is under the exclusive jurisdiction of the federal government.[10] To fill the void in the regulations, the Motor Vehicle Transport Act was passed in 1954 to empower the Provinces to regulate interprovincial trucking in the same manner as they regulated intraprovincial trucking, if they wish to do

190

so. The result has been that truckers in interprovincial for-hire trucking are subject to the regulations of as many provinces as they do business in and which have economic regulations for intraprovincial trucking. A great variety of provincial statutes exist, implemented at radically different levels. The province in which there has been least regulation has been, and still is, Alberta. Only Quebec attempts to regulate interprovincial trucking rates, while Prince Edward Island, Quebec, Manitoba, Saskatchewan and British Columbia regulate intra-provincial rates.[11]

Part III of the 1967 National Transportation Act deals with Extra-Provincial Motor Vehicle Transport. It gives the Motor Vehicle Transport Committee of the CTC wide powers to make regulations governing interprovincial trucking. In spite of this legislation, all interprovincial highway service, with the exception of passenger bus service in Newfoundland, still falls under the 1954 Motor Vehicle Transport Act and is subject to the provincial regulations. The wide powers given to the CTC have not been put into effect because of uncertainties in the Federal Government about the appropriate type and rigour of economic regulation, because of differences between the provincial views on the desirable amount of regulation, and because of opposition to centralization of control by the Canadian Trucking Associations.

The variety of jurisdictions and regulations makes it inappropriate to attempt to describe interprovincial trucking regulation in detail here. Operating authority is required for firms to offer for-hire services in most provinces, but the policing of these regulations is generally regarded as being lax. In general, interprovincial rates are not subject to control, with the exception of Quebec, although the principal carriers maintain published tariffs. The Provinces of Ontario and Alberta are examining their regulation of motor carriers, but it is unlikely that any significant extension of regulation will result. In Ontario, the use of vehicles leased from one firm with the driver coming from another firm, has been treated as exempt trucking. As a result of the excesses which are claimed to arise from this practice, the regulation of trucking by the Province is under review. The spokesmen of the trucking industry in Ontario are highly critical of the "illegal" trucking operators and of the shippers who use them. Shippers, as represented by the Ontario Division of the Canadian Industrial Traffic League, also advocate prohibition of the controversial single-trip leasing, but they are not in favour of any more government intervention on rates than the current filing provisions.[12] In Alberta, the Provincial Division of the Canadian Industrial Traffic League opposes "any change which leads to entry or route franchising or rate regulation in Alberta."[13] In general, therefore, the Canadian trucking industry operates in an environment in which there is little control over rates and frequently ineffective regulation of entry. In this environment, it is noteworthy that the trucking industry appears to be as or more concerned over the rationalization of regulation, as it is over possible industry advantages of increased regulation.

191

Regulation of Water Transport

Regulation of water transport is provided for in the Transport Act. The establishment of joint water-rail rates is governed by Sections 284 and 285 of the Railway Act. However, the coastal trades and transport in bulk on the Great Lakes are not subject to economic regulation.[14] Therefore, the main shipping service subject to such regulation is the limited packaged freight service still operated by Canadian Steamship Lines. The efforts of this company to improve technology by introducing side-port loading and using modern cargo handling techniques have not offset rising wage costs and gradually declining traffic. The service in 1976 was reduced to about two vessels, and it depended on the business of certain large shippers. The future of the business is most uncertain.

Truck and Rail Shares of Freight Markets and Intermodal Competition

While the presentation of statistical evidence about the extent of trucking operations is only a general measure of the amount of effective competition between road and rail services, it is a useful means of demonstrating the magnitude of trucking services from which competitive forces can spring. Trends in the amount of trucking can also be an important measure of share of the transport market served by trucking in competition with other modes.

Estimates of volumes of traffic by mode and market-share in Canada are only very approximate because of the diversity of sources and the unreliable nature of trucking statistics. In spite of these limitations, the data are ample evidence of the considerable importance of trucking throughout Canada. The general growth of the trucking industry in Canada has been documented briefly in Chapter II. Today, the dollar value of intercity for-hire trucking service in Canada exceeds the dollar value of rail service.

Evidence of the impact of the growth of the trucking industry on railway pricing is to be seen in the change in the importance of rate types to the railways. Table 7 in Chapter II shows that in 1974 competitive commodity and agreed charge rates, which are both used mainly when intermodal competition exists, accounted for 63 percent of rail revenue. However, while these figures are indicative of the growth and apparent overall impact of trucking, they are deficient in that they do not give any indication of the geographical distribution of trucking competition or the sectors of the economy most affected by it.

Evidence of the Range of Intermodal Competition

Two recent studies provide some evidence on the range of trucking service and rail/truck competition. They are a study by MPS Associates Ltd. for the Western Transportation Advisory Council,[15] and a study by P.S. Ross and Partners et al. for the Federal-Provincial Committee on Western Transportation.[16] The latter study was commissioned to evaluate the effects of pricing proposals brought forward by the Provinces of Alberta and Manitoba. As a part of the evaluation, the study considers the effect of changes in railway freight rates on modal split, especially with the trucking industry which provides "the most intense and pervasive competition with rail transport."[17] Both studies acknowledge the approximate nature of their data bases and the fact that the trucking statistics include only for-hire carriers. MPS estimate that private intercity trucking might "account for as much as one quarter of highway ton-miles to, from and within the West."[18]

The MPS study utilizes data to estimate the number of tons carried by rail and truck in Western Canada to, from and within the region and between the six major centres. Table 21 shows the tonnage of all commodities moved to, from or within the West by truck and the share which this traffic represents of the total carried by truck and rail. In spite of the dominance of rail in the movement of export grain and coal, and in the movement of other bulk commodities such as sulphur and potash, for-hire trucking moves 35 percent of the traffic. The truck share of the market is highest, 85 per cent, for Inedible End Products, which are dominated by sand and gravel moving short distances by truck. Overall, recognizing the substantial tonnage of the few bulk commodities moved dominantly by rail, there is no doubt that trucks carry a substantial tonnage. This has led the President of the CTC to conclude that "There is thus no doubt that with respect to all freight traffic normally considered competitive as between truck and rail, competition between the two industries in the West is intense."[19]

Table 21

Traffic in Tons Carried by For-Hire Trucking
To, From and Within Western Canada, 970[a]

	Trucking	Total Rail and Trucking	Percent of Total by Trucking
	(1ooo tons)		
Live Animals	483	704	69
Food, Feed, Beverages and Tobacco	6,106	29,985	20
Crude Materials, Inedible	9,928	38,596	26
Fabricated Materials, Inedible	15,499	29,203	53
End Products, Inedible	15,453	6,452	85
Special Types of Traffic[b]	345	2,861	12
All Traffic	37,814	107,800	35

Notes: [a]Western Canada comprises the four Western Provinces for truck data but includes that part of Ontario, west of Thunder Bay, for rail traffic.

[b]Special Types of Traffic includes Trailers and Flat Cars and Containers on Flat Cars.

Source: MPS Associates Ltd., Highway and Rail Traffic Related to Western Canada, prepared for the Western Transportation Advisory Council, 1974, Table 3, p. 21. Source data used by MPS are: the 1970 Waybill Analysis, published by the CTC; and Statistics Canada, Catalogue No. 53-224.

The freight movements are dominated by intraregional movements, which make up 90 per cent of the tonnage. This is true for both rail and truck traffic so that the modes are serving comparable and not radically different geographical markets. It is in spite of the dominance of intraregional traffic that public attention over the years has been focused on the small portion of total traffic to and from Western Canada. The share of the tonnage carried by truck in movements to, from and within the West in 1970 were 38 percent, 25 percent and 35 percent, respectively.[20] The fact that more of the westbound intraregional traffic than the eastbound intraregional traffic is carried by truck is explained by the higher proportion of manufactured goods moving westward than eastward.

In addition to traffic for all the West, the MPS study reports on the traffic to and from the six regional centres in the West. They are Winnipeg, Regina, Saskatoon, Edmonton, Calgary and Vancouver. Traffic related to those centres is 57 percent of the total regional traffic, which is significant because it excludes many movements of bulk commodities, except in the case of Vancouver to which bulk traffic moves for export. For the cities excluding Vancouver, 48 percent of the tonnage is carried by truck; including Vancouver, the figure is 43 percent.[21] For Vancouver alone, the figure is 38 percent for all traffic, but 55 percent when the bulk movements of grain, coal, potash and sulphur for export are excluded.[22]

These statistics indicate that trucking in Canada is a major component of the transport industry, certainly a competitive one, and that trucks carry a substantial proportion of inter- and intraregional traffic.

Comparative Roles of Trucking Competition in Eastern and Western Canada

Nevertheless, the observation of the large and competitive role of trucking is often made only with respect to Eastern Canada, where the share of traffic carried by truck exceeds that carried by rail.[23] The study by P.S. Ross et.al. examines truck and rail traffic for a special selection of commodity movments in which both rail and for-hire trucking participate. Table 22, drawn from that study, shows that the share of traffic on competitive commodity movements is comparable in Western and Eastern Canada. When comparable conditions are considered, the presence of trucking is as important in the West as the East. These data support the conclusion reached in Chapter II that any perceived differences between the working of competitive forces, except for those movements affected by subsidies in the Maritimes, are the result of different commodities produced and geographical conditions existing in parts of Canada. The general view that trucking competition has been ineffective in the West, is a result of the large absolute and relative size of certain commodity movements in bulk, but it should not imply the absence of trucking competition on other commodity movements.

194

Table 22

Percent of Tons for Selected Commodity Movements in
Eastern and Western Canada carried by For-Hire Trucking, 1971[a]

	West	East
Live Animals	81	84
Food, Feed, Beverages and Tobacco[b]	40	37
Crude Materials, Inedible	11	12
Fabricated Materials, Inedible	45	52
End Products, Inedible	81	79

Note: [a]The data are for a special selection of commodity movements
in which both rail and for-hire trucks participated. In
all, 308 paired highway and rail movements between the same
origins and destinations were identified.

[b]Excludes grain carried at statutory rates.

Source: P.S. Ross & Partners, et.al., Two Proposals for Rail Freight-
Pricing: Assessment of their Prospective Impact, A Report
to the Federal-Provincial Committee on Western Transportation,
September, 1974, Table 8-A to 8-E, pp. 8-3 to 8-7.

The importance of considering the effectiveness of competitive forces on a market sector basis, and not solely on a regional basis, has been made clear also by the research in this study on the workings of competitive forces. Instances where trucking is not the dominant competitive factor to be considered by the railways are found in a variety of locations and affect a variety of commodities. Shippers in northern Ontario and Quebec are often as concerned about their reliance on market competitive forces as some shippers in the West, as exemplified by the *Eastern Newsprint Case* considered in Chapter VIII. Viewing the limited impact of trucking competition on railway rates as a Western phenomenon ignores the widespread influence of trucking and the heterogeneous factors influencing the comparative advantage of modes of transport.

Comparative Advantage in Competition among Rail, Truck and Water Services

Intermodal competition is complex, as it is based on the alternate and complementary roles which the modes of transport can play in the logistics systems of user firms. The characteristics of transport service required by shippers differ greatly, depending on the commodity they ship, the location of the market they serve and the very specific conditions in the market at particular

195

times. The variety of conditions affecting the transportation requirements of a logistics system generally results in the modes of transport having complementary as well as competitive roles to play from the viewpoint of the user. For example, while rail or water transport may be used to ship basic inventory stock at relatively low freight rates, higher service modes, such as truck or air, may be used for smaller shipments meeting short-run inventory needs for which higher service levels are required. The receiver and/or shipper trade off various inventory costs against higher quality and higher rated transport service.[24] The optimum mix of modes of transport for the user is dependent on his trade-offs among the modes and his trade-off of transport costs with his inventory and other logistical costs. The level and importance of the latter can change significantly and quickly with market conditions. Therefore, the value placed on transport service changes over time.

Competition among the modes of transport when viewed from the standpoint of the logistical needs of shippers and receivers becomes complex and defies either a simple explanation or a simple rule by which an efficient allocation of traffic between modes could be achieved. The best that can be done in describing the allocation of traffic among modes is to examine in isolation some of the more important attributes of the traffic and the requirements of shippers, and relate these factors to the characteristics of the modes. Some of these factors are the same as those considered in the explanation of dynamic transport competition in Chapter IV. Because of the dominance of competition between truck and rail service in Canada, the description of the factors is confined to the relationship between those modes. The circumstances important in the use of water transport are considered separately later.

Length of Haul in Intermodal Competition

The relationship of the cost and service attributes of the modes of transport vary with the length of haul. It is considered, generally, that the length of haul over which trucking has an absolute cost advantage is restricted to short hauls. Depending on the specifics assumed as to the volume per shipment, route conditions and back-haul conditions, the length of haul over which trucking is expected to have a cost advantage may vary from 50 miles to 300 miles or even more.[25] The case studies reveal that trucking in Canada can be an effective alternative to rail transport over longer distances and for a wider range of commodities than it could ten years ago. The costs of truck transport have been held down by improvements in vehicle design, by increases in allowable vehicle sizes and weights, and by the imaginative efforts of truckers to seek out that mix of traffic to enable them to maintain profitable and relatively low-cost operations.

Transcontinental trucking is most effective in serving small-size shipments of relatively high-value goods and in this area is highly competitive with freight forwarding. Here competitive services are also available between truckers, whether operating over-the-road or via piggyback, and the railway-owned Trailers on Flat Car services.[26] However, truckers also provide an effective alternative to rail service over long distances when the characteristics of the products give the truckers back-haul traffic or a good product mix. For example, canned foodstuffs from Vancouver are good bottom freight for truckers returning to Eastern Canada with low density freight, and this compels the railways to provide competitively-set agreed charge rates. Tires shipped from Alberta to Montreal, Toronto and Hamilton are another example of competitively rated long-haul traffic.

The requirements of traffic for specialized equipment and, often, for particular service characteristics to go along with it, enable truck competition to extend over substantial distances. The movement of oil well equipment from Texas to Alberta, and of industrial equipment from Toronto to British Columbia, are examples of the competitiveness of trucking. The movements of fruit from British Columbia to Winnipeg and meat from the Prairie Provinces to Eastern Canada are dominated by truck. Rail service by refrigerated cars is too high in cost and cannot provide the equipment availability and service required by those trades. Participation of the railways in the meat trade is dependent on competition between their Intermodal Services and both the railway-owned and independent truckers. Competition for this traffic has been active, and has included independent competitive rate action between the railway Intermodal Services and railway-owned truckers.

However, the length of haul is a recognized constraint on the effectiveness of truck competition. The carriage of lumber, plywood, steel and automobiles by truck from British Columbia into the Prairies is recognized to be a more significant competitive factor into Alberta than it is into Manitoba. The effectiveness of trucking competition to Eastern Canada is greater from Winnipeg and Thunder Bay than it is from Saskatchewan and Alberta, both because of the greater distances involved from the latter and because of the availability of back-haul capacity eastbound from the Winnipeg area. A shipper of food products in Ontario found it best to ship by truck into the Prairies, but the railways moved the product to Vancouver under an agreed charge signed by the receiver. In 1974, the carriage of beer was finally lost in the majority of intraprovincial movements as the railways could no longer meet the competition of trucking, except on certain longer hauls which continued to be served by the railways under agreed charge rates. Similarly, during 1974 the railways cancelled agreed charges on cereals and related products within Eastern Canada and lost a significant amount of traffic to trucks, although they agreed with the shippers on truck competitive agreed charge rates into Western Canada and retained that traffic.

On bulk commodities, the reach of trucking competition can be considerable. In Saskatchewan, IMC trucked potash some 140 miles from Esterhazy to the

Burlington Northern at Northgate, North Dakota. Domestic feed grains, which do not come under the statutory rate levels, can be trucked from Alberta into British Columbia. In British Columbia, movements of up to 350 miles of copper concentrate from mines to Vancouver for export have only been won back from trucking by the railways through the design of competitively-priced transport systems. One mine located 130 miles from Vancouver still uses trucking services.

Freight Volume and Density in Intermodal Competition

A commodity movement which takes place in large volume through the year can take advantage of the economies of scale in rail transport. However, even on large volume movements trucking can exert a significant competitive pressure by being able to haul economically the volumes needed for small markets or by carrying those shipments on which the speed of delivery or some other service feature is particularly important. The possibility that if rail rates become too high a substantial shift to truck service will take place can exert a significant influence on the rate for the whole movement. Thus, shippers have negotiated agreed charges for traffic moving in much larger quantities than the amount which could reasonably be moved by truck, on the basis that the railways would not experience erosion in their traffic, at least in the period of the agreed charge. The movement of forest products from British Columbia to the Prairies and from north of the Great Lakes into the eastern Ontario and Quebec market area are good examples.

As important as the total volume of traffic to be moved, are the seasonality and quantity per shipment. Seasonal traffic raises problems of equipment utilization for any carrier. It appears that with refrigerated equipment, truckers achieve a better utilization than the railways and can price the seasonal movements of fruit and vegetables so as to dominate those movements. On movements of woodchips, however, the railways are better able to absorb the seasonality of the traffic than specialized truckers. A high utilization of rail equipment through high minimum weights is an important means by which the railways have attempted to meet truck competition. The rate reductions enabled by the high minimum weights offer important cost savings to shippers while the impact on the railways' net revenue is held down by the economies of full carload quantities.

The density of freight has a critical effect on the competitive relationship between rail and truck service. Very low density or "balloon" freight cannot be carried economically by truck. For example, low density containerized freight from the Orient has been more economical to rehandle and move in box cars than to move in containers. Heavy freight, for example, canned goods, which can move in shipments of about 20,000 pounds, can be attractive to truckers to provide a base load to mix with low density freight.

The mixing of freight can also be important in the effective utilization of rail box cars. For example, mixing rules apply in agreed charges on low density foodstuffs enabling better equipment utilization and lower rates than could be achieved by truck. Within those agreed charges covering a wide range of food items, the principles of price discrimination by traditional freight classification may still be present. One shipper was dissatisfied with the rate difference in an agreed charge between the rates on dog biscuits and the rates on other animal feed with which he felt the biscuits were competitive. After failing to have the railways lower the classification on the biscuits, he made an unofficial enquiry of the CTC. When he received what he regarded as a negative response, he dropped the matter.

Value of Commodities and Service Requirements in Intermodal Competition

Transport economists have long held that the inherent advantage of trucking over long distances was confined to the movement of fragile and high-value goods and service-sensitive traffic in small shipments. The case studies revealed active competition for such : shipments between freight forwarders, truckers, rail express and rail Intermodal Services. For such traffic, the railways have introduced agreed charges in Eastern Canada for the Canadian Retail Shippers Association operating through Torman Assembly Ltd. and shipping almost exclusively with CP. Out of Vancouver, the traffic of freight forwarders and pool car operators is moved under open rates for freight forwarder and pool car shippers.

However, the case studies revealed the startling significance of the competitive presence of trucking, or its potential presence, even over long hauls. Except for very short hauls, truck service cannot be a viable substitute for rail service in the hauling of bulk commodities. Nevertheless, as indicated already, the reach of the competitive influence of truck competition is much more extensive than has been commonly recognized.

High-valued freight not only tends to move in small shipments which require prompt and reliable delivery to keep shipper and receiver inventories at low levels,[27] but such freight is commonly service sensitive in other respects also. The loss and damage record of the railways was found to be a matter of concern to some shippers who felt that the railways have not been as responsive as they should or could be to damage complaints. One shipper built up a thick photograph album showing damaged shipments and poor car order before he set about negotiating a major rate and service charge. The railways responded to the threat of trucking competition on traffic they then perceived as significantly service and rate sensitive by encouraging the use of rail-owned piggyback service. A shipper of cereals and baking products was found to be making increasing use of for-hire and private trucking, partly because of rail rates and partly because of his favourable experience with palletized shipments of baking products by truck, which he argued would have been "piles of dust" by rail.

Shippers of manufactured goods for whom handling costs and inventory charges can be significant, but who ship a large enough total volume that rail service can be economical, can be influenced by very detailed aspects of carrier service. For example, factors such as the times at which rail cars are spotted at the plant can be important. Also, such shippers may find that the greater ease of loading and unloading trucks, and the lesser peaking of freight handling that they experience by using trucks, yield critical day-to-day economies which make truck service preferable to rail service.

The value placed on time in transit can vary significantly for service-sensitive traffic. For example, the benefit of clothing being available in stores at Friday noon is much greater than at Saturday noon, and certainly Sunday noon! Logistics systems are sensitive to such considerations, as was made clear in a hearing concerning Sunday trucking in Ontario. The Traffic Manager of Burns Foods Limited in Winnipeg explained that he shipped meat products hanging and in boxes to the Maritimes by rail and to Ontario and Quebec by truck. His explanation for the use of truck for two-thirds of his output was:

> We have actually a number of reasons there. For one thing we could not kill that many animals and stock them in our coolers and keep them fresh and ship everything on one particular day. We can only kill so many animals a day and they are basically designed to be held in our cooler for 24 hours and be shipped under the proper cooling arrangement. Not only that, a customer quite often demands that we ship on certain days so he can get a fresh product....[28]

Freight Rates as a Factor in Intermodal Competition

It is clear from the foregoing that a variety of service considerations are important to the competition between railway and highway carriers for shippers' business. However, the costs of the services figure prominantly in the evaluation of service alternatives by shippers. The case studies revealed that, except for instances where the railways were found to respond to service competition by the substitution of Intermodal Services for rail service, the competitive response of the railways to trucking competition was largely through competitive rate action. This competitive action was the one anticipated under dynamic competition in Chapter IV. It was only in specialized situations in the design of integrated truck-rail movements that service considerations figured prominently in the discussions of shippers with the railways. An example was in the design of handling systems for handling copper concentrate, as the loss of concentrate through spillage, wind or rain action was a significant concern of shippers.

The importance of rate competition means that at times the railways may be unable to provide a low enough rate to meet trucking competition. The loss of short-haul beer and baking products movements are examples. In other instances, the railways have been able to recapture lost traffic through a combination of technological innovation and aggressive pricing. A major traffic affected is the carriage of automobiles in tri-level carriers. A more localized example is the carriage of copper concentrate in British Columbia. However, of more importance than instances when the movement of traffic has shifted from one mode to another, are the innumerable instances where rail rates have been modified to prevent the potential development or expansion of trucking service as shippers have indicated might be the case. An example of the response of the railways to trucking competition is the movement of forest products from British Columbia to the Prairies.

Highway improvements in Western Canada have enabled the trucking of lumber and plywood into Alberta to become a reality. The economies of this movement are aided considerably by the presence of westbound grain so that full equipment utilization in both directions can be achieved. The agreed charge rates established into the Prairies have not only recognized the reality of this competition, but also the potential for the reach of trucking competition to extend into Manitoba. Competitive truck rates have been published from British Columbia to Manitoba and these have been met by agreed charge rates with high minimum weights.[29]

Such action by the railways is typical of the price responsiveness which has been present under the pricing freedom before, and to a greater extent since, 1967. It has been documented in other studies, particularly in instances where truckers provided effective competition to the railways because of available back-haul capacity. A study by MPS Associates Ltd. explains that rates on zinc smelter products moving from nothern Manitoba to Western Canadian points were reduced in 1970 and that rates on lumber from northern Manitoba to Central Canada were reduced in 1971. In both instances competition was from back-haul truck rates.[30] A paper by Professor J.D. Wahn describes the traffic imbalance of truckers leading to lower rates eastbound from Manitoba than westbound into that Province. He explains:

> ... there is a good quantity of inter-provincial freight moving westbound from Ontario to Winnipeg with less moving in the opposite direction. The effect of this is that motor carriers have excess capacity on eastbound movements and shippers in Western Canada can enjoy therefore a somewhat lower level of rates on freight destined for Eastern Canada than they otherwise would.[31]

The case studies carried out for this study revealed the continuing influence of these low back-haul rates on the level of rates in railway agreed charges. In one case, a shipper found it most economical to use an agreed charge from

Toronto to Winnipeg, but to use trucking in the reverse direction because of the low back-haul rates.

Examples of the Competitive Influence of Shipping on Rail Rates

The competition of water services with the railways is restricted geographically and is restricted to those commodity movements for which the lower rate which may be available through water transport more than offsets the service advantage of rail transport. Water competition is most likely to be effective on a limited number of bulk commodities moving in large volume. However, the case studies did reveal the competitive influence of water services on rail rates for manufactured goods on the West Coast and on the Great Lakes. In British Columbia, rail and truck service from Vancouver to Prince Rupert is via circuitous inland routes so that the use of coastal services is more competitive than might otherwise be the case. In the Great Lakes, the use of Canada Steamship Lines package service is still a factor in the negotiation of rail rates on forest products, for example, from western Ontario. However, the major effect of shipping on rail rates is that of causing the railways to reduce rates on substantial volumes of traffic which might otherwise become committed to logistics systems using water transportation. In the movement of rapeseed from Thunder Bay, the railway agreed charge was introduced to meet water competition (see Chapter VIII). On intercoastal traffic between British Columbia and Eastern Canada, the rail rates on forest products and some movements of mineral products have been held down by the potential of water competition. During 1976, the actual movement of coal by ship from Vancouver to Hamilton, Ontario received considerable publicity because it was exceptional as a Canadian intercoastal water movement. The distance by rail would have been 2,740 miles. The distance by water was about 9,500 miles.[32] In general, it is the potential of water competition which exerts an effect on rail rates. The effect of potential water competition on the rail rates on lumber and plywood from British Columbia to Eastern Canada deserves special attention because of the importance of government shipping policies which allow access by international shipping in domestic trades.

Rail rates on British Columbia forest products. Freight rates from British Columbia to Eastern Canada on forest products up to 1968 had been adjusting to the evolution of the large integrated forest product companies in the province, such as MacMillan Bloedel, Crown Zellerbach and B.C. Forest Products. Two significant changes took place in 1964. The first was the negotiation of rates on plywood down to the level of lumber rates. Previously, plywood had moved at the much higher shingle rate, in spite of the low density of cedar shingles compared with plywood. The second change was the negotiation of rates in agreed charges largely on the bases of trucking competition within Western Canada and the potential for water competition to Eastern

202

Canada. However, although the possibility of water competition was recognized as a factor, the main consideration affecting the rates to the East was the desire of the shippers to see the rates on plywood reduced, consistent with its loading characteristics. Under the agreed charges, the shippers were to move 90 percent of their shipments east of British Columbia by rail. Although the rate on plywood was now the same as the rate on lumber, the Canadian and American rate scales were comparable.

Between 1964 and 1968, no major changes in rates took place, although the railways continued to reduce some rates into Alberta and Saskatchewan to meet truck competition. In the Fall of 1967, after the American railways had increased rates on lumber, the Canadian railways notified the parties to the agreed charges that rates were to be increased, effective May 1968. The response of the shippers was to request a rate reduction to Eastern Canada on the basis of a detailed study of the economics of using ships to Eastern Canadian port distribution centres, from which products would be distributed by truck, as competitive rail rates could not be expected from the CN and CP.

This study was carried out by MacMillan Bloedel, a firm that had been active in using ships to the Atlantic coast of the U.S.A. The analysis was conducted on the basis of a lumber carrier, Japanese built and under a British flag, on long-term charter from CP (Bermuda) Ltd. Negotiations on the basis of the detailed shipping study were carried out with railway personnel in Montreal. They concluded with a rate reduction introduced immediately in a Limited Freight Tariff in July, 1968 and subsequently issued in an agreed charge. The rate reduction brought about a radical departure in the level of domestic rail rates in Canada and the U.S.A., as shown in Figure 5. The Canadian rates on plywood and lumber were reduced to a level below those in the U.S.A., and the rate of increase was held down for a number of years. The lower rate on Canadian domestic lumber and plywood was accounted for by the competitive advantage enjoyed by western Canada producers from being able to use the most efficient ships available in the Canadian domestic trade whereas the shipping alternative in the American domestic trade was confined to high-cost American flag vessels. The freight rate from Vancouver to New York was the same as the American domestic rate.

Within British Columbia, the change in the rates in 1968 resulted in the Interior producers losing a rate advantage which they had previously had over the coastal producers. However, the water competitive rate was extended to apply to the Interior producers so that they were not placed at a disadvantage.

Increases in the agreed charge rates have taken place since 1971. The negotiations for the railways have been the responsibility of the regional marketing departments, which include persons specializing in studies of the forest industry. The negotiations for the forest industry have been conducted by a special committee of the Council of Forest Industries. In view of the level of

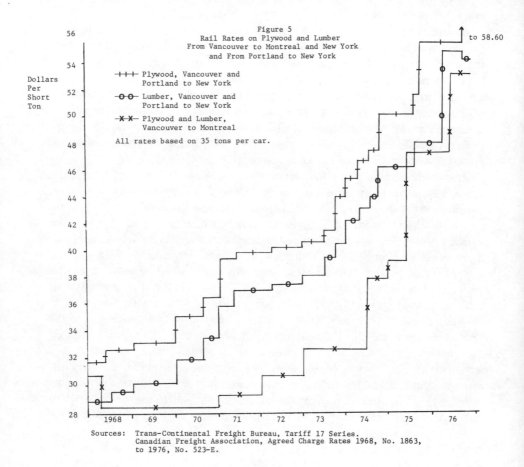

Figure 5
Rail Rates on Plywood and Lumber
From Vancouver to Montreal and New York
and From Portland to New York

+++ Plywood, Vancouver and
    Portland to New York

-O-O- Lumber, Vancouver and
    Portland to New York

-X-X- Plywood and Lumber,
    Vancouver to Montreal

All rates based on 35 tons per car.

Dollars
Per
Short
Ton

Sources: Trans-Continental Freight Bureau, Tariff 17 Series.
          Canadian Freight Association, Agreed Charge Rates 1968, No. 1863,
          to 1976, No. 523-E.

204

rates into 1974, the influence of water competition has not been as prominent a feature in the negotiations, at least up to 1975, as they were in 1968. However, both the railways and shippers now perform careful analyses of the costs of shipping before negotiations commence. Market competitive forces are also a more significant factor now than they were in the 1960's, as a result of increased competition both from producers in Quebec and in the southeastern U.S.A. The 1974 agreed charge was the first one to establish regional requirements on the amount shipped by rail. In 1974, it was 85 percent by rail east of Manitoba and 70 percent by rail in the Prairies. The decreased percentage to be moved by rail reflected the more competitive position caused by trucking, even into Eastern Canada.

Substantial freight rate increases have been experienced in the agreed charge rates in 1975 and 1976. The rise in rail freight rates have been seen by the forest industry as favorable to the possibility of utilizing ships since charter rates on dry bulk vessels are depressed relative to their 1973 and 1974 levels. The forest industry has viewed with alarm, therefore, the possibility that the restrictions of intercoastal trade to Canadian flag ships would remove the possibility of using the available shipping resources of the world and would remove the threat of such ships as providing the effective ceiling on railway freight rates.

The Practical Workings of Intermodal Competitive Forces

For a shipper currently using rail service, the possible use of alternate modes of transport is an important negotiating strategy. When the setting of rail rates is based on a shipper's claims during the negotiation of his possible use of alternate modes of transport, the issue of whether the alternative actually exists or potentially exists may be academic for the railways. Indeed, depending on the manner in which a shipper presents his case, the railway officers may have difficulty determining whether the competition is actual or potential!

Shippers make claims about the advantages of using other modes of transport. These claims vary greatly in their sophistication and the extent to which they are documented. They may be as simple as a statement that a trucking rate of a certain amount is available. They may involve the quotation of published rates, citing tariff references, or they may be substantiated by freight documents. In cases of private trucking, simple statements of the actual or expected cost of private trucking may be made or detailed studies may be referred to or even given to the railways for analysis, as was the 1968 study on the cost of shipping forest products by water from British Columbia. In all of these cases, the problems for the railways are the same. They are also the same when their own own pricing or marketing officers raise the questions of actual or potential competition quite independently of the shippers.

205

Evaluation of Shipper Alternatives by the Railways

The railways must consider a number of questions to determine whether the alternative presented by the shipper is one which he will use. The first question is certainly whether the actual or potential alternative exists. Shippers involved in, or about to be involved, in negotiations with the railways commonly contact truckers who may quote or publish rates. If the railways meet the rates, no traffic may materialize for the alternate mode. When a shipper simply claims that a trucker has quoted him a particular rate, which is not published, or claims that he can perform private transport for a particular cost, it must be a matter of judgement by railway managers whether the alternative does or could exist. The credibility of the shipper is important in such cases. When a rate for an alternative mode has been published, its existence can be verified and the railway must be concerned with the period for which the rate may be maintained and the amount of traffic which might move at that rate.

During the period of rapid inflation in recent years, the railways, in setting agreed charges for the standard period of a year, have been concerned in case the trucking rate they met would move up subsequently while the rail rate was frozen by the provisions in the agreed charge. To avoid the problem, the railways have been moving away from the use of agreed charges. However, during 1976, it became generally recognized that agreed charges for less than one year are legal and some of these have been established. Where agreed charges of a year's duration have been maintained, the railways have generally declined to meet the existing truck rate on the basis that during the year the truck rate could be expected to increase.

This movement of competitive rates in the same direction and at about the same time is to be expected. It arises from the close attention that the railways and truckers must give to each other's rates as well as to the fact that both modes are subject to the same economic forces. However, the tendency for rail and truck rates to follow one another is a source of complaints about the lack of sufficient competition in Canadian freight markets. A typical view was expressed in 1966 as follows: "... the fact is that when the truck rates went up the railroad rates went up, and the additional burden was borne by the shipper of livestock."[33] The research on the pricing process for this study indicates that the relationship between the truck and rail rates arises from active rivalry, including instances where railway-owned trucking companies are important, for example, in the movement of meat from Alberta to Eastern Canada. Whether price leadership is shown by trucking or rail is dependent on many factors which may encourage aggressive competitive action. MPS Associates Ltd. concluded that "there is no distinct pattern of leadership in truck-rail rates on Manitoba-related traffic examined".[34] The evidence of the case studies suggests that in those markets where the railways are dominant, they are the price leaders, as would be expected.

After the railways decided on the existing and probable future rates or costs of alternatives actually or potentially available to shipper, they generally considered the amount of traffic which might use the alternate route. Shippers commonly merely cited the existence of the alternative, perhaps hoping that the railways would infer that all of their traffic could move via the alternative carrier. In some cases, it was a matter given careful attention by the railway rates officers, but in other cases, the interviews left the impression that little attention was given to the amount which might move via alternative carriers. Several factors can influence the volume. The capacity of an alternative may be limited, as in the case of back-haul trucking. The amount moved by alternate modes can also be influenced by the logistical needs of the shipper. The value of trucking in a complementary role to rail service may be confined to serving small market centres and/or to meeting unexpected inventory replacement needs. In other instances, it may be economical to use only one mode of transport.

Evaluation of the amount of traffic which may be lost is particularly difficult when the shipper is considering an alternative which requires a change in a logistics system, such as additions to or reductions in the number of warehouses. Such changes, once introduced, persist for a considerable time, so that they must be evalutated very carefully by the railways and the shippers.

Competitive Actions by the Railways

The majority of the negotiations investigated for this study involving inter-modal competition were initiated because of proposed rate increases by the railways. During the inflationary period of the 1970's, this can be no surprise. However, in one case the quality of rail service was a very important factor and in one other case, it was significant. In each of those cases, the work of Inter-modal Services and other representatives from Marketing and Sales staffs in the railways resulted in the movements taking place by piggyback.

The response of the railways to the pressure of intermodal competition on their rates varied greatly. They were noticeably less ready to accede to shippers requests in 1974 and 1975 than in earlier years. In three of the cases researched, the railways were made very aware by shippers that the proposed rates would result in the loss of traffic, but the railways introduced the rate increases on the basis that they were necessary for the traffic to be compensatory. While the shippers were dissatisfied with the railways actions, the railway pricing officers expected to lose the traffic as they had been told, so that in the absence of specific knowledge of the railway costs, it may be presumed that the decisions to retain the rate increases were wise commercially and economically efficient.

In other instances, the railways indicated that, since they had taken competition into account when they set the rates, they saw no need to make further adjustments. In a few cases of agreed charges where the shipper had traffic moving from or to a number of points, only some of which were competitive, the railways indicated that they felt that overall rate levels were competitive and that if they were pushed to lower the rates on the competitive routes, they would have to examine the rates on the non-competitive routes. The obvious implication was that the latter rates would then increase. In one instance where the rate competition was from trucks seeking back-haul traffic, a rate reduction was made in the non-competitive, not in the competitive, route. This concession was made so that the agreed charge contract would be attractive to the shipper, while the railway avoided cutting rates to meet competition in a market in which it felt that it was dominant and, therefore, the price leader.

In the majority of cases and particularly those prior to 1974, the railways met intermodal competition by adjusting the rate level on the competitive traffic. In instances of lower-value commodities, the rail rate was a few cents lower than or even equal to the truck rate, although the shipment size required to get the rail rate was substantially larger, in general, than that required for the truckload rate. The adjustments of the railways were applied selectively by the railways, depending on competitive conditions. In one case, a shipper faced with a 15-percent increase negotiated on the basis of trucking competition and his increase was adjusted to 8 percent in all placed but one, in which the railways argued, correctly, that trucking competition was not effective.

Responsiveness of the Railways to Intermodal Competition

The railways generally responded effectively to intermodal competition when able to do so at compensatory levels. The rate changes proposed by the railways were made with a knowledge of competitive forces but, through negotiations, they have been requested to respond to specific intermodal competitive factors of which they may have been unaware. Under the commercial freedom available since 1967, the railways have responded to competitive pressures on routes and commodities, when applicable. In some cases, detailed studies of proposals have required considerable additional research by the railways as well as by the members of an industry group, where appropriate. However, once agreement has been reached on a rate and/or an agreed charge contract, the rates have often been implemented immediately through a Limited Freight Tariff for later publication in an agreed charge or other tariff. The experience of negotiation of an agreement with immediate and certain implementation has encouraged the development of effective organizations and the development of negotiating capability on behalf of the shippers and the railways.

There is no evidence that the railways practiced predatory pricing to the detriment of truckers, although the railways responded competitively to potential and actual trucking competition. This has presumably prevented some trucking from developing and becoming vulnerable to rail competition subsequently. The effectiveness of railway competition has been a contributing factor to the failure of some trucking firms. However, the failure of trucking

208

firms has also been caused by competition among trucking companies, and by truckers conceding too often to the demands for improved service from shippers. The support of the trucking industry for reliance on market forces both in 1966 and in 1975, as shown in Chapter IX, is certainly clear evidence that the competitive actions of the railways have not been detrimental to the vitality of the trucking industry.

The case studies include instances where rail-owned trucking subsidiaries were an important component of the trucking service available. However, the railway ownership of the trucking firms had no discernible effect on the pattern of competition. To gain their market shares the managers of the trucking and rail divisions of the CN and CP have to act promptly and effectively in their own interest, in effect, as separate corporations.

Agreed charges have been used to develop contracts with shippers which the railways have encouraged shippers to view as a package. The approach of a package contract has been used to reduce the extent to which negotiations have to deal with competitive rates on a commodity-by-commodity, route-by-route basis. The contracts also have provided a means by which the railways could meet a particular shipper's needs within the framework of a total contract, without being placed under undue pressure to provide all of the favourable rate features to other shippers. The railways have been able to respond, therefore, to the detail of market forces more effectively than might otherwise have been the case.

One important aspect of intermodal competition has not been included in this chapter. That is, where another mode of transport, generally trucking, has been used to enable a shipper to reach more than one railway to realize the benefits of intramodal competition. These examples are considered in the next Chapter.

Conclusions on Intermodal Competition

In 1961 the MacPherson Commission argued that the development of intermodal competition, because of the growth of trucking, had so changed the nature of rail transport markets as to warrant freeing the railways from restrictive regulations of their rates. The main conclusions of this Chapter are that the evidence on the significance of intermodal competition in transport markets since 1967 reveals that the MacPherson Commission was correct in viewing it as a pervasive force affecting most commodity movements and that the Commission was also correct in recommending that the railways be given wide freedom to set freight rates. The evidence of the case studies and of other published studies, suggests that the reach of trucking competition has continued to increase since 1967.

It is not possible to measure quantitatively the extent to which intermodal competition influences railway rates and services. In part, this is because of the inadequacies of Canadian transport statistics but, more importantly, it is because of the nature of dynamic competition in transport. Transportation services have heterogeneous characteristics and the demand for transport, even by one shipper, is multi-dimensional. Consequently, it is difficult to determine when modes are practicable alternatives, so that it is not practical to measure the full extent of dynamic intermodal competition. Further, intermodal competition works often through the potential, rather than actual, development and/or extension of a service. Such competitive thrusts may never be observable except through a knowledge of the workings of competitive forces in specific instances.

The importance of potential competition in transport markets has significant implications for the implementation of regulations. First, any regulations which control the development or extention of service by a mode, not only actually make the development or extension of service difficult but reduce the reach of the competitive influence of that mode through its potential development. For example, if to use foreign flag ships in Canadian intercoastal trade should require government approval, this procedure might have to be gone through by a shipper to establish the credibility of potential water competition to transcontinental railway service. Ironically, the more onerous the procedure, the more likely that shippers would have to go through the procedural costs to establish the credibility of the alternative. Having gone so far it may well be worthwhile operating some shipping to avoid the undesirable procedure on other occasions. Second, controlling the response of a mode to competitive forces is difficult when the competition to be met is potential competition. A regulatory committee may have no more evidence of the presence of competition than the statement of a shipper that a certain potential alternative is available. Therefore, considerable flexibility and ease of administrative procedures must exist if the working of competitive forces is to be efficient in the presence of any regulation of competitive actions.

The ability of the railways to respond to intermodal competition has been important to the railways in enabling them to react immediately to competitive pressures and, thereby, retain profitable traffic which might otherwise have been lost. It has also been important to shippers, as they have been able to use intermodal alternatives to gain reductions in rail rates and to stimulate the railways to more efficiency both by reducing costs and rates and by improving services.

Effective intermodal competition is likely to be associated with freight rates of the competing modes changing over time in a comparable way. The actual levels of the freight rates of competing modes may differ to compensate shippers for the service quality difference between the carriers. However, comparable freight rate adjustments must occur over time or shippers will shift from one mode to another. The shares of a market enjoyed by the modes will remain stable as long as the modes are subject to similar increases in resource costs and

210

as long as innovation brings comparable cost and service improvements to each mode. It is difficult to predict which carrier or mode is, in general, the most likely to act as a price leader because so many factors stimulate rivalry actions. However, in general, the mode with the major market share is likely to be the price leader, but it cannot ignore the competitive reaction of the competing mode or modes.

Intermodal competition is not an effective constraint on railway pricing practices on all traffic. While the major bulk commodities of grain, coal, potash and sulphur in Western Canada are the obvious examples of commodities only affected to a limited extent, or not at all, by trucking competition, it is incorrect to view the effectiveness of trucking competition as a regional phenomenon. To do that may lead to both an underestimate of the importance of trucking in the West and an overestimate of its pervasiveness in the East.

FOOTNOTES

1. See Canada, *Royal Commission on Transportation,* known as the MacPherson Commission (Ottawa: Queen's Printer, 1961), Vols. I, II, and III; A.W. Currie, *Canadian Transportation Economics* (Toronto: Toronto University Press, 1967), p. 719; and H.L. Purdy, *Transport Competition and Public Policy in Canada* (Vancouver; University of British Columbia Press, 1972), p. 327.
2. See, for example, Howard Darling, *Modal Market Shares,* An address to the Roads and Transportation Association of Canada, Montebello, Quebec, May, 1976.
3. Currie, *op.cit.,* p. 249. Currie cites *Bowlby v. Halifax & South Western Ry.,* 20 C.R.C. 231 (1916); 6 J.O.R.R. 367.
4. John Maurice Clark, *Competition as a Dynamic Process* (Washington, D.C.: The Brookings Institution, 1961), p. 56.
5. Canada, House of Commons, 27th Parliament, 1st Session, Standing Committee on Transport and Communications, Minutes of Proceedings and Evidence, November 3, 1966, p. 2,330.
6. *Ibid.,* p. 2,369.
7. Canadian Transport Commission, Motor Vehicle Transport Committee, *Report of Investigation and Decision in the Matter of an Objection by the Trucking Association of Quebec Inc. to the Proposed Acquisition of Chalut Transport (1974) Inc. by Canadian National Railways indirectly through its subsidiaries,* Decision No. MV-27-32 (M-76-2), 1976.
8. *Ibid.,* Table 2, p. 46 and Table 4, p. 50. These figures include the trucking operation of CN Express.
9. *Ibid.,* p. 71.
10. *A.G. Ont. v. Winner,* A.C. 541; 4 D.L.R. 657; 71 C.R.T.C. 225 (1954).
11. David Maister, *An Analysis of Trucking Rates in Canada* (Vancouver, Centre for Transportation Studies, University of British Columbia, 1976), p. 5.
12. Canadian Industrial Traffic League, *Traffic Notes,* July 27, 1976, pp. 4-5.
13. *Ibid.,* October 19, 1976, p. 3.
14. Contracts for the carriage of grain on the Great Lakes must be filed with the Board of Grain Commissioners to ensure that they are not unreasonable.
15. MPS Associates Ltd., *Highway and Rail Traffic Related to Western Canada,* Prepared for the Western Transportation Advisory Council, Vancouver, British Columbia, January 1974, p. 117.
16. P.S. Ross & Partners, et.al., *Two Proposals for Rail Freight Pricing: Assessment of their Prospective Impact,* A Report to the Federal-Provincial Committee on Western Transportation, September 1974.
17. *Ibid.,* p. 8-1.
18. MPS Associates, *op.cit.,* p. 11.
19. E.J. Benson "The Unknown Industry", *Manitoba Highway News,* April 1975, p. 14.
20. Calculated from MPS Associates, *op.cit.,* Table 3, p. 21.
21. Calculated from MPS Associates, *op.cit.,* Table 27, p. 92.
22. *Ibid.,* p. 95.
23. *Ibid.,* p. 101.
24. For evidence concerning the importance of the savings in time for shippers who use truck service instead of rail service between Eastern and Western Canada, see Canadian Transport Commission, *In the Matter of the Applications filed with the Canadian Transport Commision pursuant to paragraph (x) of section 11 of the Lord's Day Act, R.S. 1970, Ch. L-13: By Reimer Express Lines Ltd., and by Imperial Roadways Ltd.,*

212

Decision No. MV-LD-20 (M-74-1), March 14, 1974, pp. 16-24, 35-38.

25. The cost-competitive range of owner-operators in the U.S.A. is shown to extend to long hauls by D. Daryl Wyckoff and David H. Maister, *The Owner-Operator: Independent Trucker* (Lexington, Mass.: Lexington Books, D.C. Heath and Co., 1975).

26. As pointed out in Chapter III, railway-owned Trailer on Flat Car services are operated by Intermodal Services in both the CN and CP and these are quite distinct from, and operate competitively with railway-owned trucking services.

27. Motor Vehicle Transport Committee, Decision No. MV-LD-20, 1974, *op.cit,* pp. 16-24, 35-38.

28. Canadian Transport Commission, Motor Vehicle Transport Committee, *Public Hearing in the Matter of Applications pursuant to the Lord's Day Act in Toronto, October 26, 1973,* Case No. MV 2/73 volume 4, p. 670, quoted in Canadian Transport Commission, *Report to the Minister of Transport* Pursuant to Request of July 14, 1973, Under Section 22 of the National Transportation Act, December 3, 1973, p. 6.

29. MPS Associates Ltd., *The Influence of Truck-Rail Competition on Rate Patterns* (Ottawa: Canadian Transport Commission, Research Publication, 1973), pp. 30 and 49.

30. *Ibid.*

31. J.D. Wahn, "Selected Transportation Problems and Industrial Development in Western Canada" *Proceedings of the Seminar Series on Transportation 1973-1974* (Winnipeg, Manitoba: Center for Transportation Studies, University of Manitoba, 1973-1974), pp. 46-47.

32. "Long Way Around Pays", *The Vancouver Sun,* June 23, 1976, p. 43.

33. Canada, House of Commons, 27th Parliament, 1st Session, Standing Committtee on Transport and Communications, Minutes of Proceedings and Evidence, Statement of Mr. Gibbings, President of the Canadian Cooperative Wheat Producers, Ltd., October 18, 1966, p. 1,892.

34. MPS Associates Ltd., 1973, *op.cit,* p. 51.

CHAPTER VII

INTRAMODAL COMPETITION AND OTHER INFLUENCES ON RAILWAY RATES

In spite of there being only a few companies serving a market, or even in cases where only two firms serve a market, Clark has indicated that dynamic competition can, and often does, take place, (see Chapter IV). In the U.S.A., the importance of intramodal competition among rail carriers has been recognized in the merger cases, and these cases often provide considerable evidence on the working of intramodal competition relevant thereto.[1] In particular rate-making situations, the importance of competition between railways has been documented in ICC decisions.[2]

In Canada, much less recognition is given to the presence of competition between railways than in the U.S.A. It is a commonly held view that the railways do not engage in rate competition, although service competition between them is widely recognized. The view that there is no rate competition appears to stem from the dominance of the CN and CP in Canada, the frequency with which they exchange information and make rates in common, and the similar levels of rates published by the CN and CP, even though the similarity of rates may demonstrate competition rather than joint rate making.

Relative Importance of the Individual Railway Companies and Market Dominance

In 1975, the Canadian railway industry operated 43,941 route miles of first-main track and earned a total revenue, including subsidies, of $2,734 million. The dominance of the CN and CP is readily apparent from the distribution of revenue among the companies shown in Table 23. The CN and CP earned 90 per cent of the revenue earned in 1975.

Market Dominance by CN and CP

This dominance means that in much of Canada only the CN and/or CP are present or are actually involved in the movement of freight by rail. In Western Canada, of the six major centres, only Winnipeg and Vancouver have a railway other than the CN and CP present. In Winnipeg and Vancouver, the Burlington Northern (BN) is present in addition to the CN and CP. In Vancouver, the

Table 23

Revenues of Railway Companies from
Canadian Railway Operations, 1975
(Millions of Dollars)

Class I

Canadian National	1462.6
Canadian Pacific	1007.3

Class II

Algona Central	13.3
British Columbia Railway	50.5
Canada Southern (Penn Central)	12.9
Chesapeake and Ohio	17.4
Northern Alberta	16.5
Ontario Northaldn	28.1
Quebec North Shore and Labrador	57.0
All Other Class II	66.7

Classes III and IV	1.5
	2733.8

Source: Statistics Canada, <u>Railway Transport</u>,
          Part II, Table 1.

British Columbia Railway (BCR) is also present. In Eastern Canada, a greater number of railways exist and provide important competitive alternatives in the southern part of the Ontario Peninsula. However, in the remaining major traffic centres in Ontario, only the CN and CP are present. In northern Ontario, the Ontario Northland Railway (ONR) is an important carrier in an area dependent on forestry and mining. The railway has interchanges with the CN and/or CP systems in only three locations, but it does provide competitive routing alternatives for some communities. In Quebec and the Maritimes, the only railway other than the two main carriers serving a major centre is the Penn Central Eastern, which serves a part of Montreal.

The general structure of the Canadian railway industry is very clear. It is dominated by the CN and CP and has only few centers where other railways are present. These are either regional railways, such as the BCR and ONR, or they are northern extensions of American lines.

Legislative Constraints on Competition

The competition among these few lines in Canada operates within legislative constraints; two important ones were described in Chapter III. It was noted

216

that Section 279 gives the railways in Canada the right to agree upon and charge common rates. The right of the railways to consult, especially in a duopoly, reduces, but does not eliminate, the probability of some rate competition. Section 382 of the Railway Act, in subjecting goods carried by rail between points in Canada over lines in the U.S.A. under combination rates, as opposed to joint rates, to a thirty-percent customs tariff, reduces, but does not eliminate, the probability of American lines competing with Canadian lines.

An adequate description of the competitive relationship among railways in Canada requires looking beyond the number of carriers serving a community to the regulations affecting the access of those carriers to shippers and receivers.

Institutional Factors Affecting Intramodal Competition

The possibility of competition among railways is dependent on the ease with which a shipper may avail himself of the services of alternative railways. This is dependent on his access to originating or terminating carriers, and the extent to which he may prescribe the routing of traffic which can move over a number of competing lines. These matters are influenced significantly by regulatory constraints. Those constraints are important to the working of intramodal competition in Canada.

Interswitching Limits and Rates

In Canada, a larger percentage of rail cars can be picked up directly from a shipper or delivered directly to a receiver by a line-haul carrier than in the U.S.A. because of the more limited number of rail carriers in Canada. Traffic which is originated and is terminated by the line-haul carrier normally is charged only the line-haul rate, as the delivery or collection of a car is incidental to the line haul. In some instances, where a line-haul rate is not applicable directly to or from a plant, either a local (line-haul) rate or local switching rate is added to the main line-haul rate. For example, some rates apply on traffic moving from the U.S.A. into New Westminster, British Columbia, which is part of the Vancouver metropolitan area, that do not apply to other parts of the urban area. For rail service to be extended into those places in Vancouver either another line-haul rate or a local switching rate is added to the main line-haul rate. However, for a carrier to originate or terminate traffic for which it cannot perform the line-haul, an interswitch service must be performed. Interswitching is the movement of carload freight by the terminal carrier between the point of loading or unloading on such terminal carrier's tracks and the point of interchange with the line-haul carrier. To understand the current status of interswitching regulations and rates in Canada, it is necessary to consider some events which took place at the turn of the century.[3]

The transfer of cars between line-haul and terminal carriers was a matter of considerable controversy during the years that the railway system was evolving. Shippers often sought to obtain access to more than one railway by having interchange facilities provided and reasonable rates charged for the interchange of traffic. As a result, the Board of Railway Commissions (hereinafter referred to as the Board) was called upon to deal with many complaints regarding interchange and interswitching practices and charges. In 1907 the Board decided to consider several interswitching complaints as one case. In preparation for this investigation, a report prepared by the Board's Chief Traffic Officer was circulated to interested parties. The Chief Traffic Officer's report stated that interswitching rates had no fixed or common basis and

> ... in order to avoid the frequent complaints to the Board of excessive switching charges, and the investigations which these call for, and for the convenience alike of the carriers and the public, I believe that a uniform scale or standardization of switching tolls ought to work out satisfactorily, subject, possibly, to modifications where expectional circumstances and conditions may appear to make these necessary.[4]

The Chief Traffic Officer recommended that the then prevailing maximum rate of 1 cent per 100 lbs. be adopted and made applicable on interswitching up to four miles from the point of interchange. On July 8, 1908, the Board issued Order Number 4988 which basically followed those recommendations. However, the Board continued to receive complaints about interswitching, as Order Number 4988 was interpreted as not applying to team tracks unless the terminal carrier so desired. As a result, the Board reopened the interchange/interswitching question in 1918. This decision may be viewed as a turning point, as the Chief Commissioner speaking for the Board said:

> I am of opinion that interswitching should no longer be carried on as a matter of grace, but as a matter of right. The general order ought not to be merely a tariff but an order which provides for and compels the service to be given.[5]

In 1918 the Board issued an order to become General Order Number 252. This order was basically the same as the 1908 judgement, except that team tracks were explicitly included. There has been virtually no change in those regulations since that time except for a fifty-percent rate increase granted in 1951. The distance over which the interswitching rate and regulations apply is still four miles from an interchange point. The applicable order today is General Order T-12, issued by the Board of Transport Commissioners in 1965. With few exceptions, the interswitching regulations governing the access of shippers to railways through interswitching services are nearly seventy years old and the rates applying to the service are twenty-five years old.

The rate from or to private sidings is 1 1/2 cents per 100 lbs., subject to a minimum of $4.50 or $7.50 per car depending on the traffic, for interswitching services up to four miles from any interchange point. The application of General Order Number 252 resolved issues of interswitching rates, but the Board has heard a number of applications for new interchange facilities. No application has been made since 1967.

However, the fact that the interswitching limits and rates were set so long ago raises two questions. The first is whether mileage limits on interswitching set nearly seventy years ago are consistent with the operation of an efficient and profitable railway system in the last quarter of the century. Further information pertinent to this question is provided later in this Chapter, although to answer the question definitively requires detailed studies not carried out in this study. The second question is whether it is in the interest of an efficient and profitable railway system to have allowed the interswitching charge to stay at the same level for so long, a level which is clearly unremunerative today. The noncompensatory charge does not affect the rate paid by shippers directly, but it does cause a maldistribution between railways of the loss incurred on interswitching and encourages the continuation of inefficient car handling routes in urban areas. For example, a carrier may choose to move a car over a circuitous route in a congested urban area and transfer a car for delivery within interswitching limits, if a more direct and efficient route would require delivery beyond switching limits so that revenue-sharing on a line-haul rather than an interswitching basis would be necessary.

The continuing use of the same limits on interswitching as were suggested in 1907 means that the access of shippers to competing rail carriers through interchange points is confined to the same distance as was appropriate in 1907, that is, a shipper has access to the carriers at the interchange point as long as his plant is located within four miles of the interchange point as measured along one of the lines. Since the growth of urban communities has substantially exceeded the increase in the number of interchange points and four miles is a limited distance in the context of today's large urban areas, the percentage of shippers enjoying competitive rail service at the same rates has diminished over recent years. In many metropolitan areas today few undeveloped industrial sites are within interswitching limits. In view of the dominance of service rather than rate competition among railways, and in view of the radical change in transport markets and in urban communities, it may not be appropriate to have the same interswitching limits today as those in effect seventy years ago.

Through Routes and Joint Rates

The sections of the Railway Act under which the Board historically issued its decisions on interswitching are still virtually the same in the current Railway Act in Sections 284 and 285 (Revised Statutes, 1970). Section 284 (1) requires "Where traffic is to pass over any continuous route in Canada operated by two or more companies, the several companies shall agree upon a joint tariff...." If the railways fail to agree on a joint tariff over a route which the CTC considers a reasonable and practicable route, the CTC "may require such companies, within a prescribed time, to agree upon and file in like manner a joint tariff for such continuous route, satisfactory to the Commission, or may, by order, determine the route, fix the toll or tolls and apportion the same among the companies...." (Railway Act, Section 285 (1)).

Their ability to influence rates and to exercise control over the selection of specific routes is a matter of concern to shippers and is important in the working of intramodal competition. It was a matter considered by the Turgeon Commission in 1951. The complaints and suggestions expressed to that Commission dealt with interchange facilities, the level of rates and the position of some parties "That the railways should be compelled to quote joint interline rates over the most direct routes."[6] The Commission reported the nature of the railways' concern over the latter provision as follows: that "to quote joint interline rates over the most direct routes might mean compelling a railway to short-haul itself, and would also result in the breakdown of some existing single-line rates."[7] The Commission concluded:

> The Board has held that if one carrier has a route over its own rails which is reasonable and practicable, joint tariffs are not required. The determination of matters of this kind should be left to the Board as each case must be decided on its own merits and after a careful examination of all pertinent facts.[8]

The conclusion of the Turgeon Commission is applicable today, although there have been no applications to the CTC under Section 285. Sections 286 (1) and 287 require the filing of joint tariffs for routes from and to Canada, respectively, on international traffic.

General Order T-12 on interswitching and the rulings from the Board prior to 1967 influence the availability of competing rail services to shippers and influence the routings of traffic in the absence of competition. For example, from Vancouver CP has the short-line mileage to Calgary, but the circuitous route, via Calgary, to Edmonton. CN has the short-line mileage to Edmonton, but the circuitous route, via Edmonton, to Calgary. A Vancouver shipper on a local CN point may only have available a route via CN, through Edomonton, to Calgary. Depending on the competitive forces limiting the rates, it would be possible for a shipper located on the CN line to have a higher rate than a shipper located within interswitching limits and, therefore, able to use the CP. This could exist even if the shipper at the noncompetitive CN point was closer to Calgary, as measured by a short-line route through a CP interchange beyond four miles, than a shipper on the CN within interswitching limits of the CP. For example, a shipper at a CN local point east of Vancouver might pay more than a shipper located in Vancouver with access to the CP through interswitching. The Board has heard such cases and determined that such pricing, while discriminatory, is not unjust.[9] Whether such pricing would be found to be in the public interest since the passage of the National Transportation Act is not clear.

The various applications to regulatory Commissions and the appearance before Commissions of Inquiry of witnesses concerned with interchange facilities and rates reflect constraints on, and imperfections in, the competitive process. They also reflect the benefits that shippers know they can derive from intramodal competition and, rightfully or wrongfully, do expect to exist in rail transport in Canada. Shippers generally recognize the benefits from plant or warehouse location within interswitching limits. Achieving this ideal is becoming increasingly difficult as urban growth occurs and as industry decentralizes to suburban locations for various reasons. The case research for this study revealed instances of the working of intramodal competition and the disadvantages of noncompetitive locations.

Theoretical Considerations Relevant to Intramodal Railway Competition

The lack of a clear outcome from pricing in duopoly conditions was noted in Chapter IV. However, it is appropriate to consider pricing with two or with a very few firms, briefly here, as it may apply with specific reference to railway pricing.

The history of the rate wars and ruinous competition which took place during the early years of railroads has left a legacy of concern that price competition among railways is economically undesirable and contrary to the public interest. In practice, however, a certain amount of price competition between railways does take place in Canada, as well as in the U.S.A. The appropriate question, therefore, is not whether price competition among railways is desirable, but how much price competition is desirable. Light can be thrown on this question by considering the economic role of prices.

The functioning of the pricing system achieves the allocation of resources among different uses in both the short run and the long run. In the instance of railway services, rail freight rates influence the amount of traffic to be carried in the short run, and the profitability of this traffic guides the long-run plans of the railways. In the imperfect competitive markets in which the railways operate, freight rates are set to maximize the contribution of each segment of traffic to constant costs. The objective of each railway company is to strive for at least a normal rate of return, overall, on invested capital. However, in Canada, this level of return has been difficult to achieve because of the level of dynamic competition of various forms affecting rail freight markets and government constraints in other markets.

The right of the Canadian railways to set rates jointly allows them to price as a cartel. In this case, in the absence of any differences of cost or revenue needs among the carriers, they would price in exactly the same way as a monopolist.

221

However, should differences in costs or revenue needs exist, they might establish a mutually acceptable rate which reflects their respective aggressiveness and strength; or they might, if unable to agree on a price, engage in price competition. The greater the differences in their needs, and the greater the threat of losing the traffic for intermodal or market competition reasons as a result of collusion, the more likely that price competition will occur among them. Price competition would be economically desirable if the carriers have significantly different cost levels, so that price will reflect the relevant marginal cost of the low-cost carrier more closely, and as long as the price competition does not reduce the overall returns of the railways to an uneconomic level. However, intramodal competition which would result in traffic not moving by the more efficient route and which would imperil the overall rate of return of the railways might not be desirable.

Under today's rail transport conditions, it is not likely that the railways would engage in ruinous rate competition. First, the higher level of utilization of facilities today than that at the turn of the century in rail transport means that marginal costs are no longer far below average costs. Therefore, the range for rate cutting is less today than formerly. Second, the railways today have a much better knowledge of their costs than they did even thirty years ago. This reduces the probability of careless price cutting, unfavourable to the long-run interests of shippers and carriers. In light of these conditions, the probability of price competition between railways being desirable is greater today than it was in earlier periods.

Evidence of the Working of Intramodal Railway Competition

In railway intramodal markets, the most frequent form of competition is service competition, effective through such considerations as car supply, reliability of schedules, and loss and damage record. Shippers are very much aware of these benefits and it is for these reasons, as well as possible rate advantages, that shippers prefer a location within interswitching limits so that they have free access to more than one railway.

In this study, shippers at competitive points often indicated that their policy was to allocate a fairly equal share of their traffic between competing railways so that they would be given good consideration by both carriers with respect to car supply. However, the traffic share of individual railways was often influenced by the record of car supply and service quality that each railway maintained for the shipper. If a carrier did not respond to complaints about car supply or other service conditions, shippers characteristically indicated that they could shift a part of their business away from that carrier, but expected that they would not have to transfer away all of that carrier's business for the problem to be rectified. In no instance did a shipper completely exclude one carrier from his traffic because of poor service by that carrier, although in allocating the traffic

222

between the carriers shippers at times attempted to give the carriers the traffic on routes for which they had a service advantage. The problem of car availability, particularly during boom conditions when cars are commonly in short supply, was given by one shipper as the reason for not negotiating separately with the railways on the basis of allocating all of his traffic to one of them.

Competition Beyond Interswitching Limits

A shipper located beyond the interswitching limits does not have the capacity to use competition between railways as a basis for ensuring good service, unless some additional cost is incurred. The importance of intramodal service competition is made clear when a shipper incurs costs beyond those necessary to use an accessible carrier, in order to be served by a carrier beyond the four-mile interswitching limit. This was illustrated graphically by one case where a shipper was located one tenth of a mile outside the four-mile interswitching limit. The plant involved was large and had been in operation for only a few years. At the time of its development, the traffic manager had required that all points of agreement with the CP, as the terminal carrier, be set down in writing. The traffic was to be carried completely by CP as long as they could provide "competitive service". Subsequently, CN obtained some of the traffic on the basis of providing new equipment not available from the CP. CP initially confronted the shipper with breach of contract, but the lawyers for CP and the shipper agreed out of court that the shipper was in his rights under the contract. After further negotiations the additional switching charge was reduced from $27.00 per car to $9.00 per car. In this case, the shipper was able to obtain competitive service by viture of the details set out in a written contract. Here, because of the sophistication of a large shipper, intramodal railway competition worked in ways that were very important to the shipper.

This case also illustrates that competition for traffic does take place even beyond interswitching limits, although the extra switching charge is some impediment. In one instance, even this was overcome when the non-terminal carrier persuaded the shipper to change to piggyback service, thus enabling the CN and CP to be competitive and offer the same rate. In other instances, part or all of the extra switching charges have been absorbed, or the cost of trucking from or to the shipper's location to or from a rail yard has been absorbed in whole or part by the line-haul carrier. However, even the active solicitation of freight by a carrier beyond the interswitching limit is not a common railway practice in Canada. Intramodal competition is confined primarily to competition between carriers able to participate in a haul because a shipper is within inter-switching limits.

Price Competition among Railways

Price competition among railway carriers is not a practice which is generally

223

recognized as present today in Canada. However, in view of the concern over the presence of ruinous competition in the early days of the railways, it should be no surprise that some price competition does exist today, although it is not of the same ruinous type today as it was formerly. This is because the railways are far more highly utilized over their main lines today than in the early days of railroading. Price competition was found to exist in a number of situations.

While the majority of shippers prefer to be served by two or more railways and to share their traffic among them to gain service advantages, that does not mean that price competition among the railways is absent. However, rail-rail rate competition may be difficult to observe, for it almost never results in different rates being published. In many cases, a shipper negotiating with two railways jointly perceived that one carrier was more willing to accept a lower rate than the other. In some instances, the railway which only enjoyed a small share of a shipper's traffic undertook to attempt to achieve a more favorable rate in the expectation of obtaining a more substantial share of the traffic in the future. In Canada, this form of rate rivalry takes place in the confidential discussions of the railways as allowed under Section 279 of the Railway Act.

The most striking cases of price competition revealed in the case studies were situations in which either the CN, CP or other railways had the opportunity to develop transport systems for a shipper to move traffic under an exclusive long-term contract. For example, mines in British Columbia and Ontario, and a forest products mill and a construction project in British Columbia were all accessible to at least two railways, and negotiations on the facilities to be provided and the conditions of and rates for the transportation proceeded with the carriers remaining independent of each other in the negotiations. The planning of the transport systems was often sophisticated and involved intermodal service arrangements. There is no evidence that rates were reduced to an uneconomic level by this process. Certainly, on some of the five-year contracts signed, the carriers requested renegotiation before the contract expired. However, this appears to have been more the result of the rapid and unexpected inflation of the times rather than the result of "ruinous competition".

These examples are clearly distinguished from many railway pricing situations by the exclusive long-run contracts which were important to the provision of additional railway facilities, sometimes at considerable investment cost, for the transport service. The traffic could not reasonably be shared between carriers. The shippers were not obviously trying to "divide and conquer". In the case of the British Columbia copper mines, the presence of trucking competition, and in some cases the BCR as a competing railway, may also have added to the incentive for independent competitive action by the railways. In one case, prior to the CN and CP losing a contract to a trucker, the railways had refused to negotiate separately. The influence of small firms in causing price rivalry between large dominant firms in an industry has been recognized as a factor likely to stimulate price competition.[10]

Rate rivalry among railways serving a common origin or destination, but not both, has been known to occur. The severity of such competition was one reason for establishing stable differentials between routes to Atlantic ports. However, such competition still takes place, as is evidenced by competition between the east coast container routes in Canada and those in the U.S.A. A comparable form of intramodal competition exists in conjunction with market competition when different carriers can serve a common market. For example, in one of the cases researched for this study a movement of chemicals into the Prairies could take place either from Ontario or British Columbia. The movements would be served by different carriers who priced the traffic competitively. The rate competition in this case, as in the long-term contract cases, results in the selection of the most advantageous contract as perceived by the shipper and a single rate is published. The existence of competition is not evident from the existence of different published rates.

In some cases, the process of competition results in uniform rates. For example, in competition between two carriers, one of which has a more costly route, possibly because it is a circuitous route, only a single rate can exist. Either the rate is set at a low level by the low cost carrier so that the carrier with the circuitous route does not find it worthwhile to compete for the traffic,[11] or the rate stays at a level which can be met by the circuitous carrier which then hopes to get some traffic. Such is the case for traffic on the Calgary-Vancouver and Edmonton-Vancouver routes. The short-line carriers on these routes are CP and CN, respectively. Therefore, rates on the CN from Edmonton to Vancouver are higher than the rates at CN and CP competitive points in Calgary, although the tariff routing in Calgary shows the CN traffic moving to Vancouver via Edmonton. In the only case investigated in this research involving pipeline competition, the rate from Edmonton to Vancouver was reduced on the basis of the cost of a routing involving a pipeline movement from Edmonton to Calgary and then using the lower CP rates to Vancouver.

Even traffic moving over essentially parallel routes at the same rate may do so as the result of competitive pressures rather than inter-railway agreements. Various reasons may exist for carriers adopting different positions with regard to the optimum price for particular traffic. Costs of carriage may differ because of route conditions or traffic densities. One carrier may have cars readily available for traffic, while the other may not. For traffic with a zone origin and/or destination, one carrier may tend to get the shorter-haul traffic, another the longer. Under such conditions, either or both of expected cost and revenue levels might differ between the carriers. In Canada, such differences are normally resolved through discussions between the carriers, but in the U.S.A. the evidence of competitive action is often reported as independent rate action taken by

225

individual or interlining groups of railways. However, in Canada during 1976, the increase of rates in and into the U.S.A. under Ex Parte No. 318 before the ICC led to the situation in British Columbia in which the CN and CP implemented a rate increase which the BCR and the BN did not.

Shippers sometimes believe that one carrier is more aggressive in soliciting their business than the other. In some instances, one of the railway officers may even have reached an understanding with the shipper that if the railway can achieve a certain rate level it will get a better share of the business. Such action is only likely when the railways are negotiating with a single shipper.

Intramodal Competition between Canadian and American Railways

A further form of intramodal rivalry between railways occurs in competition between Canadian and American lines. Such competition occurs not only when the rival firms compete for the long haul on trans-border movements, but it also takes place on traffic which does or can move from a Canadian origin over American lines back into Canada. The feasibility of this type of intramodal competition is dependent on one or more of a number of conditions. Among these are: the proximity of the origin and destination points to the border; the presence of an American rail carrier at origin and/or destination points; and the availability of sufficiently low Canadian transportation costs through the use of trucking. The use of local Canadian railway rates to border points to construct a combination rate through the U.S.A. to provide an effective alternative to a direct through route in Canada is not practical because it leads to the imposition of a 30-percent customs duty under Section 382 of the Railway Act. The use of the intramodal argument involving American lines is, therefore, generally dependent on the availability of American carriers at origin or destination or the use of local trucking to or from the border. The impact of American rail competition is more effective in communities served directly by American lines. For example, the cases have revealed more effective competition in Vancouver and Winnipeg, which are served by the BN, than in Alberta or Saskatchewan, where there are no American lines. Some protection of the Canadian railway market for Canadian lines is achieved by ensuring that international rates on traffic do not apply on traffic between points in Canada over American lines. For example, Item 505 in Freight Tariff 1-X of the Trans Continental Freight Bureau prevents rates of the Bureau from being used in combination with other rates to construct through rates from points in Canada to points in Canada, via the U.S.A.

In spite of those difficulties, a number of cases revealed that the level of Canadian railway rates is to be explained by the competitive influence of rates existing in the U.S.A. In the case of the movement of canned goods from the Ontario peninsula, where American lines are present, the canned goods rates on the American railways influenced the Canadian rates into points close to the

226

border. For example, the rate differential between movements from Eastern Canada to Calgary and those to Edmonton is explained in terms of the competitive influence of American rail carriers plus trucking from Montana into the Calgary market. The same competitive influence does not extend as far as Edmonton, so the rail rates to that city are consequently higher.

In other cases, the potential use of American carriers was one of a number of arguments brought forward by shippers.

The Influence of Potential American Railway Competition

The importance of accessibility to the American rail system is demonstrated also by the attempt of Crows Nest Industries to construct the Kootenay and Elk Railway to link with the Burlington Northern to provide an alternative to the routing of export coal over the CP. The additional route was important to the shipper because an alternative rail route would provide a greater reliability of rail service, a feature sought by the Japanese coal buyers, and would provide the shipper with an alternative to the long-run contracts offered by CP and, therefore, introduce an element of price competition. A brief history of the attempt of Crows Nest Industries to gain approval for and to construct the railway is given in Chapter V.

The location of much Canadian industry close to the international border means that the use of trucking to or from the border may be possible either for domestic traffic or for international traffic. The actual movement of potash to the border by IMC was noted in Chapter V. Often, the potential of truck competition is used to get a lower rate. The use of trucking can also be encouraged by American lines anxious to realize greater mileage on their own rather than on Canadian lines. For example, Canadian lines might like to see traffic from the Maritimes to California move via British Columbia. Since this mileage would be greater than a route through the U.S.A., such a routing could well be constrained by the potential to truck the traffic into New England for furtherance by rail from there. In Winnipeg, Vancouver or another location where an American line is present but outside the four-mile interswitching limit, paying a local switching rate or trucking to the American line would be feasible. In several ways, then, there can be and is effective potential and actual competition between American and Canadian railways.

Conclusions on Intramodal Competition

The examples discovered in the field enquiries sufficed to indicate that in spite of the fewness of the railways in the market and their tendency to consult and agree on rates, much competition between railways actually takes place, especially by way of service rivalry. However, several dimensions of competition are often involved, including rate competition. Such intramodal competition extends over the border with American railroads, adding competitive alternatives for shippers in a number of instances. While American railway competition is

227

limited by the lack of rail line access to some large Canadian markets and by Section 382 of the Railway Act, the availability of short-haul highway transport at times provides the needed access at sufficiently low rates.

The incidence of intramodal competition in Canada deserves more recognition than it has generally been given. It is appropriate that the National Transportation Policy should explicitly encourage intramodal as well as intermodal competition as conditions allow. This was recommended in 1966 by the Canadian Manufacturers' Association in their brief to the Standing Committee on Transportation.[12] As Mr. Rae, Chairman of the Association, said at that time, the existence of a desirable level of competition between modes does not imply that there is a desirable level of competition within modes. Recognition that "Inter-modal and intra-modal competition should be encouraged where economic and technical characteristics permit" is included as a new policy principle in a 1975 report by Transport Canada.[13]

Adjustment of the National Transportation Policy to reflect the importance of intramodal railway competition does not imply that any action should be taken at this time in connection with those provisions of the Railway Act which restrict the amount of such competition today. However, the principal possibilities for widening shipper alternatives within rail transport deserve careful consideration in the light of current economic conditions. They are first, some widening of the interswitching limits in terminal areas to increase reciprocal switching and to make it easier for shippers to induce more rate and service rivalry between railways; second, some restriction of the legal right of Canadian railways to confer and agree on rates where there is no physical or economic necessity for joint carrier action on rates; and third, some relaxation of the restrictions on American railways meeting the requirements of Canadian shippers and receivers of Canadian originated and terminated traffic.

Action to Change the Interswitching Order

This Chapter has shown that within urban areas the levels and forms of intramodal competition are affected by existing interswitching limits and rates as prescribed in Order T-12 of the Board of Transport Commissioners. The nonremunerative nature of the interswitching rate for the terminal carriers performing the service, the fact that the four-mile interswitching limit was decided upon in 1908, and the fact that interswitching limits in Canada are much more restrictive than those in the U.S.A., all suggest that General Order T-12 of the Board is no longer consistent with the efficient working of a competitive rail system. The form and extent of the changes desirable in that Order can only be decided on the basis of a full and careful study.

Action to Limit Common Action and Agreement on Railway Rates

In Canada, the practice, both before and since 1967, has been for the rail carriers to check with each other on matters of rate determination, to agree on

228

rates quoted to shippers, and to sign joint letters of response to requests from shippers for rate adjustments. These long-standing practices are permitted under Section 279 of the Railway Act.[14] They are generally not opposed by Canadian shippers as necessarily leading to group monopoly pricing, even in markets in which rail service is the only or the most efficient mode available to shippers. Nevertheless, some exploration is desirable of whether some restrictions on the traditional joint-action practices of the Canadian railways would induce more efficient intramodal railway competition and increase the market alternatives available to the shippers.

A first point to consider is that the railway tradition of working together does not eliminate all competitive rivalry between railways. The two large Canadian railways often have separate interests and do from time to time act independently of each other. Railways usually act independently on car supply, freight schedule changes, and in their line, terminal or car investments to assure shippers adequate service. The case studies revealed instances of aggressive price competition between railways, which is a practice not recognized generally in Canada.

Nevertheless, the question of whether limitations should exist on rate making in common, when not supported by a shipper or shippers, deserves close consideration. The theoretical case for concerted action by railways on rates was stronger during the nineteenth and early twentieth centuries than it is today. In the earlier period, the overbuilt railways (constructed in advance of traffic demand) had tremendous excess capacity in line and terminal facilities. Consequently, their marginal costs were far below their average costs and they were subject to increasing returns. In those circumstances, rate competition could become ruinous. In response to these conditions, rate associations were organized by the American railways to attempt to stabilize rates and to limit rate competition. The rate bureaus operated until 1948, when they were adjudged to be in violation of the Sherman Anti Trust Act. Subsequent to that judicial determination, the railroads were given substantial exemption from the Sherman Act. Their rate bureaus were reorganized so that individual carriers were permitted to take independent action on rates if they so desired. Since the reorganization, all of the procedures of the rate bureaus have been subject to the approval of the Interstate Commerce Commission. Under railway economic regulation in Canada, joint action on rates are legal under Section 279 of the Railway Act, presumably for similar reasons as those for allowing rate bureaus to engage in concerted action on rates in the U.S.A.

Today, however, railways in Canada and the U.S.A. operate their mainline systems at levels far closer to full utilization than in earlier times, with the result that the gap between marginal and average costs has been significantly lessened. It follows that railway rate competition is far less likely to become ruinous today than in the past.

However, shippers recognize that it is necessary for railways to confer on rates involving through rates and interchange between railways. When agreed charges are negotiated for groups of shippers or an entire industry, as for the woods products industry of British Columbia, group action by the railways may be necessary as well as appropriate. Some shippers consulted in this study either did not support or were doubtful of the statement that Canadian railways should be banned from agreeing and conferring on rates. However, these shippers were unaware of any individual rate quotations by the railways. How widespread such a position is held by Canadian shippers is not known. More information on this would be desirable.

In one sense, Canadian railways might need to confer and agree on rates less than the American railways. In the West, at least, the Canadian railways seem closer to capacity than the American railways. Also, since the two large Canadian railways are both fully transcontinental in their market coverage, they should experience proportionately fewer shipments that require interchange between them than American railways experience, and should therefore require proportionately fewer agreements as through rates and the division of revenues between them. There are no truly transcontinental railways in the U.S.A., and in that country the greater part of railway traffic is interline traffic. On the other hand, the antitrust law tradition in Canada is not as strong as it is in the U.S.A.

The interview cases did not disclose that many Canadian shippers have considered the possibility of making concerted action by Canadian railways unlawful in certain situations by restricting it to through routes and joint rates or by restricting it in any other way. Nevertheless, the question is one that should be comprehensively investigated by the CTC or Transport Canada in terms of the changing conditions of railway pricing.

Action to Lessen the Restrictions on
American Railways Serving Canadian Traffic

Section 382 of the Railway Act requires that goods shipped from a Canadian origin to a Canadian destination over a continuous rail route through the U.S.A., unless moving under a joint tariff, shall be subject ot a 30-percent customs tariff. No power to waive or vary the application of this Section is given to the CTC. While this Section is a significant constraint on the competitiveness of all-rail routings through the U.S.A., the case studies reveal that it does not preclude such competition, both potential and actual, from taking place and influencing the level of domestic rates. However, even without Section 382, it appears that the Canadian railways would be able to decline to participate in joint rates over American routes for traffic between Canadian origins and destinations.

The effect of action to facilitate increased competition to Canadian railways from American carriers would obviously need to take into account various national interests. Nevertheless, if Canadian transport costs are to increase substantially because of rising demand, the "import" of lower-cost American transport service will be increasingly to the benefit of Canadian producers and consumers. This could be true, particularly, for rate-sensitive bulk commodities which might otherwise only have highly utilized Canadian railway lines available to them.

The effect of Section 382 of the Railway Act on the level and extensiveness of American railway competition for Canadian traffic is not known. In view of the varied traffic and railway conditions in different parts of Canada, the impact of the Section is likely to vary significantly on a regional basis. While all of these matters require study before any action can be taken to remove or lessen the impact of Section 382, it appears desirable to give the CTC some power to waive its application if found appropriate in the public interest.

The Extent of Competition and the Public Interest

Any action to extend the influence of competitive forces, whether they are intermodal, intramodal or market competitive forces, increases the possibility that new differences in rates will arise because the reach of competitive forces is not uniform by region or by commodity. Nevertheless, the benefits from the stimulus to efficiency brought about by competition are recognized widely and there seems to be no reason to believe that the present level of intramodal competition allowed is, and will remain, the ideal level in the public interest.

Consideration of the public interest requires that serious attention be paid to the commercial viability of the CN and CP. It is doubtful that it would be judged to be in the public interest to expose these railways to so much competition from American lines that they would fail financially. If, however, the investigations of the Snavely and Hall Commissions should lead to Parliamentary action in Ottawa to allow export grain rates to rise to levels justified by cost and market conditions, there will be less of a revenue need for the railways to avoid greater intramodal competition. The same might be said if in the future the Federal Government were to abstain from requesting rate holddowns and from compensating the railways less than fully for passenger deficits. In the absence of those burdens of government policy, it would be more feasible to allow a full range of competitive forces to work effectively.

Other Influences on Railway Rates
Through Shipper-Carrier Negotiations

The art of persuasion is vital in most negotiating situations and negotiating freight rates is no exception. It is not surprising, then, that, in addition to the arguments based on the availability of alternatives to the shipper in terms of intermodal, intramodal and market competition, other reasons for freight rate adjustments are given by shippers. Some of these are based on economic forces, while others are not at least, not as presented, although the objective is always to improve the commercial lot of the shipper.

The Role of Cost Reductions

The effects of shipper and carrier operations were matters in rate negotiations insofar as they affected railroad operating costs. The most frequent example was the negotiation of lower rates for the heavier loading of cars. The rationale for the lower rates was the need for the carrier to provide an incentive to the shipper to achieve the heavier loading and offset possible additional inventory costs associated with the large size of shipments. However, two situations were found in which the railways either would not establish a lower rate for a higher minimum weight as requested by the shipper or would not establish a lower rate although a heavier minimum weight was required. Both cases occurred during 1975. In the first instance, the shipper requested incentive rates for 120,000 lbs. and for 140,000 lbs. in an agreed charge but was refused by the railways. The grounds were that the larger cars required to achieve the heavier loading were not available in sufficient number and the railways' rate officers involved were concerned that the railways might be called on to provide a second car to handle partial shipments, under Rule 24 of the Canadian Freight Classification, when the size of the first car was not sufficient to allow a full loading of the shipment.[15] No discussion of a rule change within the agreed charge took place.

In the second case, the railways declined to grant lower rates on increased minimum loadings in new large cars on two grounds. First, the railways argued that the shipper obtained service benefits from having the large cars available so that the need for reduced rates to get heavier loadings was not present. Second, the railways argued that the high cost of new equipment removed any significant cost saving. Assuming the latter explanation to be correct, an implication is that the rates on smaller cars were not high enough to reflect their replacement value.

In the case of large shippers in particular, other considerations, such as the volume loaded and/or unloaded a month, were also related to the freight rate level. A shipper of cement achieved a rate reduction by shipping a block of cars each week rather than shipping individual cars periodically. In a few cases, shippers were able to negotiate lower rates on the basis of a higher annual volume guarantee, although it was never made clear in the negotiations that the larger volume itself would bring about lower railway costs. The importance of the railways being able to meet the needs of large shippers by passing on cost savings in rates was well demonstrated in Chapter V with particular reference to sulphur.

A seasonally adjusted rate level has also been used to enable improved equipment utilization and, therefore, enable a lower overall level of rates than might otherwise apply. The best example is that of the eastbound movement of potash. Prior to 1969, potash was priced on a seasonal basis to encourage uniform shipment, as potash is subject to wide seasonal variation in demand because of its use in makng fertilizer. During the intense price competition of 1969 the seasonal price structure was abandoned. Railcar equipment utilization then became a real problem, so the railways undertook a major study of a seasonal, "Uniflow", rate structure. Introduction of the Uniflow rate structure on movements to the American market was delayed due to hearings before the ICC because of opposition from the Santa Fe and Burlington Northern, who protested that the rate structure would break down the competitive relationship between Canadian producers and American producers in New Mexico.[16] The American carriers serving New Mexico were not faced with the same problem of car utilization as the Canadian lines, as they were able to utilize their cars for the movement of corn. In Western Canada, shipments of potash have a wider seasonal variation than any other bulk commodity except grain. Over the period 1969-1972, the average annual ratio between the maximum and minimum number of carloadings per month for potash was 2.32; for all carloadings in Western Canada it was 1.49.[17] The uniflow rates were introduced on eastbound movements of potash in Canada in 1970, with the amount of incentive varying by month but basically giving low season rates over six months. Evaluation of the experience with the system led to low season rates being applied in only three months in 1975.

Negotiation of Short-Run Rates

Shippers' requests for rates to cover special short-run situations are probably not very important in the overall level of railway business or railway pricing. However, the railway's ability to meet shippers' particular needs in special situations is valuable to shippers and a good reflection of the flexibility present in the railways' pricing systems. In one case study, a railway established a rate with a Limited Freight Tariff for a shipper with a major inventory misallocation problem. In another case the railways established a rate on what they believed to be a single movement, but which they were subsequently informed would be a consistent one. The rate when first established had led to a query from the railways' headquarters to the regional pricing officer. The regional pricing officer explained the spot nature of the movement to the satisfaction of headquarters. The subsequent renegotiation of a higher rate on the movement on a consistent basis was a galling situation for the railways' officers as well as the shipper.

Equity Arguments in Rate Negotiations

Equity arguments as they appeared in the cases were in two forms. The first of these dealt with the relationship between rates on a commodity paid by different shippers or receivers. Shippers made this comparison both in cases where they competed in the same market; for example, producers of lumber, and when they competed in different commodity markets; for example, the use of sulphur for fertilizer and in metal processing. A typical example is the relationship in British Columbia between the rates available to producers located

233

on the coast and the rates available to producers in the interior. Prior to rates becoming water competitive in 1964, the interior producers enjoyed a lower level of rates to eastern Canada than those located on the coast. The development of a water-competitive rate structure could have meant higher rates for the interior producers than those on the coast. However, since both groups of firms competed in the same market and as some of the interior firms had the alternative of making greater use of American lines, the water-competitive rates became applicable in the interior as well as on the coast. In another case researched, a firm located further from the market than its competitor was able to negotiate a rate reduction on the basis that its ton-mile costs exceeded those of its closer rival.

The railways do not always reduce their rates in the face of equity arguments, particularly if it would require the extension of competitive rates to non-competitive points. For example, in one case a shipper negotiating a downward revision in a proposed rate on the basis of trucking competition, achieved a downward rate reduction for all destinations except one to which trucking service was not available. The railways have argued that their ability to adjust to competitive conditions at specific locations is dependent in part on not extending that rate reduction widely through their rate structure. For example, the establishment of rates competitive with a routing over American lines on canned goods to Calgary has not been extended to Edmonton; the competitive rates on glass to British Columbia have not been extended to the rate structure in the Prairies; and the competitive condition at East Coast ports on automobiles, sulphur and potash has not been extended to interior points.

The second way in which shippers have raised the reasonableness or equity of railway rate increases is based on the shipper's perception of the railway's need for increased revenue. Shippers widely recognize that it is in their own long-run interest for the railways to receive sufficient revenue to remain efficient and commercially viable undertakings. However, they are naturally protective of their own profit margins, and were concerned that the amount of increase in their rates was undue and bore as much relationship to the railways' need to subsidize traffic moved under statutory rates as to the cost of moving their traffic.

Political Considerations

The last factor to be recognized as influencing rate negotiations is what may be termed "political considerations". In the case of major industries or new regional developments, shippers and carriers may be well aware of the concern of various levels of government with the outcome of rate negotiations. To the extent that this concern may be with the viability of the industry, shipper, carrier and government concerns are probably all the same.

Contact with politicians by shippers was not involved in any of the case studies researched for this study. However, appeals to provincial and federal politicians clearly take place. For example, early in 1974 the zeal of the railways to reduce the difference between rates on steel to Vancouver and to the Prairies in the face of government pressures, and the reduced competitive position of off-shore steel at that time, led to appeals by the steel users in British Columbia to the Minister of Transport, Jean Marchand "to defer such intentions (a 33 percent rate increase) until a totally integrated transportation policy has been confirmed."[18] After a negotiated settlement of the rate problem had been reached,[19] Mr. Marchand was reported in the press following a meeting with the four Western Transport Ministers as having "agreed to roll back railway freight rate increases on iron and steel products supplied by eastern Canada."[20] The changes which took place in the tariffs were those announced following commercial settlements and were not rolled back and no action was taken by the Minister in respect of these rates with the CTC.

No commercial organizational can ignore completely the political responses to their actions. At the same time, the railways cannot price with one eye on the politicians. During the conduct of the case studies it was apparent that pricing officers were expecting to work on strictly commercial bases and that significant questions of political involvement were likely to cause the responsibility for the rate negotiation to shift to senior pricing officers in Montreal.

FOOTNOTES

1. See, for example, G.A. Weston, *The Workability of Intramodal Railroad Competition in the Western United States,* Unpublished Ph.D. Thesis, Washington State University, 1965.
2. Some of these cases are cited in the Submission of Views of Railroads before the Interstate Commerce Commission, concerning Ex Parte No. 320, Notice of Proposed Rulemaking and Order, Special Procedures for Making Findings of Market Dominance as Required by the Railroad Revitalization and Regulatory Reform Act of 1976, April 15, 1976, pp. 19-23.
3. This material is based in part on R.R. Horne, *Railway Interchange and Interswitching in Vancouver,* M.Sc. Thesis in Business Administration, University of British Columbia, (forthcoming, 1977).
4. *Canadian Manufacturers' Association v. Canadian Freight Association,* 7 C.R.C., 302, p. 313.
5. *Interswitching Service,* 24 C.R.C. 324, pp. 331-332.
6. Canada, Royal Commission on Transportation, known as the Turgeon Commission (Ottawa: King's Printer, 1951), p. 107 p. 28.
7. *Ibid.*
8. *Ibid.*
9. A.W. Currie, *Canadian Transportation Economics* (Toronto: University of Toronto Press, 1967), p. 241.
10. J.M. Blair, *Economic Concentration; Structure, Behavior and Public Policy* (New York, N.Y.: Harcourt, Brace, Jovanovich Inc., 1972), p. 508.
11. Currie, *op.cit.,* p. 248.
12. Canada, House of Commons, 27th Parliament, 1st Session, Standing Committee on Transport and Communications, Minutes of Proceedings and Evidence, October 19, 1966, pp. 1926-1929.
13. Transport Canada, *Transportation Policy, A Framework for Transport in Canada, Summary Report* (Ottawa: Information Canada, 1975).
14. The CTC may issue rules and regulations under this section but none has been issued to date. Section 279 appears to be generally interpreted to allow the railways to confer on any rates as they wish — and as they do. Whether this was the intention of the Section or is the legal meaning of the Section is not clear.
15. Canadian Industrial Traffic League, *Traffic Notes,* November 9, 1976, carried a notice informing shippers that the railways planned to discontinue Rule 24 of the Canadian Freight Classification No. 22 effective January 31, 1977.
16. "Can Ross Thatcher Solve the Potash Mess?", *Executive,* August 1970, p. 23.
17. MPS Associates Ltd., *Highway and Rail Traffic Related to Western Canada* (Vancouver: Western Transportation Advisory Council, 1974), calculated from Tables 5 and 13.
18. "B.C. Contractors Sap Rail Hike", *Vancouver Province,* January 24, 1974.
19. "Railroads Relent", *Vancouver Province,* March 9, 1974.
20. "Steel Freight Hike Killed", *Vancouver Province,* March 14, 1974.

CHAPTER VIII

REGULATORY AND GOVERNMENTAL INFLUENCES ON RAILWAY RATES

Canada has gone a long way toward providing commercial freedom in rate-making for her railways and toward establishing conditions in railway freight markets that are conducive to having railway rates set by competition rather than government regulation. Commercial freedom for the railways came as a gradual process in Canada. Nevertheless, it was greatly enlarged by enactment of the National Transportation Act of 1967. A concise review of the development of Canadian regulations and of the contrast between Canadian and American regulations is given in Appendix VIII-1.

As noted in Chapters I and III, the railways have been free since 1967 to fix their freight rates on carload traffic between a minimum level of variable costs and a maximum level which is a formula amount above the variable costs in cases in which shippers can show that they are captive to railways in the sense that there is no alternative mode available to transport their traffic. If the traffic is not captive to the railways, there is no maximum rate regulation at all. In addition, the traditional unjust discrimination and undue prejudice standards which have been regulatory law for more than six decades no longer apply, though under the public interest provisions of Section 23 of the National Transportation Act some types of discriminatory rate inimical to the public interest can be controlled by the CTC.[1] The changes introduced in the National Transportation Act augment the freedom that the railways already had in utilizing Agreed Charges and in making competitive rate reductions effective immediately, although increases in rates subject to the Railway Act must still be filed for 30 days with the CTC before they can become effective and all rates and rate changes, including Agreed Charges, must be filed with that body. Obviously, the Canadian railways have been given much commercial freedom in adjusting their freight rates in both upward and downward directions, have been encouraged to meet competition, and have been relieved of the stultifying regulatory delays in changing rates that have been associated with the comprehensive and detailed regulation that formerly existed in Canada and that still substantially exists in the United States. This is underscored by the very few rate appeals to the CTC that have gone to hearing since 1967 and by the fact that there have been no minimum rate cases at all.

In addition to the minimal regulation of railway freight rates described as still existing in Canada, other important types of government influence over the railway rates continue to be exerted as in the past. These include the statutory rates on grain held to the 1899 level, the Maritime freight rate subsidies, and the expectation of the Federal Government that freight rate increases can still be delayed, as happened in 1973 and 1974, when rates were frozen at the request of the Government. While the statutory grain and Maritimes rates have been a permanent form of direct control by the Government, the rate increase holddowns have been for temporary periods.[2] Nevertheless, these types of direct governmental influence, outside the normal actions of regulatory commissions, have had significant effects on railway pricing and have limited the commercial freedom of the Canadian railways in distributing the revenue burden of fixed and common costs over their entire rate structures. They may also have affected the levels of railway investment in track and equipment to provide the transport services required by a growing economy.

The railways of Canada are generally well satisfied with their present commercial freedom to fix freight rates under the 1967 legislation and earlier enactments.[3] They would, however, like commercial freedom to be extended to the one-quarter of their freight traffic that is statutorily subject to inflexible rates over long periods of time. Thus, they strongly favor lifting the statutory regulation of grain and related rates. They have resisted attempts of some shippers and Provinces to reintroduce suspension of rate changes pending investigation of their lawfulness, as well as pressures to narrow the wide zone now existing between maximum and minimum rates where traffic is captive to the railways.[4] Presumably, they would oppose changes in the definition of a captive shipper so broad as to restore maximum rate regulation to all rates, whether or not they are set by competition. In short, they seek to preserve the existing commercial freedom and to widen it to all freight rates. They claim the existing legislation is working well for the public as well as for them, and cite reductions in rate averages or increases in average rates less than the price increases throughout the Canadian economy.[5] They are convinced that the revenue burden caused by the low statutory grain rates is more responsible for shipper dissatisfaction with value-of-service pricing of industrial products than the commercial freedom they have under existing statutes.

At least to the present time, shippers, too, generally support the basic competitive and commercial-freedom thrusts of the National Transportation Policy.[6] However, some shipper groups criticize the maximum rate standard for fixed rates and the captive shipper definition as not affording them sufficient protection from excessive rates when they have no reasonable alternative mode of transport available.[7] In addition, some shippers complain that the regulatory procedures of the CTC for appeals under Section 23 of the National Transportation Act and Section 278 of the Railway Act are too cumbersome, slow, costly and uncertain of results.[8] To the extent that regulatory protection from excessively high rates or rate increases is needed, they want it to be more easily and more certainly available. The Prairie Provinces and some shipper groups contend that the remedies for the discriminating rates, which they think hold back regional development, are too limited in the existing statutes and too slow and costly when appeals under Section 23 of the National Transportation Act are invoked.[9]

These dissatisfactions therefore suggest that some critical examination of the regulatory record since 1967 would be desirable in this work. Do the few formal appeals that have been made to the CTC under Section 278 of the Railway Act and Section 23 of the National Transportation Act necessarily imply that shippers have not had reasonable protection from whatever monopoly power the Canadian railways still possess in some of their markets to assess relatively high value-of-service freight rates and to discriminate in assignment of revenue contributions toward fixed and common costs? When formal appeals have been made to the CTC, has the CTC accorded the complaining shippers and allied groups, including the Prairie and other Provinces, reasonable protection from excessive rates or rate increases and inequitable rate relationships? Has the process of presenting appeals to the CTC and arguing the evidence in regulatory cases been so costly as to prevent shippers from seeking regulatory remedies for alleged excessive rates or discriminatory treatment except in instances in which very significant Canadian industry or Provincial interests are involved? Is the source of some of the rate adjustments complained of to be found in a lack of sufficient regulatory protection for shipping interests, or in the indirect effects of statutory rates that are required by law to be discriminatingly low? Does the experience under the 1967 Act indicate that the commercial freedom granted the Canadian railways, following the European model rather than the American scheme of tight, comprehensive and differential regulation, has been too generous to the railways, about right in view of pervasive competition in transport markets, or too little? This Chapter will be devoted to analysis of questions of this kind, though it will leave statement of the policy implications to Chapter X.

Before these questions can be answered it is appropriate to indicate the nature of shipper complaints and those of the Prairie Provinces in some detail. It is also necessary to review the rate cases heard by the Railway Transport Committee of the CTC, in order to judge the effectiveness of the regulatory protection afforded to shippers and the public interest in those cases.

The Nature of Shipper Complaints Concerning Regulatory Controls

Notwithstanding the small number of formal cases, shippers and regional groups do perceive that the commercial freedom granted the railways by the 1967 Act can be abused by the railways, though they generally support the concept of commercial freedom under competitive conditions. As might be expected, it is principally the shippers without good intermodal competitive alternatives that express dissatisfaction with the limited regulatory protections for shippers and industries under the residual regulation of maximum and discriminating rates provided by the 1967 Act. In general, such shippers are those whose plants are located in rather remote areas near to natural resources or sources of hydro power used in production of their products and who must necessarily, because of long distances to markets, rely on the railways for freight services. The shippers apparently perceive that the railways, in seeking to obtain the additional revenues to cover inflationary costs in recent years, have loaded their rates with relatively high contributions toward railway fixed and common costs because their demand for rail transport is price inelastic. They recognize, of course, the difficult position the railways are in, since they have to raise capital for additional equipment and track capacity, especially for Western Canada where the growth of bulk commodity production and traffic has been large. Such shippers also recognize that the continuance of low statutory rates on grain and related products necessarily presses the railways to seek revenue contributions to fixed and common costs wherever they can obtain them in the market. Nevertheless, the shippers largely or wholly dependent on the railways in those industries feel that they are, under the existing regulatory appeal procedure and regulatory standards, left in a somewhat helpless position. Hence, they tend to support some revision of the standard for setting fixed maximum rates and ways and means to make appeals under Section 23 easier, less costly, and more certain of results.

The case interviews conducted during 1974-75 for this study disclosed that the shippers interviewed generally were far from helpless in dealing with the railways in rate negotiations, and that few of them demanded a return to traditional maximum and discrimination controls or even expressed dissatisfaction with the commercial freedom of the railways under the 1967 Act. As is well known, however, at the Western Economic Opportunities Conference in Calgary during July 1973, the Western Provinces stated considerable dissatisfaction with what they believe to be rate inequities or anomalies and with the procedures of the CTC regarding appeals under Section 23 of the National Transportation Act, and Section 278 of the Railway Act. These were partly political in nature, a continuation of the traditional complaint of the Prairie Provinces against railway freight rates as hindering the development and expansion of manufacturing and processing industries in the Prairies region.[10]

But they were also made on behalf of some shippers and industries desirous of expanding their markets or finding new industrial opportunities.

Some shipper complaints concerning the adequacy of the procedures and regulatory provisions of the 1967 Act have been made to the Minister of Transport and are more or less confidential. Other shipper expressions of dissatisfaction have been published. For example, John Edgar, Vice-President, Prince Albert Pulp Company Limited, Montreal, made the following comments before the Canadian Industrial Traffic League in Calgary in February 1976:

> I happen to be one of those who is, for the most part, satisfied with the National Transportation Act because I believe it has encouraged efficiency over a very difficult time — a time besieged with severe inflation. Carriers, especially railways, are capital and labour intensive and thus susceptible to rising costs. As a shipper I have been greatly concerned over the sharp rise in freight rates during 1975, but since one must consider the whole problem, I had to recognize, as a general proposition, the carriers' needs.
>
> Having stated my satisfaction with the National Transportation Act, let me clarify that this concurrence is with the philosophical and policy content of the legislation. The deficiency is that it provides no effective direction, means or machinery for the enforcement of the Act or for the expeditious redress of grievances or the settlement of differences of opinion between carriers and shippers or regions. Examples are captive traffic and public interest appeals.
>
> There is widespread concern among shippers over the cost of appeal to the Commission in the case of a captive shipper and also because of the mathematical fixed rate formula to be used by the Commission. I am aware of the route open in Section 278, subsections (1) and (9) of the Railway Act for a captive shipper. However, some thought might be given by Government, carriers and shippers alike to some informal procedure whereby any shipper might have a rate adjudged by a third party without formal proceedings and their attendant high costs. I believe a captive shipper should have the right of a reasonable rate based on a judgment that has regard for all the facts of his particular situation rather than a fixed formula of 150% of variable costs the resultant rate from which would be readily calculable by the carrier.
>
> Most probably, shipper appeals would normally be

launched under Section 23 of the National Transportation Act — the public interest section. There is of course no substitute for a fully researched and properly prepared case competently presented at a public hearing and thus the judicial process ensures a forum for all that can be said for or against a given question. Lord Darling once said that the courts are available to all; so is the Ritz Hotel. My experience in Prince Albert vs C.N.R. is that only the most tenacious would take a Section 23 case to the C.T.C. given the current procedures. It is a costly and time consuming affair not to mention its attendant frustrations. Some way must be established to enable shippers to have access of appeal to the Commission within a reasonable cost and time framework.

While these are problems to be resolved, this does not mean that we must scrap the Act — we need to improve it. Let us not now throw out the baby with the bathwater![11]

The Canadian Industrial Traffic League (CITL) represents the industrial and commercial shippers of Canada, with some 1,000 members representing some 500 companies and their subsidiaries across Canada. The member companies are shippers and receivers of all kinds of goods shipped in quantities ranging from small shipments to truckloads, trainloads, and shipload quantities, and they pay about one-half of Canada's total intercity freight bill by road and rail carriers. Hence, the views of the CITL on freight rate issues and railway commercial freedom are significant. In a recent statement to the present Minister of Transport, Otto E. Lang concerning the 1975 Policy Reports of Transport Canada, the CITL responded with a statement that also calls for some examination of the captive shipper description and the legal maximum rate formula in the Railway Act, but then went beyond this rate issue to comment on the state of Canadian transport and other key questions related to the railways' use of their commercial freedom. As to that and other specific rate issues, the CITL said:

> iii As it concerns the examination of the present legal minimum and the present legal maximum freight rates by railways, the League has consistently voiced its concern regarding the equity and effectiveness of the present legal maximum rate formula established for railway "captive shippers". We believe the formula must be thoroughly reviewed and in addition that the present description of what constitutes a "captive shipper" be examined for possible revision and clarification.
>
> iv With regard to the Railway Cost Disclosure Act: The

242

League is concerned as it relates to the release of railway cost information, particularly to the uninitiated. Railway costing is an extremely complex subject, and in our view can best be dealt with by the professionals of the railways and the Canadian Transport Commission.

v The League is intrigued by the plan of providing special rate officers in the field. However, it is not clear to us what role they are to play.

vi The League takes strong exception to the criticism of the fact that some rail rates are lower for a longer haul vis-a-vis a shorter haul. Legislation to remove this alleged irritant could interfere with the natural forces of the market place and would remove the right of industry and carriers to negotiate rates, based on sound economical practices, without which neither could participate in the business. Furthermore the contribution of the retained business can only benefit Canadian industry, including that located at intermediate points, by reason of the improved revenue of the carrier. In our opinion objections to the long haul-short haul provisions seem inconsistent with the request for wider application of rate groupings.

vii We note a study is being made on the question of rates for raw materials versus finished products. We agree this is a complex study and are very desirous of contributing to such a study.[12]

The CITL shares the concern voiced by John Edgar, whose Prince Albert Pulp Company was actually involved in a Section 23 case, over the definition of captive railway shippers and the equity and effectiveness of the maximum rate formula in Section 278 of the Railway Act. Hence, it appears that there is wide industrial-shipper support for a thorough review and possible revision of the two related subjects. In addition, however, the League challenged the statement of the former Minister of Transport (Mr. Marchand) that transportation in Canada is in a "mess". Inferentially, this critical comment is in support of Canada's wide commercial freedom for the railways, as the League suggested that if the Ministry of Transport wanted to see a mess in the transport industry "it need look no further than some railways in the United States which have been brought to their present sorry state [bankruptcy] largely by over-regulation and Government interferences."[13] Elsewhere in the statement, the CITL indicated that it had supported "the approach under the National Transportation Act 1967, where National Policy has been kept separate from National Transportation Policy." The statement continues by emphasizing "that

243

regulation be restricted to the minimum to assure protection of the public interest." Nevertheless, the CITL would have the shipper access to the CTC "eased so that appeal is more readily available and at reasonable cost levels."[14] All together, those statements call only for some revision to strengthen shipper protection, not to reverse the long-standing competitive freedom and deregulation policies with respect to the railways.

The CITL makes it clear, moreover, that some revision of the minimal railway regulation provided by the National Transportation Act such as may be needed to strengthen the hand of captive railway shippers would not alone settle the controversy over freight rates before the country. The reasons are that the relation of freight rate differences to regional economic development has become an emotional and political issue, and that a significant part of the problem of inequitable freight rates arises from the long-standing policy of holding grain and related rates to very low levels by statute. Hence, the CITL seems to be suggesting that perhaps such factors, rather than the commercial freedom of the railways, are the real factors contributing to current freight rate issues.

The CITL cautioned against more Government involvement in transport and the use of transport to attain national objectives as possibly placing too much reliance on what transportation and lower freight rates could do to stimulate economic development of various regions in Canada. The CITL, emphasizing that improvement in rail transport efficiencies had occurred since 1967, cautioned that more Government involvement would not be effective unless restricted to areas of proven need. Some of those areas are suggested by the following quotation:

> The reference to rail freight rates being an emotionally charged issue has our support. However, the question of anomalies, we submit, is one of allegation only and is a prime example of emotionalism in reference to rail freight rates. The examples of so called anomalies which came out of W.E.O.C. did not, we understand, stand up to close scrutiny and information that we have and from our own knowledge would suggest that the term anomaly was incorrectly applied. If there are anomalies we are unaware of them and we would hope that any such situations would be given a more accurate appraisal before being termed anomalous.

> We are pleased to note...that it is felt that the blanket use of freight rates, either in the form of "freezes" or "subsidies", is inefficient and is not the major factor in development and that subsidies can be better identified and distortions avoided where they are paid directly to the industry in question. We

244

underline this because it is four square with The League's Transportation Policy. We feel that one of the most dramatic applications of this statement is to the Crow's Nest Pass Rates. It would appear these rates are non compensatory and have obviously led to a cross subsidization situation of growing proportions. It would seem to us that overall equity must prevail and if losses are found to be a fact, such Crow's Nest Pass Rates must be adjusted upwards to a compensatory level and if, in the public interest, such an increase is found to be detrimental to the producers, consideration then could be given to paying them a subsidy directly from the public treasury.

We are pleased that the grain handling system in Western Canada is currently the object of government inquiries. The League is ´aware of the formation of two Commissions of enquiry dealing with branch lines (the Hall Commission) and the cost of transporting export grain by railways under Crow's Nest Pass Rates (the Snavely Commission) .... We fully agree that the overall approach to freight rates must be one of their being equitable; equitable to both carriers and the users. In the League's view, under no circumstances should carriers be forced to provide transportation below compensatory levels.[15]

If the quoted views of John Edgar and of the Canadian Industrial Traffic League are representative of all shippers except those whose rates are held down by statute, it would seem that in the perception of the shippers a large part of the rate issues are political or are based on misconceptions of the real problem so far as regulation and commercial freedom are concerned. According to commercial and industrial shippers, the opportunity lies in making existing minimal regulation more responsive to captive railway shippers and in removing long-standing statutory rate holddowns that create rate inequities.

The Specific Complaints of the Prairie Provinces about Railway Rates

The long-standing specific types of rate complaints of the Prairie Provinces were summarized in Chapter I and some of them were examined in Chapter II. In addition to historical resistance to general or horizontal percentage rate increases which affect the Western Provinces more than the Central Provinces because of the long distances from and to the Prairies, there are today three types of railway rate relationships to which the former Provinces object and which for many years they have made efforts before Royal Commissions on Transportation, before the regulatory body, and by political action to have changed.[16] One rate relationship of concern to them is higher rates on finished or processed goods than on raw materials. This was the concern of the Prairie Provinces in *The Rapeseed Case*. Another rate relationship of concern is the higher railway rates to short-haul points than to long-haul points, as where the rates on steel products are higher from Hamilton, Ontario to Edmonton than to Vancouver in spite of some 600 miles greater distance to Vancouver. A third rate relationship to which they object is the relative lack of blanket or group rates in the West as compared with Central Canada. These features of the rate structure were examined in Chapter II.

Along with percentage increases in railway rates from time to time, the first two types of rate differences are the most significant causes of the continuing discontent of the Prairie Provinces with respect to railway freight rates.[17] Higher rates on finished products than on raw materials can, to an extent, encourage processing to take place in Central Canada rather than in the Prairies, because the raw materials utilized in such processing move from the Prairies to processing plants in Ontario or Quebec. Higher railway rates to Edmonton than to Vancouver can influence to some extent distribution to interior points to take place from Vancouver rather than from Edmonton and can lessen the market area for manufacturing plants located at Edmonton. Hence, since such rate differences often do not appear to be in accord with the differences in railway costs, the Prairies contend that they are rate *anomalies* or rate *inequities* and that they constitute unjust discrimination that prevents distribution, processing and manufacturing industries from locating or from expanding in the Prairies. The lack of blanket rates, that is, rates that are the same from all points within an origin territory or to all points within a destination territory, is alleged by the Province of Alberta to prevent industry from developing in the small cities and towns that have rates to their markets higher than the key rates to the same markets from the principal city or cities within the same geographical area.[18]

Setting aside the important question of whether freight rates and differences in rates are actually significant factors in the location and expansion of manufacturing and other secondary industries, the Prairie Provinces perceive that railway rate regulation in Canada has continuously failed to eliminate the rate anomalies and inequities which they believe have hindered industrial development in the Prairies. As their pleadings to several Royal Commissions on Transportation clearly reveal, the Prairie Provinces were strongly dissatisfied with the small progress made toward reduction or elimination of rate disparities by regulatory legislation and by the Board of Transport Commissioners before the passage of the National Transportation Act. This was especially the case for long-short haul discrimination in transcontinental rates.[19] Since this and other types of railway pricing which they perceive as being harmful to them have not been eliminated by the growth of intermodal competition or other competition under the wide commercial freedom granted in 1967, the Prairie Provinces are also dissatisfied with remedies provided under the existing legislation. Indeed,

246

they have expressed strong dissatisfaction with the rate of progress of the CTC in adjusting the relationship of the rates on processed goods and raw materials (as illustrated in *The Rapeseed Case*) so that the rates on articles processed in the Prairies for markets in Central Canada will not handicap the growth of the processing industries of the Prairie Provinces.[20]

As to the remedy of intermodal competition, the Prairie Provinces contend that the forces of intermodal competition in the long-haul transcontinental markets to and from the Prairie centres, although helpful in limiting railway rate anomalies, are insufficient. Compared with the strong and effective intermodal competition in transport markets for the same commodities involving shorter hauls up to 600 or 700 miles, it is argued that the limited presence of effective intermodal competition on longer hauls for some manufactured goods is the basic reason for the higher rates and revenue contributions to fixed and common costs to and from the Prairie producing locations.

At the Western Economic Opportunities Conference, the Western Provinces strongly criticized the National Transportation Act of 1967 for not explicitly containing a policy principle stating that regional development is an objective of transport regulation.[21] In effect, they sought a policy of using railway freight rates as a tool to promote industrial development, including development of processing industries, in the West, particularly in Alberta, Saskatchewan and Manitoba.

Up to a point, the pressures of the Prairie Provinces coincide with those of railway captive shippers for some regulatory reform aimed at strengthening of shipper protection and access to the regulatory remedies of the 1967 Act. But the complaints of the Prairie Provinces go far beyond those of the shippers, for those of the Prairie Provinces fundamentally challenge the value-of-service rate structures and pricing by the railways and even the continued commercial viability of the railways. For example, Alberta's Equitable Pricing Proposal, which advocates rate equality on a cost basis, would substantially reduce many railway freight rates and the general freight rate level, for it would virtually require that railway rates be placed approximately equal to long-run variable costs.[22] And since this would ignore the railways' need to discriminate in setting freight rates as to revenue contributions toward fixed and common costs, this would mean that the railways could operate profitably only if they were subsidized for their fixed and unassignable common costs or if their rights-of-way were taken over for government support and operation. Manitoba's Destination Rate Principle would have less effect in reducing the railway rate level, but would require that the lowest basis of railway rates for any commodity to a particular destination be the rate basis for all originating points shipping that commodity to that destination.[23]

It can be readily understood that such proposals go far beyond those of the Canadian Industrial Traffic League in suggesting somewhat greater regulatory protection of railway captive shippers. What the Prairie Provinces have done, after decades of discontent with the discriminatory pricing policies of the railways and with the slow progress in getting those policies changed by the regulatory body to meet their specifications, is to call for fundamental change in both the railway rate structure and in the traditional institutional arrangements of the Canadian railways. Though such vast rate structural reform conforms to the prescriptions of some welfare economists, they are unlikely to receive endorsement by the industrial shippers of Canada, the railways, or even the Federal Government.

The issues over the rate disparities that allegedly retard industrial development of the Prairies, and over the alternative rate structures proposed by Alberta and Manitoba at the Western Economic Opportunities Conference at Calgary in July 1973, led the Federal-Provincial Committee on Western Transportation to sponsor a large-scale study. A consortium of prestigious consulting firms studied the economic effects of railway rate reductions and rate structures that would reduce or eliminate rate disparities, substantially by relating railway rates to cost of service (instead of value of service). The conclusions reached on the effects of freight rates and freight rate disparities on industrial development in Western Canada were essentially similar to those reached by the CTC in regard to the specific rate anomalies examined in Chapter II. The general finding in that comprehensive Report was as follows:

> Although western provincial governments have not provided specific figures concerning their goals with respect to industrial structure or acceptable patterns of employment, it is clear that some shift in the relative significance of agriculture vs. manufacturing is a strongly held belief. Associated with this is the conviction that this will reduce the degree of instability experinced in the past relative to central Canada.

> Transportation appears to be so important in western Canada that it is natural to seek "redress" along these lines. However, our general finding is that even substantial reductions in railroad freight rates, unless sharply differentiated between in and outbound traffic, and less widely diffused among all parts of Canada, will do little in the way of changing the industrial structure of western Canada. The determinants of industrial location and relocation vary substantially among different types of industry, as noted in Chapter 5, but in general changes in transportation charges do not loom large. There are exceptions, as already noted, but even large reductions from present rail freight rate levels would not be sufficient in themselves to induce a large expansion of secondary manu-

facturing in western Canada. They could, in fact, for reasons already noted, retard such development.

This general finding should come as no surprise. Numerous observers have come to the same conclusion in the past.[24]

Brief Review of Regulatory Rate Cases since 1967

There have been very few formal appeal cases for shipper protection under the provisions of the National Transportation Act of 1967 and the Railway Act, as modified in 1967. Up to the present, only one formal application has been made to the CTC for a fixed maximum rate under Section 278 of the Railway Act, and there have been only three appeals heard under Section 23 of the National Transportation Act for adjustment of rates thought to affect the public interest adversely. During 1976, at least one additional application to appeal under Section 23 was made to the CTC. Though of less interest to shippers than to competing modes except when discrimination might be involved, there also have been no minimum rate cases under Sections 276 and 277 of the Railway Act. In addition, an appeal whose effect would have been to suspend or postpone a railway rate increase on domestic traffic in the class rate and noncompetitive freight categories, to be effective on January 1, 1975, was taken to the CTC and the courts,[25] and an appeal has been taken to the Governor in Council contending that the decision of the CTC in *The Rapeseed Case* under Section 23 was inadequate to remove all of the prejudice to the public interest involved in that case. Though there have been numerous informal queries for information and informal complaints to the CTC concerning freight rate changes and increases and some of these have been referred to the railways for attention, the record of the nine years since 1967 reveals little formal case activity compared with the ICC situation under the more comprehensive, detailed and restrictive regulation in the U.S.A.

The fewness of formal CTC appeal cases does not necessarily mean, however, that the recent Canadian regulatory record is one of inadequate attention to shipper and Western Provincial rate problems and complaints. First, the rationale of the 1967 legislation was that competitive forces could now set most railway rates and that wide commercial freedom for the railways was essential for competition to work effectively in transport markets and for commercially viable railroads to be able to give adequate and efficient railway services over the long run. Under those concepts, it would be surprising if there were as high a relative frequency of formal rate cases in Canada as in the U.S.A. during the same time period. Second, in Canada there was a Government freeze on rate increases by the railways that applied to non-negotiated rates for two years, 1973-74, and there also were continuing statutory rate holddowns and rate subsidies, governmental actions not found in the U.S.A. Third, the formal appeal cases that did arise under Section 23 involved important industries in Canada, that is, woodpulp and newsprint, and also a test case over the issue of the regional development effects of lower rates on raw materials than on processed products from the Prairies to Central Canada.

With the extension of the commercial freedom of the railways in 1967 to include a great deal of freedom over assessment of rates above variable costs, the regulatory procedures were changed significantly. It now required the working out of regulatory procedures and experience relevant to the new, more limited regulatory authority over railway rates, and this would obviously involve test cases and much time to find workable regulatory procedures acceptable to the parties. Looked at with those factors in mind, there may be nothing wrong or unusual about the fewness of the formal appeal cases before the CTC so far. To the contrary, this fact may indicate that the widened commercial freedom is working more or less effectively in spite of the rapid rate of inflation to which both railways and shippers have had to adjust and the statutory and other rate freezes that have channeled the railways' actions in their pricing of freight services under constrained market circumstances.

Nevertheless, there are, as noted above, both shipper and regional dissatisfactions with railway rates under the commercial freedom provided in 1967. Some of these may represent continuation of regional attitudes toward the effect of freight rates on regional economic development that have lost most of their relevance under the competitive organization of transport, and the inflationary influences, of the present era. Others may represent serious regional or shipper rate problems that do require effective and expedient regulatory action, and, of course, the shipper complaints summarized above reveal that shipping interests would like to have the formal regulatory remedies available more speedily and with less cost. Hence, it is useful to review the regulatory cases before the CTC, not in terms of a complete legal, economic and technical analysis, but to ascertain whether the residual regulation under the 1967 legislation worked substantially as intended in the cases brought before the CTC.

Cases of Suspension of Filed Rate Increases

Unlike the power of the ICC to suspend filed rate reductions pending investigation for up to seven months, Canadian regulatory statutes do not presently allow the CTC to suspend railway rates for investigation of their lawfulness prior to their taking effect. The CTC, however, can, upon complaint and *prima facie* evidence, investigate such rates to ascertain whether they exceed variable costs, as Sections 276 and 277 of the Railway Act require. The CTC can extend the 30-day notice period before a rate increase can go into effect, but the Supreme Court of Canada has held that the CTC cannot postpone the effective date if the rate-increase tariff has been filed properly and has given the required 30 days' notice.[26]

250

Notwithstanding the enlarged commercial freedom given the railways, the Governments of the three Prairie Provinces recently sought suspension and delayed application of a rate increase filed by the railways. Thus, when the railways filed new tariffs on November 22, 1974 to increase by 25 percent the rates for domestic traffic in the class and non-competitive freight rate categories, those Governments on December 24, 1974 filed an application with the CTC to request that the effective date, January 1, 1975, be extended to March 1, 1975. In that application, the Prairie Provinces contended that the rate increase was prejudicial to the public interest on various grounds and they sought additional time for negotiations on the phasing-in of the increase sought. This was the first such application related to a freight rate increase since 1967. The rates to be increased had been subject to a "voluntary freeze", requested by the Federal Government in 1973, which expired at the end of 1974.

At a two-day public hearing, the application to postpone the effective date of the rate increase was supported by Ontario and the Atlantic Provinces Transportation Commission. The CTC's decision of December 31, 1974 postponed the effective date for one-half of the increase until March 1, 1975, with the other half to become effective on January 1, 1975 as scheduled. The Commission directed that the Prairie Provinces and the intervening Provinces in support of the application report on the progress of negotiations or discussions with the railways on a continuing basis.[27]

Clearly, the action by the Prairie Provinces represented an adverse reaction to a 25-percent rate increase in one step after the expiration of the rate freeze which they had sought. It may also have been a move by those Provinces to restore the suspension power over rate advances that had existed before 1967, in order to limit the upward rate freedom of the railways in the future. As a minimum, the Provinces sought to delay inevitable rate increases resulting from the freeze and inflation, and to obtain another opportunity to negotiate with the railways for a lesser rate increase or for the increase to be phased in gradually.

Whatever the objectives of the Prairie Provinces, the railways did not accept the CTC's decision of December 31, 1974. Instead, they appealed it to the Federal Court of Appeal. The railways argued that the Commission had no power to postpone the operation of a freight tariff duly filed and published under Section 275 of the present Railway Act, as the rate-increase tariffs had been. The Court held unanimously that the CTC order should be set aside, as Section 275(2) did not empower the "Commission to make an order postponing the effective date of the whole or part of a tariff which has been regularly filed and published or to set a new date for the coming into effect of the whole or part of such a tariff."[28] However, a majority of three of that Court held that the CTC had power under Section 275(2) to enlarge the minimum 30-day period before the rate-increase tariffs could become effective, and suggested that the CTC should consider whether the application of the Prairie Provinces justified

251

such action. On February 5, 1975, the CTC set aside its previous order, but postponed the notice requirement to February 28, 1975, a total of 98 days from the date the tariffs were filed.[29]

The railways appealed to the Supreme Court of Canada the majority judgement of the Federal Court of Appeal that the CTC could enlarge the notice period before the rate-increase tariffs could become effective. And the applicant Prairie Provinces cross-appealed the unanimous decision of that Court that the Commission had no power to postpone the effective date or to set a new effective date under Section 275(2). The Supreme Court agreed with that decision of the Appeals Court which stated that the CTC did not have the authority to postpone the effective date of or suspend it either before or after it comes into effect, pending investigation. Further, the Supreme Court concluded that the changed wording in the Railway Act introduced in 1967 was intended to facilitate accomplishing the purpose stated in Section 3(a) of the National Transportation Act — to prevent regulation from restricting the ability of any mode of transport to compete freely with other modes. Hence, the Supreme Court considered that the CTC had no power to postpone the 25-percent rate increase by its order of December 31, 1974, the last day before the effective date of the tariffs.[30]

Manifestly, the attempted abridgement of the additional commercial freedom granted the railways in 1967 was found by the Supreme Court of Canada to contravene, in effect, the policy of Parliament, as expressed in the National Transportation Act, to deregulate so that transport competition might work effectively in the market. And that Court implicitly recognized that railways, with their fixed and common costs and excess capacity, cannot compete effectively with other modes unless they have upward commercial freedom to adjust rates as well as their traditional downward freedom to adjust rates to compete with other modes. Thus, the Prairie Provinces failed in their attempt to restore aspects of rate regulation that had existed prior to 1967. So long as the Parliament retains the policies expressed in Section 3 of the National Transportation Act of 1967, this judicial interpretation will plainly be in line with the commercial freedom granted by that Act to the railways to price their freight services with a minimum of restrictive regulation.

Fixed Maximum Rates – The Domtar Case

A Canadian shipper critic of the maximum rate rule provided by Sections 264 and 278 of the present Railway Act, Arthur V. Mauro, Executive Vice President, Great Northern Capital Corporation Ltd., Toronto, implicitly forecasted that there would be few cases where the CTC would fix maximum rates for captive shippers after the enactment of the National Transportation Act. Mauro made the following statement to a group of transport specialists in the U.S.A. in 1970:

... The [Royal] Commission recommended that a shipper

252

declare himself captive and thereby gain the benefit of the new maximum rate. The legislation as passed does not permit such self-declaration and a shipper must establish that there is no alternative, effective and competitive service by a common carrier other than rail.

In short, the legislation proceeded on the basis that there is no traffic in Canada which is captive to any specific carrier and that even those shippers who were shipping under Class Rates or Noncompetitive Commodity Rates must prove that there is no alternative, effective, and competitive service before they can obtain the benefits of the maximum rates established pursuant to the formula.

It seems incredible to me that a shipper should be required to establish a right to a maximum rate. As indicated in the Royal Commission Report the maximum rate formula was to be an alternative to the Class Rate structure. All shippers in Canada had a right to a Class Rate and this right did not entail an obligation to ship a given proportion of their goods. Under the new rules, if a shipper applies for a maximum rate and establishes his claim to such treatment, he is required to ship 100% of his traffic by rail.

The new legislation introduces into the Canadian regulatory structure an alarming concept in ratemaking. Class Rates have been effectively done away with. A new maximum rate formula has been introduced based on a mythical 30,000 lbs. shipment. Shippers must establish their right to a maximum rate and then enter into a contract with the carrier to ship 100% of their captive traffic. Shippers are required to open their books to the railway and the regulatory agency to make certain that they have in fact shipped 100% of their goods and are liable for the difference in rates plus 10% as liquidated damages if they fail to meet this test.

It is the first time to my knowledge that a shipper has been required to enter into a contract in order to obtain a rate to which he has a right by law and in excess of which the railways have no right to charge. We have effectively introduced into maximum rate control the concept of an agreed charge.[31]

How widespread this critical view is among Canadian shippers is not wholly clear, though it could be said that the 1967 legislation did abolish the previous maximum rate regulation and, therefore, the shipper's statutory right to a maximum fixed rate unless he actually is in a captive railway situation. Whether

253

or not the *prima facie* proof of captivity to rail transport required to obtain a fixed maximum rate, and whether or not the conditions to be specified for such a fixed rate, are too difficult and exacting is a matter that the Ministry of Transport presently is studying. Judgement of those questions will involve the entire policy of setting the railways free to price their freight services except when the shipper truly faces a monopoly or when public-interest discrimination is involved.

Nevertheless, there has been only one application to the CTC for a fixed maximum rate in the ten years since the 1967 Act was passed. That appeal was by Domtar Limited, a large producer of pulp and paper, chemicals and building materials. The traffic in question was chlorine received by Domtar in tank cars of 55 tons from Standard Chemical Ltd. under Agreed Charge 953. The signatories to the Agreed Charge were the main chemical producers; Domtar was not a signatory. All rates in Agreed Charge 953 were set on a formula by which the rates were related to first-class rates, depending on distance. For example, up to 150 miles the rates were 30 percent of Class 100 rates as given in CFA Tariff 83-8; for mileages between 151 and 300 miles the rates were 35 percent of Class 100 rates as given in that tariff. The Agreed Charge was first established in 1960 because of truck and water competition.

In July 1970, Domtar and Standard Chemicals negotiated with the CN and CP to get the rates on chlorine from Beauharnois, Quebec to Cornwall, Ontario (approximately 90 miles) and to Windsor, Quebec (over 284 miles) reduced on the basis of the competition from private trucking. During communications into September 1970, the railways refused to adjust the rates in response to that argument. On March 21, 1971, Domtar applied to the CTC under Section 278(1) of the Railway Act to determine the probable range within which a fixed rate would fall. Domtar believed that, in spite of its trucking argument to the railways, trucking over the routes proposed had turned out not to be feasible for safety reasons and, therefore, they were eligible to apply for a fixed rate. Further, since they were not a party to the Agreed Charge, the question of the applicability of Section 278 of the Railway Act to a rate under the Agreed Charge part of the Transport Act would not be relevant. With a knowledge of the probable range of the fixed rate, Domtar would have been able to choose between proceeding with the maximum rate application or continuing to incur the cost of the Agreed Charge rate as signed by Standard Chemicals. Rather than receiving information on the probable range of the fixed rate, Domtar was summoned to Ottawa for a Hearing before the CTC on December 2, 1971, attended by representatives of the railways and several Provinces. The CTC viewed the application as an important test case of a number of aspects of Section 278, but no decision on the eligibility of Domtar to be given the probable range of a maximum rate under Section 278(1) of the Railway Act has been handed down. The chlorine has continued to move under the Agreed

Charge rates and the rates have been subject to increases since 1971.

Hence, very little can be said about the handling of the case. However, the case appears to provide clear evidence of the difficulty associated with the application of Section 278 of the Railway Act. Not only do difficulties exist in the legal interpretation of the statutes, but also in reaching a judgement as to the meaning of "... no alternative, effective and competitive service by a common carrier ...".

The Rapeseed Case

The first case in which the CTC's Railway Transport Committee decided to grant leave to appeal railway rates under Section 23 of the National Transportation Act was *The Rapeseed Case;*[32] the second case was *Prince Albert Pulp Company Ltd. vs. CPR et al.* In both these cases, much time was spent determining the procedure to be followed in verifying applications for leave to appeal under Section 23, and to the nature and quality of the evidence required to substantiate the claim that acts, omissions or effects of rates of carriers presented a *prima facie* case that the public interest had been prejudicially affected.[33] *The Rapeseed Case* is significant not only for those procedural reasons, but also because it directly involved one of the key complaints of the Prairie Provinces against railway rates, the relationship between the rates on raw materials and processed products, that is, the rates on rapeseed compared with those on rapeseed meal and oil on movements from the Prairies to Central Canada.

On October 14, 1970 the Saskatchewan Wheat Pool, Agra Industries Limited, Co-op Vegetable Oils Limited and Western Canadian Seed Processors Limited applied to the CTC under Section 23 for leave to appeal, on the grounds of prejudice to the public interest, certain rail freight rates for movement of rapeseed, rapeseed meal and rapeseed oil to or from their plants located in Saskatoon and Nipawin, Saskatchewan, Altona, Manitoba, and Lethbridge, Alberta. On December 23 of that year the Provinces of Alberta, Manitoba and Saskatchewan intervened in support of the application, and on April 13, 1971 four eastern processors intervened in opposition, followed by the Provinces of Ontario and Quebec, also in opposition.

At the Winnipeg hearing on April 29 and 30, 1971 on the *prima facie* showing, the four applicants claimed that their rail transport costs were as much as twice those of the eastern processors, and that their eastern competitors in Canada had alternative sources of raw materials, soya beans, from both the U.S.A. and Canada. They contended that the rail freight rates, therefore, could discourage rapeseed growing and processing in Western Canada. They further stated that their efforts to negotiate lower rates with the railways to enable them to compete on more equitable terms had not succeeded, as the railways had either refused to negotiate or neglected to grant sufficient rate reductions. The

Prairie Provinces requested the same rates on rapeseed products as on rapeseed, a request which meant that the Crow's Nest Pass rates should apply as they did on rapeseed to Thunder Bay and Armstrong and for export to Churchill, Vancouver, and Prince Rupert. The CTC on November 2, 1971 decided that the *prima facie* case had been made and ordered a hearing on the merits of the appeal.[34]

Hearings on the merits were held at Saskatoon, Toronto and Ottawa between April 24 and July 21, 1972. More than 5,000 pages of transcript and 100 written exhibits resulted, attesting to the significance of the issues to the parties and the care that went into preparations for this first test case under Section 23. An Act of Parliament on August 1, 1961, had added rapeseed (but not rapeseed products) to the commodities covered by the Crow's Nest Pass rates, which had originally applied to grain and flour but later were modified to apply to grain and grain products generally. However, the railways had not voluntarily extended those low statutory rates to rapeseed products, the nub of the appeal regarding rapeseed and rapeseed products rates.

The evidence of the Western producers showed that 75 percent of the consumer market for edible oil products was located east of Manitoba, and that they were dependent on the eastern markets to obtain the economies of scale that their plants made possible. Although only one eastern processor, Canlin of Montreal, was crushing rapeseed from the Western Provinces, the other three were getting ready to crush rapeseed in substantial quantities. For a decade the western producers had been seeking lower railway rates, both domestic and export, in view of the alternative sources of raw materials available to the eastern processors. But the freight rate officers had been unwilling to act clearly, promptly, and unequivocally on those requests. During the hearing, the request to reduce rates on rapeseed oil and meal to the rapeseed level was amended to one that sought a finding that the existing rates were prejudicial to the public interest and an order prescribing lower but compensatory rates.

The Eastern processors were solidly opposed to the relief of lower rates on those processed commodities, the Province of Ontario requested dismissal, and the Province of Quebec asked that the market balance of the eastern and western processors not be disrupted. Obviously, the case involved market competition between the two regional sets of producers, with the Prairie Provinces seeking to obtain rates that would increase the markets for their processors and the Central Provinces seeking to protect the existing share of the market of the Eastern processors. Thus, the case can be regarded as a classic case of geographical competition between producing regions for a common market, similar basically to the market competition between California, Texas and Florida citrus fruit growers for the markets of New York and Chicago and other populous centres in the northeastern U.S.A.[35]

The Railway Transport Committee of the CTC found that the domestic rates on rapeseed meal were prejudicial to the public interest under Section 23 and that they must be reduced. The Committee directed that the rates on rapeseed meal from the Prairie plants to Montreal be reduced to the level of the rates on rapeseed, and that such rates to other destinations in eastern Canada be based on the feed grain rates, at specified mark-ups over them. As the railways had voluntarily reduced the domestic westbound rates on rapeseed oil and meal before the Committee's decision was issued, no further action was ordered on those rates.[36] However, the Committee did not find the eastbound domestic rates on rapeseed oil prejudicial to the public, because "the freight rates on rapeseed oil are substantially lower than those applicable on other similar movements of vegetable oils",[37] being at the same level as in 1968 for shipment to jumbo freight cars and lower than in 1959 in standard tank cars. Freight rate neutrality, a concept advanced by the Province of Saskatchewan, did not require those rates to be changed as no bias was created against the natural advantages of the Prairie crushers. Convinced that the long-term prosperity of the Prairie processors lay in development and growth of an export market and finding that the railways had not developed a complete export rate structure on rapeseed meal and rapeseed oil, the Committee considered that omission as prejudicial to the public interest under Section 23. Hence, the Committee directed the railways to develop a satisfactory export rate structure within 30 days.[38] The railways complied with the order of the CTC by filing rapeseed meal rates, both domestic and export, and export rapeseed oil rates with the Committee on July 25, 1973, and these were approved on August 2, 1973.[39]

Though the decision of the Railway Transport Committee was generally favorable to the Prairie interests, there was not complete satisfaction with the results. Shortly after approval of the new rates by the CTC, the Prairie rapeseed processors protested to the Committee that the railways had failed to comply with the directions given by the Committee in filing the rates approved by the Committee. This prompted the Committee, after a conference with all parties on November 2, 1973, to issue its own export tariffs for rapeseed oil and rapeseed meal. These were established on December 12, 1973, with higher rates for movements in covered hopper cars than in box cars due to a cost differential.

Another complication arose because the railways gave notice to an eastern processor (Agrabec, successor of Canlin) of cancellation on October 25, 1973 of the Agreed Charge of 44 cents per 100 lbs. on *rapeseed* from Thunder Bay to Montreal and suggested a new rate of 59 cents. As this Agreed Charge was the basis of the domestic rapeseed rates to Montreal, the suggested change would affect both rapeseed and rapeseed meal rates to eastern points. Hence, this railway action was also discussed at the Ottawa conference of all parties mentioned above, where it was agreed that Agrabec and the railways should attempt by negotiation to find a satisfactory rate. A new rate of 57 cents was proposed by the railways to the Committee, with the 44-cent rate continuing until April 30, 1974. Shortly before that date, the railways alleged that the 44-cent rate was not compensatory under Sections 276 and 277 of the Railway Act, and the Committee decided to investigate this issue, ordering that the rate remain in effect meanwhile. The railways subsequently cancelled the Agreed Charge of 44 cents but published that rate in open tariffs, to apply only in boxcars not exceeding 40'7" in length; they simultaneously reduced the rate on meal published in open tariffs for similar movement and published a new rate of 59 cents for movements in covered hoppers. Previously, the higher rate on rapeseed meal did not differ by type of car. Covered hopper movement is the preferred method of movement.[40]

On March 15, 1974, the Prairie processors exercised their right under Section 64(1) of the National Transportation Act to appeal the CTC decision to the Governor in Council, to alter in various respects the CTC orders pursuant to its decision in *The Rapeseed Case* of June 27, 1973. The appeal was not against the CTC's findings of prejudice to the public interest, but against the rates established by the railways or the CTC under that decision. In one respect, the appeal challenged the CTC's finding on prejudice — the finding that the domestic rates on rapeseed oil did not create an unreasonable discouragement or an unfair disadvantage to the Prairie processors. They stated that those rates were so much greater than rapeseed rates that an unreasonable discouragement and an unfair advantage resulted. They also challenged the additional charge by the railways of 15 cents per 100 lbs. for domestic rapeseed meal carried in hopper cars, the preferred conveyance, and alleged that the railways failed to reduce export rates on rapeseed meal and oil to eastern and Pacific ports. They asserted that the Committee had failed to act on the 15-cent differential in domestic meal rates for covered hopper cars, and complained of the export rates prescribed by the Committee as including such a differential and of several other adjustments in export meal and oil rates too detailed for mention here. They also complained that the CTC erred in its original decision of June 27, 1973 in view of the 3 1/2 years that had ensued and cited voluminous evidence.

The appeal to the Governor in Council was supported by an appeal by the Prairie Provinces filed with the Governor in Council on the same date. Those Provinces likewise accepted the CTC's findings with respect to prejudice to the public interest. However, they, too, objected to the differential for covered hopper cars in the domestic meal rates; to the export rates on rapeseed meal and oil; to the failure of the Committee to reduce export rates on rapeseed products to the rapeseed level; to the failure of the Committee to compare domestic rapeseed oil rates to eastern Canada with rapeseed rates and to reduce the former to the rapeseed level. In these and other respects, the Prairie Provinces contended that the CTC had failed to remove the unreasonable discouragement and unfair advantage that were found prejudicial to the public interest. The Province of Ontario asked for dismissal, arguing that the appeals were premature,

258

as the CTC's decision was an interim one and it had continued its investigation of the contested rates. Ontario argued that the CTC had gone some way in giving the Prairie interests the relief sought, and that ordering rates on raw materials and their products to be the same would be adopting a new ratemaking principle of doubtful validity. The Province of Quebec also objected to establishing equality of rates for rapeseed and rapeseed oil as a principle, and claimed this would create an *undue advantage* for western processors and would limit the cultivation of rapeseed in Quebec. Quebec desired that the decision of the CTC be upheld.

The reply of the railways was similar in principle to that of the Province of Ontario, and it also asked for the appeal to be dismissed. They requested no intervention by the Governor in Council, holding that the Committee was entrusted by Parliament to make expert analyses and reach conclusions as to whether there is prejudice to the public interest in railway freight rates. Moreover, the railways contended that the relief requested from the Governor in Council was not the relief actually requested of the CTC.[41]

During April, 1976, more than two years after the appeals to the Governor in Council, Transport Minister Otto Lang announced the decision of the Governor in Council. It was that domestic rapeseed oil rates from the new and old processing plants in the Prairies be reduced to the minimum legal level under Sections 276 and 277 of the Railway Act. This appears to mean that such rates, if materially above the variable cost to the railways, must be reduced approximately to that level or to a level slightly exceeding the variable costs of the railways. Without a detailed analysis of the present rapeseed oil rates and current railway long-term variable costs of transport using the appropriate equipment, it is difficult to comment on the implications of this order. One thing that can be said is that it will give the problem of ascertaining those variable costs to the CTC. Another is that ascertainment of the minimum legal level of such rates will take much time and will be highly controversial. So it is likely that the proceedings in this case that already have gone on for six years will continue for some months, possibly years, in the future.

Following the decision of the Governor in Council, dissatisfaction continued to be expressed from Prairie interests. As a result, Transport Minister Otto Lang published two telexes sent to the three Prairie Ministers responsible for transportation. In the first telex, Mr. Lang concluded by noting an alternative to the proposed solution, as follows:

> In order to reduce inequities between raw rapeseed and its processed products, the alternative open to the government is to allow the rapeseed rate to rise also to the compensatory level by a change in the law. Such action would encourage Prairie crushing of rapeseed by completely removing the

> freight inequity. I would be interested to learn as soon as possible if you support this course of action.[42]

In the second telex, Mr. Lang sought confirmation from the Prairie Ministers concerning their real objectives by concluding with the following question:

> Please confirm that you agree that compensatory rates on rapeseed would produce an equitable relationship between seed and oil, but that you are really seeking additional subsidies instead.[43]

Considering the new regulatory situation in Canada and the wide commercial freedom granted the railways in 1967, six or more years may not be a grossly excessive time for the CTC, the Governments, and the shipper and carrier parties to spend in the test case under Section 23 of the National Transportation Act.[44] After all, the Prairie producers and Governments were given sizeable rate concessions in the original decision in *The Rapeseed Case*. They got equality in domestic rapeseed meal and rapeseed rates, though to obtain this took about three years. Moreover, they got some other rate concessions and continuation of the CTC's investigation. They did not win all they wanted from either the CTC or the railways, that is, they did not get equality of rates for rapeseed oil and rapeseed. And they got some things they did not desire. For example, they got the cancellation by the railways of the Agreed Charge basis of rates from Thunder Bay to Montreal, a part of the total charge on carload movements of both rapeseed and rapeseed meal to eastern centres, which brought about increased railway charges for the preferred movement via covered hopper cars.

Nor did the CTC promise the Prairie interests that its decision would imply that all rates on processed commodities would be equalized with the rates on the raw materials from which they were made. This principle, if widely adopted, could have substantial repercussions in terms of regional interests concerning the location of industries and also with respect to the revenues of the railways. Hence, it demanded careful and exhaustive examination, a process through hearings before the regulatory body that necessarily took much time, as all the interested parties had to be given the right to be heard, to submit evidence, and to engage in cross examination of witnesses. It can also be mentioned that the facts of record seemed to indicate that rapeseed processing had been expanding in the Prairie plants under the contested rates and rate relationships.[45] This implies that sophisticated economic analysis of the relation of rate differences to locational advantage and disadvantage was crucial to a competent regulatory decision, and that there may be reasonable questions raised regarding the assumption that the rate differences were controlling factors in location and growth of the rapeseed processing plants.

Clearly, *The Rapeseed Case* does indicate that the regulatory process was working responsively and probably about as expertly as might be expected to resolve the type of railway rate issues that the commercial freedom granted to the railways had left to Commission economic regulation. True, the western interests were not fully satisfied with the CTC's decisions and orders, but it would appear that all parties were heard thoroughly, had their pleadings and evidence considered, and obtained a reasoned decision from the CTC. Moreover, the partly dissatisfied Prairie interests had the benefit of an appeal to the Governor in Council, attesting to the significance of *The Rapeseed Case* to inter-Provincial and Provincial-Federal Government relations as well as to the shippers and carriers directly involved. But can Commission regulation function expertly and equitably and without uneconomic political interference with railway pricing and commercial viability if there are frequent recurrences of appeals from decisions of the CTC to the Governor in Council in the future?

The Prince Albert Pulp Company Case

This was the second case in which the Railway Transport Committee decided to grant leave to appeal railway rates under Section 23 of the National Transportation Act of 1967.[46] Unlike *The Rapeseed Case,* this one did not involve the relationship between the rates on processed commodities and the raw materials from which they are made. Rather, it basically concerned the issue of group or blanket rates and whether the rates from a nearer origin group were prejudicially out of line with those from a more distant origin group. Thus, the principal question was whether the railway rates for the carriage of wood pulp from the mill of the Prince Albert Pulp Company Ltd., located near Prince Albert, Saskatchewan, were not a sufficient amount below the rates from a competing pulp mill located at Hinton, Alberta for the Markets in the four Midwestern States of Minnesota, Wisconsin, Michigan and Ohio. The additional mileages to the common markets ranged from 420 to 453 miles.[47] The Prince Albert Pulp Company Case was also unlike the earlier Section 23 case in that it involved the complication of international joint rates between Canadian and U.S. carriers, and therefore the extent of the jurisdiction of the two regulatory bodies, the CTC and the ICC, over foreign railways participating in joint rates. For this reason, the proceedings of *The Prince Albert Pulp Company Case* do not provide as good an indication of how well public-interest shipper protection is working under the regulatory remedies available under Section 23 as do the proceedings of *The Rapeseed Case.*

The CTC granted the Prince Albert Pulp Company Ltd. leave to appeal under Section 23, and the CTC maintained that it had jurisdiction to entertain that Company's application for leave to appeal joint international railway rates under the public-interest provisions of that Section.[48] Notwithstanding, the circumstances in the case were such that the relief from the public-interest prejudice sought by the Prince Albert Pulp Company Ltd. depended very largely on the success of the negotiations between the shipper and the Canadian railways, on negotiations between the Canadian railways and the American railways participating in the joint international wood pulp rates, and on the decisions of the ICC relative to its jurisdiction over the American railways participating in the joint international rates. In these circumstances, the CTC performed the significant function of encouraging the necessary inter-railway negotiations and of standing by to employ its undoubted regulatory power over the Canadian railways and its power over the American railways to the extent that such foreign railways are within its jurisdiction because of involvement in joint international rates with the Canadian railways.[49] Consequently, this discussion will rely largely on the decisions of the ICC, as it is understood that the shipper and the Canadian railways resolved the issue of public-interest prejudice in terms of the ultimate ICC findings. The ICC, on December 24, 1974, found that the assailed carload rates on wood pulp from Prince Albert, Saskatchewan to destinations in Minnesota, Wisconsin, Michigan and Ohio were unduly preferential and prejudicial, and it entered an order to require removal of the unlawfulness found to exist under the Interstate Commerce Act.[50] As the removal of the prejudice by the American railways took care of the public-interest rate appeal of the Prince Albert Pulp Company Ltd., the Section 23 case before the CTC apparently required no further action by the Railway Transport Committee.[51]

The Prince Albert Pulp Company Case involved competition of differently located Canadian producers of wood pulp for common markets in the U.S.A., principally in the Midwestern States of Minnesota, Wisconsin, Michigan and Ohio. Interestingly, though other producing locations and markets were involved at least in making railway rate comparisons in relation to distance, the intense market competition was between the two wood pulp producers located in the Prairies. These were the complainant in Prince Albert, Saskatchewan and North Western Pulp and Power, Ltd., in Hinton, Alberta. On April 20, 1970, the Prince Albert Pulp Company formally complained to the ICC that the joint carload rates on wood pulp, minimum 120,000 lbs., maintained by the defendant Canadian and American railways "fails to give full recognition to the complainant's geographical advantage by reason of its relatively close location to the market area."[52] The Province of Saskatchewan intervened in support of the complainant and the Province of Ontario and North Western Pulp intervened in support of the defendant railways, thus in opposition to a rate reduction from Prince Albert.

The example of the market competition for the Midwestern U.S.A. market for Canadian wood pulp has been referred to in Chapter V. Hence, only the bare essentials will be mentioned here. Prince Albert Pulp and North Western Pulp were shown to be two of the five largest Canadian sellers of sulphate wood pulp in the U.S.A.[53] Of those, only Prince Albert Pulp was exclusively a market mill, one that sells pulp on the open market. Canadian pulp sold in that manner is sold on a delivered price basis, that is, the price to the customer includes the freight to the buyer's plant. Hence, Prince Albert Pulp Company's marketing was extremely sensitive to freight rate differences, even though its "Arctic white" pulp is a fine grade of bleached pulp made from spruce trees. Prince Albet Pulp completed building its mill at Prince Albert in 1968, and expanded daily productive capacity by 50 percent in 1969. Its sales to the four-state Midwestern U.S.A. region amounted to 44.2 percent of its total sales in 1970, a decline from 1969. The evidence showed that "intense competition" existed between Prince Albert Pulp and North Western Pulp, with both firms selling at several points in the four-state market area.

The ICC found the rates from the Prince Albert mill to the four-state U.S.A. area to be 40 or 80 cents less than the rates from Hinton, Alta. to destinations in Minnesota and Wisconsin, but the same to those in Michigan and Ohio. The railways gave no explanation of the reasons why the rate differentials were not extended to the Michigan and Ohio points. The ICC described the western rate structure for wood pulp and its several origin groups as follows:

> The assailed woodpulp rates may be described generally as the western and eastern rate structure. The western rate structure, which includes all Canadian origins in Manitoba and provinces to the west thereof, was established by Canadian railways prior to World War I. It was created to promote the sale of woodpulp in excess of Canadian needs to distant markets in the United States and to attain this end the rate structure involved broad origin groupings which are similar to the American transcontinental rate structure. Prior to the building of the mill at Prince Albert, three rate groups were in existence: the Port Alberni group along the Pacific Coast of British Columbia; the next easterly inland group which includes Prince George, British Columbia; and still further east, the Hinton, Alberta, group. Finally, after various unsatisfactory negotiations with complainant, the defendants established in 1968 the assailed rates from Prince Albert which are in most instances 40 cents less than the comparable rates from the Hinton group. Shortly thereafter, defendants added The Pas, Manitoba, to the Prince Albert group upon the completion of a new mill at The Pas.[54]

The ICC found that the Prince Albert Rate group was not shown to be unlawful. It was in line with the equalization of rates over a large area that had been approved in several cases in the American transcontinental rate structure to place all producers on the same footing in a given market even though relative distances from competing origins were ignored to some extent. Nevertheless, the ICC found the existing differentials in the rates from Prince Albert were unduly prejudicial to shippers at Prince Albert and unduly preferential to shippers at

Hinton, and the ICC directed that a favourable differential of $2.00 per ton (instead of 40 or 80 cents) for Prince Albert rates with respect to Hinton rates would remove the undue preference and prejudice. Such a differential would create eastbound rates-with-distance relationships that would about match those existing on westbound pulp traffic under the existing differentials between the Hinton and Prince Albert rates on pulp traffic to western markets. In reaching those conclusions, the ICC found, among other things, that no evidence existed of differing transportation conditions to justify the relative level of eastbound rates from Hinton with respect to those from Prince Albert, and that an injury to Prince Albert Pulp Company from the existing preferential eastbound rates from Hinton could be presumed to exist and to comprise the injury essential to finding undue discrimination under Section 3(1) of the Interstate Commerce Act.[55]

Though the precise role of the CTC is somewhat unclear in the final result accomplished by *The Prince Albert Pulp Company Case*, it can be concluded that regulation to provide shipper protection from unjust discrimination under American regulatory law and from public-interest prejudice under Section 23 of the National Transportation Act had worked in this case of international joint railway rates. No doubt, this was one of the reasons that John Edgar, Vice-President, Prince Albert Pulp Company Ltd., stated recently, as quoted above, that the National Transportation Act should be retained, although he would like to have the Section 23 appeals by shippers to the CTC made less costly and time-consuming under that provision. It may be that it is considerably easier for shippers to make formal complaints to the ICC and to prove undue prejudice under the traditional unjust discrimination control standards of the Interstate Commerce Act.[56] However, without an analysis of the effects of the possible application of the simpler American standard on commercial freedom and the viability of the railways, no conclusion can be drawn.

The Newsprint Case

The Newsprint Case is the third Section 23 case in which the Railway Transport Committee has decided whether or not to grant leave to appeal under that provision of the National Transportation Act. Like *The Prince Albert Pulp Company Case*, this case involved international joint rates by Canadian and American railways, the relative jurisdictions and regulatory powers of the CTC and the ICC, and market competition. Like the former case, it involved rate and transport issues of one of Canada's most important industries, the newsprint industry, which long has found its most important market in exports to the U.S.A. Moreover, as in *The Prince Albert Pulp Company Case*, to find workable solutions for the complaints of Canadian shippers required negotiations and agreement between the Canadian and American railways on the international joint rates as well as some actions by the two regulatory bodies.

264

As in the previous case, the ICC appears to have been the regulatory body to make the decisive regulatory decision. This was because it has the power to order the removal of any unlawful preference and prejudice caused by joint international rates to the extent of the participation therein of railways subject to ICC jurisdiction *on movements within the U.S.A.,* and because the ICC is the *only* regulatory body with power to order American railways to adjust their domestic rates on movements wholly within the U.S.A. on a finding of unlawfulness.

The basic complaint of the Canadian newsprint shippers was that their share of American markets had been subject to some decline in recent years. This was largely because of the development of a newsprint industry in the South, and allegedly because of the lower railway rates from southern producers to common American markets than from Canadian producing points to such markets. Therefore, if the domestic American railway rates from the southern mills to domestic markets were to be found unlawful or to be prescribed, such regulatory action would necessarily have to be by the ICC. Neither the ICC nor the CTC have the power alone to prescribe joint international rates for application partly within the other country. But the CTC can set aside, on proven complaint under Section 23, joint international rates that do not conform to the standards required by Canadian regulatory law.[57]

A full legal review of the law relating to the CTC's jurisdiction with respect to joint international railway rates would go beyond the scope of this Chapter. However, it is important that the nature of rate making with respect to international joint railway rates be understood. Hence, the following quotation from the CTC's report in *The Newsprint Case* is pertinent:

> These proceedings are also a graphic illustration of the limitations under which the Committee must exercise its jurisdiction over joint international freight rates. Rates such as those in issue in the present case are founded upon agreement between the railroads who participate on both sides of the international boundary, and, in the absence of such agreement, it is impossible for either the Committee or the Interstate Commerce Commission, acting alone, to require them to be set at any given level. It is only when all roads agree or when the two regulatory bodies exercise their jurisdiction concurrently with the same result that railway companies in Canada and the United States can be required to issue a tariff containing a joint international joint rate.[58]

On May 7, 1970, a number of Canadian pulp and paper mills filed an application under Section 23 with the Railway Transport Committee for leave to appeal certain railway freight rates on the movement of newsprint from their

265

mills in Eastern Canada to markets in the U.S.A. They alleged that in establishing those rates, the Canadian and American railways involved had restricted their ability to compete in the American markets, and for that reason the rates were prejudicial to the public interest as contemplated by Section 23(2) of the National Transportation Act. Specifically, the rates complained of were those from their mills in Quebec and New Brunswick to destinations in the Official Territory and adjoining areas in the U.S.A. The principal complaint was "that the rates in question are so much higher than those paid by newsprint producers in the Southern United States, that Canadian mills are at a severe competitive disadvantage in areas within the United States that have been traditional markets for the Applicants' products."[59]

The rates complained of were joint international rates. The railways strongly argued that the CTC lacked jurisdiction since the Committee is not empowered to order any change in freight rates for the movement of traffic over lines beyond the Canadian border. The Railway Transport Committee, after consideration, dismissed the Motion of no jurisdiction in a decision on June 21, 1971. In December, 1971, the Provinces of Ontario and Quebec entered the proceedings as intervenors. A hearing was held on December 20, 1971, and on May 26, 1972, the Committee issued a decision finding that a *prima facie* case had been made and granted leave to appeal.[60] After a pre-hearing conference and a decision on procedure, the Committee held hearings on the merits during two periods, November 14-December 5, 1972 and March 1-16, 1973. The evidence alone amounted to 3,064 pages of transcript, and there were over 130 written or printed exhibits. The CTC's investigation, as required by Section 23(3), continued until March 31, 1975, and a Report on the evidence and investigation was issued on October 20, 1975. A decision has not been issued by the CTC. Contemporaneous with the application to the CTC, the concerned pulp and paper mills brought a formal complaint case before the ICC, requesting the same rate scale (the AP&PA, or Southern long-haul scale) for their products as that requested of the CTC. The ICC heard its case during 1973 and 1974, and issued its decision on reconsideration after appeal on December 16, 1975.[61]

The importance of the American market for newsprint and the effect of freight rates in reaching that market were points emphasized by the Canadian pulp and paper mills, which complained to the CTC and the ICC that international joint railway rates were restricting their markets. They stated to the CTC that the demand for newsprint produced by Eastern Canadian mills comes principally from the American market, in which some loss of their market share had been experienced in recent years. And they explained the significance of freight rates on their exports to the American markets as follows:

> The Applicants say that the controlling factor in
> determining how far afield a mill can profitably sell its product

is the cost of freight to a given market. If freight costs increase more in the case of one shipper than in another, the first shipper finds that he is either forced to retreat from that market or reduce the price of his product. As a result of the *ex parte* rate increases that have applied to rates in both the United States and Canada, the Applicants have had to pay higher rates than before; thus the absolute increases in rates charged to Canadian shippers have been greater than to newsprint shippers from the Southern United States. With the spread that has grown over the years, the Applicants say they have become less able to compete at the more distant market points and have either been forced out of these markets or have had to sustain a reduction in profit on sales in those areas. This situation is compounded by the distance factor, since the markets from which the Applicants are now being excluded are those at the greatest distance from their mills. In 1934, these routes bore the highest absolute rates... Each time a new *ex parte* increase is levied, the Applicants claim that the Southern United States' mills significantly improve their selling positions, especially in markets in the southern part of the Official Territory.[62]

Considerable data on market-share trends in the newsprint markets were given in the CTC's report in *The Newsprint Case*. They revealed the following trends: (1) Neither the market share held by Canadian mills, nor that held by the complaining applicant mills, changed significantly during the 1963-1972 period; (2) overall, the market areas in which the shares of Canadian and complaining mills have experienced reductions in their market shares are those where a local newsprint industry has developed; and (3) the market share of the complaining Canadian mills has declined in the South census region of the U.S.A. in that ten-year period. The economic reasons for this market-share decline in the southern U.S.A. markets were summarized as follows:

On the other hand, the market share of the Applicants, in the South census region, declined by almost six percentage points in the ten-year period between 1963-1972. The reason for this is that, not only did new technology permit the growth of a Southern newsprint industry but, concurrently, the South became the fastest-growing newsprint market in the United States. The results of the locational advantage of Southern producers became obvious during this period. As already stated, the share of the Southern market enjoyed by Canadian and Applicant mills, while showing a small absolute increase, has shown a decline on a relative basis.[63]

As an intervener in support of the complaining mills, the Province of Ontario emphasized that the economic well-being of the newsprint industry in eastern Canada is important to the public interest and thus that relief from the railway rate relationships was justified under Section 23 of the National Transportation Act. That Province described the grounds for shipper complaints, as summarized in the Report on *The Newsprint Case,* in the following terms:

> The main point of this case, in Ontario's opinion, is that the Respondents [the railways] have not preserved the rate relationships established in 1934 by the Board of Railway Commissioners, which they could have done by setting reduced rates to restore the competitive position of the Applicant mills....
>
> The increases in the rates that have been put into effect by the freight conferences of the United States railroads, and accepted by the Canadian railways, have directly contributed, Ontario submitted, to a decline in the sales of Canadian newsprint in the principal United States markets. Thus, these rates have been responsible for unreasonably discouraging export trade in newsprint from Canada to the United States, especially from the region in which the Applicants have their mills. If more equitable newsprint rates, that reflect more completely the distances and tonnages to be moved, were implemented, the Applicants would be able to broaden their markets; at present it is the Applicants' competitors who are able to expand.
>
> According to Ontario, market competition, as the railways have considered it, has not been an effective determinant of freight rates. Consequently, the Applicants have not been able to reach their traditional markets at a competitive price, and have lost a number of them. Where competition between transport modes does not act as a factor in controlling rates, Ontario believes the regulator must step in. The decision in this case must weigh the effect on the carriers of a reduction in rail revenues as compared with the benefits to the industry in Canada and those who use rail services for export shipments.[64]

The railways, the respondents in *The Newsprint Case,* agreed that some decline in the market share of the complaining Canadian mills in the American market had occurred since 1949. However, they contended that there were good economic reasons for some decline in the Canadian mills' market share in the following explanation:

> This increase in capacity in the United States occurred with the construction of modern, efficient mills in an area where power, wood, and labour costs are lower than Quebec, as are transportation costs, according to the Applicants. In light of this growth, the Applicants admitted that it was not to be expected that Canadian mills could retain the 80% share of the United States market which they said they had in 1950. Furthermore, the absolute amount shipped by Canadian producers to the United States market has increased; since 1962 the tonnage supplied from Canadian mills has gone from 5,228,000 tons to a projected 6,950,000 tons in 1974.[65]

The Railway Transport Committee of the CTC did not render a decision on *The Newsprint Case* in its report of October 20, 1975, but rather requested the parties to file submissions within a 90-day period on the new material that the Committee's continuing investigation had introduced since the hearings had closed. For this reason, whether the CTC found public-interest prejudice in the Canadian or the joint international railway rates on newsprint cannot be stated with certainty. However a careful reading of the report suggests that the CTC will not make such a finding. Another possibility is that the CTC will hold that it is effectively powerless to order a reduction in the joint international rates to offset the intermodal competitive-compelled lower American domestic rates from Southern mills to southern and border-state newsprint markets; powerless for the reasons that the American railways would not agree to such an adjustment, that the ICC did not find undue prejudice caused by their domestic newsprint rates as alleged by the Canadian newsprint complainants, and that without the concurrence of the ICC, the CTC could not alone order a reduction in the joint international rates.

As suggested above, the ICC decided negatively on the complaints of the ten producers and shippers of newsprint located in Eastern Canada in *Anglo-Canadian Pulp & Paper Mills, Ltd. v. A&RR Co.*, decided by Division 1 on December 16, 1975. The ultimate findings of Division 2 were: (1) that the existing newsprint rate structure had not been shown to unduly prefer United States and Midwestern Canada newsprint mills and to unduly prejudice the complainants'/interveners' mills located in Eastern Canada; (2) that the comparative rate evidence failed to demonstrate that the newsprint rates from Eastern Canada were unjust and unreasonable; and (3) that the initial decision had properly made the same findings. The ICC ordered that the Canadian shippers' formal complaint be dismissed.[66]

On the Section 1(5) issue of the *unreasonableness* of the rates complained of, specificallythat the rates from Eastern Canada were generally the highest of any relevant newsprint rate level, distance considered, the ICC found that the comparative rate facts of record did not verify the shippers' contentions. According to the record, in hundreds of instances the Canadian shippers had railway rates available on newsprint shipments to points in the U.S.A. which were lower, distance considered, than the rates available to competing American newsprint mills and those in Midwestern Canada.[67] From Quebec, Quebec, to Chicago, Illinois, 989 miles, the effective rate, minimum 100,000/120,000 lbs., was $14.00 per ton, considerably lower than the rates for shorter distances from 10 competing Southern and Southwestern U.S. mills and Midwestern Canadian mills. The rates from the latter origins ranged from $15.40 per ton from the Midwestern Canadian mills to $16.20 to $20.20 per ton from the American mills for shorter distances ranging from 620 miles to 960 miles.[68] Referring to a principal contention of the Eastern Canadian mills that their rates were unreasonable as compared with those from Southern and Southwestern American mills, the ICC indicated that the record showed a pattern of rates from the latter which were sometimes lower and sometimes higher than the rates from the Eastern Canadian mills. The ICC also found that the lowest ton-mile rate from any of the origins to the three major destinations, Detroit, New York and Pittsburgh, was from a point in the Eastern Canadian Grand'Mere Arbitrary Group; and that the lowest rates on newsprint from Eastern Canadian mills were invariably lower than the corresponding rates on paper and paper articles to New England and Trunkline destinations, and usually lower than such rates to Central Territory.[69]

The ICC was no more favorable to the Eastern Canadian newsprint shippers and supporting intervenors on the Section 3(1) issue on whether the proof had been sustained for holding that the newsprint rates from Eastern Canada caused undue preference and prejudice. The ordinary proofs required in such cases were four: (1) that a difference in the level of rates exists in favor of the preferred points; (2) that the difference in rates was not justified by transportation conditions; (3) that there was a carrier or group of carriers that effectively participated in the prejudiced and preferred traffic; and (4) that the prejudiced party or parties suffered actual or potential injury. With respect to the first proof, the ICC readily found on the rate-distance evidence summarized in connection with the reasonableness issue that "there is no pattern of rate levels on newsprint from eastern Canada being consistently higher than the corresponding level from mills in the United States and midwestern Canada."[70] Even if a substantial rate disparity against the Eastern Canadian mills had been shown, the ICC concluded that the allegedly lower rates from Southern-U.S.A. mills would have been justified by the differing transport conditions involved. This was because the evidence showed that severe truck and barge intermodal competition from mills in the southern part of the U.S.A. had forced the railways to put in an incentive rate structure for an average loading of 150,000 lbs. per car. Hence, these substantially different transport conditions would have rebutted the contention that transport conditions affecting movements of newsprint from Eastern Canada were substantially the same as those affecting movements from the southern American mills to common markets in the South and border markets.[71]

The key finding of the ICC on the Section 3(1) issue, though, was that the Commission could not find from the record "that the allegedly prejudiced Grand'Mere/Arbitrary mills have suffered actual or potential injury as a result of the existing newsprint rate structure."[72] This important finding was based on several facts. First, the Eastern Canadian shippers' own evidence showed that in absolute terms their newsprint shipments to the U.S.A. had increased by almost 500,000 tons between 1963 and 1972; from 1,173,000 tons in 1963 to 1,359,000 tons in 1972 on shipments to the Northeastern United States, "the natural market for eastern Canada mills"; and that even to markets in the South where domestic newsprint capacity had been greatly expanded, the Canadian shipments had increased from 392,000 tons in 1963 to 427,000 tons in 1972. In the latter markets, the ICC said that the Eastern Canadian mills were penetrating the natural market for the Southern U.S. mills.

The ICC further said that the reductions of the share of the total American market for newsprint that have been experienced by the Eastern Canadian mills "have come about as a result of factors other than allegedly prejudicial railroad freight rates."[73] From 85 percent of the newsprint market which American producers had in 1913, the share fell to 27 percent by the 1930's due to intense Canadian competition. When the efforts to develop a newsprint industry in the South succeeded with the opening of a mill at Herty, Texas as a result of a technological innovation that made possible the production of marketable newsprint from southern pine, and with development of other mills in the American South and Southwest, the structure of the newsprint industry had markedly changed. This development of production in the South and Southwest was aided by rapid growth in population in the South between 1930 and 1970. Hence, the decline in the Eastern Canadian mills' share in the market in the South (from 21.2 percent to 15.5 percent between 1963 and 1972) was due, the ICC stated, to (1) the emotional advantage of a "homemade" product; (2) the economic advantage of a more adequate supply of lumber closer to the mills in the South than in Eastern Canada; and (3) the advantage enjoyed by the Southern U.S. producers of being closer to the growing Southern market.[74]

In the light of the facts of record and the locational and market factors summarized above, the ICC found that the Eastern Canadian shippers and their interveners had not proved their   allegations that the newsprint rates from Eastern Canadian mills were prejudicial to them while the rates from the Southern U.S. mills were preferential to their American competitors. The ICC reached the following conclusion on the economic and prejudice issues:

271

In light of the growth of the South as a newsprint market, the development of substantial producing capacity there which enables the newsprint mills in that region to serve the market area in which they have a natural advantage, and the various other advantages enjoyed by the Southern newsprint industry, the record is persuasive that regardless of the prevailing rate structure on newsprint, the complainants can no longer expect to dominate the U.S. market for newsprint as they have in the past. Therefore, their showing that their share of that market has been eroding does not demonstrate that the existing rate structure on newsprint results in undue prejudice to them or in undue preference to their competitors."[75]

Whatever one's reaction might be to some relative erosion in certain markets in the United States for Eastern Canadian newsprint, it cannot be doubted that the regulatory process is still working as to international joint rates in Canada under the 1967 Act very much as it did before the enactment of the National Transportation Act, which gave a substantial increase in commercial freedom over pricing to the Canadian railways. In a rate issue involving one of the very important export manufacturing industries of Canada and its capacity to sell newsprint in the significant markets in the U.S.A., the CTC did grant an appeal under Section 23 to the shippers involved; did make a large-scale investigation of the facts involved in the market share and marketing problems of the Canadian newsprint idustry in Eastern Canada; and apparently did seek to resolve the issues through agreements between the Canadian and American railways participating in the international joint rates. In view of the fact that the facts found by the ICC, and presumably equally available to the CTC, did not show the substantial rate disparities alleged by the Eastern Canadian shippers and supporting Provinces, and of the fact that the key competition in the American markets came from the Southern-U.S.A. producers who enjoyed truck and barge intermodal competition, it is unclear what more the CTC could do. Certainly, the CTC has no power to prescribe domestic railway rates from the Southern U.S.A. mills to domestic markets, so the matter was really in the hands of the ICC. There is no evidence that the ICC did not consider the relevant factual evidence for finding unlawfulness under Section 1(5) and 3(1) of the Interstate Commerce Act. Hence, since the actual processes open to the complaining Eastern-Canada newsprint interests were utilized fully, it is difficult to reach any conclusion other than that the available regulatory process and potential regulatory remedies were not denied to the Eastern Canadian shippers and their Provincial supporters.

Direct Statutory and Executive Control
of Railway Freight Rates and Rate Levels in Canada

As noted in Chapter I and earlier in this Chapter, the Federal Government in Ottawa has long influenced the level of some highly significant railway freight rates in Canada. This has been done by specifying the level of certain railway rates by statute, as in the case of the Crows Nest Pass rates on grain and related products, held to the 1899 level by legislation passed by Parliament. The level of railway rates has also been lowered by statute with payment of rate subsidies to the railways and competing modes of transport, as in the case of the railway rates from and within the Maritimes;[76] and feed grain rates have also been lowered by Federal rate subsidies, though a lowering and partial abandonment of these rate subsidies has recently been announced by the Federal Government.[77] Holddowns of general railway rate increases have also been legislated or directed by the Federal Government, with rate subsidies temporarily paid to the railways. Since 1967, this has occurred with the rate freeze of 1973 and 1974, which applied to the non-negotiated types of railway rates. As noted above, the decisions of the CTC can be appealed to the Governor in Council, as happened in *The Rapeseed Case*. Hence, both in the past and today, railway rates have been strongly controlled in certain sectors of the Canadian economy by direct statutory or directive control by the Federal Government. This, of course, reflects the great economic and political interest that Canadians have shown in transport supply and in railway freight rates from the beginning of the Confederation more than a century ago. The amounts and the economic effects of railway rate subsidies paid by the Federal Government of Canada have recently been examined by Howard J. Darling in his report on *The Structure of Railroad Subsidies in Canada.*[78]

In spite of the critical importance of rail transport to shippers and the economy, the strong view of shippers has been that government play no greater role in the determination of rail rates than is the apparent intention of the current National Transportation Policy. However, as indicated earlier, shippers do have some dissatisfaction with the working of existing regulatory constraints. The attitude of most shippers has been in strong contrast to the position of Provincial Governments on two recent matters of Government policy.

The first is the amendment to the Railway Act passed in March 1975, as Bill C-48, to allow the Provincial Governments to obtain railway cost information on a confidential basis through the Federal Minister of Transport. The latter Minister may furnish the Provinces with the costs of certain railway operations or the costs of particular commodity movements, but this information must be kept confidential except that it may be used publicly in any proceedings to which it is relevant, under the Railway Act, Transport Act or National Transportation Act. In opposing the amendment to the Railway Act in a letter to the Minister of Transport, Jean Marchand, the Canadian Industrial Traffic League stated:

> The Canadian Industrial Traffic League wishes to record with you Sir its opposition to this particular Bill.
>
> Besides being ambiguous as to the need and as to the end use of any railway costs which would have to be released under Bill C-48 our concern is such cost information could be misused by the recipients having a detrimental effect on the proper management of our Canadian railways.
>
> In our League's view our Canadian railways, generally, are well managed under the system of free enterprise. Interference in their management can only have an adverse effect on their operations which is considered by this League as the best railway transportation system in the world.
>
> In railway service pricing consideration must not only be given to operating costs to perform the service but also to competition of other modes and to market competition. Costing figures are meaningless to the uninitiated; full knowledge of what was behind the production of costing a move must be fully known; such costing figures for one move cannot necessarily be used to determine the costing of another move.
>
> In our League's view, Mr. Minister, the railways in Canada have acted as good Canadian corporate citizens and as such have continued in the development of our country. To impose outside management of their affairs is contrary to Canada's slated national transportation policy.
>
> The passing of Bill C-48 would be, in our view, a retrograde step in the continued establishment of a sound and economical railway transportation system.[79]

Some shippers are opposed to the cost disclosure requirement for the railways, as they see tha it could lead to the requirement that they, too, be expected to disclose their actual costs. This might be a natural consequence in a rate case involving the ability of a shipper to serve a market profitably in face of market competition. However, some shippers support the cost disclosure for the railways, but oppose any suggestion that shippers be required to reveal their costs.

The reason for Bill C-48 was primarily the concern of Provincial Governments over freight rates which they believed could be contrary to their interests.

Whether they expect rates on major traffic to be cost-based is not clear. Whether they believe that the railways lose traffic by overcharging and whether they are unaware of other remedies in the National Transportation Act and Railway Act are not clear either. But it would appear that the Federal and Provincial Governments anticipate becoming more involved in matters relating to the cost of transport than they have been.

The second example of action by the Federal Government opposed by the majority of shippers was the rate freeze. The rates were held down at the request of the Minister of Transport from July 1973, although increases had been delayed since 1972. As early as January 1974, some shippers were letting their views be known. In another letter to the Minister of Transport, Jean Marchand, the Canadian Industrial Traffic League requested the Minister to consider "immediately rescinding" the freeze in view of the "detrimental consequences" to the carriers and shippers, in the long run, of such a selective price control programme.[80] The CITL recognized that the unpleasant economic reality of rising rail costs and rates would have to be faced, and gradual adjustment would be more efficient and less emotional than large sudden increases.

One result of the freeze was a number of subsidy payments. Thus, $41 million were paid to the railways for revenue foregone in 1973; $118 million to the railways for revenue foregone in 1974; and $10 million to truckers and $3 million to water carriers and non-federally regulated railway companies.[81] The payments to the trucking industry and water carriers were approved in March of 1976, so tha Government appears not to have planned for the effects of direct government intervention in railway rates on other modes of transport.

The payment of subsidies to carriers for resources, facilities and services provided as an imposed public duty is recognized as desirable in the National Transportation Policy. Unfortunately, the principle has not yet been applied to the most critical area of government interference in freight traffic – the carriage of grain and related products at statutory rates.

The Commission on the Costs of Transporting Grain by Rail, known as the Snavely Commission, was undoubtedly established because of the railway and industrial shipper criticism of the economic effects of continuing the 1899 level of statutory grain rates; effects on railway investment and capacity and on the high value-of-service railway rates paid by industrial shippers on many industrial goods. The Snavely Commission report throws decisive light on one of the long-standing issues of direct legislative control of railway freight rates. The task of the Commission was "to establish revenue and reliable cost data pertaining to the rail movement of grain and grain products as defined in Section 271 and Section 414 of the Railway Act."[82] The Commission interpreted its terms of reference as placing outside its jurisdiction "the revenue need of the railways" beyond the coverage of the full long-run variable cost of the grain traffic. Therefore, the Commission did not include system constant costs in the calculation of the cost of statutory grain traffic.[83]

In this respect, the recommendation of that Commission on costing differs from that of the MacPherson Commission, which recommended that payments should be made to the railways "as a contribution to constant costs".[84] However, a part of the terms of reference of the MacPherson Commission was explicitly concerned with the burden imposed on the railway by law for reasons of public policy.[85] The conclusions of the Snavely Commission leave as a matter of public policy the question of whether the burden of constant costs should be borne entirely by those shippers who are required to pay rates commercially, or whether a contribution to constant costs should also be made by, or on behalf of, the traffic moving now under statutory rates as a matter of public policy.

The question of constant costs notwithstanding, the Snavely Commission concluded that in 1974 the carriage of grain and related products at statutory rates imposed a substantial financial burden on the railways. The total cost of transporting grain by rail was estimated at $234.4 million. The total value of related freight revenues was $89.7 million; of government subsidies to branch lines and the cost to the government of covered hopper cars, $55.4 million, leaving the railways with a revenue shortfall of $89.3 million.[86] The loss on statutory grain must be growing under inflationary pressures, and it carries serious implications for all shippers, the railways and the whole National Transportation Policy of placing reliance on commercial forces in the provision and pricing of railway services.

It is clear that, in spite of the wide commercial freedom given to the railways to price most commodity movements on a commercial basis, direct government intervention with respect to railway rates has continued to be important since the passage of the National Transportation Act. The losses incurred by the railways in the carriage of grain and related products at statutory rates and the rate freeze of 1973 and 1974 both had serious implications for the efficiency of the railways and other modes of transport and for the financial burden on the carriers and other shippers. The passage of Bill C-48 to enable the disclosure of railway costs to the Provinces could either bring about more pressure from the Provinces in the future for cost-based rates, or it may provide the Provinces with a better factual understanding of the relationships between costs and rates and mitigate ill-founded political tirades against transport rates and policies.

Finally, it should be noted that the existing legislation provides wide powers for the Federal and Provincial Governments to have studies undertaken by the CTC and/or other persons to investigate a wide range of matters concerning the working of transport regulation. In Chapter II, it was suggested that the absence of an effective mechanism by which specific and relatively minor matters could be addressed gave rise to the extreme emotionally-based complaints of the Provinces at WEOC. Such a vehicle for dialogue between the federal and provincial levels of government is provided now by a number of

276

Federal-Provincial Committees on Transportation. However, it should also be pointed out that the existing legislation contains provisions to allow a wide range of matters to be studied if the Provinces, the federal Minister of Transport, or the CTC had chosen to initiate studies through the duly constituted means. The complaints about particular freight rates at WEOC were precisely the type of complaints the CTC was set up to hear. However, no such complaints were made to the CTC, and the issues of freight rates and transportation policy became highly politicized.

Summary and Conclusions

This study is concerned primarily with how competitive forces in transport markets have worked out in Canada since 1967 and whether reliance on competitive forces has been beneficial to consumers and the major parties involved. Neither of the two primary questions can be analyzed fully without some consideration of the long-standing and continuing direct statutory and other government-directed control of railway rates. Because of the voluminous nature of the economic and political literature on the subject of direct statutory or other direct control of railway rates, this consideration was best accomplished in several other Chapters, particularly Chapters II and III, which describe the key traits of the railway rate structure and the governmental constraints on railway pricing, respectively; and Chapters IX and X, which analyze and reach conclusions on the effects of commercial freedom and competition on railway rates under the National Transportation Act.

The review in this Chapter of regulatory and governmental influences on railway rates reveals that neither shippers, railways nor the Provincial Governments are wholly satisfied with the working of regulatory and government constraints on railway pricing. The Prairie Provinces have expressed dissatisfaction with the National Transport Policy and with the relationships of rates, have opposed rate increases, and have sought means of requiring information on the costs of railway operations and services. The railways and most shippers have opposed all of these positions taken by politicians and have sought to prevent the government freeze on certain freight rates and to eliminate the distortion of the freight rate structure caused by Crows Nest Pass and related rates. Shippers have not been wholly satisfied with the working of the limited constraint provisions on railway rates. They would like to see revisions to Section 278 of the Railway Act and means by which applications to appeal under Section 23 of the National Transportation Act can be dealt with in easier and less costly ways.

The existing regulations leave power in the hands of the CTC to control public-interest discrimination in railway rates and to set maximum rates when shippers can prove they are in a railway-captive position. The establishment by shippers and intervening Provinces of a *prima facie* case of injury to the public

277

interest, required for the granting of leave to appeal under Section 23 of the National Transportation Act, may be a more difficult task than that of entering formal complaints under the control standards in existence before 1967. But once that has been done, the processes of CTC regulation, or of CTC and ICC regulation of international joint rates, continue much the same as they did before 1967. A reasonable conclusion to draw is that, under the remaining regulation of railway rates for the protection of shippers and the public interest under the National Transportation Act, the Railway Act and the Transport Act, the serious railway rate problems of Canada's shippers have been receiving appropriate regulatory attention since 1967. Also, the regional complaints of the Prairie Provinces have received much regulatory attention in *The Rapeseed Case* and in additional voluminous research and sophisticated research undertaken by the CTC or initiated by the Federal-Provincial Committee on Western Transportation.

The real difference in the experience with regulation since 1967 is that there are fewer formal railway rate cases, because the regulatory remedies have been limited to important public-interest discrimination cases and to railway captive shipper cases involving maximum rates. This seems to have been the design of Parliament in enacting the 1967 legislation. Aside from finding ways to make the regulatory remedies available to the shippers and the Provinces in easier and less costly ways, a decision to increase the incidence of maximum rate regulation or to change the basis for regulation of undue discrimination should be based on whether an economic case exists for reducing the wide commercial freedom granted the Canadian railways in 1967. This central issue will be dealt with in the final Chapter.

FOOTNOTES

1. A.W. Currie, *Canadian Transportation Economics* (Toronto: Univeristy of Toronto Press, 1967), pp. 226-229.
2. Howard J. Darling, *The Structure of Railroad Subsidies in Canada* (Toronto: York University Transportation Centre, October 1974), pp. 11-13, 33-36, and 65-70.
3. *Report of the Royal Commission on Transportation,* known as the Turgeon Commission (Ottawa: King's Printer and Controller of Stationery, 1951), February 9, 1951, pp. 85-86, 89-92, 94-95, 269-271; *Report of Royal Commission on Agreed Charges,* W.F.A. Turgeon, Commissioner (Ottawa: Queen's Printer and Controller of Stationery, 1955), February 21, 1955, pp. 17-18, 21-22, 30-31, and 35-36; and F.S. Burbidge, President, Canadian Pacific Limited, "A Look at Canadian Pacific Today," paper before Eighth Annual Meeting of The Thunder Bay Chamber of Commerce, January 16, 1973, pp. 8-9.
4. See the judgement of the Supreme Court of Canada on May 20, 1975 in *Canadian Pacific Limited v. The Governments of the Provinces of Alberta, Saskatchewan, Manitoba and Ontario and The Atlantic Provinces Transportation Commission et al and the Canadian National Railway Company v. the Same Parties,* pp. 3-4 (mimeo copy).
5. See J.H. Morrish, Vice President, Marketing and Sales, CP Rail, and D.P. MacKinnon, General Manager, Marketing Service, Canadian National Railways, "The Only Thing Wrong with Simple Solutions Is the Lack of Simple Problems," and address before the 18th Annual Traffic and Transportation Conference, Canadian Industrial Traffic League, Winnipeg, February 21, 1974.
6. The Canadian Industrial Traffic League, "A Statement of Position Prepared for the Honourable Otto Emil Lang, P.C., M.P., Minister of Transport Concerning 'Transportation Policy — A Framework for Transport in Canada'," January 13, 1976, pp. 4-6, and 9-12.
7. *Ibid.,* p. 9. See letter of January 31, 1975 from R.A. Cushman, Manager-General Distribution, Aluminum Company of Canada, Ltd. to the Hon. Jean Marchand, Minister of Transport, Ottawa.
8. See address of John Edgar, Vice-President, Prince Albert Pulp Company Limited, "Governments' Role in Transportation," before the 20th Annual Traffic and Transportation Conference of the Canadian Industrial Traffic League, Calgary, February 26, 1976, pp. 9-10.
9. See Verbatim Record of the Morning Session of the Western Economic Opportunities Conference, Calgary, Alberta, July 24, 1973, pp. 59-100.
10. Submittal of the Premiers of Saskatchewan, British Columbia, Manitoba and Alberta, *Transportation,* to the Western Economic Opportunities Conference called by the Federal Government, Calgary, July 24-26, 1973, p. 3. See "West premiers mould rail stand," *The Province,* September 27, 1974, p. 19.
11. John Edgar, *op.cit.,* pp. 9-10.
12. The Canadian Industrial Traffic League, *op.cit.,* pp. 9-11.
13. *Ibid.,* p. 11.
14. *Ibid.,* p. 4.
15. *Ibid.,* pp. 4-5.
16. Howard J. Darling, "Transport Policy in Canada: The Struggle of Ideologies versus Realities," in *Issues in Canadian Transport Policy,* edited by K.W. Studnicki-Gizbert (Toronto: MacMillan of Canada, 1974), pp. 3-46.
17. See Letter of July 19, 1973 from Transport Minister Jean Marchand to E.J. Benson, President, Canadian Transport Commission, specifying 11 rate comparisons "cited by Western spokesmen of differences in freight rates that in the eyes of Westerners are not

economically justified." Only two of the 11 rate comparisons comprised rate group issues. Letter contained in Appendix A of the CTC's *Report to the Honourable the Minister of Transport Pursuant to his Request of July 19, 1973 under the Provisions of Section 22 of the National Transportation Act,* December 3, 1973.

18. *Ibid.* An example cited was steel sheet railway rates from Hamilton, Ontario to Edmonton, Alberta of 246 cents per 100 lbs., while the rate on steel sheet from Hamilton to Redwater, Alberta, was 251 cents. For an excellent study of blanket or group rates in the U.S.A., see Stuart Daggett and John P. Carter, *The Structure of Transcontinental Railroad Rates* (Berkeley, Calif.: University of California Press, 1947).

19. See *Turgeon Commission,* 1951, *op.cit.,* pp. 30-34, 44-62, 77-82, 96-101, 116-118, and 269-273; and *Report of Royal Commission on Agreed Charges,* 1955, pp. 9-11, 26, and 38-46.

20. WEOC, *Verbatim Record, op.cit.,* Morning Session, July 24, 1973, pp. 60-80, and 87-88.

21. *Ibid.,* pp. 79-87 and 89-98.

22. F.H. Peacock, Minister of Industry and Commerce, Government of Alberta, "The Equitable Pricing Proposal" presented to the Western Economic Opportunities Conference, Calgary, July 24, 1973. This was supported by a 103-page study done by the Transport Research and Development Division of that Department, *The Equitable Pricing Policy, A New Method of Railway Rate Making,* Edmonton, July 1973.

23. Province of Manitoba, "Destination Rate Principle", a proposal to WEOC, at Calgary, July 1973.

24. *Two Proposals for Rail Freight Pricing: Assessment of Their Prospective Impact,* a Report to the Federal-Provincial Committee on Western Transportation by P.S. Ross & Partners *et al,* September 30, 1974, pp. 12-11 and 12-12.

25. *The Eighth Annual Report of the Canadian Transport Commission, 1974* (Ottawa: Information Canada, 1975), pp. 7-8.

26. See the judgement of the Supreme Court of Canada on May 20, 1975, *op.cit.,* pp. 3-7.

27. *The Eighth Annual Report of the Canadian Transport Commission, 1974, op.cit.,* pp. 7-8.

28. See judgement of the Supreme Court of Canada on May 20, 1975, *op.cit.,* p. 3. The Federal Court of Appeal judgement was entered on January 25, 1975.

29. *Ibid.,* p. 4.

30. *Ibid.,* pp. 5-6. But the Supreme Court said, pp. 5-6, that it was not necessary to decide the issue of whether Section 275(2) gives the CTC power to extend the 30-day notice period; but that Court noted that the extension of the period of notice would have to be made before the effective date, as Section 274(4) authorizes a tariff to come into effect on that date; also that the CTC "did not purport to extend the period of notice prior to January 1, 1975." Compare the comments in the Report of Railway Transport Committee in *The Newsprint Case,* cited below, pp. 75-78 and Appendix 4, pp. 12-29.

31. Arthur V. Mauro, "Conglomerates — Is Regulation Necessary", *ICC Practitioners' Journal,* September-October 1970, pp. 956-957.

32. *In the Matter of the Application and Appeal of Saskatchewan Wheat Pool, Agra Industries Limited, Co-Op Vegetable Oils Ltd. and Western Canadian Seed Processors Ltd.,* pursuant to Section 23 of the *National Transporation Act,* decided by the Railway Transport Committee, Canadian Transport Commission, June 27, 1973, hereinafter referred to as *The Rapeseed Case.*

33. Canadian Transport Commission, Railway Transport Committee, *Report on the Hearing and Investigation into the Application of Anglo-Canadian Pulp and Paper Mills*

et al. v. Canadian National Railways et al. (The Newsprint Case), October 20, 1975, Appendix No. 2, pp. 3-4.

34. CTC, Order R-13001, November 2, 1971. The Railway Transport Committee found that the railways had "revealed a persistent unwillingness ... to react clearly, promptly and unequivocally to requests from the Applicants for more favourable freight rates." Decision in *The Rapeseed Case, op.cit.,* p. 53.

35. See Truman C. Bigham and Merrill J. Roberts, *Citrus Fruit Rates* (Gainesville, Fla.: University of Florida Press, 1950), reviewed interestingly by John P. Carter, *Land Economics,* August 1950, pp. 312-313.

36. Decision in *The Rapeseed Case, op.cit.,* pp. 54-56.

37. *Ibid.,* p. 57.

38. *Ibid.,* p. 58.

39. Railway Transport Committee Order R-16824 and Order-17016, respectively.

40. Based on information obtained from the Canadian Transport Commission in interviews in Ottawa during March 1976.

41. *Ibid.*

42. Transport Canada, *News,* No. 49/76, May 6, 1976.

43. Transport Canada, *News,* No. 58/76, May 21, 1976.

44. See "Reply of July 19, 1973 from Mr. E.J. Benson, President, Canadian Transport Commission, to Transport Minister Jean Marchand's Letter Concerning Freight Rate Appeal Provisions of the National Transportation Act," pp. 4-14 and 18-30.

45. Decision in *The Rapeseed Case, op.cit.,* pp. 4-14 and 37-39.

46. Report of Railway Transport Committee, *The Newsprint Case,* October 20, 1975, *op.cit.* Appendix No. 2, pp. 3-4.

47. The difference in the mileage ranges from Hinton, Alta. and Prince Albert, Sask. was taken from Table 1 in *Prince Albert Pulp Co. Ltd. v. Canadian Natl. Rys.,* 349 I.C.C. 482,487 (1974).

48. Decision of the Railway Transport Committee on June 21, 1971, *In the Matter of Section 16 of the National Transportation Act between Prince Albert Pulp Company Ltd., Applicant and Canadian Pacific Railway Company et al, Respondents and The Governments of the Provinces of Alberta, Manitoba, Ontario and Saskatchewan, Intervenors,* contained in the *Report in the Newsprint Case, op.cit.,* Appendix No. 1, pp. 22-25.

49. Report of Railway Transport Committee, *The Newsprint Case, op.cit.,* pp. 77-78.

50. 349 I.C.C. 482, 490-494 (1974). Also see an earlier decision in 349 I.C.C. 447 (1973), which contains the statement of facts, conclusions, and findings of Administrative Law Judge Warren C. White from his initial decision of July 18, 1972.

51. In the Report on *The Newsprint Case* of October 20, 1975, *op.cit.,* the Railway Transport Committee stated on pp. 77-78 as follows: "Prince Albert Pulp Co. Ltd., on the other hand, reported that some issues had been resolved, and progress was being made in discussions with the Respondents relating not only to the increase of 10% in rates *but to the main issues arising in its case under Section 23.* The Committee has been advised that Prince Albert Pulp Co. Ltd. and the Respondents *have settled all their differences, and that it is not intended to proceed further with that case under Section 23."* (Emphasis supplied.)

52. 349 I.C.C. 482 (1974).

53. *Ibid.,* pp. 483-484.

54. *Ibid.,* pp. 485.

55. *Ibid.,* pp. 491-493.

56. But see *Anglo-Canadian Pulp & Paper Mills, Ltd. v. A&RR Co.,* 351 I.C.C. 325, 335-340,

where the ICC found that the Canadian shipper complainants had not proven factually that actual or potential injury to them existed under the standards of Section 3(1) of the Interstate Commerce Act. Less complicated standards than those of Section 23 of the 1967 Act do not eliminate the requirement of proof for a finding of undue prejudice. This can be difficult to sustain.

57. See 349 I.C.C. 482-493 (1974); and Report of Railway Transport Committee, *The Newsprint Case, op.cit.,* pp. 83-85.
58. *Ibid.,* p. 78.
59. *Ibid.,* p. 4.
60. *Ibid.,* p. 4 and Appendix No. 2.
61. *Ibid.,* pp. 5-6, and 351 I.C.C. 325 (1975).
62. *Ibid.,* p. 10.
63. *Ibid.,* p. 32.
64. *Ibid.,* p.15.
65. *Ibid.,* p. 18.
66. 351 I.C.C. 325, 342-343 (1975).
67. *Ibid.,* pp. 327-328.
68. *Ibid.,* p. 329.
69. *Ibid.,* pp. 330-335.
70. *Ibid.,* p. 336.
71. *Ibid.,* pp. 336-337.
72. *Ibid.,* p. 337.
73. *Ibid.,* p. 338.
74. *Ibid.,* p. 339.
75. *Ibid.,* p. 340.
76. The subsidies to reduce freight rates below their normal level on certain traffic within and westbound from the Maritimes is not dealt with further in this Chapter. For a description of these subsidies, see Howard J. Darling, *The Structure of Railroad Subsidies in Canada, op.cit.,* pp. 13-26.
77. See "Feed freight aid to B.C. reduced", *The Province,* June 1, 1976, p. 7. Effective Aug. 1, 1976, "the freight rate subsidy of $6 a ton and less will be eliminated in Ontario and western Quebec ..., and other rates will be adjusted accordingly." In B.C., the rates will be reduced by $4 a ton but the rates in Eastern Quebec and the Maritimes will remain unchanged due to heavier reliance there on outside supplies of feed grains. One effect may be to increase livestock production and meat processing in the Prairies.
78. H.J. Darling, *The Structure of Railroad Subsidies in Canada, op.cit.*
79. Canadian Industrial Traffic League, Letter from the President of the League to the Minister of Transport, Jean Marchand, February 10, 1975.
80. Transportation Newsletter (Vancouver: Westrade Publications, 1974), January 28, 1974.
81. The amounts of the subsidies were obtained from the following sources: Order-in-Council, P.C. 1974 — 2/801, April 9, 1974; Recommendation of Transport Canada to the Governor in Council under P.C. 1974 — 9/2876; and Order-in-Council P.C. 1976 — 503, March 2, 1976.
82. *The Commission on the Costs of Transporting Grain by Rail,* known as the Snavely Commission, Report to Governor in Council, Vol. 1, 1976, Appendix B, p. 1.
83. *Ibid.,* pp. 60-67.
84. *Royal Commission on Transportation,* known as the MacPherson Commission (Ottawa: Queens Printer, 1961), Vol. 1, p. 65.
85. The terms of Reference of the MacPherson Commission were, in part, as follows:

> to consider and report on ... the obligations and limitations imposed upon

railways by law for reasons of public policy, and what can and should be done to ensure a more equitable distribution of any burdern which may be found to result therefrom...

Ibid., Appendix A, p. 1.
86. *Snavely Commission, op.cit.,* Table 10, p. 207.

APPENDIX VIII-1

RAILWAY RATE REGULATION IN CANADA AND THE U.S.A.

The railways of Canada have enjoyed far more commercial freedom to compete with other modes for freight traffic than have railways in the U.S.A., and they have enjoyed their greater sphere of commercial freedom for a much longer time than their American counterparts. Except for some quite modest regulatory relaxation in application of minimum rate control by the ICC in recent years, American railways won their first real commercial freedom in competitive ratemaking in 1976 when the Congress enacted the Railroad Revitalization and Regulatory Reform Act of 1976. Whereas Canada has allowed wide commercial freedom for the railways to adjust freight rates both in upward and downward directions for almost a decade, and this freedom began to emerge several decades earlier, the process of liberalizing transport regulation has just begun in the U.S.A.

There are several reasons for this contrasting situation. First, Canada, as a prominent member of the British Commonwealth of Nations, has looked to the actions of Great Britain for a regulatory model, and in that country deregulation of both the railways and the road freight carriers began in 1953 and almost complete deregulation was accomplished by 1968.[1] Second, Canada, unlike the U.S.A. in the regulatory acts of 1935 and 1940, never fully adopted the theory of utilizing comprehensive regulation of all modes as a tool for achieving economic coordination of transport.[2] Therefore, entry control and minimum rate regulation for all surface modes did not early become prominent features of the Canadian regulatory structure as they did in the U.S.A., and there were far fewer occasions in Canada for the regulatory body to interfere with competitive rate reductions by the railways to protect the share of the market and revenues of truckers after road transport had developed. Third; although all Provinces except Alberta have some restrictive entry and rate control of intra-Provincial trucking and all Provinces have exercised some control over inter-Provincial trucking, there was no act until 1967 to authorize Federal regulation of the trucking industry; and Part III of the National Transportation Act has not yet been used to regulate trucking.[3] The Provinces can and do regulate inter-Provincial road carriers, but their regulatory bodies cannot restrict railway rates on inter-Provincial traffic as that traffic of the railways is exclusively under the jurisdiction of the federal Canadian Transport Commission. Consequently, the railways of Canada have been left relatively free to adjust their rates to meet the competition of other modes all along. Nevertheless, it required the Transport Act, 1938 and the National Transportation Act, 1967, as well as some rulings of the Board of Railway Commissioners, to bring about the wide commercial freedom that now exists for the railways.

Commercial Pricing Freedom under Traditional Railroad Regulation

Both in Canada and the U.S.A., the railways were subjected to comprehensive regulation that considerably limited their freedom to fix and change their freight rates during the 1920's and 1930's, when intermodal competition from highway and other modes had not yet developed and become significant in transport markets. Briefly, in both countries the railways were required to charge reasonable rates — rates that were not unjustly discriminating or unduly prejudicial — to shippers, communities or ports or between competing commodities; they had to file their rates with the bodies established to regulate the railways and change them only after giving 30 days' notice; their rate increases, and later their competitive rate reductions in the U.S.A., could be suspended by the regulatory body (for seven months by the ICC) and investigated upon complaints by shippers and other parties as to their lawfulness in terms of the statutory regulatory standards; and the regulators could prescribe maximum and nondiscriminating rates, or equitable discriminating rate relationships, under those standards, and even minimum rates in the U.S.A., beginning in 1920.[4] In Canada, the railways were permitted to confer and agree on rates. In the U.S.A. this was unlawful under the antitrust laws until 1948, though tacitly the railways were allowed to do so through their rate bureaus.

The purpose of those regulations, given here only in broad outline, was to afford shippers protection from monopolistic abuses by the railways, that is, from excessive rates and unjust discrimination.[5] It was not to eliminate value-of-service pricing by the railways, but merely to prevent its abuses. Thus, the railways' commercial freedom was circumscribed to protect shippers and the public from unjustifiable and inequitable simple or cartel monopoly pricing. Limitation of the railways' commercial freedom was not done primarily to prevent the railways from engaging in ruinous competition with one another or to prevent predatory or other competition by the railways with other modes, although the filing-of-rates and adherence-to-filed-rates requirements and the tacit or explicit acceptance of concerted action did enable the railways in both countries to engage in cartel pricing.[6] Regulation in the U.S.A. early contained provisions to assure separate ownership of domestic water carriers, intermodal connections, and differential rates for water carriers to keep competition viable between them and the railways. There were some differences between the traditional railway regulation of the two countries that need not be of concern here.

Under such circumstances, the lack of commercial freedom in ratemaking, though vexatious to the railways, did not constitute a significant drag on the railways' ability to obtain the revenues needed from value-of-service rates to become commercially viable concerns. Of course, excess profitability was limited by regulatory action under the traditional scheme of railway rate regulation, but the value-of-service rate structures, the state of the economy, the stage of development of the railways, and the overbuilding of railway capacity were probably more decisive factors in railway profitability in both countries. After the rapid development of competing modes following World Wars I and II, the competitive situation faced by the railways changed drastically, earlier in the U.S.A. than in Canada owing to an earlier development of modern highways there. To obtain revenues adequate to cover costs and provide some return in the widening competitive markets, the railways now had increasingly to make their rates competitive with those of the truckers and other modal carriers. During the early period of development of road transport in the U.S.A., the intercity truckers were not under Federal regulation and even today there are very large exempt areas in the regulation of motor and water carriers. Similarly, in Canada inter-Provincial and some Provincial trucking were not regulated or were controlled only to a limited extent. And in both countries, the private carrier trucks have not been under economic regulation. Thus, the railways of both countries have had to meet intermodal competition to survive in the modern transport markets. In this context, where regulation imposes differential social-service burdens on the railways and subjects them to restrictive regulation of their competitive rates compared with other modes, the railways can experience severe difficulties in adjusting their rates competitively in intermodal markets. The extent and nature of the commercial freedom that regulatory law and regulatory commissions allow the railways can become crucial factors in the ability of the railways to survive over the long run and to supply sufficient and technologically modern service to shippers, the economy and consumers.

Evolution of Commercial Freedom to Price Railway Services in Canada

The development of the wide commercial freedom to price according to market forces presently accorded the Canadian railways was a gradual process. In addition to the authorization to assess competitive rates flexibly if the Board of Railway Commissioners permitted under the Railway Act, 1903, commercial freedom was brought about by the decisions and regulations of the Board of Transport Commissioners and its predecessor and, more importantly, by legislation, principally by The Transport Act, 1938 and the National Transportation Act, 1967. As the essential nature of the railways' competitive freedom has already been described, only the evolution of the major features or steps in freeing the Canadian railways to price competitively with other modes will be given here. A full tracing of the history of railway commercial freedom is beyond the scope of this Appendix.

First, it is significant to note that Section 274(1) of the present Railway Act authorizes the railways to utilize competitive rate tariffs, defined in Subsection (3) as "a class or commodity rate that is issued to meet competition." This would appear to encourage the railways to reduce rates to meet intermodal competition. And though all railway freight tariffs must be filed with the regulatory body and be published, and all rate-increase tariffs must give at least 30 days' notice before their effective date (Section 275 (1) and (2) of the Railway Act), Section 275 (3) states that a freight tariff that *reduces* any rate "may be acted upon and put into operation immediately on or after the issue of the tariff and before it is filed with the Commission." Section 275(4) further makes the filed rate the lawful rate on the effective date of the tariff unless and until disallowed by the regulatory body. These current provisions definitely permit railways to place competitive rate reductions into effect without delays and regulatory interference, that is, without suspension pending investigation of their compensatory nature and without delays that the investigatory process necessarily involves. Hence, the types of regulatory interference, *on protests of competing modes,* that have often thwarted railway rate competition against regulated truckers and water carriers in the U.S.A. have been avoided.[7]

It is not clear whether previous to 1967 the Board of Transprt Commissioners had the power to set minimum railway competitive rates to limit intermodal competition as had the ICC. However, Section 277(1), put into the Railway Act by the 1967 legislation, grants the CTC the power to "disallow any freight rate that after investigation the Commission determines is not compensatory"; and Section 277(2) directs the CTC, upon complaint containing *prima facie* evidence that a filed rate is not compensatory, to investigate such rate to ascertain if it is compensatory, that is, whether "it exceeds the variable cost of the movement of the traffic concerned as determined by the Commission", as specified in Section 276(2) and (3). Such minimum rate regulation, definitely provided after 1967, would hardly delay competitive rate reductions by the railways or obstruct economic rate competition by them with other modes since rates lower than the relevant variable costs would not be profitable. This type of minimum rate control is compatible with effective intermodal rate competition, but in the U.S.A. minimum rate regulation by the ICC frequently disallowed railway rate reductions to meet motor or water competition when the competitive rates were above railway variable costs, and even when they were above the railway full costs.[8]

Canadian railways have been authorized to utilize competitive rates flexibly in meeting intermodal competition without being subjected to rate suspension or delays in making the rates effective for at least three decades, and probably much longer. Thus, the Royal Commission on Transportation headed by W.F.A. Turgeon reported in 1951 that "The Railway Act of 1903 recognized competition, and the present Act still provides authority for tariffs of competitive rates under Sections 314(5) and (6), 328(c), 329(4), and 332.[9] And the Turgeon Commission reported that in numerous judgements, the Board of Transport Commissioners had held "that it is entirely within the discretion of a railway company whether it will meet the competition in tolls of other transport agencies, subject to the prohibitions in the Railway Act with respect to unjust discrimination."[10] The discretion referred to also meant that a railway need not reduce a rate to meet intermodal competition, and that it could restore any competitive toll to its normal level when competition ceased. As the decisions of the Board of Railway Commissioners cited go back to 1910, it seems clear that the Board disallowed a railway competitive rate only when it caused unjust discrimination to shippers.[11] Noteworthy is the Turgeon Commission's conclusion in 1951 rejecting a proposal that the Board approve competitive railway rates before they became effective on the ground that this "would hamper the railways in their efforts to increase their revenue."[12] It can be concluded, therefore, that the Canadian railways have long enjoyed freedom to offer shippers competitive rates to compete with truck and water carriers, and that they may quickly and flexibly make competitive rates effective with a minimum of regulatory interference. Objections of the competing modes have had little standing, a situation strikingly different than that in regulation in the U.S.A.

In addition to having long-standing authorization to utilize competitive rates to meet intermodal competition largely without regulatory hindrance, the Canadian railways were authorized by Part IV of the Transport Act of 1938 to make contracts of agreed charges with shippers. An agreed charge contains a rate or rates agreed upon by a carrier for the transport of all or any part of the goods of any shipper or group of shippers. The Canadian authorization followed similar legislation in Great Britain in 1933, but was more restrictive in its protection of shippers. As enacted in 1938, an agreed charge had to be approved by the Board of Railway Commissioners before it could become effective; approval could not be given if the Board found that the competitive objective of the railway could be attained by a special or competitive tariff; and where the transport services were to or from competitive points or between such points on the lines of two or more railways, the Board's approval could not be given unless all railways joined in making the agreed charge. In addition, the agreement had to be filed with the Board, public notice given, and other shippers in comparable circumstances were accorded the right to apply for a similar fixed rate if their business would be unjustly discriminated against. Within an agreed charge, the carload rate for one car could not be greater than the carload rate for any greater number of cars.[13]

In the *Report of Royal Commission on Agreed Charges* in 1955, Commissioner Turgeon commented on the reasons for Parliamentary authorization of agreed charge contracts that gave contracting shippers competitive rates lower than the rates in competitive and other tariffs provided they agreed to ship all or a stated percentage of their traffic by railway for a specified period, usually one year. Noting that it was recognized in 1938 that the use of competitive rates did not suffice to arm the railways against truck competition, Commissioner Turgeon stated:

The railways point out that Parliament enacted this agreed charge legislation in 1938 for the express purpose of helping them to cope more effectively with carrier competition, especially truck competition, which was making serious inroads upon their business by methods which they themselves were prevented from following by the restrictions of the Railway Act. The record shows that this new practice has been of valuable assistance to the railways...[14]

Further commercial freedom to meet intermodal competition with agreed charges was granted to the railways on the basis of the findings and recommendations of the second Turgeon Royal Commission. Because of regulatory delays occasioned in making agreed charges effective under the original requirement of Board approval, Commissioner Turgeon recommended that legislation be passed to eliminate the Board's prior approval and to allow an agreed charge to become effective 20 days after the date of filing with the Board (to take place within seven days after the agreement was made).[15] This was accomplished by amendments to Sections 32 and 33 of the Transport Act on July 28, 1955. These amendments also permitted water carriers to become parties to agreed charges if they had through route arrangements with rail carriers; allowed other shippers with the consent of the carrier to become parties to an agreed charge by filing a notice of intent with the Board (but their earlier right to oppose it before the Board before it became effective was removed); after an agreed charge had been in effect for one year, allowed any party to withdraw by giving 90 days' notice to the other parties; and, after an agreed charge had been in effect three months, allowed any rail or water carrier, association of such carriers, or any association of shippers to protest to the Minister of Transport that the agreed charge was unjustly discriminatory or placed a carrier's or shipper's business at a disadvantage. The Minister might then, if in the public interest, refer the matter to the Board for investigation and action to vary or cancel the agreed charge.[16] The right of truckers to protest agreed charges was denied in the 1938 legislation because they were not considered to be under federal jurisdiction. Truckers were given the right appeal any competitive rate by Section 277(2) of the Railway Act in 1967, possibly including an Agreed Charge, which they considered to be below the lawful minimum level (the variable cost to the railways handling the traffic) specified by Section 276 of that Act.

Manifestly, then, the Canadian railways have long enjoyed almost complete commercial freedom under Canadian regulation to make rate reductions to meet their intermodal competition. In addition, they have the agreed charge, which binds to rail for an agreed period a contracted amount of the traffic of a shipper or group of shippers in return for the lower competitive contract rates. Thus, they have been able promptly to engage in price competition with other modes and, in addition, to temporarily protect the traffic given the low competitive agreed charges from further diversion by other modal carriers' retaliatory price reductions.[17] This stay of continuing competition with other modes, however, only delays truck price competition for the duration of an agreed charge. And the fact that the percentage of traffic to go by rail is often below 100 percent, say 70 percent, frequently allows a considerably area for further truck competition within that time period. Since 1967 Canadian railways have been subject to regulation of minimum competitive rates, but the variable cost standard prevents this from becoming a competitive handicap in their competition with other modes. Moreover, the dropping of the specific dsicrimination prohibitions of earlier regulation further freed the railways to price competitively with other modes. As compared with the American railways, the Canadian railways have been fortunate, indeed.

In addition, as noted above, the Canadian railways were largely freed from traditional maximum rate regulation in 1967 except where shippers can show that they are captive to the railways. And since fixed rates for captive shippers, when prescribed by the CTC, are 250 percent of variable cost based on 30,000 lb. carloads, the railways even here are largely free to price without rigorous maximum rate control. Hence, the Canadian railways have wide commercial freedom, both to reduce prices to compete with other modes and to raise prices above variable costs to obtain revenue contributions toward coverage of fixed and common costs.

Commercial Freedom to Price Railway Services in the U.S.A.

Until the Motor Carrier Act of 1935 and the Transportation Act of 1940 were passed, the American railways were comparatively free to reduce their rates to meet highway and waterway competition. The minimum rate power given the ICC in 1920 was rarely used, and in the early Great Depression years the ICC allowed many railway rate reductions to meet intermodal competition.[18] But after intercity trucks and nonbulk water carriers in interstate commerce were placed under regulation in 1935 and 1940, respectively, the ICC frequently interfered with railway rate reductions by suspending them for months or years pending investigation, and often after such delays finding them below reasonable minimum rates and requiring the railways to assess higher competitive charges.[19] These suspension and decisional actions were generally invoked by complaints of regulated motor and water carriers that the railway rate competition would be destructive to them and to their market opportunities. The rationales given by the ICC for limiting railway rate competition with other modes were that "destructive competitive" would otherwise result; that each mode, even the high-cost mode, should be given a reasonable opportunity to share in the traffic (fair-sharing); that the low full-cost carrier should have the traffic, not the carrier with the lowest relevant marginal cost; and that unlimited rate competition would break down the value-of-service rate structure.

Aside from the questionable economic validity of such official assertions, the effect of the ICC minimum rate regulation was to allocate an unduly high proportion of the high value traffic to the regulated motor carriers (regardless of their higher unit cost levels) and to give much of the bulk goods traffic to the inland water carriers. Over time, this regulatory process and denial of competitive freedom to the railways misallocated traffic, placed emphasis on service competition that inherently favored trucking, reduced the ability of the railways to hold high-rated profitable traffic, and contributed to declining and low levels of railway returns, eventually even to bankruptcy of a number of northeastern railways, including the Penn-Central.[20] These effects prompted economists, government departments and ultimately Presidents, beginning with President Eisenhower in 1955, to recommend varying amounts of deregulation to allow the pervasive competitive forces to work efficiently instead of inefficiently and to allow the privately-owned railways to save themselves financially, to invest in modern technology, to render adequate and efficient service, and to become fully competitive to the advantage of shippers and the general public.[21]

Until 1976, all efforts of the Executive Branch, the railways and the economists and some shippers to bring about regulatory reform by granting the railways commercial freedom to price their services and compete effectively with other modes failed in the Congress. This was due principally to the organized opposition of the regulated trucking and water carrier industries that have benefited from larger shares of the traffic and revenues than they would have enjoyed under full economic price competition in intermodal markets.

Compared with the commercial freedom that Canadian railways have long enjoyed under the National Transportation Act and earlier acts, only modest and somewhat provisional commercial freedom has recently been granted to the American railways by the Railroad Revitalization and Regulatory Reform Act of 1976.[22] Under that Act, railway rates are not to be found to be unjust or unreasonable on the grounds that they are too low if those rates are equal to or exceed variable cost; and no rate is to be found unjust or unreasonable on the ground that it is too high unless the Commission finds that the carrier has "market dominance" over the traffic. And no rate of a railway is to be held up to a particular level to protect the traffic of any other carrier or mode of transport, unless the Commission finds that such rate reduces or would reduce the going concern value of the carrier charging the rate. Any rate equalling or exceeding variable cost is considered to contribute to going concern value. As an experiment for two years, the railroads may raise or lower specific rates by as much as seven percent from the level in effect at the beginning of each year, without suspension by the ICC and regardless of the reasonableness of the proposed rate. However, the ICC continues to have the power to assure port equalization and to suspend rates because of probable violations of Sections 2, 3, and 4 of the Interstate Commerce Act, the personal, unjust, and long-short haul discrimination provisions, or wherever the railway is found to have market dominance. Limitations are placed on challenging a proposed railway rate that involves a capital investment of $1 million or more by a railway, shipper or receiver. And railway rate bureaus are no longer permitted to agree or vote on single-line railway rates, a provision designed to stimulate both intermodal and intramodal railway competition.

Clearly, this new commercial freedom for American railways has features that follow the Canadian model. Thus, the use of railway variable costs for testing minimum rates is virtually the same as in Canada after 1967. However, the directive to the ICC not to hold up a competitive rate that is profitable to a railway to protect the traffic of a competing carrier or mode is unique to the Protective and restrictive American regulatory scene. These provisions should prevent the most questionable "fair-sharing" allocations of traffic by the ICC, and remove many, but not all, of the past regulatory impediments to economic competitive pricing by railways with other modes as in Canada. With respect to maximum rate control, the new American scheme is similar to the Canadian one for captive shippers in that no rate is to be found unreasonably high unless the ICC finds the railway has "market dominance". The experimental permission for railways in the U.S.A. to raise or lower specific rates by up to 7 percent for two years contrasts with the almost complete freedom of Canadian railways to raise their rates, except that they may be challenged after the rates go into effect under the captive shipper or Section 23 provisions of the National Transportation Act.

On the other hand, rate increases on other than competitive traffic have been temporarily rolled back in Canada by legislation or Executive power, something that does not occur in the U.S.A. Another difference is that the new American legislation retains the strong specific discrimination prohibitions and controls of earlier acts and the suspension power with respect to most rate changes, whereas in 1967 the specific unjust discrimination clauses were eliminated from the Railway Act and were substituted by the more difficult-to-invoke public-interest appeal provisions of Section 23 of the National Transportation Act.

Notwithstanding, considerable commercial freedom has now been granted to the American railways, although still far less than that enjoyed in Canada by the Canadian railways. How workable this commercial freedom might be in allowing full economic price competition between railways and road and water carriers can only be determined after some experience with the relaxed railroad regulation and the variable cost, market dominance, and other standards specified in the 1976 Act. Manifestly, however, Canada has provided a model for regulatory reform and liberalization in the U.S.A., although the American regulatory scheme gives far more specific regulatory attention to inequitable discrimination in railway rate making than the Canadian scheme.

FOOTNOTES

1. *Report of the Royal Commission on Transportation,* known as the Turgeon Commission (Ottawa: King's Printer, 1951), p. 88; and *Report of Royal Commission on Agreed Charges,* W.F.A. Turgeon, Commissioner (Ottawa: Queen's Printer, 1955), pp. 33-35. See Raymond L. Cannon, *The Economics of Deregulation of the British Motor Freight Industry,* M.A. Thesis, Department of Economics, Washington State University, 1973, pp. 1-11; and for the European emphasis on competitive freedom for the railways, see "Reply Statement of James C. Nelson" before the Interstate Commerce Commission, Docket No. 34013 (Sub. No. 1), *Cost Standards in Intermodal Rate Proceedings,* Railroads' Reply to Submission of Other Parties, Appendix C, April 30, 1970, pp. 5-13.

2. See *Turgeon Commission,* 1951, *op.cit.,* pp. 276-280.

3. See *Report of Royal Commission on Agreed Charges,* 1955, *op.cit.,* pp. 24-25; and Richard Schultz, "Intergovernmental Cooperation in Transportation: The Case of the Extra-Provincial Motor Carrier Industry in Canada," paper before the Joint Session of the Transportation Research Forum and the Canadian Transportation Research Forum, Toronto, November 4, 1975.

4. See the judgement of the Supreme Court of Canada on May 20, 1975, in *Canadian Pacific Limited v. The Governments of the Provinces of Alberta, Saskatchewan, Manitoba and Ontario and The Atlantic Provinces Transportation Commission et al and the Canadian National Railway Company v. the Same Parties,* p. 5, where it was stated that previous to the enactment of the National Transportation Act, the Board of Transport Commissioners was given by the *Railway Act,* R.S.C. 1952, c. 234, Section 328(1) and (2), the power *to postpone or suspend* the effective date of any tariff before or after it came into effect. The Court noted that those provisions were repealed by the National Transportation Act and not re-enacted.

5. *Report of Royal Commission on Agreed Charges,* 1955, *op.cit.,* p. 20.

6. See James C. Nelson, "The Changing Economic Case for Surface Transport Regulation," in *Perspectives on Federal Transportation Policy,* edited by James C. Miller III (Washington, D.C.: American Enterprise Institute for Public Policy Research, 1975), pp. 7-25, particularly p. 10.

7. James C. Nelson, *Railroad Transportation and Public Policy* (Washington, D.C.: The Brookings Institution, 1959), pp. 43-44 and 138-147. Also see Ann F. Friedlaender, *The Dilemma of Freight Transport Regulation* (Washington, D.C.: The Brookings Institution, 1969), pp. 23-27 and 90-99.

8. *Ibid.,* p. 43, footnote 18, and p. 44, footnote 21. Also see J.R. Rose, "Regulation of Rates and Intermodal Transport Competition," *I.C.C. Practitioners' Journal,* October 1965, pp. 11-26; and George E. McCallum, *New Techniques in Railroad Ratemaking* (Pullman, Wash.: Bureau of Economic and Business Research, Washington State University, 1968), pp. 115-127.

9. *Turgeon Commission,* 1951, *op.cit.,* p. 84.

10. *Ibid.*

11. *Ibid.* See confirmation of these points in John B. Rollit, "Aspects of the Railway Problem," *The Canadian Journal of Economics and Political Science,* February 1939, pp. 44-45.

12. *Turgeon Commision,* 1951, *op.cit.,* p. 86.

13. *Ibid.,* p. 88. Statutes of Canada, 1938, 2 George VI, Chap. 53, Part V, Sections 35 and 36.

14. *Report of Royal Commission on Agreed Charges,* 1955, *op.cit.,* p. 13. Also see p. 26.

15. *Ibid.,* pp. 35-38. See *Turgeon Commission,* 1951, *op.cit.,* pp. 93-94, for data on

regulatory delays encountered in obtaining Board approval of agreed charges.

16. Chap. 59, An Act to amend the Transport Act, 3-4 Elizabeth II, assented to 28th July, 1955; and Canadian Industrial Traffic League Inc., *Canadian Traffic and Transportation Management,* Volume Two, Subject Fifteen, pp. 12-14. See A.W. Currie, *Economics of Canadian Transportation* (Toronto: University of Toronto Press, 1954), pp. 224-231.

17. *Report of Royal Commission on Agreed Charges,* 1955, *op.cit.,* pp. 21-26; and A.W. Currie, *op.cit.,* pp. 298-301.

18. James C. Nelson, "The Changing Economic Case for Surface Transport Regulation," *op.cit.,* pp. 9 and 13; and his paper, "New Concepts in Transportation Regulation," in *Transportation and National Policy* (Washington, D.C.: National Resources Planning Board, May 1942), pp. 197-237.

19. James C. Nelson, *Railroad Transportation and Public Policy, op.cit.,* pp. 138-142.

20. *Ibid.,* pp. 36-40, 191-192, and 195-230. Also see Ann Fr. Friedlaender, *The Dilemma of Freight Transport Regulation, op.cit.,* pp. 66, 87, 98-99, and 101-103.

21. James C. Nelson, "New Concepts in Transportation Regulation," *op.cit.,* pp. 236-237, and his "Revision of National Transport Regulatory Policy," *American Economic Review,* December 1955, pp. 910-918; Dudley F. Pegrum, *Transportation: Economics and Public Policy* (Homewood, Ill.: Richard D. Irwin, Inc., 1963), pp. 504-508 and 585-600; *Transportation Act of 1972,* Hearings before the Subcommittee on Transportation and Aeronautics, House of Representatives Committee on Interstate and Foreign Commerce on H.R. 11824, H.R. 11826 and other bills, 92nd Cong., 2d sess., Parts 1-4, March 27-May 12, 1972; and "Freedom from Regulation?", *Business Week,* May 12, 1975, pp. 74-80.

22. Public Law 94-210, 94th Cong., S.2718, approved by President Ford on February 5, 1976.

CHAPTER IX

ECONOMIC AND INSTITUTIONAL EFFECTS OF COMMERCIAL FREEDOM AND COMPETITION IN CANADIAN RAIL FREIGHT TRANSPORT

Almost a decade has elapsed since the passage of the National Transportation Act in 1967 greatly reduced the regulatory constraints on Canadian railways, as had been recommended by the MacPherson Commission. The Commission had argued that the general pervasiveness of competitive forces had removed the necessity for the comprehensive and restrictive regulation of railway rates characteristic of the U.S.A. and of previous periods in Canada. This study has described how the forces of intermodal, intramodal and market competition have affected particular railway rates and rate levels through the processes of railway market research and shipper-carrier negotiations. However, the important question raised in Chapter IV still remains to be answered. Has the working of the dynamic competitive forces in the Canadian economy over the last decade produced in larger measure the benefits to be expected from effective competition whenever it takes place? Overall, has the wide commercial freedom for carriers in Canadian freight markets assured shippers and the economy adequate and efficient railway services and facilities to meet the traffic demands of a growing economy, to encourage service-improving and cost-reducing technology in transport, and to assist in bringing about an efficient allocation of resources within transport by assigning to each mode that traffic and those transport and distributional functions for which it is best adapted and most efficient?

This Chapter emphasizes analysis of the question of whether the economic effects that have been occurring indicate that dynamic competition has been working as would be expected from the extent to which the prerequisites of effective competition, outlined in Chapter IV, were found to exist. In short, the interest here is whether the presumption of workable competition stated there can be confirmed as workable or effective competition on the whole when all available facts are considered. This Chapter also examines the evidence concerning the changes which have taken place, and are taking place, as

295

organizations and procedures adjust to reliance on dynamic competitive forces. Achieving the potential of competitive results with a minimum of regulatory interference is sensitive to the effectiveness with which institutions adjust and perform. The results achieved by the commercial system, largely unconstrained by regulatory forces, are expected to have significant implications for political views concerned with railway regulatory policy.

Criteria for Assessment of Economic Effects

The assessment in this Chapter of the economic effects of relying primarily on the working of dynamic competition to regulate Canadian rail freight markets requires an explicit statement of the objective assumed for the working of freight markets. The objective assumed for the desirable working of the transport markets can be simply stated. It is that the transport industry should be economically efficient, that is, make the best use of available resources within and between modes of transport and in transport, as a whole, compared with other sectors of the economy.

Important assumptions must be recognized for such a statement to be a useful practical guide for assessing the performance of the existing markets. First, it is assumed that the objective of efficiency can be most closely realized by pursuing a policy of commercial viability in the operation of transportation services. That means that in the case of Crown Corporations, they should strive to earn a normal return on capital and be guided by the same commercial considerations as private corporations. This appears to be the case currently for the CN (and that the authors endorse wholeheartedly). Second, it is assumed that Government can achieve socially desirable results, not achievable through reliance on commercial forces, by appropriate interventions. However, the achievement of social and political objectives can be most effectively realized by intervention into the market system in the most direct way possible, and not through indirect means such as the use of transport to achieve non-transport social objectives, such as the redistribution of wealth.

The objective assumed here is consistent with the current statement of National Transportation Policy. This reads in part:

> It is hereby declared that an economic, efficient and adequate transportation system making the best use of all available modes of transportation at the lowest total cost is essential to protect the interests of the users of transportation and to maintain the economic well-being and growth of Canada....[1]

In the policy review process of the last few years, changes have been suggested for the statement of National Transportation Policy. While it is not certain what changes, if any, will be made finally, a statement of February 1976 reads in part:

National Transportation Objectives

3. (1) It is hereby declared that:

   (a) an efficient total transportation system for Canada providing accessibility and equity of treatment for users is an essential instrument of support for the achievement of national and regional economic and social objectives;

   (b) it is the responsibility of government to attend to the provision of the transportation system described in paragraph (a); and

   (c) achievement of the transportation system described in paragraph (a) requires the integration of services provided through the most appropriate modes for each service.[2]

It seems that only the first paragraph in this statement is really an objective while the others are "means". The need for an efficient transport system is still recognized, although it is not clear what is meant by "providing accessibility and equity of treatment for users". However, it seems likely that the objective of efficiency guiding the analysis in this Chapter is still compatible with the possible revision of the National Transportation Policy.

Stating the objective for the analysis is much easier than identifying and using criteria by which to judge how well the transport system is performing. This task requires the identification of results which can be measured and the employment of measures by which the level of accomplishment can be assessed. The realities are that the complexities of the workings of the national transportation system, plus the authors' own inadequacies and the limited resources available to them, preclude the generation of data appropriate for precise scientific measurement. The authors are confident they are not alone in this problem. As a result, the means by which to assess how well the system is performing is, simply stated, the exercise of "judgement". The criterion applied is whether the present reliance on the workings of competitive forces in railway markets is, in the authors' judgement, working well and whether there are any aspects in the workings of this system which could be improved by greater or lesser government constraints. While it is acknowledged that fuller and more authoritative analysis is possible than that accomplished here, the authors are convinced that the essential nature of practical economics precludes a wholly quantitative approach to the measurement of economic performance.

Many difficulties are encountered in finding economic effects. First, there are many imperfections in competition in Canadian transport, as noted in Chapter IV. Second, because of those imperfections, the rigorous tests of economic performance under perfect or pure competition and static conditions cannot be relied on wholly to indicate whether transport competition is effective or not. Dynamic conditions of competition are the ones that exist in the real world, and the effectiveness of these competitive conditions must be measured by broader

297

and less specific tests of economic performance. Finally, the data that reveal the economic effects of competition, such as the relation of rates to marginal and average costs or the influence of differences in rates on industrial and regional development, are inadequate for precise measurements without very detailed and time-consuming investigation far beyond the resources available for this study.

For those reasons, the analysis in this Chapter is in terms of whether the effects noted from the information available, including the case studies of shipper-carrier rate negotiations and the considered opinions of knowledgeable parties, have been the types of effects that are to be expected from the efficient workings of dynamic competition in transport markets, particularly in railway markets. The conclusions in Chapter X are concerned with whether changes might be considered in existing constraints on railway markets, to encourage greater efficiency, and with the general implications of the findings on economic performance for public policy.

A basic assumption of the analysis in this Chapter is that transport markets are, and necessarily must be, a mixture of competition and monopoly influences even under the widest commercial freedom. Therefore, the influence of market forces on railway rates cannot be expected to yield the perfectly efficient results that can only be attained under perfectly or purely competitive markets.

Realization of Economic Effects
According to Perfect or Pure Competition

The effects of perfect or pure competition, in theory, were noted in Chapter IV. Thus, when the firm and industry are in competitive equilibrium, price will be equal to marginal cost and also to average total unit cost, and marginal revenue (the competitive price) will be equal to both of those costs; uniform rather than discriminating prices will prevail, with price discrimination taking place only in limited true joint-cost situations; the firm's output will be at the least-cost level of utilization of plant and equipment and firms will be operating at the optimum scale for the firm, so that the average total unit costs will be minimized and prices will be as low as possible; and the returns to capital and entrepreneurs will be only the competitive returns necessary to attract those factors to the enterprise, with the result that no monopoly profits will be earned. Clearly, these effects imply the attainment of maximum efficiency in production and the use of resources, and prices that yield the maximum economic benefits with the technologies available for production at any given time.

While those effects from perfect or pure competition are obviously desirable for society to achieve in transport and other fields of economic activity, they are unattainable in all respects in Canadian railway transport. Though competitive forces of several kinds are found to a greater or lesser extent in nearly all transport markets, they are not sufficient to equate all railway rates with the relevant unit costs. Nor, given the economic characteristics of railways mentioned in Chapter IV, would it be economic to equate railway rates with marginal and average total unit costs under the traffic and utilization conditions that typically obtain in railway transport. Hence, railway freight rates cannot be expected to be uniform prices, but rather must necessarily be discriminating prices far beyond the limits imposed by the existence of true joint-cost situations.

In actual fact, railway freight rates have varied between variable cost levels and 250 percent or more of those levels in Canada as in the U.S.A. Because of errors made in adjusting rates or lags in adjustment to changing cost and other circumstances, some railway rates have been below variable costs and others above variable costs but below the levels that market demand and the low levels of railway profitability would justify. How many uneconomically low rates, made by the railways and not by statute, there are in the Canadian railway rate structure is not known, but such rates should be raised to profitable levels to reduce the burden on other traffic and to avoid the waste of scarce resources. Except where noncompensatory rates are retained on large volumes of traffic, as by government intervention, little or no complaint has been raised about uneconomically low rates. Rate proposals from the railways based on over-estimates, or even normal estimates, of the optimal discriminating prices lead to shipper protests. These have normally been resolved through negotiations, but on occasion they have required regulatory action. Far more attention is given by shippers to their problems with high rates than is customarily given to low rates, with the exception of substantial government rate hold-downs.

Rate discrimination should be held to the minimum required for normally profitable railway operations, with sufficient profitability to draw the necessary capital into the business. In earlier times, commission regulation was relied on to limit discrimination to economic levels, but in Canada today the principal reliance to achieve such limitation is on the widespread active competition in transport markets, along with the remaining regulatory controls described elsewhere in this study. In spite of the pricing freedom of CN and CP, their overall rates of return have certainly not been at monopolistic levels.[3] Table 16 shows that the highest annual return on the net railway investment of CP since 1959 was 5.6 percent. For that year (1974), the Snavely Commission estimated the cost of capital for the CP as 11.31 percent after taxes,[4] so that it may be judged that the return on capital has been below competitive levels. However, there are so many contributing factors to the inadequate rate of return, including rate holddowns and services provided in the public interest without full compensation that these low returns cannot be attributed to excessive or ruinous competition. Indeed, the fact that the Canadian railways strongly support commercial freedom in rate making indicates that they believe they are better off under the competition that exists than they would be if they were under more comprehensive regulation, as are the U.S.A. railways. They believe, also, that with the commercial freedom they now enjoy and with economic compensation for noncompensatory services provided in the public interest, they "know of no reason why railways should not be able to meet the demand for their service including the replacement of plant and the provision of new capacity as and when it becomes necessary."[5]

Generally, the Canadian railways have supplied all of the freight services demanded of them by the Canadian economy, as competitive firms under perfect competition would do.[6] However, their efficiency in producing such services, though increasing considerably over time, probably has fallen short of the perfectly competitive ideal, as recurring or long-term excess capacity and areas of insufficient equipment or line capacity reveal.[7] On the other hand, no perfect adjustment of supply to demand can be expected in railway transport because of the highly variable nature of demand and the durable and fixed nature of the plant — not to mention governmental restraints on abandonment of unprofitable services and light-density lines. Moreover, under perfectly competitive conditions firms adjust production to the prices the market clearly fixes for them. In railway transport, as in many types of modern industry, however, the firms must negotiate with their customers and fix prices, taking into account all relevant demand and demand-elasticity factors, as well as unit cost changes in a complicated structure of fixed, common and joint costs. Again, even with the most alert managements and refined market analyses, it cannot be expected that perfectly efficient prices could be set in an industry in which the firms serve so many diverse markets, commodities and shipments, and face such highly sophisticated dynamic competitive elements.[8]

Hence, even though the Canadian Government has given the railways a wide amount of market freedom, and though competition in one form or another generally prevails in transport markets today, it would not be logical to conclude that the policy of commercial freedom and competitive rate setting in Canada has failed because the complete beneficial results of perfect or pure competition have not been realized. A realistic and pertinent analysis of the economic effects of commercial freedom for the railways should look instead to how the dynamic forces of transport competition operate in spite of market imperfections, and to whether those forces bring about, to a reasonable extent, the types of beneficial effects that perfect and pure competition would yield if those market states were possible. To achieve the desired results requires that the institutions be adequate and responsive to the competitive demands placed on them.

Institutional Effects of Commercial Freedom in Canada

It is difficult to achieve substantive changes in large organizations and complex procedures in a short period of time. Views of the people within large organizations take a considerable period to change or evolve and the working of an organization takes much longer to change than that required to complete the physical appearances of a reorganization. Institutional changes evolve rather than occur dramatically.

When examining the effects of commercial freedom on railways, shippers, and government organizations in Canada, it is necessary to recognize that prior to 1967 the influence of competitive forces on the railways had increased greatly and the railways had been given significant freedom to respond to them. The increase in the free working of market forces was associated with the evolution of the characteristics of railway and shipper organizations away from those the era of effective railway monopoly. The passage of the National Transportation Act permitted a considerable amount of commercial freedom. This accelerated institutional changes and contributed to the development of a degree of sophistication that has enabled the organizations to deal with the opportunities, requirements and limitations imposed on them by competitive forces.

Railway Organization and the Across-the-Board Pricing Method

A long-standing basic criticism of railway pricing, one that was frequently voiced in Canada before the period of the MacPherson Commission and the passage of the 1967 Act and that still is strongly stated by shippers and economists in the U.S.A., is that regulated railways have relied too heavily on horizontal, or across-the-board, general rate increases to obtain the needed revenues, both in times of depression when traffic volume is low and in times of inflation when costs increase rapidly and rate adjustments lag behind cost increases. Generally, this pricing did raise some or all of the additional revenues needed, but it neglected to price individual commodity movements in particular markets according to the specific demand, competitive, and cost factors in those markets.[9] Although, typically, some adjustments or holddowns were included by the railroads and the regulators to reduce the differential impacts on shippers located long distances from their markets and who faced market competition, generally price increases of this kind quickly or gradually priced the railways out of many markets where alternative modes were actually or potentially available to the shippers. Even though some or all railways subsequently adjusted rates competitively to meet competition and to reduce the traffic-loss effects, those efforts were frequently too little and too late. The long-term result of excessive reliance on horizontal rate increases too often was loss of the high-revenue-yielding types of traffic, especially high-value manufactures, to the for-hire and private trucks. Since railways frequently have lower unit costs than the trucks except in small shipments and over short distances, such losses of the profitable

301

carload traffic in manufactured goods not only undermined railway profitability but also contributed to an inefficient allocation of traffic between the modes.[10]

Heavy reliance on general pricing by horizontal percentage rate increases was strongly encouraged by the comprehensive and restrictive railway rate regulation that formerly existed in Canada and still prevails in the U.S.A. It was also the most practicable method for the railways to adjust their rates as long as they had a highly centralized and small staff responsible for setting rates. As the Canadian railways recognized during the 1950's, responsiveness to market forces required a reorganization of their marketing and pricing activities.

In Canada, but not in the U.S.A., the self-defeating reliance on general rate level increases was ended with the rate freeze during the investigations by the MacPherson Commission (1959-60) and by the enactment of the National Transportation Act in 1967. Since 1959, the Canadian railways have not raised revenues to meet cash-flow and financial needs primarily by horizontal rate increases. However, during 1975 and 1976, they raised many of their freight rates by considerable percentages or amounts in some broad market actions to catch up and keep up with inflation after the 1973-74 rate freeze ended as noted in Chapter III. This rejection by the railways of the use of general rate level increases can be attributed to their commercial freedom since 1967 to adjust specific rates and agreed charges quickly and freely. And knowing that they must depend on themselves, rather than on regulatory decisions and orders, to obtain from the market the revenues needed for viability, the Canadian railway managements, as noted in Chapter III, have organized market research, cost research, marketing and distribution efforts, and sophisticated pricing and demand-study techniques to enable them to price dynamically, competitively, and profitably in individual markets.

Clearly, one of the most significant gains from commercial freedom and the lack of protective and restrictive regulation in Canada has been the encouragement that those conditions have given to sophisticated pricing in particular markets and to the creation of effective organization for research and innovation in the marketing and pricing in railway services. The magnitude of the benefit which Canada enjoys in these respects is reflected in the uniform rejection by shippers and carriers in Canada of any form of "ICC regulation."

Greater Self-Reliance by Shippers and Attention to Transport Alternatives

The granting of greater commercial freedom to the railways in 1967 also had institutional effects on many shippers. Under a system of greatly reduced reliance by shippers on regulatory suspension of railway rate changes and protective orders with respect to alleged unreasonableness of rate levels and relationships, the shippers must necessarily exert more sophisticated and stronger efforts to find workable alternatives to railway services. It has become more important to develop negotiating positions involving selective analyses of the probable effects of rate changes on their production, markets and profits, and to compile the evidence of the actual and potential alternatives to railway transport open to them. The possibilities of operating their own trucks and of cooperating with for-hire truckers in furnishing traffic for back hauls are among the shipper activities that have been stimulated by the necessity for being more self-reliant in finding solutions to shipper rate and service problems. And as noted in Chapter III, shippers have adopted more industry-based approaches for negotiating rates with the railways, thus assembling countervailing market power and a more comprehensive research basis for effective negotiation. The case studies revealed a number of situations in which presentation of evidence to the railways that the shippers could organize shipments by another mode or combination of modes was effective in limiting proposed increases in railway rates. In this way, the competitive market forces are effectively brought to bear on railway rate making, as they should be in competitive theory. The favourable results obtained by well informed and organized shippers has encouraged other shippers to increase their research and negotiating efforts to the general betterment and efficiency of the competitive process.

There is an organizational and manpower cost to shippers resulting from having to depend more on their own close analyses of the market, on well-prepared negotiating positions, and on their ability to present their actual and potential alternatives to the railways. However, this cost must be compared with the expense of litigation in a more rigidily regulated environment. Also, wide benefits are realized by shippers who have placed emphasis on acquiring greater knowledge of transport and distributional alternatives, of railway unit costs, cost factors and cost findings, and of the underlying economic forces affecting transport supply and efficiency. Such effort can only improve the economy which shippers attain in the planning and conduct of their wide range of logistics functions. In turn, the greater sophistication of shippers in conducting transport and rate analysis and in presenting their alternatives to the railways also stimulates the latter to conduct more sophisticated pricing and costing analysis.

Indeed, the gains from the significant institutional changes brought about by the greater commercial freedom for the railways under the 1967 Act have been recognized by the Canadian Trucking Association. In its comment on the 1975 Transportation Policy reports of Transport Canada, that Association stated that greater commercial freedom aided in keeping ton-mile costs down for shippers and gave railways the flexibility and assurances to take new approaches to their problems, and that the greater competitiveness of the railways induced the truckers to become more efficient and sophisticated. The CTA statement was as follows:

Comments on the National Transportation Act and findings of the MacPherson Commission can be endorsed in general. The National Transportation Act may be deficient in failing to create a framework for dealing with passenger transportation adequately. It may also be true that the MacPherson Commission, having discovered the phenomena of intermodal freight competition, let out a shout of "Eurkea" and drafted a report calling for more of the same. But implementation of the basic MacPherson philosophy calling for greater freedom probably saved the Canadian railways from total collapse along with some of their American counterparts. The National Transportation Act offered the railways the flexibility and incentive to invest in new equipment and in new approaches with some assurance that an adequate return could be earned from exerting initiative. It is this fact as much as anything else which has allowed the railways to keep a lid on ton-mile costs for the past eight years despite extreme inflationary pressures. In turn, the increased competitiveness of the railways undoubtedly spurred-on the truckers to become more efficient and more sophisticated. It may be true that the competitive framework outlined in the National Transportation Act is not the whole story, but at the same time, it would be wise not to discount the significance of the changes introduced under the National Transportation Act which still have significant implication for most of the freight moving in this country.[11]

Reform of the Surface Transport Regulatory Body in Terms of Modern Needs

Another institutional change brought about by the grant of greater commercial freedom to railways in 1967 was the reform in the organization and functions of the regulatory body. Under the comprehensive regulation of railway rates to limit the effective monopoly power of the railways during the railway era, the regulatory body, the Board of Transport Commissioners, had to have a large legal and technical staff to hold hearings, to make regulatory investigations, to prepare reports and decisions, and to engage in legal actions before the courts. While those types of activities were clearly necessary when there was limited intermodal competition to the railways, it was recognized by the MacPherson Commission in 1961 and the Parliament in 1967 that Canadian railways no longer possessed the market power, except in limited markets, to discriminate unduly in rates or services or to assess excessive charges. Hence, the reorganized regulatory body, the CTC, was relieved of most of such case and legal activity.

The recognition that there was no longer a public need for full regulation in

Canada made it essential to have the regulatory body concentrate on the functions that were still useful and required in the public interest. Except for the question of whether transport policy research should be located in the CTC or Transport Canada, which is being resolved in favor of Transport Canada, this reassignment of functions has been accomplished. The CTC is still equipped to hear, investigate and decide the relatively few rate issues that the competitive market forces do not resolve satisfactorily and that are of real importance to the public interest or to captive shippers. As the analysis in Chapter VIII indicates, the CTC has dealt with the meritorious Section 23 cases successfully and probably in the public interest, albeit over an extended time period. In addition, it appears to have been used efficiently by the Government to administer the rate subsidies under statutory rates and rate freezes. Again, Canada is far ahead of the U.S.A. in reform of the surface transport regulatory body and in limiting it to the regulatory functions still required in the public interest.

Of course, there is not complete satisfaction over the attitudes and work of the CTC in relation to its research and advisory functions or its regulatory functions.[12] As noted in Chapter VIII, shippers would like easier access to the CTC in the filing of rate investigation appeals under Section 23; would like the *prima facie* proof procedures to be less time-consuming and difficult; and some shippers would like more mediation of rate disputes and additional CTC pressures on the railways to negotiate fully and effectively with shippers. On the other hand, the wide support that shipper groups continue to give the commerical freedom and liberalized regulation philosophy of the National Transportation Act implies basic support for the changed and more limited regulatory functions assigned to the CTC. Shipper advocates of regulatory change seek to have relatively minor changes in the existing statutes made and more substantial changes in the structuring and working of the CTC to enable it to be more responsive to the diverse demands placed upon it under today's market conditions. It must continue to be the agency to administer regulatory statutes and to respond to fine points of law often raised by the complainants and respondents themselves. Yet it is expected to accomplish its judicial tasks in a fair, quick and inexpensive manner consistent with the pressing needs of commercial forces! That is a large task and one that perhaps cannot be accomplished to the complete satisfaction of all groups. However, the CTC has been less sensitive to the need to innovate than have the carriers and the shippers — less responsive to the need to change in order to meet the requirements of today's competitive transport markets.

Realization of the Beneficial Economic Effects
under Workable Dynamic Competition

Though railways do not operate under perfect or pure competition and their markets do not yield all of the economic efficiency results of those ideal market states, Canadian railways do operate, price their services, and utilize scarce resources under widespread dynamic competition. Earlier Chapters have shown that railway rates and services are widely subject to the full range of constraints of market forces. The essential reality of effective competition in transport markets is the degree to which rivalries between different carriers and modes, different products, different regions, and different sources of supply, as well as the locational alternatives of individual producers, all work to impose the discipline and the incentives of dynamic competition on the railways.

The types of economic effects to be expected from workable dynamic competition are similar to those to be expected from the ideal states of perfect or pure competition, with the differences that the beneficial results of the latter are not likely to be fully experienced under the former, and that there will be some "wastes of competition" and some monopoly practices as dynamic competition works with market imperfections. On the other hand, dynamic competition encompasses changes in the arts or technology rather than requiring static conditions. Hence, under dynamic conditions of competition consumers and the economy will experience new products, new services, more productive capital goods, and more efficient ways for producing goods or services from time to time, types of real gains that are generally regarded as highly beneficial even though other goods and services, older technology and capital, and some entrepreneurs and labor are displaced or placed in an inferior market or earnings position.

Tendencies toward Correspondence of Rates with Costs
and Less General Rate Discrimination

If dynamic competition in transport is workable, it would be expected that rates would tend to come into closer relation with the relevant costs of service over time, and, as a corollary, that the range and frequency of discriminating rates would tend to lessen over time, except for their natural continuance in true joint-cost situations. What do the available facts reveal? The evidence assembled is of three types. The first is the evidence on the workings of the railway rate-making system which is suggestive of results. The second evidence is that provided by the statistical analysis reported in Chapter II. The third is the general evidence of changes in the structure and level of freight rates over time, also reported in Chapter II.

From the evidence provided by the case studies for this research, there is good reason to believe that the railways are now as attentive to cost considerations in pricing as it is reasonable to expect large railway enterprises to be. They routinely carry out costing calculations for the pricing officers who are setting rates. The pricing officers are now sensitive to the responsibility which they have to ensure compensatory rates. Normally, those costing analyses are based on the use of the Quick Costing Formulae of the railways, but the officers have available for use, in appropriate instances, methodologies that "represent a degree of sophistication and precision that puts Canadian National and CP Rail at the forefront of railway cost ascertainment."[13] However, the research for this book has not attempted to ascertain the detailed correctness of the railway costing procedures for pricing purposes. In particular, it is not possible to conclude whether the means of adjusting system costs to local situations, or of adjusting long-run costs to short-run situations, or of costing and associated capital budgeting procedures, are correct. However, it can be concluded that the costing systems employed and the costing information available to pricing officers are good and meet the requirement of effective costing for efficient market performance as well as can be expected at this time. The development of this costing system has been an essential component of the sophistication of the marketing and pricing system of the Canadian railways, initiated during the 1950's to assist the railways in responding profitably to competitive forces affecting specific commodity movements.

The availability of the cost informaton is certainly the first requirement in achieving an efficient relationship between costs and rates. However, without specific and detailed knowledge of the margin of contribution to constant costs made by specific traffic, it is not possible to ascertain how closely rates approach relevant costs on various traffics in Canada. It is easier to ascertain whether pricing methods are likely to produce desirable results with rates below costs than with them substantially in excess of costs. The case studies reveal instances where the railways have insisted that rate increases have been necessary to keep rates at a compensatory level and instances where the rates were raised knowing that traffic would be lost as a result. In cases where rates were set on long-term contract under conditions of intramodal, intermodal and market competition in the late 1960's and early 1970's at what turned out to be noncompensatory levels, the explanation seems to be that the contracts did not allow sufficient flexibility to cover the effects of the inflation actually experienced. In the case of some coal traffic, a lack of appreciation of the track maintenance costs of heavy unit trains was also a contributing factor.

This is not to deny that the railways have been delinquent of accepting uneconomically low rates in some instances in relation to calculated or calculable costs, and that reliance on historical cost for assets requiring replacement has resulted in uneconomically low rates in some instances. The latter problem has become obvious over the last year or so, and has resulted in the adoption of replacement cost as the basis for pricing decisions. An example of the railways raising rates rapidly from an admitted noncompensatory level is the charges for weighing cars. The noncompensatory interswitching tariff is an instance where the railways have not been as active as they should have been in getting the CTC to raise the level of those charges. However, if the railways have been errant under their own responsibility through uneconomically low pricing in certain instances, the Government was probably even more errant through the rate freeze of 1973 and 1974. Further, the greatest burden of uneconomically low rates are those on statutory grain and those on passenger services; in the latter case the railways receive eighty percent of any loss in subsidies.

Overall, then, it appears that the commercial system has produced good results with respect to the relationship between costs and rates, and it has been government intervention which has produced extremely bad and damaging results. This conclusion from the facts demonstrates that under today's conditions there is no evidence that the railways have engaged in predatory pricing and demonstrates the much greater flexibility of the commercial system than the political system in responding to economic forces.

Evidence on the level of contribution of rates above relevant costs is not deducible from the case studies except to the extent that the case studies demonstrate the effectiveness of competition when the full range of market constraints is considered. However, the results of the statistical analysis and other data in Chapter II confirm the expectation that the result of competition has been to produce more cost-based rates.

This result is evidenced by three types of data. First, the Waybill Analysis data for the years 1951, 1963, and 1974, shown in Chapter II, reveal that a far larger proportion of Canadian railway rates were of the competitive type in 1974 than in 1951, which means that they have   become   nore subject to being set by the forces of competition   over time.   Thus, in 1974 competitive commodity rates and agreed charges accounted for 63 percent of rail revenues and 45 percent of rail ton-miles; they were 13 percent and 11 percent, respectively, in 1951 and 51 percent and 34 percent in 1963. This does not include the revenues and ton-miles of a large number of non-competitive commodity rail rates which have been strongly subject to market competition, and even to some carrier competition. Class rates have generally been thought of as monopoly-type rates, but whereas 22 percent of rail revenues and 9 percent of rail ton-miles came from class-rated traffic in 1951, only 3 percent and 1 percent, respectively, came from such traffic in 1974. Clearly, though those data tell only a part of the story, as the force of market competition in limiting non-competitive rail commodity rates (27 percent of rail revenues and 36 percent of rail ton-miles in 1974) is left out, they clearly imply that rail freight rates today are set by one or more types of competition in most cases and further than they are becoming generally to be like competitive prices. Though the forces of dynamic competition were bringing this about before the 1967 Act, the wider commercial freedom since then has continued that tendency.

Second, the Waybill data show the positive effect of competitive forces in preventing railway rates from rising to the levels that would be expected because of the inflation in the economy since 1959 and because of the revenue needs of the carriers. The average revenue per ton-mile for railways increased from 1.12 cents in 1949 to 1.79 cents in 1959, years during which comprehensive rate regulation by the Board of Transport Commissioners was in effect. On the other hand, from that level in 1959, the average revenue per ton-mile declined into the mid-1960s, then rose slightly to 1.55 cents in 1968, about the time the National Transportation Act became effective, after which there was another decline through 1971, with a subsequent slight rise to 1.46 cents by 1973. After 1974, when the recent rate freeze ended and the inflation rate in the Canadian economy rose, the average revenue per ton-mile for railways rose rapidly. The average revenue per ton-mile for 1976 will probably be shown to exceed the level of 1959 when the Waybill data are available.

Recognizing the inflation which has occurred since 1967, the level of Canadian freight rates has behaved rather well. Imperfect as the Waybill data are, as noted in Chapter II, they confirm the probability that overall the extent of price discrimination has decreased under reliance on dynamic competition.

Third, when railway rates are becoming more competitively set and less related to the varying elasticities of demand under monopoly conditions, they are also logically becoming more closely related to cost of service and less discriminating. The definite implications of the statistical analysis of Waybill data given in Chapter II was that over the period 1956 to 1972 the railway freight rate structure had become more cost oriented in Canada. Furthermore, that regression analysis showed that the impact of the value of commodities on the level of freight rates had decreased over that time interval. There is little reason to doubt that this lessening of discrimination because of the widening of competitive forces has been continuing since 1972. And in the U.S.A. the revenue burden studies of the Interstate Commerce Commission and the Department of Transportation have revealed that over time the dispersion of discriminating railway rates above and below fully allocated costs has lessened, although this tendency has been considerably retarded by restrictive regulation of rail and truck rates. This confirms that dynamic competition, even under restrictive minimum rate regulation, has been lessening the range of discrimination and bringing about a movement toward competitive cost-based rates.[14]

The fact that dynamic competition does not completely eliminate general railway rate discrimination except for true joint-cost situations, as theory indicates should take place, is explained by the seasonal and cyclical variability of the demands for rail freight service, the necessity for railways to be geared up in car, line and terminal capacity to meet peak demands without excessive car shortages and blocked train movements, the durable and fixed nature of railway capital facilities, and the immense capacity and size of their movement units when used efficiently. In short, the continuance of considerable general discrimination in rail rates reflects the stimulation that excess capacity continues to give for relating rates to the value of service as low as the relevant marginal cost, as well as the need to fix some rates above average cost to ensure the commercial viability of the railway enterprises. In Canada, the necessity of general discrimination in railway rates is strengthened by the continuance of the financial burdens placed on the railways by government policies with respect to unremunerative passenger services and statutory grain rates.

The Wide Choice of Economic Services

In Canada, shipper choice is unaffected by restrictive minimum rate and other regulatory constraints that reduce shipper choice to decisions made entirely on the basis of service quality because a parity of the rates of alternative modes is maintained by cartel-like regulation. This benefit of reliance on competitive forces to achieve the development of economically based competitive services can be appreciated best by a brief comparison with the U.S.A.

In the U.S.A., ICC regulation has induced rail-truck rate parity pricing on high-value goods and has limited competitive rate cutting by the railways, and sometimes by motor carriers; and this profit-protection regulation, unless private carrier trucking can be utilized, often denies shippers a real choice between the services of those modes, a choice that reflects both relative service quality and differences in rates corresponding to differences in ton-mile costs.[15] In the U.S.A., this virtual confinement of shipper choice to service alone in the case of high-value commodities has cost the railways large amounts of carload traffic of manufactured goods over medium and long hauls and the high revenues associated with it, and has contributed significantly to their low earnings levels and to the social cost, estimated at billions of dollars, of misallocated traffic and resources each year.[16]

The case study data of this work reveal quite clearly the effectiveness with which the railways have used their flexibility in pricing to meet intermodal competition. In many instances, the rates agreed on with shippers as necessary to move traffic by rail have been put into effect *immediately* by the issuance of a Limited Freight Tariff. The contrast of this experience and that existing in the U.S.A. is one which was made pointedly by shippers and carriers on numerous occasions. The case studies also reveal the great benefits enjoyed by Canadian shippers since 1967 from being able to negotiate the design and pricing of rail services tailored to their needs. These activities have taken place through the versatility allowed in the current regulations and put into effect through the transportation and logistics planning capability of the railways' marketing departments. The development of intermodal transport systems, the combination inbound and outbound rates, the use of volume-based rates in

310

terms of cars per shipment, the employment of annual traffic guarantees in tons, and the development of unit train systems are all examples of services with their own unique characteristics and rates which have proceeded on a strictly commercial basis. The result has not only been a transport industry in which the shippers have available a range of choices among modes based on the costs and needs of the various carriers, but also a railway industry able to design specific services for shippers and to price those services according to their cost and value.

The Level of Service Provided under Dynamic Competition

In view of the foregoing, it would not be surprising to conclude that the level of service is generally considered by shippers to be favourable. However, the evidence from the interview programme for this study is not sufficient to reach that conclusion, since the objective has been to study pricing rather than service quality per se. Nevertheless, in only two instances did shippers indicate that a lack of receptivity of the railways to service complaints was a significant concern to them. On the other hand, a number of shippers were complimentary about the effectiveness of the railways in the development of special rail and inter-modal transport systems. In the case of the sulphur industry, effective working of the distribution and rail transport system has been difficult to realize and has given rise to accusation of performance failure on the part of shippers and carriers.

Important support for the conclusion stated above is the study by Bruce Mallen and Jean Francois Pernotte of shipper attitudes by means of some 500 interviews conducted with buyers of freight transport throughout Canada between July 1970 and June 1971. Their study provides some useful conclusions with regard to service levels. Mallen and Pernotte concluded as follows:

> Incidentally, among the truly captive rail shippers, there is no widespread feeling that the railroads are taking undue advantage of such captive situations — at least in terms of service.

> In general, it may be said that a large majority [of shippers] are fairly satisfied with the service they obtain from the various carriers they use; this holds true for all three modes.

> Water, truck and rail are rated in that order. However, since respondents only rated those carriers that they themselves were using, the higher truck score (versus rail) must be understood as a result, to a great extent, of the possibility of selecting the best truckers (as perceived by the shipper) from a relatively wide choice. In other words, a shipper is usually not in a position where he must do business with what he considers to be a poor trucking company.[17]

311

While the Mallen-Pernotte study revealed that shippers reported absolute and relative drawbacks in the services rendered by the railways, as well as by other modes, many of them reflected the basic economic and physical traits of each mode that cannot be eliminated. For example, some recurrent car shortages are inherent in the railroading that necessarily experiences peak and off-peak seasonal and cyclical demands. If sufficient capacity were provided to meet all peak demands, huge investment costs would be incurred and higher rates charged to shippers.[18] Where the supply of specialized cars is deficient, this often reflects low statutory rates and, as well, low levels of railway earnings compared with costs of replacing equipment, especially equipment with seasonal or cyclical demands.

An aspect of rail service not studied in the Mallen-Pernotte study or here is the question of the maintenance of services on uneconomic branch lines. However, this is an issue in countries with liberal regulation, such as Canada, stringent regulation, such as the U.S.A., and complete government ownership, such as Great Britain. The issue of branch line abandonment is one of those difficult instances of the public's interest in preserving the production of goods and/or services which can no longer be produced commercially. Public decisions on these issues should be put into effect with the minimum distortion possible to the allocation of resources through the market process.

Enjoyment of the Full Benefits of Dynamic Technological Competition

In Canada, as in the U.S.A., there has been a long-term expansion of intermodal competition based on the introduction and development of new technologies of transport during the past 75 years, the growth of which has depended in large measure on public investment in ways and terminals and financing from user fees or general taxes. Over several decades, technological competition in transport has been quite effective in improving services, in reducing the cost of transport, in offering shippers and travelers service and rate alternatives, in providing for peak demands and for emergencies caused by war, strikes and weather, and in being responsive to the locational needs of firms, communities and regions. Among the most appreciated and widely enjoyed benefits of technological competition in transport have been faster passenger and goods transport, more comfortable passenger transport and less breakage and damage for fragile and high-value goods, greater flexibility in schedules for passengers and goods transport, and far more service and rate alternatives open to shippers and travelers than during the railway era. Technological competition has also created many social-cost, environmental and conservational problems for society which recently have been given more attention in Canada and elsewhere, but the overwhelming beneficial effects of technological competition over the long run is a matter of common knowledge.

The freedom which the railways have enjoyed since 1967 has assisted the

312

railways materially in introducing new technology because they have had the freedom to introduce the rates or rate structures necessary to make it commercially worthwhile. They have not been inhibited in their pricing proposals for particular shippers by the complaints of other carriers or modes or the complaints of other shippers. There is no doubt that this has yielded material benefits in the effective utilization and development of technology for both the carriers and the shippers. For example, the low-cost movement of sulphuric acid in unit trains has enabled substantial advantages to be derived in the economies of scale in production. Many other volume movements have been associated with similar benefits.

Although no effort was made to determine specifically how much of the gains of productivity in Canadian freight transport in recent years were due to the wider commercial freedom given to the railways in 1967, Transport Canada, in its 1975 Freight Report, published a chart which showed that the Canadian railways had achieved marked gains in productivity between 1956 and 1972. During that period, the index of real net output per person employed by the railways rose from 100 in 1957 to about 300 in 1972; and railway ton-miles per ton of freight car capacity rose from around 7,000 ton-miles in 1962 to more than 11,000 ton-miles in 1972. Transport Canada forecasted "that the railways will continue to increase their productivity, measured in ton miles per constant dollar of operating expenditure, at the rate of about 2.25% per annum."[19] Cited as factors were expected technological gains from introduction of more unit trains, more containerization and piggyback operations, more widespread use of large ships, rail cars and trucks, and the possible introduction of rail electrification. And in the following statement, Transport Canada revealed that technological change, which dynamic competition and commercial freedom logically stimulate, had been the principal source of the major increases in productivity in freight transport in the past:

> Major increases in productivity have been achieved over the past decades by the introduction of more efficient propulsion units (rail dieselization, jet aircraft), larger vehicles (100-ton hoppers, 25,000-ton lakers, jumbo jets, larger, multiple-trailer trucks), improved handling (unit trains, containers, piggyback operations, etc.) and more productive equipment in general.[20]

Transport Canada also indicated that increases in freight-service output with the given infrastructure, such as railway line and terminal facilities, will not be as easily accomplished in the future as in the recent past, because the rising levels of traffic forecast for the future will utilize excess capacity and come up against capacity limitations. This, of course, means that railways will have to be in position to make sizeable capital investments (estimated to be twice to three times the present annual level) to expand capacity at strategic points as well as to substitute more efficient rail cars, train movements, and motive power for existing facilities. Transport Canada made an interesting point as to the future rate implications of the earnings requirements for providing the necessary capacity expansion and desirable technological changes, in the following terms.

> The other major implication of lessening rates of productivity increase is that a major means of stabilizing transportation costs and therefore rates will no longer be as effective in this regard. Rates can thus be expected to rise, in future, more in line with the general cost of living, rather than lagging behind the cost of living as has been the case during the past decades.[21]

Pricing Flexbility Required by the Railways for Viability and Capital Investment

As shown by the sizeable rate increases the railways successfully made during 1975-1976, the present commercial freedom they have is obviously conducive to raising rates to obtain greater revenues and earnings to support, through investment, the technical change and capacity expansion required over the next decade or two. Parenthetically, it also is conducive to reducing rates in those markets where lower, but profitable, rates are essential to meet intermodal or market competition, or where lower rates are necessary to stimulate new enterprises and regional development that promise to be able to contribute profitable business to the railways in the future. Without judging whether the Canadian railways overreached themselves in the 1975-1976 rate increases in terms of the economic situation of some of their shippers or the industries they serve, which the new Section 23 cases in 1976 might suggest, it is clear that essential rate increases were made without regulatory delays and were made in terms of the conditions of particular markets and of particular shippers.

In view of the railway capital needs widely recognized by shippers as well as by Transport Canada, this flexibility in rate adjustments is a real advantage, at least up to the point where the railways can operate with normal competitive returns and make the most productive and essential investments. Of course, the railways will have to avoid raising particular rates so high as to injure their shippers in their ability to produce and market goods and to provide productive employment, or to drive profitable traffic to other modes as has happened to a considerable extent in the U.S.A. due to regulation and general rate increases. Both the need for additional earnings to support investment and the need to avoid unprofitable and uneconomic rates require, too, that the railways examine their competitive and other rates to eliminate real-loss rates, to obtain as much revenue from each item or class of traffic as demand and competitive conditions will justify, and to discourage altogether traffic that cannot pay the relevant marginal costs, or much more than such minimal costs in cases where rail capacity has become insufficient.

Placing the Canadian railways in a better position to price flexibly and sophisticatedly to changing market and general economic conditions, as the 1967 grant of wide commercial freedom has done, does not necessarily mean that the railways will actually earn a competitive level of returns or returns sufficient for commercial viability and essential capital investment. Since 1959, the return on net railway investment for CP is shown in Table 16 to have ranged from a low 2.3 percent in 1962 to a high of 5.6 percent in 1974. Citing the low return of CP, and CN's average net income before interest on debt of a little more than 1 percent on its consolidated assets in 1971 and 1972 and a negative return of 1 percent on shareholders' equity held by the Government of Canada after payment of debt interest, J. Heads commented in a paper before the Transportation Research Forum as follows:

> Canadian experience has shown that freedom from regulation will not necessarily solve the financial problems of the railways. Although the railways have received [some] compensation for services provided as a public duty, particularly in respect of passenger transportation and branch lines, the industry has not been able to generate sufficient funds to produce rates of return which would attract substantial new investment. Theoretically, this can be attributed to a combination of a failure to reduce costs following deregulation; a failure to exploit fully the new flexibility in pricing; and possibly the development of new supply and demand conditions that make it impossible for railways to earn rates of return considered normal in other industries.[22]

To examine fully the theoretical explanations cited by Heads would require a comprehensive and detailed investigation of CP and CN's productivity and cost-reduction records and of the results of their pricing and service policies far beyond the scope of this study. Some comments can be made, however. It is true that railways throughout the western world have confronted difficulty in earning normal rates of return in recent decades other than in times of war or other special demand conditions, and many have been in a deficit position for many years.[23] The rise of new modes of transport whose basic investments have been publicly-owned and financed by special and general taxes has definitely changed the demand and supply conditions in transport in a manner unfavourable to railway profitability. But there are many reasons for the unprofitable performance of the railways, some of which are clearly beyond the control of the railway managements.

Canada, which has released the railways to attempt to earn normal returns and which sensibly operates its publicly-owned CN system with this objective in mind, has set up the market circumstances for testing whether railways, when free largely to operate like other businesses and when managed and operated efficiently, can earn normal returns. The executives of the Canadian railways are confident that they can earn a sufficient rate of return to support the needed expansion of railway capacity. Certainly, since 1969 the CP has achieved a higher return on capital in each successive year until 1975 when the return of the company dropped by 0.8 percent.[24] This record must be viewed against the increase in the cost of capital over the period and the burden placed on the railways by the unsubsidized carriage of statutory grain at a loss and by the performance of passenger services at a loss. Only eighty percent of the passenger loss is covered by a government subsidy (although there is no allowance for subsidizing passenger commuter services). Had the CP received the extra revenue on grain estimated by the Snavely Commission to be necessary to cover long-run variable costs, and had a full subsidy been paid on passenger service, the return on the net railway investment of CP in 1974 would have been 7.8 percent.[25] This return would still have been earned during the second year of the rate freeze on non-negotiated rates, a time when the profits on some long-contract traffic and agreed charges were suffering from the effects of unexpectedly rapid inflation. It is also true that still in 1975 and 1976 the increasing sophistication of the railways in the costing and pricing of their services was causing them to look more closely at the profitability of some of those services.

It seems, therefore, that it was too early to reach conclusions, such as were suggested in the Heads paper, that deregulation and commercial freedom do not solve the financial problems of the railways. As Heads states, it is true that granting commercial freedom alone will not make railways in the modern competitive and varied capital circumstances achieve normal rates of return for competitive industries. But less regulation and wide commercial freedom do provide the railways with the market opportunity to accomplish such a feat, provided Government also relieves them of unprofitable statutory rates, compensates them fully for social transport services, allows them to adjust plant and services in line with present and future traffic demands, and assesses fully economic road and other user fee pricing on competing modes using public facilities.

Conclusions on Economic and Institutional Effects

Dynamic competition and wide commercial freedom for the railways in rate making have not given the Canadian economy, the shippers and the railways the ideal beneficial effects of the ideal states of perfect or pure competition. The reason is plainly that all the conditions required for full competitive efficiency do not hold in railway transport or in transport markets as a whole, partly, because of the large role played by the railways in carrying freight traffic. But this result does not mean that dynamic competition in Canadian freight transport and wide commercial freedom for the railways have failed to attain significant economic and institutional achievements.

In terms of beneficial institutional effects, those conditions have put an end, probably a permanent one, to reliance by the Canadian railways on across-the-board increases in freight rates as a method for taking care of their revenue needs. Adequate revenues are required for continued viable operations, for the investments required by future freight demands and for realization of productivity and service gains from application of new technology. Thus, the many difficulties for shippers, communities and regions, particularly those located great distances from markets, occasioned by the horizontal rate increases after World War II until 1959 have been avoided. This does not mean that rate increases have been, or can be, avoided during periods of general inflation in the economy or when the freight demands exceed, or threaten to exceed, the capacity of railway facilities to handle the traffic offered. It merely means that in the period since 1967 the railways, with the rate flexibility they have been given, have sought the necessary increases in freight rates in a much more sophisticated manner by adjustments related to the demand and supply conditions in particular markets, giving close attention to the competitive alternatives open to shippers, to the effects of rates on the traffic and the needs of the shippers served, and to the carriers' need for making all traffic offerings pay at least the relevant variable and capital replacement costs and as much more as would be consistent with earning an overall normal rate of return. In this respect, the Canadian railways are far ahead of the American railways which still rely heavily on general rate level increases and still confront continuing financial difficulties from loss of traffic to other modes because some of their traffic becomes overpriced relative to the competitive alternatives open to shippers.

Just as wide commercial freedom and liberalized regulation have required the railways to adjust their organizational structure, their research and costing efforts, and their marketing activity to engage successfully in sophisticated competitive pricing, the Canadian shippers, too, have had to rely on themselves more in negotiating with the railways, in looking for alternatives to railway service, and in organizing for countervailing power in their negotiations with the railways. No longer can they utilize delaying tactics before a regulatory body, such as rate suspensions, to avoid solving their own transport problems. While this can often be frustrating to some shippers, there is much evidence that self-reliance has been generally workable in stimulating shipper analysis and presentation of data on alternatives and effects to the carriers, and in obtaining reasonable rate consideration from the railways. Where the railways prove unable to meet or neglectful of shippers' interests, shippers appear to have been successful in finding alternative solutions.

317

In Canada, liberalized regulation and commercial freedom have necessitated reform of the regulatory body. In addition to responsibility for the continuing, although more limited tasks of rate and service regulation, the CTC has important responsibilities in the administration of public policy with respect to subsidization of branch lines and passenger services required in the public interest. The CTC also has important functions in various aspects of transportation research and in providing technical advice to shippers and the Government of Canada.

While all of the ideal results of perfect or pure competition have not been achieved, many of the types of effects and benefits to be expected of workable dynamic competition have been achieved under the liberalized regulation and wide commercial freedom for the Canadian railways. There is evidence that a closer correspondence is gradually taking place between rates and costs and that general freight rate discrimination may be lessening as would be expected from effective competition. More of these desirable results would take place if statutory rates and barriers to railroad facility rationalization in terms of today's traffic needs would be removed, or at least adjusted to allow more profitable and efficient operations to take place. Shippers have a wide economic choice of alternative freight services, not only among road, water and rail services, but also in the significant sense that choices can take place as between high-quality serivce at high rates and low-quality service at low rates, the rates in each instance corresponding fairly closely with costs. Thus, Canada may have avoided an excessive emphasis on service competition at parity rates between road and rail, conditions that have brought huge misallocations of traffic in the U.S.A. and financial difficulties for the railways in that country. Though there have been some shortages of freight cars and delays due to congestion, generally satisfactory freight services have been supplied by the Canadian railways under liberalized regulation and wide commercial freedom. Until 1975 and 1976, these services were supplied at low rate levels, generally, in a period of inflation. Though there can be a question as to whether there was some underpricing of railway service, the Canadian railways have the pricing flexibility, both for meeting intermodal competition and for pricing for sufficient returns, for commercial viability and capital investment. Finally, these conditions appear to be conducive to continued enjoyment of the remarkable benefits of dynamic technological competition in transport.

FOOTNOTES

1. Canada, *National Transportation Act,* 1966-67, c.69, s.2, Section 3.
2. Canada, Transport Canada, *Refinements of Concepts Workshop* (Ottawa: mimeographed, February 19, 1976).
3. Canadian Transport Commission, Railway Transport Committee, *Anti-Inflation Report No. 1, Monitoring of Increases in Railway Freight Rates under the Anti-Inflation Act and Regulations,* August 1976, pp. 9-15, 18-19, and Appendix "D" and Appendix "E".
4. Canada, *Commission on the Costs of Transporting Grain by Rail,* known as the Snavely Commission, Report, Volume 1, October, 1976, p. 93.
5. F.S. Burbidge, President CP Ltd., Speech to the North American Railroad Public Relations Association, June 26, 1975, as reported in *Traffic Notes,* Canadian Industrial Traffic League, September 9, 1975, p. 7.
6. Transport Canada, *Transportation Policy, A Framework for Transport in Canada, Summary Report,* June 1975, p. 15; and *An Interim Report on Freight Transportation in Canada,* June 1975, pp. 14, 21, 26-27 and 51.
7. *An Interim Report on Freight Transportation in Canada, ibid.,* pp. 5 and 21 and figure 10.
8. For an excellent statement on the difficulty of estimating costs, see the *Snavely Commission, op.cit.,* pp. 197-198.
9. James C. Nelson, *Railroad Transportation and Public Policy* (Washington: The Brookings Institution, 1959), pp. 327, 330-332, 337-344 and 373.
10. *Ibid.,* pp. 31-40.
11. Canadian Trucking Association, *Statement of Position on Transportation Policy,* Submission to Transport Canada, May, 1976, p. 5.
12. J.W. Langford, "The Canadian Transport Commission: Restructuring for Effective Regulation of the National Transportation System," *Transportation Policy: Regulation, Competition, and the Public Interest,* edited by Karl M. Ruppenthal and W.T. Stanbury (Vancouver: Centre for Transportation Studies, University of British Columbia, 1977).
13. *Snavely Commission, op.cit.,* p. 46.
14. Interstate Commerce Commission, Bureau of Accounts, *Distribution of Rail Revenue Contribution by Commodity Groups,* 1961 and issues in other years. For discussion of the retarding effects of restrictive rail-motor carrier regulation on the lessening of general rate discrimination on high-value commodities, see Ann F. Friedlaender, *The Dilemma of Freight Transportation Regulation* (Washington: The Brookings Institution, 1969), pp. 57-61.
15. Ann F. Friedlaender, *ibid.,* p. 59; and James C. Nelson, *Railroad Transportation and Public Policy, op.cit.,* pp. 39, 43-44, 46-47, 50-51, 57-60, 116, 133-134, 142-147, 191-192, and 349-353.
16. Ann F. Friedlaender, "Issues in Evaluating Transportation Regulation," an address before the National Symposium on Transportation for Agriculture and Rural America, New Orleans, Louisiana, November 15, 1976, pp. 1, 3 and 6.
17. Bruce Mallen and Jean Francois Pernotte, *Decision Making and Attitudes of Canadian Freight and Cargo Transportation Buyers* (Montreal: Sir George Williams University, June 1972), pp. 24-25.
18. *Ibid.,* p. 27. For peaking traffic flow tendencies, see *An Interim Report on Freight Transportation in Canada, op.cit.,* pp. 10-11 and Exhibits 6 and 7.
19. *An Interim Report on Freight Transportation in Canada, op.cit.,* pp. 21 and Exhibit 10.
20. *Ibid.,* p. 20.

21. *Ibid.,* p. 21. On p. 48, an estimated capital investment requirement for Canadian railways during the 1976-1990 period of $9 billion to $15.7 billion, or approximately $600 million to $1,050 million per year, was given. As noted on pp. 50-51, this creates cash flow problems as the railways have been spending only about $320 million per year in recen years.

22. J. Heads, "Lessons from the Canadian Deregulation Experience," paper given before the Transportation Research Forum, October 10, 1974, pp. 6 and 7.

23. James C. Nelson, *Railroad Transportation and Public Policy, op.cit.,* Chapter 7, pp. 193-230; and Department of the Environment, *Transport Policy, A Consultation Document* (London: Her Majesty's Stationery Office, 1976), Vol. 1, pp. 49-50, and Vol. 2, pp. 77-87.

24. See Table 16, Chapter II.

25. Estimate supplied by Office of Comptroller, CP Ltd., Montreal, December 1976.

CHAPTER X

CONCLUSIONS AND IMPLICATIONS FOR REGULATORY POLICY IN CANADA AND OTHER COUNTRIES

Canada, like other countries has been seeking transport regulatory policies that are compatible with the competitive organization of transport and the competitive transport markets that have become the prominent features of transport in the past half century. In 1967, Canada passed the National Transportation Act, which adopted a competitive philosophy and abandoned in large part the comprehensive regulation that had grown up to deal with the monopoly conditions formerly existing in railway transport, particularly with rate discrimination and oppressive rates. That Act widely extended the commercial freedom of the railways to make rates, subject only to limited rate control to assure that rates are not set below variable costs, that captive shippers can appeal for a maximum fixed rate, and that cases of public-interest discrimination or ommission by the railways can be investigated in appropriate cases by the regulatory body. Except for statutory rates and a rate freeze at the request of the Federal Government, the Canadian railways since 1967 have adjusted their freight rates flexibly in negotiations with shippers and with a minimum of regulatory cases.

The workings and degree of success attained in Canada's experiment with much enlarged commercial freedom for the railways, allowing them to operate and price efficiently in a competitive environment, has been of great interest within Canada as well as in the U.S.A. and other countries. The railways naturally hope that this freedom in the market will enable them to operate more profitably while meeting growing competition from other modes and sources. The shippers generally support this experiment, but some wonder if the forces of competition are always adequate to give them reasonable rates, and some question whether the regulatory controls remaining are sufficient for adequate shipper protection from unjust discrimination and unnecessarily large rate increases during inflationary times. The Western Provinces continue to feel that their industrial development has been retarded by rate difficiencies and discrimination and that competitive forces do not sufficiently limit railway rates,

321

particularly in the Prairies. In the U.S.A., where comprehensive regulation of intercity freight transport has not been relaxed very much and where significant segments of the railway industry are in serious financial straits, there is great interest in whether Canada's wide commercial freedom for the railways, provides a workable model for regulatory change in that country.

The Objectives for This Study

A major purpose of this study was to throw factual and analytical light on the actual workings of railway rate making under the wide commercial freedom and transport competition that exist in Canada. This involved determination of the nature and general extent of the transport competition that prevails in the Canadian economy, with attention to all types of competitive forces, not just to those of an intermodal character. This also involved examination of the way rates have been made by the railways and negotiated between the railways and the shippers, including the organizational devices and procedures that have been developed both by the railways and the shippers to bring about realistic consideration of both carriers' and shippers' needs and to facilitate the full operation of the forces of competition, via the alternatives open to shippers, in railway rate making. An essential part of such analysis is to consider whether the remaining regulation of railway freight rates, affecting those rates not limited sufficiently by competitive forces, has been adequate as an effective substitute for workable competition in such cases.

This Chapter will state the authors' conclusions. They will deal with how competition actually works; whether the arrangements for shipper-carrier negotiations of rates are workable or need some improvement; what types of economic effects have resulted from the dynamic competition that has existed and whether they have been beneficial; and whether the residual regulation of railways rates by the CTC has been effective. In short, it will state the authors' conclusions on the successes or failures of Canada's experiment with reliance on competitive forces to set and limit railway rates under wide commercial freedom and a minimum of regulatory control.

Finally, this Chapter will state the authors' conclusions on the implications of the record with respect to revisions, if any, that may be essential in the current scheme of liberalized but minimal regulation of railway rates in Canada. The authors, of course, are aware that Transport Canada has been considering with carriers and shippers some proposals for making some changes in the present scheme of regulation. The suggestions to be made here will bear on those proposals, but are not to be considered as specifically designed as an evaluation of Transport Canada's proposals. Rather, they are the outcome of this study of how competition has been working under the liberalized regulation since 1967, and of independent factual investigations made of the shipper-carrier negotiating process in specific cases and of possible ways that competition can be extended in some areas. Unavoidably, such inquiries, and the conclusions reached, will have implications for the regional issues over freight rate differences and discrimination and their effect on regional industrial development. However, the main objective of the study was not to deal specifically and in detail with those problems, as they have been addressed by the Snavely and Hall Commissions and by the vast factual studies of the impacts of freight rates on industrial location and development that were conducted by consultant groups after the WEOC meetings in Calgary in 1973.

The implications of this study stated for the U.S.A. and other countries are made in recognition of the importance of regulatory issues in the U.S.A. and in some other western countries. One of the authors has made a number of studies of American regulation and its economic consequences for the railways, for other modes, and in terms of efficient or inefficient transport in that country.

How Transport Competition Works in Canada

The transport competition which has so rapidly and fully developed in freight markets in Canada in recent decades can best be characterized as dynamic competition, in the sense developed by J.M. Clark of Columbia University. It is far from static, as technologies within each mode and between the modes have been constantly changing, the logistical systems and emphases of shippers on service quality have been changing, and the competitive services and other appeals of the alternative carriers and modes have been changing. New carriers, both modal and intermodal, appear on the scene from time to time, particularly in highway transport or in rail-truck combinations. In addition to its dynamic character, competition, as Clark recognized in modern industry, arises in several dimensions, that is, in service quality and differentiation, in selling and rate negotiating appeals, in cost reduction from more efficient technology and methods in producing transport services, and, of course, in price.

Both actual and potential competitive appeals can be made in all those respects and they can present shippers with alternatives to existing services or those of any one mode. Even the shippers can, and do, create alternatives to the railways and other for-hire carriers by engaging in private carrier transport by truck or water. As emphasized by Clark with respect to industrial markets, the pressures from *potential* competition are very real, and often powerful, in transport markets. Also in transport, competitive forces are not limited to direct competition between carriers or modes. As shown in Chapter V, there are also very powerful and widespread forces of market and locational substitutional pressures that impact strongly on railway rates, especially in the case of non-competitive commodity traffic. Only in the limited number of railways in Canadian markets, and in the practice of their conferring on rates, are the conditions for Clarkian workable dynamic competition violated; notwithstanding, intramodal railway competition in service and technology continues,

323

though price competition between the railways is subdued. All in all, transport competition for freight is dynamic, many-faceted, and far more present in Canadian transport markets than is commonly thought. Neglecting all but inter-modal competition markedly short-changes reality.

While not all of the prerequisites for perfect or pure competition exist in Canadian freight markets, the essential ones for workable dynamic competition do obtain widely. The increasing amounts of railway traffic and revenues that come from the competitive-type rates, the competitive commodity rates and the agreed charge rates, as shown in Chapter II, certainly indicate that carrier competition has had a wide impact on railway rates. More and more railway rates have to be competitively set. And when one considers the tremendous volumes of non-competitive commodity traffic that are subject to strong market competition (such as coal, potash and sulphur), it becomes apparent that most Canadian railway traffic today is subject to dynamic competitive forces, an environment in which competition is likely to be effective and workable, though not perfectly so as in the ideal models of perfect and pure competition.

Moreover, as was shown in Chapter III, the organizational and institutional changes made by the railways and by the shippers in recent years have both been responsive to growing competitive elements in transport markets and conducive to dynamic competition working effectively. Though the railways started to reorganize their marketing, research and pricing organizations two decades ago to be in a position to meet and deal with rapidly growing competition, they have increased this emphasis under the wider commercial freedom after 1967. They now analyze their competition and shares of the market, the suitability of their services in terms of the shippers' needs, the variable costs of their services relative to the costs of efficient carriers in other modes or of private transport, and they design price and service offerings to the shippers and make competitive thrusts selectively in particular markets. Each major railway makes thousands of specific cost analyses on competitive traffic in particular markets each year, and makes that cost information available to regional pricing and market staffs. Much decentralization in pricing has occurred, which makes meeting competition more flexible and timely in local situations.

Shippers, the larger ones in particular, have long had traffic managers and rate clerks. In recent years, however, they have developed more sophisticated trans-port and logistical staffs and have engaged in considerable research to find effective alternatives to railway services where service difficulties arise or their transport costs might be lowered. They increasingly measure alternative transport services in terms of their advantages with respect to inventory and warehousing savings as well as with respect to rate savings. Thus, the shippers have increasingly placed themselves in a position to play the competitive game. And as the rate negotiations examined in the case studies for this work have revealed, there is much evidence that, through their own studies of the market and their rate negotiations with the railways, the shippers have been utilizing the existence of the actual and potential competitive alternatives available to them rather effectively in dealing with the railways on rate and service matters. The shippers have been very active in their search for alternatives and they are skillful, individually and in industry groups, in presenting them to the railways. The railways can no longer afford to be sluggish in examining the competitive elements in their markets; indeed, they must respond to them selectively and vigorously by adjustments in their rates and services.

Thus, there are many and varied forces of dynamic competition presently working in Canadian freight markets and they affect, in one way or another almost all of the railway markets. Even in the so-called non-competitive markets, in which large volumes of freight move at so-called non-competitive commodity rates, the cases and illustrations cited in Chapter V reveal that railway rates in those markets are also largely set in terms of competitive influences. Nevertheless, the intermodal and market competitive forces work more forcefully in some markets than in others. Markets which are subject to little or no competitive forces, however, appear to be exceptional in today's Canadian freight markets. The problems which they raise for shippers, arising from freight rate discrimination or railway omissions not in the public interest, can be resolved with the remaining regulatory procedures open to the affected shippers and regions under the National Transportation Act, Railway Act and Transport Act. Except for these limited situations, dynamic competition is omnipresent in Canadian freight markets.

Effects of Dynamic Competition in Canadian Freight Markets

The effects of dynamic competition noted in the preceding Chapter, while not entirely those of perfect or pure competition, are the types of effects that can be expected from effective dynamic competition for shippers, carriers and the general public.

In the first place, the institutional developments and effects that have taken place under the wide commercial freedom for the railways in Canada have been conducive to the effective working of dynamic competition. As noted above, both the railways and the shippers have become well organized internally to negotiate rates and services within a competitive framework, one in which there can be assurance that all actual and potential competitive alternatives will be taken into account. In addition, there has been a notable reduction in reliance on across-the-board rate increases by the Canadian railways, with a distinct substitution of selective rate adjustments in particular markets made in terms of their demand and supply conditions. This selective-market approach in pricing makes dynamic competition more workable, because it avoids the overpricing of railway services in many competitive markets and thus the stimulation of uneconomic competition between the modes. In the U.S.A., where general rate

325

level increases are still relied on as a result of the comprehensive regulation applicable there, the costs of uneconomic competition from the overpricing of many railway services continues, a result that Canada's railways have avoided in favor of sophisticated competitive pricing that is more effective in bringing about efficient traffic allocation and in taking care of both railway and shipper needs. Finally, the grant of wider commercial freedom to the railways and the reduction of detailed regulation has occasioned a reorganization of the regulatory body, the CTC, enabling it to perform the limited regulatory functions that remain significant in today's competitive transport markets. This does not mean that the performance of the CTC in its reduced regulatory responsibilities, in its research and advisory roles, and in its specially assigned technical functions, such as administering the payment of rate subsidies, has been exemplary in all respects. It does mean, however, that Canada has limited the CTC to regulatory functions that do not interfere with the effective workings of dynamic competition in Canadian freight markets today. Again, Canada is ahead of the U.S.A., which has yet to fully adjust ICC regulation in terms of the reduced regulatory requirements under workable dynamic competition.

In the second place, as far as the research done in this study has disclosed, the types of economic effects to be expected from effective dynamic competition do exist under the wide commercial freedom for railways in Canada. Under workable competition, as under perfect competition, rates would tend to come into closer relation to costs and rate discrimination would tend to lessen.

There are several types of evidence which suggests that those tendencies have been operating. First, far more attention has been given by the railways in recent years to assure coverage of relevant unit costs and avoidance of loss rates when competing for traffic, when considering new traffic, or when deciding whether to continue to participate in existing traffic. Though the railways have erred at times in accepting unprofitable traffic by basing rates on original costs rather than replacement costs or by failing to anticipate sufficiently the cost increases due to inflation, government intervention in the form of maintaining low statutory rates has been a more prominent force in the continued carriage of traffic at unprofitable rates. Second, several types of evidence of a statistical nature, though not specifically showing the relationship between rates and relevant costs, do reveal that a result of the dynamic forces of competition is more cost-based rates. The statistical analysis in Chapter II of the factors in railway rates indicate that cost has been a more important factor in rates while values of commodities have been becoming less significant. The Waybill data summarized in that Chapter clearly show that more of the railway ton-miles and revenues have been accounted for by the competitive types of rates as time elapses. They also show that railway rates have not risen to the extent that would be expected from inflation in the economy, an indication that

326

competition was limiting rates severely until the large selective and catch-up rate increases of 1975 and 1976 (after the rate freeze) occurred. As railway rates have become more competitively set, more cost influenced, and less related to the varying elasticities of demand under monopoly conditions, they have necessarily tended to become less discriminating.

Of course, dynamic competition has far from completely eliminated general rate discrimination other than in true joint-cost situations. Nor should it be expected to do so, so long as railways continue with excess capacity, highly fluctuating levels of traffic, and a significant element of fixed costs. In those circumstances which still apply in Canada, a good deal of rate discrimination is essential for the commercial viability of the railways, and its continuance is strengthened by the financial burden placed on the railways by unprofitable statutory rates and passenger train services that are not fully compensated.

Under effective competitive conditions, with many carriers and several modes in freight transport markets, various grades and types of service would be offered from which shippers could choose at prices that would reflect the varying cost of the different types and qualities of services. Under the wide commercial freedom for railways in Canada and the minimum rate standard of variable costs, both the railways and other modes have been free to provide shippers with a wide range of economic choice among the modes based on the costs and the needs of various carriers. And shippers can freely choose whether a superior service at a high rate or an inferior service at a lower rate will best serve their needs, a choice that is often limited in the U.S.A. because of restrictive regulation that promotes parity rates and service competition. In addition, the evidence from the case studies and studies made by other researchers suggests that the level of railway service available to shippers under commercial freedom has generally been satisfactory and sufficient, except for the recurrent car shortages and line blockages due to poor weather or mountain slides, which are more or less inherent in railroading. Where significant shortages of efficient large freight cars have occurred, this has been substantially brought about by unprofitable statutory rates that do not induce and support railway investment for the large flows of traffic involved.

The conditions of wide commercial freedom for Canadian railways are favorable to the continuance of dynamic technological competition, intramodally and intermodally. Such competition in the past has promoted better services, cost and rate economies, and continued effective rate and service rivalry between carriers and modes, with the benefits widely accruing to shippers and the general public. Because large investments in new, efficient equipment and other facilities are often indispensable to service improvements and cost reductions, the freedom that the railways have to design rates has substantially assisted them in introducing new technology. In the past, rapid productivity gains have been made by the railways, largely from the technological improvements they have made. Transport Canada has reported that very large investment needs exist for the Canadian railways if they are to avoid a lessening in productivity gains and rates rising faster than the cost of living in the future. Obviously, the capital requirements for those investments will require profitable operations by the railways.

Finally, the commercial freedom of the railways has been conducive to the pricing flexibility and sophistication that seem essential if the Canadian railways are to generate cash flows required to make the investments that will be needed to continue making productivity gains and to expand their facilities where needed. Rates of return have not been high for the Canadian railways, but, at least for the CP, some improvement has recently occurred. With government action to remove the losses of statutory rates, to compensate the railways fully for rendering social transport services required by government edict in the public interest, and to adjust user fees to assure that the modes using public facilities pay fully for way services, the Canadian railways, with their commercial freedom continuing, should be able to obtain the earnings level necessary for the attraction of capital for urgent and well-paying investments.

The Implications for Regulatory Revision in Canada

The workings and the institutional and economic effects of dynamic competition under commercial freedom for the railways, as provided by the 1967 legislation, thus appear to have been generally beneficial to the railways, the shippers and the general public. Nevertheless, there have been some issues and problems which shippers and regional interests have carried to the CTC for regulatory investigation and action, though such regulatory appeals have been minimal in number in the last decade, as mentioned in earlier Chapters. This fact seems to be a further indication that the effects of dynamic competition have been beneficial and that the incidence of its benefits has been rather general. It is possible, though, that there would have been more regulatory appeals for fixed maximum rates had not the proof of captivity to railways been so rigorous and the legislated maximum rate so high. Moreover, as to Section 23 appeals to the CTC, the requiremens for showing a *prima facie* case of injury to the public interest and the time and cost involved in hearings and the presentation of evidence may have limited the number of appeals. Another explanation, though, might be that the dynamic competitive forces under wide commercial freedom and rate negotiation procedures induced the railways to keep their rate increases relatively low when adjusting to inflation, so that shippers did not have urgent reasons to appeal more frequently to the CTC either on Section 23 grounds of public interest or for a fixed maximum rate under Section 278 of the Railway Act.

The Effectiveness of the Regulatory Role of the CTC in Shipper Protection

In any event, the discussion in Chapter VIII deals comprehensively with the CTC record in the three major Section 23 appeal cases that have been heard, decided or resolved by compromise after hearings and investigation by the CTC. There is no need to summarize here the issues, facts, decisions and other outcomes of those cases, *The Rapeseed Case, The Prince Albert Pulp Company Case* and *The Newsprint Case,* or the one maximum rate appeal, *The Domtar Case.* The last case was also reviewed and commented on in Chapter VIII.

Some useful things can be said about these cases at this point. There were some questions about the time that was involved and the cost to the parties and to the Government of regulatory proceedings, and there was some dissatisfaction by the Prairie interests and the Prairie Provinces in the application of the Section 23 relief only to rapeseed meal in *The Rapeseed Case.* Nevertheless, the CTC handled the Section 23 cases competetently in terms of the facts involved and the limited extent of its regulatory authority over the American portion of international rates or American rates for hauls wholly within that country. The decisions or other outcomes of those appeal cases were in line with what might logically have been expected of a regulatory body in view of the facts and factors involved. Substantial relief to the Prairie milling interests was granted in the CTC decision in *The Rapeseed Case* as to the relationship between the rate on rapeseed meal and rapeseed, that is, the rate to Central Canada on rapeseed meal was ordered brought down to the rapeseed level. This relationship should lessen the incentives to ship rapeseed in raw form for milling into meal in Central Canada near the location of the significant markets. In *The Prince Albert Pulp Company Case,* the joint action of the CTC (largely through negotiations) and the ICC lowered the rates from Prince Albert, Saskatchewan to the American Midwest in relation to the rates from competing Alberta mills, thus giving the Prince Albert location a rate advantage for being substantially nearer to those markets. Finally, in *The Newsprint Case,* the newsprint mills in Eastern Canada did not obtain the full relief they sought from differential rates to significant U.S.A. eastern and midwestern markets. But this was because the ICC, not the CTC, had the power to make the critical decision of whether the American domestic railway rates were unduly discriminating in allowing the new and expanding southern-U.S.A. mills to market their products in border cities along the Ohio River and in other eastern- and midwestern-U.S.A. markets. As this was a domestic rate issue wholly under the jurisdiction of the ICC, and the decision reached by the ICC seemed in accord with both the facts and the Interstate Commerce Act's standards for unduly discriminatory railway rates, it would be difficult to conclude that the regulatory process in Canada had failed in this case. Competition from truckers and barge lines had an impact on the American rates from the southern-U.S.A. mills to the border-city markets along the Ohio River, while this competitive force was absent or of less intensity from the

Canadian mills. The American railways responded to this difference in competitive conditions and to their own incentives for giving developing mills the opportunity to obtain market shares reflecting the closeness of the southern-U.S.A. mills to the domestic markets. While the outcome was not favorable to the Central and Eastern Canada mills, it must be recognized that, in such circumstances, there likely can be no regulatory solution for their export marketing problems.

As the one maximum-rate case under Section 278 remained unresolved, with no decision from the CTC and with no pressure from the shipper for a decision, the regulatory process was not fully utilized. Hence, little useful comment can be made on that case, except to say that the CTC might well be better off had it handed down a decision or made some announcements on the progress of the case. A question about this area of regulation in Canada that is more interesting than that of whether the regulatory influence was entirely helpful concerns why, in almost ten years, there have not been more appeals for maximum rates under Section 278. The answer is not solely because the maximum level is so high.

Certainly, as to the Section 23 cases, the conclusion can be reached that the CTC responded to the appeals made, dealt comprehensively and thoroughly with the issues, studied and heard the facts, and made decisions or exerted influence of a sound and useful kind. That the CTC's role in those cases has been criticized as being insufficiently responsive to shipper appeals, as requiring too much time and cost for hearings, investigation of facts and resolution of the legal issues, and as imposing to difficult *prima facie* tests for hearing an appeal on its merits, is understandable. Those things that could be done to induce a more responsive attitude by the CTC, to make it easier for shippers to gain access to the regulatory adjudication of meritorious rate issues, and to make the entire process less time-consuming and formal while preserving due process, should be done. However, to deal further with the procedural issues of CTC regulation is a legal and technical matter beyond the scope of this study.

Consistency of CTC Regulatory Role with
Dynamic Competition and the 1967 Act

The authors conclude that, with respect to the cases which the CTC has heard, investigated and acted upon, the limited regulation of railway rates and rate relationships contemplated under the 1967 Act has been working about as well as might be expected. If the process and legal tests for appeals to the CTC have limited the number of appeals to serious issues affecting true captive-shippers and public-interest-discrimination and omission situations, this is precisely what the Parliament must have had in mind in reducing regulation from the former comprehensive restrictive type of control to the liberalized residual regulation in Canada today. If the procedures for making and investigating rate appeals under the standards of Section 23 and Section 278 have unduly limited the number of meritorious cases that do go before the CTC, then some moderate adjustments in legal procedures might be called for to facilitate more cases of the meritorious type being heard and investigated by the CTC. However, having limited grounds for appeals to the regulatory body and limited regulatory and investigatory powers in the hands of the CTC with respect to railway rates is truly consistent with the overall workability of dynamic competition under wide commercial freedom that this study has found in Canada. Therefore, care would have to be exercised to avoid opening the regulatory gates to hundreds or thousands of rate complaints each year, to rate suspensions, and to other aspects of comprehensive restrictive regulation that are hardly compatible with the effective working of dynamic transport competition and the financial and commercial viability of the Canadian railways.

The need expressed here for the exercise of caution, even in any moderate modification of the rate regulation established in 1967, is based fundamentally on the principal findings of this study. They are: (1) that the dynamic competition in freight transport in Canada under the present wide commercial freedom for the railways has been workable overall during the past decade, in spite of the considerable inflation that has occurred in the Canadian economy, the continuation of unprofitable statutory rates, the 1973-74 rate freeze, and the fact that shippers primarily have to resort to rate negotiations with the railways and to depend on their own initiatives to develop alternatives for solution of their rate problems; and (2) that where serious public-interest issues about railway rate relationships have arisen that affect shippers in reaching their markets and affect communities and regions interested in industrial development, and where such issues cannot be resolved by negotiations with the railways, appeals to the CTC, though they have been very few, have been effective in giving regulatory protection to the shippers, communities and regions involved and in obtaining the reasonable rate adjustments that could be expected under the factual and legal circumstances. In short, both dynamic competition and residual, but limited, regulation have been working well in Canada, though not without some problems that may need regulatory or legislative attention.

Strong Shipper Support for the Philosophy and Workability of Limited Rate Control of the 1967 Act

It may be of considerable interest that the Canadian Industrial Traffic League has sounded a similar note of caution to Transport Canada in commenting in November 1976 on certain regulatory policy proposals that Transport Canada had previously circulated among shippers and shipper groups for comments. The League strongly endorsed commercial freedom for railway rates and retention of the existing regulatory controls without much enlargement. This is apparent from the following statement of the League in its submission to Transport Canada:

331

The League has continually supported the approach, under the National Transportation Act, 1967, where National Policy has been kept separate from National Transportation Policy. C.I.T.L. is fearful that more Government involvement in transportation and use of transportation to attain national objectives, may very well put too much reliance on transportation for the development of various regions in Canada. This could lead to disproportionate benefits being expected from transportation alone and could possibly detract from the real needs of a region.

The League does have concern over the degree of involvement by Government in attaining the objectives stated. The League is convinced that these objectives, to a large degree, are being realized under the National Transportation Act in response to the normal pressures of the competitive system, today. The League believes that it is chiefly in those areas where competition is not an influencing factor that Government should play a role in the attainment of its objectives. As stated before, C.I.T.L. believes this is the spirit of the present Act.

The League cannot help being concerned that possible changes in the Transportation Policy, the National Transportation Act and other relevant Acts might be made without due regard to consequences that could result from a completely needless upheaval of a transportation system that is generally working well for everyone concerned.[1]

The C.I.T.L. stated its opposition to basic legislative change in the existing railway rate regulation with respect to regulatory prescription of maximum/minimum rate levels in specific terms. In its statement on this subject, this powerful group of industrial shippers cautioned against re-introduction of the restrictive regulatory influences that have been associated with comprehensive rate regulation, such as those that existed before the 1967 Act. Also made clear is the League's belief that rate making under the normal influences of the market place gives adequate protection to all concerned, if regulatory protection is given to captive shippers. The League's comments were as follows:

The League wishes to record with you that it is unalterably opposed to formula rate making per se, and that it firmly believes rate making under the normal influences of the market place is the best method for all concerned, with protection being provided to Captive Shippers.

C.I.T.L. is of the opinion there is no justification for the

332

expansion of a Maximum Rate Formula to other than Captive Shippers; that Transport Canada must determine how a Captive Shipper should be clearly defined and should direct their attention to this vital problem.

The League's concern over the proposal to expand any Maximum Formula approach to all shippers is the real possibility of some shippers indiscriminately approaching the Canadian Transport Commission, in this regard, thus placing an extra burden on this regulatory body.

The League can agree that there is a need to develop an adequate definition of railway costs, one that is administratively feasible to implement. C.I.T.L. cannot quarrel with the suggestion that the 1969 Railway Costing Order be revised and updated for this purpose.

The League has no objection to the proposal to establish a Minimum Rail Rate Provision based on Variable Costs, as redefined under the new proposed Costing Order, to ensure that rail rates are compensatory to the railways. In other words, C.I.T.L. agrees in principle with the present provisions of the National Transportation Act that a rail freight rate "shall be deemed to be compensatory when it exceeds the variable cost of the movement of traffic concerned as determined by the Commission." However, the League does question the need for enforcement by means of penalties against the railways.[2]

In raising questions with regard to proposals for changes in the determination of fixed maximum rates for captive shippers, the C.I.T.L. also showed concern that rules to lower the maximum rate to somewhat below 150 percent above variable costs for a 30,000-pound carload might seriously reduce railway revenues. And the League also questioned the view "that long/short haul rates are necessarily discriminatory in railway freight pricing," and expressed fear that a prohibition of the practice would cause a substantial diversion of traffic from the railways, interfere with natural forces of the market place and remove the ability of shippers and railways to negotiate rates that would insure that both would participate in valuable business. If the long- and short-haul rate practice were to be ruled out except for exceptions required by competition, the League would be concerned over the restrictiveness of the CTC criteria for granting exceptions and whether they could be granted expeditiously to facilitate competition and shipper measures to protect their markets.

All in all, the C.I.T.L. was not favorable to much change in the regulatory powers and standards currently in force under the 1967 Act. On the other hand, the League heartily endorsed proposals to speed up Section 23 appeals and to enable the CTC to be flexible and more informal in its procedures; but the League warned against a proposal to authorize the Governor in Council to provide policy directives to the CTC. The following statements of the League clearly reveal those views:

> The League supports an amendment to Section 23 of the National Transportation Act to establish time limits for the handling of freight rate cases, under this section, at the "prima facie" stage.

> C.I.T.L. endorses the proposals to enable the Canadian Transport Commission to be more flexible and informal in its hearings, stipulating that the C.T.C. is not bound by unnecessary legal or technical rules of evidence.

> The C.I.T.L. is unsure of the intent and ramifications of the proposal to authorize the Governor in Council to provide policy directives to the Canadian Transport Commission. In any case, the League can certainly agree that any directive to the C.T.C. should not be relative to any specific case pending before this regulatory body.[3]

The several statements quoted above constitute strong endorsement by the organization representing Canada's industrial shippers for the policy of leaving the limited regulation under the 1967 Act almost intact. However, this powerful shipper group would favor reasonable measures to make cost determinations more useful and readily available for regulatory and other purposes, and to make access to the CTC easier, to make the procedural requirements for regulatory cases more informal and easier to meet, and to speed up the CTC determinations of whether to grant an appeal for investigation and adjudication, especially as to Section 23 cases. Implicit in this endorsement is the view that the shippers, through rate negotiations with the railways, and with the aid of the pervasive dynamic forces of competition in the market place, can continue to obtain reasonable and nondiscriminatory rates from the carriers, quick adjustments in rates needed to meet their competitive threats, and careful consideration by the railways of their rate and logistical needs.

The observations might be made, however, that many of the C.I.T.L. members are large firms, well capable of developing alternatives to railway service and of presenting their well-researched cases to the railways. Those firms are often located in the larger centers of the developed regions of Canada where they enjoy intramodal and intermodal alternatives and where market competition may also be an effective force. On the other hand, the case interviews for this study revealed situations where agricultural shippers, who often market through cooperatives or other large-scale agencies, also enjoy the advantages of having actual and potential alternatives to the railways and have been capable in negotiating rates successfully with the railways. Small shippers have access to agreed charge rates negotiated by large shippers with the railways by signing an intent to be included. There are, of course, industry organizations to represent small shippers. Notwithstanding, there are some truly captive shippers, including large corporations in the resource-based industries, that are located on only one railway and far from their markets. Such shippers often have plants in remote areas near resources that become diminished when processed, and are engaged in the process of mining, refining or milling at locations that are beyond the range of efficient trucking. The League is certainly aware of those situations, and would retain fixed maximum rates and Section 23 controls to enable such shippers to call upon the CTC for regulatory remedies if the railways overprice their services in terms of shipper commercial and competitive necessities and prove to be intractable in rate negotiations.

Although the sizeable rate increases during 1975 and 1976, which the railways have deemed essential to their financial viability, have stimulated some additional Section 23 cases to be filed with the CTC,[4] the case interviews did not disclose many captive-shipper or other situations in which the shippers could not negotiate reasonable limits upon rate increases, a time schedule for their gradual application, or other arrangements to reduce the adverse effects on their businesses of the rate increases.

Strong Railway and Trucking Support for
Limited Rate Regulation under the 1967 Act

The railways, like the shippers, have much at stake in the extent, practicability and effects of rate regulation. Their commercial and financial viability is directly involved, and their futures as dynamic, well-managed, and technologically efficient concerns are at risk. The Canadian railways strongly endorse the continuance of the wide commercial freedom and limited rate regulation established in 1967 as essential to their finding basic solutions for their competitive-earnings and captive-investment problems. In a recent interview Dr. R.A. Bandeen, President of the CN, stated:

> ... I think the legislation of 1967 (National Transportation Act) is by and large pretty good. It was considered at that time to be the most advanced in the world in regulating transportation, and it still is to a large extent. It gave a degree of freedom on the rate side and in certain aspects of the operation which I think will eliminate the need for future commissions in that area.
>
> It also enunciated a principle which I think is important, that if a non-commercial service is required for national purposes, the government should pay for it. That principle has

335

been applied to anything that has occurred since then, and I
think future situations that may arise will be met in that
fashion. The government will meet with the carriers, shippers,
customers and other people involved, and determine on a
policy of underwriting the situation.

The difficulty is the old situations that existed before the
NTA. How do we move to put them on the same basis? This is
really the difficulty with all the commissions that are going on
right now. But the situations are being tackled. Old obligations
that have developed historically to run non-commercial
operations are being tackled one at a time — the holds on
branch lines in Western Canada, the Crowsnest grain.[5]

In connection with government requests for rate freezes, Dr. Bandeen stated:

... that is something that I doubt we'll get into, I hope we
won't get into, again. If a situation occurs in the future, I hope
the price will be discussed in advance, and the method of
payment. I certainly don't think CN will knowingly get into a
non-commercial operation in the future without having
established the ground rules in advance.[6]

Like railways in other countries, the Canadian railways have had to adjust to
the coming of new modes, new technological competition, and the growing
insistence of shippers on being rendered faster, more dependable, and more
flexible service. With labor and capital intensiveness, the Canadian railways have
had especially difficult problems during recent wage, interest-rate and general
price inflation, and they have had, in addition, the special problem of having to
render large blocks of freight service at unprofitable statutory rates and to
provide some social services of transport for the public at losses which were not
fully compensated by the government. Notwithstanding all of those problems,
the Canadian railways have maintained financial viability during the last decade
and have found their commercial freedom in rate making quite helpful in doing
so. Though not earning adequate competitive returns in their railway operations,
they express greater hopes for their future under existing liberalized regulation
and commercial freedom than under any return to comprehensive regulation and
limited commercial freedom. The present freedoms of the Canadian railways in
the market place are the envy of the American railways.

Consequently, both of the significant parties directly experiencing dynamic
competition under wide commercial freedom want those conditions to be
continued. Transport Canada and the Parliament would have to show real
evidence of the failures of those conditions during the decade since 1967 to have
a persuasive case for making basic change in existing legislation to enlarge the
regulatory role of the CTC and to move back toward comprehensive, detailed

and restrictive regulation. This study did not find such evidence in the actual workings of dynamic competition in Canadian freight transport under the present wide commercial freedom for the railways.

As noted in Chapter IX, the Canadian Trucking Association, too, has endorsed the operation of the 1967 legislation, as it applies to railways, as beneficial to the trucking industry as well as to the railways. The truckers apparently believe that it assures them that the railways, including the nationalized CN, will be required to stand on their own feet under wide commercial freedom; also, the truckers believe that they are well protected from any predatory rate competition by the minimum rate standard that railway rates must be in excess of variable costs. As noted elsewhere, they have the right to protest competitive railway rates for which they have evidence indicating they might be below variable cost. There have been few protests or inquiries of that sort to the CTC.

Of course, there are problems, in a country with the geography and scattered resources of Canada, in obtaining sufficient and efficient transport for the northern underdeveloped regions. Comprehensive and detailed regulation of the railways, however, cannot make them more capable of assisting, via low rates, in the development process in such areas. This is because the railways can no longer obtain, under the dynamic competition to which they are subject, the high profits in their operations in the southern developed corridor of Canada that would be necessary for use in cross-subsidizing railway service and extensions in the remote and less-developed areas. Nor, if they were able to do so, would it be economically desirable for government to influence the railways to assist regional development in this way rather than to use public subsidy funds. Governmental subsidies that are well conceived and administered, and limited to the amounts truly essential for the purpose, would be a far more effective way to help development in the northern regions.

The Problems of the Prairie Provinces' Concerns with Railway Rates

In countries like Canada, Australia and the U.S.A., the regions depending largely on extractive industries naturally compare the incomes, job opportunities, and population growth in their home regions with those indices of economic well-being in the industrial and highly populated regions of the nation. And noting less industrial development in the home regions, they tend to seek to attract processing and manufacturing industries, too. Where these do not develop as rapidly as anticipated or not at all, the barriers to fuller industrialization are looked at. Differences in railway freight rates, whether they involve undue discrimination or just the greater distance from and to markets, easily become, in the minds of those interested in regional development, *the* barrier to the desired development. Because the railways formerly had much monopoly power over rates and services, and the rationale for the complicated rate structures was

337

hard to comprehend without sustained study, the belief that freight rate differences, or anomolies, were responsible for retarded industrial development spread and took on a political flavor.

So it was with the Prairies in Canada. Many people and the provincial governments in the Prairies have long contended that freight rate differences and discrimination against Prairie locations have retarded or prevented the development of processing, manufacturing and commercial businesses that otherwise would have occurred there.[7] The nature of their rate complaints have been summarized in Chapters I, II, and VIII. The dissatisfaction with freight rates has prompted the Prairie interests and provinces to take a vigorous role before the Board of Transport Commissioners in horizontal rate-increase cases and in other railway rate proceedings prior to 1967. Their efforts have sought to prevent burdensome effects on Prairie enterprises and to lessen or eliminate long- and short-haul rate discrimination and other rate differences regarded as undue discrimination that were thought to limit artificially the industrial opportunities of the Prairie region. Moreover, Prairie interests took active roles before several Royal Commissions on Transportation, including the MacPherson Commission, in seeking regulatory policies that would limit the rate differences and anomolies of which they complain. Some gains have been attained in the elimination of unjust discrimnation through regulatory action, a recent example being the CTC's decision in *The Rapeseed Case.* But the Prairie rate complaints have continued, and from their point of view, have been insufficiently resolved.

The issues over the continuance of rate anomolies under liberalized regulation and wide commercial freedom became hot political issues in 1973, at the WEOC meetings in Calgary. One outcome of the discussions between the Western Provinces, and Federal officials, including Prime Minister Trudeau, was the financing of large-scale consulting studies to ascertain the extent to which freight rate differences might logically or factually influence industry not to locate in the Prairies. Large sums were allocated by the Governments for those studies. The study by P.S. Ross *et al,* as noted elsewhere in this work, found that transport rate costs were generally only a small percentage of the final destination value of processed or manufactured commodities; and that except for a rather limited number of types of industrial production, railway rates could not be the determining factors in industrial location decisions affecting the Prairies.[8] The subsequent MPS Associates study, based on estimating the freight rate cost of identical industrial plants located in the Prairies and Central Canada, did reveal that, for serving the national market, a plant located in the Prairies would generally occasion higher transport costs in shipping its products to the major Canadian markets, compared with a comparable plant located within Central Canada. This, however, was basically due to extra costs occasioned by the greater distance to markets from the Prairies than from Central Canada as the largest markets were in the latter populous area; it was not basically due to

338

inequitable or anomolous freight rate differences.[9]

The implications of both of those comprehensive studies were basically negative to the idea long held in the Prairies that freight rate differences and discrimination have actually been the controlling factor in whether industrial plants locate in the Prairies or not. The study by P.S. Ross *et al.* however, did find a number of types of industrial products for which further analysis of all the industrial location factors, including freight rates, might disclose that some industrial opportunities for development in the Prairies would be encouraged to an extent by freight rate adjustments. The MPS Associates study, clearly shows that the higher rates for locations in the Prairies result from the higher transport costs occasioned by greater distances to the large national markets, cast attention to the fact that, so far as transport is concerned, the real barrier to further industrial development in the Prairies is distance to markets, not anomolies or unjust discrimination in freight rates. What those and other studies have accomplished, then, is to place emphasis on the need to pinpoint the rather few rate relationships that truly may be a barrier to industrial development in Western Canada.

This does not mean that the Prairies do not have some legitimate complaints concerning the effects of some railway rate differences and relationships on their industrial and job opportunities. This was shown by *The Rapeseed Case* and *The Prince Albert Pulp Company Case.* There may be some long-short haul rate relationships, once justified by import or other competition affecting the Pacific Coastal cities but not the Prairie cities, that may need revision because of changed competitive circumstances or because the railways erred in adjusting the rates lower than necessary at the port cities and higher than reasonably justified at the Prairie cities. The record of the CTC since the 1967 Act reveals, however, that for the most part regulatory remedies already exist, in Section 23, for railway rate relationships that conflict with the public interest or other standards. Effort to make the filing and hearing of Section 23 appeals more rapid and practicable would help in redressing rate relationships that unduly handicap industrial development in specific cases in the Prairies. How to lessen the concerns of Prairie intersts that long- and short-haul discrimination in railway rates exist in cases unwarranted by competitive conditions, without placing undue constraints on the ability of the railways to respond to competitive forces, is complicated, and this study has not reviewed all the facts and factors that would have to be considered in reaching a conclusion on what should be done in the way of legislation. As the C.I.T.L. has stated, because the competitive ability of Canadian shippers and industries are involved as well as the ability of the railways to participate in traffic, the issues should be carefully studied before drastic changes in the existing regulations are made concerning long- and short-haul rate relationships.

The agricultural and other interests in the Prairies have long had the advantage of the low and unprofitable statutory rates on grain and related products. On the other hand, the railways and other shippers, particularly those of manufactured and processed goods, have experienced the disadvantages of those rates. The railways have encountered difficulties in financing more efficient railway equipment and added capacity. And the shippers of industrial products have possibly experienced higher rates on high-value products to cross-subsidize the statutory-rated traffic, as well as instances of inadequate railway equipment and capacity for shipment of their products. There is also evidence that the low statutory rates, themselves, have encouraged the flow of Prairie materials to Central Canada for processing there, rather than in the Prairies. What would be of assistance in solving these problems would be for the Government to remove the cross-subsidy to the statutory traffic in some appropriate way. This could be done by eliminating statutory rates and allowing those rates to be adjusted on commercial considerations as in the case of other traffic, and, if need be, by paying Governmental subsidies to the direct beneficiaries of the current statutory rates as long as that may be deemed desirable for the economy of Canada and in the public interest. The recent report of the Snavely Commission could serve as a basis for progress with respect to statutory rates. Then, the railways' need for rate discrimination would be lessened.

Considerations for the Improvement of the Working of Dynamic Competition

During the research for this study a number of means have become apparent by which improvements can be brought about in the working of dynamic competition in transportation markets under limited regulation. Some suggestions are made in various chapters, but it is appropriate to provide a brief synopsis here. It is important to emphasize that these are suggestions of means by which improved efficiency could be achieved and, while the merit of some proposals can be agreed on generally without further study, the merit of others can only be established after full and careful study. The suggestions cover a wide spectrum of phenomena which, for convenience, can be dealt with under two headings: (1) means to improve the rate making and negotiation process; and (2) means to improve competitive conditions in Canadian rail freight markets.

Means to improve the rate making and negotiating processes. The suggestions for improving the rate making and negotiating processes are diverse and reflect the diverse nature of the activities. First, the railways should make a greater effort than they have in the past to ensure that shippers are aware of railway officers to contact for the purpose of discussing rates, whether or not the notices of rate changes are sent out through the Canadian Freight Association. Second, the Canadian Transport Commission should develop, and subsequently maintain, railway cost indices. These should be developed in conjunction with the railways and shippers with a view to their use as bases for rate escalation clauses in long-term contracts. They should not be considered as providing a basis for normal changes in freight rates or the periodic revision of rates under long-term contracts. Third, since perceptions are important, the Canadian Transport Commission should drop the designation "non-competitive" from its description of "normal" commodity rates in the *Waybill Analysis*. Fourth, the railways and Transport Canada must ensure that the cost of major capacity investments in particular regions are, and are seen to be, financially viable on commercial grounds so that shippers in other regions do not believe they are being called on to pay cross-subsidies. This applies especially to system improvements where statutory-rated grain is a major component of the traffic. Fear of such cross-subsidy can be a real source of concern to shippers facing rising freight rates. Fifth, shippers should ensure that applications to the Canadian Transport Commission for leave to appeal under Section 23 of the National Transportation Act "put a convincing case for the need for a hearing"[10] in terms of the financial and economic implications of a railway omission, act or rate. It is not enough to complain that a freight-rate increase is so high as to be unreasonable. If the Canadian Transport Commission is to be more responsive it must be able to see a basis for a shipper's complaint in terms of commerical and economic effects and not be left wondering if the application is really a part of the negotiating process. Sixth, and last, shippers and the railways should give consideration to the use of further non-judicial proceedings to resolve commercial differences. This idea appears to have some support among shippers, railway officials, and government officials and deserves brief elaboration.

When negotiations between shippers and carriers break down, use of a third party may be an efficient means to seek a satisfactory conclusion. Such an approach should not be viewed as "a cheap Commission" but as an opportunity for a third party, familiar with the economics and practical matters of transport, to participate either by holding discussions to assist the parties in reaching agreement, or by carrying out a study and making recommendations, or both. Such work could be done by an independent transport economist, by the rate-consultant officers of the Canadian Transport Commission, or by appointment of a person under Section 81 of the National Transportation Act. The approach would be most likely to succeed in cases involving one shipper or one group of shippers and the railways. It would be less likely to be of assistance when market competition gives rise to conflicting interests between railways and between shippers.

Means to improve competitive conditions in rail freight markets. Little restrictive regulation exists on the working of competition between the railways and other modes of transport in Canada. However, restrictions are placed on the amount of intramodal railway competition as noted in Chapter VII. These restrictions warrant study. First, there is no doubt that changes are needed in the rate for interswitching as set down in General Order T-12 of the Board of

Transport Commissioners, and it seems desirable to undertake a study to determine the appropriateness of the four-mile interswitching limit set down in the same order. Second, it is not clear that in today's conditions the railways should be given the exclusive power to decide if they will make rates in common or if they will compete, as is given to them by Section 279 of the Railway Act. Third, shippers are hindered from taking advantage of services available over American lines by Section 382 of the Railway Act. The need for this protection warrants study, especially if Canadian rail rates are forced to rise because of capacity limitations on Canadian lines.

Conclusions on Implications for Regulatory Policy

The shortcomings of this study result from having inadequate data for a detailed analysis of some questions; its strengths lie in its close look at how dynamic competition works and how rates are negotiated between railways and shippers. The study's final conclusions can be stated simply. First, the dynamic competition in Canadian freight transport under the wide commercial freedom for the railways provided by the 1967 Act has proved workable in promoting efficient transport, sophisticated and efficient pricing of railway services, adequate service for the most part, competitive levels of railway rates, and some lessened rate discrimination in railway pricing, as well as in maintaining the commercial and financial viability of the Canadian railways. The economic results have not been perfect, but they have been good. Second, dynamic competition and wide commercial freedom have been conducive to the railways and the shippers making the institutional changes that are essential for the making of freight rates that conform to competitive standards of efficient pricing under today's conditions in Canadian freight transport. Third, the residual and liberalized regulation of railway rates retained in the National Transportation Act of 1967 has proved to be reasonably workable and to meet reasonably the need for regulation of railway rates under today's conditions. However, some changes can be made to improve the access to the Canadian Transport Commission and to make regulatory appeals easier to make and regulatory investigations and proceedings less time-consuming and costly. Finally, this study does not find that there is any need for Canada to return to comprehensive, detailed, and restrictive regulation of railway rates.

Some Implications for Regulation in Other Countries

Although the U.S.A. preserves privately-owned railways to a far greater extent than does Canada, that neighboring country has experienced similar problems with respect to its railways and some unique problems as well. The American railways, too, have lost much of their market share to other modes. They also have had to face dynamic intermodal and market competition, and, with so many railways, considerable intrarailway competition as well. They have had to adjust to those technological and competitive conditions, and to water

342

carrier competition operating without payment of user fees, far more than in Canada. To a greater extent than the Canadian railways before 1967, the American railways have had their flexibility in competitive pricing severely handicapped by comprehensive and detailed restrictive regulation. This regulation continues except for some modest relaxation and provisional commerical freedom granted by the Railroad Revitalization and Regulatory Reform Act of 1976, as described in Chapter VIII. Uniquely, the American railways have had protective regulatory influences that have misallocated high-value traffic from them to other modes. Many influential people, including economists, believe that the American railways would be far better off under wide commercial freedom similar to that which has existed in Canada since 1967 than they have been under their current highly regulated conditions.

The Canadian experiment reveals that wide commercial freedom does not place shippers generally at a disadvantage in dealing with the railways, although there is the problem of having some captive shippers. Shippers generally obtain adequate service, and innovative services, at competitive rates. The Canadian experience also shows that commercial freedom for the railways can be compatible with the legitimate role and interests of alternative modes. There is little evidence that dynamic competition under wide commercial freedom in Canada has led to ruinous or predatory competition under the variable-cost standard for minimum railway rates. It would seem, therefore, that the success of the Canadian wide commercial freedom for the railways under liberalized rate regulation gives some real assurance that liberalization of railway rate regulation in the U.S.A. might be highly workable for that country as well. It might, by promoting flexible and efficient railway pricing and by reducing the need for horizontal general rate increases, improve considerably the market position of the railways, particularly for medium- and long-haul manufactured-goods traffic, and thus their financial viability over the long run. It might also make a considerable contribution toward reduction in the economic costs of regulation, including those from misallocation of traffic and resources within the transport sector.

Most other countries principally have government-owned railways, in many cases operating with large annual deficits. But for these countries, too, the issue of the extent to which government intervention is desirable in setting freight rates is important.[11] For them, the Canadian experience can reinforce the need for arrangements to compensate the railways from public funds for the losses occasioned by the continued rendering of social, non-remunerative transport services. It also can throw light on some of the ultimate consequences of governmental holddowns of railway rates, by statutory or other influences, on capital formation and on the provision of efficient equipment and sufficient facilities. Finally, the fact that Canada's nationalized railway, the CN, has been subject to the commercial and management rules applicable to an efficient privately-owned railway might serve as a model for improving the performance and financial viability of nationalized railways in other countries.

FOOTNOTES

1. Letter of November 4, 1976, from A.A. Landry, President, The Canadian Industrial Traffic League, Toronto, Ontario to N.G. Mulder, Assistant Deputy Minister, Strategic Planning, Transport Canada, Ottawa, Ontario, p. 4.
2. *Ibid.*, p. 2.
3. *Ibid.*, p. 3.
4. One of these is the Canadian Cellulose Company application for leave to appeal to the CTC, pursuant to Section 23 of the National Transportation Act, the acts, omissions and/or rates of the Canadian National Railway Company with respect to logs shipped by rail by Twinriver from Terrace, New Hazelton and Kitwanga, British Columbia, to the woodpulp mills of CanCel at Watson Island, British Columbia. This case is in its preliminary stage.
5. R.A. Bandeen, "CNR's Efficiency Orientated Boss," *Winnipeg Tribune,* October 29, 1976, mimeographed reprint.
6. *Ibid.*
7. See Howard J. Darling, "Transport Policy in Canada: The Struggle of Ideologies versus Realities," *Issues in Canadian Transport Policy,* edited by K.W. Studniki-Gizbert (Toronto: Macmillan Company of Canada, Limited, 1974), pp. 3-46; and F.W. Anderson, "The Philosophy of the MacPherson Royal Commission and the National Transportation Act: A Rectrospective Essay," *ibid.*, pp. 48-65.
8. *Two Proposals for Rail Freight Pricing: Assessment of Their Prospective Impact,* A Report to the Federal-Provincial Committee on Western Transportation by P.S. Ross & Partners, MPS Associates, Ltd., R.L. Banks and Associates, Inc., Trimac Consulting Services Ltd., the M.W. Menzies Group Limited, and George W. Wilson, Indiana University, September 30, 1974.
9. MPS Associates Ltd., *Transport and Regional Development in the Prairies,* prepared for the Ministry of Transport, Federal Government of Canada, Vols. I and II, December 1975, released by Transport Canada in October 1976. See Ken W. Stickland, *Freight Rates and Western Canada,* Alberta Rural Development Studies, sponsored by the Rural Education and Development Association and Alberta Agriculture, October 1976, pp. 11-14.
10. Canadian Manufacturers' Association, excerpt from a proposal to streamline Section 23 procedures, quoted in Canadian Industrial Traffic League, *Traffic Notes,* June 18, 1974, p. 7.
11. *The Benefits and Cost of Government Intervention in the Normal Process of Setting Freight Transport Prices,* Report of the 22nd Round Table of Transport Economics, Paris, 1973, European Conference of Ministers of Transport. For information on how deregulation of transport works in Australia and on the need by Australia's state-owned railways for the application of the commercial and management rules used by efficient, privately owned railways, see James C. Nelson, "The Economic Effects of Transport Deregulation in Australia", *Transportation Journal,* Winter 1976, pp. 48-71.